Also by Eliot Wagner

Grand Concourse

Better Occasions

MY AMERICA!

Eliot Wagner

KENAN PRESS
New York

Published by Kenan Press
A Simon & Schuster Division of Gulf & Western Corporation
Simon & Schuster Building
1230 Avenue of the Americas
New York, New York 10020
KENAN PRESS and colophon are trademarks of Simon & Schuster.
Designed by Dianne Pinkowitz
Manufactured in the United States of America
1 2 3 4 5 6 7 8 9 10

Library of Congress Cataloging in Publication Data

Wagner, Eliot.
My America!
I. Title.
PZ4.W132My [PS3573.A3834] 813'.54 80–14122

ISBN 0–671–25332–8

TO DAVID MARK SCHIER

And thou America . . .
. . . Thou, also thou, a World,
With all thy wide geographies, manifold, different, distant,
Rounded by thee in one—one common orbic language,
One common indivisible destiny for All.

And by the spells which ye vouchsafe to those your ministers in earnest,
I here personify and call my themes, to make them pass before ye.

Behold, America! . . .

WALT WHITMAN
Leaves of Grass

1

"HYMIE, HYMIE HYMIE HYMIE, IT'S TIME HYMIE—"

Every morning she Hymied him, his Golda, his little woman, to paling gaslight and sleepy voices. But ah, sweet slumber, and never sweeter than those extra minutes that sent you late to the shop. And that must have been a sweet dream while he dozed, because when he decided to wake he woke up happy.

Alert.

From a room like a box, with only an inside window cut through the kitchen for a little secondhand air steamy with oatmeal now, he could smell it out: spring in September!

He threw the covers aside, jumped up to the washbowl—and hello looking glass! Girls—who could blame them?—envied him that complexion and those long lashes. From boyhood he'd had the white streak in the beautiful head of hair he combed into winning waves. "Oh you look so mature Hymie," they used to rave. Now it was "Hymie how young you look!" "Charmer," he kidded his reflection, but it was true: the charmer of Essex Street. He centered his tie under the starched collar and went in with good-morning kisses.

For his wife; for their sixteen-year-old darling Naomi; for Leah eighteen their eldest who had to smile when he kissed her, hard-boiled as she considered herself. He rumpled his son's hair too, Danny's, but the elderly snotnose barely a bar mitzvah was a lip curl artist.

The father's appetite stayed fine regardless—take his word—for the tasty breakfast that Golda served him. He good-heartedly waved, even if Danny didn't, when the boy climbed out of their street-level window in a head start to his Saturday job. Ambition, you had to admit, the boy had. Might it take him far. Again Hymie waved as his young ladies—two dolls: one light, one dark—left by the long way around, the black hallway to the bright street.

"Hymie—"

Hymie smiled at his wife—let the rich get heartburn—and took his time.

Till finally—"Hymie"—he dabbed at his mouth and pressed Golda's dear calloused fingers that lovingly pressed back.

And outside Hymie took his bowler off to the golden Sabbath, the teeming sidewalks and the tenements crisp with sunshine. Black threadbare gaberdines also shone in two streams of misery: pilgrim beards to the synagogues and consumptive types drawn like puppets toward the West Side factories.

And look!—Hymie ducked across the way fast—phlegmy and spitting in the gutter but no consumptive that barrel chest, the old workhorse just turned boss, his brother-in-law Frank. What are you pondering Frank, gold in the streets? Hymie grinned crossing back. If he'd known the world on your shoulders glues your eyes to the pavement he would have stayed on this side in the first place.

At Gertrude's Hymie ran up the steps two at a time—the husband only shouldn't have dragged her to *shul* yet—and almost knocked down the husband. Hymie steadied Kass, he begged Kass's pardon, he picked up Kass's prayer book, he asked if Kass was all right. The young-old giant, the sour scholar, touched his lips to the prayer book so God shouldn't be sore, then gave Hymie a hard nod.

Oh owl with the hooked nose, the glasses, the round drooping puss, are you a wise old bird! Hymie was a stranger to Kass, but Mr. Kass was no stranger to Hymie. Hymie knew him, knew him inside out courtesy Gertrude since the beginning of summer. Stopping in front of the dry goods store to point out hubby waiting on trade she'd shaken Hymie a little that night. Was it a bitch playing tricks? Size the husband had. But Hymie'd cracked, "Any friend of yours is a friend of his?" Gertrude had shrugged, "He's nearsighted," and that had tickled Hymie so much that he'd given her a sly tickle right there on Orchard Street. Had she been indignant! And she'd meant it—a respectable girl. Lucky Hymie, that Kass was one of those dawn to midnight gold miners. Fool's gold, with better than gold in his own bed!

A twist of the bell handle—now let her be home—and Hymie was surprised to see the door open up and Gertrude walk away lacing her corset. The edge in her voice—"What's wrong now, you forgot something?" —was a new tune to him.

Kass, she thought!

"No," Hymie hugged his sweet soft darling, "I remembered something."

Gertrude turned in his arms—"You?"—with those lovely eyes wide.

"The one," he kissed her, "and only."

"No—not here."

The girl was right, sensitive. The sofa was better. In here she slept with her husband. Hymie maneuvered her toward the parlor.

She giggled "Hymie!" but wrenched away. In a moment she had her skirt on and was buttoning his last week's present the white silk shirtwaist. "Pretty? No long faces," she stroked Hymie's. "You know we go to *shul* Saturdays."

"Cross my heart, I forgot."

But always, always, his little Sabbath observers put up a delicious struggle. That was why years ago he'd taken a job with Feldman the American. For the husbands Sunday work, Saturday pray, and—even-steven—for Hymie Saturday work and Sunday play.

Hymie—"My holy lady"—kissed Gertrude's shirtwaist over her breast.

She pulled back—"I'm some wife"—in such sweet affliction.

"Walk you to *shul.*"

And Gertrude could only shake her head in teary happiness, he was so kind. But a foot out of the flat and the funny girl's fresh worry was neighbors. So he let her go first—all his!—with the fascinating twitch of the hips under her long black proper skirt. And again side by side with him she was all shame and blushes on account of housewives who didn't know them from Adam!

So for fun he began talking her into skipping *shul* for their park, their room, and before he knew it they were at the synagogue porch. "Hymie—" she begged, but her hand kept squeezing his in spite of outrage and shoves too from religious dogs in the manger whose way in they were blocking.

"Come darling," Hymie said.

"He'll be home by noon."

"You'll be home before noon."

Ah, worried as she was, she asked, "Yes?"

When a dig in the ribs whirled Hymie around furious.

To the gloating eyes and yellow-stained beard of his father. And Mama.

"Welcome to synagogue," the old man cackled. "God must be honored —a rare treat for him."

Hymie managed a smile. Thirty years ago when Papa would catch him Hymie would smile like that. Then it was for sneaking a garment from his own workpile to his brother's, and the punishment, the smack in the face, would come down and turn his smile to tears.

His father leered at poor flustered Gertrude.

"Who's this?"

To say something, Hymie said, "You remember Leah's friend Bessie."

Gertrude ran mortified up the steps as fast as her skirt would let her, while Hymie's mother beamed a sunken-gummed smile after her. But Abe Share studied his son like a hard line in the Law.

"That was Bessie?"

"Who then Abe?" Rivka wanted to know. "You heard what Hymie said."

"What Hymie said!"

"Never mind." Rivka Share slipped her hand under her youngest son's arm. "Come Hymie, help Mama upstairs."

That had been close! But for the first time in years Hymie found himself facing the dais, the Ark and a few hours of prayer. He threw plenty of tender glances up toward Gertrude in the women's balcony, but Gertrude ignored them, and with every glance he lost his place in the prayer book. "Idiot," his father kept rumbling, "where are you reading?" So Hymie wound up praying and swaying along with the best of them, including star chanter Kass.

The final amen and Hymie edged into the crowd that pushed him toward Gertrude coming into the vestibule.

"It turned out okay," he winked.

She mustn't have heard right, although she answered what he would have said next. "I can't, I won't—I'm sick of the lies, the hiding. . . . How can you even ask me, here!"

She hurried away. But from the porch sure enough, where he waited for Mama, didn't he see Gertrude craning around for him even with her husband beside her down there. Hymie shaped on his lips, *Tomorrow*, Gertrude shook her head no, and four-eyed Kass saw nothing.

Still there she went, and the sun kept shining but with not quite the sparkle. So Hymie kissed Mama goodbye—"See what a nice boy he is?" she smiled to Papa while the son grinned—and went to pick himself up half a day's wages in the factory.

And there it was, like always, the grind and rattle of industry, the stink of cloth, dust and honest sweat, of gas leaking and machine grease. He winked democratically—he felt sorry for them, to tell the truth, the hard workers—at the cutter with the long knife, the pressers like ghosts in their vapors, his fellow operators hunched at their machines, and scrawny Feldman the boss.

"Good afternoon," Feldman said.

"God should forgive you, making poor Jews slave on the Sabbath. I had to run here from *shul*."

Feldman waved him into the office. "How do you like this pattern? From Spitz."

"I give him credit, robbing the rich."

"Never mind wisecracks. For wisecracks I can go elsewhere."

But Hymie's few magic strokes of the crayon brought the pattern to life.

"Ah," Feldman murmured, "I see—"

"Sure you see. It's there now."

Feldman leaned back in his swivel chair and he slapped the desk.

"So what do you say, Share? When are you going to behave yourself and show up every day and be my designer and make money?"

Hymie tilted his bowler and laughed. "Everyone throws gold in the streets—I should only bend down and pick it up. Today you, yesterday your former sweater my brother-in-law Frank. How come?"

"You need Frank like a hole in the head."

"I need Frank like I need you, but listen, he offers me money."

"Oy Hymie, Hymie. Okay, I'll raise you a nickel a pair of pants."

Who could outfox the foxes better than Hymie? Never for a second would he consider leaving his little Feldman, let alone to clap himself under the guardian eye of Golda's brother.

"Feldman, you're as good as a brother. In-law. Ten cents and I stay."

They settled for six and a half.

Immediately that raise began burning a hole in Hymie's pocket. He pumped the treadle, but the hours dragged, the sun still gilded the cobblestones. Then the factory windows across the way clotted red, and—at last, at last—paled to a diamond twilight that meant freedom was near.

After work Hymie bought a snappy checked suit at Axelrod's, a lovely worsted, not like Feldman's junk. He bought himself a new cane too with a brass tip like gold.

Wait till Gertrude got an eyeful of this!

In the kitchen on his way out next morning he tried out his new clothes on the family. Golda was setting little goldenhair's hair, Leah was elbow-deep in laundry and never-crack-the-face Danny was muttering to "Sweet Sue" and strumming the bar mitzvah ukulele from his sisters so low you hardly could hear him.

They'd raised a joyless son, not from any example of Hymie's.

"Sing out," the father encouraged him, "like Ukulele Ike in the *Follies*!" —and oops, a slip. Where did they come to the *Follies*? Only Hymie went.

So for his pains he got a silent look from the son and the heaving of Leah's slim back over the scrubbing board. But Golda said, "Hymie, you're gorgeous!" and Naomi, "Papa I have to kiss you!" He bent to his strawberries-and-cream darling while Golda beamed.

Poor Golda! That brown rag she wore you wouldn't want to wrap onions in. He was down to his last tenner today—the new outfit. But next week. Next week he'd take a few dollars and buy her something pretty!

And—his eyes were as bright as his narrow black pointy shoes—he gave Leah a hug.

"Is it a suit?" he boomed.

The girl was bound to turn. "A suit-and-a-half," she had to admit. "From your shop?"

Now why did she have to go and ask him that? He hated to lie and they made him. "Where else?" Otherwise she'd add extravagance to her list of the father's shortcomings.

Because they knew—partly. They knew he had a way with cloth, an eye for design. They knew he could do better for them if he tried.

About the money they didn't know. The girls with their bookkeeping, the boy with his part-time job in some law library—all told they earned less than what Hymie had to spend on himself every week. He loved them, he wanted to move them to a better neighborhood, larger rooms, uptown maybe, Mt. Morris Park; he wanted Golda to buy them nice things instead of stitching together remnants off Rivington Street pushcarts; he wanted them to have meat on the table a few times a week; he wanted . . .

But he also wanted Gertrude. Before Gertrude he used to want Freda; before Freda, Ullya; and before Ullya—he himself had lost count.

After all, the fourteen dollars that a good tailor brought home he brought home too. The other nine from his special ability, wasn't he entitled to use them for his special needs?

Outdoors he flashed his stick at weather turned gray. On a northbound cable car he picked his way over legs, plumped to a place and, as he dug for his nickel, winked at the conductor riding the running board. And the man? With a sneer as black as the bushy mustache—"We ain't got all day now, mister, we ain't got all day"—he rattled the fare cup.

Why were they all so miserable, humanity?

And at their bench in Madison Square Park, Gertrude too? Look at that frown! But the faint fuzz along those dark pretty cheeks always excited him.

He struck his vaudeville stance—his son with the gloomy uke should watch him some time—with the cane under the arm and pointing up happily.

"Is it a suit?"

She stared at the washed-out lawn. But Hymie sat down and toyed with her forearm. He wanted her upstairs already in their hotel room with the rich festooned draperies.

She moved away from him!

"What?" he asked in astonishment.

"I shouldn't have come. I shouldn't be here."

He kissed her earlobe. She twisted free.

"I know, that's all I'm good for."

"What would I do without you?"

"What you do all the time. What you'll do after you leave me today."

Hymie laughed. "What'll I do? I'll go home and eat."

"If you loved me you'd take me away."

Ah—demands now! Hymie slouched back and flicked a wrinkle out of his trousers leg. A man like him, Hymie Share, needed to put up with demands? And maybe he'd mistreated her? How many times from that very curb had he handed Gertrude into one of those hansoms for a drive uptown like a society beauty with her swell!

Gertrude said, "You would, if you loved me. You'd take me where we could walk in the street together without being ashamed to meet people—"

Hymie became curious. "Where, for instance?"

"Anywhere. Chicago—"

Chicago! Golda was overjoyed to have him home a couple of nights a week and an occasional Sunday, and for this one he was supposed to fly to Chicago! Then maybe to China? He winked at a brunette passing and those cheeks curled far from insulted.

And him stuck with Madam Chicago! He felt like letting her have it, right across that obstinate puss. But his eye ran down the plump figure and he kept his voice smooth.

"All right, Chicago."

Then her gratitude, the eyes swooning up at him, melted his heart. In their bed overlooking the park she chattered her happy plans and Hymie felt sad that soon, most likely, he wouldn't be able to see her any more.

By themselves after supper Golda told Hymie, "You haven't been honest with me. That hurts."

The shock hung a silly grin on his mouth.

"Frank was here," Golda continued.

Then that skunk must have seen him yesterday, trailed him to Gertrude's. . . .

But no. As far as the brother-in-law could bubble over he'd been bubbling over with the new business finally set up. He'd dropped in for tea and talk, and Golda had had to say, "I'm sure you'll make a success, Frank, I'm proud of you." Naturally she would mean it and big-hearted Frank would repeat to her his work invitation to Hymie—with a plus. "He could break in to become a partner after a while. Meantime I could give him even a little more than by Feldman. Twenty-five, I could pay."

Big-mouth! What Hymie had kept quiet all these years became public knowledge. Oy Frank, fools are born not made. But what could you expect, a Frank Trachtenberg to conceive of what it was to be a Hymie Share?

But Golda said, "Frank doesn't know you've been fooling your wife about your wages, I didn't let on."

Then Hymie didn't feel so proud of himself. He was thankful for the dim gas jet in the silence. He unfocused his eyes and his wife seemed far off, lumpish, like the chipped sink, the rust-bellied stove, the gashed icebox. Once his mother had caught him spilling his milk out and while she'd scolded him he'd sat like this, trying to amalgamate with the shadows. Now he stole a wistful glance at the window. Outside on fruit boxes under the lamplight the neighbors were enjoying the evening.

Golda had to laugh. "I'll bet when you were a little boy and you pulled a face like that your mama hugged you and gave you candy."

Hymie was startled. "That's exactly what she did. After I threw the milk out of the window and she hollered at me. She gave me a sheet of sugar buttons."

Golda couldn't resist kissing him. "Although," she said, "I shouldn't. After all, you're a grown man. But I must say," she affectionately added, "you don't look a day older than the boy I married—and your wife looks many years older than she did at her wedding."

It was true, an eye-opener. He'd been enjoying himself and she'd grown old. "Golda!" he was heart-wrenched. He banged the table. "I'll be different. Yes! My mind is made up. I'm going with Frank. I'll show him. I'll be a partner yet! What do you think of that, Golda?"

He pulled her to his lap and there was kissing and grabbing like a honeymoon all over again.

"We'll be rich yet, Golda. You'll wear silks. The girls too. I'll send Danny to play his ukulele in college."

And on the side—why not?—he saw that brunette in the park, a brougham, drawn curtains. . . .

Later though at Frank's the future began losing its glow. Golda and Frank's Rose with a chest like a mountain beamed to the words of wisdom while Frank paced his dreary roomful of green mohair and raved about machines. Frank's eyes glittered!

But how about Gertrude? Tomorrow poor Gertrude would be there waiting, and Hymie'd be in Frank's loft.

Hymie's eyes moistened.

Suddenly . . . silence.

The three of them were looking to Hymie's lips. Who? What?

"Er, hah, yes, I see. But tell me Frank, when can we figure on retirement?"

They all laughed thank God.

Some joke.

Frank said, "We can figure on work, Hymie, hard work. That's all I can promise."

And—the shop at dawn or the day won't count—the party broke up early.

Work work work work!

"Isn't it wonderful?" Golda whispered in bed. "It's like a dream!"

Some dream—a nightmare. She hugged him to do him a favor, but even apart from his long afternoon with Gertrude, he couldn't.

No more days away from the machine. No more glass of tea in a sunny café. No more yelling the horses to the Sheepshead finish line. No more East River on sultry mornings while the suckers sweated in the garment lofts.

He was a member in good standing now of the suckers' union. President!

And no Gertrude.

A tear—he couldn't help it—trickled along his cheek. He could have run, with Gertrude. But he hadn't. Family comes first. And this was the reward.

Get rich! His wife, his children, his brother-in-law: always they'd dangled that plum in front of his nose. Now he could eat it, worm and all.

He groaned when Golda woke him, an honest groan, and turned over, sick for sleep. "Hymie—" He ground his teeth, he breathed curses. "Hymie," she kept at him, "Hymie—"

Tugged at his shoulder!

"Let go of me!"

It was as black as midnight, the kitchen window reflected the gas jet, and she was the aggrieved one!

He touched water to his throbbing forehead with daughters to drive him crazy chirping away at the breakfast table. And on the cot in the corner Lord Daniel slept on.

Bleary, weak as Hymie was, he sipped coffee. The gas jet became pale in the morning light and the girls left. But the persecution continued.

"Hymie—"

"You require your million immediately? You can't wait one more second?"

God in heaven forgive him, that woke the son. And Danny's stares—Hymie'd had them up to the ears.

Like last month he'd taken a well-earned day off for a dip in the river and climbed out blowing and dripping near the deep thinkers on the pier. With one foot in the grave most of them, they sweated over does society corrupt the individual or vice versa. Two minutes of that were enough to send you right back into the water. But he'd been caught on the eye of an interested listener: this same know-it-all with the same stare.

Hymie'd found himself stammering, "N–no school today?" And the wise guy had dryly announced, "Summer vacation Papa, since two weeks ago." Then he—the father—had had to make up excuses about slow at the shop!

Now Hymie warned his son, "You mind your own business." So, "Hymie," his wife pinned his arm down for a lecture, "nobody wants you to do anything you don't want to do—"

A lie!

"Leave me alone, I know what I'm doing!"

He glared at his son, but the son ignored the father, finished breakfast, grabbed his books, gave his mother a kiss and hopped out of the kitchen window into the street.

"He'll break a leg like that one of these days," Hymie muttered, "the smart aleck."

Himself, he felt his way muttering and cursing through the dark stinking hall. And with all his care he tripped over the single step out, turned a wild cartwheel and yelped at the sidewalk swinging to meet him head-on.

The doctor's needle put Hymie to sleep but he had bad dreams: Golda nagging, nagging; Frank promising hard work; sewing machines. Then he woke and saw . . . Mama? Her round face was full of anxiety, he broke into a cold sweat. He'd been hurt bad then?

"Mama—" his voice shook.

She squeezed his hand.

"You'll be better soon, darling."

But Golda hung over him like doomsday. Was Mama lying to spare his feelings? He moaned, "What did the doctor say?" And what a relief—the doctor had said that in a few months he'd be as good as new. You could see the guilt on Golda's face. She knew whose fault it was!

No Frank today! And no apologies!

That night Papa came for his say. With the wagging whiskers and the small shiny eyes he looked as mean as the billy goats that used to roam over the East Side and scare Hymie when he was a little boy.

"Idiot! What did you break your leg for, a vacation?"

Hymie just lowered his eyes while Mama took his part.

"Abraham, what makes you say such things? Can't you see he's in pain?" Papa flapped a hand in disgust and left the sickroom. Mama said sadly, "Everything is a joke to him, this too."

Only to him. To the rest this was no joke. Even Leah said it was rotten luck. And did her duty toward her father.

And Hymie knew how to show appreciation.

How many times did he apologize to Mama or Golda for calling them. How many times did he thankfully stroke Naomi's cheek or try to kiss Leah's fingers.

Danny—Danny was Danny. He'd run you an errand but he was too big for thanks, the snotnose. "It's okay Papa," he'd interrupt, with that face (*Faker, get out of bed*) Hymie could read like a book.

To a father with a leg in a cast!

Just the same never had the house been so lively. Even Hymie's brother Willie visited all the way from Orange, New Jersey. Men dropped in from the factory. Feldman himself brought a bottle of schnapps and consoled Hymie that before he knew it he'd be on the job again.

Hymie only smiled, winked to Golda and smacked his lips over Feldman's liquor.

Frank also came, and talked business. Cutter this, machine that, Rosenthal temporarily, a young fellow, as designer and to help . . . Fascinating. Once Frank's hard chuckle—"Look, I put him to sleep"—woke Hymie up.

Hymie'd make believe he was sleeping though when Frank pushed money into Golda's hand. Good. If not for them would Hymie be on his bed of pain?

Yet how far did Frank's pittances go? Danny's shirts that used to be Hymie's were threadbare. Naomi had been due for a new coat and went to work shivering rather than be seen in that horse blanket of an old one.

But Golda managed to mend the shirts a dozenth time, and when it snowed Naomi shed a few tears and the old coat was brought out of tar paper. So, Hymie took note, with all their complaints they could get along. His one regret was—doctor's orders—the only meat in the house had to be for his plate.

So when Golda decided to go into the hairdressing business at home—the children naturally were against it—Hymie enthusiastically volunteered to print the window sign. "Nothing doing," the son put his two cents in. But the sign went up—MADAM SHARE, BEAUTY SALON—a lovely sign!

Effective. Through the hole in the wall between Hymie's bed and the kitchen he watched shows as good as the *Ziegfeld Follies*, some of the best-looking women in the neighborhood with their hair down. Afterward—"How is the foot, Mr. Share?"—they'd pay their respects while Golda stood by proudly.

One girl though was quiet—never a word while Golda snipped away or afterward, but her eyes were continually drawn to that inside window. You smiled at her she'd blush and turn right to her baby playing with its toes in a carriage.

This girl hurried away one morning and Hymie called to Golda sweeping the clippings up, "That's Nadelman the watchmaker's wife, isn't it? A fine good-looking man."

"The only fine good-looking man I know of around here I'm speaking to now. That was Kirschner the poultryman's wife, poor child."

"Isn't he doing so well, Kirschner?"

"He sells chickens all right. Only, for my taste, he isn't much of a man with his thick lips and blue chin . . . How's my boy?"

Hymie'd never felt better, but—"Getting along, the same as usual"—don't tempt fate was his motto.

"If any ladies come in for haircuts," Golda pinched his cheek before she went shopping, "tell them please wait?"

But how often could these ladies afford a haircut?

So with nothing to do mostly but read the papers—some nut went up in an aeroplane to California then he ate an orange, or else the cloak-and-suitmakers struck and a new day was dawning for the poor sweated suckers yeah yeah—Hymie had plenty of time to daydream. And for this purpose, to his surprise, Gertrude Kass was a flop. Hard as he tried to bring back that moaning and twisting, the naughty light on her body, nothing stuck—"If you loved me"—but that selfish mouth.

Kirschner the poultryman's wife with the shy wandering eyes, the billowing shirtwaist, the full swishing skirts—she fit better.

Oh to be on his feet!

A lot doctors know. Not till way after the new year was Hymie able to swing outdoors on crutches. And what a pleasure: the people, the noise, even the garbage! And when he went back to bed there were still a few hairdressings in the kitchen.

Till his son—oh that fella had a wonderful life ahead of him—called another family council with the father permitted to eavesdrop from the bedroom if he wanted to.

The prodigy was sick of—sick of, at fifteen! Of Uncle Frank's handouts. Of—the expert on women—his mother waiting on a bunch of fat slobs. And he particularly was sick of that card in the window.

He yanked it down—warped, dusty, to make your heart bleed—and ripped it in half. Golda cried out, Naomi squealed. Leah of course took Danny's side. And the first two, even with their little noises, did you hear them argue?

Hymie pulled himself out of bed, limped to the girls' cubicle and slammed himself in. Murmurs. Exclamations, protests, an actual sob. By some miracle the father's feelings were finally being considered? He opened the door a crack.

Listen to what the crying was all about. His son—and Danny himself kept shouting he wasn't that marvelous a scholar—was switching to a full-time job and night classes! They should cry so loud at the father's funeral God forbid.

And if the genius was so smart how come Golda's customers still rang the bell sign or no sign? If she was out Hymie'd tell them, "What did I need it for? It was her pastime." But an easy dollar lost was his private opinion.

He was in bed yet one morning when he called "Come in" to a timid ring. And oh ho—a go-cart came, a kicking baby came, and the delicious figure and scared gray eyes of Kirschner the poultryman's wife came. Hymie sat himself up with a twinge so slight that flopping back to the pillow with a groan was pure inspiration.

Kirschner the poultryman's wife came running.

"Medicine," Hymie croaked, "near the washbasin—"

The medicine, pfui, he hadn't tasted for months. But she helped him sit up and ah, did she smell sweet, with that soft arm supporting him—it was worth it. He sighed thank you and let his head droop to give her a look at that profile. Then, with her helping hand, he sank slowly back. He tried holding on to those lovely fingers, but she slipped them away.

"You're right," he murmured, "you should go. No more hairdressing anyhow."

She was upset but to Hymie's pleasure she made no move. "I'd better wait," she felt obliged to say, "till . . . Mrs. Share gets back—"

Hymie's hand found hers. "You're an angel—"

But that rotten drug was pasting his eyes together. He yawned, he patted her wrist, he dozed. . . .

". . . the ambulance—"

"What ambulance, when ambulance?" Hymie woke up and sat up. "What for?"

The women stared.

"What for?" Golda said. "We thought you fractured your leg again."

"The way he fainted," the girl all but whispered.

"Nothing," Hymie said.

"You're sure?" Golda asked him.

"Sure? Sure I'm sure!"

"Isn't he brave! Dora, how can I thank you?" Golda clasped the girl's waist. "Come, I'm going to do your hair—for friendship."

Dora blushed and she ran out with the baby while Hymie gazed lovelorn at that firm young back. The door shut and he jumped out of bed to head for the kitchen window.

"Where do you think you're going?"

He'd forgotten Golda was home!

"You get right back into bed and take care of that leg."

Whew—so she hadn't guessed. Though outside would have been nice, instead of a stuffy bedroom. But that had been a nice little visit with Dora too; and Leah and Danny—were they shocked finding the father on his back when they got home from work. First whispers with Golda, then the worried questions to him concerning his health.

Hypocrites!

Other nights they asked, "Walk far today, Papa? . . . With your stick?" "No, with my wings." "Oh ha ha ha—why Papa, that's marvelous."

Leeches, the pair of them. Were they lacking a roof over their head? Were they begging for bread? Every second the father was out of the shop was like a year off their lives.

So take notice—and don't rush me!

Golda at least didn't rush him, she even carried it to the other extreme keeping him a whole week in bed. But at the end of that week, in the spring, in the sunshine, there across the street airing her baby, looking and (he could tell) waiting, with frightened eyes, stood his—his Dora!

"I didn't see you outside," she said when he went to her, "I was worried—"

"I'm fine, thanks to you."

Dora blushed, and Hymie casually told her how you get broken legs in the gold rush—the whole story. Was she indignant! She forgot to be frightened.

"Money is not everything."

Hymie didn't disagree. He tickled her gurgling baby under the chin—even infants loved him!—and, "But I'm keeping you from . . . whatever you have to do," he gave her a wistful smile.

"You aren't."

She only wanted him to stay, to talk, but to be first to say goodbye has an advantage.

And see, how she was there the next day, and the day after that? He met her every day, to stand in the sunshine with and fill her eyes with sympathy.

Yes, he remembered himself for her as a skinny kid that lived in a sweatshop. Sewing and Hebrew school, Hebrew school and sewing, beatings from the father, then from the teacher. Five brothers—three of them sickened into yellow-faced corpses.

"And do you know something? I was scared, seeing them in their shrouds like that, one after the other."

Dora was so attentive, so heart-stricken, he found himself making things up.

"I had dreams. In the middle of the night the Angel of Death sat on my chest and wagged his finger at me. 'You're next,' he'd say, 'watch out!' He resembled my papa."

"Terrible," Dora caught at her throat, "terrible—"

And Dora—Hymie asked her one day—what about her childhood? Just a childhood, she told him, not like his. She grew up, she found a job in a department store, her father brought Joe Kirschner around, Joe was very good to her, they married. . . .

"And he's still good to you."

"Yes, he's a good man, he works so hard, he comes home so tired—"

"Ahh . . ."

Ahh, he could almost taste the wonderful hours ahead, ahh . . .

But the morning arrived when he was reminded of his near and dear.

At nineteen a bitch. He hated to say it even to himself, but that was his Leah. He heard her voice loud on purpose to wake him up early in the morning for no reason. Or was there a reason?

". . . Shush!" Golda said.

Leah said, "Let him wake up. It's about time he woke up, and went to work."

"Be still. It hurts him to walk."

"Except—" you could count on the son—"when there's someplace he wants to go."

Naomi pitched in, "He's a darling anyway."

Anyway!

Golda agreed. "I always called him that."

"Save me from such darlings," Leah kept it up, "I'd sooner stay single all my life."

"Wait, you haven't fallen in love yet," Golda said, "like I did." And his wife added, "Not that I'd want to wish my life on you."

Hymie sprang up and yanking his pants on he banged the bad leg against the bedstead.

"For God's sake Papa," Leah the bitch changed her tune, "if your leg still—"

Golda pleaded with him, Naomi. "Papa—" He swept Naomi's hand off his arm.

"You'll all be rich. Let's hope you'll also be happy."

He stomped out. But in the old streets between the sickening factories pain slowed him to a hobble. He had to hold his ears against screeching axles, teamsters bawling, hooves ringing off stones. He dragged himself two flights to Frank's loft and there were the curved spines, the sighing irons, the rancid sweat.

At the cutting table his brother-in-law stood paralyzed with joy at the sight of him.

"Well," Frank located his voice. "You're better."

Better!

And in place of the golden promises of last year Frank offered alibis: a going concern, didn't know (with a chin massage), his designer Rosenthal, commitments.

Hymie wound up at a machine—thank you Frank, thank you for the favor—and pedaling was like knives through his leg. Sure mutter, look daggers at the big boss the office side of the partition with blubber-lip Rosenthal, but Hymie's bones were doing the breaking. Still he kept on. A man mustn't deprive his family of their satisfaction! Nausea though and cold sweat stopped even him. He propped himself on his feet, the operators asked what was wrong.

Frank and the assistant? Not a glance.

Only at Hymie's humble tap on the jamb did they turn, the industrialists. Sick as he was, Hymie forced a smile.

"You'll pardon me for disturbing you. I just wanted to let you know, I'm leaving. There seems to be something wrong with my leg."

Frank stood there with his face creased. Hymie was a liar to this son-of-a-bitch? But—"Well, you tried"—a day's torture was estimated at a five-dollar bill.

Hymie was sorry to disturb his wife too in the kitchen humming over her soup greens without him in the way. One look at his face though, his brimming eyes, and she cried out.

"Sha," she stroked his forehead, "sha," after she put him to bed. "It was a mistake, you won't go to work again till you're all better . . ."

Even they, even his family, had learned something. No more questions, no more complaints now all his weeks in bed. And only when he was well enough to get up did Golda announce that the next day they were moving to Hester Street.

"To the Pig Market!" Naomi wailed.

"And no arguments please."

Master Attorney-at-Law Wet-Behind-the-Ears Daniel had to cross-examine his mother till she admitted she was exchanging janitress services for rent-free in Hester Street. Shocking!

And in the full heat of summer—move a muscle and you were soaked through and through—Golda helped the mover load up the wagon, that was part of her bargain with him. But it was not right.

Dora Kirschner eventually did show up with the baby in the go-cart down the busy street and—so happy, so excited—waved to him from a distance. Closer, she saw Golda and turned and hurried away. Just as well. How could he stand and talk with Golda killing herself?

Poor Golda. In the new streets the gutter was so high with slops you couldn't see the cobblestones and the pushcarts were so packed together that the teamster could barely squeeze through. In Essex Street the hallway was dark? In Hester Street it was dark and besides the sink overflowed. Cats—the house stank with them. What did they feed on? In these holes could mice live too? Hymie felt like ordering the mover one two three about face—back where we came from! But what could Hymie do?

He was rich only in pain.

In pain he had to stand by while Golda unstacked the chairs to dig the makings of a meal from heaped barrels. All in this heat that left Hymie mopping his face exhausted.

Naomi came in from work first, looked around, and cried on her mother's shoulder poor child. Danny and Leah swallowed their bite of supper and pitched into the unpacking like they were fighting a war. And for Leah the father was excess baggage.

"Go out," she said, "find a cool breeze—" And tittered, maybe to hide the hate that made her voice shake. But she didn't fool him. The father heard.

"Thank you, but there seems to be something wrong with my leg."

And would he have enjoyed a dip in the river! Taking a dip just such a night a year ago he'd met Gertrude Kass. That night also the sky was like brown felt over the tenements. Children slept half-naked on fire escapes and rooftops then too, and on the recreation pier with their parents nodding on the benches. Hot! Even the chessboards had been folded and the players had sat staring across the thick river, at what, black smokestacks in Brooklyn? Hymie'd been poised to dive when he saw this girl watching him. He'd laughed, "Come on in," and ignored the dirty looks from the watchdogs with their kids. And she'd come over, Gertrude, to tell him she had no suit on. As he'd dived she'd gasped, so for a joke he'd swum awhile underwater. Then he'd climbed out dripping and laughing and she'd told him he'd scared the wits out of her vanishing into the black that way. . . .

But that was a year ago. Tonight his happy family straightened the furniture out and sweated over hot tea that was supposed to cool them off according to Golda. He cracked a joke, they sat like at a funeral. What did they want?

"Here."

He laid Frank's fiver of last month on the table, and the four of them put down their glasses of tea and goggled at him like he was a thief!

The hell with them, he went to bed.

Fine thanks!

And since that was their attitude—he woke to the hot gray light filtering through the flat's one window—he saw no reason why he shouldn't go for a swim this morning. He peeled off his union suit and put the bathing suit on under his shirt and pants, hid a towel in his back pocket—and found Golda on her hands and knees scrubbing the outside hallway.

She would soak the brush in the bucket, let it drip, then bear down with a grunt on the filthy tile. She stopped to wipe her forehead, Hymie shook his head over her hard work he wished he could help her with and he softly shut himself in the flat again.

He sat and perspired in front of their view, a smoke-stained air shaft. He had no way of knowing if the sun was out but at least there was no rain. After a while he took another peek at the hall—and the coast was clear. So he sneaked out and he beat it from Hester Street. Nearer the river he sniffed good brine and walked even faster.

The water was churning with swimmers Danny's age and Hymie knew some of those kids, Danny's friend Lefkowitz over there, Cohen. So? They'd tell on him? Let them tell. He came up spry and spouting, as good as the best of them. On the shore factories and tenements sprang at the blue sky; the masts of a sailing ship rose bone-white in the sunshine!

Hymie roared "My America!"—and if the kids laughed let them laugh!

The tide rolled under him, smooth, sweet. He tried kicking, and in the water the game leg felt good.

Wasn't that wonderful! He had to tell someone!

He wheeled pumping hard, and swam back to the pier in long easy strokes.

And dressed, and all but ran to Essex Street he was so impatient to get there, to bring Dora the love and tenderness welling up inside him.

She opened the door and her eyes were bright, almost feverish. She gazed at him, she couldn't move! He had to lead her by the arm into Kirschner's very neat little parlor.

"Baby asleep?" he asked.

"I never thought I'd see you again," Dora said, "I missed you."

"I missed you too, I missed you—" He bent to kiss her, she didn't resist.

But she looked up at him anxiously when he let her go, she murmured, "This is wrong, isn't it?"

"Darling," Hymie almost in pain he loved her so much brought that dear burning face to his lips again, "love is never wrong—never."

2

OH HOW DORA CLEANED NOWADAYS—SHE POLISHED THE house! She kept her ironed and fresh white muslin curtains in tucks and the sun pouring over the Essex Street pushcarts three stories down shone red-gold lights on the mahogany and little rainbows on the cut glass in the cabinet. But on the Lower East Side dust gathered always. With the dining room spotless she went back to the bedroom with her mop and rags and she hummed and polished. She owed her husband a sparkling house.

Then—how quiet Sammy was—the kitchen again, and there legs straight out he sat on the red-dotted yellow linoleum, her little man, her rose on rose, her sunlight on sunlight, glassy-eyed, rubbing his gums over his spoon. "Hard work," Dora said, "drumming on a pot so long," and he smiled to Mother in the doorway and crawled to her in a flurry of hands and knees to be gathered up for a big kiss.

"But," Dora crooned in chubby's face, "it's lunchtime, and he's so good, he doesn't even complain!"

Sammy let off a string of cheerful syllables and reached for his mother's nose. What could she do but squeeze him? Had she always loved him this much? More every day it seemed. With Sammy on her arm interestedly watching she warmed some milk. Then she poured and placed it within reach on the kitchen table and sat down, still with Sammy, in the shadows behind the wide-open window, where she could see into the yard without being seen. The world, the alley—she gave Sammy her breast—was so full of sunlight and still so warm for so late in October! Her clothesline between her house and the one opposite sparkled like snow with this morning's laundry. And oh was that lady at the window talking to somebody on this side ugly, with the creased face and her wig on cockeyed! Dora giggled, and Sammy grinned up around the dark nipple on the white breast. Ah, the lady was bragging about a grandchild.

". . . and smart as a whip!"

Dora said, "I don't want to be smart Sammy, do you?"

Sammy had been more passing the time than sucking and at the question pushed himself away altogether. "Ack," he said, which meant milk in a glass. So again Dora squeezed and kissed him and slipped him into the high chair.

"You *are* smart, but I'm only a woman, so . . . I'm only happy."

While she fed Sammy milk and mush the barley soup on the stove began steaming. Dora poured half the soup into a jar for Joe, the rest was for . . . Also she filleted three herrings, one for Joe, one for . . . and one for herself. The last two she put back in the icebox. But time and again she'd begged Joe to come home for lunch and a nap instead of never leaving the store from morning till night.

"No," Joe always said, "I have to be there and see what's going on."

So, since Joe wouldn't, there was no reason why . . . you know . . . Such joy whenever she felt Hymie's name, joy overflowing, touching everything: the woman down there, the red bricks and the fire escapes, the wash waving, the blue sky when you bent your neck up a bit. Touching Sammy? No, Sammy was her joy in himself.

Sammy slept in the carriage through the hubbub of Rivington Street as Dora brought Joe his lunch.

"Here lady, sweet white little loaves only two for a cent!"

Dora stopped at the pushcart. Other wives got these rolls three and sometimes four for a cent, but she never could bargain. She bought rolls for Joe, and for . . . They'd be the sweetest, the rolls for . . .

" . . . Ah thank you, young mother. Eat them in good health."

So she knew that she had been overcharged.

Joe had started with a small store but his market now was enormous, full of ferocious women and the smell of singed flesh. Being there made Dora feel so . . . unhappy. Chickens squawked in their coops indignantly, each on a different note, and her husband's workers would grab them by the legs and turn them upside-down for those terrible women to poke at. Dora shivered and looked the other way. It took some moments of being jostled in the doorway (because never, never would she bring Samuel into that place) before she managed to catch the eye of one of the pluckers who sat up in the loft at the end of the long counter. "Hey boss, there's your missis!" that woman shrieked above the grief of the chickens.

Eventually Joe came, tall and skinny just like her father, but with blue-grained close-shaven cheeks, cool blue eyes, a cap and a white bloody apron. Even now, two years married, her face at the sight of his fine market offended him. But he could laugh it off.

"Like medicine Dora, hah? It keeps you alive but the taste makes you sick."

"I'm sorry, Joe—"

He fondly touched Dora's chin and then sleeping Sammy's.

"Joe are your hands clean?"

Now, Kirschner asked himself proudly, was there a son better taken care of than his? "They're clean, they're clean." The dish of herring that Dora handed him started his nostrils tingling, his mouth watered. "You'll bring him back later, when he's awake?"

"Certainly." She did every day.

Still, Dora wished that she wouldn't have to go back, that place made her so faint. Even on the way home she felt slight nausea. But with the perambulator left under the stairway this armful of the good sleeper Sammy with the toasty face against hers was a comfort up the three flights, heavy as her boy was becoming. She was trying to manage her keys, baby and shopping, and a man running downstairs stopped right behind her. She stood trembling. But—

"Hymie!"

Hymie lifted his bowler, "How do you do?," quickly replaced it, kissed Dora and carefully transferred Sammy to his arm.

"But what—"

"Open, open—"

In the mild light of the kitchen Hymie looked at his darling with the heart-shaped face and the little nose that curved in. "You're not well!"

"It's only the chickens."

And Hymie found himself sore at Kirschner, he, Hymie, who laughed at husbands, even felt sorry for them they were so pathetic. Also, the thought of taking this wife away crossed his mind, of taking care of her. Though how could he desert poor old Golda?

Dora fed him lunch in her beautiful clean kitchen, barley soup, herring to make your mouth water and sweet poppy-seed rolls while he explained the stairs surprise, though who'd guessed his sensitive girl would be scared? None of their business, the neighbors, that she had a dear friend who lived only to run to her. So he'd come via the rooftops from the next block, Norfolk Street. And from the roof you see the sky spread out—over chimneys, water towers, the new Woolworth Building downtown!

Dora forgot her roll, her coffee; she listened enchanted.

Today he'd been on the roof early and enjoyed the street from the edge: people thick as flies swarming around; black shawls, white shirts, brown derbies, caps, back and forth at the pushcarts alongside horses and wagons —fascinating! It makes you think.

"What did you think?"

"I thought, 'When is Dora coming already?' "

So she kissed him.

He also thought—and it was on the tip of his tongue but he didn't say it—that of the women and women he'd been with, never had he so much as considered keeping comings and goings secret, except from Golda. The opposite, he used to march in with pride let smirk who smirked, a lady-killer. Sometimes calling on one he'd find the next in an encouraging glance from that one's neighbor. The others all wanted: flattery, presents, good times, screwing. Or for some bargains, like Gertrude, you should go change their lives for them. But the heart of an angel with flaring anger for his near and dear, his charming family all for themselves? Such a girl never, ah, never had he met before.

She said now, "It's true, if a neighbor told Joe, he wouldn't understand."

More and more Hymie's heart overflowed!

"God put one innocent on earth—and my privilege to meet her! What wouldn't Joe understand?"

"Why, that he's my husband but you're my boy. Since you, I have two boys."

Well, a darling tells you that after lunch—one thing leads to another. Was this something new? Yet even bed with this girl was different. The physical part no, though as to this he was far from the captain courageous of five or even two years ago. Dora's boy yes, but oy, age, age . . . But not counting his wife—a wife should be modest and more modest than Golda they'd never made them—he'd always been the connoisseur of the voluptuous curve and that lost look in their face in half-light half-shadow. In hotel rooms at night he used to keep a small lamp on for this purpose. Now, with Dora, he pulled down the green shades and climbed into bed in his union suit. When they'd made love, he kissed both her eyes and drew the blanket up to her armpits.

"You're so kind, Hyman—"

Ah how she gratified him with that appreciation that made no demands. Even in respect to her modesty she asked nothing. Only, after their first time together, when others parade themselves let alone show you modesty, he'd caught such pain, such embarrassment in her glance—misery you could say—he'd figured here it comes, another one full of boring she-shouldn't-haves. Then he'd seen she was blushing, china pink from the face down, all over her body.

He had asked, "What, mamaleh?"

She'd only shaken her head but she'd been too ashamed even to face him. Yet she hadn't wanted to cover herself—she'd admitted later—if he wanted her . . . uncovered. With a gush of tenderness that was new in his life he'd said, "Mustn't catch cold mamaleh," tucking her in.

At age forty-three to be in love like a boy!

After Sammy woke up and was cooed at and tickled and diapered and dressed, Dora brought him back to the market for his father to play with while the mountain goat Hymie leaped over the roofs. In the bustle of Grand Street Dora, Sammy and Hymie got together again and running over the cobblestones to a downtown trolley they almost ran into a closed auto that chugged by drays and hansoms while people watched in the sunlight.

"Get there fast in your coffin!" Hymie yelled.

Then Hymie astonished the meat-faced conductor on the streetcar by hoisting Sammy go-cart and all onto the rear platform.

"Yez can't bring no carriages on!"

Sammy began puckering up at the red angry face over the black uniform. Passengers stuck their noses out, Hymie shook his head at the man. "Ts-ts-ts, scaring infants—" Even Dora's eyes sparked. Hymie asked, "Do you have change, mamaleh? Here . . ." he pushed the dime Dora gave him into the man's receptacle.

The conductor wagged his thumb Sammy-wards. "And what about that?"

"Mister," Hymie laughed, "you want fare from a ten-month-old baby?" He pushed down the motorman's stool for Dora to sit on. "Money money —that's all you hear in America." The stymied conductor—now was there an actual regulation against carriages?—went off after easier fares. "All the same," Hymie told Dora, "I could use some money, instead of taking . . . such dimes."

"Oh no, I do the laundry myself now instead of sending out wetwash, and that's how I save. So it's really my money."

"And what's yours is mine?"

"Of course."

Did you ever see such a girl? Him, when he looked at her, it was as if he had never seen a woman before. And how pale that face still was on account of her good man's chicken market! This could not, must not go on.

He said, "Mamaleh, would you like to live in Chicago?," then felt slightly dizzy. Supposing she said yes?

"Is it nice there?"

"They say that there's a lake like an ocean."

"And here there's only an ocean?" She looked up with that innocent face, that sweet smile. "I'd rather be here, where you are."

Whew! "Wouldn't I be there too?" he could laugh.

"But Joe's business is here."

Hymie's joy filled the trolley, welled into Grand Street and up over the clothing stores, soared through the El tracks into the sunshine! He squeezed Dora's face.

She said, "You're so happy!"

"Your fault mamaleh—you teach me."

"Yes? What?"

What he had known all the time: it's a hard life so why make it harder? He answered her, "That there's goodness on earth. Hey mamaleh, do you hear me philosophize? With your help I'll grow up to be as wise as my son yet!"

In Battery Park they strolled with other couples at leisure along white sandy paths between green lawns. At the water's edge Hymie all smiles in his tipped-back derby lifted up Sammy, who pointed chubbily out at the blue bay full of sailboats and side-wheelers. Gulls swooped along a fresh breeze, and a full-masted schooner sailing past Castle Garden into the narrows slowed as the wind shifted. Soon the boat was overtaken by a tramp steamer with a thin line of smoke blowing shoreward. Dora kept beaming at her two boys.

Hymie suddenly turned to her.

"And out there in Europe there's a war on. Lunatics! What could they want?"

Hymie wanted—four dollars. He had to repay the two dollars his daughter Naomi had staked him to with great trepidation, he had to (be fair) bring Golda home a dollar, and the fourth dollar would be for perfume for Dora. Plus fifty cents for himself for a rainy day, make it four-fifty that he wanted.

So now he stood himself on Sixth Avenue corner Fourteenth in his new business venture. Well, God was good and had declared all-year-round summer because Hymie Share was in love. And matching the weather was the trayful of color hanging from the straps around his neck. Ties.

"Ties ladies—stripes, flowers, rainbows. Ties for your hubbies, or even better your boy friends . . ."

They smiled, some stopped, with the pinched waists and the fruit on their hats. Salesmanship was his dish it seemed. And think of all his black years at sewing machines before his leg went and broke!

Yes, you didn't need to go to Chicago. Dora had changed his whole life right here at home! Who knew him wouldn't believe it nor from his lips would they hear it, but he'd tossed a whole night over the subject of money and early this morning had actually found his feet leading him bad leg and all to Houston Street and the treadle. But he'd managed to control that insane impulse, remembered his pal Horowitz with the nice ties sweatshop on Baxter Street, and picked up this display. He also could have picked up Miss Debby Horowitz, a wild one, devouring him with black shining eyes while she worked at the dining-room table with the rest of the Horowitzes, stitching in larcenous high-sounding Sixth Avenue labels.

"All day at this?" Hymie'd jollied her.

"Nights off though," she'd said.

But strange, how immune he had become to such good-enough animals.

Horowitz said ten cents a tie was a good peddling price, but for the fancy Sixth Avenue shoppers Hymie found ten cents meant cheap. A cop chased him, Hymie came back and there was another tie peddler there with a short beard and a black beaver hat. Both the beard and the hat had seen better days.

"Beat it," the guy said. "New York is too small for you?"

Hymie laughed. "Who said we're competitors? I got a fifty-cent line." But Hymie moved along to the middle of the block, outside The Big Store with the winter line of velveteens in the window and the dummy propped up against a papier-mâché tree. But look at that hat in the display—a sweep of roses—perfect for Dora! Now say, Captain of Industry there with the black sideburns, the cane and the long driving stride, pull out your handkerchief and drop that nice fat bankroll of yours on the sidewalk for a man who knows how to use it.

But the industrialist God keep him in good health did not require his handkerchief and the pleasures of his bankroll stayed his own problem. Eh, who cared? At thirty cents—suckers—Hymie's dime neckties sold, but how long it took, how you had to wheedle these people. Even without the gold watch in his vest Hymie's rumbling stomach told him it was way past noon already and he should be at Dora's. But forgetting the dollar for Golda what he made so far would only pay Naomi back with not enough left over to buy the hat.

"Here gents, here ladies, all patterns, all colors, pure silk from China!"

Finally, finally, with the golden dust of late afternoon teeming high on the buildings and the street of hacks, trolleys and autos in deep shadow, he sold two ties to a young dude and four to a not-so-young smiling lady and had a pocketful of silver and paper, enough even to give Golda some. He was folding up the tie tray when this round-shouldered runt stuck his face in. The man rubbed this tie, that one, he squinted.

"Mister, we're closing up for the day."

"What, you're rushing me?"

Hymie shut the tray and with the man's voice behind him—"Lunatic, misfit!"—dashed into The Big Store, past the fountain with the marble pillars around it, up the grand staircase and over to the hats. Out of habit he gave the salesgirl a wink and got a look hard as the Blarney Stone from those green Irish eyes.

"Who needs you, darling?" Hymie said pleasantly. "Just that hat downstairs in the window . . ."

Which naturally was not in stock. But for his money he found a genuine black velvet with a ruby plume.

"This one is fine, dear." Hymie paid her. "Just say thank you, and smile."

"Drop dead," the girl muttered.

Hymie put on a stern face. "Call the manager."

The girl went pale, Hymie laughed and strolled out with his tie case and the hatbox.

All of a sudden Sammy felt himself swung up from the go-cart and Mama didn't so much as look at him in her arms. Then they pressed indoors to a twilight where great big birds in cages shook wings, snapped beaks and hissed at him. He began whimpering and only then Dora kissed him, and even then in distraction.

"Sha darling, sha—"

She carried Sammy past the cashier, the shouting at the counter, the squawks from the coops . . . and no Joe till the back, in a stall with the slaughterer and a customer with a black shawl on her head watching to make sure that they didn't switch chickens on her. From a young pullet hanging upside-down on a hook over a trough blood burst on the knife. Dora's head swam, Sammy bawled, Joe turned and was angry.

"Wild horses can't drag you over the doorstep, and now I see you back here?"

"Nobody," Dora just managed, "knew where you were—"

Another salesman rushed in, another pushing housewife with a fat bun of hair, another doomed screaming hen. Sammy threw his head back and wailed.

"You waited this long," Joe pulled a nickel-plated watch out, "you couldn't wait five minutes longer till I got back front?" He lifted his hand and Dora flinched, she shut her eyes to be hit. Joe stared. "Are you sick? What's gotten into you?" He moved Dora forward with howling Sammy and shoved the pullet at a plucker up in her perch.

"I, I—"

But Dora didn't know how to lie. She wished that she was dead, like that chicken. She was without life anyway. All day long and no Hymie, all these hours to wonder, then fear, where could he be, what could have happened to him? What could she imagine but what had happened before, that that family of his had hurt him again, crippled him (God forbid!), the older daughter especially that she'd never laid eyes on but knew so well just the same. All right, being in love Dora was prejudiced. But leave Hymie out of it. An older sister to take a younger sister and cut her beautiful hair off for the sake of a wig business? That, Hymie had told Dora indignantly, had been Leah's shameless act on his dear little Naomi! How could such greed exist, to hurt others, possibly even—kill them? Worst, Dora didn't know what to do, how to find him, she didn't so much as know what number house he lived in on Hester Street. That was why she'd brought Sammy into the market, to have the visit over with and rush home in case Hymie was there. Now though, she saw God was punishing her. It wasn't enough to keep the house very clean. She began blinking.

"All right, all right," Joe softened, "no tears. Take him home. It's too busy anyhow," he couldn't help another criticism, "the night before Shabbos."

Free! She was full of new hope. But three steps into the mass of push-carts and women, peddlers in black coats and derbies, and a firm hand on her sleeve stopped her.

This elderly woman with a shopping basket and wisps of gray hair leaned to pinch Sammy's cheek. "And how are you, Master Kirschner?"

Embarrassing—Dora mumbled how are you—to know the woman, yet not to know who she was.

"Surviving," the woman said, "with war there, layoffs here, and my husband making a profession of that bad leg of his."

Golda Share! Dora clasped her own breast with a sinking fear. "Your husband's not well?"

"No, except for that he's fine."

Then where was he? Oh God, run over? While Golda went on, about . . . hair? . . . business? . . . her older daughter's? . . . Dora imagined horses, a lumbering wagon, screams, grinding wheels—

" . . . your friends don't wear wigs," Golda was asking, "they aren't that Orthodox?"

Golda smiled, and was waiting. Dora forced her lips up and vaguely shook her head.

"I didn't think so." Golda bent over gurgling Sammy, who was quite pleased with her. "Goodbye fat little darling!"

Dora pushed through the crowds. Across the way from her house she peered up at the roof wishing intensely to see Hymie waving to her, but the sun was blinding. She ran upstairs carrying Sammy, and at the landing—no one. She unlocked the door, yet couldn't bear to give up. Children yelled, a truck backfired, "Susannah," a woman called. But no footsteps, no Hymie trotting down from the roof. Sammy grunted to be put on the floor. Dora reached into the flat and handed him down to her immaculate linoleum, but he began crawling straight back out to his mother.

So she had to go in.

The slanting rays showed up dust on the dining-room table, but she hadn't the energy. Dully, she sat herself on a hard chair. Sitting you didn't see the dust, the mahogany shone.

Something terrible must have happened, what else could it be? And if this went on how could she stand it?

She sprang up and grabbed her coat from the wardrobe to search, to try to find him.

The doorbell grated.

Hymie slipped in—"Surprise!"—he held up the hatbox. "Open it, it's for you. And here . . ." From the tie case he selected a navy blue with light polka dots . . . "just right for your Joe, it's on me, big business, I'll tell you—" Then he saw her wet eyes.

He stepped back, he cradled that dear face in his palms. "Why?" his throat filled, seeing that pain, "why are you crying?"

"You're well," she barely could say.

He felt tears rising too, the first time ever for somebody else. "Stop, darling . . ." The things that he'd given her, that she hardly knew she was holding, he relieved her of, he set aside on a chair. "Look, I was your boy, now you're making a girl out of me. . . ."

And they laughed clasping each other's hands tight, and they cried . . . don't ask them why.

3

TWO YEARS AFTER (BUT LIKE A FOREVER) RIVKA SHARE'S Abraham he should rest in peace left this earth, Rivka came in from business with the pretzel basket sold out thank God, cold as the weather was. And what, a letter? Yes, her name on the envelope, all she could read in English, and on the stamp the King of England an old friend, not that she saw him that often. But how often—she opened to the Yiddish inside—did you see a Gentile with a beard since the war? She read, and thought, then realized that the landlady was still standing there with her well-nourished face, her curiosity, and her small smile to show that she wasn't curious. Rivka should sin by causing a fellow human to die from anxiety?

God forbid!

So Rivka said, "You'll find space here for an immigrant, my widowed cousin Gittel I haven't seen all these years since," she sighed, "I left the old country, Kadzyrnye? And oy—Gittel's Reisel is a poor orphan—you'll take them on trust until they become settled?"

The landlady—she enlarged her smile slightly—knew a good joke when she heard one.

"They're due soon?"

"Any day."

"Very fortunate, to get out with the war hardly over."

"Such fortune you shouldn't know who to wish on. They barely escaped with their lives from those murderers, the Reds and the Whites."

But from bitter experience the landlady knew this old woman with the widows! To this day it bit at the landlady's heart the way at no extra cost Rivka Share had moved that Bertha Axelrod into her room. Her room? Into the landlady's flat! Argument—if Mrs. Share for instance had claimed she'd rented a whole room, not just room for one person—that, the landlady could have easily dealt with. But the stream of soft words! A Jew must be charitable, a Jewish woman even more so, and especially to a widow only forty years old—such sorrow, with a boy to raise, a true Artur Rubinstein, Isidore Axelrod, remember that name—a musical genius! That had been the old lady's trick.

"A boy here too!" the landlady had cried out.

"Not here, of course not. In Europe to study."

Followed by effusive blessings and thanks before the landlady had known what was happening. Then a *nu*, and the conversation had been over.

So now—live and learn, "Reds, Whites, let my enemies mix their heads up with colors," the landlady escaped with her life also.

A fine woman, that landlady. With Abraham, with all his faults, Rivka had not had to deal with such fine women. But never mind, with a furnished room, what to eat, a coat to put on your back now in winter, and at almost eighty years old more or less, a person could not complain.

So she let the landlady go and kept the murder part of Gittel's letter to herself. She would shed a tear about it to Bertha, when Bertha came home. And in her room, a small room but big enough for a chiffonier, a wood stove, her bed, and the two chairs poor Bertha slept on, Rivka unwrapped her shopping—a cracked egg, a piece of fish, a thimble of butter—took a small pan out, a dish and a fork, and was ready to cook.

But that ruffians should come, soldiers they called themselves, and murder a darling man, Gittel's Elya. How could God make such creatures? Rivka remembered Elya as a little boy in their village, then more clearly as a young man with honest eyes at his wedding, that was how he looked in a picture in Rivka's drawer. Him, actually, she didn't remember well from the wedding. But herself—this minute she could see herself there in the hall with the company, the music, dancing, laughing! Now, she old, at the end of her lifetime, with her beautiful hands not so beautiful, they were speckled and trembling, and her own groom, her Abraham regardless, gone, and Gittel's poor Elya murdered. Who knows what sins we are atoning for?

The door opened and, though how far could you go in this room, Bertha rushed in, tall, thin, pale, just a shawl over her shoulders in winter, with her basket of merchandise—thread, needles—not that empty, her lips a rich blue from the cold and poor health, her blue eyes elsewhere, a driven woman.

But when Rivka clucked her tongue, "A bad day?" Bertha was calm. "Not so bad, Mrs. Share."

"You mean Mama."

"It's true, you're as kind to me as a mama could be."

"You're kind to me too, or else you'd say Grandma. You ate?"

"Yes. Do you have a toothpick?"

"An old woman warns you, God punishes liars."

"In this world, or the world to come?"

"The world to come, naturally. Where is there room for more trouble now?"

Both fondly smiled, and to explain her not unusual little white lie Bertha drew out of her reticule and offered Rivka—a letter.

"Good news?"

"Sweet and sour, as always."

"Better than mine. See—would you believe it?—tonight I have mail too. But first we'll eat, then you'll read your letter to me."

Bertha's eyes filled. "As if it weren't enough, your taking me in with no rent. I wouldn't, you understand, eat what you work so hard for and I can never repay, if not for . . . my Izzy. . . ."

On the stove the fish sizzled, Rivka divided a roll.

"You'll repay, how many times must I tell you? At my funeral, while I hover a minute till the blessings free this poor soul, remember I'm counting on you, you'll be my agent there—you'll be sure they have the right rabbi, and everything proper!"

Poor soul, they both thought. The poor soul was Bertha. Would she last to see Rivka's funeral?

As long as Bertha ate the scrap of fish and sucked the delicious warmth of her tea through the sugar cube that she held between her teeth, she could bask in this pure comfort and not think. But her thoughts came back full force, oppressive, like the hall oozing green mold where she rinsed their few dishes under the common faucet. One hundred dollars. Where could she possibly find one hundred dollars? But she had to find it, Isidore's teacher said that one hundred dollars was essential for Isidore's career. He had to give a recital if he was to establish himself as a prodigy. Now, peddling, Bertha saved six, sometimes eight dollars a week. But the World War that had made this windfall possible had raised food prices too, and she begrudged every penny she had to spend on such nonsense. Her earnings were just enough to pay for Isidore's room, board and tuition the three months he'd been on the other side. She had made up her mind to live on two rolls a day and some tea, and it had worked at first. Only now, the whole day long, her stomach grabbed into knots. All that she could think of was eating. A woman would say did she have a spool of this or that thread, and Bertha might stare and make the customer angry, "Madame does not answer questions?" or altogether lose her.

And the cold. Maybe she would have to give in and buy a brazier. But then there'd be the cost of charcoal to burn in it. If she had a spot in the sun there in Orchard Street to stand in with her merchandise, the winter was bearable. Still by four in the afternoon she'd be clenching her teeth against the vicious air. What would she do if what had happened today kept on happening? In midafternoon, with a hazy sun still in the sky, chills had suddenly run through her—uncontrollable spasms. She'd had to give up her good place on the corner and run into a tenement. There too icy dampness had knifed her shoulders, and a whiff of bread baking had brought her down to a cellar, then to a subcellar where the bakery was, with one bare bulb hanging, and the hot ovens.

They'd looked at her, the baker, his man helper and a young woman helper, at her . . . ghostly figure, her basket, her calm blue eyes. Some calm—it had taken all her willpower not to shiver in front of them.

The baker had nodded toward her basket. "You must be doing some business if you have to bring that down here."

But when Bertha had spoken, her teeth had knocked together. "I took a chill. Can I stay for a minute?"

"Do you cough?"

She'd prayed God give her strength not to. "Thank God, no."

Under the gas pipes there had been an upended fruit crate with the baker's black derby hat on it. He'd hung the hat on a gas meter. "Liebeleh, give her tea." He'd inspected a trayful of hot rolls and Bertha had thought she'd die looking at them, breathing in that awful sweet steaming fragrance. She'd been sure he would offer one, but she'd say no, she couldn't accept more for nothing. Then he'd passed the tray to his man helper in exchange for an empty, and—stupid woman—she'd felt aggrieved.

"Husband sick?" the baker had asked Bertha over his shoulder.

"He died eight years ago."

"No sons?"

"One," she'd said proudly, "studying music in Paris."

"Out of your blood."

"He's my blood. But he thinks his father left money."

"Out of your blood just the same."

The baker's young wife had laughed handing Bertha a glass of hot tea, "The big socialist. We have two children—"

"Boys," the baker'd said.

"—and he's planning another new world for them."

"He's a good man," Bertha'd said, "thank you both."

People were good to her. Of course, there was the landlady. Her ill will terrified Bertha whenever, like now, she had to pass through the flat from the outer hall to Mrs. Share's room. The woman had that peculiar expression, the stare of a cat with a sparrow just beyond reach. The woman could, when she wanted, throw Mrs. Share out and Bertha along with her. But so far she only watched, with that not quite a smile, and made you shudder. The landlady though wasn't that important. In a pinch Bertha could find some cellar to sleep in, like the one with that bakery perhaps. Her weak body was her worst enemy. Still a body could be useful, Jewish women became whores and stood on the Bowery. If she were younger that would be a way to make money.

Rivka was very angry at Isidore's letter. "That's some teacher he has. One hundred dollars! A crook I'm afraid. Should a mother go skin herself? What good would she be then? So you'll write and say, 'Dear Isidore, tell your teacher that we're poor people, you'll be a prodigy a little later.' "

Bertha was hardly listening. A glance had shown her that what this message from Liverpool to Mrs. Share meant was—now none of this dizziness, no fainting please, no outright begging!—these two cousins were on their way, she'd have to move out. And with the reality at hand, not just make-believe, her body worn out like one of those swaybacked draft horses with all its ribs showing told her that a single night in a cellar and in the morning she wouldn't get up. So she'd have to find a place of her own at two, three, four dollars a week. . . .

"What is wrong, darling?" Rivka laid a motherly hand on Bertha's. "You're not well?"

"I'm fine." She kept the blue-eyed gaze clear. "Don't worry Mrs. Share, I'll be out before they get here."

"Out? Out where? Shame on you Bertha, you thought that's what . . . why I showed you . . . Now be sensible mamaleh. Where would my cousins fit, say God forbid I didn't have you? One under the bed?"

The blue eyes stared, then all of a sudden seemed they would pop. Bertha caught at her own throat and lurched into racking coughs, spells, one worse than the other. Rivka knew that cough well. Her Abraham had died of the tailors' disease, fast, all at once. And while she was undressing Bertha to put her to bed, that crazy landlady—every misfortune—came banging on the door and would have marched in if Rivka didn't always take care to keep the latch on.

"You better get her out of here quick," the woman sounded high-pitched, insane. "This is not a pesthouse!"

"A person can't cough?" Rivka called good-humoredly. "And next will it be against the law to sneeze, God bless you?"

"No lung cases in my apartment!"

"Apartment, did you hear her? Well, Mrs. Abraham Share, what would your husband with his sour smile say to that? Without him you've come up in the world—not in a corner of a Clinton Street flat, but in an apartment!" The threats and mutterings died down and Rivka tucked Bertha in. "And you, Mrs. Axelrod, in Gan Eden mustn't your husband be proud of you?"

"Thank you, thank you," the blue eyes smiled weakly. "It's just a chill—"

Ah see, asleep, the poor thing, she couldn't hold her eyes open.

So good—Rivka put out the bedding and lay down on the two chairs in the dark—let her sleep for the both of us. How much do aching bones sleep anyway, eighty-five years of age? Now America was a fine place, where you look the policeman straight in the eye and for fifteen cents, oy, sometimes a quarter, he lets you stand with your basket, the same as in the old country only there it was kopecks. Her two sons, even Hymie, you never see in the synagogue. And the grandson, such a good boy as Danny was with his hard work and studies, to play the balalaika and sing—and not Jewish songs—was his heart's one desire. Just the same here at the Gentiles' Easter you don't shiver in the cellar while the pogromniks parade through the Kadzyrnye mud behind their evil-faced priest and their dolls and their saint's bone from the Polebsk monastery to beat out Jewish brains, to murder a Gittel's Elya for no reason. In America live die, cough don't cough, the worst that bothers you is a landlady.

Only so crowded, so full of Jews! Or if not one thing, then another. Orange, New Jersey, where her son Willie lived was a countryside like Kadzyrnye to make your heart melt, only so far away.

"Must you go so far, Willie," Rivka had asked him years ago, "such a fine tailor, to wait on roughnecks?"

"They're w-workingmen, M-mama, they're not r-roughnecks. And M-mama," he'd begged her with such pain, "d-don't m-mention t-t-tailoring any more, don't remind me of those p-p-prisons we grew up in—"

So what mother would want her boy unhappy, even if he must be so far away? But could you send two frightened women, with every cause to be frightened, to live with a bachelor over a saloon? Fine, if God were to use such a means of sending Willie a wife, but Reisel was too young and Gittel was too old. Also—why, Rivka did not know—Willie was not receptive to a wife. Last year she'd had Danneleh write Willie a postcard come have supper with your mama and meet a young very sweet widow, Bertha Axelrod, and Willie answered he'd come but please no ladies Mama. Well, God punishes pride and Rivka had been a very proud young woman with five sons, so God took three from her, and the fourth went to New Jersey.

Then where was left for the wanderers? One place, Rivka's son Hymie's house. And her granddaughter the young businesswoman Leah on Hester Street, how happy was she going to be with such a conclusion, that her father's house was that place?

Daredevils, women in love. First Dora had to bundle up Sammy and walk Hymie part of the way home in the dark, a love convoy. Then as their little troupe came closer and closer to spy street she kept calmly walking. Maybe with more peddlers slapping themselves to keep warm than there were last minute shoppers, she didn't recognize Hester Street. She wheeled the go-cart one-handed and the other hand was tucked under Hymie's embarrassed arm.

"Do you know where we are, mamaleh?" he asked her.

"Together."

In a world of her own. Of such stuff they make heroes. Hymie, his motto was run away and live to love another day. But at the corner a glance that the coast was clear and he removed the incriminating evidence in her little glove from his arm by way of his lips. Then he went through the motions of taking his handkerchief out and blowing his nose.

Just in time. Crossing from his house Mama came. So now he had three innocents, counting Sammy.

"Mama, you're branching out with two baskets!"

"Mine, and my friend's, she has a slight cold. And do you know, Hymeleh, even when she's better I think I'll still take out two. You can't imagine what a business I'm doing!"

"To spend on her own funeral," Hymie light-heartedly told Dora. "Isn't that so, Mama?"

"Ah," Rivka sighed, "to find the right place, the right rabbi. Last Tuesday Lazinsky from the Rutgers Street *shul* buried an old woman my age." She made a face. "A fine reputation, but in love with his own voice. It's not easy, young lady, even to have a funeral."

"Mama, do you know Kirschner the poultryman's wife?"

"Stay healthy, beautiful young lady with a fine son. . . . What is your name, little boy?" "Sammy." And wrapped up tight with his arms sticking straight out as he was, Sammy half-buried his face in Mama's fur coat while he kept a smiling eye on the grandma. "Modest," Rivka observed, "as a young man should be. And you have another, I see, soon on the way."

Dora blushed all over, but Hymie's mother was so nice! So Dora confided, since it was—she just knew it!—Hymie's love child she was pregnant with, "I hope," in nearly a whisper so Sammy whose cool cheek she stroked holding him close wouldn't hear, "I won't love the new one too much. I mean even more than—" Her eyes gestured.

"No no," Rivka said, "a mama loves all her sons. And if she should love one best? Tell me darling, your name is . . . Dora, in these hard times, for a friend, Mr. Kirschner might let you find a nice little pullet wholesale maybe every two weeks?"

Innocent number one exclaimed, "Why I'd be—"

"Mama, I'm surprised." Hymie should become a go-between for the chickens, and innocent number two Mama would praise him to his family? "Saving even on food? I, Hymie Share, tie salesman, will take care of your pullets, Mama." And he slipped Mama a quiet fiver.

"The tie business is going well, Hymie?"

Hymie laughed. Rain or snow you visit Dora in this fair weather trade. And hours? Variable according to cash on hand. "Better than the tailors' disease that God spared me from in my future, Mama."

Rivka pressed her son's arm, "Ah then, listen . . ." and told him a story of pogroms and two poor immigrants.

"Of course we'll take them in Mama. We'll have a hotel in the kitchen!"

"Young mother," Rivka said, "God send you many sons like my son here!"

"Oh how I wish it!" Dora was in an ecstasy.

Hymie laughed between his two admirers and gave the horizon another quick scan for spies. . . .

Danny on his usual mad dash home from work pulled up in a hurry and guiltily crossed the street at the sight of his old man with this girl friend at a broad-backed lady peddler's baskets. Only, what was Danny guilty of? *He* never put that big belly on her, though his goddam little hard-on starting up wished he had. But the open gall of the bastard, to haggle for gewgaws for his cunt on their own corner. Yet in spite of his old man that girl's face got Danny: sweet, innocent. Jesus, you saw it and didn't believe it. Were women like that?

But crap on the both of them—he was putting an end to this, once and for all. He was gonna bring Ma out and show her. Ignorance might be bliss, but who could stay ignorant about this shameless prick? Get rid of him, who needed him, throw him out in the street!

"Ma," he burst in, "put your coat on."

Golda said, "It's not cold here at the stove."

"You're going to see him with your own eyes—out there with his girl friend."

And for Danny's pains?

"When I need your advice master I'll ask for it. Right now with your permission I'm making supper."

And what did his sisters the wigmakers have to say while they were stitching hairs from the wrong end of the horse to nets stretched over wooden heads that fit right into this family? Naomi the weeper's blue eyes immediately filled as expected. But how about Leah the instigator? She'd sung Danny to sleep in his cradle with complaints about their old man and now her high sign was a headshake: No, lay off Ma.

Danny stood there indignant like a chicken ready for slaughter, not knowing where to head next. He lunged for his schoolbooks under the sewing machine.

Leah said, "Eat your supper first, Danny, don't be an infant," but Ma kept mum.

"Eat hell—what we need here is some backbone!"

Naturally, as if he were watching it all with himself main ham in a movie, he slammed the door. A wind like ice slammed him back so he gave the necessary curse, but neither wind nor dark of night could keep his eye from wandering to that corner. The corner was empty though—just bent passers-by—no old man, no cunty. But sure. That pair had to get back to their fun again. And here Danny stood in that guy's cast-off overcoat!

Danny ran back in, threw the coat off—"Not on my pelt!"—scattered his books back under the sewing machine and dug his life's savings out of his mattress on top of the wardrobe.

Leah—"Don't be a dunce"—took hold of him.

"Lemme go."

He rammed into the cold again in a thin freezing jacket with his scarf playing tricks in his face. He didn't give a damn. Next stop Mottke the Thief's on Orchard Street for a nice new coat to match his father's—except Danny'd worked and worked hard for his!

"God in heaven," Mottke mumbled, with his old horsy face, "the way you bang on the door is enough to give heart trouble. The cops, I thought." At the kitchen table the Mottke family stared up like idiots while Mottke took Danny through to the airshaft showroom where the stolen goods hung. Mottke struck a match but before he'd touch it to the gas jet, "You got money?" he had to ask.

Danny flashed the miniature bankroll. "Weighing me down."

"You're Hymie Share's boy?"

"I'm my boy. What's for sale?"

"What you want, is for sale."

To Danny's relief all Mottke had was for greenhorns—sleeves over the hands, or just reaching the elbows. Meanwhile the fence lectured you, with no extra charge.

"Why are you so angry, young man? . . . A good fit, don't exaggerate. . . . All right, look, here's a real buy, for a prince, with a belt in the back—"

What could Danny say? This was like custom-made. Yet . . . Though he dreamed of millions he didn't care that much about money and at ten bucks for a Fifth Avenue overcoat who could argue? Yet down to his guts he was against what he was doing, squandering his college and law school dough. And in the same guts he didn't believe there'd be law school, maybe not even college. What was the matter with him?

Mottke smoothed down the garment and stood back in admiration, envy even, of this face like an Irisher, a chip off the old block, with money in the pocket and his America. Mottke didn't keep mirrors where the racks were. Why confuse customers? But a fit like this you could show in the looking-glass. He dragged Danny to a bedroom, sighed and turned on still one more gas light.

Who was this third party Danny saw—another customer, another accessory in crime? Then Mottke also entered the picture—a mirror, and that was Danny himself, with a girl's face you could love?

"The girls," Mottke the mind reader said, "will be likewise easy for you."

Danny whipped around to his father's clothier. "What do you mean likewise?" And began ripping the coat off with the bottom button still buttoned.

"What could I mean?—oy God in heaven don't tear the garment—handsome goods handsome face oy oy oy!"

Halfway downstairs Danny could hear, "Come back young man—nine seventy-five, nine fifty! Oy, what could be eating him? . . ."

And right you are Mottke. Was Danny a kid to fly off the handle that way, or a guy sixteen years old? Again and again, Yom Kippur and January first alike, he did penance for furies like this, resolved to curb his own impulses, not to be like his old man. In half his daydreams he was counsel for the defense, loaded with arguments to save the next Lefty Louie or Gyp the Blood from the chair. The other half he was featured at Proctor's Twenty-third Street Theater, the sweet singer with the dreamy uke. But here's what he really was: a half-assed comedian who tried sincerity on God.

"Listen, self-control, not just because the Talmud says be hard to provoke and easy to pacify, but for my own good."

Then God was supposed to shake His head, "There's a smart honest boy, and a scholar into the bargain. I'll give him a hand."

But if Danny knew he wasn't a scholar and never would be one and not so smart either, God didn't know?

The wind banged in his face, his scarf flapped, he had to hold his cap down with raw fingers. Snow began dancing and his insides were growling. But it wasn't the weather or his belly that misted his eyes. The Orchard Street peddlers were packing up and the sidewalks emptying fast in the dark. And he?

He needed Sylvia to sit with in some warm place and tell this stuff to, hold her hands, soak up her sympathy. . . .

Some sympathy. But he raced to look for her.

The Settlement Saturday night dance Sylvia's dancing, Sylvia's laughing, Sylvia's singing along had all been for the benefit of Cheesy Charlie the cheese salesman. But why criticize Charlie, not that Charlie would give a damn. So Charlie wasn't a sparkler—a steady guy, old, in his twenties, with a good job selling cheese. Who sparkled, Danny? They'd begged him to come on sing and, the melancholy Dane, he'd said "Not in the mood." Or did Sylvia sparkle, for that matter? There were three ways you could walk alongside her: in dead silence, or else you could wisecrack and she'd compliment you on your dry humor, Danny the dry humorist, or—Sylvia was as good as a song sheet—you could listen to her render the popular tunes of the day. So what was so great about Sylvia? His horny pal Lefkowitz said that the red hair catches the eye and the big tits do the rest. Don't lie, Danny didn't mind those breastworks a bit, but it was that face that got him, that looked . . . intelligent, as if she could be . . . loving. And she could be. Maybe she'd felt sorry for him toward the end Saturday night. She'd joked, "Own the subway yet, Danny?"

"I got a small deposit down on a wheel."

"I love your dry humor, Danny. Let's dance."

A kind word from Sylvia and up pressed his hard-on in joy. But in that crowd who could see, and her fragrance had been like heaven. She gathered her tawny hair like a crown, and she was slim, oh, with slim ankles and feet!

At the Bowery now he posted himself beside the kiosk under the El with two cents in his fist. In case she did come down from the station on her way home from work he was buying a paper. Not that it fooled her. Early this week, "I bet you must know all the news," she'd given him that sly smile of hers.

But waiting for her he broke into song—*Sylvia let me pay the debt*—he was so happy.

He was in voice tonight too, though at home he'd gotten into the habit of singing low because he didn't want his old man to hear him. Jesus, he loved the snow flickering down, the glints on the derby hats, the zircons like diamonds in the jewelry windows, girls' ankles, their narrow shoulders bent against the cold that kept him shifting from foot to foot—he loved it all!

Of the kiss
I stole from thee . . .

A girl clapped her hands right in front of him and Danny gaped like a man who'd just waked up.

Sarah Bialek—"Don't you recognize your own cousin?"—gazed overjoyed at him. She was cute too, the whole five feet of her, with the doll of a face and brown curls snow-tipped now that fringed a red cloth hat, but this finished Sylvia for tonight because Danny hated that sort of thing, talking to one person and keeping a lookout for another. That was Sylvia's specialty.

Danny said, "How are you, third cousin twice removed?"

Sarah smiled, "You do the removing, not me."

"I thought it was fate."

" 'I am the master of my fate'—with a little outside assistance."

"You don't need any assistance," he kidded her, "an expert bookkeeper like you."

"For what I have in mind I need assistance."

"What do you have in mind?" he asked innocently.

"Were you waiting for me?" Sarah kept teasing him.

"I uh," Honest John stammered.

"Dope, you're supposed to say yes. But you shouldn't be waiting for anybody in this cold, dressed like that. You could get pneumonia and die. Then I wouldn't speak to you any more."

They both giggled, and Danny thought what the hell.

"Call for you after supper, okay? We can take in the show at the Fourteenth Street Roof Garden."

"You won the lottery!"

"Nah, I quit school tonight. I'm spending my savings."

He showed his money and she looked quickly around.

"Put that away—do you want your pocket picked? And you put that money back in the bank, you are not quitting school!"

"How many times must I tell you, Sarah? I stink at the underlying causes."

Sarah laughed. "You just need some coaching. Listen, come home with me, we'll have supper. My mother and father are in the store."

Danny grinned: now he had her. "And skip school?"

Sarah threw her head back to laugh this time. "No, don't skip school. I'll see you later—in your overcoat."

"I can't wear that, it was my father's. We had a big fight at home, me and Ma, over one of his girl friends. I mean it was one-sided, with me cast as usual as the idiot son."

"Poor Danny." Sarah patted his arm. "Don't think about your father so much, think of yourself. Meanwhile, till you buy a new one, put on the coat."

Now why couldn't Sarah be Sylvia?

At school before class Mr. Komsky the history teacher with the joking eyes and thick hair was in the hall with the teacher next door.

" . . . do is try," Mr. Komsky shrugged, "to tell 'em what's what."

Danny wished he knew what was what—about anything. His family had him cast for genius and when he denied that he was they called it modesty. Sure, daydreams, banner headlines: VERDICT FOR STANDARD OIL OF NEW JERSEY, MAJORITY OPINION BY CHIEF JUSTICE SHARE. But for his mother, his sisters, his cousin Sarah—even Grandma for chrissakes—that wasn't a daydream, that was things to come. And here in History, the lawyer's subject, he could learn facts but never figure out why. Gee . . .

Oh sweet Sylvia, know thou this . . .

As a flourish to the under the breath lyric, his empty stomach trumpeted up a belch. Lazarus an older guy next to Danny shot him a stare—and remember Lazarus was hard of hearing from a going over from the pogromniks before he came to America.

"Repletion," Lazarus scolded him, "no wonder you can't concentrate on your schoolwork."

"Just the opposite," Danny cracked. "I'm a prisoner of starvation."

"That'll take you far too. You were born here so you don't know your advantages. But let me tell you, ten years ago I disembarked from an Ellis Island barge and it was like the gates of heaven opening up."

Danny said, "I like the U.S.A.," though he'd never given it much thought one way or the other.

"And the U.S.A. doesn't owe you any thanks for liking it," Lazarus said.

But the majority of the class were bedbug boys and not such boys either, twice Danny's age. They knew all the whys and laughed Lazarus down like a freak. Lazarus'd challenge them what was wrong with America and no matter how many facts or statistics he cited they'd keep repeating, "Too many bedbugs," till one night Danny got sore. "Scratch yourselves quietly why don't you." So Lazarus took Danny under his wing. Still the reds did have a catchy theme song they marched around Union Square May Day.

A-rise ye prisoners of star-va-tion . . .

That sent the thrills down Danny's spine, especially during his eighth hour of typing absence reports at the Rapid Transit Harlem Division time-keepers' office. Near six one evening the timekeeper Fernald overheard "The International," sotto-voiced as it had been.

"Hey," Fernald announced to the rows of bent backs, "we've got a socialist in our midst."

No one was interested. Fernald was the office drunk, Danny worked hard and—give him credit with these Quinns and Kellys—at least he didn't look Jewish. He'd checked in two years ago with his name, face and recommendation from Shannon the Suffolk Street district leader and except the timekeeper Mr. Feinberg they'd taken it for granted he was an Irish kid. Danny'd said yes to Mr. Feinberg's conspirator question *"Bist a Yid?"* and Mr. Feinberg's side of the mouth follow-up had been, "Keep it under your hat, they never forgive you for it." But Danny'd said, "I got nothing to hide." "Help yourself," Mr. Feinberg had shrugged. And who wanted swarthy little Mr. Feinberg to hide behind, the lunch hour Jew peddling costume jewelry, condoms, and dirty pictures he'd drive Danny mad with a glimpse of? Nobody else had asked Danny what his nationality was but after a while Mr. Byrnes the supervisor began showing him off to the higher-ups as "My excellent Jewish office boy." So Danny's would-be protector Mr. Feinberg must have spread the word.

Fernald had kept it up that day though with "If you don't like it here" and so forth and so on till Mr. Byrnes had shut him up. But the half-hour to closing, Danny'd typed away daydreaming red flags and barricades with himself personally mowing down Fernald.

"Death!"

That shout out of Mr. Komsky brought Danny back to class with a throbbing headache.

"Learn from those fellows," Mr. Komsky preached smiling, singsong like a rabbi, "learn from the enemy."

The Reformation was the topic, the fellows were Calvin, Luther and Knox, according to Mr. Komsky a great double play combination. While Danny'd been wool-gathering, the socialist Sohmer had claimed that they'd reformed papal corruption to do their own exploiting.

So Mr. Komsky'd howled "Death!" like an Old Testament prophet and given Danny the usual headache.

Mr. Komsky sat at the edge of the desk and confided that with his City College degree in his pocket, the back pocket, inconspicuously, he'd wanted to see the world. So he'd shipped out on a freighter as seaman tenth class—a special rating for City College men. When third mate Flanagan observed that Mr. Komsky was a man of the people, the Chosen People, he chose Mr. Komsky to scrub his way over the ocean blue. And what if the cook had a tendency to flavor seaman Komsky's food with a dash of galley floor? A day on your knees and it tastes better that way.

But land ho—Geneva ahead!

The Marxists guffawed and Danny lifted his brows at Lazarus, who dryly whispered that the Swiss have no coastline. Now Jesus Christ, Danny knew that. What was wrong with his brain, outside of this pounding headache?

In the Geneva public gardens—park, that meant—velvet lawns, plenty of flower beds but no bedbugs, two or three bees to sting you into the realization that the marble frowner on a pedestal one end of the blue shining pool is John Calvin.

"The question is, class, why is he frowning? And the answer is he knows something not even Sohmer knows."

Sohmer dared Mr. Komsky with a tilt of his fat face. "What don't I know?"

"That we die."

"That's news?"

"Till you live as if you know it, it's news."

"Ah please, Mr. Komsky. Calvin just lived to look down from heaven and enjoy everyone else burning in hell. We can do without frowning spirits like that."

Now how in the name of Jesus did Sohmer figure out all this stuff? Danny's temples hammered away. And suddenly Mr. Komsky was on top of the desk waving his arms like a monkey!

"Predestination, exploitation, success—that's the enemy's idea of life. But don't underrate him—that's the life that you're living." He jumped down and chalked on the blackboard.

CALVIN = DEATH!

"So? You prefer life? Live for life. How many lives have you? Nine like a cat?—but don't go home and throw your cat off the roof. You've got one—count it—one. And what makes that one important? Death! Then perform that difficult feat, walk that tightrope—and without landing on my head." The finger swooped down at Danny and the jolt as he ducked sent his brain crashing. "Live for that one life, Share! Not mine," Mr. Komsky chanted, "not Lazarus', not even Sohmer's—yours!"

The Marxists—"Anarchy, anarchy!"—went into an uproar. The pair of class anarchists—"The only solution!"—were shouting back. But up on the desk again Mr. Komsky with windmill arms outshouted the bunch of them.

"Facts, facts—stick to the facts!"

At the end of the period Danny asked Mr. Komsky what he'd meant, exactly.

"Why, you have to figure out what means most to you with least harm to others—and do it."

If that was all it was, anyone knew that.

But Mr. Komsky left you so worn out that Danny sat dazed through Latin. In Math he put his example on the board and spent the rest of the hour salivating over whether he could hold out for Sarah's—she was sure to insist that he have supper—or give in and buy a hot dog from the Greek outside the school.

Danny voted to hold out but his stomach voted to give in.

In a brown glint of slush under the school portico he slung the dangling sauerkraut into his mouth, but the headache sickened his appetite. Another fact as he tramped back to the East Side in a soft hiss of snow was that he'd been a damn fool to leave that overcoat off.

But how could Sarah answer the fact that he hadn't had the faintest idea of what Mr. Komsky'd been driving at, simple as it was, till Mr. Komsky had told him! Crazy Komsky, waving his arms up there like Jeremiah. Danny kept giggling and every giggle stabbed at his brain.

Maybe that plus snow in the face took him a block beyond Sarah's in spite of the fact that her building stood out like a lighthouse next to the stretch of rubble where the tenement next door had collapsed last year, burying seven. Sarah lived on the ground floor and you could see her lights on. He went in though he'd sooner have taken his stupid head home to bed.

He rang, knocked, rang—and nothing. The hallway crackled with noise, but not from Sarah's. In the empty lot with plenty of skidding he climbed a snow-piled slag heap under her window and looked in.

Asleep!—her arm on the dining table, her head on her arm, cute, all dressed up in blue. He trotted back, rang, knocked, then banged like a maniac and the door gave way—and Sarah slept. His aching head spun. Gas? The jet whispered evenly—no leak. He crouched close to make sure that she was breathing.

She was breathing, her cheeks were sleep-flushed. Her breasts rose and fell.

Top speed so she shouldn't wake before he could beat it he tore a sheet from his notebook. *Dear cousin twice removed, you sleep so nice I couldn't bear waking you.* A lie, what the hell. He stuck the note in the crook of her arm, whipped out the gold watch Uncle Frank'd given him for becoming a man and hurried to the East Side Settlement in case Sylvia was there.

Nobody was there except the usual mob of intellectuals just out of the lectures—*From God to Evolution, Love in Shakespeare, The American Purpose*—also the usual, on the bulletin board every night.

" . . . murdered the Czar and his family."

"I'll light a candle for the son of a bitch."

"Excuse me, murder begets murder."

The noise, the pushing—guaranteed headache in case you were short of one. Arms flailed, you got poked by elbows. The big corridor was nice and warm though; Danny hated to plunge back into the cold again.

But he did, and Sylvia's house also met all his expectations. She was there, Cheesy Charlie was there, long Solly Brown the condom kid from the drug business was there, and her parents were there listening from the kitchen. As usual she gladly admitted Danny to the retinue for an hour of wisecracks, dumb cracks or no cracks, the high point of which was a joke so good by Solly that Solly laughed till his nose ran which sent even steady Charlie into hysterics. What more could you ask, a piece of green cheese from the moon?

Sarah woke from so thick a sleep she thought she'd overslept and was late for the office. But sitting up? She stared at the couch and the little cactus pot on the cut-glass cabinet, and . . . Danny—

This piece of paper fluttered down to the linoleum.

She read it, and—oh my God!—rushed for her hat and coat, forgot galoshes and went three wet steps through crusted snow without them when her cousin Leah, Danny's guardian angel—of death, the way she looked at you if you came near him—occurred to her. So she detoured to Papa's grocery for an unburnt offering to Leah. Papa sat reading a paper behind the counter on the store's only chair, Mama bundled up like a barrel sat on a box in front of the counter with the other barrels—of beans, chick peas, polly seeds—and they both breathed frost.

Only in Sarah's family did both parents stay in the store all the time because the husband had to have company.

"Close up, folks. Even the mice won't come out to shop for cheese in this weather."

Papa read, Mama breathed frost. Of their three children only two, their sons the lawyers (when visiting), required answers. But when Sarah dug deep into the polly seeds poor Papa's eyes that were crawling out at life anyway all but reached over the counter at her.

"So much, for the house?"

"It's okay Papa—for cousin Golda's house, not our house."

"Since when cousin Golda?"

"She runs after the boy there," Mama explained.

"Thanks, Mama."

"That ladies' man," Papa squeezed his face up, "like the father?"

Sarah—expense was no object—also scooped up a bagful of coffee beans, pushed both gifts into her pockets, gathered the dishes from her parents' supper that she'd brought down before, and teased Papa with some steps toward the door.

"What," Papa rose to the occasion, "stealing the merchandise?"

Sarah—"That much less for me to chip in this week"—weighed and paid for the parcels.

"Instead of wild goose chases going on seventeen," Papa tied the score fast, "take this advice since you won't take any other. Find a rich man to marry. A poor one you'll flay alive!"

Now look at these shoes full of snow. The second time out of the house and still no galoshes. But it was late, she shouldn't have been going to Danny's at all. What they'd think of her. But falling asleep! How could anyone be so stupid? Darn that job of hers with today's ten hours' billing, darn cooking, darn cleaning. Yet she still had to smile over that angelic boy and his note. He was so funny, handsome and lovable!

On Hester Street in the cold stink of his hallway she unbuttoned each shoe and tapped an avalanche out. Then she took a deep breath—but not through the nose—and twisted the bell key. The whir hadn't died down before Naomi threw the door open.

"Oh," Naomi was close to tears, "it's you—"

"Crying? I can't be that bad."

Naomi sat Sarah down knees to knees with her on the two cots that filled up the sisters' room.

Naomi—"I thought you were Phil"—gave Sarah a letter from under the pillow. "We're getting married as soon as he's discharged. . . . Don't look at my finger, Sarah, there's no ring—"

Phil was in the American Expeditionary Force and they'd only met at an East Side Settlement House dance just before he was shipped. Even then he'd wanted to marry her, except without the ceremony. He'd said there wasn't time—and there wasn't—so they'd have the ceremony when he came back.

"You didn't believe that, did you Naomi?"

"I believed it, I still believe it, but you know I couldn't do anything like that."

"Whew!"

Now Phil was fighting the Bolsheviks, though as far as Sarah could read he was doing none of the fighting and all of the complaining—marches, rations, snow, cold, and no one spoke English, especially the English—love, photo enclosed.

"Where's the photo?"

Naomi produced it from the next-to-the-heart shirtwaist pocket. You saw a log fence, a front yard and a hut, all covered by a white fluff of snow and a dull sky. A bleak scene, and Phil well-wrapped in the foreground, with a heel on the bottom rail and his elbows on the top rail of the fence, with his military coat slanting toward and his chin slanting away from the camera, didn't enliven the prospect. What could you say?

Sarah said, "You're in love," and gave her cousin a kiss.

Naomi brightened immediately.

"How did you know?"

"Gypsy blood. But why were you crying? The letter doesn't say to expect him yet."

"I was wishing so hard for him and then the bell rang. We had a tumult before. My grandmother is wishing some European cousins on us and my mother agreed and there's no room to breathe here as it is. I have to marry and get out."

And Naomi was nineteen, three years older than Sarah—a woman, supposedly. Sarah listened for Danny, but the muffled talk and occasional shouts all came from the airshaft, not a sound from inside.

"Home alone?"

"Are you kidding? The wig factory's full blast in the kitchen—Ma and Leah. I was at it too—and I'm so sick of it! But we're running out of orders, no more Orthodox immigrants thank God. We're starting an entirely new business and I can hardly wait—electric lamps, and lampshades. Leah's boy friend knows the electric part. Do you think Phil is handsome? I mean, in a different way?"

"Handsome is as handsome does. But why wait for Phil if you want to marry and get right out?"

"What about love?"

"Here," Sarah held out a bag, "have a polly seed on that."

In the middle of the room the sons in skullcaps and prayer shawls, so many good sons, sang the prayer for the dead around their mother's bier. Rabbi Nachman with glasses and closed eyes prayed at the head of the coffin draped black with a white Star of David. Further back other men prayed, and still further, on plank benches along the walls, the women sat weeping, moaning, with black shawls.

The rabbi was dignified—good; and slightly gray—also good; not too young but not too old either, a perfect age for a rabbi he should live and be well on the day God forbid you need him. He began the speech for the departed, "A woman of valor," and Rivka shed a tear too, as much as you could do for a stranger. More and more Rabbi Nachman pleased her, enumerating the virtues of the old woman who had died. If he was slightly long-winded, he was sincere, and not with general statements that meant nothing. This was a woman who had raised sons, and not simply sons but pious sons. They stood here, you saw them, with their loss in their faces. And not simply pious sons, but honest hard-working sons, like Rivka's sons. And not simply pious and honorable and hard-working sons, good parents themselves, but loving sons. And while we are not commanded to love, only to honor—Rabbi Nachman quoted the Torah chapter and verse, and . . . ahh . . . added three references from the Talmud—in this instance the love could not be helped for a mother who had earned love so well. She came to America a stranger, a greenhorn, and she protected her children until they could protect themselves. She worked beside her husband, the rabbi said, and the rabbi could and did tell how this woman worked, how she suffered, how she sacrificed herself gladly for family, for friends, even for strangers. And holiest of all, she didn't know that she sacrificed. What we must call sacrifice, to her was a joy!

Now Rivka's eyes really filled. She had found him! She had found her rabbi for her own funeral! Well, this woman who died yesterday—may God preserve her good soul in heaven—clearly she was a saint. But a rabbi who could do a saint justice you could also count on to say the best for a sinner.

The men raised the coffin, they carried it out, the rabbi followed swaying and chanting, then the rest of the men went, then the women. Ah, Rivka wished she could say a word or two to the rabbi right now, to tell him, fine beautiful dignified man, that she wanted him at her funeral, not for charity, thank God she had money saved, but to put her soul at rest as he had done for this woman this morning.

Only, outside, it was not proper to interrupt the rabbi beside the hearse with one of the sons. The mourners helped one another over the snow into machines to the cemetery: so modern, enclosed like real carriages! Though to tell the truth, for Rivka's part she would have liked old-fashioned carriages and black shiny horses with a black plume waving when they walked and shook their head yes. But the hearse pulled away with its chained wheels churning the snow, then the other machines, and they went slowly, dignified. Rothschild himself in fact could have asked for no better. . . .

Aahh!

It was like waking up, back in the raw day with snow banked in the gutter, but Rivka could hardly wait to share the good news with Bertha.

"My rabbi is found! Tonight," Rivka dragged out the baskets and beamed at her young friend, "you'll hear all about it."

"I overslept." The poor weak child pushed her leg out from under the featherbed. "Today I take my own basket."

"Mistress," Rivka said, with a warted hand on her friend's chest, "you'll give an old woman battle?"

Bertha cried; she cried lately.

"We'll take care of you," Rivka said, "and of Isidore too."

Bertha lay back and stared at the smoky ceiling with plaster shreds hanging. "I must really be dying," her voice was calm again, "if you tell me these impossible things."

"With such dying the Angel of Death would have to find a new business!"

But through snow flurries in a cold that could freeze your heart to an icicle Rivka and her two baskets went not to the pretzel bakery but in the other direction. At the Henry Street Nurses' Settlement she gave the young lady Bertha's name and address.

Rivka said, "You were so nice to my husband. But I called you too late then."

The next day Rivka set up business on the snow at the foot of her own stoop, she shouldn't miss the nurse. First of all the way Bertha could brood now, and despair, you didn't scare her in advance with the Settlement. Then you had to hear what the nurse said, or Bertha might make up a white lie. And then, God forbid, who knew what would happen if their crazy landlady had to let a nurse in?

"Here pretzels, Jewish people, to warm the mouth and make the stomach rejoice. . . . Here ladies, all color spools, sharp needles that stitch by themselves. . . ."

A good thing Rivka did set up trade. The nurse with her black satchel didn't come till it was dark almost, a gloom that made you fear the worst.

"Tiptoe, please," Rivka whispered to her, "we have a landlady."

Bertha sat up straight. "I sent for no nurse."

"But darling, she's here already, so many flights. Don't disappoint her."

What could Bertha do but smile, though, "I'm sure I won't," she said bitterly.

But the nurse said, "The red throat's not serious. You only need a good meal."

"I eat well."

"She tells white lies, young lady," Rivka put in a friendly two cents.

The upshot was Bertha had to report to the Settlement next day.

Rivka asked in the morning, "Can I trust you to go, darling?"

"I have no other hope, Mama."

And even that hope, that the Settlement might do something for Isidore, how much of a hope was it? Did they have money there for piano recitals?

And downstairs in that razor air if Bertha hadn't had Rivka to lean on she would have fainted. Then between the walk to the Henry Street Settlement and the time they spent there, it was a lost day. Worse than lost. Bad enough the insult of a bag of food Rivka accepted, bad enough the Settlement woman nagging Bertha that to live you must eat. But who needed that fine advice to bring Isidore home from Europe and let him help support her, New York had music schools!

". . . and she just would not understand," Bertha kept shaking her head to Rivka all the way to Clinton Street, "that you cannot work at a job and be a musical artist at the same time."

To show their heart was in the right place the Rapid Transit Harlem Division gave you five minutes of company time to wash up in before you knocked off at six. Danny the sport gave 'em back two of those five tonight finishing what he had in the typewriter. Covering the machine and putting away tomorrow's reports only took forty-five seconds, but Mr. Byrnes at the head desk killed the rest with the wave of a hand.

"Bad news, Danny." He passed the week's big twelve bucks over. "We're letting you go."

Danny was stunned.

"Did I do something wrong?"

"Nothing personal. We're just cutting down. In fact drop in tomorrow. I'll have Miss Myer type you a reference . . . oh, and you better let me have your subway pass now."

So the next day Danny had to ride the El uptown on his own nickel. And he had to stand too till Forty-second Street, so the Company couldn't be that down on its uppers. Sliding the ice downhill on the gray day toward the train yards, he happened to overtake that kid Reilly the beanpole who sat on his ass up in the Planning Department, planning his horse picks for the New Orleans Fair Grounds. He was a careful worker, this Reilly, with his desk facing the door. The door opened, the drawer opened, in slid the Racing Form till he saw whether friend or foe went there. Such were the requirements of his boss, Mr. Kehoe the architect. Reilly was errand boy, sometimes downtown to the main office with blueprints but mainly to buy the architects cigarettes or lunch or some beer in the saloon in case they felt thirsty.

"Too bad, huh Reilly? You got some new job in mind?"

Danny's blue eyes showed sympathy, Reilly's showed suspicion.

"What's wrong with the job I got?"

"Didn't they tie the can on you yesterday?"

Now Reilly's thin vacant face looked really worried.

"No. Why the hell should they? I do my duties. You hear anything?"

Odd. Danny's brains danced in such anger that he could hardly see straight. His former boss Mr. John Francis Byrnes marched into the office with the gall to give him a cheerful good morning and for better or worse Danny had no voice to reply with. Yet all the while there was this midget perched in his head that wanted to know why all the fuss over a job he hated? But an hour of waiting for Mr. John Francis Byrnes and even the midget was ready to call it a day.

Then the very second Danny's thighs flexed for the stomp through the office gate and fuck you Mr. Byrnes, the boss calmly dictated the letter. Miss Myer a well-stuffed type exactly Danny's old man's taste took Mr. John Francis Byrnes's dictation both on and off duty so they said. But heading back to the typewriter she had a wink for the condemned man and when the letter was ready she hung out her arm, squeezed his claw with her shirtwaistful lurching up in his face and with a miss you forever expression in the big brown eyes she swore that she'd miss him.

Now what the hell was that for? One thing he knew—since he was able to lie thanks, he'd miss her too—he had his voice back.

So at Mr. John Francis Byrnes's desk he enjoyed the tan thinning top of the boss's head till the pale no longer friendly eyes were kind enough to tilt up.

"I was just wondering," Danny croaked while the midget jumped back in place and announced, hey, you're turning baritone! "how come I was laid off and Reilly upstairs wasn't?"

"That's life. And let me give you a tip, Buster. Keep complaining and you won't get very far."

Danny was close to tossing back the reference letter for Mr. John Francis Byrnes to stick up his ass, but the midget advised him don't be a shmuck.

With the troops coming back and all these older guys looking for work, it turned out that the shmuck was the midget. Danny couldn't find a job anywhere.

"So you know what that letter's good for," he told cousin Sarah twice removed a Saturday afternoon she caught him under the El again waiting for Sylvia.

"Sure—lunch at my house," she took him by the hand, "and this time you're not getting away."

"Who wants to? No school Saturdays."

"Aren't we lucky school is an Orthodox Jew?"

The way she made Danny laugh!

The cold sun in the icy blue sky stretching over the tenements sliced out perfect shadows of the El pillars and tracks. Danny had his cap pulled way down and his collar way up as they walked, but while the winter air skinned the back of the hand Sarah held, Danny's palm sweated in hers and embarrassed him all hell. Sarah wasn't embarrassed though, she just held on.

"You bought a new overcoat," Sarah observed.

"You mean tent. You want to join me inside?"

"Any day."

"You'd fit too. Your idiot cousin. I was ashamed to go back to Mottke the Thief, so I wound up with this."

"You'll grow into it—"

"So my mother said and I yelled at her."

"—by 1929."

They went into one of their giggling fits.

Sarah's ma fat-faced cousin Mary with the crinkly brown wig mumbled that her daughter had to cook French toast for lunch on the Sabbath with an iceboxful of things to eat.

"But she works half a day on the Sabbath, cousin Mary."

Cousin Mary intoned, "The Talmud says work is an exception."

"Mama eavesdrops on the Talmud," Sarah giggled, and she and Danny were off again, choking, because she got in, "Ssh, no laughing when my papa's asleep—or awake."

When Sarah's father strolled in yawning after his nap the free lunch was over but he could take in the remains still on the table and he gave Danny a nice surly nod.

"He looks just like his father," Mr. Bialek described the specimen he was looking at, "to the boyhood gray in the hair! Also a lady-killer, I see."

"Wanted by the police in six boroughs," Danny said.

"And with Share's exact same dry humor."

Sarah loudly wanted to know if Danny happened to have his ukulele stored away somewhere in that overcoat.

"What for?"

"The Fourteenth Street Roof Garden. Remember? You did me out of it last time, when I fell asleep. Amateur matinee today."

"What do you think, I won a lottery?"

Sarah's eyes opened wide as if she'd just won one. "He remembers what

I say! But I win every week—the Saturday afternoon prize in my office. See?" She took out her pay envelope, while her mother watched with pained eyes. "One dollar I keep." Sarah offered it to him.

"I'll take you," Danny was shamed into saying. "Who needs your dirty money?"

"See, Mama, don't have an apoplexy," Sarah laughed. "We'll stand in the back, Danny, and maybe we won't have to buy anything."

At the Roof Garden the amateur act before Danny wasn't that bad. The guy juggled, tap-danced and sang—simultaneously. Yet the hoots and catcalls were awful and a pro with a hook yanked the poor guy off the stage. And look at those meatfaces with derbies with their dames and their booze down there at the tables under the fake sheltering palms.

"Not me," Danny told Sarah in the wing opposite. "Let's go."

"Not you. They'll love you."

A few trial strums to make sure Danny wouldn't wipe out the instrument and the band's banjo player lent Danny a uke, the emcee winked at the crowd, "A sweet singer from Belfast," and Sarah's Sarah-killer went on so grim, so handsome, so cute she could have run out and kissed him. The crowd laughed and he looked back at her what was so funny, so she blew a kiss, and he strummed, and he sang.

Be kind when you hear me sigh,
I'm a roman-tic kind of a guy,
Sure as there are . . . heavens above,
We were meant for love . . .

The front tables clapped, the back ones hadn't heard him too well—but a sport at a table halfway along between the wall and the pillars stamped and yelled like a cheerleader, then turned and pointed.

"My son the sweet singer!"

People laughed, but there stood the tie salesman, next to his big-bellied whore, the schnapps glasses and, on his whore's lap, her baby busy smearing its face with ice cream.

Danny ducked back in the wing, where Sarah kissed him and he hardly noticed. "Come on, let's beat it," he said. But she didn't budge except to kiss him again. "I said—" he started over.

"We're staying for your first prize. You're only the escort."

"My drunk and disgusting father's out there with his broad and her kid—maybe his kid for all I know."

"Then don't say bad things about your kid brother. I like your father, he claps so loud."

"That just proves that you're female."

"And proud of it."

"I wouldn't be so proud."

But Danny peeked out front and his father must have come to his senses, that table was empty. And when the crowd picked the winners, Danny's claps did win third prize—a bunch of bananas from the Roof Garden's fake banana tree.

"Have a banana," Danny told cousin Sarah.

Sarah—"Gladly"—peeled and munched it on the way home while she planned Danny his singing career.

"Yeah sure," Danny said.

"You'll see. You just do what I say—about everything. Of course," Sarah added, "you'll keep going to school."

"Hey, you're practical!"

"That just proves that I'm female."

At Danny's house too after he left Sarah—kisses, pride and banana-peeling by Ma and his sisters. No career planning though. That encouragement—okay Mr. Komsky, what's the underlying cause?—came privately later from his old man.

"Beautiful! Didn't I always tell you sing loud? And still louder will be still better. The Palace is a big house, when you get there. Third prize only—they must have tin ears! By the way, no sense mentioning me there clapping. It was on my route, so I dropped in to see what the talent was."

"Why should I mention what Ma has no interest in hearing? I won't mention that woman either."

"Woman? What woman?"

"Come on, Pa. The woman with the kid, Kirschner the poultryman's wife."

"Kirschner the poultryman's wife?" His old man looked honestly mystified. "I never saw her there."

No wonder Ma had no interest in hearing. This guy could twist you into a pretzel.

But to get along that's what you need: absence of shame. Sure, daydream: the silver-toned minstrel inundated by swooning girls and you turn them all down for Sylvia. But where do you catch the train to that destination? Even Sarah agreed that Danny wasn't the one to wander around restaurants with a uke in one hand and a hat in the other till vaudeville came after him. He had no job anyway, so he put himself through the misery of a few booking agents. He hung around like a dope in their waiting rooms, resenting the actor clients and the good looks they knew they had, and resenting the pretty faces there too that kept dragging his eyes like a magnet no matter how hard he fought it. The wise guys he got in to see smoked their cigar and said he had a nice voice but didn't he ever smile? Smile or no smile, they weren't short a boy tenor right now, they'd let him know if something turned up.

4

THIS STOP TO RESTOCK AT HOROWITZ'S, HYMIE GAVE HOROwitz's cousin Debbie with the black burning gaze a slow smile that took in the bare neck, the mouth-watering swells of the shirtwaist, the light coil of hair that—with poor Dora in her ninth month for God knows how long—he could already visualize on a pillow. Long ago this flame who stabbed neckties with her needle had tipped him off that her nights were free, but what time do you meet her? So he filled his tie cases at the round table full of Horowitzes and sighed, "From early morning to late at night, hah Mrs. Horowitz?" to the cinder-sharp presiding spirit.

"For us, yes. She—" Mrs. Horowitz nodded toward cousin Debbie without missing a stitch—"gets her beauty sleep."

"A half day only till nine?" he laughed.

"Till six, what do you mean?"

"All right," Hymie winked straight at Debbie, "let it be six."

Then what a day on Fifth Avenue in the slush outside the big stores—ties, tiepins—he sold himself hoarse. At noon he rushed down to Dora's and she was well, thank God. He fondly stroked her big belly with their baby still inside, then he swung the old baby Sammy aboard his knee for a ride. Busy! He helped Dora prepare Joe's lunch and kept out of sight when a boy from Joe's market came to pick up the lunch and find out how Dora was. Next it was Dora's turn on Hymie's knee—as far as he went with her these recent months—and he made her smile at the idea of still another pre-birthday-for-baby-to-be celebration at the Roof Garden. Finally, in no hurry at all, he cautioned her.

"Be careful, be careful with yourself, darling. If you're here, I'll see you later, otherwise in the hospital."

But downstairs he went a mile a minute back to Fourteenth Street. He waved, he shouted, he sold ties left and right, till dark began to thin the light in the streets. He shut his cases—one was heavy, two were a ton, but heavy expenses heavy expansion—and next he sped to the Bowery with too much to do and not enough time to do it.

Under the El he rushed into Grogin's Imitation Jewelry Wholesale Only to buy a couple of pins, one for Dora and— Why a couple? One for Golda too? Were his brains in a mix with all this hurry! No—it came back to him—for that Debbie Horowitz. But suppose in spite of her fiery glances the young lady hadn't received the message? Then he'd give the present to Golda.

Grogin's stuff was so inexpensive though—ruby settings, black opals, purple amethysts, diamonds even if they didn't look real—that Hymie bought a handful. Make everyone happy! At Himmel's Fine Jewel Cases a few doors away Hymie boxed his purchases on the best blue imitation velvet, with expert hands wrapped them in gift paper and plunged his face sweating like summer into the cold wind again.

On the East Side in Shapiro's live chicken market—not Joe's; in the old days Hymie would have bought straight from the husband for fun, but now who needed it?—Hymie picked a fine bird and winked at the hag who sat plucking.

"Quick, darling, quick, my mama is hungry."

"Let her slice your throat and fry you for supper then."

Witch. Such ugliness was depressing. But Miss Debbie Horowitz's curving breasts wanted *his* lips on them!

At Dora's the new baby was still in no rush to join the party. "And who can blame him," Hymie brought out an . . . emerald, "with such nice present accommodations?"

"Hymie dear, this baby does not know what he's missing!"

But Hymie could have passed up the no rubbers, face flushed and wet feet lecture his darling had to give him before his laugh and his joke got him away.

Mama he tracked down on Rivington in the slush, with pretzels left. So he bought out her stock—"No no Hymeleh," "Yes yes Mamaleh"—and, "One spring chicken for another," dropped Shapiro's chicken into her basket.

Did Mama give him a kiss!

The home reception had more variety. Naomi loved her brooch and pinned it on right away, Leah didn't and laid hers on the table, and Golda liked hers but she shook her head. From Danny he got a sharp look, a pity. The son was out of work and brought home nothing. Did Hymie give sharp looks?

As to six o'clock Debbie, how could Hymie have been so dumb? Leah and Golda were first starting to serve supper now. He could as easily have let Debbie know 7 P.M. Would she wait?

In the olden days, wait, don't wait, there's a long line behind you girlie. These days, he had to notice, young and old in the cafés, on the streets, in a live chicken market, weren't always that thrilled by his smile. And even the mirror by the wrong light could be depressing.

So he didn't know whether she would wait, and you can't rush your family's supper.

But all good things come to an end; finally his son put on that comical overcoat, gathered his books from under the sewing machine, one by one, slowly, and crawled out to night school. Only then, with the women ready to resume getting hair over the whole flat with their wigmaking, did Hymie tap down his derby, button his pearl-gray overcoat, tuck his stick under his arm and casually stroll out.

Was his heart hammering—like his first girl! Sure she'd be there—his stick swung—and be there all the better for him, in half-hope, half-despair: ripe! How long had he been only with Dora—three, four years? She should only get through this childbirth. . . . But oy, was it slippery and dark, with a freezing wind from the river. And no sooner thought of than he slipped on the icy pavement, and—he could have broken his other leg—just regained his balance.

Who'd wait an hour on a night like this? Who'd come out? He should have stayed home and the hell with that one. Funny, when he first met Dora winter had never come—always sunshine.

There are omens.

On Baxter Street under the lamppost, right in the crosswinds—was she anxious!—she did a little dance in the cold hugging herself and squinted into the shadows. For him!

Hymie marched forward—to a Chinaman, in a dress, a funny hat, and a queue.

Common sense said Canal Street, the Actors Café, to warm up with tea, where many a time the oglers had taken him for an actor. But eh, his heart was heavy. He looked for Debbie anyhow—not that he expected to find her—in the vestibule of Horowitz's house and even up the slippery stoops of the houses next door. Then he actually took two steps toward home, but that hair—over chairs, tables, in your soup when you ate, in your tea when you drank—and his three women hot and heavy at it with the weaving needles.

He turned toward Canal Street after all.

The trees in the square around the corner from Baxter shone like silver and under lamplight the icy branches glittered like diamonds, better than Grogin's Imitations. Gold in the streets and to be picked off the trees almost, but in his pockets none. Yes, depressing but true, money counted. With money like in the olden days, he would have gone straight from work to Debbie and blown himself to a meal without second thoughts. And with money you could find a worldful of Debbies.

From nowhere—hey!—came a good punch in the arm. He had his stick up to defend himself, and . . . Debbie! . . . white, drawn, shriveled with cold. Those black eyes glared.

She said, "You have some damn nerve!"

"See—I'm a hero! I thought it was some thug after me—and I stood ready to fight! You ate?"

"My fingernails."

Hymie slipped his suede-gloved hand under the arm of this morsel and drew her close.

"Come."

Rivka started the chicken as quick as she could so Bertha would eat a good supper when she came home from business. But Rivka needn't have hurried. The stove crackled, the pot boiled, the tiny table was set with a white cloth. And Bertha?

She only shouldn't have collapsed in some corner.

The key picked at the lock and Bertha with hollow cheeks but happy blue eyes stood for a second to breathe in that ecstasy of warmth and cooking chicken.

"More from the Settlement House, Mama? I'll be corrupted with luxury!"

"This," Rivka was glad to be able to tell the truth for a change, "is from my son Hymie."

The blue eyes clouded. "Then I must pay for my share." Bertha went to her purse.

Rivka waved aside that idea.

"You must tell me where you were so late."

"Listen, Mama." Bertha sat down and clasped both Rivka's hands. "My worries are over. I've struck a gold mine!"

"Where darling? I'll bring a big bag."

Thanks to Rivka Bertha had regained her strength and it was such a snap peddling now—cold, dark: they didn't matter—that when night fell she went into the tenements and knocked on doors. So you got three insults for every spool of thread sold, so what? With the miraculous food Rivka brought home free from the Settlement House, Bertha was drawing a little ahead of Isidore's room, board and tuition expenses in Paris, a little closer toward Isidore's concert. Well tonight she'd knocked on a door and although the man laughed in her face with a roomful of women sewing, some at machines, some by hand, he invited her in. They did piecework and a day's peddling paid more. But at night, with empty streets and no buyers, she could go to this man and earn as much as a dollar!

"What, to pay for your coffin Mamaleh?"

"No, don't worry, Mama," the blue eyes shone. "I won't be sick any more. I can't afford to be sick."

What good did arguing do, when it was a question of Isidore?

The first days of Bertha's collapse Rivka had brought her extra for supper, the larger portion small as it was, had tried to coax her to eat, get better. Bertha? She'd cried, refused, then to humor Rivka she might take a bite. Oy, had the heart twisted to see those vacant eyes, those wasted cheeks.

"Be a good girl," Rivka had sat by her.

With an effort Bertha had brought herself back, and apologized, calmly. "I'm sorry, my mind was with Isidore. . . . Mama, even if I did eat your supper—I'll sound like a monster—look how little it is. I'd still never get well."

"Trust in God Mamaleh, with whatever little it is."

"I trust in Him," Bertha had smiled, "but He won't trust me with a hundred dollars for Isidore."

Could that have gone on? While Bertha slept the sleep of exhaustion, Rivka had reached like a thief into the mattress and stolen from her own funeral savings. The next night, like a magician, she had uncovered her basket and revealed treasures: shoulder cuts, soup greens, potatoes, hot rye bread spicy with caraway seeds.

Bertha had eyed it with suspicion.

"Where does it come from?"

"From the Settlement House, where else? They want you well not a patient."

You could see the blue eyes thinking.

"You became a beggar for me."

"Not a beggar exactly. How can they know if nobody tells them?"

"All right."

And Bertha had eaten herself if not back to good health, at least out of sickness. And now, with a full month of winter left, to spoil everything with work that that poor body could never endure, from before dawn to buy for her basket to late at night sewing collars?

"Mama," Bertha laughed, "I am well. Besides, this has to be done."

So the funeral money kept on melting, though that was the least. If God let Rivka live until she died, money is replaceable. But who could replace Bertha? Also, if the worst came to the worst, Rivka still owned her grave. Her son Hymie would see that she had a good Jewish funeral. So there wouldn't be frills, luxuries, particular prayers, particular sayings. What were they anyhow, but a weakness to give in to.

Bertha should be well only.

But in no time the joy in those blue eyes at money accumulating for Isidore burned like a fever. And one night while Rivka dozed next to the stove still heating Bertha's supper—screams, curses!

Rivka looked in the hallway at the landlady's finger pointing straight at her.

"Out! I'm giving you notice before this witness. Out of here by the end of the week!"

A child from Bertha's sweatshop stood there scared and confused, with Bertha's full weight on her. Bertha's head drooped, her mouth trickled blood, her eyes were half open and rolled back.

In the morning Rivka said to the Settlement House nurse, "Now it's a matter of life and death," and the nurse agreed. Still, thank God, with rest, Bertha would recover. Then, a different young woman from the Settlement

House said, they would place her where she would stay well, say as a domestic in Denver, with good food and air, and money to send to her child.

"For her sake," Rivka whispered to the young woman, "the child above all—"

Rivka stayed close to Bertha, giving medicine, helping her sit up to taste broth, fending off the landlady, making jokes. But Rivka's heart was like the heavy sky over the buildings. Better Bertha anywhere than no Bertha—was there a comparison? Yet to lose Bertha wasn't so easy.

At sundown while Bertha napped Rivka locked her in and went through the cold to synagogue. Upstairs in the women's section she sat in the last row and prayed.

> *King of the Universe, who creates day and night, who brings the new seasons, and ranks the stars in the sky. You are blessed oh Lord, our redeemer. Heal the sick and the sick at heart, make them whole again. . . .*

At the end of the service Rivka wiped her eyes and blew her nose and left with her heart at ease.

Stock clerk, conductor, laborer, cashier: answer the ad or tramp the agencies in the Nassau Street canyons and the jobs were all filled, hard times and the soldiers back. For Danny what the opportunities boiled down to were barboy at Uncle Willie's saloon in Orange or shipping boy in Uncle Frank's clothing factory. Grandma'd nagged one and Ma'd nagged the other. An equally appetizing third choice was to be the whole shipping department for the lamp company Leah, Naomi and Leah's boy friend Jack Berger had just started.

Naomi was desperate to have Danny work here, at least to give it a try. Who'd want to be stuck at Uncle Willie's out in nowhere New Jersey? And who'd want to go to Uncle Frank's and work in a factory?

Danny was amazed. "What do you call this?"

They'd rented a small loft on West Street overlooking the piers, the freighters, the whole waterfront tumult. Even now in winter with windows shut trucks and drays rumbled right through your bones, longshoremen and teamsters fractured your eardrums with their yells and a fishy tang crept up your nostrils. Inside under the windows only Leah was bent over a machine. The second machine waited for Ma's finishing the final wig orders to join the new enterprise, the third was Naomi's. Lamps packed, half-packed and ready to be packed were scattered along a pair of raw shipping tables, with boxes stacked or tumbled nearby. Jack Berger, the curly-haired supersalesman with a smooth face and smooth talk, welded shade frames together when he wasn't outside trading back-pats for orders. Berger also fooled around with a metal file that flashed sparks and was giving Danny a headache already.

"This is *our* business, it's different," Naomi explained. "And look at the river—we have a view."

"Indoors too," Berger flipped a wink at the kid brother and turned on his best Don Juan smile for the kid sister.

He probably shouldn't have. His file stopped sparking, the lights went dead, the machinery ground to a halt and the kid sister piled on him.

"Yes, indoors he can look at you blowing fuses! Mr. Manual Dexterity what good are you? Who needs you as a noncontributing partner at our expense? Why don't you go way and earn a living somewhere?"

"Because, shrew," Berger smiled imperturbably while he looked for a fuse, "I have your pretty face and good humor here."

Danny was set to tear this guy apart but Naomi beat her brother to the punch. "You know what you're good for?" she shouted into Jack Berger's face. "If the business fails with you working for us and we want a good fire."

She snatched at the fuse Jack held but he caught her wrist and grinned in her eyes, the he-man with the rolled-up sleeves and white muscles.

"All right children," Leah said, "business before pleasure."

What sense that remark made don't ask Danny, but it worked. Berger let go and Naomi stamped to her machine and sat glaring, waiting for him to replace the fuse. Leah reminded her that she'd been about to show Danny how to wrap lamps.

"I'm not taking that guy's lip," Danny told Leah.

"Nor will it be offered. Help us out a few days till Mama's ready, then we'll see."

Well why not? Orange was in New Jersey, one factory's as bad as another, and West Street's in the same town with Sylvia. So after the few days he was too pooped for school? Who needed school—though by now he was smart enough to keep this under his hat as far as his mother and sisters were concerned. Nobody expected Quality Lamps to flop. It was understood he was being broken in for bigger and better things.

Yet pooped as he was by the time Leah freed him from crating brass torches weighted like murder weapons, he flew east like a bird to the El stairs at the Bowery. Yeah, to find Sylvia. Why? His one wish was to steer clear of her. But his legs had a mind of their own. Now with his collar up and his hands deep in his pockets he knew how to wait craftily, across the way outside Grogin's Imitation Jewelry Wholesale Only, so's not to be embarrassed by Sarah who'd know exactly why he was there. And who wanted her nagging him to keep after those useless theatrical agents.

"Smile," Sarah'd smiled, "if they want you to smile." She'd touched Danny's dimple. "You have a nice smile."

"I did smile. They've shown me the door, you want me to go back and laugh?"

"No, just go back and keep smiling."

Ever since that bananas episode Sarah called him Sweet Singer, and he'd told her he'd had enough of that little joke.

"But it isn't a joke," Sarah assured him. "When you sing my heart melts."

How could you not like Sarah? But a train rumbled overhead, crowds poured down the stairs and he stretched his neck looking for Sylvia.

There she was!

He almost got himself killed dashing through traffic and earned plenty of dirty looks while he pushed and twisted between people. But he caught up to her, that coppery hair under the big fruity hat, the slim shoulders in the green coat with the fur collar.

His voice sounded to him like somebody else's, panting and idiotic, "Just home from work?" as he jostled himself next to her. Her stare and lift of the cheeks showed all the joy a bad smell can bring you. And with her—no stranger—was long Solly Brown the condom kid, in full regalia of black derby and black velvet collar. From Solly it was a tilt of the chin for small fry and back to big business with Sylvia, as if Danny didn't exist. How or why Danny's legs moved he didn't know. Soon he was outpaced and he actually stood still a minute with his misery grin, blocking the sidewalk, the jostler jostled.

He might have kept up with Sylvia and Solly instead of crawling along. Their way was his way, toward home and supper. Only he had no appetite.

Jesus, did he hope Ma would wrap up those wigs soon! He just couldn't wait to beat it away from that goddam factory and get out to Jersey!

Jack Berger naked alongside naked Leah heard wedding music drift up from the Broadway Central main ballroom and murmured against Leah's cheek, "Why don't we get hitched?" while he lazily drew his finger between Leah's thighs. Leah's lids were half-shut, but, "What . . . have you got . . . to offer?" she asked in rhythm with what she was doing.

Jack flipped himself over on her, made a vise of his hard chest and arms and rammed her. But you couldn't faze Leah. She was top dog at the end, or should he say bitch?

She leaned over him in his collapsed state. "Anything else?"

"Short dark and handsome," Jack pecked up a kiss at her, "you sure know how to screw."

"Assume that I've curtsied."

"Well, I have my superb conversation to offer."

"You mean on your war exploits?"

"What's wrong with my war exploits? How about my no man's land wriggle face to face with that wriggling kraut." Jack laughed. "Was he surprised when he got it!"

Leah yawned. "But I'm not. That's the tenth time he's been killed and he's still wriggling."

"You should have seen his entrails, poor guy. . . . Say, you're wriggling nicely, as good as he was. Come here, I'll show you how I stabbed him in the belly . . ."

After that demonstration Leah smiled down again. "Why get married? Isn't this married enough?" She cast the amused glance over the Oriental rug and real mahogany bureau of the pretty room she'd teased Jack into taking her to. "Home was never like this."

"Well dear, for one thing, when we're married I won't have to blow a day's pay on one night's screwing."

"You don't have to now. We could have gone to your flat."

"What? And let all the neighbors know my intended's a whore?"

Leah nimbly jumped out of bed and started to dress. "I'll marry you for your humor."

Jack jumped up too and he surrounded her with arms and kisses. "Okay, so that misfired. When you're in love," he reached under her chemise, "you can ignore the duds."

Leah's body was tense, undecided, then gave in. She laid her head back on his shoulder.

"Who's in love?" she asked.

"I am."

"You don't know what love means."

"Then in my ignorance."

Leah laughed, "You're a wonderful salesman though," and went back to bed with him.

"Then you'll marry me?"

"No darling," she flicked a naughty tongue at his lips, "I'm not in love either."

Did you ever see such a bitch? She really could frustrate you if you brooded about it. But Jack wasn't a brooder. The brooders were back in France in the cemeteries, beneath the crosses row on row. By the time his battalion had gotten over there, the war had almost been over though of course nobody'd known it. Maybe straight infantry would have worn him down, with minenwerfers and shell-hole stinks. As it was the few weeks he'd been up front he'd hated the icy drafts through the trenches, all his life he'd been very susceptible to colds. But it had been a real kick to discover that for him the bombardments had been one great big Fourth of July—big flaring lights, little ones, mortar sparks converging around shell holes. And he'd liked his detail: Western Union boy, sitting on your ass mostly at company quarters. And when he'd had to get off his ass to crawl between trenches and actually looked that sentry gun in the eye, his gun had gone off first. Hadn't he felt pretty good, opening up that Dutchman's face! But what used to was used to was, now it ain't. Now, he had a sneaking suspicion that his little bedmate's gentleman's agreement to partnership for him if the lamp business clicked was, as it stood, nothing for an ex-doughboy to stake his future on. Because not only was his little bedmate no gent but she was coarse enough to remind him, if the occasion rose, that he wasn't the only doughboy who'd come home from war. In New York if you had a product to sell there was no shortage of salesmen. So the safest arrangement would be a marriage contract—not that he was a bit mercenary. Outside of the hotel rooms it pays for, a suit and a dinner or so, money didn't mean a damn thing to Jackie boy. He liked her, possibly even loved her, though in her half-assed way she was right—who the hell did know what love meant? But he was already twenty-three years old and a bed in the Broadway Central should leave him broke for the rest of the week?

Still this kid tickled him, and in more ways than one. Screw a dame then utter the word marriage? Why they'd trample you in the stampede to the rabbi. Leah was different, he'd give her credit for that. But no trifling, honey, with Mama Berger's starry-eyed boychik.

"I may propose to Naomi, dear, unless you've reconsidered."

"I almost *could* love you," Leah threw herself on his vanquished form, "you're such a dreamer!"

Gee the snow was pure in the morning! How come going to work Naomi had never noticed that, or the way the factories—yellow, brick-red, brown—took on color? Even the air had color—pearl-gray blasts from the nostrils of the truck horses the trolley sped past. Listen, she knew why. She was no dope even if her family unanimously thought so. She was happy!

But what did they take her for, some kind of tramp? Couldn't they trust her, not even Papa who she'd stood up for always, no matter what anybody said?

"A day and night on a train, to run after a bum? No!" Papa had stuck up his hand. "Only a bum would send after a respectable girl—I have experience, I know!"

"A-men," her wise kid brother had gulped a swallow of coffee to mutter, and stupid her—"You shut up"—had burst into tears.

But now she was happy, and glad she hadn't shown them Phil's Pittsburgh letter. *Come out, de luxe accommodations, and we'll enjoy that little ceremony we skipped two years ago. . . .* If they'd known she was going there to marry him on his weekend pass from that slow creeping Camp Haley that never discharged a person they would have dissuaded her easily, because she wanted them to be at her wedding. She and Phil would have a real wedding in New York when he was a civilian again. Also the prospect of being in bed with a strange man called your husband still scared her. But what kind of idiot was Naomi Share, after all the wishing and hoping and suffering, to behave like a ninny? Now she knew she wasn't a ninny, and Papa would find out that Phil wasn't a bum. And meanwhile she loved the snow, the fire escapes, all these old buildings! She loved stupid old New York, she almost hated to leave it, even for a weekend.

Yet at Penn Station—PITTSBURGH, the board over the gate said—what turmoil Naomi felt inside, what joy to be going! On account of the tip she hadn't dared look at the porters, and on the train her suitcase—she hoisted it toward the overhead rack but she was too short and it was too heavy—suddenly took on life and flew up.

Her helper was old, about forty, and not much taller than she, but broad-shouldered with a friendly rubbery face that made you smile. All the window seats were taken, but he insisted that she sit in his. Naomi couldn't stop thanking him.

The man said, "That much gratitude? And I had you pegged for over eighteen."

"Had me pegged? I am over eighteen. I'm partners in a lamp factory!"

The man laughed out loud.

"One sure thing, you're you."

Naomi blushed and she pasted her face to the window just as a trainman sang out, a whistle blew, steam hissed and the platform began gliding past. Concrete panels slipped by, and now and then a dull light.

"Don't want to miss that tunnel," the man kept teasing her.

But, "It's my first trip," Naomi kept looking away from him.

"Not to Pittsburgh I hope?"

She looked at him slightly annoyed. "Why not to Pittsburgh?"

"Hardly a pleasure, the town of smoke and black curtains."

"Oh I'm not going for pleasure," she set him straight, "my fiancé is stationed there."

Another big joke for him. She excused herself and took out her Booth Tarkington, which she couldn't read out of excitement at the snow-patched meadows, towns and, eventually, mountains flicking past the corner of her eye. The suitcase man invited her to the dining car for lunch, luckily she had sandwiches with her. After dark though, the train slowed down at a black flashing river laced with black metal, Naomi gasped at a city flaming to an oven-red sky, and the man got even on her.

"That's Pittsburgh, don't get burned."

She thought her shoulder would fall off from the old suitcase with iron corners and thick straps bouncing against her thigh in the enormous station with soldiers everywhere but not her Phil. But Phil was where he'd promised to be, outside the exit gate, and—with the khaki overcoat unbuttoned, leggings crossed, visored hat tilted up—completely absorbed in a magazine. Naomi stationed herself in front of him.

"It's me."

Phil looked up lazily, "Ah," and gave her a light kiss.

"Say," she laughed, "you'd think we were married already."

"Already?"

"There's something missing in your kissing."

"Oh, that'll come later."

But Naomi surprised Phil by throwing her arms around him for a good juicy one now. Then, "Am I too forward?," worriedly.

"You really are happy."

She exclaimed, "I am!" all the louder because she wasn't so sure.

"Most women I've met like to conceal their emotions—not that my female acquaintanceship is all that extensive."

"That's good. So you won't have that many of them to give up."

But although Phil offered to buy her a gardenia when she stopped to look at a flower shop window (she refused) and brought her to an insanely expensive restaurant for dinner where a string trio played "Poet and Peasant Overture," she really did not know what she was doing in Pittsburgh. Unextensive as his female acquaintanceship was he kept bragging about it. One woman had treated him to a dinner here, another—the trio playing the "Bolero" reminded him—had put a Victrola record of that on to keep time to some kind of rhythms exercise—whatever that meant—that they were doing. Three waiters served you but Naomi didn't like the meal here with the meat in some sauce like poison, she didn't like the "Bolero," and she didn't like Phil calmly telling her about machine-gunning Bolshie prisoners, leaving wounded to freeze, and the marriage offers he'd had from Russian women on account of his charms and his American citizenship. He sneered at everything, even at himself. Would she like him better tomorrow?

A foot in the lobby of the hotel he took her to—top hats and ermine, thick Persian rugs, potted trees, leather furniture—and she refused to go a step further.

"It's too expensive, Phil, I can't afford it."

"Just follow the bellhop. Ladies' Day."

"But it's too expensive for you too, Phil."

"I'll get my money's worth."

That meant, upstairs in a room that could have held the whole four rooms in Hester Street, with a bed large enough for five sleeping sideways, that he expected to sleep with her!

"You were just fooling," Naomi said, "about the wedding ceremony?"

"Ceremony," Phil corrected her. "This *is* the ceremony."

And he reached for Naomi, not that she let him come near her. Now tell her this. Why, in a family that never cried, was she a born crybaby? He bent to kiss her moist eyes, she pushed him away. "Let's not wrestle," she said.

"I never intended to. May I ask what made you travel to Pittsburgh?"

She sniffed, she couldn't help it. "Some crazy notion, you sounded so refined—and all those letters, the last especially. Well," she took another dumb sniff and picked up her suitcase, "goodbye—"

"Sit down, Naomi. . . ."

So she sat, she was so depressed, and while trolleys ding-donged outside and the radiator mewed he spun her a long line about men, women, physical, love.

"What's love?" she asked dully.

He stuck his hand on her knee and drawled, "I'll show you."

"You don't have to." She stood up. "It runs in my family, so I ran here . . ." She put her coat on. "We both made a mistake, I'm sorry."

Did he heave a sigh! It was the most energy she'd seen out of him all evening including the seduction speech. Was he at least going to offer to leave and let her sleep here?

"I suppose there's no point of my trying to persuade you further? Okay," he opened the door for her, "never let it be said of Phil Stein that he forced a maiden to stay against her will."

So—at the elevator she flicked her finger at a jade-green glass lampshade and it rang out like a bell—I ran to a bum, Papa, just as you said.

You couldn't find out from anyone—the chambermaid, the elevator man, the doorman—whether there was such a thing as a women's hotel in Pittsburgh, not too expensive. The chambermaid said the Y, but that sounded like Christians. Maybe the men knew, but they began with leering wisecracks as if she was some sort of . . . creature. She waited for a trolley and a cop eyed her up and down, she didn't dare ask him.

In the terminal on the bench nearest the all-night ticket window she happened to look up once and out of the ground sprang some man with a "Hello, dearie." So she sat eyes down, collar up, with a tight grip on her handbag and suitcase. Then she had to pick a subject to think of to keep her dumb eyes dry. Imagine what a tear would encourage in this place.

See how right Papa had been? No no no, no Phil—not about Phil. Last month before she and Leah had rented the loft, their business had seemed to have failed without even starting. Glass shades had been the problem. Glass cost a fortune, it was hard to assemble and a million companies were making glass shades. Worst of all they were breakable. So, Papa'd told her. . . . But shouldn't she have known what Phil was from his cleverness? If you want to marry a person don't you say . . . So Papa'd told her what did they need glass for, use satin. And what kind of credit did Papa get for that good advice? Leah'd said Papa had a lot of talent, too bad he's a lazy . . . Bum—Naomi shivered—Leah'd called Papa.

This waiting room was so cold!

If the train ever came the first thing she'd do at the factory was send Berger to canvas orders from big hotels for lamps with fabric shades, unbreakable. None of them had thought of that either. So see, her trip west hadn't been foolish! Wait till Papa heard this idea, he'd crack his sweet joke to her. "Such brains with such beauty is absolutely against the law." Against the law, Papa!

Why couldn't she find someone like Papa?

Those tears. Again she swallowed, again gulped them down.

And all this time only ten minutes had passed. She'd be going home to people who loved her, even if they did say dumb things about any boy she happened to care for. But what of her poor cousin in Europe, a father murdered, nowhere to go and loving cousin Naomi fighting tooth and nail against taking her in?

"Reiseleh," Naomi whispered without moving her lips, "forgive me, I love you—sail quickly, I can't wait to meet you—"

As soon as Naomi had recovered physically from her sparkling travels—mentally, what boy could you trust now?—she ran to Grandma's to prove what a Good Samaritan she really was at heart, how anxious she was for Reisel to come stay with them. Grandma didn't know, she showed Naomi the latest from Gittel, Reisel's mother.

> I'm still living—if you can call this living—in the same London attic in a swarming neighborhood known as Whitechapel where the streets creep with filth. Rivka, I never complain, but any time I stand up here I knock my head on the ceiling. Terrible birds gabble at you, and when you wake they stare in from the windowsill even before the first streak of light. And Reisel encourages them, Reisel speaks baby talk to the birds. "Good morning," she chirps to them, "how are you this bright London morning?" in fog-drenched Britannia where your heart and bones ache.
>
> Rivka, why did I have to leave my home, why did I have to leave Kadzyrnye? Is it my fault that my husband left me? I didn't write this before while I hoped for better. Now I have no hope, except you Rivka.
>
> If I were a businesswoman I would have stayed in Kadzyrnye, but my business was to be adored, catered to. That, it happens, was how my darling father raised me. Where was it my place to run a lumber mill and a warehouse? My daughter though had a different kind of father—more like husband and wife than father and daughter if you ask me. Well, I picked that Elya Leben to marry—my mother's choice, not mine: poor, a clerk of my dear papa's, a nothing. But I never threw any of this up to Leben, and I won't complain to you now. That wishy-washy Leben I married humiliated himself, gave bribe money, to get his daughter into Gymnasium in Wladkow. "Brilliant," he kept pestering me, "isn't Reiseleh brilliant?" So why didn't she stay in Wladkow in the Gymnasium since she was so brilliant? Why did she throw up her studies that made everyone else on earth her inferior, why did she come home in such a hurry to Kadzyrnye after four years? If I asked that once in those days, I asked it a thousand times. And you know what Leben's clever reply was? "They have no more to teach her." The father wanted the daughter home, he had her home—no skin off my nose. Then he made her a business partner. The room off the dining room in our house had been good enough for my father's office. Those two—my husband and my daughter—moved the office to the warehouse. Anything so as not to be bothered with me. All right, no skin off my nose. But, brilliant daughter and fine businesswoman, the soldiers are gone and the pogromniks are back in their huts and your father has deserted us, so why don't you run the business? I asked her that at the time, a sane question, and the deranged girl screamed that the warehouse was a cinder, the mill a shambles. Lies—not even worth my going out there to see if they were lies.
>
> Rivka, she's crazy, but maybe you can write to her. For her, Whitechapel is beautiful—with rooftops, chimney pots and smoke in every direction. She stands flowerpots on the windowsill and every day she waters those leaves thick with soot. I beg her, "Throw those awful plants out, they'll take revenge." "Learn from them Mama," she instructs me, "they survive in adversity." Her addled brain loves Britannia so much she speaks

only English, even to me. "Britannia is kind to us, its stepchildren," she tells me. "Though they dislike us, though they serenade us *No Jews allowed down Wapping*, they do not murder us." Let her be the stepchild, full of gratitude to her father's low-class cousins who bless us with their landlord's attic at our expense. Our proud Reisel takes turns squatting in filth like a janitress, scrubbing all the halls not to speak of the stinkhole that everyone goes to on the first landing. In between she flirts on a bench over shirtwaists with her fine pauper cousins sewing beside her. Me they make fun of. Rivka, in Britannia the very sparrows are evil. Leave half a quarter of butter, an egg and some milk in the window box, the birds open the box, eat your bitter, suck your egg and drink as much of your milk as they can reach in the jar. Evil, evil. Dare speak of this and my daughter's cousins laugh and wink and tell me, "Today shut the box, don't forget." And in the neighborhood, our fine Native Quarter with the fine privy smell, I pass by and people laugh at me too. Not enough Leben deserted me, I try to sleep and he comes jeering at me with his two mouths, one in his face, one in his throat. Or else he keeps agents downstairs slandering me, laughing that I'm to blame. Most of the time it doesn't matter, but sometimes I overhear terrible schemes about me from those agents whispering and then I don't dare take a breath. I wish to God, if there is a God, I could get away from here while there's a chance. Already there's a pogrom in the streets, with Cossack shouts that have me frantic. I went to hide in the cellar, so naturally the cousins laughed. "England is on strike," they try to delude me. Rivka, God knows I can recognize a pogrom when I hear one. I am at my wits' end, Rivka, America the golden land is my only hope now.

Rivka, please please please, write a few words and do what I cannot, put some sense into that crazy head of my daughter's so I can come to you? Please, Rivka? . . .

Crazy Naomi started gulping and mopping up tears.

"I knew," Rivka said, "you have a good heart Naomileh. I knew you didn't mean this sufferer shouldn't come to your house."

"I don't have a good heart. I have a bad heart."

"So you shed tears? Last week my friend Bertha went away, God knows where, to Denver, she only should get her health back. The conductor wouldn't let me on the platform. Then I explained, I had to make Bertha comfortable, so he let me. In the train was a very nice black man, the porter, he brought a pillow for Bertha and he promised she was in good hands, no one would receive better care. Then, everything was finished except for me to get off the train, and Bertha looked at me with her blue eyes.

" 'Mama,' she calls me Mama, 'let's have a good cry.'

"So I made a joke, 'All right, you begin, I'll join in.'

"She wrinkled her face, but you think that she could cry? It came out a smile, with damp blue eyes. My eyes also were damp. With so many tears inside that's all we got out, Mamaleh. Ah, better to be young and still have tears left. Even this Reisel had a few tears for poor Elya, for her poor father."

"Even? That poor girl! But I don't understand from this letter. You said they killed her father?"

"They killed him, they killed him. Gittel can't bear to think of it."

"Oh my God. Write to Reiseleh, Grandma, make her come. Tell her you can really be happy here, if you meet the right man. Or you can make money—whatever you want!"

Rivka gazed out at the cold cobbles in sunlight, odds and ends in the gutter, children chasing—each other?—and as usual women with arms hooked in shopping baskets though it was Sabbath and a whole hour to sunset yet before a Jewish woman should shop. Eh, you felt tired all the time at her age. Gittel was right, Kadzyrnye had been better. But Kadzyrnye was from long ago, finished. . . .

"I don't know about that modern daughter, whether they'll come."

"No no, she will Grandma, if you tell her it really is different. I know what I'll do—I'll write to her myself!" Then Naomi was worried. "Is a letter to England very expensive?"

5

FINE START.

In the milky air outside Orange station Danny saw some small stores, a few shoppers, a touring car, a horse scattering oats as it swung the feedbag up in front of a wagon—but no Uncle Willie.

So Danny disgustedly set out on foot with his suitcase in one hand and his uke case in the other.

But say, this small town wasn't bad, with the smell of earth damp from melting snow you still saw on a rock here and there, white, gray or red wooden houses with homey porches and tan grass from last summer. Trees—along the street, on lawns, in back of houses—had bumpy branches, about ready to bud. Nice. Just the same it was a long walk to Uncle Willie's, Danny wasn't certain exactly how long. He'd been there once in his life, a few years ago, to bring Grandma out, and had he made that trip indignantly. What kind of guy, the question had been, was an uncle who wouldn't move himself to visit his own mother? And in advance Danny had answered what kind of guy would you expect your father's brother to be? Their simple motto was Number One first.

Uncle Willie had been right there at the station in his delivery wagon though that afternoon, and firm believer as Danny was in guilt by association, it was tough to associate his uncle with his old man in spite of the family resemblance. They both had gray hair, but the Hester Street dude's was primped whereas Uncle Willie's stood up like short grass. Hymie was willowy but Uncle Willie looked pounded down and hammered together in some blacksmith's shop. And the old man had a nice healthy complexion—why not, outdoors at leisure when he wasn't in bed with some frail—and Uncle Willie looked scorched as if he'd been through a furnace. Then there was the talk, Danny's razzle-dazzle old man and Uncle Willie the stammerer.

Uncle Willie had steered Grandma around the side of the saloon, which had seemed more like a barn, and sat her down under a shade tree between a flower garden and the edge of a pond. Uncle Willie didn't talk much but he had been fast with the lemonade that hot day. Danny had swallowed his down and been surprised to see Grandma sipping hers. Kosher was a big issue for Grandma on enemy territory, which stretched practically everywhere outside of her own room. At some clan gatherings Grandma could drive a suspected housewife cousin crazy by toting her own hard-boiled egg, roll and even pinch of salt for when dinnertime came. Did Uncle Willie run a kosher saloon?

Danny never in the world would have spoiled Grandma's lemonade by asking, but—Jesus, what a Grandma!—she read your mind.

"Danneleh, you see your uncle," Grandma had smiled, "but you don't see the kosher dishes, the kosher food he keeps especially for your grandma so she shouldn't go hungry in case she pays a visit."

So there was more to Uncle Willie than met the eye.

And Uncle Willie sure didn't make it easy for anyone to get drunk. Now the sidewalk turned into a dirt road, damped down and hard, and bare woods either side with a sweet smell of wet fallen leaves. But no saloon.

A wagon loaded with egg crates came creaking along, and the farmer pulled up at Danny's question.

"Saloon?" the farmer echoed him.

"Willie Share's."

"Oh, Willie's. You passed it a way back. Climb on." The farmer looked like a peddler, only with overalls on under his coat. "Trying the liquor business before Prohibition sets in?"

"I'll just be helping my uncle."

"One more helper," the farmer chuckled. "That's Willie. Ask your uncle about the time he went hunting."

The farmer let Danny off at a rutted side road and clucked the horse around a curve out of sight. Now—nothing but thick woods—that guy was either a wise guy or had made a mistake. But it was great! On impulse Danny put down his baggage and began shinning up a tall tree. A crow gave him hell, others chimed in. Danny gave them some nice loud caws back and a small cloud of them wheeled up overhead. Jesus! Halfway up Danny pressed his cheek against the brownish-black patterned bark he squeezed tight.

He said, "I love ya, tree!"

On top he swung his leg over a branch and—how do you like that!—Uncle Willie hid his saggy clapboard barn of a saloon on a rise against the overcast sky. Hey and the crows had announced Danny! Some dumpy woman shielding her eyes at the saloon door was waving to him. Had he met her when he was a kid? She had on a thick lumpy sweater, her hair was in a loose knot. To play safe he waved back and the woman waved again and ducked into the barn, or saloon. That pond glinted at the foot of the slope, gray-green in the middle and deep green at the edge, though there was no green around to reflect.

So this was what the country was like in winter!

He shinnied down, grabbed the bag and the uke, and when the woods opened up there were Uncle Willie and that elderly woman at the door waiting. The puffy motherly face with a snub nose beamed at him.

"What did I say, Will? He's the spit and image of your brother. In fact, my first thought was what's Will's brother Hymie doing up in that tree?"

Who was this stupid dame anyway, with the unfunny jokes and the standard Jewish busybody delivery, only Gentile?

Willie said, "Aw A-anna, he doesn't resemble his f-father one bit. B-besides, you haven't seen H-hymie in twenty years."

"Handsome Hymie."

And from the teasing voice and out-of-place girlish smile on the saggy cheeks, Danny figured this was his uncle's girl friend. What could Uncle Willie see in a dame like this? At least Danny's old man's following had looks.

Willie grinned at his nephew.

"So you climbed a tree."

Before Danny could fish up any alibi he found himself grinning too.

Uncle Willie asked, "Wh-what do you have there?"

"Oh that, that's just my ukulele."

"G-gonna play for the guests a little?"

"Sure, if you want me to."

The guests were a knot of long-mustached Italians waving their arms around in some foreign argument while they hit the free lunch. Trotting upstairs behind Uncle Willie Danny'd already cast himself as the Young Orange Troubadour strumming "La Paloma" out of his uke. "*That's a sweet voice,*" one of the Italians would say.

Seemed Danny was to sleep in a harness room with saddles and straps hanging and—Jesus!—free-zing, since the little black stove was cold. But his room—to himself!—and enormous, with a glimpse of the pond with its rich gray-green winter glint through branches scraping the windows.

Uncle Willie—"G-gonna s-stay?"—was watching him.

"What do you mean? And how! This is great." Danny took a few sniffs. "Smells like a horse."

"Named Rosa. You play piano too?" Uncle Willie's blue eyes smiled at you though his mouth didn't, exactly the opposite of Danny's old man. "We h-have a p-piano downstairs."

Danny hadn't noticed it on the way in but there it was, old and beaten, in a lonely corner far away from the bar. But Uncle Willie gently uncovered the keyboard, sat down and, by ear, with his iron fingers, played a tune with a one-line lyric—"Just a kiss, just a kiss"—he half-sang half-talked. Then he winked at his nephew.

"Th-that's my repertory."

Anna polishing glasses behind the bar called out, "Ain't he swell?"

Swell? Danny'd never met anybody like him before. The new school term began and how could you ask a guy who was giving you room, board and ten smackers a week to keep a glass clean and play your uke whether you could take weeknights off and travel to Newark to finish up your diploma? So Danny kept his mouth shut and the next thing he knew Uncle Willie was ordering him to hitch up Rosa and drive over to register in the county high school—days!

"What are you paying me for then, Uncle Willie?"

"F-for what I ask you to do."

"If I were some stranger you wouldn't make this arrangement."

"Th-that m-may be so. B-b-b-but you aren't some stranger. Y-you're," Uncle Willie's swarthy face creased into a grin, "my loving nephew."

That was how Danny had signed his job negotiation letters from New York to Uncle Willie.

So, Abe Lincoln with a regular homework pad instead of a shovel and charcoal, Danny trudged a couple of miles into town every morning and went to school with kids of his age who seemed to him at least five years younger, soft kids, even those from the farms. They were hicks. But not Carrie the farmer's daughter. Her old man, Mr. Baum, was the chicken farmer who'd given Danny the ride his first day in Orange, and Carrie was sharp, and skinny, with light-brown hair cut short à la mode, maybe ahead of the mode. "They're wearing their hair like this now," Carrie told him.

Danny took a look at the other girls, with hair long, or braided, or in buns like his Ma's and sisters'. "Who's they?"

Carrie—"Not them"—shot a glance of contempt at where he was looking. But Danny interested her, she told him, because he'd achieved her ambition—except in reverse. Imagine anyone going from New York to Orange, New Jersey!

"What's so great in New York," Danny wanted to know, "the stink in the hallways?"

Carrie said, "You're a damn fool," the advanced girl with curse words. "Theaters, parties, big buildings, a chance to do something."

"Like what?" Danny challenged her.

"I'm not sure yet. I was only three when I left. I'll find out when I get back there."

Meanwhile every morning Mr. Baum driving Carrie to school on his egg wagon began overtaking Danny toward the end of the trip.

"Why don't you come with us rather than walk?" Carrie called down. "You could have an extra hour for pleasant dreams."

Danny blurted, "I don't dream."

"Daddy Moishe, you think he's normal?" Carrie asked.

"He's a real country boy," Mr. Baum the little humorist Danny would have liked to take a slug at chimed in, "right from your hygiene book."

Idiot Danny burned red. The truth was, wet dreams aside, he wanted to dream of Sylvia and never did, maybe because when he concentrated on her for that purpose before he dropped off the thoughts were all so dry and grinding. But what else could they be? Ten P.M. sharp Uncle Willie would make him call it quits at the bar and go up for his eight hours' sleep. But sometimes Danny'd sneak down again and out the back way to lean against a tree in the cold and open his arms to a skyful of stars, the moon, silver clouds drifting. Jesus Christ was he in love with the firmament! Of course five minutes of that with nothing over the black sweater that kept you warm enough in the saloon and your teeth began to sound like a crap game. Besides, the firmament wasn't enough. You wanted coppery hair, a slim face, gray loving eyes to love the firmament along with you.

So he wrote Sylvia all about this marvelous place, his swell uncle, how she ought to come out here and he'd show her. He played it smart for once and didn't say that he missed her. He just said he could pick her up on a Sunday, the saloon was closed then, and it was a nice ferry ride. His Aunt Anna was a swell cook, then he'd see Sylvia home after dinner.

And for three weeks he'd lived and died for the mail.

Carrie on the other hand caught him in the stream of kids leaving school and said, "How come you never ask me for a date?"

"How can I when I work every night?"

"Your uncle'll give you a night off. He only keeps you there for charity anyway."

"So say we make a date. Then you'll tell me sweet things like that, that you've heard from your father?"

"You're a smart boy, that's why I like you. We could go to the pictures, you treat since you work, and then you could buy me a hot chocolate in Andersen's."

Danny had to laugh, Carrie laughed along with him.

"You're an out-and-out gold-digger."

And she got her date. See, Sylvia?

The movie was a Hoot Gibson to Carrie's disgust, Wild West with plenty of galloping. Over the hot chocolate in Andersen's with the wireleg tables and chairs full of Sunday night kids, Carrie complained, "The girl didn't even get a kiss out of that ungraded hero."

"Sure, he kissed her at the end."

"Nah, that was the horse he kissed, she just got in the way."

Plenty of laughs, Carrie, but to her kissing was serious. Danny had to catch up on homework so at the farm gate he said no to her invite in and gave her a so-long peck on the lips.

Carrie said, "And what's that supposed to be?" took plenty of time drawing him close, and cemented her mouth to his. In the night all cats are gray, yet through two coats—his and hers—he could have diagramed skinny Carrie bone by bone and dark as it was he was still kissing that shrewd and sort of hard face with the bent bony nose. No good trying to imagine that it was Sylvia any more than he'd been able to with the mud-colored whore across the tracks he'd visited with Swedlow, Musaracca and Blum from school to prove what? That he was a man-about-whorehouses? For thrills Carrie's kiss equaled the whore's lay and they both equaled the log rail Carrie had backed herself up against.

Finally she let him go, explained, "That's a kiss," and ran toward the light from the farmhouse windows.

"Gallop you bastard, run your heart out, drop dead!" Danny laid a neat sidearm flick of the whip on the mare's muscular flank and if Uncle Willie's whiskey barrels were rattling in the back of the wagon the hoofs and wheels scattering pebbles drowned out the sound. Trees flashed by, meadows and farms spread out on both sides of the road. "My America!" Danny let out a yell.

Lunchtime with the usual Eyeties at the bar who'd have drunk their pay up in cheap whiskey if Uncle Willie'd let them, Uncle Willie had told Danny, "Bring down your uke." Danny had made a face, but Uncle Willie had said, "S-sure, go ahead," and had sat down at the piano and begun his one-tune repertory. So with the uke Danny'd chimed in on Uncle Willie's millionth chorus of "Just a Kiss" and then had sung "La Paloma" solo to the railroad workers as dreamed. After a few *zitti zittis* from Anna you're being entertained, the shouting subsided, and Danny could have kissed that rich black handlebar mustache that applauded, "Thatsa sweet voice."

Then the Italians resumed the full-blast arm-waving, and Uncle Willie and Anna when she wasn't pouring were the audience for the rest of his stuff. Uncle Willie asked for five encores of "Meant for Love" to figure it out on the piano—and Danny even smiled from deep down south.

Watch out Palace, here I come!

Wouldn't Sarah be proud of him! And Jesus, he hadn't even said he was leavin'. He'd have to drop her a postcard.

So into Orange and back Danny let loose that joy, and though he walked Rosa the last half-mile, Uncle Willie wanted to know how she'd gotten so sweaty.

"She ran away with me."

Uncle Willie looked Danny straight in the eye.

"Y-you m-m-mean you ran away with her."

Uncle Willie made him cool her down like a thoroughbred racehorse, some punishment. Danny loved this roan mare Rosa, named, Uncle Willie said, in memory of a great woman, some dead Bolshie or other. Danny not only walked her but groomed her, mucked out her stall and fed her some sugar cubes. In the middle of carting off the manure—"Be kind . . . when you hear me sigh"—he remembered an afternoon date with Carrie, so he gave himself a quick grooming and ran.

But on Mr. Baum's porch nobody answered his knock. The barn was empty: no horse and wagon. At the pasture fence Mr. Baum's cows gaped at Danny like a couple of Hester Street fishwives with horns, and at the coops the dumb red chickens and their grand stink huddled together scared as if Danny meant curtains. The joint looked deserted.

Danny lifted his head just in time to see a back upstairs window slam down and Carrie dressed as an Indian wrapped in a blanket wave him up. When the explorer discovered her room she was in bed wearing rather than covered with the same red-and-black blanket. She patted the mattress.

"Sit down."

"You sick?"

"No, I'm asleep. Hear me snoring? You smell sweaty."

"I was grooming the mare, and it's not like roses here either."

"Thanks. I have la grippe."

"Maybe I'd better go then."

"That's not necessary. You're the one boy I could allow into my bedroom when I was in bed like this and not have to worry."

That—"You want rape?"—got Danny sore. He gave the cover a jerk, unrolled her, and there she lay looking kind of pathetic with her bony chest half-bare in a green-trimmed flannel nightgown. She said, "Eek," and he half-heartedly lunged at her breasts—practically nonexistent from the quick feel he got.

Then followed the "After I trusted you," and so forth and so on.

"I don't care," Danny said, "whether you trusted me or didn't trust me, but I'm sorry I did that. In my family the height of hilarity is to call me a chip off the old block, because my father is a big woman man. But I don't believe in that stuff, I like you and . . . so I'm sorry."

Look at this! Tough Carrie showed two tears in that sallow face.

"Excuse me," she took a swipe at the moisture, "it must be the fever. You are not a chip off the old block. I never met anyone as nice as you before."

Danny gazed at her with new eyes. If only she was less skinny.

There is a Dame Fortune, she smiles or frowns, and when you're more or less fifty the smiles become scarce with no frowns shortage. This had struck Hymie over and over, and never more so than right now. His Dora bleeding to death in a hospital from his child—boy, girl, he didn't know which—and suddenly Mama was here bothering him with some relations he'd never seen and never wanted to see.

"From Britannia," Mama said. "Reisel writes that they're sailing on the *Empress of Liverpool.*"

Therefore Hymie should stand ready, a reception committee for greenhorns whenever the boat docked, to accompany Mama to Ellis Island, welcome the newcomers to America the beautiful that was closing in on him tight, open the golden door of Hester Street to them. Certainly while Dora bled, while his heart bled, Ellis Island was not going to be on the program. He wasn't in a position to refuse here at supper in front of his wife and daughters, but he didn't agree either.

"Grandma—let me go with you!" Naomi begged for the favor.

Leah stared at her. "With those back orders piling up at the factory?"

Count on Leah, and count on Hymie's luck. He was like a curse to himself and a worse to Dora. Hope, but how much hope could there be? All day long Joe Kirschner sat at her bedside, a man who normally wouldn't trust his workers with a chicken feather, let alone with a cashbox. So in the maternity section Hymie had to snatch a look from the corridor at his beloved because the husband was planted inside. Not a flower was Hymie able to bring his Dora, he couldn't touch that white hand, he couldn't whisper courage to that poor half-alive face.

It was not permissible for his Dora to die and him not say a word!

"Golda," he said after supper, "fix me a jar of chicken soup, for my friend Glantz in the hospital."

With a straight face, "She makes pants?" his charming Leah asked.

"Glantz is a watchmaker. God should spare him his life."

Mama said, "I'll pray for your friend. Let them also change his name in the synagogue, Hymileh, it sometimes helps."

Not a bad idea. Hymie didn't consider himself that religious, but recently he felt through and through there was more to the universe than his smart atheist chums were so sure about in the café on Grand Street. He'd give the name change suggestion to Joe Kirschner along with the chicken soup. And he'd go to *shul* himself—that wouldn't hurt either—and pray for Dora.

Damn him if taking Mama home to the new room on Suffolk Street Hymie didn't catch sight of his blazing-eyed bitch Miss Debbie Horowitz shadowing him! The nerve! She was the first he'd told Glantz was sick! From across the way she stuck to you like a gnat, close to the stoops, the buildings, a real shadow, skimming the pools of lamplight at the corners. Drop dead, he had Glantz on his mind, Dora. Oy, and Mama's greenhorns yet.

"Mama," he carried her basket with Golda's soup tucked in and he supported her arm as they crept along in the chill, "is the new landlady still an improvement?"

"*Is* she. An angel from heaven, not like in Clinton Street. Thank you, Hymileh, how could I have made that move if not for you?"

"What, Mama? How much did I carry? A few little things. Only Mama, about Ellis Island, if I could tell you what a whirl my head is in on account of poor Glantz. You think that maybe Willie could take you?"

"Certainly, why not darling, with such a worry?"

Now this was what you call a woman, his mama, not like that nut chasing him in the dark.

He came down from Mama's and Debbie Horowitz girl detective was still on duty across the street and ready to join him. He'd show her a join. He set off for the Delancey Street trolley with a stride that broke Debbie into an immediate trot and she ran straight up against two men walking.

Let them keep her, with interest—she could wear them out too! At Delancey, a spurt a jump and a shove and Hymie just caught the trolley.

It took most of the ride west to get his breath back—that crazy woman! Even at Broadway, transferring uptown, he felt . . . not sick exactly, but not well either, sick inside for Dora, and also—the way his heart thumped unevenly—really sick?

Then the hospital was full of sick people, in the hallways, the rooms, the wards. Dora still lay like a dead one with the cover up to her armpits and her eyes closed, that poor innocent face. Kirschner with his blue-grained jaw stared at the bed rails above Dora's pillow like the Angel of Death. And she had even worse company, a white-haired Methuselah with a turned-down mouth, heaving sighs, mourning in advance. Was he insane? Hymie felt like grabbing him by the collar and giving a heave he'd remember—and the husband along with him.

Instead Hymie played it dumb, he paid his respects to the old man. "Mr. Kirschner? My mother heard Mrs. Kirschner was . . . And I was in the neighborhood . . . So she sent a small jar of . . . " He put down the chicken soup.

The old man said, "This is Kirschner. Me, it's my daughter. You're the same age I am, your daughters should have better luck, if you have daughters."

"Where there's life," Hymie shook his finger, "there always must be hope."

Dora's father let out a groan. "You see hope there?"

"You'll have time," Kirschner turned on the old man, "to cry later." But the doctor had said—the doctor'd put it that way, Kirschner told Hymie—they'd have to hope for a miracle, she'd already had three transfusions.

"Did you try changing her name in *shul*?"

Kirschner jerked his head at his father-in-law. "He took care of that nonsense."

"They changed it to Hudl," the old man said.

Moron! The Angel of Death would be fooled by Hudl? How could his darling survive with these two as helpers? Hymie stood, he kept silent, he concentrated on Dora. *You must live!* With all his strength, all his energy, he sent her this message, over and over toward those blanched cheeks, those waxen eyelids.

Dora's head moved, she sighed. Was there faint color returning? *You must live, darling!* Her head moved back, the lids didn't open. Still—

The old man just mourned, but Kirschner, he also thought he'd seen something and he looked up at Hymie. *Dearest, live!* Hymie nodded.

"You could ask the doctor—"

Kirschner said, "You'll be here a minute, mister?" and hurried out. The old man, the father, didn't know he'd just been insulted, didn't see—*Live live live, dear girl!*—the life pouring back into his daughter, the life Hymie wished her, willed for her! Dora's lids fluttered, she stared at Hymie like she was dreaming. Hymie gave her a smile like an angel and then crossed his lips with his finger.

He touched Methuselah's shoulder—the same age I am, hah!

"Look—"

Methuselah raised his head and his eyes almost popped out.

Hymie said, "You'll give her some chicken soup," and he slipped away.

Hymie Share the Angel of Life—that was him! But don't worry, he could give credit where due. First thing in the morning he would be in *shul* thanking God. There could be relapses, too.

Now—he sprang out in the cold again, who had patience for trolleys!—where was his little detective with the black eyes and white body? He could have used her! God was he happy—he felt like twenty-one!

He absolutely had to see Dora.

About-face, he marched back, just in time to be a shadow himself and watch the visitors drag out of that gray comfortless building. The two killers passed right by him, Joe and the father-in-law, and to Hymie's surprise Dora's father was a tall man, the same height as Joe. Upstairs he'd sat shriveled, here he was like an arrow, he could have been Joe's brother. That made two Hymie had brought back to health!

Joe was bubbling over, "What happened to that—what was his name, with the chicken soup from his mother?"

"He appeared, he disappeared," the father-in-law bubbled with him. "And you still believe in nothing, Joe?"

"I believe, I believe."

Forgetting your gloves was an elevator pass and to the nurses Hymie could pose as Dr. Life with the silver hair, walking stick and pearl-gray overcoat. In the room Dora wasn't ready to polish the furniture, but her eyes brimmed with happiness.

"I was dreaming of you," she said, "then I woke and felt better."

"Yes darling," Hymie rejoiced with his own damp eyes, "I brought you roses, but you can't see them."

"They said," worried, "I'm too sick yet?"

"No," he stroked his finger along that soft skin, "because they're in your cheeks."

She had the strength to press her hand against his.

"Sit down, Hymie."

"No Mamaleh, I have to look like I'm going."

And sure enough a nurse popped her head in to ask him what he was doing there. So he formed a kiss on his lips for his convalescent and followed that tough white-capped string bean down the hall. Lean as she was though a certain twitch of the hips under the uniform made you feel like being her patient for a few minutes. Surely a young woman in this line of business would have a bed at her disposal?

"Are," Hymie caught up to her, "you going off duty soon?"

"Long after your bedtime, Pop."

In Yiddish he told her pleasantly to sink into the earth and in Yiddish this Irish mutt returned him the compliment. Eh, let her take that ugly mug to surgery, maybe they had a cure for it.

So what was the alternative? The fountain of youth, Miss Debbie Horowitz. The only trouble with her was that the real fountain of youth is youth and this one could wear you out. But tonight he was the Lion of Judah! He hopped two trolleys to Baxter Street and his siren's light shone in the window. If a heavy father answered, excuse me wrong flat.

Debbie's pout answered over her sexy wrapper.

"Go to hell nine o'clock."

He grabbed her wrist. "I'll see you downstairs, spy."

Kid speed, in no time those heels came pattering down the staircase. Listening, nurse? What had annoyed him taking Debbie home the other night, the clinging vine with the shivers, tonight excited him and he circled that limber waist.

Debbie said, "Murderer."

"I bring life."

"She'll die, the one you went to before."

"Pray she doesn't, or you'll die with her."

"You'll run begging to me when you have nobody else."

"Yes, I'll spy on you, I'll trail you, I'll follow you in the shadows."

But look at this. Across the way from the Bleecker Street fleabag he was taking Debbie to, he saw his daughter Leah come out of the place with a man.

"Wait," Hymie said.

"Another one?" Debbie cackled in her obsession. "Do you think you're fooling her too?"

Then Debbie was wise to his mattress shortcuts with her? But maybe not. Anyway, who cared what she meant. If he'd been by himself he would have given this daughter of his a good piece of his mind, and this big-mouth bum from her factory too, this Jack Berger wise-guy. Naomi you could forgive, a good loving child, even if she'd been too smart for her own good, running off God knows where against the father's advice. And what happened in Pittsburgh? Her lips were sealed. Let's hope, God willing, that nothing happened. In seven, eight months, we'll see. But Leah, his Lady Virtue with the sarcasm? Two-faced! And not even with pleasure. Hymie held Debbie back in the shadows, and between the entrance lights of the hotel his fine daughter and her lamp salesman were giving it to each other hot and heavy. Or rather Leah was hot with a mouth like bullets and she was listening to no sales talk from the salesman. And in the meantime a father could be stuck in the cold a whole night.

"A shrew," was Debbie's comment. "That's your taste?"

"My taste is angels, like you."

"Who is she?"

"My aunt."

Debbie laughed. "Did you say aunt?" and damn him if her hand didn't slip inside his coat right to his member!

Thank God Leah finished her say, whirled and click-clacked away, and left Berger to stare after her, strike a match at a cigarette and saunter off in the opposite direction.

In an airshaft bedroom, finally, Hymie had Miss Debbie Horowitz twisting like a chicken on a spit, without a sound, exciting as the first time and with no cheating required on his part. And this glutton, this white-bodied athlete, claimed that she'd been a virgin till she met him!

Hymie let her have virgin again, then, relaxed, half-awake, he murmured, "What's gotten into you girls, what mania? Was it the war?"

"What girls?" She pushed Hymie off her and sat up, Debbie ferocious. "Never lump me in with those aunts. I'll have you, or you'll rue the day you set eyes on me."

"You think that I'll leave my wife for you?"

"You're too soft. You'll never leave her."

"Then Miss Greed, how will you have me?"

"She'll leave you."

Debbie laid hands on Hymie, slid her thigh over him—two minutes after a session! Now right here with the high-powered ass and belly on top of him, yes you Debbie sweetheart, was the one who was going to be left—the second that his Dora was better!

Nobody talked to anybody in the agency waiting room, as if they were enemies, dog eat dog, the actors, showgirls, specialty acts. Danny slouched ankle across knee in the torture chamber and tried to look nonchalant though no one gave one little damn how he looked or even knew he was there. His eyes kept swimming the expanse of plush maroon carpet to that doll with a cap of hair blue-black as plumage and with a pair of beautiful dark impatient eyes that flicked past him once as if he was part of the furniture. Naturally the eyes smiled and looked demure—onstage—when an international profile Edwin Mulholland strolled in with an agency toady. But Mulholland—why dislike him? he could act—noticed her eyes the same as she'd noticed Danny's.

But it was a bright sunny day, almost spring. You practiced smiling at the skyscrapers outside the windows and they smiled straight back. At the saloon last week Uncle Willie and he had pruned away bruised maple limbs and shrub branches, and though Danny'd started with a lot to learn about sawing, toward the end Uncle Willie said he was getting there. He was also doing okay in school: no East Side Bolshevik geniuses teaching or learning in the fresh air of Orange. He even bragged law school next and impressed Carrie.

"I'll be the lawyer's wife," she said.

"I thought you were going in for big things in the big city."

"Ain't that big enough?"

So Danny was set for a profession and a skinny nut of a wife. Then why was he here? He was here because . . . he didn't know why he was here.

Grandma wanted an Ellis Island escort—old country cousins due on the *Empress of Liverpool* full steam ahead—and Uncle Willie'd volunteered Danny. Danny wasn't too keen on it, meeting two old women, but you couldn't say no to Uncle Willie and you wouldn't say no to Grandma. So this morning he had put on his one and only suit—Anna had pressed it for the occasion—and in the saloon Anna couldn't have beamed at him harder if she'd been his own mother.

"You'll never see him again Willie," Anna joked. "Those New York girls'll never let him get away twice."

"He won't let a g-g-girl come between us," Uncle Willie'd grinned like sunshine. "W-would you? . . . S-say, he's thinking it over!"

Behind Danny's red face there had been a thought—king of the dopes—Sylvia.

Then Uncle Willie loaded him down like a greenhorn with jars of honey from last year's hives—some for Grandma, some for Ma and some to dispose of any way Danny saw fit. The "saw fits" made him think of Sarah for the first time in months. Jesus, some cousin he'd turned out to be, not a goodbye to her and just one postcard in answer to one she'd written him.

And much as he loved the country, what spray, what sunlight at the bow of the ferry churning the North River, with ocean liners in port whistling and streaming up smoke and overhead gulls squeaking, gliding, flapping and stumbling into the green-and-gold breeze. He'd taken a quick look to make sure no one was close and cupped his hands for a yell—"New York, that's my town!"—at the gingerbread skyline.

So a wise guy wind made him eat his own words. He had the uke along. That was when he decided one more shot at the theatrical agents.

West Street had been all push and tumult, longshoremen shouldering bales, teamsters backing their wagons flush with the loading platforms. Between piers the sun teemed on the river. A wagonload of fish had shone like silver. Danny's nose had been full of waterfront smells, his eyes full of light, and boy—he'd known through to his bones that this was his day!

In the factory though, the dark of the stairway'd made him a blind man, he'd had to grope his way up. And a step into the loft—more people less space, a burst of noise, a sweet stink of machine oil, girls bent stitching shade hems, some guy enameling frames—and if it had been anything but a social call he'd have just backed quietly out. Only—he blinked at the racket—where were Ma and his sisters?

But in the daylight beyond the electric dimness of the wrapping tables where two kids were busy at the job he'd handled solo—home sweet home! Hester Street had been sweatshop and West Street was big business, but there'd been Ma over the same old sewing machine and there'd been Leah and Naomi, two heads together, only in a glass-partitioned office and at books not wigs, with Jack Berger's head the third for a crowd.

With plenty of eeks hugs and kisses they'd surrounded their pride and joy and been presented with honey and the news he was joining vaudeville.

Ma—"Really?"—had doubted it, Naomi had squeezed his hands, "Remember, you always have us," and Berger's "See you at Proctor's" didn't sound like a date. Just Leah had said, "Don't pay any attention to these disloyal people—you go and wow them Danny!"

He'd guessed they'd all meant well, but the parties of the first part had had the exact gauge of the agencies uptown. The opener had given him a half-chorus audition then the phone rang. The next two hadn't been looking for Irish minstrel types. The fourth'd said he had talent leave his name with the girl. The fifth had been a bald Greek with old-fashioned sideburns who'd sat there and encouraged Danny through three full tunes. Had the hopes shot sky-high while that guy'd thought it over! Danny'd sat back with the ridiculous grin he'd stuck on for all of them and his heart galloping like Rosa the mare when he'd let her loose out in Jersey.

The man confided, "The trouble is, we got singing acts. Maybe you could spice up the songs with a contortionist routine, you got the build. Say roll yourself up in a ball with your head between your legs facing the audience. Then you play your uke and you sing . . . I admit an act like that would take plenty of practice."

"Nah, and at the same time I could unbutton and button my fly."

But it had been a relief to stop grinning for a minute. Just the same he hadn't given into himself and his temper, the excuse for avoiding what he disliked, and he'd unleashed the grin again here in this Show Time Agency reception room plush as the Ritz. The receptionist was a nice kid and she'd sworn that even if she did send in his name no one at the Show Time Agency ever talked to an act off the street. But Sarah was forever pushing him to be pushy, so he'd kept his thirty-two white horses shining upon their red hill till the girl did send his name in.

Yet even Sarah, certainly Sarah, wouldn't want him to be a complete idiot, and facts were facts. You saw the whole waiting room—except you—change faces in the course of a couple of hours and you could admit the receptionist may have had something there and that it was breeze time—a hot breeze of course.

Into cool sunlight. You did have to push to get ahead in the big town—agencies, lamp factories, jammed-full sidewalks. The trouble was, he was the pushee.

Then came this goddam fool urge to run after Sylvia. He hugged his uke case to his chest and swiveled between other morons—they moved just fast enough to stay in your way—down to where Sylvia worked in the clothing district. How come, lovelorn minstrel? He hadn't thought of her for months out in Orange. On the corner of Seventeenth Street and Sixth he resumed his typecast role: prize schlemiel. He craned his neck for her as if he had a date with her there, while the home-goers spun him around like Uncle Willie's weathercock in a high wind. Finally one large chap pushed Danny into the gutter and, instead of swinging, Danny quit. He'd had enough of Sylvia and the big town. He chased down to find Grandma in case by luck the greenhorns might be landing today. Then Ellis Island and tomorrow he'd be back at Uncle Willie's saloon.

They were doing all kinds of sowing in the vegetable garden now: beets, radishes, lettuce. Early this morning—that'd been a crisp tasty sunlight—Anna'd been on her hands and knees peeling winter mulch off her flower garden between the house and the pond. And the pond had mirrored the long trees and sticky buds in the still of the morning. A half-day away and Danny even missed nutty Carrie. Yesterday she'd been in her yard with a knife and an outraged chicken she'd pinned down on its side.

"Here," she'd offered Danny the knife, "kill this chicken."

"Kill it yourself. I have no grudge against it."

"Tan-capped sparrow." She'd meant Danny, he'd had his cap on. "Maybe if you had your uncle's shotgun you wouldn't be scared to."

That was her old man's crummy Baum joke.

Ten years ago, after a planting, Uncle Willie'd walked out with his shotgun because the crows ate up his seeds three meals a day and snacks. Uncle Willie said the crows ought to be big city birds they're so smart. One guy lays chickee in a treetop out of range and barks to the rest of the gang that you're coming along. But Uncle Willie'd been new there then. Meanwhile a pheasant had followed behind him like a pet dog. Uncle Willie'd stopped, so'd the pheasant. Uncle Willie'd started, pinhead'd also started.

"S-s-skiddoo," Uncle Willie'd told that dumb bird, "I'm not hunting you."

Up had popped a woodchuck that likewise had enjoyed Uncle Willie's plants best. Uncle Willie'd taken a quick shot at him, and another, and the gun'd misfired both times. The woodchuck had done a brown dive into the woods, the crows'd given Uncle Willie the horselaugh, and the pheasant'd hung around looking stupid.

Uncle Willie'd waved the gun at him, "I s-said s-skiddoo!" and nearly'd jumped out of his own skin when that gun went off. Then Uncle Willie'd been stunned to see the bird on its back. Had the poor guy fainted? But he'd picked up that limp body and there'd been blood on the wing . . . fatal accident.

Uncle Willie'd said, "Wh-what was he but a red-faced chicken with a long tail, and I'd s-slaughtered plenty of chickens in my time. S-so why did I feel so bad?"

Worst, starting that day a pheasant Uncle Willie'd been tossing corn grain to had quit showing up. So that had been the guy, following Uncle Willie because Uncle Willie'd been feeding him. And that had been the last time Uncle Willie ever had taken a gun out. . . .

So Danny'd suddenly pushed one hand inside Carrie's sweater, grabbed the back of her neck with the other and stuck a kiss on her mouth, not of love—far from it. The chicken'd run away fast, but Carrie'd pressed her skinny bones against Danny, held on good and long and gotten him so excited that it had been embarrassing—but not to Carrie. Would you believe that she gave him a sly smile and took a flick at his jigger? Next she'd casually strolled after her chicken and, among all those red chickens, caught it with one magic dart of her wrist.

In spite of his principles Danny had tried to follow up on this new-style chicken flicker. But, "Nix," Carrie'd said, "you'll just have to cool down for five years till we get married." With another lightning move she'd stabbed the chicken right in the head and it'd gone limp as a soggy banana. Danny'd felt like taking a real dive at Carrie and the hell with it all. Instead he'd gulped like a ninny.

"You're a killer."

Carrie had smiled up at him sweetly.

"The quicker the kill, the easier the pluck."

Jesus it made Danny hot now just thinking of Carrie! And stupid, over a dame as skinny as that.

He drifted through the hubbub of Essex, Suffolk, Norfolk Streets, full of people and pushcarts but no Grandma. The sun was beginning to peter out at the housetops, the air became sharp. Wide Delancey Street was much lighter and after a block or two the crowds weren't that thick. What if he uncased his ukulele, laid his cap on the sidewalk for pennies and, the Irish troubadour from County Bar Mitzvah, sang the housewives a tune? Yeah, sure. Crosstown over black piers and warehouses a red sun was slipping down for a dip in the river.

Jesus Christ, were his feet really carrying him west toward the Bowery station to gape like a clown for Sylvia? The hell with that! Where was he?

The lamppost said Clinton Street. Whew, that was close. He'd forgotten about Grandma, the idiot grandson. Clinton Street was her street, his feet must have been getting smart for a change.

Grandma wouldn't be home yet. From the top of her stoop he watched the derbies go by with the long yellowing whiskers, kerchiefed women with kids, and, in the shadows when the street lamps came on, girls home from work.

Just one he wanted, to fall in love with.

But he was freezing his ass off and still not a sign of Grandma. Upstairs he knocked and Grandma's landlady with the black hair and crazy eye glittered at him.

"Oh poor boy, your grandmother's dead. Her leech died, so she couldn't bear life without her."

He stared dumbfounded till—moron!—he could have socked his head. Grandma'd moved. With all due respect to Grandma there'd been a letter to Uncle Willie what a great guy her son Hymie was, carrying her featherbed, her teakettle, her dish and her spoon the five big blocks to Suffolk Street.

Danny beat it quick from that maniac.

At supper Naomi couldn't have been more sympathetic, indignant even, about Danny's music adventures, especially the Greek contortionist item.

"Oh sure, they enjoy tying you up in knots. You can't trust any of them." Her brother was pleased she said that, but underneath she was thinking of herself and love. Love tied you up in knots and made you unhappy, all you could trust was work. So you went to work, and here was love again—Jack Berger—and her present predicament. Why did Jack have to be so cute and lazy? Why had he had to be Leah's boy friend? Leah, not she, had invited him into the business and on top of that promised him a partnership with the hitch when profits warranted.

"Why begrudge me my laziness," Jack had grinned at the sincere talking-to for his own good that Naomi'd given him, "if I'm lazy at my own expense?"

Of course, it was at their expense too. But as Jack pointed out, what did profits warranted mean to a guy like him? He didn't sneer at gold, he'd admitted, otherwise who'd care about partnership? But gold wasn't his prime interest. So she'd bit, knowing very well what the answer would be, and asked what was.

Jack hadn't hesitated. "Well, you," he'd said seriously.

And if that was "Nonsense," as she'd immediately said, how come her . . . joy!

Just the same, she'd tried not to come out like sunshine, interests weren't the point. The point was, she was asking him to stop welding frames afternoons—they had Taks and Kammerman to weld frames—and use his valuable time selling such-and-such places Quality Lamps.

"I'd rather," Jack had said, "weld lamps and watch you."

"With one eye, and the other on Leah?"

"Leah gave me my walking papers because both my eyes tend to be on you."

"But," Naomi had forced herself to say, "we're in business, Jack. You'll make me give you your walking papers on the business side."

"Don't do that," he'd leveled those gray eyes on her. "I have to see you."

And he'd brought in orders from the Astor Hotel, then the McAlpin, and he'd been careful to break the good news each time when she was alone in the office. She'd had an urge to kiss him, but he would have taken that personally. Had she been excited!

"Get more! I feel so greedy!"

"I don't," Jack had said quietly.

"Then you'll be rich in spite of yourself."

"I don't want to be rich, I simply want to marry you and live happily ever after." How had he sensed she was going to answer by gaily calling Leah in from the shop? "Wait," he'd leaned close.

"Don't you dare," she'd whispered.

"Kiss you? Nobody's kissing you. Smell that booze on my breath? That's the New Yorker order—a three hours' lunch, or shall I say imbibing, with the manager and two boob assistants. Drinking isn't my sport, I like my mind clear. Unfortunately I didn't work out for your sister. How it happened after that would be hard to say, but I love you." He'd winked. "If the same goes when I'm sober, I'll let you know."

The next day he had let her know, and more confusion—he'd still started out with Leah—more joy. Three little words, eight little letters, but none of the cagy boys it had been her luck to meet had ever said I love you to her. At night she had happy dreams of searching for him up and down ritzy hotels . . . and finding him. He was so loving—in the dream too—so handsome. "I owe you a kiss," she'd say in the dream, and they would kiss. Then in real life also.

So Naomi had put it straight to Leah, was her sister finished with Jack? Leah'd laughed, "I am, but his heart belongs to another."

"Who?"

"Quality Lamps."

Sour grapes, but Naomi'd decided to keep on meeting Jack away from the house to avoid further comments. With the dishes done she pinned down her cute green velour hat with the rose on it, did over-the-shoulder poses at the looking-glass in the new green coat she was just nuts about even though the fur trimming was pussycat, and lied that she was going to the Settlement House.

"Have fun," Leah gave her a wink, "but don't get serious."

Danny's heart lurched—Settlement House. Then there was a dance on, Naomi didn't doll up like Astor's pet horse for lectures. *Just happened to walk my sister here*, he'd say to Sylvia if she was there. "Naomi, just a sec, I'll go with you." But the door slammed, so he made a dash for his coat.

"Slow down, innocence," Leah said. "She has a date with my ex."

Golda said, "I'm so worried about Naomi with that one."

"What's that guy doing, a family tour?" Danny jabbed his arm into a sleeve. "I'm bringing her back!"

"You just stay put, Master Temper," his sister said. "Naomi will bring herself back, just as she brought herself back from that shrewdie Stein in Pittsburgh. She's very practical."

"Then why all the remarks if she's so damn practical?"

To his amazement that floored them. Leah glanced at him, then at Ma, and she and Ma both began laughing.

"What's the gag? I'll pull it on the Show Time Agency tomorrow and maybe they'll talk to me." He had them doubled up. "Spill it for chrissakes, let me in on it."

Leah could barely point. "You look so . . . stern."

Go figure dames.

Including Grandma, who he found home finally after supper. Uncle Willie sends honey, and what's her answer?

"Ah Danneleh, good sons make a mother's life sweet."

Why the plural? Did Uncle Willie add up to twins? For Grandma the other good son was Danny's old man, and Danny had to sit there in Suffolk Street and smile like at the agencies. How could she compare the two of them? Danny wasn't religious or not religious. But Grandma was religious and his father had her fooled because he might have walked her to *shul* last Rosh Hashonah? Uncle Willie never went near a *shul*, but if you were religious you could take him as a model.

Danny hadn't been able to figure out Uncle Willie and Anna at first, in fact they'd embarrassed him by letting him see for himself. But what he'd seen was that they were married, minus the marriage. Anna'd remarked to Danny that they hadn't married because Uncle Willie didn't want to hurt Grandma's feelings by marrying a Gentile. Then last week Uncle Willie went to market, Anna was tending bar with Danny as barboy, and the road workers drinking became pretty merry and stood Anna a few. So Anna'd turned mushy, hung her arm on Danny's neck while he dried glasses and said it was her fault Willie and her were not man and wife. She'd been married once, she'd said, to a very brave guy named Coker who'd been at San Juan Hill in the Spanish-American War. But peace finished Coker. He drank, then he quit talking, then gave up eating, and to this day he was in the crazy house. And know who visited Coker? Not her. She'd stopped visiting Coker because her second husband, Riley, didn't approve and she'd gotten out of the habit. But Uncle Willie had stammered, "Y-you can't let the poor guy s-simply r-r-rot there," and he visited Coker, brought him clothes, little pastries she'd baked.

Not that Riley had been her actual husband. That is, he was, but it had been a common law marriage, till Riley'd kept getting so tanked she'd had to walk out on him. Yes, Anna'd told Danny, Uncle Willie used to keep pestering her straighten out her life and make an honest man of him. But all that stuff made her dizzy, getting Coker annulled, and besides, why hurt Willie's mother? This way Anna stayed out of sight the once in a blue moon Grandma came out, and no harm was done.

Danny'd said, "If you made him an honest man you could still stay out of sight and no harm would be done."

That was where Anna had blown herself to a drink.

"You're an ace at logic," Anna'd laughed, "even better than your uncle. He doesn't want me to hide."

Okay, so Grandma didn't know this. But she knew everything else about Uncle Willie. How could she go so wrong?

Still, between Danny's father, the greenhorns—yes, expected, but God knew when, on those terrible boats that crowd you like animals underneath—and her friend Bertha in Denver, Grandma was preventing him from making a jackass of himself at the Settlement House tonight much as he wanted to.

"Bertha," Grandma said, "keeps house for good people, and she writes and of course doesn't complain. But, you should never have to learn this, Danneleh, to live with the rich a person has to humble herself."

"I'd spit in their eye."

"At eighteen you spit, at thirty-eight, Danneleh, you swallow. That proud spirit has her son to live for. Ah, it should only not kill her. . . . How she would have enjoyed this room, so spacious—"

Like any good grandson, Danny admired the spaces, none too large, between the chiffonier, the bed and the chair, and he kept quiet about his saddle room ten times this size at the barn. And that swung Grandma into a rehash of Saint Hymie the moving man.

But Grandma kissed him good night and he strolled through the cool streets—stars like pinpoints, not the New Jersey splashes across the sky—to the Settlement House anyway.

Lefty Lefkowitz—"You cheap son of a bitch, not even a card saying having wonderful time wish I was there?"—clapped both Danny's biceps. "Gettin' much out in Jersey, at least big tits to look at, like Sylvia's hair is like the night?" Lefty ducked Danny's feint. "She got what she deserved though—Solly the condom kid. They're engaged . . ."

Just as well, so don't cry.

But in the house he felt so lousy that he grabbed a jar of honey and astonished Ma and Leah—"Where are you going at this hour?"—by dashing out again. He deserved some credit with his cousin Sarah for that contortionist agent, and—he had to smile though at the stuff he gave her: bananas, honey . . . some nourishment—he put on speed toward her house. At the empty lot he saw a light in her window for the wandering boy and in the hallway he gave her bell key a happy flip.

What looked out at him but Cousin Mary's moonface with a sort of victory glint. Danny said his piece anyway, "Sarah in?" and Cousin Mary mimicked him, "No Sarah's not in." Then she hoisted one fat cheek with real pleasure, sang "What did you think, she sits home waiting for you? My regards to your mother," and left him holding the honey.

6

TO CROWN IT ALL IT WAS TEEMING. THE STREETCAR WOBbled through zany gray sheets of rain, which finally slapped the trolley rod off the overhead line. The car squatted God knows how long on lower Broadway while the motorman put on his fisherman outfit and went to stamp around on the roof.

Rivka murmured, "Oy."

And kindhearted as Grandma was, Danny knew that oy wasn't for the Irisher doing the rain dance upstairs. The pair of poor fish marooned in New York Bay—if Ellis Island was still afloat in this deluge—were her worry.

Okay, but why his?

Leah had calmly told him why his. Their father, with a lifetime of practice, had wriggled out of what he'd preferred not to do. However, you didn't register such complaints with your grandma.

Just the same, Danny morosely asked, "How will we know them?"

"They wear tags there, Danneleh," Rivka smiled through narrow eyes at her grandson, "like the best merchandise."

"Very nice."

"That's why, poor things, they shouldn't be kept waiting like this."

Was he being blamed yet? No, Grandma dipped into her canvas carryall, with such trembling hands that Danny glanced at that face full of lines, seams, old warts and kindness, really saw it so that it clutched his heart. Sure, why not Ellis Island? Grandma brought up a studio photo from the old country, with Russian on the back. This mild young guy with a neat mustache and dark suit faced the camera from a chair in front of a stage flat with a dim garden scene. But at his shoulder this beauty stood with light hair piled up—and for Danny it was love at first sight.

With a sense of loss, as if this one had been his girl, not Sylvia, and had gone and gotten married on him, he couldn't let go of the picture.

"How young she looks there," he heard Grandma sigh, "like a child. Yet on her wedding day Gittel was far from a spring chicken. In Kadzyrnye she was old to be single, a spinster already. Through those years she could have had anyone—but Gittel loved a party, she loved to dance! Then her father, he was my Uncle Strool-liebe, kept saying what was the rush. Poor man, he didn't live to see his daughter a bride. But the second that the mourning for him was over—my Aunt Pearl, Gittel's mother, didn't let grass grow under her feet—Gittel was married to Elya Leben, her father's clerk. What a surprise, that they picked a dreamer. Elya was well known for walking in the woods with a European book in his hand so wolves would find him and he would have to climb a tree till a carter drove by and whipped them away. Besides, he wasn't a dancer. That sly flirt Gittel would say, 'He'll dance,' and set all the hens cackling. But if one of the mean ones would say, 'You'll have plenty to teach a boy so much younger,' Gittel would get on her high horse. 'First I'll teach you arithmetic,' she would say, 'if his twenty-two minus my eighteen makes him younger.' And it's true, in our family we always look younger—but unfortunately," Grandma laughed, "only to seventy-five. Or else, it's so long ago maybe I am mistaken, maybe Gittel was younger. Elya never did dance, but Pearl and Gittel made a good choice anyway. He kept up Strool-liebe's business, day and night in the warehouse, better even than my uncle himself when he was alive. For Elya home was just eating and sleeping. Ah Danneleh, how long ago, how long ago. Alexander the Second was still Czar, or was it Alexander the Third God should forgive him for his sins against Jews. . . ."

Alexander the Second! Jesus Christ, Danny was in love with a historical character!

Grandma had asked cousin Gittel for a more recent picture, but Reisel whose only love was Britannia and the cousins to flirt with had refused to have pictures taken. "So, with a difficult daughter, at Ellis Island we'll have to go by the tags they put on them, in case we ever get there. Danneleh, is your grandma tired out from this electric car! They went better with horses."

"Grandma, how old is the daughter?"

"How old could she be? I heard Gittel had to wait for even a daughter. Do my elderly eyes deceive me, thank God is that man back?"

But if somebody is eighty or ninety like Grandma, how old is not old? Grandma remembered the girl in the picture's wedding! The motorman's shiny slicker streamed water, the car hissed, shuddered and screeched, and hooray—they were off, to the old ladies from the old country.

On the ferry gangplank he paused to inhale the rain skidding over the bay, curling the whitecaps, waves riding waves along the sidewheeler, and the wind almost blew him and Grandma into the drink. Gee, the top deck bow would have been nice, the Iceland fisherman grinning into the storm, Mr. Christopher Columbus. As it was, Danny hustled Grandma a back-breaker seat on an inside bench and balanced himself in front of her on a packed shelter deck with the windows steamed over so you couldn't see where you'd been or what you were heading for.

At Ellis Island immigrants stood hunched on the pier, under umbrellas or derbies or shawls, soggy, with soggy boxes, suitcases, bundles. The rain became needle-fine, hardly enough to shrink your one suit up to your wrists if you hadn't been drenched through to begin with. From other gangplanks new greenies were being unloaded, and, the far side of the boardwalk, at Hotel America with its turrets, white facing and red brick a dismal gray in the drizzle, still more greenies all laden filed in and out. Beards wild or trimmed; clean-shaven; fuzzy mustaches, waxed, walrus; ritual wigs sticking out of kerchiefs, high natural hair, wide-lidded bonnets. So what did they all have in common, these greenhorns?

No tags.

"No name tags, Grandma."

"Don't be angry, dear. In my day they pinned tags on."

You could tell who were the guards though. They wore the raincoats. Danny stepped forward ready to battle one of the brogue boys—"All right, step lively . . . All right, step lively now"—but the guard wasn't battling. He pointed Danny to a wing of the palace.

Only, inside, it looked like a Carrie Baum chicken coop, except with people, Jesus Christ—people! Danny thought of his historical sweetheart and saw red.

"They got some hell of a nerve!"

"Danneleh, tell their name to the policeman—"

Over the hubbub the guard let loose a "Leben!" with a roar like Farmer Baum's bull when Carrie shut him out of the cow pasture. He bellowed another name, and another—name after name. People in the coop jumped up, they craned, waved, exclaimed, grabbed baggage. But who would cousins Gittel and Reisel wave to, if no one knew anyone?

Danny spotted a likely pair—"Leben?"—one old, one middle-aged. These two exchanged a mistrustful glance with each other and kept moving . . . when out of the blue Danny found himself smothered with Yiddish kisses.

"I could have recognized you among a million!" this withered doll in green with plenty of leg showing swore to him. The cheeks were talcum-white and as rumpled as if she'd swum to America. "Do you believe in reincarnation? You're the exact image of my papa, except—" she reached, Danny ducked, but she stroked his chin—"except Papa wore the loveliest beard. . . ."

"Oh Mamá, introduce yourself," a fahncy accent half-Jewish and half-British burst in, "de young man does not know you."

"How can he not know me? I mailed them a picture." She slurped him another smacko. "Rivka sent you?"

Grandma toddled up, "Gittel?," and the character gaped.

"You're Rivka? What happened to you in America? You look like ancient history!" And without so much as a handshake for Grandma the benefactress, "Reisel, here's your cousin Rivka, slightly decrepit," Gittel tittered, "but at least say hello to her like a person instead of standing there with limp wrists."

But the kid, the Cinderella with red curls crowning her mourning shawl and with a set of round breasts you only wanted to lay hands on pushing up a black shabby coat, stooped to Grandma. "May I kiss you, Baba Rivka? May I thank you, thank you, for all of your kindness to us? . . . " Next this man-to-man angel held her hand out and gave Danny's a shake. "Ond you, young man, for setting us free."

"Then that really is Gittel?" To think of that picture then to watch the mamá trying to wriggle away from Grandma's hugs, blessings and one-sided kisses, you felt sorry for Gittel. "But is she your actual mother?"

"Why should she not be my mother? She admits it herself."

"Because she dates back to Czar Alexander and you're about sixteen years old."

"How old?"

"Sixteen."

"What?" she stayed happily deaf.

Danny grinned, "You heard me, sixteen," and Jesus, he loved her already!

"What is your name? . . . I do not care that they call you Danny. I prefer Da-ni-el. Daniel in the lion's den! Thank you, Daniel," she giggled, "though often I feel more like sixty. However, your compliment sounds sincere, not like those of my East End tailor cousins, although they are good souls for roughnecks."

"Rivka, didn't I tell you?" Gittel broke loose and pointed. "She's after your grandson!"

Yeah? He wouldn't run fast. But nah, look at her blush and go for their baggage. Gent Danny beat her to those four bulging suitcases—"Be careful of my beautiful dresses," Gittel bragged, "she'd have gotten rid of them if I let her"—and he staggered to the pier burdened down like a jackass. But what the hell, to be thanked by Reisel again!

The rain had thinned and the skyline loomed mistily the far side of the water. Reisel gazed—what a face!—with her eyes shining.

"Mountains," she murmured.

"Buildings," Danny told her, surprised. "You saw the skyscrapers from shipboard?"

"I forgot for the moment. You should not have reminded me."

"She saw nothing from shipboard," Gittel chimed in. "Too busy chasing sailors and *Yidlach* in steerage."

Reisel muttered, "The scum."

"But I saw Sandy Hook, then the port, then—I'm so happy Rivka!—Madame Liberty!"

Steel-gray water sucked at the pier, Reisel with the faintest of smiles kept staring out at the bay. Danny wanted to hold her, comfort her. As it was he defended her against the old glad-rag doll.

"Reisel never belonged in steerage."

"Who belonged there," Gittel laughed nastily, "I perhaps? But I happen to know how to make the best of things."

Not like Reisel, Gittel kept up the squawk while Danny lugged her stuff onto the ferry. Her daughter'd bartered away not only clothing but some of their most valuable possessions on the *Empress of Liverpool,* Reisel's earrings, Reisel's cameo, Reisel's exquisite gold watch. And for what? Potatoes, because Princess Rose would not consume unkosher food!

"Ah Gitteleh," Rivka smiled, "you should be proud of her."

"Of her manias? Her father deserts her, and . . . "

"Deserts me?" Reisel crinkled her face. "To God my dear papá deserted me."

" . . . and," Gittel plowed on, "at twenty-one suddenly—from the opposite extreme, the freethinker, she thinks praying will bring him back?—she turns to religion."

"Gitteleh, where else can we turn?"

"Who had to turn anywhere," Gittel puckered up ready to cry, "when we could have stayed home in Kadzyrnye?"

Twenty-one, Jesus, what a blow, she was older than he. Danny felt shriveled. Reisel was sitting next to him on the ferry bench, but—twenty-one—she might as well have never left England. Yeah, he could live in the same house with her, care for her, know her better than anyone, what chance did he stand? She'd figure him for a kid.

Reisel sprang up. "Let us go outside and see your skyscrapers."

"I know 'em all—Woolworth, Standard Oil, Bankers Trust!"

And in the spray of rain before they even reached the bow, Reisel smiled shyly, beautifully at Danny.

"Thank you, Daniel."

"What for?"

"For taking my part." She fetched out a studio portrait. "View me as a long-nosed English lady."

"With your short nose?" He wanted to kiss it. But take a gander at this! In front of a painted rose garden Reisel not only stood smiling and beautiful, breathtaking in a broad-brimmed summer hat and slender print dress, but the unhappy lady posed on a cane chair was Gittel! "My grandmother said your mother said you said you wouldn't take pictures."

"I?"

She had enough snapshots in that bag to stock an album, all ages and scenes: braids, fluffy hair, coils, a baldy infant pointing at you from her proud papa's arms, even a gray country house with a patio. He sneaked a shot of her in bathing dress into his pocket. "Which do I keep?" And damned if she didn't hand him the house.

"Before," her lips moved, "the animals came."

"One of you, I mean."

"Ve shall take one together."

How do you like that! Maybe she didn't figure him for such a kid!

So—fair's fair, since he'd asked—he sneaked the abducted shot back into the pack. And at Battery Park he still was so overjoyed that for the first time in his life he hailed a four-wheeler. As the coachman slung up the baggage Danny had this pang for the chunk of his infinitesimal savings the extravagance was going to cost him. Even a taxi would have been cheaper, and Grandma's thought was couldn't they manage by trolley. The worst was that Reisel's "So your streets really are paved with gold" sounded a little too wise for his taste.

Gittel was the impressed one. She pushed her wrist under his arm in the cab and let it be known that in contrast her daughter's generous London uncle had transported them to the station in a wagon like peasants. Reisel only played her mysterious smile on the damp overcast half-empty cleft of Wall Street, and as they jolted over the cobbles past the warehouses east she said nothing either. But at Hester Street with its pushcarts and its mud puddles, its crowds and its noise, with the coachman snapping his whip and barking down curses, her smile became grim and Danny's eyes opened.

Jesus Christ, he'd never seen this before, he'd simply lived here.

Reisel said, "You did not care for London, Mamá."

"Wet blanket, can't you see we're just passing through?"

"Not passing through so fast," Rivka laughed, "but soon you get used to it."

"No need getting used to it," Danny snapped. "We're moving."

And—nowhere to dodge—was rewarded with a wet loving smack on the cheek from his new girl friend Gittel. "Danneleh! Of course he wouldn't let me stay in such a Gehenna, sweet boy, he knows I'm too sensitive—"

Grandma was surprised. "You're moving? Where, Danneleh?"

"Far—and fast."

Yeah, he'd been shirking his responsibilities as man of the family, but the time had come to take hold. Number one, he was going to learn the lamp racket—and not at the shipping tables. Jesus, rich!—driving his wife Reisel, and the hell with the age difference, in a long closed car with a chauffeur. Meanwhile a move to say Harlem, with trees and open green you could see from your window, might keep Reisel with them. A seven room flat—okay six, he'd sleep in the parlor, which would still be an improvement over the kitchen cot here—and there'd be space for everyone. And if luck really kept rolling Danny's way, Mr. Hymie Share might just decide not to join 'em, might just stay put in Hester Street near his lady love with the belly!

Reisel woke first. When she turned on the kitchen gaslight, Naomi and Daniel were still asleep on mattresses across parlor chairs, handsome, two fine profiles on their pillows, innocent—unlike herself—Reisel could tell.

They had not been seized by barbarians, polluted by beasts, as she had. That however, what had happened in Kadzyrnye, had been her punishment. No girl in Kadzyrnye had had a father like her father. "You have a good little wife helping you there," a Gentile said to Papá in the warehouse. Papá had beamed, "That's my daughter." How proud Reisel had been to be mistaken for Papá's wife! Her pride, her sin. Why should Papá have paid? That her mother was a jealous light-minded woman who tried to match her with oafs was no excuse for Reisel. Possibly in Kadzyrnye, certainly in Wladkow while she was in Gymnasium, her ideal must have existed if only she had looked. In any case, even if her ideal had not existed, there had been the good young men—Silber's Joseph, Rappaport's Yankel—her dear concerned unselfish Papá had suggested. She had asked herself, marry, leave poor Papá to her mother? But perhaps she had been the selfish one, not wanting to leave him, not wanting what as a Jewish girl it had been her duty to want: a husband, and children? Why else, after the mill and warehouse were plundered by their fine peasant friends, then by troops, then set afire by bandits, why else had the day dawned for horses to pound into Kadzyrnye again with Reds, or Whites—who knew which, and what was the difference? That day, no matter how humble her selfless father had been, standing on the carpet that covered the trapdoor to the cellar, the Revolutionaries, White or Red, the idealists aflame with their pure world, were too clever. They slit her dear Papá's throat, and they dragged her out of the cellar. Thank God that they had not searched to her mother's hiding place. Where Reisel had found strength to be silent, she knew. God had granted her strength. While the Revolutionaries, the idealists, tore off her shirtwaist, her skirt and her chemise, she had fought them hoping to die and had drawn blood from a hand, an animal face, but had never uttered a sound. Otherwise her mamá, poor scared hen, would surely have rushed from behind the woodpile to be plucked, perhaps God forbid slaughtered. Thank God too Reisel had not seen her dear papá—God Himself could not have helped her from crying out then—till the Revolutionaries, the world-savers, had finished with her. One detached a bayonet to cut her throat also, and—"Cut"—she had stretched her neck out for him.

"Don't spoil good meat," another Revolutionary had laughed. "We'll stop in on the way back."

Of what had been left they looted what pleased them, but thank God they had not had time for her other skirt and shirtwaist in the chifforobe. She had cleaned herself—on the surface: the inside would be filth always—dressed, and called to Mamá that they were gone. But, but . . . Then she had flung herself over Papá, with his frightened face, his wound, and his blood.

The children of Israel were stiff-necked, she among them. God had spared her, against her will, for repentance. She lived in a murderers' world, where murderers, the Gentiles, had every convenience. For Gentile women in her case the Gentiles maintained hermitages. Being Jewish, she would be her own hermitage, to live God's life while she breathed and only hope to die without pain. Her mother had grown so bizarre in Whitechapel, the insistence Papá—that papá of Reisel's who gave his life for them—had abandoned them, that the quirk had finally shone through as a message from God sending Reisel for penance to America.

Yet last night her cousins, in misplaced kindness, had made a fuss about her sleeping on chairs. The boy, already in love with her, insisted she take the kitchen cot, chairs were perfect for him.

"And I," Mamá had reminded them, "will sleep standing up."

"No Mamá, you will sleep on the cot and I shall be comfortable on other chairs in the parlor."

But that had shocked her cousins though they did not say so, that she should share a room with Daniel, even a room connected by a doorless doorway and an indoor window to Mamá in the kitchen, even with a dining table intervening in the parlor itself.

"What improvement is that?" Naomi had asked. "Reiseleh darling, take my bed."

Reisel would not, in Hester Street for atonement. She had smiled.

"You are even more proper than the English. This young man is holy. Unless," she had asked Daniel, "my sleeping in the same room will offend you?"

His sisters made fun of this idea she had of Daniel. He made fun of it himself, which only gave Reisel the greater certainty she was right. In the end this handsome sweet holy young man and his kind prim little sister had stretched out where they were now, the parlor side of the indoor window, Mamá had slept in Naomi's bed, and Reisel on the cot in the kitchen.

All, they were all generous, even the older sister, Leah, who was poisoned with cynicism, and the father, not unkind but foolish. The grandmother was holy. If Reisel had come alone, she would have chosen to live with the old woman. But Golda Share had already been good for Mamá. Mamá. Mamá had marched in holding her nose, as she had marched in at Whitechapel. But here, as if that were an everyday posture in the land of Columbus, Golda had kissed Mamá and said, "Gittel, how are you?"

"How am I?" Mamá had gone straight to the oval glass in the parlor. "Gray from my troubles!"

Golda had assured her, "Then you've come to the right place," and in moments had had Mamá toweled and Mamá's hair lathered and rinsed with a dye. When the job was done, "Why Golda," Mamá had regarded herself in the looking-glass with great pleasure, "you're almost better than Sheindl!"

"Sheindl?"

"My maid in Kadzyrnye." Then Mamá had patted her hair. "Danneleh, do you like the new style?" Nor, "And how about you, what do you think young man?" had she failed to flirt with the father.

Leah had sweetly smiled, "Don't you want my opinion? It's lovely."

"So how is it my fault," Mamá had pointed at Reisel, "that her father left her?"

Reisel had said, "You know that it is not your fault, Mamá," but just the same her mother had sat down to brood and Golda had joined her to hold hands with her and cheer her.

Perhaps in return Reisel could be of help to the weak ones, like Leah and cousin Share, who, she could tell, did not know God.

The Shares were surprised, yawning and rubbing their eyes in the dark, to find the table set, an oatmeal pot steaming, water boiling for tea. Golda kissed Reisel and explained that New York can't wake up without coffee, but otherwise— Then, over coffee, or tea, Reisel surprised them still more.

"Where," she asked, "is the synagogue?"

They looked at her like crazy. Then Naomi thought of a reason. "The year of mourning's not up?" she sympathetically asked.

"It's up," Gittel sipped her tea with her finger stuck out, "even for runaways. In Kadzyrnye she never opened a prayer book. Now nothing else but."

"Is it far?" Reisel smiled.

"It's not far," Hymie swallowed his oatmeal, "I'll take you."

Before angry Danny could pipe up never mind, he'd show Reisel the *shul*, this wonderful kid Reisel herself told his old man, "Oh no, you must not trouble yourself."

"No trouble, I go there to pray."

"Father!" Leah played shocked. "Ends justify means, but that's sacrilege!"

"No sacrilege," Hymie turned to this new princess in residence that God must have sent to him or else why would she be here? "I also was not a regular synagogue-goer. Then a dear friend of mine, Glantz, was on his deathbed—"

"Of childbirth?" Leah asked.

"Get used to us, Reisel," Hymie smiled. "We're like vaudeville. Glantz was extremely close to death and I prayed to God let Glantz recover, I'll attend synagogue every day."

"God kept his part of the bargain," Reisel said, "so you're keeping yours."

"More or less," Hymie let the joke be on him.

Because this was a sharp one, he saw, this Reiseleh. Try her with her own weapons and you could wind up in thin slices, like a limp dish of noodles. And that holy stuff last night, volunteering for a platonic sleep with his son—she'd really meant it. What a tidbit to have dropped out of the sky to a cot in Hymie's own kitchen!

In his youth he'd preferred them slim like this, filled out of course where it counted. That was why when Mama brought him Golda to marry he had put up no objections. But as soon as the honeymoon had been over—if you could call that a honeymoon: boy, had he been fooled!—his tastes had changed. Fat no. Yielding, like Dora with her rosy-cheeked loving face and, above all, her sweet, loving nature. Other women made difficulties, Dora smoothed difficulties out. Roly-poly Sammy, that bright child, had he learned to stop, look and listen and to tell all about it! Dora had needed no explanations. Without discussion she'd found an Irisher to watch the child while she "went shopping" a few hours sometimes. Better still, she wasn't forever pushing him to his hotel room of olden times over Madison Square Park. He'd say, "Let's go, Mamaleh," she'd go. Otherwise a matinee, a nice lunch, a sit in a park, suited her just as well. Not like that panther Debbie from the Central Park Zoo, where the keeper needed a gun for protection. But Dora and Debbie, some comparison. Dora knitted sweaters for him, scarves, neckties. Debbie the all-night wrestler used to demand, "What did you bring me?" not that he didn't enjoy bringing, to whoever it was.

Once he'd teased Debbie, "I brought you love, what more do you want?"

"Something to prove love, you liar!"

Yesterday he and Dora had met to sit in Madison Square Park for an hour but the rain had driven them up to their room. First, Dora rehearsed everything their baby had done: how she tried to turn over, how she shook her rattle, how she cooed with pink smiling gums when Dora lifted her. Her name was Joyce, their joy, Dora's and Hymie's. But the father saw the baby so seldom!

Dora'd said, "You'll see her every day soon, when Sammy begins school."

Hymie'd kissed Dora for that, leaned back in his armchair and snapped open his newspaper. Reds shipped back to Russia, good riddance to bad rubbish; a million Model T Fords expected this year, they should crash into each other not him; peace treaty goes to the Senate, let his enemies knock their heads together. He'd yawned, exchanged a smile with Dora over her knitting for Joyce, and never stopped thanking God that he had his Dora to smile to. The long weeks of her convalescence he'd gone to *shul* religiously. He wasn't fooling around, not with God, and not with that demon Debbie—call it superstition if you want, her curse Dora should die. Even after the crisis he'd begged God to listen to him not to Debbie, and—let this Reisel make fun of him—God listened. Still, a person is human. Dora recovered, he stopped going to *shul*, even though one prayer—to be rid of Debbie—God left unanswered, unless His answer was no. That girl pursued Hymie, she haunted him. Hymie's last time buying ties at his pal Horowitz's, before all eyes Debbie had jumped away from the work table and chased after him into the hall.

"Are you crazy?" he'd whispered.

"You be in the park tonight," she'd shaken her scissors in his face, "if you don't want your married whore's eyes out with these."

He, Hymie Share, had lived to be intimidated by a female! He'd shown up at Columbus Park, near her house, as ordered. Who knew what this possessed woman would stop at? The next ties he bought were from Aaronson on East Fourth Street—a good distance away. Then he'd had to run into Horowitz in the café and lie he was out of the tie business—embarrassing, with his display case right there under the table. Worse, he could not walk the streets with a free mind. He was on the alert all of a sudden, like William S. Hart in the moving pictures, sneaking through Indian territory. More than once, more than twice, more than three times, Hymie'd caught sight of that Apache on the warpath and just escaped.

Yet, yet Debbie had aroused his boyhood taste for a panther, one long twisting muscle to grab against you. Sometimes, true not so often nowadays, darling as Dora was you wanted the other, who made you set your teeth and sent your blood running wild whether you liked it or not.

So what a gift from God if, just occasionally, Hymie could go somewhere with this angel Reisel with the same straight build and full chest as that devil Debbie, because otherwise, thank God, there was no resemblance between them, coarse, black, sweaty Debbie and this pure flame of red hair. Far be it from him to lead a woman astray. If Reisel said no, then no. But from religion could come sympathy, and from sympathy—who knows?

The girl would like to get to a synagogue, he told her where the Essex Street Synagogue was. She went, he let her go. He also went, he didn't catch up to her in the street and he didn't interfere with her worship by smiles, or even a nod, to upstairs where the women sat. He ignored a scowl from God's representative on the Lower East Side, Golda's cousin Bialek the groceryman, avoided the eye of some Rivkin from the tailoring days, and thanked God for blessings received: for Mama, for Dora, for Naomi, for Golda. Last but not least he prayed for a let-up from Debbie the wild woman. Apart from Debbie, the text expressed his actual feelings:

> *Happy are we! how goodly is our portion, how pleasant our lot, how beautiful the world we have found!*

At the end, with all his willpower devoted to keeping his eyes off the balcony, he folded his prayer shawl slowly to give Reisel a chance to come down for the accidental meeting in the vestibule.

Rivkin asked him, "Somebody died, God forbid?"

"Knock wood, no."

"Then why are you here?"

Hymie eyed the man sternly. Man—the foolish son from the pictures in the Passover prayer book, with his round idiot face and whiny voice.

"To pray, what else?"

Unlikely but possible, Rivkin's pushed-out lower lip meant. "Me," Rivkin said, "I lost my wife, three weeks ago."

Hymie gripped Rivkin's arm with real feeling.

"That's a blow. I'm sorry to hear that."

Rivkin shrugged. "While she was alive she made life a hell for me."

And Hymie was wasting time with this imbecile? He grabbed the tie case—let Rivkin gape—and he rushed out after Reisel.

What a day! Sun poured down the streets. A fresh breeze inched cottony clouds across a blue smiling sky. So far, among the hard workers streaming west to the Elevated to enjoy a day indoors, no Reisel—but he knew he'd see her. In fact he had a happy sense that all this had happened before—and just the way that he wanted!

Ha!—there stood Reisel in her greenie black coat and old-fashioned ankle-length skirt, examining ginghams in a window.

"First God," Hymie grinned, "but clothes a close second."

Reisel said, "We must live in the world."

Who could ask for finer encouragement?

"Not in this cheap junk though. Come, I'll buy you better."

"I can buy myself better, thank you. But are you an expert?"

"So expert that I could have made millions."

"Then why did you not make them? You could have given me one million."

Listen to that! And she strolled along willingly beside him. To improve the good start he opened his old tale of woe: a slave to a family, an accident, a rich hypocritical brother-in-law. And Reisel was paying attention too, deep attention.

And out of the ground, with her white face and her black snapping eyes, sprang Miss Debbie Horowitz, a plague from God for his sins, whatever they were.

"One more cousin?" Debbie cackled, so close you could feel her enraged breath. "Live forever, golem," she all but spit at Reisel, "in your mourning costume!"

Reisel became as pale as the other and her lips moved silently. *Hear oh Israel, the Lord our G–d, the Lord is one.*

"Scat, bitch!" Hymie flung that devil away by the wrist.

"You be there tonight."

"Away lunatic—drop dead!"

"All yours will die—and you'll be there!"

People were stopping. Hymie hurried Reisel away, they were both shaking. She said, "You know such women?"

"Insane. I used to buy wholesale ties from her cousin."

"Oh."

So you don't fool Reisel that easy. But outside of crazy Debbie, popular with the ladies was usually a boost. Except Reisel's next move was to free her arm from his hand.

"She has the evil eye," Reisel shuddered.

Hymie smiled, "Do you believe in such things?" though since he'd been carrying on with Debbie he himself wasn't sure one way or the other.

"Do you think soldiers came to my house by chance back in Kadzyrnye?"

"Ah, when your poor papa was killed. Some Gentile sent them?"

"A Jewish woman!"

"Who? Why?"

Reisel—"Let's drop the subject"—stared straight ahead.

Could you believe her? But why would a Jewish woman—? Out of jealousy? Or was this a nut too, like Debbie—or like her own mother? Though for a nut Gittel wasn't so dumb, the way she'd made eyes at him. Gittel set her sights high.

"So why do you not return to tailoring," Reisel asked, "now that they use electric machines and you do not have to treadle?"

"I've grown to like outside work better."

"Do you work every day?"

"When I want."

"Paradise!"

Oy sharp Reisel—who gets you is entitled to a real victory smile. And in front of Mottke the Thief's house Reisel looked up the stoop, at bedding sunning from windows, then at Hymie. "What is this Mottke?"

Hymie had to explain about lucky Mottke, fine garments, low cost.

"Cousin Share," that beautiful face with the red curls under the black brim of her comical hat stared him straight in the eye, "stolen goods, things belonging to others, do not interest me."

"There are stores nearby too."

Reisel gave him a sweet pursed-up smile that with any other woman would have meant kiss me. "Where?" she said.

So don't lose hope!

And the next morning this jewel who woke up first and served breakfast shone even by gaslight. No more mourning clothes, but the pearly filled-out shirtwaist he'd brought her to at Finkelberg's on Orchard Street yesterday, the blue skirt that showed those breathtaking legs halfway up to the knees. Today she woke them up without coffee! And what did she say while Golda and the girls oo'd and ah'd—Gittel had other business suddenly—and Hymie's son stood dumbfounded? "I'm his creation," her smiling glance flicked at Hymie. Hey, there can be too much success. The whole jury switched eyes to him, the vote was guilty and his son the judge sentenced hang by the neck. So Hymie laughed in full hope of good things to come and explained that Reisel meant Finkelberg.

So, Leah thought, their devout cousin was already a chum of their father's. That open face with the demure eyes and delicate features you'd swear belonged to a young lady who'd slip into bed only alongside the man she'd marry—and post-, not pre-rabbi. But young ladies can be surprising, take Leah Share. Who would have dreamed a short year ago how nice it was to be naughty? Not that Leah was irrevocably opposed to virtue with the right man. She'd gladly marry him if she ever found him, but not a duplicate Papa. She'd been amazed—or had she?—to find herself in bed with Jack Berger the famous night of the day many months ago that

Quality Lamps became a reality. That had been a total seduction, from soup to nuts, to relish as long as she lived. The soup had been clam chowder in a sawdust-strewn restaurant downstairs from the loft, and ended her kosher status. Then Jack had fed her fat oysters—"Aphrodisiac," he'd winked at her—and white wine. But if Jack had meant the aphrodisiac he had underestimated a hard chest and muscles. Had that been delicious, his grip on her waist, that thigh to thigh walk in the cold after dinner, the pauses for cool kisses, the hilarious little room—no bedbugs, just one small tired roach on the pillow trying to catch forty winks—where she'd been only too happy to deposit her virginity. Why had beautiful Jack with his flat stomach and round thighs with the frisky little fellow between them had to . . . really prostitute himself, trying in bed for a business advantage! And on top of that, courting Naomi on the supposed sly. What did he think Leah was, a saint God forbid? Compared to Naomi Leah knew she was plain Jane but she had her vanity. Besides, Jack's basic crush was Jack, just as Papa loved Papa. And these self-lovers did gall you. Imagine Jack's quietly arguing, when she gave him hell and broke off their relationship, that he'd asked her to marry him, so what did she want?

"I want you to leave Naomi alone," she'd told him.

"As a clean-living American boy ain't I entitled to a loving spouse and so forth?"

"At least you're honest if and so forth means a share of the business."

"Such was your promise."

"When profits warrant."

"There'd be no profits without me."

"Don't flatter yourself, buster. You can be done without—in the business as well."

Poor kid, that had really upset him. He hadn't quite succeeded in keeping his voice level. "You mean you're giving me notice, in front of a Bleecker Street layery?"

She'd snapped at him, "You just behave yourself at that factory," and walked out of his private life—except insofar as she was Naomi's big sister.

Well here was Reisel, synagogue one moment, Hymie the next, and come-hither eyes on full-time duty. Possibly it was just flirting—one Finkelberg's shopping spree does not a clandestine relationship make, especially if announced by the weaker vessel. But if the hint of depravity in this paragon could give Papa such a high complexion by early gaslight, shouldn't she also do wonders for the blood stream of Jack the rover? To make it a crowd even little brother Danny had been smitten since yesterday, and—"Are those your working clothes, Reisel?"—was drinking her in as if she were God's latest invention. So how immoral would it be to employ Reisel at Quality Lamps Light The City (Jack's slogan) where Jack could see her and Naomi could see them both? If that was pandering, it was pandering to obvious inclinations. And if Leah was wrong, as had been known to happen, if new coz was too good to be false, then virtue would be rewarded by regular hours instead of a sweatshop.

"False feathers," Gittel commented.

But her daughter—"These are just clothes to seek work in, Daniel"—charmed the hope of the Shares almost to extinction.

Leah shot a glance to Naomi as if to say, *Not hiring her?*, and enjoyed her sister's dilemma. The lamp business had been Leah's idea, with urging from Jack. Till they'd gone into it, and even after, she'd been chief cook and bottle washer and Naomi tagger along whose South Sea isle had been that lout Phil Stein. Why, the kid had even tried to draft Danny into the business on the expectation that she'd soon be Mrs. Phil the lout and out of it! But with Naomi's return from the Pittsburgh mystery jaunt the tables had turned. Naomi had seized the reins and Leah had been perfectly happy to give them up in her heady beginnings with their ace and only salesman. And one thing Jack had taught Leah: the best things in life really may be free. So now Naomi was boss and chief penny-pincher and she had Leah's sincere leave to enjoy it. And as boss she could now fire Mama's big slow soft protégée Sadie Kominik the shade trimmings botcher to make room, as you could see she wanted to, for Reisel who had her bewitched too.

The bewitcher left for the synagogue with Papa in not too distant pursuit, and Leah lent a little encouragement to the kid sister.

"Be as tough as your job, sweetheart."

"Yes, I know," Naomi gloomily murmured.

So farewell Sadie, and Jack take care!

And—victory is ours!—at the end of the morning service Hymie's proud beauty was waiting for him! While pitiful Bialek his wife's cousin's husband the groceryman glared from the synagogue porch, the best-dressed peddler in lower Manhattan—derby, stick, slim dark coat—skimmed down to . . . she herself had said so . . . his own creation in a new beige spring coat and elegant cloche hat with a feather. Hymie raised his hat, but before he could tell Reisel she was the best-dressed woman in the Essex Street congregation, not to mention the youngest by fifty years, she posed him a question.

"Why do you attend synagogue?"

"Yesterday Rivkin, today you?" he laughed. "To pray."

"And what do you pray?"

"I prayed," he smiled boyishly, "you'd be waiting."

Reisel gave not quite a smile. "Well, thank you for the compliment. Since we also live in our bodies, if you were your son's age that might be a reason though not a good one. But for you, cousin Share—"

"Call me Hymie."

"All right, Hymie. Do you not see that entering a house of God for flirtation is an insult to God?"

"Flirtation yes, tender affection no."

"And you probably once brought tender affection to that demented woman of yesterday? . . . No no, do not answer. You certainly do not have to answer to me. But what do you think God is?"

"Reiseleh," Hymie grinned, "am I a rabbi?"

"Nor am I. But clearly, God is not an old man with ears, nose and a beard."

"To tell you the truth I always pictured Him that way, like my father, and they both scared me stiff!"

Oh love's old sweet song—Reisel's eyes filled!

"Poor cousin Hymie. I had a father very different from that. Then your father was harsh to you?"

Was he in his element! Through your boyhood your papa whipped you, and through your manhood you whipped your papa. For Reisel Hymie trotted out everything, from the three small shrouds to a smack in the ear.

"Still," Reisel said, "it was your father, and he had to eke out a living in this hard land."

"A living out of my hide, and Sol's and Joe's and Morris's and Willie's, and then he'd go pray morning noon and night?"

"There your father was wrong so do not, in your own way, emulate him. Prayer, synagogue—in themselves they are not sufficient. Our good deeds make God good. . . . Hymie," she gave him a short, manly handshake, "I must find work."

Bakeries, coffee, he wanted to learn more from her—no, she had to run, which way was Fifteenth Street where Daniel said the shirtwaist manufacturers were?

"Which way is easy." He pointed uptown. "But why not take the road to riches in the lamp industry?"

Reisel knew why not. Naomi would want her in the lamp business but the two sisters had exchanged a glance and nothing was said. But Leah's behavior was no news. Reisel had endured jealousy in London, in Kadzyrnye, in Wladkow, so why not here the worst of all her sojourns, supreme in filth both material and spiritual?

"I was not asked," she said.

"So that makes two of us. . . . It must be work, immediately, not coffee? . . . Then come, my friend Bert Mintz on Fifteenth Street is in shirtwaists."

"See?" Her brown eyes were delighted. "You can be a good man!"

See?—step two of Reiseleh converting him into a saint while he converted her to the human race.

Rome wasn't built in a day!

7

"COME ON LEAH, HONOR DICTATES, THE TALMUD SAYS, and I love ya."

Al Greenfield had popped the . . . protest, you had to call it, in Leah's warm lazy sun-beaded bed in Bank Street. Sweet muttface, he certainly did appeal to your maternal instincts—not to mention the other instincts—standing up or should she say lying down for morality, with his rough-grained cheek on her shoulder, a chest as good as sculpture and a white belly with most delicate light strands of hair fanning out to his springy spigot.

"You have a beautiful foot, Al."

"I thank you, and so does my foot. But you haven't settled my fate."

And so decent!—four months' hard work to unveil those doggy-brown curls from their ritual skullcap and even today she wouldn't have succeeded without plying him with enough Passover wine at don't ask how much the bottle to make him, as he'd been quaintly apologizing for an hour or so, "lose control." And next, the Talmud admonished, tardy as it was came marriage.

"Why," she kidded Al, "buy a cow when milk is so cheap, dear?"

Al though was too full of Talmud and Torah for such nuances, and he only laughed. "Seriously Leah—"

Seriously she did want to fall in love, marry, share books and thoughts. But you can't force love and, sweet as Al was, who wants to settle for humdrum? So she kept teasing him.

"But I left home and took this apartment so I could meet you in sin, not holy deadlock."

And no joke that had been, her kid sister and brother's baffled stare to hear she loved them a million but thought she'd improve her reading habits in a place of her own in the Village instead of moving along with them to Tompkins Square. And leaving Mama had been a dozen times tougher.

"Go right ahead," Mama had sadly intoned, "carry my folly one step further."

"Mama," Leah'd taken her hands, "your folly will have to shift for itself, I'll be too busy to carry it."

And Mama got the drift a lot faster than little Al here. Her eyes had opened up wide, "Are you sure?," and brightened into happy connivance. "You'll take care of yourself, evenings especially?"

Leah did love that Mama!

Al reminded her, "But you already lived here last spring when we met at that party, Leah."

Leah slid level with him and, lips to lips, asked, "Must you be so scientifically literal?"

Her well-knit baby gathered her up—"My little girl"—and Leah lost no time swarming over him. When she finished swarming, "You're very lustful," she still kidded him.

"That's it," poor Al was half proud half worried. "That's why we have to get hitched, Leah."

"And face the world honestly!"

She reached a bare arm and raised the blinds to her balcony over her landlord's nice backyard garden. The August sun varnishing the gingko rushed onto the parquet alongside the bed. Al leaped up galvanized—"You'll be dispossessed!"—remembered himself, and crouched to the window with a modest hand shielding dickey bird like Adam kicked out of Paradise. He let the blinds down again and Leah couldn't stop laughing.

"You don't love me," she said, "you love my apartment."

He snuggled into her breast, "Baloney . . . ," dozed, and gave a start.

"Can't you sleep, dear?"

"I begin to, then I get this fear that I'm dying."

Her heart went out to him so, she was almost ready to devote a lifetime to hushing him in a room stirring with summer. "Sha, sha, little boy, sleep now, Leah's watching. . . ."

Soon Al slept like an angel in the vague murmur of her charming apartment, so sweetness was for once the beneficiary of pure gall. Because if not for a big wild-haired penniless Narcissus named Carl Baer without even (pardon the expression) a pot to piss in she would have probably still been living with the family and thinking up home late from fun alibis for them. Her Carl, Carolus Magnus as he chucklingly called himself, was preoccupied with the revolution and the universal strawberries and cream diet to come, so he had no time to waste on questions like food and lodging. But he forever bitched about the Bleecker Street hotel she treated him to that she'd thought perfectly adequate for her to graduate in.

"For chrissakes Leah, I'm a poet—I can't make love in this squalor!"

Oh he'd make love. Virility he had, women chased him. His ex-wife was an M.D., a society woman who had found him too slippery. Yet at a party, with one glance the first time Leah saw him, she'd caught him!

And he'd been better than night school with his tips on what authors a real Villager would be reading, though doing her that service—or anyone any service—had been the last thing on his mind. For self-absorption Carolus was incontestably Magnus, Papa himself couldn't hold a candle to him. Carolus had been a sensation at his own engagement ball at the ex's parents' stone house in Fairfield Connecticut with a three hours late lumberjacket and sneakers act—and the girl had seemed to be put out! The people's bard with poems in *The Liberator* didn't pass such tidbits along as funny either, just to show that all the disagreements had been on the poor lady doctor's side. He'd just been himself.

Nevertheless right's right and once the eyes were opened what self-respecting girl wanted to conduct her love life in Bleecker Street? So she'd searched out this pretty flat and, to corroborate the convictions of Carolus Magnus (rapidly dwindling to Carolus Minimus) on the perversity of women, would not tell him where she had moved to. What self-respecting girl wanted him as a boarder?

And darned if she didn't find him moping outside Quality Lamps in West Street one twilight, waiting to track her home! For fun she'd put that formalities loather through a "My friend Carl Baer the poet," to Mama, to Danny, to Naomi, to Reisel, and she had to admit Carolus had never displayed his winning grin better, especially for the two girls. When the family went its way she'd kidded Carolus that he'd met them all now, except the one she was beginning to think she really took after. But you couldn't kid Carl. What did he care who she took after?

He'd said, "Let's go eat."

Well, you can't let a poet starve. She'd bought him dinner and wine at Fisherino's downstairs from the loft and between bites and sips he'd entertained her with his grievances against that MacDougal Street bunch who'd promised to put his play on and weren't putting, his so-called friend Krimsky who'd sent him packing for the sake of a totally uninteresting girl not that Carl had much to pack, and Leah's mistrustful immature bourgeoise lockout self. Then Carolus'd picked his manly teeth while Leah's and so forth self had paid the bill.

"Let's go to your place," he said, "but I have to stop at Occult Arts to pick my things up."

"Occult arts?" Leah slapped her thighs in absolute helplessness while Carolus Magnus grinned. "You wouldn't stop at anything! But," she wiped her eyes and held out her hand, "goodbye and good luck, Carlie, I hope the Provincetowns do your play."

He'd taken her hand and his other arm he'd laid on her shoulder. "Stick around," he'd headed her south, "there's a party on at Meserole's studio. You'd better get some wine to bring along though."

And at Meserole's, where in no time Carolus Magnus had a blonde, then two blondes simpering up at him, Leah had found herself this well-knit and medium-rumpled wallflower under a Lower East Side skullcap, little Al

Greenfield brought there by a friend Judah who loved to dance and at that very moment had been two of the legs making the Jane Street flat tremble. And after a poet, someone more in the science line was refreshing.

"In Connecticut," sweet Al had confided, "they used to call me the Rat Man."

"Why that's what my escort's ex-wife used to call him in Connecticut," Leah'd said brightly. "How did you earn the title?"

Al couldn't have been more won by Leah's winning ways. His rats had short legs and long tails. At Cornell he'd been in the agricultural school. In the army—latrine engineering, still it's important for armies—he'd come out as captain. In Connecticut—on the spot training: infested houses and restaurants—he'd taught the local health men the mind of the rat till they knew it as well as he did. Now that was his job in New York.

"And how," Leah had asked, "did they like your skullcap in all those places?"

"There may have been a fist fight or two, but they got used to it."

"I don't think, Al, you know the first thing about the mind of the rat!"

"You mean the other kind," Al had laughed. "It's true, I don't really."

And now Al—he slept on so darlingly in the last pink rods of evening—whose suspicious kosher throat you could hardly force food down, wanted to mismate himself with her when the perfect match for him was Naomi. However—you had to smile—Leah's last idea of a match had been happy Jack Berger and Reisel the inviolate virgin!

Poor Jack, did she call him happy?

A lunchtime Naomi was out, Leah in the office and the shop empty except for Ma, moonstruck Danny, Reisel, their kosher salami sandwiches and Reisel's Shakespeare—an affectation if Leah ever had seen one—handsome Jack had wandered in and tossed his order pad on the desk with such gloom that Leah'd felt sorry for him.

"Cheer up, Jack."

"Shut your mouth, hypocrite."

"It wasn't me," Leah had said. "I didn't persuade Naomi against you. It's true I tried, but—"

But Jack had walked out on her with that obstinate resentment, even his back looked resentful. And—what a funny world!—Leah was innocent: all that needless plotting! Naomi for some odd reason worshipped Reisel, she'd had to have her at Quality. Once Reisel was there to look Jack over, poor Jack, what chance did he stand? Reisel's meek eye would dart at you—and you were pinned down like a butterfly. Leah'd had her own taste of that before the getaway to the Village. Friends, shows, moving pictures—any old excuse for your evenings was good enough for the family. But from Reisel—rarely, true, but not rarely enough—would flick that glance of pure curiosity as to what a loose woman looks like close up.

Yet give Jack credit. He'd guessed the wrong enemy, Leah instead of Reisel, but he'd fought it out like a man. In front of Naomi he'd made a lunch date with—of all people—their brother. Danny himself would have gotten out of it. All he wanted for lunch was a work table, a salami sandwich and a redheaded immigrant. But Naomi's eyes had begged him say yes.

And Jack's story had been convincing, perhaps even true. Leah'd given him the gate, and his motives dating Naomi had been as unkosher as the steamed clams he and Danny had been pitching into—pique, and worse. The worse, Jack preferred to drop, because his hope and belief were that he and Danny would be brothers in the not distant future. But the more he saw of Naomi, that beautiful kid, so loving, so straightforward, the question wasn't was she the girl for him but was he good enough for her?

Jack had said, "You're young, Danny, but you're no kid. Did you ever find your whole life revolve around one person?" "Every day," Danny had said, but he hadn't said who either to Jack or to Leah—as if he'd had to.

So while Leah'd been changing that night to meet her moocher the poet, Naomi still with the rest in the kitchen had asked their brother how he'd enjoyed his lunch.

"I enjoyed it, Naomi, but I didn't like it. The first name may be Dan but the last ain't Cupid."

Then, "It could be," from that bitchy tease Reisel.

"Well kiddo," Danny had said, "he really loves you. That's what you want to know?"

"Sincerely?" Naomi'd asked.

"Yeah, he's sincere."

Naomi'd soaked this up the way that grass soaks up water. Then Leah had been treated to the doubtful pleasure of her own opinion from Reisel's lips.

"Sincere yes, for Naomi today, another tomorrow and still another the day after tomorrow."

"Mention a man and she runs," Gittel had suddenly piped up on the side of Jack whom she had never laid eyes on, "even for someone else."

And behold—the meek Reisel could spark like lightning.

"How dare you lie to our cousins who have befriended us. As to myself, since you are my mother I do not complain. But as to others I never deceive them! A good beautiful woman like Naomi can always find a truly good husband."

"Don't bite my head off," poor Gittel had pouted, almost cried, "I have enough enemies without you—"

Naomi had motioned Reisel into the parlor where Leah had been eavesdropping, so Leah'd gotten out and fast. But the dining table that night was where Jack's goose had been cooked. And cooked well, or all a mistake? Either way, she would have to get this lovable sleeper Al together with her kid sister—in proper attire of course, from skullcap to toe.

Though the mechanics might not be easy.

At the railroad station in Orange Danny grabbed a taxi and the hell with the dough. If he made it back to Tompkins Square by say four o'clock,

Reisel still might be in the park. What a girl! How anyone could read in that bedlam around the tiny playground crawling with kids and mothers was beyond him. But Sundays she always squeezed into that corner of the park near the memorial statue for the children who died on the excursion boat *General Slocum* that burned to a hull with practically the whole neighborhood on it.

"It reminds me," Reisel'd explained, "of the afflictions of others."

Had that made him sick! "You need extra afflictions? Take mine." Of course he'd wound up apologizing.

Then—you say curl up with a book—she'd bend over her book, her Shakespeare, with the smiling excitement he used to see on Naomi over a letter from Phil the drag Stein, where you half-expected the page to go bare the words were sucked up so. But early this morning—Danny had been heading for Orange for the stuff he'd left there—he'd tried without the slightest hope of success to coax Reisel to come along.

He had blurted, "You'll always have Shakespeare," and had immediately wished he could take that back. But—whew—she'd let it pass with a would she not like to go but how could she?

Sure how could she, with a rag in her hand and a rag on her beautiful head for Sunday cleaning. Jesus Christ, a lamp factory all week, then this?

"You're not the maid," he'd said.

"Nor are my cousins." With that body meant to be held, loved, adored, she'd stretched to dust the top of the china closet. "But they help just the same."

Gittel meanwhile the second that this subject was broached had hidden herself in their room with the white and green shades both pulled down and the curtains drawn in midsummer. You don't want that Kadzyrnye spy perched up on the roof across the park to see what you're doing—or not doing. Cousin Gittel might be crazy but she wasn't so dumb, lounging around in total exhaustion. Still it took a lot out of you, a three times a week walk to the library with Russian police eyes trailing you all the way so you had to stop and be merry with total strangers so they would help in case that guy tried to arrest you. Luckily, since he never did, you could come home, curtain yourself in, turn the electric light on in broad daylight and lose yourself in a romance. "Pity her," Reisel said, and that was fine. But then to send Danny completely out of his mind Reisel would fight to chip in extra for the electric bill on account of her mother.

Reisel and Grandma—how come the ones you care for most drive you the craziest?—made a good pair. You saw Reisel up with the sparrows to escort Grandma to the Essex Street Synagogue because the rainy day the *Empress of Liverpool* unloaded Gittel on them seemed to have given Grandma the old rheumatiz. So Grandma had been wincing around ever since, but if you tried to buy her out of the pretzel business you got not only a refusal from her but a sermon from Reisel that you must let Baba

Rivka take her peddling baskets out even in pain since she wishes it. On top of that you had to battle Grandma into accepting a few bucks a week.

"Grandma, will you put this money away, or must I rip it up in small pieces?"

Finally Grandma would kiss his red pounding forehead and take the dough. What a good young man he was—big fuss! Then, did he still play on his . . . balalaika, sing those songs? And she was happy to hear the answer was no. So for a few lousy bucks and no minstrelsy, Grandma would tell Reisel and Reisel would give him that "holy person" business again.

"What must I do to prove I'm not," he'd asked Reisel no kidding, "sock you one on the jaw?"

"That means . . . strike me? Even if you could, what would it prove, since you are replenishing Baba Rivka's funeral savings which went, you know, to her friend in the Wild West, in Denver. Both you and Baba Rivka have been a lesson to me. When my mother and I move to our new flat, I am hoping that she will join us."

"What new flat? You're not moving to any new flat."

"What did you say?"

"I said you're not moving."

"Well Daniel, I hope you and I shall never be at a great distance from one another."

Did you hear that! Didn't that mean she . . . ?

In the park Reisel would take Shakespeare notes in her tiny handwriting while Danny struggled looking up words in his Shakespeare that he'd bought to try to keep up with her. But they'd also walk to the piers, where Reisel's eyes would flash over the river.

"I am the Lion of Judah, and the river is my dog! And you, Daniel," she'd tease him, "are you a lion or a chicken?"

So he'd gone at the lion for a kiss, but it's hard to scale a fence leaning toward you or kiss a girl leaning away.

Reisel'd said, "I did seem to suggest that, while not intending to. Still, you must not, Daniel," but so sweetly, lovingly almost, that he would have jumped off the dock next if she'd said so.

Then Naomi would recruit her for gatherings or parties. Or Reisel would ask Naomi to accompany her to a museum or concert, and Naomi didn't really care for that stuff any more than Danny did but she'd bargain—she'd go to the Metropolitan Museum with Reisel if Reisel agreed to a double date.

How come after all that hullabaloo the foursome never included Jack Berger?

But whoever it did include made Danny sick. What could you do though, hoard Reisel like wartime sugar? So far these guys Danny's sister dug up, presentable grown men much as you loathed them, only suited Gittel not

Reisel. Yet how long could that keep up? Reisel was bound to meet one who would bowl her over. When she was out Danny drifted around in poker-faced misery. But when she was home safe, sleeping a few rooms away from him, off he'd zoom into a future with her in a Pierce-Arrow sedan, Delmonico dinners—*a kosher menu, waiter, for captain of industry Share's wife*—and box seats in Carnegie Hall since that was her sole idea of music. . . .

Now in Orange he paid off the taxi down the road from Uncle Willie's so he wouldn't have to explain it, slung his jacket over his shoulder, rolled up his sleeves and made tracks past heart-piercing patches of forest sunlight he was walking too fast to enjoy. At Uncle Willie's path through the wood the crows in the distance—"Hey Frank, hey Frank"—had a big shindig on.

Only on the grass in front of the saloon it wasn't crows. Sunday suits and celluloid collars, shiny foreheads, pinch waists, light dresses down to the ankle—an old-fashioned bunch, working stiffs and their missuses but not the Italians, all holding glasses and not exactly pie-eyed but not sober either, with loud talk and loose laughs. Anna sailed out of the black saloon through her mob of pals slapping and catching at her and threw her arms around Danny. What had he fallen into?

"You came to my birthday!"

His heart sank. He'd never get back to Reisel in time. Anna stuck a strong whiskey kiss on his lips.

"Guess my age."

She struck a pose with her finger under her plump chin and grinning Uncle Willie came up and laid his arm across Danny's shoulders. What the hell. He'd sit in the park with Reisel next week. Danny said, "Twenty-nine," and got another big kiss straight out of the bottle.

"Willie, where'd you ever get a handsome nephew like this?"

"Wh-wh-why he looks like my brother."

"Now Jesus," she drawled, "wasn't that what I said all the time and you kept disputing me? Well, whoever he looks like, I've been lucky with the men in my life. You should have seen Coker in his blue uniform—oh he was a soldier! I should never have let him take his discharge from the army to marry me, but I was in love with that pushed-in ugly mug of his, you know, ugly-handsome. Now here's your uncle, twice as ugly—and twice as handsome, my teetotaling private in overalls!" Anna presented lips and Willie gave her three fast salutes on the mouth. "I'd better fix Danny a drink before we run dry." She weaved her way back to the saloon.

Danny said sternly, "Anna's drinking a lot."

"Sh-sh-she's not a sot. B-birthdays are harder for women." His uncle rumpled up Danny's hair. "Wh-wh-what did you quit school for?"

"I didn't. I transferred back and got my diploma. It was as quiet as Orange, they'd thrown the Bolsheviks out."

Back in New York Mr. Konsky the history teacher had been axed, with his drilling into you that used to give Danny headaches. Flanagan and Sohmer were in jail Danny'd been told. Some of the classes had been half empty. The papers said that they were deporting a shipload of Bolshies back to Russia. Quiet or no quiet and nasty as those bedbug boys had been, Danny felt kind of sorry for them.

Not Reisel.

"Good!" she'd sung out like a trumpet. "Good for those murderers. Let them go where murder is the law of the land!"

"Those guys," Danny'd objected, "are not murderers."

Had Reisel glared! "Innocent!" she'd snarled. So she could snarl—and at him too. "Innocent in the worst sense—ignorant!" Imagine, tongue-lashed by Reisel. He couldn't have felt worse and she must have seen that, because she'd calmed down. "May God only never let you experience, Daniel, what they are. . . ."

But with Uncle Willie, Danny seemed to be on the capitalist side.

Uncle Willie said, "You have to be for the w-w-workingman, Danny."

"I am the workingman, Uncle Willie."

"Y-you?" Uncle Willie grinned. "Wh-where's your ukulele?"

Danny shrugged. "Home under the bed."

Anna stuck a tumbler in Danny's hand with enough whiskey to sink a man-o'-war.

"Aw, y-you know he doesn't d-drink."

"For my birthday he drinks. Come on handsome, put mud in your old Aunt Anna's eye."

Danny wet his lips with that poison, and Anna dragged him by the hand to every man, woman and child on the premises. And damned if it wasn't one big family affair, from uncles and aunts down to dogs and cats and good eaters all of them, with the two-legged ones washing down Anna's food with Uncle Willie's dwindling supplies.

Disgusting, and the men kept bothering him drink up kid. So finally to shut their mouths he drank up kid and it went down like suicide. And in Tompkins Square Park was Reisel.

But then gradually the green air shimmered in a golden stillness, and he sat down to enjoy it from the doorstep. A chunky little striped orange cat with hazel eyes mewed at him, and Danny swung and nearly missed a pat at his own knee for the cat to hop up on. The cat obliged and curled up, and Danny began stroking him. The roses beside the doorway were drunk in the sun—and that perfume. . . . "In London," Reisel had smiled at him, "they called me Rose. . . ." Danny's eyes narrowed like the cat's as he worked the cat's fur.

Ma'd said, "If I moved even in the middle of winter it would be hot."

Hester Street moving day had been early May and like summer. He and Reisel reached for the same carpetbag; her bare arm touched his, like silk. Reisel had smiled.

"This bag is mine. I must bear my own burdens."

But he'd borne that burden, and that touch. With the whiskey, the roses, the sun, he felt it now, silky as grass, Rose-Reisel. . . .

"Like pussy?"

Out of nowhere he had a cousin or niece up close with teasing eyes, hazel like the cat's only she scared the cat away with the touch of an icy gin glass or maybe it was her ugly mug with the fade-away chin. On top of that she'd brought her own audience, a guy and dame to enjoy the show.

"I bet them," the tip of her toboggan nose almost touched Danny's nose, "you'd be good at puss-in-the-corner."

Danny had all he could do not to shove chinless aside and hang one on her pal the grinner. As it was he gave her the ice cold treatment till she stuck her tongue out, rolled off a Bronx cheer and swayed away laughing with her assistants. Then she kept grinning back at him from the edge of the crowd, so go try for that mood, the nice feeling he'd had till she'd barged over.

The shadows weren't that far along the grass yet, his gold bar mitzvah watch said . . . three. With luck he could still get back and find Reisel downstairs. He stood up, almost fell down, and did some swaying himself through the crowd inside the cool dusky saloon. But at the stairs—"S-say, D-danny"—he made believe that he hadn't heard, he started up anyway.

Brushing off Uncle Willie? That booze sure corrodes the mind in a hurry. Dizzily, Danny looked down.

"C-c-come on."

And Danny took his second deep breath for no Reisel today.

Uncle Willie picked his few tunes out of the piano and Danny sang a real whiskey tenor, just for themselves with Anna's gang full blast indoors and out. Then Uncle Willie sat him down at a table for a bite of corned beef and cabbage and Danny discovered he'd been starving to death. He plowed through two servings.

"S-sing much at h-home?"

"Not too much."

The truth was, Reisel did not approve of popular tunes of the day, she said they were for frivolous persons. Beethoven was her meat. In Kadzyrnye the vandals had splintered her grand piano and thrown the pieces out of the window. She hoped, she'd tittered, when she was rich in America, to buy a modest piano, an upright. Count that hers as soon as Danny would have the greenbacks. Meanwhile was he supposed to admit he was frivolous? So he'd kept his mouth shut, and singing in the bathtub—and not too loud—about summed it up.

"H-h-how do you like the f-f-factory?"

Another embarrassment. Originally he'd told Uncle Willie the factory stank, how do you explain it was great now? Danny himself didn't know why. Sure, since Reisel came she'd made the loft . . . fragrant—like the flowers outside here. Sure, it was worth anything to get there first mornings, shape frames or stitch shades or enter bills with one eye on the door and see Reisel stride in from *shul* with that face, that smile, that dear pal of a nod.

And sure, "I thought," Jack Berger had stuck his hand out to Danny on

Danny's first real day as a lamps man, "you were something like me, no lover of factories."

"What I love is the dough."

Jack had granted, "She is the temptress," and had willingly settled down to teach Danny lamp wiring.

Among less spic-and-span daydreams Danny did spin himself five-figure earnings—but to his amazement he enjoyed wiring lamps! And the business in general gets a grip on you. Who'd rearranged the machines and tables so the work whizzed along from one step to the next and got finished faster? Who even read an accounting book—Naomi and Leah's paperwork was bad enough without doing it twice—and cut the bookkeeping in half? Yessiree!

So, "I guess West Street fooled me, Uncle Willie. There's more to it than meets the eye."

"As long as you l-l-like it, D-danny, that's what counts."

Outdoors the pond reflected darkening fern in a red gash of sunset. The air smelled sweet, pure, and he wished Reisel were there to breathe it with him. And crap, had he had to be impolite to that girl while he was under the influence? For all her gaiety he'd probably hurt her feelings. The crowd under the trees had thinned out considerably but he didn't make her out anywhere in the twilight. . . . But hey—he knew a girl in the neighborhood: Carrie Baum!

There was still light in the sky over the treetops but the shortcut to Carrie's was pitch black. He didn't get bitten up too much though by twigs and mosquitoes and he came out singing near the rank chicken coops and the porch lit by the parlor.

Be kind, when you hear me sigh,
I'm a roman–tic kind of a guy . . .

But his knock hung a foxy face he could have done without on the door screen: Mr. Baum.

"Carrie—"

A Hester Street "What?" sailed down the stairs.

"The Messiah has risen."

The foxy mouth grinned at its own joke, but Danny didn't. The face disappeared, heels clacked down, and Carrie's face with the hair curled in papers dented the screen. She came out—"Where the hell have you been, you bastard?"—and stuck her hands on her hips. Then she sniffed a few times, like Towser. "Hey Daddy, he's drunk!"

"So? Who tells you to mix with the saloon element?"

"Who'd mix with this bum? Lips that touch liquor shall never touch mine."

And she latched on so tight for one of her serious kisses that Danny's short branch sprang up against clothestree Carrie. She felt it okay too—that's what the victory smirk meant.

"Well," she said to his blushes in the dark, "that takes care of the greetings and salutations. Sit down, we'll rock awhile and catch up on what's new. . . . Oh you don't have to squeeze into the corner like that—I'll fit in." She cuddled close with her curlers in his face and her arms across his lap just missing his half-mast jigger. "See, I'm not that fat yet—though I'm beginning to fill out a bit. Look . . ." She put his hand on her breast but brushed his good hold away. "You have some nerve. First insults—not even a so-long—then you try to take advantage of me because I'm innocent? . . . I had to visit your uncle the hunter's low-life establishment to find out what was what, and you know how his . . . lady friend loves me."

"They needed me in the business at home."

"Sure, night and day. What do you think, you can fool me, Carrie Baum? But I forgive you. Just work hard and get rich."

He had to tell her for honesty's sake, "I don't expect to be back though," and she laughed in his face.

"You know what you are? A kid."

"Yeah? How come?"

"I'll tell you in 1929. In the meantime kiss me kid, nothing makes me sick." And they were glued together again with a new twist, Carrie's inquisitive tongue tip playing tricks . . . then drawing away to edge out a sly smile. "I'll dig you up whenever I like," she told him, "whether you come back or not."

"You know," he gave her tummy a good rub, "you have filled out—"

"No cursing please."

Others, a pat on the behind shortens the trail, but for a girl like Reisel: finesse! Therefore mornings, since Hymie tested her and she didn't mind, he'd overtake her for the walk—wind, rain, heat of day: immaterial—to the Essex Street Synagogue. And you don't scare the girl with heavy romance. You tell a joke, or an interesting happening, or you discuss Gittel's health. Or, finally, like today, you comment that was a fine-looking young man that brought her home last night, with Naomi and the other boy.

"Ehh!"

"Ehh?"

"He was a nice boy but not my type."

"And what is your type, Reiseleh?"

"My type is religious, spiritual, and—" she flicked him that smile, that long-awaited signal!—"of course handsome."

Hymie had everything he could do not to take off the straw lid pointing up and smooth back that rich hair of his.

"I owe you thanks," he said, and what could she do? She laughed, "You're welcome, but why are you thanking me?"

"Who's made me into a Jew if not you?"

"And how does the new Jew differ from the old heathen?"

"In life," he slanted his best love-look at her, "in hope."

And why not, at the end of summer though you'd never guess it in this steamy sunshine, with a sporty checked jacket and white flannels, a Dora in your present and a Reiseleh in your very near future? Ah happy day— "And what is your hope?"—the dear young woman prompted him with brown smiling eyes.

He whispered to her, "You're my hope," practically under Bialek's pop eyes and squashed angry nose in the synagogue vestibule. As Reisel turned to the stairs Hymie pressed her hand and once more she smiled those brown eyes at him. How he survived the service he didn't know, and Bialek or no Bialek he sped out to catch her—she could call up the lamp factory with some excuse—for an eight hour honeymoon!

The synagogue emptied—even Bialek let loose his dirty look and went back to sell eggs—and no Reisel. So Hymie shot into the synagogue and Methuselah the caretaker with the scrawny beard gaped at him. Hymie patted a pocket. "You saw a wallet?"

"What would I do with a wallet, put my millions in it?"

What you could do, Methuselah, instead of shuffling around with the same prayer book all morning long, is put a broom in your hand and sweep. Then if somebody has to make believe he's looking for something under a front bench he doesn't have to pick up half the Lower East Side real estate in his trouser cuffs.

Hymie straightened and managed a look upstairs where the women sat. Tired benches. A fast departure for Reiseleh, go figure. But at Tompkins Square that night she was cheerful, she still had smiles, for him, for everyone.

This morning again that damp sunshine that already had him setting the tie cases on the pavement and wiping under his collar with the freshly ironed handkerchief dear Golda had just given him with the kiss goodbye. But a block along and better than ocean breezes—Reisel waited!

Did he rush down to her! And just like yesterday she smiled in his eyes!

"Will you do something for me?"

"As much as I can—more even!"

He grabbed her hand, which she neatly slipped free.

"Then honor your white hairs."

"How can I honor them better than by honoring your red ones?"

"And Golda's gray ones?"

Aha, first the misgivings, then the yes. "I hold Golda sacred," he set her mind at rest.

"I do not believe you hold her at all."

Hey innocence, you look in at keyholes? But at a moment like this—he grabbed her hand again, again it slipped away—who cares! "Pity Golda's poor boarder then," he laughed.

Reisel's own mother had stopped sleeping with Papá long ago in

Kadzyrnye, so Reisel knew some women were heartless—not that you could compare her dear Papá with this poor buffoon for whom she saw less and less hope.

"I do pity you, Cousin Share. Therefore—"

"Not Cousin Share—Hymie."

"—Therefore I advise, why not suffer a little? It will be good for you."

Hymie exclaimed happily, "I suffer, I suffer!"

Hopeless, but Reisel made one more effort. "Do you not consider Gehenna?"

"I'm too young," if she wanted to swap jokes for a minute, "to consider Gehenna."

"One is never too young, and you especially are not too young. Good day Cousin Share, and please do not follow me, either now or in the future."

Was she serious? That's how it looked, with that man's stride away and him grinning here like a fool. Not a fool, fooled, by an old maid's six months' siren act. His forehead felt sick with sweat, cold in the heat. He took the handkerchief out. And dragging Golda in. To gall there's no limit. An eerie waft of steam—the kitchen, with Golda pressing?—made him look up . . . and did he jump back just in time! Idiot street cleaners hosing down Avenue A full of people and traffic! Things weren't bad enough, they tried to muddy your flannels for you?

Suddenly did he have a yen for his lunatic Debbie, and he strolled downtown past East Fourth to stock his cases in Baxter Street. And free of the holy spinster he could enjoy the fuzzy sunshine and enjoy even more the sheep's eyes he picked up from housewives along the way—not such old hens either, those sheep! And like magic, at Dora's street, Essex, the haze lifted and even the pushcarts sparkled in yellow sunlight. An old barber slouched under his awning, and Hymie—"Good morning Papa," dropped in for a trim. His white hairs! In the mirror in the shade inside the store his white hairs still crowned those slender good looks, so let her go to hell though he wouldn't wish anything bad on her. The old barber plunged a hand into that mane.

"Premature, hah?"

Hymie smiled, and after the trim he gave the old man a tip that set off thanks and whiskbrooming Hymie had to laugh his way out of the store to escape from. White hairs! In the candy store Hymie picked up a pink rubber mouse for the baby, and then it was over the roofs and downstairs to Dora's. She shone, and her house shone. Her pretty face was glistening from work, and the way, in the shadows, she filled out that green wrapper, he was tempted.

"So early?" She anxiously touched his cheek. "Are you well?"

"Only sad, to be stuck selling all day. Short of funds."

"Oh—" Dora cheered up and she reached her bare arms around his neck—"I have funds."

How could you not adore her? He drew the shades and they made love then and there, in the half-light on the sofa. Suffer, suffer—the sage Reisel. She should know the suffering it took—you could go crazy!—to hold yourself in with Dora to save for Debbie. But he suffered and he fooled Dora, she was satisfied, and together they touched foreheads over Joycie's crib while he dangled the toy mouse for the baby to catch and gurgle at and try to eat.

"My joy," Dora whispered, "every minute more like . . ."

"Like?"

". . . like my boy, with—oh!" she pressed her whole self against him—"your boy's body!"

Hey Reiseleh!

In Baxter Street his poor bald sallow-faced hunched pal Horowitz was bitter.

"Back in the tie business?"

Hymie winked at him. "Up to the neck."

Debbie at the table with the women and needlework didn't need winks. She knew why he was there.

Gehenna, so soon? By six in the blast of home-goers he also was rushing home, with cases empty and pockets full. Gittel setting the table shrieked, then tittered, "Oh it's you," when he passed through to leave the cases. Then she primped her hair.

Primp, for all the good it will do you, wrinkled doll. And there, so help him God, stood her daughter in twenty years, maybe less, dried up inside now already. And that's where Gehenna is—inside you, Reiseleh. She'd been born with it, with red hair for camouflage. Him, he sauntered lightheartedly toward Columbus Park, Debbie's, yes, the land of Columbus to use Reisel's expression, that his cousin frittered away!

His fiery-eyed one was smarter, in the park ready and waiting with her little smirk. Debbie left her bench—no begging required—and grabbed his arm like a lifeline.

She said, "I knew you'd be there this morning."

"A message from God?"

"Not from God."

"Then guess where we're going, witch."

How could she guess? Since he'd never taken her, had she ever been in a taxi before, in a Weinerschnitzel and wine restaurant where Dutchmen played waltzes, in the Madison Square Park Hotel high upstairs instead of Bleecker Street with roaches big as mice and mice big as rats? His gypsy glittered tonight, naked in front of the window with the city stretched twinkling beneath them. Then she left the shades up, so look in, keyhole Reisel, watch Debbie play boy, dog and Frenchwoman! In a pink lamplight—"I've made you newborn, not like that mud doll of yours with the red mop on top!"—Lilith arched her breast and bare belly against him.

Hey, Reiseleh?

But oy, the morning. He got up a broken man from that circus. Between holy Reisel and glutton Debbie they'd ruined his plumbing! Then came a week, two weeks, three weeks of excuses to Dora. Debbie he avoided like cholera. He earned useless money selling ties, he turned it over to Golda. Nights he stayed home listening to his insides and from his son the industrialist shot glances What are you doing here? Worse, his wife and his daughter Naomi pestered him see a doctor.

"Who's sick?" he shouted.

But had he brought on—or rather, had the saint and the gypsy cursed him with—a serious disease? And would you believe that the saint sneaked in where he moped by the window and with her Judas smile and soft voice dumped philosophy like coals on his head?

"Cousin Share you should not live by extremes. It is not right, since you are ill, that you should not have yourself taken care of."

"I'm well!" he clenched his teeth.

In desperation he arranged to meet Dora to prove it. And knock wood, waiting in the hotel—you can be sure a different room than with Debbie—he felt more like himself again. The curtains fluttered, the sun shone, downstairs the park was a promising if still slightly worrisome green, with plenty of life passing through. Then came Dora's tap on the door and she threw herself at him like a drowner that pulls you down too.

"Hymie—"

Whatever it was, good it would not be.

In the street yesterday with Joycie and Sammy a young woman had threatened her, "Pray for the orphans, your days are numbered already," then called her a . . . bad word. With what eyes that woman had looked at them! Sammy'd held on to Dora—

Was Debbie real, or a devil from a grandmother's tale? And was he really sick or was there a curse on him? Who knew, with a clammy forehead and a limp hand? And he had a dry throat to croak through.

"A lunatic—"

"That's what Joe said, but—"

Or—"You told Joe?"—was Hymie the lunatic? Next maybe Hymie's name and address to Joe and a knife in Joe's hand with her regards? And at thirty years old innocence blushes—or was it stupidity?

Dora blushed, if she had done something wrong. But she'd been so scared, not for herself, for the children. What would they do without her? Besides, Joe's dark frown had not been for Dora. He'd kissed her and comforted her, more than usual. He had called that woman a . . . bad name. In bed in the dark he'd held her, her dear Joe. Should they begin another baby, he'd asked, to grow up and laugh at its mother's orphans' curse story? Yes, she'd shaken her head yes . . . and fallen asleep snuggled up to Joe.

She'd waked this morning and Joe'd stroked her cheek and she'd been so happy! Then that woman's mean laughing eyes had come back and weighed like stones on her. She'd kept this woe to herself, she didn't want Joe going to business worried for her sake. And now her Hymie, poor white-haired boy, how drawn he looked, pale. She shouldn't have told him either.

"You're not well," she touched his forehead.

She too? "Leave me alone!"

Dora did just the opposite, she tried to console him. "It was lunacy, that woman," she fondled him, "I'm sorry I told you, darling—"

So why did you tell me! But Hymie kept his trap shut—the way she should have done. Then, in bed, for the first time in his life he was a cripple. Nothing! Dora kept telling him that it didn't matter, she didn't care.

It mattered!

Days, nights, he stayed the same, with whores, with fingers, no matter how hard he tried. Debbie—what else?—must have worked something on him. He prayed in synagogue, in more than one synagogue. No use. He finally went to a doctor but made the long story short. The idiot tapped, the idiot poked, the idiot said, "Well, as you grow older . . ."

Debbie had cursed him all right, let God strike her dead. But to come home to the other one, Saint Reisel, in *his* household?

He loathed the sight of her!

8

THE SECOND SARAH WALKED INTO THE EAST SIDE SETTLEment House with Joe Seiden to have her feet stepped on to music, she caught sight of Danny Share from behind and her heart almost stopped.

To the humiliation, after he'd disappeared, of no one home at Hester Street but her cousin Leah with the furry purr—"Danny doesn't live here any more, didn't he tell you?"—the pain had been added, a real ache like sickness, that he hadn't thought enough of her to bother telling her. Not a word. Dumb Sarah, she'd turned red as an Indian but murmured where did he live? so Leah could wave toward the world outside and smile cattily, "With his uncle."

What uncle, which side of the family? Why did people like Leah leave her helpless? Naomi and Golda would certainly be told about pants-crazy Sarah. How could she have gone back and faced them to ask where Danny was? So dope fiend Sarah had gone back and faced them and found out where Danny was.

Well, if you care you care, so she'd written a funny note on a Statue of Liberty postcard.

> *Dear cousin still more removed. Who'll win bananas for me if you're washing musical glasses in a country saloon? Will you be home in time for the Prohibition Law?*

He'd answered too, just like him, with a blue fuzzy postcard labeled "Watchung Mountains." "I'm sorry," he'd sandwiched between he was glad to hear from her and he was hers sincerely, "it was all of a sudden. I do sing a little, for laughs, no bananas, not even peanuts." So she'd kissed his handwriting and written back. "A little song is better than nothing. Are people allowed to hear you?"

Then silence—until even dumb Sarah had studied forgetting him. And this was how she passed the first test, all but dragging poor easygoing Joe through the press in the corridors and the stairway to try to catch up to Danny.

"Hey," laughing Joe squeezed her waist, "you can't wait to dance with me, huh?"

And although the dance was in the upstairs gym, to Joe's further puzzlement they got off at one. And to his complete amazement they were settling down in a lecture room full of people.

"Hey we're lost!"

"No we're not. Self-improvement."

"But," Joe kept laughing, "I'm too soft for these hard chairs."

"You're not so fat," Sarah absentmindedly patted his arm. "You have a long way to go."

"I'll get there," Joe happily promised her. "What's the lecture about?"

Sarah had taken back seats to make it a chance bumping into Danny on the way out. Only—why did she have to be so darn short—where was he?

Joe nudged her and repeated his question.

"Deep things," Sarah kept looking.

"Then I'll have to float around on the surface."

Sarah turned to him smiling.

"Say, that's pretty good, Joe."

Joe squeezed her hand.

"I know you appreciate me."

That good-looking Mr. Schnee—though he didn't have Danny's looks—introduced the topic, *The Merchant of Venice*, and a stout grinning man who looked like a fish hawker.

Joe whispered, "Watch how well I sleep sitting up."

"You'll listen, it's good for you."

"Who was Shakespeare, the author of *The Yiddish King Lear*?"

"Ssh."

Well, Joe'd heard of Shakespeare but that was about all, if you went to work back when Noah's Ark made its first Coney Island excursion and you finished eighth grade in continuation school. Yet the lecture was swell. This old geezer in front of the blackboard jumped right in with was Shakespeare an anti-Semite?

Joe whispered to Sarah, "Was Shakespeare Jewish?"

"Shut up, Joe."

"Then what else could he be," Joe shared the fun with her, "but an anti-Semite?"

The geezer said Shylock, so what do you know, that's where Shylock came from—that Shakespeare son of a bitch! Except that the geezer, with a wisecrack here and a quotation there, proved that not only was Shakesie not an anti-Semite but this play was anti-Gentile and 100 percent for the Yids!

By the question period though, the camp chair was really cutting into Joe's ass. "Let's dance," he whispered to little Sarah.

"Ssh, the best is yet to come."

From the hand wavers rose a redheaded queen like a movie star with a meek voice part ritz and part greenhorn who began her own lecture.

Joe kidded Sarah, "That doll, you mean?"

Sarah craned—and next to the redhead speaking sat Danny! Was he with her, the way he looked up bewitched at her? But so did the middle-aged man to the redhead's left, yes, her father, it had to be. Which would mean Danny was here alone. Sarah gasped, "Yes, that doll"—with this idiotic elation!

Reisel wonder of the lecture hall supported her theories with Shakespeare from memory and Danny was prouder than when they'd handed him his diploma last summer. In fact she beat the diploma by a mile. At graduation there'd been Ma, Grandma and the girls all beaming at him, Gittel's—hey!—slobbering kiss, Reisel's funny hearty handclasp. But the fellow grads—not many he'd known—had mostly been day kids who'd had it soft, the M.D.'s and lawyers to be, and to round out the crowd there'd been his old man.

Now what would Hymie have been doing in a school auditorium a long hot afternoon, watching his son graduate? My ass! Watching Reisel. Danny hadn't thought of that then, he'd given his father the benefit of the doubt. Someone congratulates you, you say thanks. But the paternal counsel tonight had been the tipoff.

Tonight with dusk over the cobbles and the empty loading platforms of the West Street docks Ma and the hired help had knocked off and Reisel and Danny's sisters were leaving. Him, one leg was aiming toward Reisel, the other was staying put. He'd figured another half hour would do the pagoda lamp he'd designed and was finishing up. Jesus, there was more to lamps than he'd ever imagined! They had their geometry: shade height equals base height or the product looks lousy. And sometimes to get the trimmings and color right took sleight of hand. Which was fine from seven-thirty to six, but not when you wanted to pack it in and ride home with Reisel. So he'd kept tacking green silk onto the elegant curve of the frame, they'd left, and his stomach had churned.

But if he'd gone with them he wouldn't have met Mr. Schnee on the trolley and Mr. Schnee wouldn't have told him of the Shakespeare lecture he ought to take in. Danny himself, he wouldn't have crossed the street for a Shakespeare lecture, but Reisel said Shakespeare was her English professor. So without even a sniff at the withering grass in Tompkins Square Park that gave him a nice homesick feeling for Orange he'd burst upstairs with the news.

Reisel'd said, "Of course I must go, Daniel. Will you accompany me?"

"Will fish swim?"

So the visiting Leah had exchanged glances with Ma, that was their prerogative. Him, he was a citizen and an overjoyed one, to be going somewhere with Reisel. But it wasn't his old man's prerogative to corner him with advice on the sly.

"Keep away from that girl if you want to save yourself heartache."

Danny'd pulled free. "Where's your rent?" he'd given his father the cod eye.

Hymie'd shrugged, "A word to the wise," gone back to the front window to nurse his mysterious ailment till supper, and left Danny at the edge of a pounding headache, a corker.

But—slow thinker Danny with your sledgehammer pulses—the word to the wise meant that Beau Bummel had made his play. Sure Reisel had blocked that pass, but his bastard father had thrown it. Danny had to get this guy out of here, tears or no tears from women! One thing sure, the walk to the Settlement with Reisel next to him, the sweet pools of lamplight, the nippy fall air—they'd all been poisoned for him. He was used to Reisel in silence, she'd meditate, he'd dream. But this trip—and Ma's chocolate cake, his favorite, had been the dessert—he'd had gall with his headache, his mouth had been bitter with that son of a bitch. At Houston Street Reisel grabbed his arm and a flivver shaved by him.

"Daniel, what is the matter?"

"Anyone in my family," he'd burst out, "ever annoy you?"

"Of whom do you speak?"

"Must I say it out loud?"

"You need not have said it at all," she'd reminded him, not unkindly. "But listen, Daniel, there is no use judging—what shall I say?—certain people, if you do not wish to drive yourself crazy, you understand?"

"Why?"

"Because our law forbids us to and we are a people of laws. Without law in our life and law in our spirit what are we? Wild bestial Cossacks!"

Danny'd had to grin, headache or not. "Who, me?"

But, "It is no laughing matter," Reisel had been stern.

"Okay. Then those laws don't go for my father?"

"If your father is what you say he is, he is not that way only since yesterday."

"You're darn tootin'."

"Consequently why did your mother not leave him? I would never have stayed with such a man!" And before Danny could take her up on that, she'd added, "As you make him out to be."

So it was Ma's fault? Figure out Reisel. And he would have told her too, but that beautiful head had stayed bent and brooding until they'd reached the Settlement. There, in the crush like pounding fists against Danny's head, Reisel had cheered up.

"So many crowds!"

How come her once-a-month English mistakes filled Danny's heart with her? And hey—the headache had vanished!

"Shakespeare never said that."

"I have said something wrong?" She'd smiled, and he'd been happy almost to tears. "I count on you to correct me, Daniel."

But Reisel was the expert.

And now, in the harmless little girl voice that tickled him so, she was proving to the congregation that in *The Merchant of Venice* government of the Gentiles, by the Gentiles and for the Gentiles—Danny's wisecrack in her ear when the old boy up front had started—shall not perish from this earth. Sure, Shakespeare let Shylock have a nice Jewish speech. What of it? His Gentiles were punks, but they were okay to each other. The Jew was the guy starving for that pound of unkosher meat.

"Consequently although Shakespeare is the greatest of poets, even greater than Tolstoy whose Christianity confused him sometimes, we should not be so foolish—" and the way that mild voice suddenly clanged out—"as to place trust in Gentiles in our inevitable hour of need!" And she sat down muttering.

The tumult, the shouts: not all the Bolshies had been deported.

"Bigot!"

"Reactionary!"

"You're in America, not the old country!"

"Religion separates—the working class stands together!"

Yeah, take a stroll to Mulberry Street where the dagos hang out, or west along Bleecker and say hello to the micks—and on the balls of your ass you'll find out how the working class stands together. But who cared, let 'em shout. What did Danny have to do with the working class except work? The mystery to him was old roly-poly's cheerfulness in front of the room through the whole commotion, as if that's what he'd come here for. The noise petered out, roly-poly thanked Reisel for starting it—"You do Portia honor"—choked off a new Bolshevik uproar—"With such dialectics the class struggle is in the safest of hands"—and left 'em smiling when he said goodbye.

Sarah's coat and purse fumbles brought her into the aisle perfectly, but Danny only mumbled "Excuse me" when she bumped into him, so she had to catch at his sleeve.

"Haven't we met?"

Her heart gave a catch too the way his face lit up, he seemed so happy to see her—

But in the shuffle she introduced Joe, and Danny introduced that . . . redheaded genius. Then how he beamed. That's what he was happy about. No—or rather yes and no. He was glad he and Sarah had run into each other—but just glad.

In the big gloomy ice cream parlor down the block you'd have thought that Danny'd become drunk on a few sips of soda. At least Sarah had never heard him talk like this before.

"According to Euclid," Danny said after they'd worked out that she and

Reisel were not related, "cousins to the same cousin should be cousins to each other."

"Your theorem is entertaining, my friend," Reisel said, "but not very logical."

So he'd gotten it from her. But cheer up, Sarah old girl, you have Joe, dear old Joe happily slurping Reisel in with his eyes along with the happy slurps at his soda. And smile.

Sarah smiled, the woe stayed inside. "Do you teach?" she asked Reisel.

And darn that girl, she smiled too, and so friendly, so openly, that how could you hate her, even with that dumb she meant smart handsome Danny doting on Reisel with his motionless spoon in his hand while the ice cream in his soda melted away.

"I teach trimmings to cling to lampshades," Reisel joked, then explained, "What I can teach has no connection with livelihood."

Sarah really had the worst possible luck. Even when Reisel bragged how smart she had been in Gymnasium—only why couldn't she have stayed in Europe?—she bragged with such innocent pleasure, like a kid, that you had to smile along with her.

Yes, Reisel had made her dear papá send her to Gymnasium in Wladkow, exactly as her mother had done with Reisel's grandpapá except that Mamá had gone there to flirt. At home Reisel had learned Hebrew and Russian. In Gymnasium she had become their best English and French scholar. To her regret she had only a smattering of German and so could not read Goethe's *Faust* in the original, although she understood that as a man Goethe had been far from exemplary, living with women he was not married to.

Joe Seiden grinned, "I'll take that job."

"You might not enjoy it," Reisel glanced at Joe, "as much as you may think."

She went on to tell Sarah that her professor of English, an anti-Semite supreme even among anti-Semites, must have been one of that sort, although at the time—she had been brought up so sheltered—she had not comprehended what his kindnesses signified, nor needless to say had she responded except by excellence in study to his tenderly calling her his "Biblical Jewess."

"But," Sarah asked—and darn it, her uncontrollable eyes flicked over to Danny—"if he loved you and never came out and said so how bad could he have been?"

"While I was good, how could he be bad?"

"Just the same," Sarah smiled at Reisel, "I feel sorry for him."

"Because, thank God, you do not know him, or anyone like him. It is true nevertheless that he led me to Shakespeare."

"Your one real romance."

"That also is true," Reisel smiled without surprise at the small explosion of jealousy. "I think Shakespeare is like me, though irreligious I am afraid."

That catty remark had slipped unawares out of Sarah and see how nice Reisel was? So could you blame Danny for loving a nice beautiful red-headed genius, even if you could swear that the nice beautiful redheaded genius didn't love Danny? Anyhow, no use crying over spilt milk. Just go jump off the roof.

Walking home after they had left poor Sarah and the clown Joe, "She cares about you," Reisel told Danny.

"Nah, not like that. We're just cousins."

"As you and I are."

"Yeah, as you and I are."

Reisel could see that he was angry and angry because she was . . . the special thing to him, as nice little Sarah was not. And Reisel was pleased. So? At times Scripture refers to heaven before earth, but at other times to earth before heaven. Thus we are taught that nature and spirit are of equal importance in God's eyes. Should she then deny her humanity? She was superior, as Daniel recognized. Consequently why should she not be pleased . . . to be preferred?

Naomi's first thought the snowy afternoon Jack turned in his order book and demanded a check for one hundred and thirty-eight dollars and twenty-one cents for final payment in full for his services was he still loves me. Otherwise he would never have been spiteful enough to get the arithmetic right—she checked it over at once—correct to the penny. Her next thought, worriedly, was that he'd take all their business to some other lamp company.

"But why go," she said, "just to—" She caught herself before the get even.

"Don't worry, hon." His handsome face was a mask. "I won't cost you one cent."

He still hypnotized her with the wavy hair, the straight nose and the white forehead, he made her heart beat. Oh damn him, damn Leah! After Naomi had broken off with him she'd seen the twinkle in his beautiful brown eyes just once more, at lunch in the downstairs restaurant—and they hadn't been twinkling at her. The girl he'd been with—brunette, bold and handsome, as if he'd shopped for Naomi's exact opposite—he'd placed facing the door so you couldn't possibly miss her or the message: You're not the only oyster in the stew. Danny'd been with her that noon because Reisel had been home with a sick headache and he'd asked Naomi what she'd expected, she'd given the guy the gate. Just from her expression her brother'd said that, she hadn't spoken a word!

"You're creeping into my love life?" she'd snapped. "Do I creep into yours?"

"Mine?" he'd tried to dirty joke his way out. "You mean those old blondes on the Bowery?"

"Remember," she'd given it to him, "I'm still your sister. I don't have to listen to that kind of talk!"

In the evening Reisel's headache had seemed to disappear while Naomi had sat on Reisel's bed for more lovelorn advice.

"That woman was nothing, another animal. He wishes you to be jealous, and to give him a sign. Just the same, were you to have married him he would still have such animals. He is himself somewhat animal. . . ."

And in your heart you knew Reisel was right—and too bad for you.

Now Naomi asked Jack, "What are you going to do?"

Jack grinned lovelessly and he really shocked her. Liquor was outlawed, so the liquor business for him: easy hours and sales, high commissions, early retirement. The shop clatter, the people working beyond the partition glass, became blotted into a silence, she was so scared for Jack. She was hoarse saying, "You want to frighten me."

"Frighten you, hon?" Jack would not soften one bit. "Why should I?"

He did hang around poolrooms with all sorts of low company. Why did she want so to protect him?

"You're kidding, Jack, aren't you?"

His grin did soften. "No."

"But you could get killed, becoming mixed up in gangs."

"I didn't get killed at Ypres," Jack bragged, "the Germans got killed."

Naomi blurted, "Jack, I'll make you a partner."

"The hell you will. Did you suppose I'm a guy women can twist around their little finger any time they decide to? Write your name on that check."

She sat stunned while Jack went into the shop, shook hands with Danny and ignored everyone else, dented his fedora, fitted it on and walked out. Danny already was breaking the news to Leah and Reisel, then Ma. They all glanced in Naomi's direction, so she had to resist jumping to the window for a last glimpse of Jack. From her desk you could see the snow fluttering past the panes to the cobbles, drays and piers, but dammit, you couldn't see the sidewalk below.

Who wanted a man, her eyes filled, who sat with brunettes facing the door? The only thing was, where would she find another salesman like him?

Leah adored the snow winking past the corner lamplights and fluffing over the sidewalks. The Village looked villagey as an old-fashioned post-card! Suppose she were to run into Jack Berger now, after that performance of his at Quality? Would he stop, would he talk to her? Yes—and she bet more than talk to her if she wanted, that handsome lecher. . . .

She didn't run into him though and on the whole that was best. No sense reaching back. At Waverly Place she pointed one galoshed foot toward the doorway of Bessie—what was she thinking!—Be*t*sy Gould's knickknacks oops Occult Arts Shop and . . . Henny Lieber? But the trouble with Henny was that whenever you went there he was one of the boys in the back room behind Bessie's cretonne curtain of privilege. Yet Lieber looked so honest with the wide mouth, square dimpled chin and Dutchy blue eyes—another Jew with a Gentile in the family woodpile. Last week Leah'd been fanning her face between two fires in that windowless stuffy rear enclosure Amy Lowell had once sanctified by sticking her head into—a glass of Bes, Be*t*sy's admittedly free wine, and a Krimsky canvasful of yellow, red and green splotches.

Next thing she'd known, "Nice painting?" Henny Lieber'd been testing her.

"I hope it's not catching. It reminds me of when I had scarlet fever."

"It could be fatal," that's when the dimple had come out, "if Krimsky heard you." Then the dimple had gone back but the blue eyes had stayed lively while he'd waved at the paintings screaming from all four walls and asked wasn't it a shame since it was Betsy's good nature to exhibit her friends' things for sale that she should keep the back room a secret from the world at large?

Now had that been criticism? The laughing eyes had seemed to say so, but just then Bessie had black-widowed in to reclaim her property with an imperative whisper. Henny had said, "Speak up, Betsy, so a person can hear you." Bessie had not spoken up, but Henny had excused himself just the same and gone into the shop with her. Later he'd strolled back and proposed a Saturday tour of the galleries to Leah, but she'd been noncommittal. Was there such a man shortage that she needed to play stand-in for Bessie?

So now Leah pointed the galoshes away from Bessie's toward Eighth Street and a movie, and at the ticket booth she all but had the coin out of her purse when Henny Lieber walked out of the theater.

"Leah, don't you dare go in there!"

"You think I won't like the picture?"

"I'd hate to think that you would."

"But I'm in flight," Leah said, "I'm tricking a nice boy into marriage—with another girl."

"Leah that's marvelous! I'm in flight too, for almost the same reason. Let's run together."

"Run to Bes pardon me Betsy's?" Leah gave him a test.

"No. That's where I'm in flight from."

Henny gripped her arm—and it felt nice, even through gloves and coats!—and marched her to the three-steps-down speakeasy on Grove Street, where he gave the password. Leah though was the one that the man at the peephole said hello to letting them in. The room was dazzling with mirrors and cozy with talk, but Henny sorrowfully shook the snow off their coats and ordered her Orange Blossom and his Scotch. "Prohibition an infant," he told her, "and already you're famous here."

"Yes, they sweep me out. Though you suggested the place, I didn't." But the Dutchy-blues were studying her in dead earnest, and there are such things as jokes carried too far. So Leah shrugged, "You'd be famous here too if you'd dropped in with a friend in a *yarmulke* and—"

"What's a *yarmulke*?"
"Aren't you a bar mitzvah?"
"I know what a bar mitzvah is, though nobody had one in the Lutheran Orphan Asylum on Amsterdam Avenue where I grew up."
"You sit at this table drinking Scotch and tell me you're a Lutheran?"
"Formerly, but unaffiliated right now. As a Lutheran I always felt God kept too close an eye on me."
"A *yarmulke* is a skullcap Orthodox Jewish men wear for the same reason. So if you'd brought in the friend with a *yarmulke* that I did, to trick him into marriage . . . with somebody else . . . and he'd only trust plain seltzer—because who knows, bootleg slivovitz could be distilled from pig's feet—the doorman would remember you too."

Actually Al had asked the waiter where the brandy came from and been told to take his comedy act to the Palace. But Al had really meant it, the waiter'd talked to the manager, and to bring the skit to a climax the manager'd tried to buy Al off as a prohibition agent. Leah'd then led an anthropological round table discussion with Al's skullcap as evidence. Even so, her Orange Blossom had taken next to forever to come, so Al must have been subject to further scrutiny before he'd been cleared as just an honest citizen breaking the law.

"Between your seltzer," Leah'd told Al, "and my Beef Bourgignon—" never would she forget Al industriously gathering peas from his plate in her house like a pearl diver with his clever fork not even touching the dietarily unclean beef in the stew—"we can't possibly marry. I'd die of thirst and you'd die of hunger."

"Make fun of me if it gives you pleasure, Leah," Al had gloomily watched his seltzer go flat, "I'm an easy mark."

He was touching, and the next thing Leah knew she'd be touching him, the worst thing possible. The lift of a finger and one more marriage proposal. Yet even in the first few weeks when the romance was hot she'd let him know she wouldn't be forsaking all others in any future she knew of. Back from all others—Mama's once a week, a movie, the so-called artists behind Bessie's trinkets store, Russek's for shoes, or her friend Ivy Mason —she used to find her faithful hound Al on her doorstep. Then he'd cross-examine her lying down, and she'd been patient, she'd explain she didn't explain. She'd offered just the girl for him, a delicate blonde five feet tall, beautiful, serious, thrifty and basically kosher, and he wouldn't listen. He'd barely glanced at a snapshot of Naomi. Eventually—who wanted this after a day at the factory?—she'd said, "Al, hadn't we better break up?" and the breakage had been awful to contemplate. But from then on when he phoned she'd say she was busy. Why busy now, he'd plead. She hadn't been busy six, four, two months ago. "We're too different, Al." Of course she never should have used the endearing word Al. But she was fond of him, like a mother. "I'll be around," he'd insist, and she'd laugh, "I won't." Ivy Mason called kindness the worst cruelty and reminded Leah that Al's manly assumption was her reverting to orthodoxy. But Leah hadn't the heart to disappoint him, she would wait around. Which proved Al's point. Why had she stayed if he and she were that different? "Why why why why?" she'd laughed. Finally though, she said she wouldn't be around and she wasn't around. A pretty picture, Al's detailed account by phone the next day: his ringing the bell and no answer, his reconnoitering in the cold, craning up at dark windows back and front. And yesterday, "I have this date for tomorrow," he'd rung her to threaten her!

"With the rabbi's daughter? That pretty one with the black curling lashes in your Palisades picnic snapshot? Keep the date, Al, and her too if she's as nice as she looks."

Silence.

Then, "I'm sorry that I ever went to that party last year where we met, Leah. Goodbye."

"If he didn't matter to her," to quote Al, why the blues and guilt afterwards?

But tonight doing the dishes and picturing Al all kosher and cozy with his little rabbinical wifie, Leah had actually burst into song.

Life's a lark,
I'm as free . . . as that bird . . .

Then that nemesis phone had begun ringing and she'd run.

At twenty-four a girl doesn't spill all the beans, but she served some to Henny. "A relative of mine by marriage," she rounded out the sad tale, "was a bargain basement playboy, and my contempt for him Henny, my whole girlhood long, you wouldn't imagine. Now in the wisdom of age, I see—"

"You see," Henny happily filled in, "playboying isn't all play?"

"I see—don't look—that you've been tracked down."

"Tracked down?" Henny did look and saw lean Bessie Gould spidering toward them in a snowy black felt helmet. "What do you mean?"

What Leah meant was, for instance, the way he sprang to his feet like Bessie's jack-in-the-box. "Betsy! Let me hang up your coat."

Bes—Be*t*sy let him and shook out her hat to Leah's lap, and—"Oh, darling—" started spanking the snow off Leah till Leah grabbed Bessie's hands and laughed, "Whoa—" at which Bessie appropriately bared her horsy teeth. Two-faced Henny with sincerity stamped on each face instantly offered Betsy a cocktail.

"I certainly will have a Manhattan, though I'm mad at you Mr. Lieber—and you too, Leah—for deserting me in my direst need and trundling off to speakeasies."

Betsy had sorely missed . . . both of them. Krimsky'd been in complaining how could his paintings sell if she never allowed any live customers in to see them, and he'd ended by calling her a lousy Philistine, her, who'd given up her father's fifteen room duplex at 1000 Madison Avenue for art's sake!

And the devious Henny who'd said the same thing as Krimsky but with a little less punch, now said, "Shocking. I wouldn't have believed it of Krimsky." Amen Henny, shocking was the word and disgusting an even better one. Leah was pretty disgusted, not to say bored, while Bessie throated grievance on grievance about Krimsky, intertwined with Henny's evasions about dynamics of balance in the Krimsky productions. But Bessie's begrudging Krimsky her free wine and cheese nibbles was the absolute limit. Leah pushed back her chair and murmured early rising tomorrow to work for her food and drink.

"Oh, good night dear," Bessie said. "Occult Arts opens late, though I'm beginning to wonder why it opens at all."

"No, it's a lovely shop, don't you think so Leah?" asslicker Henny came through, and Bessie, "You appreciate it more than I do, Henry dear," panted for more, which Henry dear was pleased to deliver, dragging out of Leah that Betsy's knickknacks—rings, earrings, pins—were lovely. And why shouldn't they be, Leah was too polite to add, with lawyer Gould financing, no matter how reluctantly, the European trips that his daughter Bessie made ostensibly to pick them up.

Say, Leah hadn't had to be so polite. Since Henny refused to let her walk home alone and Bessie could hardly wait to get more snow on the black felt chapeau, Henny went for their coats. Then Bessie suddenly bent close and breathed eye to eye at Leah: "Please in the future pursue your nympho activities elsewhere than in my shop. Is that clear?"

"You mean I nullify your Occult Arts? But never fear, darling, you're welcome to all the odds and ends there—present company included."

The sweatshop door opened and Debbie lifted full lips to Hymie, but when he bent the kiss thinned to that teasing smile of hers. Peculiar, that she should be in a men's suits factory with tailors hunched pumping treadles: up down, up down. Scrawny Feldman the boss waved from the office, but Hymie had other things on his mind. Naked, free—what a pleasure!—he sailed straight up into Debbie and rode that twisting form. The sly smile asked, "Do you like maiden nipples?" and melted into thin air.

He woke vaguely excited, then the dream drifted back and he came to with a vengeance—dancing, ready, like Big Red at the post out at Jamaica.

Was this real or was he still sleeping?

Real!

And overdue—he didn't owe gratitude! This minute he could have used Debbie, if you could make that witch disappear afterward like in the dream. He had Dora—better than Debbie—and her smooth round belly with poor Joe's baby inside, if she was okay. Otherwise—he'd see, otherwise. The main thing was *he* was okay. Imagine: yesterday gray gloom, today fully restored!

Like old times he hopped out of bed, washed, and smacked his palms over the breakfast party. Hey, the shock on the Unholy Inquisition—his son's puss, Golda's, even Naomi's—that the father was well and stirring. They liked sick, drag yourself, bring home dollar bills, move your lips by a gray window like his pal Gittel. He'd get home, she'd perk up and roll those old eyes at him, so last week out of pure misery he'd called her bluff. When he caught hold of her backside had she climbed her high horse out of reach, with her wells, what do you means, who do you thinks. But now he smiled and who smiled back, who sensed his vigor? The wrinkled prune at the table and the juicy peach at the stove!

"I am pleased," the young one handed him oatmeal, "to see you in good health again." And "Aren't we happy this snowy morning!" the old one simpered.

And what do you know, it was snowing—a white steady fall, with the windowsill thick already. You could hear slaves shoveling, he'd thought coal. Well watch out, he might melt that snow without coal! After breakfast he wrapped himself up and he was first to the door, ahead of Reisel even who sped on angel's wings.

Daniel the wise flipped after him, "Selling snowshoes?"

He laughed, "Flexible Flyers."

The whole world had come to life, even the dead ones with umbrellas, round shoulders and baby steps in the snow, and you had to smile how the trees across the street in the park held up their arms with white sleeves on in surprise at the prisoners in lockstep along the shortcut to the El. Ah, and out of the house went Reisel—what a waste, the way her leg swung under that slim curving green coat of hers with the fur on top—to give God her regards. And look—at the far side of the virgin-white lawns: Debbie!

Spying, still spying? He'd teach her spying—with a twist of the wrist. And hey, Dr. Pecker with the cure for what ails you stood straight at attention! Hymie started after the witch in such a rush he almost ended up on his ear.

Then what a ceremony!

This snotnose and his girl friend had to prop Hymie up as if he only lacked crutches. You got books scholars? Look in your books and mind your own business.

"You okay, mister?"

He could have mistered that miss with the blonde bob and the baby-blue eyes where his mister would have done the most good. "Okay, okay," he finally escaped from their clutches.

Meanwhile—Debbie? He'd have known the black coat and snow-trimmed toque anywhere, and instead—a bush with white cotton stuck on the twigs. So where was Miss Witch hiding with her quick gypsy body? At the corner that cunning face of hers popped out between white shaggy umbrellas.

The will-o'-the-wisp, you got there and she'd vanished. Or was she trailing him? He went slow, he shuffled his feet in time to the walking dead all around him. Oh when he had her indoors he'd thrash her till she wriggled for mercy. Then he'd give her—and with pleasure!—some mercy. But the crowds thinned out—Second Street, First; Stanton and Rivington—and no sign of her.

Let her go to hell with her appear disappear!

In a burst of affection he ducked into a bakery and bought Dora a bagful of the cookies she'd been having a yen for, this latest pregnancy. With his scarf flying he ran two steps at a time to the roof of the house behind Dora's and he wanted her so much that in the stinging swirl and high drifts of snow he nearly walked off the edge! Drop in, the jagged snow-dusted crates smiled up at him from the bottom of the airshaft. The next step, as the joke went at the National Burlesque, would have been a lalapalooza! But—in Dora's building he stamped and swatted and dug snow out of his shoes—his trousers crease was still perfect. Dora let him in and Joycie in diapers reached up to "Unckie." Minus Debbie he told Dora his story—"So," at the lalapalooza, "wasn't God saving me for you?"—and she threw herself with a cry, belly and all, into his arms.

"Hymie, never come that way again."

But Joycie, with her grin surrounding the pink mouse Hymie'd brought her a long time ago, also wanted to play. An infant was supposed to be up this early? So what could Hymie do? He had to grin too, calm himself and, with Dora lovingly watching, play with the daughter instead of the mother. "Taste a yen cookie, Dora," Hymie winked while Joycie giddyapped on his knee.

"I lost the yen," Dora smiled with moist eyes, "now that you're well—"

Now that he was well, "Madison Square Hotel later," he kissed her ear.

If only she herself were well, with her stupid, difficult pregnancies. But Hymie was so happy, her joy, she didn't tell him that. Besides, by the time that Samuel had lunch and went back to school this terrible blizzard should have stopped blowing.

And it did!

Without traffic the air was so fresh and still, the streets shone a billowy white with icicles sparkling from the fire escapes. Even pulling bundled-up Joycie on the cute sled Hymie had brought Samuel when Samuel was his sister's age, and carrying Joe his hot lunch, Dora felt so . . . happy! She hardly ached. Yes, at the market with those sad awful chickens and their screeches the smell did make her slightly faint, but when didn't it? Joe scolded her she should have stayed home, but how could you go uptown to Hymie if Joe was eating in some greasy lunchroom? Then Joe gave her a kiss anyhow—"I'm glad you're here now"—and a twinkle of his gray eyes.

God in heaven how lucky she was, to have Joe and Hymie! And at three o'clock to have Samuel. He raced in with his primer and wet gloves from snowballs, charged around the living room with a grin and his eyes shut—"'*Where are you going?* said the cow. *Moo moo,* said Dickey Dare'"—kissed Rosie from upstairs there to watch Joycie, and "Going out to get rid of your belly?" ended up in his mother's arms.

Dora and the twelve-year-old Rosie both blushed and Dora gathered her smallest young man against her fur coat. "A brother, or another sister?"

"A sister. I'll diaper her and stick pins in her."

Did Dora squeeze this little boy! Wait till Hymie heard that cute saying, and Joe.

But the crowds jostled you so in the narrow path between snowbanks that those stupid pains started again, not labor, under the shoulder blades. Then, no taxis, and trolleys stuck in deep snow that men were shoveling. She dragged herself to the Bowery and was so slow climbing those El flights that she'd only reached the turnstiles and the conductors were clanking the gates shut. The waiting room made you sick with its stink, and—she had to laugh—the platform made you sick with the cold. The worst was the train didn't come and poor Hymie was already expecting her. Then uptown at Twenty-third Street the only way was to walk. With legs like stone and her back a torture Dora reached the hotel but she stopped just long enough in the lounge not to look awful for Hymie.

And what did her dear boy tell her?

"Other women grow ugly when they're pregnant—and you bloom!"

He was forever saying nice things to her, certainly. But he draped a lovely crimson silk scarf on her shoulders—he'd been selling ties in the Fourteenth Street subway station, her sweetheart, for her—and in the looking glass with her white-haired young man smiling behind her she really was blooming: bright eyes, cheeks full of color. You were sick and, like magic, well!

"You make me bloom, darling."

With the shades down, in bed, the sweetness was always close to unbearable, but today she gasped in real pain. Thank God Hymie took the cry for excitement, kissed her and drowsed. When he woke though he went up on his elbow, he couldn't believe his eyes.

"What, Mamaleh! You're sick, and keep quiet?"

She tried to think of apologies, but did you ever see such a Hymie? He was dressed in a moment, he dressed her and he ran out. With no cabs in New York, he had a cab waiting. Under the blue of the street lamps the winds sent snow twisting like the blizzard all over again, but at the doctor's Hymie insisted on waiting in the white howling street for her sake, so the doctor shouldn't get any ideas. And Dora came out blooming and beamed at him from the stoop.

"See how healthy I am?"

He brought her home around the corner and wouldn't let her go till she assured him she still felt fine. How could you feel otherwise with him asking like that? In the house she pressed a kiss and a whole silver dollar on Rosie, and she was showing off the scarf to Rosie's admiring eyes when such a shower of pain exploded in her insides that the whole world went black.

Two children weren't enough for Kirschner? He had to go jeopardizing his wife's health? What kind of man was that? He, Hymie Share, just the opposite. After yesterday's scare how could you be heartless and fool around with Dora before the baby was born? But that was if you had self-control!

Still, what a nuisance—right away that bitch in heat Debbie ran through his mind—the second a man was finally himself. But—learn, Joe—the main thing was Dora. Toward the end of the last pregnancy Hymie'd let her alone, and she'd been so grateful, adoring. Then came Joycie—and a new honeymoon! Of course this time—stupid Kirschner—she was far from the end yet.

So maybe she herself wasn't ready for Hymie to leave her alone? If so, who was he to fight nature? He marched cheerfully through the rosy white morning, but the trip across the roof was in knee-deep crusted snow. Who wanted to hang over the ledge like an icicle to see whether she was coming back from taking Sammy to school? And the truth was, he couldn't tell from the roof who was who in the street any more, even men from women—his eyes, something. All he could make out was figures rushing around, one like the other. So he went down, tapped on her door, waited, listened in the brown hallway—and nothing.

And hey—did he just get an idea! Instead of the street you peddle ties in the houses and you start with one foot in the door. He should have thought of this long ago! Later he would stop by at Dora's.

Only, the young mamas would open barely a crack and right through the nose their husband didn't need ties. Idiots, without looking how do you know what stands there? The two or three that did let him in, they had a ties obsession. Wink, joke, ask if such a good-looking girl spends the whole day cooking and cleaning, they keep squeezing material. Finally he laid a hand—friendly, no more—on the shoulder of one in a slob outfit that, while she bent over the case, climbed up two solid thighs like a prayer feel me. And did she give him a "What is this?" as if she was face to face with the Rape Fiend of the Lower East Side.

Sickening!

And even more sickening were the grandmothers who invited you in, sat you down, bought ties, offered tea and—with their shameless old eyes—anything else you wanted, completely without pride!

Hymie was proud, proud to have Dora! These specimens could take a good lesson from her. The sky was still light but the streets were getting dark, like the snow underfoot. This late Sammy would be home, a young man you couldn't put uncle stories over on any more—and a blabbermouth if ever Hymie had met one. But Hymie had to see his darling, he had to!

Yesterday he'd bought cookies for her, today marzipan. Yesterday a red scarf, today, from the same store, a yellow and green like springtime. What did he live for if not her happiness?

His own footprints in the snow led him over the roof in the twilight, and—ah, she was home now, with the door slightly ajar for him. But to be on the safe side, she might have company, he twirled the bell key.

What? He'd come down the wrong stairs? This looker answered, tall, ash-blonde, you knew her . . . and didn't, like in a dream. He squinted, only the number on the door was too dim.

But the ash-blonde said, "This is it, to our sorrow," and took the bag of marzipan from his hand. What? People on boxes, torn lapels, shoeless? Hymie's insides felt as if they were emptying. Kirschner stared out of a face like a ghost's, the old man, Dora's father, moaned like one, with a plain young woman holding his hand. The ash-blonde sat down by Joe and looked like him a little. So that was the sister-in-law.

Joe said, "I'm telling you, I as good as murdered her, Millie."

"Nonsense. These things happen to women."

Hymie's legs were like water, the room danced in the gloom. An armchair was vacant and he fell into it.

"I remember you from the hospital," the old man groaned at him. "You saved her that time. This time you're too late."

"But—" Hymie croaked.

But the hateful ash-blonde, the sister-in-law, what did she care with her loud voice? She went on to prove that what had happened to Dora, the hemorrhage, was not Joe's fault, that it was not Joe's fault that Hymie's darling, Hymie's Dora—could you believe this?—was dead. Joe kept nodding as if he was praying, but Hymie couldn't bear his darling in such a . . . creature's mouth.

He got home, don't ask him how, more dead than alive himself. Luckily nowadays the Inquisition wasn't inquisitive, the policy was to ignore him when he came in, except Naomi and she was locked in her room. If he wanted to cry there was the toilet, if his son ever came out. But who could cry? He found himself in the dark, in shirtsleeves, staring into the courtyard with the snatch of street under lamplight. Living ones passed by—why not her? Yesterday fine, today dead? How could that be? It couldn't be. Only it was. Had he hung his jacket up, and his overcoat? He couldn't remember. The toilet clicked open, so he went and passing the best bedroom—designated by his son for the prize guest and her mother—his dull eye fell on the beauty Reisel—she lived, why shouldn't she?—in front of the mirror brushing her hair. She stopped brushing, she turned, she came to him.

"Cousin Share, you do not look well now. Has something bad happened?"

Then his face wrinkled up, "Oy—" the groan escaped without his expecting it.

"What, Hymie?"

He threw up his hands, "Dead, they say," and his hands slapped down again.

"Glantz?"

"Glantz."

He started to cry and she drew him into the room, sat him on the chair and herself at the edge of the bed.

"How?" she asked full of sympathy, not like that ash-blonde at . . . "Talk, cousin. Of that old illness?"

"That old illness," he could barely echo.

"Dear cousin, death cannot be helped, we must endure it."

Hymie slipped to his knees and he shed tears in her lap like a baby.

"Sha, sha dear cousin," she stroked his hair, "sha—"

And all of a sudden, between her warm lap, the strokes and his misery, he became so excited that he didn't know what he was doing. He grabbed her up higher, he pressed kisses on her though she was twisting away, and he had half thrown himself over her—when he was sailing, like in a dream: wall, ceiling, you couldn't tell which was which. She glared down at him like a prizefighter.

"Did you think, chicken," she hissed at him, "if the murderers had sent only one of their beasts after me, my poor papá would be in his grave and I here in this horrible land?"

He stumbled to his feet, he stammered excuses, apologies, but he could have saved his breath. In the doorway his whole family gaped with his son the fury foremost, and next came a regular Saturday night Thalia melodrama with the father cast as the goat. Cold hearts, cold people! He'd lost Glantz, his only Dora, but his wife stood there like a death in the family.

"I am to blame," Reisel said, "I am still young and judged poorly. Besides, it is time my mother and I find a place of our own."

Gittel sang, "Over my dead body," and patted Hymie on the cheek. "Silly boy, didn't you know she's a prune with slapped faces all over Europe?"

Some consolation, and who heard that but Hymie? Next—Hymie couldn't believe it—his son was sending him packing . . . and with physical threats if he was slow about it! Golda—"How could you shame me so?"—was like the song, she couldn't say yes she couldn't say no, but no no equaled yes. And Naomi, she held hands with her mother.

Oy Dora, are you somewheres watching this?

Filth!

A rusty stovepipe hardly warm to the touch, a gray sheet, a gray pillowcase, a map of grime on the window, black snow on the outside sill of the black airshaft bedroom his beloved ones had driven him to—and without a bite to eat even! The twenty dollar bill that his son the hero had pushed at him he'd turned his back on. He should have ripped it in pieces! The gas jet globe—who used gas nowadays?—cast a faint lemony light though maybe not faint enough. You hung your coat on a nail, you walked the three paces alongside the bed, at your wits' end you sat down—and look. Was Hymie's eyesight playing him tricks, or a brown stain on his pants taking exercise?

A bedbug!

In his fury to grab it, crush the life out of it the way he should with his enemies, the thing fell down and melted into the brown filthy boards. But there it went, full speed! He stamped and missed, and again, and a third time. They banged up from downstairs, he gave one more stamp for good measure. But you want bedbugs, Hymie knew where he could find them from the nights here with Debbie. He lifted the mattress—mattress: straw inside sacking—and they swarmed out of the slats. He banged them, smeared them, erased them!—and scraped open his knuckles. . . .

What, he should bend still sore from that two-fisted punch in the chest by Saint Reisel, bleed into a trickle of water in a filthy Bleecker Street sink and whimper like a dog out of sheer aggravation while that bitch Debbie the witchcraft queen should loll in Baxter Street enjoying her accomplishments? He yanked his coat off the nail—the loop ripped, who cared?—and ran down the stinking stairs into the street. Snow blew in his face? Let it blow, he'd give her blows!

He pounded her door. A runt opened: the father. Behind him in the parlor was Miss Squint with a towel on her head, and Mama's melon face stuck out of the kitchen. Hymie walked in—"Excuse me"—pulled off his belt, and—"Murderess"—missed the first swipe at those twisting hips.

"She's dead?" her mouth twisted up too. "Then next you!"

Hymie chased her, caught her, and even with those claws down his face held on to her and walloped that backside of hers. Between her screaming and him seeing red, his arm already felt like a ton before the parents' yelling came through.

"For all three of us—" that was Mama. And the father: "Now you pick on old men? What did you do to the old man, you whore you!"

From such a father was it a wonder you had such a daughter? Hymie let go of Debbie with her wet hair hanging down, and she bounced up laughing.

"He won't be old much longer."

Hymie spit and so did the parents: give them credit for that. If ever there was an evil eye, it shone out of her kisser. But this time—Hymie glared at them all and reeled back into an icy wind his parched throat drank in like water—his wild member throbbing up against his overcoat assured him that the spell was not working. At Bleecker Street the Irisher landlady on guard sewing in her closet-sized parlor gave him a come-hither twinkle in case he was in the mood for dumpy. But better in the world waited for Hymie Share, Dora would forgive him. All their years together —what a loss, you felt sick—that poor dear sweet girl never knew the meaning of the word jealousy, not like the rest of them, his wife included.

The bitch Debbie'd fixed his cheek good. But then—Hymie washed down the gashes in the Irisher's cold water—he had fixed her ass good she'd discover when she tried sitting. He brushed his hair into place, dusted his coat and suit, and, after the smarting let up, patted talcum over his growth of beard like years ago with a date and no time to shave. In that parlor the landlady was only too glad to sew the overcoat loop and—surprise—she offered him tea, or even a drop of something stronger if he liked. For this time he thanked her and swung his stick to the Actors Café. At a front table sat Oltarsh the spear holder with Madame Nadler the has-been.

The comedian Oltarsh, no wonder they never let him talk on stage, said, "Don Juan ran into a fighter."

"A tigress," Hymie acknowledged, and Madame Nadler began looking interested.

"You've met?" Oltarsh asked her.

"Don't name Madame Nadler to a humble admirer," Hymie put on the charm, "right up to *Love and Lace* in the fall."

"Sit down and tell me your name," Madame Nadler, even-steven, put on her charm, "and then tell me more."

So this redhead was hefty, with the red out of a bottle, not like the bona fide, the desirable, the genuine redheaded Angel of Consolation Miss Reisel Leben? Hah! Miss Leben was fake, fake angel, fake woman, and this actress—you didn't need eyeglasses to tell—was the real thing. So Reisel the circus strongwoman, with so much pride in catching a man off balance and knocking him over, your chicken has wings—and watch him fly!

Dora darling, how I miss you. You'll understand. . . .

9

THE SONG IS OVER BUT THE MELODY LINGERS ON. HERCULES Junior cleaned out the stable—what a relief that guy was gone—but it still smelled of horse. The morning after the great eviction Ma carried her black crêpe expression on the trolleys to West Street with Naomi matching her gloom for gloom. In the shop Danny hardly had time to get his hands full of rough castings to be ground and bored when Leah caught him for some grinding and boring.

"Did you really have to throw Hymie out? Oh buzzie boy, what a kid you still are!"

"You say so," he raged red, "after preaching to me from kneepants up chop Mr. Deadwood off the tree?"

"I know, but . . . sermons like that, it's better to forget them."

"You mean absence makes the skin grow thicker? But I didn't move to the Village, I don't have your advantage."

"Nobody's forced to stay, Danny dear."

"What are you talking about, Leah?"

Naomi also came out of the office for a free swing at the unanimous pariah with brass mountings up to his chin. She didn't see why he'd had to make a big issue of a small misunderstanding. Small misunderstanding? His old man down for the count like Gorgeous Georges Carpentier in the Dempsey fight? What did they want, the Battle of Gettysburg?

And Sunday morning with the sky and the streets one gray swab of snow, and for four Sundays after that, Reisel left for early synagogue services—let do the housecleaning who would—and didn't get home till dark. No need for jealousy, though Danny was too dumb to be jealous. He could hate her, he could feel like grabbing that slender round-breasted body and plowing right through her in pure anger. And he could hate himself for being so stupid as to have fallen in love with a dame who spun you like a top. But keeping up a grudge against other guys was harder to manage, especially like now, when there were no other guys. She was searching for somewhere to move to from Tompkins Square, and no use arguing with her.

"I moved here for your sake," was finally wrenched out of him.

"Since you wished the credit for it, you ought not to have mentioned it."

That, her business voice in the factory, her book in the shop lunch hours or at home after supper, her polite voice at home, finished her off as far as he was concerned.

Didn't he wish it did.

Then one bright March morning in West Street with the teamsters swinging their loads to sunny platforms and on the river a blue tide twinkling off tugs, freighters and ocean liners, he passed Reisel taping frames by the window as if they were her religion—half-lowered lids, a furrow on the high forehead—and her comic hand snaked out to slap his arm.

"Say," Reisel's eyes darted a smile, "you were to bed early last night."

"I had a headache."

"From stuffy rooms of card games with ne'er-do-wells."

"Ne'er-do-wells? They did well yesterday. How do you know where I was?"

"Come see the flat that I have taken on Norfolk Street," she struck him with lightning. "I have left a deposit!"

"On some dump?" Migraine dots were dancing already. "And to prove what?"

"No no, not a dump. You will see."

Dump was palace compared to what she'd dredged up, high-stooped dilapidation sagging between a bridal gowns to rent window and a gravestones store. Her find opened into the parlor, where you struck a match right away because daylight didn't filter that far in. The roaches gave you an over-the-shoulder glance that said mind your business and plaster reached out like man-eating plants. But it had its advantages.

"Hall toilets," Reisel was proud to point out, as if your nose didn't tell you, "not yard ones as at Hester Street."

"That's why we quit Hester Street."

"Daniel, you will help me fix it up, eh?"

So that's what this Sunday invite had been for.

"No."

"We cannot allow Baba Rivka, your grandmamá, to move into unsuitable rooms, Daniel."

Danny-el, Reisel burned you like hell. Running away from you and no way to stop her. Stop her? You could only praise her. To watch Grandma's snail pace with the pretzel baskets used to be enough to do the entrails once over lightly. Then a couple of months ago age had tripped Grandma up on an icy sidewalk. Slow as she'd been before that, the fall had come near stopping her altogether. She needed someone to wait on her, not pretzel baskets. Danny'd already gone through the motions of begging

Grandma to share Tompkins Square with the Shares but Grandma and he had both known it was only motions. How could she and Ma live together? Grandma thought that her favorite son, Hymie, was a sterling character whose wife didn't appreciate him. And now could Danny say come on Grandma, move in, no cause for conflict, that sterling character has been kicked out? And here was Reisel, with a loony mother to cope with, taking in Grandma. It was a real kindness.

"You're so damn clever."

Reisel's merry "Blame on my genius" with the grammatical shortcut hit him like a warm gush in cold water. And, "Say, Daniel," old fella, old pal, "you know I can no longer, much as I might wish to, remain at Tompkins Square. How could your parents be reconciled in my presence?"

"No one wants to be reconciled."

"Ah," she reproached baby boy Daniel, "your mamá does."

No, Ma looked down in the mouth but that was because she was like dumb Danny, a dreamer. Underneath you knew what was what. But he wouldn't argue with Reisel.

"Come," Reisel gave him another wind around her little finger, "I shall tour you."

The rattrap had other positive features, a window in the front and a window in back. The front, boy, Norfolk Street—kids, pushcarts, peddlers, women with limp oilcloth bags, a bedlam—the world at your fingertips! What more could Gittel desire? Reisel, though she had her fears, hoped her mother would like it. In the rear you had laundry crisscrossed between buildings like flags on the Fourth of July, and, with some argument, Baba Rivka had accepted the backyard bedroom for herself before Reisel rented the place. What a saint Baba Rivka was! The beautiful little room—Baba Rivka had called it beautiful—with the inside window would be perfect for her, she'd argued. But Reisel had had none of that. Reisel had been sorry, she was not that unselfish. The beautiful little room with the inside window (that stinking closet, she meant) would be hers to meditate in, and to sleep in undisturbed by loud snoring! Also it would be Baba Rivka's duty to pray with her, read the papers with her and discuss with her.

So what could you do with Reisel except love, honor and obey her, go home, change into old clothes, buy a scraper and plaster and attack those five disgusting holes-in-the-wall?

"Thank you, thank you Daniel, what would I do without you? Thank you for helping me."

So the next Sunday, moving day, he rushed down to Norfolk to help without her even asking and he found out what she could do without him. BOOKBINDER FANCY BOOKBINDING, DUANE STREET the wagon was printed that blocked the gutter between the two rows of pushcarts lining the curbs, with a truck behind honking and teamsters roaring like feeding time at the Central Park Zoo. Danny'd met that man once at Tompkins Square and completely forgotten him. As a by-product of a Naomi double date—

indirect, Naomi didn't bother with over forties—Reisel had gotten this old guy with gray in the hair, a twinkle of tan in the eye, a cigar in the mouth and pink in the cheeks. But there he stood—"Just a few minutes, boys"—as calm as his dapple-gray nag with the oats bag on. He jockeyed a table over the wagon flap to his shoulder, then—joy! "Daniel—" so the cigar knew Danny's name, which wasn't mutual—"who would I rather see?" What, was what he meant: another shoulder.

He laid the table across Danny's back—and Danny cooperated! although pink cheeks cigar did pick up a couple of chairs himself. On the stoop next to the wedding gowns window Gittel stopped them. She had left complaining from Tompkins Square, "My daughter's my punishment, I don't know for what." But here, "I adore wedding gowns, don't you Danny?" she giggled at the table-backed turtle peering up at her. "I'll get one and we'll start over again, all right, in the country?" Then she stuck her tongue out at Danny sidling around her. "Rubin," she switched grooms, "all right?" So Rubin, very good, had been hanging around Reisel long enough for first names with Gittel.

"All right, but first settle down in the city, Gitteleh."

She pouted, poor old girl.

The furniture was unloaded and Norfolk Street jammed with traffic up to the corner but Rubin was in no rush to leave. After a second offer of a cigar to Danny—"That's right, you already don't smoke"—Rubin watched him put up a bed and asked, "How's business?"

With the Quality Lamps staff pared down to the family, Taks the framemaker and terrible Gable the salesman Danny had to step double-time to keep treading water. But Gable with his slow talk, his shrewd fat-lidded eyes and his beer belly would assure you leave it to Gable. The panic would end any day now, just a postwar adjustment. Gable was a salesman okay.

"Rotten. Can you say the same?"

Laughing Rubin could not. His business was good even in bad times. "But knock wood, how can a man go wrong with bookbinding when his ancestors select him the name Bookbinder?" And blame-on-genius Reisel hung on his words. Then a stern cop strolled in about the horse and wagon and business was good with him too. Rubin passed him a few smokes, winked him half a buck for something to wash the smokes down with in prohibition, and the two birds of a feather walked out together.

Danny told Reisel, "And you take furniture from him, huh?"

"You are a man, do not speak like a boy. He is kind to me, as you are. The furniture is from the Salvation Army, and," with the smile that made slavery a privilege, "you will now go escort Baba Rivka to her new home."

So Danny escorted Baba Rivka in maddening slow motion to her new home, hustled the two blocks back to Suffolk Street twice for her bags—mostly paper—and bedding, and went out again to corral Gittel the stray around the corner on Grand Street at still another rabbi's for a divorce from her dead husband. Then at last with Reisel's thanks floating him he caught her hand—she let him—grinned, "Let's sit down a minute, and discuss," and before the no too much work reached her lips, back strolled Bookbinder in his best Sunday tweeds.

"Ah, still here, Daniel? Have a cigar—"

Grandma wound up in the front room after all. Gittel had only been on the new block a few hours and already could report that people were pointing at her. "She killed the Czar," she heard them whisper about her. What she hadn't found out so far was which ones were the Russian agents. Then she spotted one in the house: Grandma, because Grandma remarked what a nice room Gittel had, always interesting things to watch from the ground floor, neighbors to talk with. Gittel stared at her, "So if you're off duty the ones outside will still watch me?" and marveled, "Who won't the Russians hire next!" So with a Russian spy in the family Gittel would have none of the exposed front room. She holed up not only in the rear but in the rear windowless cubbyhole.

From then on Danny'd gulp supper at Tompkins Square, brush his teeth for the dream kiss, keep a blind eye to Ma's long face at his nightly desertion, run to Reisel, and find Bookbinder. Play hard to get, that you were there to visit Grandma, and Reisel would queer that act with her eyes amber-green like a cat's and her face glowing.

"Baba Rivka is in her room and will be glad to see you."

"And," Danny would mutter, "how about you?" stupidly, after a day at the shop together—though with Reisel's proper behavior there, no further apart could any two people have been.

"I—" nice block on that kick!—"am always glad."

So in that interesting front room Grandma thanked God for sending her His angel Reisel. In Grandma's old age she had become . . . indolent, she slept all hours till eight o'clock in the morning. That meant she had to pray alone mornings. But evenings Grandma would sit with her ritual wig and Reisel with a shawl on her head and they would pray together. In place of Bertha—alive and well, thank God, in Denver—the merciful heavens had sent Reisel to Grandma to put at rest her fears about that famous funeral: the Star of David draped on the box, Rabbi Nachman, a nicely trimmed grave, pebbles later so the concerned soul would know of visits.

Meanwhile the concerned soul was worried had Danneleh had a quarrel with his father?

"Yes, every day, Grandma. We quarrel about who's first to the bathroom." Then Grandma gave him the it ain't no joke look, so he figured he'd close the question with a half-truth. "What should we quarrel about? Of course we don't quarrel."

A few days later at West Street Reisel said to him, "Accompany me somewhere after work."

Where wouldn't you accompany Reisel? Well, there was one place, the one she'd picked on—to visit his old man. But she cut Danny's squawk short. Last week she'd been astounded by the apparition of Baba Rivka wrapped up to venture into the bitter cold she had not set foot in since the day she'd moved from Suffolk Street. Danny had told Baba Rivka there was no quarrel. His father had told Baba Rivka there was no quarrel. Naomi had told her, Reisel had told her. But—the experienced Gittel knew how to keep Russian spies off balance—in nasty detail Reisel's mamá had filled in a lie that Reisel had transformed Daniel and cousin Share into each other's bitterest enemy. Therefore Baba Rivka felt so blue that she was paying a visit to Hymeleh and to Danneleh to see with her own eyes that poor Gitteleh had made up that terrible story. Only Reisel's logic—"Suppose while you are visiting them that they are visiting you?"—had forestalled that walk which could easily have brought Baba Rivka to her good funeral. Three times—three nickels thrown out—Reisel had telephoned cousin Share at his hotel. Three times a woman had answered. To catch cousin Share leaving the hotel in the morning meant to sacrifice the morning prayer which gave Reisel strength. One mitigation: she would not expect him out in bad weather, and she'd thanked God for the few days of rain which followed her promise to Baba Rivka to arrange a visit to Tompkins Square. Then yesterday alas sunshine, spring rippling through bright nippy air. But no cousin Share. Early was too early for him and late was too late, although the Broadway Central lobby had been overrun with his replicas. Let them see a woman alone and they accosted you, persecuted you into the street to see what they could accomplish in their lives.

Naomi had been so upset at the thought of meeting or even speaking on the phone with the woman her father lived with that Reisel had not pressed her. Nevertheless Naomi had agreed that should her father come to Tompkins Square for a visit from Baba Rivka, Naomi would take Golda somewhere beforehand, to a movie perhaps.

So old handyman Danny made the fourth phone call, got the woman—"Allo"—his old man, and an of course . . . with coach Reisel hissing in your ear, "Since I do not trust him to sustain a resolution from noon till seven o'clock, tell him we will call for him."

The elevator cage in the Broadway Central was full of mirrors, Reisel in all of them along with the hungry envious eye of the operator whose monkey suit was so tight it seemed painted on. Did Danny feel proud, posing as Reisel's boy friend with the homburg! And ha ha, Reisel's eye caught the elevator man's in the glass, flashed and outfaced him.

"My first step," she announced on the royal red carpet leading to his old man's playground, "in a house of prostitution."

"Quit it Reisel. This is a respectable hotel, outside of my father."

"The vile see life in their own image, while you—" she slapped his arm, ran and merrily called over her shoulder—"are blinded by decency. . . ."

Overjoyed Danny joined the chase, made a high speed right turn down the corridor . . . and doors and red carpet. He tilted his homburg, he scratched his head.

"Boo!"

Reisel popped out of a broom closet, flushed and beautiful.

"Say, Daniel, what do you think of the Disarmament Conference?"

"It's left me defenseless."

"Where is their door?" she sparkled at him.

A knock roused wolf bays, a "Shut up!" and a yelp.

"Don't you dare keeck him, Hymie!"

"Don't you dare keeck him—lock him up and I won't keeck him."

Hymie flung the door wide and glared. Who? What? He squinted. Two actor friends of his boring consort he'd leave in a minute if he had where to go? Then his eyes cleared and he remembered the date with Mama.

"Hansel and Gretel! Come in, meet the witch."

"Who's a weetch?" from the boudoir.

"You hear her French accent? Because they let her walk on in *Oo La La*."

"How can you say that? I lived fifteen years in Parees."

"So go back, give my regards to the frogs and take your husband along with you."

"Hee hee hee, Hamlet is my pet not my husband—exactly like you."

And with a tan pony-sized animal trotting beside her this small rack of butterballs in a kimono floated out brushing down long black hair.

"My God," Reisel muttered, "Jews with a dog!"

"Don't call Hamlet a dog, darling. He's a darling boy, better than human!"

"Hear O Israel!"

"I tell you," Hymie insisted, "he reminds her of her husband with the square nose, Nadler the noble Dane from Hotzeplotz he should rest in peace and how he survived so long with her was a miracle." Hymie lifted his arm and Hamlet worriedly backed to their mistress, who smacked a kiss to his nozzle.

"I am dumbfounded," Reisel said.

"Well you," Hymie said, "you would be, by a kiss."

"Don't you kees, dear?" Madame Nadler asked.

"Not dogs."

"Or men either," Hymie said.

"He's jealous! He went after a redhead not as kind as I am!" Madame Nadler clapped hands "—though I'm brunette these days you see, for my role. And what does she need you for," Madame Nadler puckered up and kissed Hymie, "when she has this beautiful boy."

Kiss shmiss, Hymie shrugged. "Me in the mirror, te—five years ago."

So Danny'd had enough from old man spats in the fancy rust velvet smoking jacket with the matching rust fifty-yard-long cigarette holder from his fat friend.

"Ready, Father?"

Madame Nadler threw up her hands, "Without an aperitif, or a cordial? Unheard of!" and went tilt like a doll.

"The kosher Madama Butterfly," Hymie said.

"He came to me ig-no-rante," Madame pecked Hymie another kiss, "but I've taught him evree-thing."

A cat in a black tux with a dickey and four white gloves strolled in from the boudoir, looked at the outstretched Great Dane, looked at them and sprang to the sofa. Reisel sprang off.

"A menagerie! Daniel, cousin Share, let us go."

The courtier Hymie rose with a little bow to change from his lounging jacket and Madame Nadler tittered, "Cleo and Hamlet get along very well, like cats and dogs, or, if you prefer, like me and that man inside, who's so vain he never mentioned he has a beautiful son whose name no one tells me and a daughter-in-law who doesn't ap-pre-ciate the animal kingdom."

Danny told her his name and Reisel's into the bargain, and Reisel, "We are cousins," set the . . . woman straight.

"Is Dan-nee your cousin, or are you only his cousin?"

"I do not understand you."

"They're cousins, they're cousins," came the voice of experience from the boudoir, "and they'll stay cousins, believe me."

And to bear Hymie out, the cat sprang at the dog's thumping tail—yelps, snarls, flying fur, Madame's laughter—Reisel screamed and hid behind Danny and Danny moved his arm back to hold her . . . and gripped air. And at Tompkins Square with himself and his father at home in shirt-sleeves, damned if Danny the maid wasn't privileged to serve tea not only to his old man, Grandma and Reisel—but to Rubin Bookbinder! Bookbinder had driven Grandma and Reisel up.

"In your horse and wagon?" Danny asked not too pleasantly.

"In my new Dodge sedan," Bookbinder announced proudly, added a sales feature, "Completely enclosed," and—"Have a cigar, Daniel? Hymie—" extended an invite for a ride Sunday, plenty of room in the back seat next to Gittel. For tonight, with Hymeleh and Danneleh proven pals, Bookbinder took Reisel home with happy Grandma.

So—Danny'd had plenty of practice along these lines from way back, with Sylvia—forget Reisel, busy yourself. Noontimes on West Street in the suddenly hushed shop with everyone else out except Leah in the office and doleful Ma at lunch who you'd try to cheer up in a loud hearty voice, let Reisel stick to her book you couldn't unglue her from. Danny, he'd gulp down his sandwich and piece of fruit and go straight back to work and a rip-roaring headache for the afternoon. After his supper gulp he'd run to Lefty Lefkowitz's for pinochle, bridge, poker, casino two- or four-handed, rummy, in a pinch pisha-paysha—whatever whoever was there would play for money. If he lost, he got a headache. If he won, he won. He hated nights the gang—and he along with them—dated girls they hoped would want to be ganged, or picked up dollar blondes on the Bowery.

And Bookbinder whizzed Reisel off in his flivver with Gittel in back to Jersey in spring, Rye Beach in summer, Valhalla in fall to look at the damn dam, and who the hell knew where in winter?

But self-discipline pays. A couple of aspirins and the eyestrain headaches from not looking at Reisel in the shop would be gone before supper. Now and then of course you found your eyes on her anyway, and one bleak dark day with lights on in the shop he felt so sad for her, the way that she was bent over that stupid frame. It seemed such a . . . waste, in this shabby tumult. And just then, as he stood there staring with the factory climbing all over him—lamp bases with off-center bores, the lathe man complaining, late shipments, overdue bills give and take—Reisel turned as if he'd called to her the length of the loft . . . and oh, that expression of hers: Thank you for caring about me, do not be angry.

Sunday as soon as he could decently leave Ma alone he was in Norfolk Street—to hear from Grandma how beautiful Reisel had looked, with a flower face on top of rugs and blankets she was wrapped in in the machine, how Rubin cranked and every child in the neighborhood had a wonderful time waiting till the machine shook like a cat somebody threw water on, and how the machine roared like a lion and rode away with the three of them.

"Rode away where?"

"To the country."

So when Danny could decently get away from Grandma and run after Reisel, he had the whole U.S.A. to choose from. He chose Orange with Uncle Willie and Anna as a destination, so the trip wouldn't be a total loss.

He loved the ferry with the white swath across the December-gray river to the piers and flatlands of Jersey. Today though, in case Reisel was there, he was busy squinting into autos packed three abreast to the stern, and all he saw was some suspicious squints back and the oily blue sloshing around in the ferry slip. From the train in Jersey he gloomily studied the road, but the light on the few sedans chugging past wagons and teams turned their windows into tawny mirrors reflecting bare trees.

Looking for Reisel? Save your eyesight, Danny-o.

Uncle Willie'd covered his artichokes and carrots bed, but—Liberty Hall—a tan skinny rooster and a half-dozen red chickens were busy uncovering it. In the back Anna was pouring grain in the feeders while Willie the practical farmer was hanging suet strips for wild birds.

"Willie," Anna rushed to smother grinning Danny against the denims, the sweaters and that big motherly bosom of hers, "break open a fresh bottle of gin—the prodigal son is back on the premises!"

Anna did break out the gin—home brew, guaranteed, from her own tub—but she was the only drinker in that little crowd.

"A shame," Anna said, "we might have been rich. Our old barn—look how your uncle took the trouble to ruin it—would have made the perfect speakeasy. Even when we were a saloon people had to be sober to find us." But Anna's eyes shone the way Uncle Willie'd turned a barn into a house with rooms, built a ceiling, and broken through for a bay window where you sat and watched the stray chickens eating up next year's peas. Orange flames cozily licked the logs in the fireplace, and you almost wished there was no New York.

"S-speakeasies are against the law," Willie said.

"He likes the law," Anna winked, "if he agrees with it. When the law threw his socialist hero in jail he didn't like it so much."

"Not the l-law, the injustice. Y-you don't put a man in j-j-jail because he's a pacifist. They should have put the D-duponts in jail, the K-krupps, not Eugene V. Debs. F-f-fifteen million people killed in the war, Danny—for what? Imagine it, as if they'd wiped out N-new York, Chicago, Philadelphia, Pittsburgh—"

Yeah yeah, that wiped out the whole National League and half the American: no more major league baseball. On the hearth the embers twinkled, bark snapped, yellow blue orange flames curled over the logs. Light faded and beyond the rumpled pond and splintery treetops a cold sky thinned to a pale edge of green. Bookbinder didn't exist, Danny just longed for Reisel. But Uncle Willie was off ruining the pleasure at a gallop, like the Bolshies in the old days in high school. Workers without work, Ku Kluxers, the Red Menace trick—the same old horseshit that trotted you back to the same old stable. Even Anna gagged at the workingman spiel.

"How about the workingman who voted for Harding to get even on President Wilson?" she defied Uncle Willie to tell her. "Who wanted the anti-immigrant law if not the workingman? Where do they recruit the Jew-haters? The workingmen in my family know that the Elders of Zion—they mean the local chicken farmers and Mr. Friedman the grocer in town—are stealing the bread out of their mouths. Being my husband, you of course are exempt. The workingman!"

"Th-th-they're fooled, it's c-capital's interest to fool them," Uncle Willie patiently answered. "B-but they'll learn. Th-they'll learn that they'll eat when we have production for use instead of for p-profit."

"Ah come on Uncle Willie," Danny couldn't hold it in any more, "say Debs and your Bolsheviks—"

"Socialists, D-danny—"

"What's the difference?" Danny waved his hand to forestall the explanations he'd heard time and again. "Say they took over and I bust my gut to share my profits with bums—not that there are any profits. Would that hurry up my Pierce-Arrow for me? Or get it for me at all?"

That surprised Uncle Willie. "What do y-y-you need a P-pierce-Arrow for, Danny?"

"To take my girl for a ride—and why not?"

"Didn't I tell you," Anna sang out victorious, "that that Carrie Baum would catch up to him?"

That surprised Danny. "She's the last thing on my mind."

And blue Monday night, in the rain too, he was down at Norfolk Street and the first thing on his mind—and Jesus Christ, Monday even, Reisel opened the door and there were the other happy two, in the kitchen with the tea glasses still on the table, Gittel with the smirk and Bookbinder with the Corona! Danny tilted his chin and headed straight for Grandma back in bed with the *Forward* and, courtesy Reisel, custom-made eyeglasses, not off a Rivington Street pushcart. Grandma'd said God had taken away most of her hearing, but Reisel had given her back most of her sight. Danny'd paid for the eyeglasses, but if you want credit don't ask for it—you won't get it anyway.

"Good news," Danny yelled, "in the paper, Grandma?"

But Grandma had a new hard luck story from her friend Bertha Axelrod in Denver to pester him with. The Axelrod file was tremblingly brought out to a slow loop-the-loop of Danny's guts, while in the next room the parlor games seemed to be turning into . . .

" . . . look drawn, Reiseleh," apple cheeks with the smile said, "from your factory. . . ."

" . . . her little sick spell last year and she didn't have what to send her son Ilya in Paris? Now he calls himself Ilya," Grandma's smile was so kind you had to smile with it. "We ran from Russia, he finds a Russian name will help. Ilya packed himself up and went to find out why his mother was robbing him of his inheritance. Ah, good silly Bertha, to bring a boy up in a fairy tale of money his father left him. . . ."

" . . . open a bookstore," Reisel was setting Bookbinder straight, don't ask Danny about what, "with extras from your factory like the leather-bound set of Dostoievski you gave me, for which as I told you I am grateful. Dostoievski would be my favorite did he not hate Jews. And you would place me as manageress . . ."

" . . . not exactly to say his mama robbed him, but to say however she threw away his money he needed it for his work."

"Work?" Danny said.

"To play the piano."

"Sounds like play."

" . . . Dostoievskis were not from Bookbinder's Bookbinding, since you corner me. But you need bookstore managing, Reiseleh, like . . ."

" . . . is Ilya's picture—handsome too, with his dimple, but not as handsome," Danny's cheek—what an idiot he was!—got a stroke from Grandma better than credit, "as my Danneleh, or as good, either . . . Ilya knew you can't squeeze blood from a stone or money from a mama with the tailors' disease in Denver. So on the spur of the moment he gave a concert on Bertha's mistress's piano that Bertha says those rich people use mainly as furniture . . ."

" . . . that you are selfish?" Reisel said.

"No, I didn't know that I was selfish," carefree apple-cheeks answered. "I thought just the opposite. Where do I . . . ?"

" . . . Ilya would do his mother's boss a favor, he could be Ilya's benefactor, with money. And either from the concert with Ilya's beautiful playing, or else for Bertha's sake, the mister gave him . . ."

" . . . I did not invent men and women," Bookbinder laughed. "Besides, for that simple purpose—if I understand you—there are only too many women . . ."

" . . . Bertha was so proud. She got up out of bed all better. Ilya was also proud of himself. Almost the minute he walked off the train in New York he sent a postcard, from a fancy uptown address. A famous pianist was teaching him . . ."

"But do you hear me, Reiseleh dear, proposing to them—God forbid?"

"And I do not wish to hear your proposals to anybody!" Reisel's voice rang out.

" . . . but now four months already with no letter from Ilya. Poor Bertha is back in bed, under a nurse's care, poor child . . . collapsed . . ."

" . . . to the wrong girl," Gittel piped up.

"All right Gitteleh," Bookbinder asked, "will you marry me?"

Now if you had them both by the neck, which would you squeeze harder, Ilya or Bookbinder?

" . . . to play second fiddle, Rubin," Gittel reproached him, "even if it wasn't just a joke at my expense . . ."

"*Blue air*, Bertha writes, *green pines, birds in sunshine, everything to get well.* But the poor girl is frantic. *Is Ilya well? Where can he be? . . .*"

" . . . stitching lampshades in a loft," Bookbinder kept at it. "So Reiseleh say yes like a sensible girl and the three of us—"

"Get out!" Reisel screeched. "Get out of here with your loathsome cigar!"

"But Reiseleh, you always liked . . ."

"Must I throw you out!"

" . . . So Danneleh . . ."

"Good night Gitteleh . . . Baba Rivka," Bookbinder yelled for Grandma's deaf ears. "Daniel . . . Reisel, be well . . ."

The door closed on Bookbinder, but Danny's elation—"I'll see that this bum Ilya writes to his mother, Grandma!"—did not last long. Reisel was on top of them, flushed, almost disheveled.

"Bonehead you will do nothing of the sort to indulge your bad temper! I will take care of this as of everything else. You get out too—I have a sick headache!"

Danny's "Don't ask me twice," set off his own headache. He kissed Grandma deafly beaming on the two lovebirds she considered as good as a pair, but before he could make his getaway a demolition clang in the rear sent him and Reisel both running to see which ceiling had fallen down. But it was only Gittel trying to back up her door with her bedspring. Last week she'd soaped the floor for Grandma to slip on and die of a broken hip and that hadn't worked. Bookbinder had just been dismissed, Danny—this made sense—she considered a ninny. So with no hope of escape from Norfolk Street which she called Whitechapel what was left but to barricade herself against Grandma the secret agent?

"Barricade yourself," Reisel made it a fairly clean sweep, "I do not care!"

Gittel began sniffing, "I know you don't care—"

With the migraine bugs swarming along with him to Lefty Lefkowitz's he wished he had some loving lap to bury his bonehead in. But whose? Lefty's mother with the black hair and pink powdered cheeks was delighted to see him. Lefty's father rubbed his hands together at the prospect of matching wits with draw poker Share, and Lefty and the boys raised a shout, where had he been? Wherever he'd been, they found out where he was now. He couldn't lose, not even his headache. When the game broke up he rushed his full pockets and full bloom migraine home to—you bet, expect Naomi to stay home with Ma once—Ma alone nursing her chin on her palm in the dark next to the window.

But—he kissed Ma, then made a desperate dash with his nausea to his pajamas and bed—maybe there is some sort of divine justice. Sure, Naomi shot out every night chewing her last bite of supper, but that was to the Postgraduate School to stock up her brains gratis on inventory control, packaging hints, and whatever else might hold down costs at Quality and eke out profits in the absence of the sales their star Gable didn't bring in. Furthermore, as Naomi'd pointed out crisply, she did stay home with Ma whenever she could, and also, she hadn't been the one to throw Papa out. Of course Papa out was more or less equal to Papa in, but who knew better than Ma's boy that things like this were . . . mainly mental. So Danny-o, do as you would be done by.

Therefore merry Tuesday night the minute Ma went to plant her miserable cheek on her fist Danny went after her.

"Ma."

"So long."

"Charlie Chaplin is a dud next to you, Ma. What are you sulking here for?"

"You run, I'll sulk."

"What's in the dark street down there that's so fascinating?"

"Bare trees."

"Did you finish the papers?"

"Yes. A dirigible burst down in Virginia. Things burst."

"Why sit around nights, Ma?"

"I'm tired of dancing."

"You never see Uncle Frank any more. Put your coat on, we'll look him up."

"I've already enjoyed my sister-in-law Rose's crystal chandelier and her size fifty-two mink. Likewise I'm able to dispense with her broad smiles of sympathy."

"But she can't give any others, Ma. Her face is too fat. *She* needs the sympathy."

"So do I."

"Then I sympathize with you."

"Not yours."

"In that case," he dragged her up by the arm, "I'll show you none," and back to the kitchen, blushing, tittering—that was more like it—like a girl. Out of the cabinet came the cards and he thumbed 'em a professional riffle. "Casino, a nickel a hand."

"Don't do me favors."

"Shut up and deal."

And Danny-o was a clever one. He sprinkled his losses with a win here and there. "Some card sharp," Ma made fun of him and when they called it quits she honestly believed she'd outplayed him two bits' worth. Then he and his date sipped coffee and discussed the dirigibles that made it to their moorings.

So with a card game Tuesday, a movie say Thursday, Leah's Friday visit, other nights Ma started to look up neighbors, or even Aunt Rose's chandelier. And these card games also took on an unexpected interest for Danny, playing to lose by the skin of your teeth. And the more he didn't wear out his welcome at Reisel's, the more human Reisel became at West Street.

And the day dawned that she greeted him at the shop as if she'd never thrown him out of her house. "Say, Daniel, accompany me lunch hour to Ilya Axelrod who still does not write to his poor mother."

"To indulge myself," he kidded her, "in my bad temper?"

"No," she laughed, "to defend me if necessary. You will wait in his hallway since we do not wish to antagonize him, and should you hear me go Eek you will break in with your muscles."

The girl who handled Hymie Lady-killer Share by a kayo in one, drafting you as bodyguard? It beat an apology!

But—some hallway, the top floor of a Central Park South château, with a private elevator and two period chairs—he waited through ten minutes of dead silence, then heard a few piano notes, and then a whole concert he could have done without. Danny, lunch, West Street? She was having her fun inside. And the hell with the keeping under cover gag when the prodigy—and snotty too, with his tall dark and handsome glance at the trespasser—finally decided to let her out. And hear the goodbye: pals. The door shut, and besides the concert and whatever else had gone on in there, Reisel all smiles held up her trophy a sealed envelope. She'd gotten him to write on the spot.

"What," Danny asked miserably, "did you need me here for?"

"Because, good beautiful Daniel, with you here I did not feel alone with that kept, lying boy, magnificently as he may play Beethoven."

At the elevator door her contemptuous lips kept moving though she did not speak, and Danny's joyful modified hard-on went to full mast under his spring coat when she leaned against him full weight as if she were dreaming. He didn't move. He just let her lean . . . delicious seconds, until the elevator woke her.

For the first time he really saw himself standing beside Reisel with the organ playing the Wedding March.

God didn't intend Danny for Sarah, so why did He have to play these dirty tricks on her? Because she didn't believe in Him? But she kept that to herself, she didn't try to persuade others. That she was a ninny, all right, that wasn't God's fault. When Danny moved out of the neighborhood two years ago no voice from On High had ordered her go home by two trolleys and a half a mile walk instead of by the fifteen minute El that let her off a couple of blocks from home. Nope, Danny took trolleys and the inspiration had been entirely her own. But wind and rain, hail and dark of night, and never a glimpse of anyone resembling Danny, had stayed this courier of the weepy heart, even idiot Sarah at last, from riding trolley cars and anxiously gaping around and shivering and freezing at Twenty-third Street and Avenue A where you transferred.

Why couldn't God mind His own business?

No. He brings over that beautiful brilliant redheaded greenhorn. Then he sends her to the Essex Street Synagogue, Sarah's father's stamping ground morning and evening every day of the week God gave Sarah's mother health to watch the grocery store. Why on earth would a genius like Reisel be in *shul* all the time too, instigating pious resentment on account of her brains and good looks among the fishwife widows and old women up in the balcony? And why did Sarah's father have to be an old woman, the stern dignified Lazer Bialek? Why his darned outrage at the postwar short skirts and at the sinful legs that ran out of them? Mama solemnly said the Talmud said. But that only meant that Pa said the Talmud said. Even from Sunday school at age twelve which thank God had seen Sarah's last yawns in *shul* if only in the basement classroom under the *shul*, Sarah knew that whatever the Talmud said it said a lot more than that. You dwelled on what bothered you.

Lazer Bialek had slipped out of the old country a shadowy step ahead of the Czar's conscription vultures, but you couldn't exactly call him a peaceful man. "Let them rot in the ground," had been his prayer for the Czar and the Czar's family after the Bolsheviks finished them, "and—" as far as gratitude went—"the murderers too, all anti-Semites!" Yet he'd never stopped feeling homesick for holy Bialystok in this unholy America where, for instance, your blessing from God, the daughter you'd slaved to raise to her present glorious estate, comes in smiling from shopping one Saturday with a new dress on up to the belly. "Prostitute!" Papa had waved his eating utensils in the kitchen at supper. "Go walk on the Bowery with the rest of the whores!" He'd made Sarah cry, though he'd given her something else in common with Reisel, if Reisel's having and Sarah's not having Danny counted as something in common. Papa called Reisel Danny's father's whore, not to her face of course. Such intimate language was reserved for Papa's immediate family. If only Sarah'd been able to believe that last message from God she would have run straight up to Tompkins Square and never mind trolleys. But, as Sarah's Joe laughed, her father couldn't tell the difference between a whore and Lillian D. Wald of the Henry Street Settlement.

"And if he saw my tries," and Joe had taken a try, blocked as usual, "at under your skirt, he wouldn't be so loose with his language."

Still you didn't want to flout God altogether just in case he existed, so it had been back to the trolleys for little Sarah and—no Danny—she hoped that God at least was having more fun out of it than she was.

Then home from the office a wintry night she warmed the supper Mama'd prepared and when she brought it down to the store for her parents the indignant customer shouting across the counter at Mama, a bulky little man with his overcoat collar up, was actually Papa, just back and refreshed from evening prayers. Mama looked stunned, confused and to blame.

"Open scandal," Papa was spitting it out, "between your Share playboys—and a good third to go with them, their redheaded whore that they took into the house! It's the neighborhood's pleasure, all over the synagogue, how the two of them fought with fists over her, father and son, over the son's wife—from the whore's own mother."

Sarah went pale, numb. Danny married. The statue of misery stood holding a pot of dead chicken in cooling soup while Papa's oration continued in a dim distance.

"Your relatives! Your fine cousins! The son would have altogether murdered the father God forbid and good riddance with your family in the papers if the cops hadn't rushed in to drag one to the hospital and the other to jail. And with that, with their charmer," Papa somewhere out there was coming to the point, "with their redheaded whore with legs, hypocrisy with eyes looking down at the ground, I, what I am, have to pray with in *shul*!"

"What relatives?" Mama finally gathered her wits. "Even the mother, a cousin how many times removed?"

"Three," Sarah said, proving that even with her goose cooked a dead chicken can cluck. Although three was Danny. Danny's mother was two.

So a humane knock on the head and your troubles are over. But that was for regular chickens, not for Sarah. For Sarah God pulls His fast ones. With a family grocery store you never starved till it failed and you were also alone in the house most of the time. That night Joe Seiden came over and Sarah threw herself at him.

Joe gave a guffaw. "Hey, lemme strip down for action—"

"No, I'm your dead weight," Sarah hung on, "and you have to support me. We're getting married."

Joe didn't mind hugging his little virgin, even through clothing layers. He popped her a merry kiss.

"When, now?"

"No, this is Tuesday and we'll need time to plan," the passion kid Sarah breathed in his face. "Saturday night." And that moonface had never looked jollier as Joe took off, shook out and neatly hung up his good winter overcoat. And Sarah, "So get off early Saturday, don't forget," stood by to spring at good old Joe again.

Joe smiled himself to the couch, crossed his leg on his thigh, slapped the pillow beside him for Sarah to come join him and gathered her close. Then he wheezed, "The off early's a cinch, but don't go and lose your job."

That was the night of the snowy day Joe was fired from the fruit store. And there were so many more important things God should have had on His mind, like the grim gray payday last month when she handed over three dollars less to Papa and Papa wouldn't believe her pay had been cut. Papa'd accused her, honest Sarah Bialek, of lies, misrepresentation, theft, with him barely keeping his credit up with the wholesalers. Sarah begrudged her boss, Mr. Schwartz, those three little dollars considering the price of the thin Havana cigars and the *Ziegfeld Follies* tickets he sent her for on her lunch hour. But a glance at her ledgers would have shown God that Mr. Schwartz was telling the truth, who bought pocketbooks these days, who had what to put in them? Or if God got off the El at Bowery station he would have seen not only her poor papa's whores that whole dreary winter and not simply beggars, but men without work begging, Jews too.

That same night, after Joe left, Sarah jumped up from deep sleep on the couch into the black of the parlor and a continuing dream of Danny still in their bed asleep and their baby crying. She stared dopey at a strip of light under her parents' door. And sobs. Who was sobbing?

" . . . live to grow old . . ."

"Sha, sha, Lazer, sha—"

" . . . eating the food off the shelves," Papa sobbed, "off my store shelves I won't have much longer . . ."

"Sha, sha—"

" . . . Bolsheviks . . . Ku Klux Klans to kill Jews, better die in Bialystok . . . a heart dried up . . . in *shul*, with . . . that woman—No," Papa crooned like a mourner, "no no no—"

Oh God, Sarah felt her heart breaking. She tapped at Papa's door, to go in, to touch his poor face.

The light went out. Pitch black.

So Papa cried, and God let him.

Therefore, as they used to say in geometry, it should have been no surprise that God brought Sarah and Reisel to the same bargain counter at Hearn's on Fourteenth Street a couple of paydays later though it did take some doing. If Reisel was religious why was she shopping on Saturday? If Sarah couldn't forget redheaded Queen Reisel, Reisel could easily have forgotten brown-haired plebe Sarah. Therefore . . . why did Reisel's eyes light up bright as the windblown March sunshine outside, why did she hold her hand out and say, "How are you, Sarah?" and tell Sarah, "Come, I know where the real bargains are"?

Reisel brought her to the store basement and winked. "The best resides always under the surface." Then, "Look, Sarah—" Reisel held up a white cotton blouse, sleeveless for tennis Lower East Side, with red trimming. "Fifty cents and size nine, perfect for you, when summer comes as it will. Here, try it on—wait!" The arm with the tan fur cuff snaked into the pile. "Here is another—" blue—"and still another—" white again with blue trimming. "I have an instinct for these. And fifty cents!"

Ridicule? Was Danny's wife making fun of Sarah's indecent poverty? But Reisel giggled, "Forgive me, I am so proud of my treasure hunts," and went so far as to blush. "For myself nevertheless," her lovely fingers continued to send blouses flying, "I find nothing. I am now out of fashion." She spread open her coat and she showed that svelte figure, including the legs that scandalized Papa. "Too big in the chest."

Such talk! Was Papa right? Right or not, if not for God, *shul* and Papa congratulations wouldn't have been in order and the word Danny would absolutely not have passed Sarah's lips.

As it was, she began, "But your new coat's lovely, and—"

Reisel beamed, "It is not new, I have altered it."

"—and," Sarah stumbled along, "my cousin Danny is lucky."

"Why," Reisel became stern, "is he lucky?"

"To be married to you. I mean, I want to wish—"

"I am married to no one. Has Daniel implied— No? Then?"

"My—my father," Sarah blushed to the throat, "goes to your synagogue—"

"And heeds busybodies there. He should not do so, with respect to your father . . . Eh, cheer up, Sarah. Though our parents' sins are not ours we often are called on to atone for them, just as I have enjoyed an afternoon's shopping while you will pay for the blouses. Goodbye, I must run home now to Baba Rivka." Reisel pressed Sarah's hand, and, "Of course," paused with that flitting smile to do herself justice, "you will own the blouses."

The blouses fit, oh did they fit! Summer, Sarah is ready! And only four months to go, four months to find Danny so he could see her in them. Because if Reisel could suppose Danny and his removed cousin Sarah saw and spoke to each other, Reisel was definitely not mistress of all his comings and goings!

That was how for the third time God's rubber ball Sarah happened to bounce back to the Twenty-third Street trolley, the Avenue A transfer and the man or rather girlhunt for Danny Share since he was still single. But while God obviously wasn't going to let her forget Danny, He wasn't sending her Danny either. So since she was shameless in private—thoughts, wishes, daydreams—why not in public? Mr. Schwartz's secretary Celia

Kampf had exorbitant tickets for sale for a charity bridge party at someone's fancy apartment on Riverside Drive. Sarah had already refused, since charity began at the grocery and there was nothing left over. As a result Celia had cut down her good mornings to a thin unpleasant twist of the cheek. Impetuous Sarah handed over two dollars for two tickets and only then wrote the funny note to Danny which she'd sworn she'd never again write after the last funny note a few years ago. Even George Washington looked doubtful on the pink two cent stamp she stuck on the envelope, and it seeped through to that microscopic organ of hers called her brain—her wishes to horses machine—that what she had to look forward to was ten days of lunchless lunch hours (she couldn't face another deficit payday with her father), no answer from Danny, and a long evening of bridge across a table from Joe to regret her two dollars in.

Did Danny live in that particular mailbox? His answer posthaste—the second of her stack of two love letters or rather love cards, this one with Grant's Tomb on reverse—asked how she knew that he was a contract bridge fan.

Surprise on surprise.

Sarah thought she'd take a beauty nap before the big game, and who knows with that Danny, if Mama hadn't been up from the store a minute and against her better judgment let him in Sarah might have waked up with another note on her chest been here and gone. Mama was worried you could lose Joe this way, but Mama was wrong. You couldn't lose Joe. Joe'd taken a post office examination and foresaw a marvelous career, funny Joe, as a government man with a bag on his back. June groom he took for granted.

Sarah'd asked, "And who'll be the bride?" because by then God, Papa and Reisel had reinfected her. Joe had almost dropped off the couch in merriment. "No I mean it," Sarah'd insisted and even tried to explain, "Woman is fickle." That had been one big joke to Joe. Yet while she'd sat grinning—impossible not to—at Joe's hilarity, she'd had a sudden pang of the heart which told her she wasn't fickle.

"Joe, suppose we did marry and I was unfaithful. What would you do?"

"Spitballs at ten paces."

"No, really Joe—"

Joe grinned like bright weather. "Who with?"

"Handsome—" and the exhilaration, to talk about Danny!—"with blue eyes with a twinkle and a straight nose with a lilt at the tip."

"What," Joe guffawed, "a nice Jewish maiden doing it for a Gentile?" then made a lunge at her. "What for, when you can do it for me?"

Body and soul, her Joe.

So Sarah'd caught twenty winks in the dark on her parents' double bed when her shoulder was shaken. "Your big shot," Mama hissed into Sarah's dazed ear and though the intent was sarcastic it came out respectful. Then you stumbled into the parlor rubbing sleep out of your eyes and saw why: young Rothschild parading a fawn-colored suit, a high white collar and a fat knot in his velvety tie. Tossed to a chair at the round dining table where he'd caught her asleep last visit were his tweed coat and his high-crowned tan cap.

"You've made good at the Palace!"

"You mean bad at the factory." But Danny hit his troubadour stance.

> *"I care not, like knights of old,*
> *Who gets rich . . . and piles up the gold,*
> *I just wanna . . . get the girl*
> *And be ha–a–a–ppy—*

making bridge contracts."

Mama shook her head and walked out on the act, so Danny finished palms up to Sarah, "Ya brings out the minstrel in me," and shook hands with her. "Came too early, woke you up, huh?"

Now who did this darned friendly handclasp remind Sarah of? Oh yes, darn it—Hearn's Department Store, blouses, Reisel. Still, those twinkling blue eyes . . . Sarah held onto the fingers, the hand, till Danny pointed at it.

"Can I have a loan of this?"

He sat Sarah at the table and casually took a small blue and white box out of his pocket.

Dopey Sarah exclaimed, "A present!" and Danny was embarrassed.

"Cards." He shuffled them. "Pre-game huddle."

Some huddle, though Sarah drew her chair as close to his as she could. There were bidding methods, he explained when Sarah defined bridge as something you crossed to visit cousins in Williamsburg, Brooklyn.

"But," he said, thick Danny, "why a bridge party if you don't know any bridge?"

"For a worthy Jewish cause . . . What cause? Sarah. How do I know what cause? . . . Here—"

He examined the tickets, "A dollar?," and he had to be generous, the friendly booby: friendly was all he was. "You can't pay for this." He dug out two dollars but Sarah folded her arms. "Come on, take 'em fifth cousin."

"I keep telling you third but I wish it were three hundredth."

"What's the difference, take it, it's still in the family. You're poor and I'm," he cheerfully told her, "partner in a business—on its last legs!"

He began pushing the bills at her, she pushed them away, they giggled, their fingers tangled. Oh what a good time she was having! Then she stupidly said, "I have my pride, sir. Besides, I'd prefer the diamond you were promising me."

And, "Oh yeah, diamonds," he stupidly remembered and off he went:

responses, hearts, spades— "I respond," Sarah said—singletons, doubletons, honors, tricks vulnerable and invulnerable, above and below the line.

"I'm trickily vulnerable," she interrupted again, "above the line, darn that line!"

"Don't worry, you'll catch on," Danny laughed, "as long as you're willing."

"I'm willing."

"Whereas Reisel claims cards are childish."

"I'm childish."

She must have been, to endure hours of bridge even if in a rich lovely overheated apartment she could have lived in with Danny, with pictures and bric-a-brac, an India rug and two wide couches that people quit the card tables for eventually and necked on but not her partner or the middle-aged fanatics—two schoolteachers wonderfully mated—he had drummed up as small-stakes opponents. Sarah was dummy a lot, a natural role, and she could enjoy Danny at play and her co-worker Celia enviously staring at Danny. The coffee and cookies were nice too, but there was too little heart and too much hearts, and ugly discussions between the schoolteaching wife and husband after each hand they lost.

"Danny," Sarah finally lied, "I have a headache—" And the sweet kid, what anxiety!

"Not migraine?"

Cuddling against Danny on Riverside Drive with March winds rattling branches under the street lamps and frothing the black Hudson more than made up for bridge. But she had to assure Danny her headache was gone and that got him started with depressing enthusiasm on Reisel's headache theories. The run-of-the-mill ones—factory headaches, ten minute meals, no fresh air—he knew himself, but nobody could equal Reisel on cards headaches.

" 'Cards—' " and how perfectly he could mimic Reisel's half-English half-Jewish accent!—" 'are a fever of the soul and meditation is the sole antidote.' "

"I know another antidote," Sarah said. "Kissing."

So Danny laughed, brushed her lips with his and resumed his darned entertainment. "Then how come no winning headaches? Simple. 'In winning you are filled by a pretended attainment. Headache fills up the emptiness when you lose.' "

"The sweet singer? You? Empty? Why Reisel's nuts, Danny, smart and beautiful as she is!"

Danny squeezed her. "You'll have to write me a testimonial, Sarah."

Voluntarily Danny squeezed her!

10

WAS GOD STILL FOOLING AROUND?

Criticize Reisel and Danny squeezes you. Shiver on the El platform and he takes you under his coat. God had even sent a thickset middle-aged man to the 125th Street station to stare at Sarah and glance to see how Danny qualified. And Danny had even gone fishing for her Joe status.

"How's Moe?" he'd asked, and Sarah had merrily tossed Joe to the March winds, "No headache of mine."

Only where was the phone call that would get her fired so she could live happily ever after? On the train she'd jotted down the forbidden Chelsea 4067 of Schwartz's Handbags, no personal calls in or out. Why had she brought up that silly rule to joke at to Danny? Bubble with love and everything seems to dance right out.

Danny had smiled, "How can I phone you there then?"

"You get Central and you just say this number."

"But—"

"Though I'd hate to tell you," she'd shone up at him, "what happened to the last girl Mr. Schwartz caught receiving calls."

Danny—"What?"—had really looked worried.

"She got married to the personal caller."

"Say," Danny'd watched her stuff away her envelope scrap and pencil, "there's that old postcard that I wrote you from Orange."

"Yes," over the dam, "I always carry my most precious possessions along with me."

"You're a card," modest Danny'd grinned.

"Two of clubs."

"Ace of spades."

She'd wanted Danny to say queen of hearts, but how often do you get what you want—such as a telephone call at Schwartz's Handbags? Never. Her record was clear. She remained Mr. Schwartz's good girl, too good in fact. After Mr. Schwartz laid off Betty and Gertrude he reached to assure Sarah with a chuck under the chin that business would have to get a lot worse before she ever went. And the very second she'd been thanking him for the assurance she'd been stooping to transfer a piece of paper from the floor to the wastebasket and missing the chuck. Neatness counts. "Ya done right," Joe had said while being moderately fended off on her sofa, "give those guys a chin and they take the whole body." The following week the good girl's bad pay had gone down three dollars, but what had she cared once Danny'd squeezed her? She'd even said, "Listen Joe, I'm in love with another man," not that that burned any bridges.

She must've been too forward with Danny. Or backward. Mr. Schwartz went out of the office and she boldly whispered Quality Lamps's number to Central. God, let Danny answer. But a girl answered—Leah, Naomi?—and Sarah hung up as red as if they could see you by phone.

Type him a letter here anonymous on the outside and love on the inside? Or forget love. Another card party, Bialek residence, centrally located. Who else played cards?

Joe.

Dear Danny, let's go for a walk now that the weather is still so cold for April.

Still he'd squeezed her, voluntarily.

April showers bring May flowers, but April snows? Warm furry flakes twinkled like gold under the street lamp with Papa in *shul*, Mama in the house cooking supper, and Sarah minding the store. God's white penmanship, because for her to be minding the store God had to have crazed three separate customers. Late this afternoon one after another those insane women had barged in to sell groceries to the grocer. Each had wanted Papa to take back leftover matzos from Passover. Take back matzos! Never, never—as Papa had shouted to the first two—never in the history of matzos had this happened before. When the third woman had trailed in snow and claimed that Mama'd promised, Papa'd put on his coat and hat and pushed his collar up. "Even she," Papa had screamed pointing at innocent Mama, "would never have told you any such lie!" And to Mama, "She thinks it's you—you argue with this lunatic!" And off he'd crashed to synagogue an hour early to ask God who'd sent plagues to Pharaoh why this plague. So Mama had been an hour late starting supper.

Next, God sent—or at least didn't prevent from getting to Rivington Street at this dark hour—the kid with the Sunset picture show posters. He sloshed into Katzenstein's the tailor across the flickering street and the hand of God—of course invisible—slid last week's features out of the window and jiggled in this week's. Sarah ran to the door.

"Hey kid—you with the posters!"

Oh stupid, he gaped with snow on his cap. She swung her arm, and, slowly he plodded over.

"Your fadder don't take in no coming attractions."

"I take in coming attractions."

Sarah yanked the kid in, pulled a card from under his arm and propped it in the window against the corn flakes that gave no nourishment anyway.

"Where's my pass?"

It was a kid who breathed through his mouth, you had to drag everything out of him. His fingers stuck out of torn mittens so he didn't have to pull off the mittens to fumble the pass to her: Admit Two Free.

"Thanks, that's a good boy. . . . Wait, where are you running?" Sarah scooped a handful of figs off a string and poured them into the kid's pocket herself, he was just the type to drop them right on the floor. "Don't eat them all at once—you'll get sick."

Sunset, be my sunrise.

Dear Danny, she wrote leaning over the counter, dear Rudy, dear Valentino—that beautiful hair-greaser was nothing beside her, beside someone's, beautiful Danny with the clean brown wavy hair—dear Rudolph Valentino in *Faust,* dear Faust whoever that was exactly, *Imagine the luck!—a pass for the Sunset, Admit Two Free, for Saturday night and Valentino in* Faust. *I'm one free. Are you too free?*

The dreamy blue snow melted away overnight, the poster lasted two days before Papa noticed it in his open graveyard for last year's flies. Then God said unto Papa, "Lift up thine eyes." The dead flies stayed put, but the poster: rrip, rrip, rr—

No matter how hard anybody hated the movies—dirty pictures full of half-naked women—they could not rip that cardboard quadrupled.

"God give me strength," Papa ground his teeth. "Who let this filth into my grocery?"

Mama was sure Sarah'd done it but Papa couldn't be positive about Mama. Sarah admitted nothing with a mind weighed down by nothing. Nothing from Danny. And mail delivered seven times daily and three times Saturdays. But Sarah game to the finish took a deep breath to tell Joe no couch Saturday night when Joe fascinatingly said, "No couch this Saturday night."

"How come?"

"They're short a weekend man in the Essex Street Fruit Market. I said, 'No dice, Sarah needs me more than you do,' but people go down on their knees with tears in their eyes and beg you, 'Two bucks—' can you be heartless? So, good ol' Joe, I gave in."

"You did the right thing, Joe."

"You're one in a million, Sarah. Soon as I'm appointed a city official, Clerk Grade Two, believe me darling you're getting that diamond ring and the magnifying glass that goes with it, and then'll come wedding bells."

"Meanwhile," idiot she, still with her sweet singer, the Fourteenth Street Roof Garden and the amateur prize years ago, "you can bring me a banana on Sunday."

So Saturday Sarah took her old pal hapless Hilda, Admit Two Free but buy your own popcorn. The bill led off with a jolly dependable Fatty Arbuckle Joe short. Valentino Danny who only had to breathe and you were a goner was the main feature. Oh to gauzily perish and sail a final reel celestial shaft up to heaven while Danny Valentino in a black cloak below stretches loving if tardy arms after you . . . Ah . . . and wet blankets say that movies have nothing to do with real life! The screen, yearning chords from the pianist, tears delicious as chicken fat—what a menu for the price of admission!

Arm in arm she and Hilda sniffed final sniffles into the lively night air, but at Canal Street, at the Actors Café where they were due to meet Joe and the lackluster Murray Kaye Joe was bringing for lackluster Hilda, Hilda wrinkled her face, squeezed a yawn out, and thought she would not go in, it was so late! . . . "What," Sarah kept a good hold on her, "and disappoint two lovely boys?" And if Sarah's hunch was right—and she'd been just feeling it in her bones, that's why she'd picked this place—the third lovely boy would be here, her sweet singer, better than actor, and Hilda could have the other two lovely boys and all the actors. Not even Joe and Murray were in the half-empty café though and poor shy Hilda had to be wrestled out of another getaway try.

"Sit down. There must have been a rush on bananas in the Essex Street Market, and you know why bananas are so much in demand?"

"Why?"

"That's a good girl. 'Because they have no bones,' " Sarah quoted the popular tune of the day, "and no bones no hunches. Enjoy the actors, like the one walking over to us."

Which proved Sarah's bones had been half right, or maybe some smaller fraction, guessing Danny when they should have guessed the offstage scandal of the Essex Street Synagogue, Danny's father.

Hymie in his dove gray varsity suit, flowered tie and starched collar had become such a regular here as a result of Madame Henriette Nadler that this was his club. He wanted a glass of tea, he ordered. If not, not. Through eyeglasses for only this purpose or the theater, he kept a keen eye on who came and went, and tonight he'd been half-listening to Spielman the human interest man on *The Day*, a plump lecher that women wanted no part of. Spielman sipped tea and dropped nasal tidbits about lunatics in the highest positions, the President of the United States for example.

". . . a lady in his closet, stark naked. Nice work eh, if you can get it?"

"Sure," but Hymie's mind and eyeglasses had been on those two girls—the small doll, Golda's cousin, and the other, the scared one, with not so much of a face but ah, what a figure!—and he'd slipped his glasses into his pocket, "provided that you want to stuff ladies in closets. . . . Excuse me."

He shouldn't he knew: Spielman watching was as good as a Western Union to Henrietta. But let Spielman see, let Spielman's mouth water. Sarah if Hymie wasn't mistaken was a sharp little piece, and he'd had enough of that kind. Give them goods by the bale, not quality. So directly from the health of Sarah's father old man Bialek he hadn't seen, knock wood, since the synagogue days, also knock wood, he aimed his conversation and the cane chair more toward Hilda Klainvogel.

"Your father," he took a stab, "was in the clothing business?" as who was not? "He worked for . . . what's his name?"

"Wolfe?" Hilda was surprised into saying.

"Of course Wolfe! I know your father, if he'd remember me, from years back, sure, Klainvogel. He goes to *shul*, doesn't he?"

Hilda's eyes filled. "My father died." She sighed, sobbed almost. "Two years and three months ago."

"Ah," Hymie was moved, the poor girl, he honestly was, and laid consoling fingers on Hilda's arm. "Such a fine man!"

And Hilda who turned stiff as a board if some . . . nobody touched her elbow to dance—not that they did often—felt so . . . warm, so . . . grateful to Mr. Share. He'd suffered too, you could tell by his worn . . . beautiful face, so sincere, so refined. Not like those heavyset brutes her mother boastfully paraded into the house since . . . Papa died, with her sarcastic suggestions—"You take the father, I'll take the son"—to ridicule Hilda.

Sarah, she sat amazed, holding in a big smile for Hymie and real tears for herself. How he resembled Danny! It was like having the image of Danny years later next to you, only with the edges blurred, the cleancut slippery.

"Yes," Hilda said, "my father was a fine person, and good—not like some others. He could bring half the synagogue home for supper Friday night after services, much as my mother begrudged them. She'd snap out remarks in front of them all to embarrass him. But she couldn't embarrass him, he was too . . ." her face crinkled . . . "gentle."

"A gentle man," Hymie did remember someone like that: it must have been Klainvogel! "A real gentleman, and you remind me of him."

"I do?"

Those wondering eyes lifted up to Hymie's to be told more, and he felt himself falling in love, in spite of Madame Nadler and her suite in the Broadway Central Hotel. "Like father, like daughter, the same beautiful soul," he swore and, engrossed as he was, just then noticed Golda's snotnose relation with the big grin. Let her grin, for all the good it would do her. "Your father's very words practically, many times in the shop . . . But listen," this other—and who'd sent for her?—had wisecrack written all over her face, "have you seen *Such a Peach*?"

"Sarah?" Hilda asked and no kidding.

"Sarah," he winked at that girl, "is a well-known peacherino. But I meant the show next door in the Civic Theater. Here," Hymie dipped into stock, "here's a ticket."

Hilda blushed, "But don't, d-don't you want to use . . . ?" She broke into a cold sweat like at dances, she couldn't help it and she hated herself for it.

"For my own use?" Hymie helped her out. "I know that show by heart, as good as the actors. An acquaintance of mine plays the grass widow, a bit part," he yawned, "Madame Nadler. Though," he perked up, "Reisenfeld is worth watching—the ingenue. I still might go see it again."

"Cousin Hymie," the wisenheimer finally couldn't restrain herself, "you must be mad at your relations. Don't I get a ticket?"

Sarah had to smile even wider, he seemed so truly surprised.

"Didn't I hand you one? Here."

And look, the way she compared it with Hilda's, whether they were both the one date. Yes, Smarty, they're both the one date. So? "You still live in the same house Hilda, as in the old days?"

"No, after my father died we moved to Stanton, near Clinton Street."

"Oh, the big red house there on the corner."

"No," Hilda said, "the one next to it."

Well Smarty, how smart are you if Hymie Share wants to see someone again? He shook hands with Sarah first—she was after all a relation—then with Hilda—Stanton near Clinton—and he went back to Spielman.

And why why why God, in case You were listening—Sarah had another of her little onesided theological discussions—didn't you add up Danny and his father and divide by two? And Monday Danny's postcard arrived, the Woolworth Building in color, shooting out of the clouds. Thanks, he really appreciated her asking but he'd seen *Faust* uptown at the Lyric, great movie, he knew she'd enjoy it. Could anyone deny that if God existed He was torturing her?

Lay off!

You think He'd listen?

Just when you supposed—and you without your umbrella—the waves of rain were washing your mind of trolleys, transfers and periscopic scanning of desperate Avenue A home-goers for a lucky glimpse of Danny . . . an arm in your arm all of a sudden and a golden umbrella over your head.

Sarah's heart—Danny?—almost jumped out of her rain-blackened coat into the lamplit splashes on Twenty-third Street. And another arm in her arm, umbrellas bumping like halos?

One shining blonde face was cousin Naomi's. The other—cut it out, God—auburn-fringed, was Reisel's!

"A person could drown," Naomi said. "What are you doing here?"

"Drowning. Be careful I don't pull you down with me."

They giggled into the skittering downpour and toward the downtown trolley car where Naomi ten times as tough as Sarah'd have guessed shoved herself and Sarah on first. Then Naomi blocked off a frantic man to save Reisel a seat. Poor man, he had to give way to a woman and his thanks from Reisel were a muttered "Good only for lust and rapine."

"Don't you hate men?" Naomi exclaimed.

"No," Sarah said, "I adore them."

"Who doesn't? But look at my brother—"

Sarah's gymnastic heart took another leap. "Where?" She quickly searched but could make out nothing but wet surly coats steaming the aisle.

Reisel good-humoredly smiled, "In your mind's eye, Sarah"—the dirty genius—and Sarah idiotically blushed.

"At the factory," Naomi explained.

Just before five she and Danny were at her desk checking invoices when their salesman terrible Gable loomed up. Do you think Danny would stay five minutes extra and not leave her alone with that dinosaur? Reisel was a darling and waited out in the shop, she didn't have to be asked. But Danny ran right out on time if not ahead of time the way he'd been doing lately. Fine example, wasn't it, for a partner? He said if the workers didn't like it they could and so forth, and he and Leah would both rub it in you hired Gable you fire Gable.

"And they are correct!" Reisel burst out in the streetcar rattle and screech. "Since at last you bring it into the open you should dismiss that anti-Semite with his evil cat's-eyes which harbor criminal thoughts!"

"But he's Jewish," Naomi none too strongly objected.

"His is the worst kind, I have learned to my ruination."

How could Naomi admit she'd hired Gable just because he didn't look or act Jewish, yet was? Even at the original interview Gable hadn't concealed his sweet personality. He'd looked over their line and said, "Cheap stuff, but it's good enough for the Jews." "I don't like such jokes," Naomi had said, and Gable had laughed, "I'm a bar mitzvah." Then it had struck her, since most of their customers were Gentile, that this slightly piggish-looking tower of fat might be useful. Jack Berger had once mentioned to her that the Gentiles began by taking him for a Gentile. Most of them eventually would make a kikes crack in his presence and he'd let 'em know, "I'm a Jew," straight in the eye. Handsome Jack—she could just see that gaze of his—when he said marry me Naomi why hadn't she said yes! But Gable had kept a pleasant face on, he was certainly expert in lamps and he had the best testimonials. She herself knew Gable's last boss Canavan died and the & Co. died with him. And again, Canavan. For an Irishman to employ a Jew the Jew had to be good. Only was Gable really Jewish? Naomi'd worried the question till Leah'd lost patience, "Then tell him take out his jigger and prove it," and made Naomi burn red. And—the worst uncertainty—was Gable a really good salesman?

"Only this?" Naomi would thumb through the few orders.

"Only this?" The ugly stare scared you. He stood there like a mountain. Maybe she'd put a pink slip in his next pay envelope, Your services are no longer required? As if he could read her mind he'd slowly relax and rejoin humanity. "Billy Sunday himself couldn't drum up more orders the way business is if he decided to enlighten the Gentiles by lamp."

"Billy Sunday?"

"The Gospel preacher."

Where did a Jew come to Gospel preachers? Was Gable really a Jew?

Whatever he was, more and more he gave her the shivers. Tonight she should have canned him but hadn't had the nerve. Just the opposite. All the nerve had been on his side.

He'd had the unheard of gall to plump his empty order book on her desk and demand—not politely request—an advance against nonexistent commissions! Her electric bulb on a string—Danny made fun of her economies and she doubted now that this one was worth it—cast more shadow than light and that mammoth had hulked there with his lunatic glare. Scared as she'd been even with Reisel's angry eye fixed on Gable from outside the office, giving him money had of course never entered her mind. But how did you go about saying no in face of that threat that could throttle you with one paw, do whatever he wanted to you while Reisel watched screaming?

Suddenly Gable had made a motion and Naomi'd gasped. He'd reached for a cigar in his pocket. Then he'd bitten the tip off, spit it on the floor, grinned, "See a mouse?" and eased his bulk to the edge of her desk. His fat-lidded eyes had been enjoying this and Reisel had seemed to be busying herself with a lampshade and not even looking.

Naomi's "No mice and no advances" had been hollow as husk.

"Worse off than I am?" fat Gable'd laughed. "Is that possible? Tell you, get rid of the holy Jewess lurking out in the shop and I'll blow you to dinner—maybe more if you're nice to me."

Imagine that tub pressing against you, kissing you!

Thank God—"No thank you"—she had had her full voice again.

He was so big he'd seemed to get up in sections. "So you won't help a man spend his money. The ex-wife would like that, good for the alimony." He'd winked, "Sure now?" leered, "Don't look so scared, honey, nobody bit you—though not for want of trying," and he'd ambled away.

What a relief that had been!

Only now did it strike Naomi like the clear ding-a-ling of the motorman's bell in the rain that the advances, both cash and otherwise, and the jack-o'-lantern expressions, had been a smart sales act to confuse the main issue: that order book without orders.

She said, "I'm firing Gable tomorrow, Reisel." And, no more than half-joking to Jack's original enemy, "Will you get me back Jack?"

"Good riddance to that born gangster too."

"I'm still carrying the torch for him, Reisel."

"Douse your torch in this deluge. Daniel should be salesman."

Sarah bent around Naomi to ask, amazed, "Danny? Danny Share?"

"Why not," Reisel's smile flickered, and she mimicked, "Daa-nee?"

"He's no more a salesman than I am Helen of Troy!"

"Would you like to be—" smiling, so darn superior!—"Helen of Troy? You are attractive enough, Sarah . . . But is Daniel to remain a factory drudge then, a—" Reisel laughed—"greenhorn born in America?"

Because the day Reisel had stepped off the boat at Ellis Island who had been the greenie but her cousin Daniel, a fine boy but a primitive whose one desire had been to perform in music halls! True music had been a closed book to him, and even—for all his studies—books a closed book. While with her influence—he was not educated, hardly that, but at least owned a Shakespeare, could find his way to the gods in Carnegie Hall and, most important, was getting an inkling of what God is. Ah, it was not for her to mark down her good deeds—that was God's business. But though Daniel might not realize it, his best friend was Reisel.

". . . You should see," she therefore continued over the din of rain and trolley to little Sarah, who certainly had Daniel's interests deep at heart if she only knew what they were, "how harried, driven, his factory tasks make him. I understand," Reisel smiled, "that he bears no resemblance to salesmen we are accustomed to at Quality Lamps or Schwartz's Handbags since he does not qualify as cheat, bully or smooth talker. But rectitude and intelligence may have their place too, as my sainted papá demonstrated trading in lumber with the respect even of the anti-Semites. Why should not Daniel be a real businessman with equal respect instead of pitching himself into daily grime with the rolled up sleeves of a laborer? Our work has its effect on what we become."

Sarah muttered, "I don't know what to say," because how could you say the boy is a born troubadour doing everything wrong? Would she herself want Danny a troubadour in the same way her grandfather had been a Talmudic scholar, studying in back of the store while Grandma sold groceries, the hereditary Bialek pursuit? Ridiculous, there was no such thing—unless . . . unless it was Danny's father, the songless troubadour. But who'd want that for the Danny you couldn't seem, darn it, to help loving?

"Well," Reisel said gently since Naomi, you could tell, was won over, "it is so."

"But," Naomi pondered, "who would do Danny's work?"

"I!" Reisel was inspired. "I shall be your new foreman!"

"Oo Reisel—that's a pip of an idea!"

"Blame on genius."

The bristle-beard with the moist derby straphanging above them shot a last insane glare at these girls who'd made him stand dead on his feet the whole trip downtown. "Witches!" he sprayed at them. "You have men at your mercy even for work in hard times?" And he swayed toward the exit.

"Us?" Naomi said.

"The Three Fates he meant," Reisel laughed. Then she sympathized, "Poor man. In the old country they murder you. Here life is hard. Suicide is forbidden. What is left?"

Sarah asked, "Ride trolleys and hope?"

The three of them giggled.

"You crook!"

Naomi in the office let Gable have it and loud enough so they heard her all through the factory, even over the ear-splitting whine of Benny's lathe. Leah looked up from the work she was laying out. Reisel and the other lamp draper turned. Danny and the two shipping boys he was herding—yeh yeh Danny knew that before President Warren Gameliel Harding and normalcy they'd had three shipping boys and that this McCarron order was as big as old times and enough to kill a horse let alone a couple of dumb oxes—even they stopped and turned. But nobody fazed Lew Gable, especially not a little girl with a silky gold cap of hair. He eased himself tolerantly down to the edge of her desk.

"That loud noise just now couldn't have passed those highest grade ruby lips?"

"Well I have only myself to blame for hiring you, you crook. It shouldn't have required a gypsy to figure you out. Why just looking at you . . . And he sits grinning, when I could throw him in jail."

Of course she couldn't throw him in jail. A few weeks ago she'd come in ready to fire this crook with crook written over his beady-eyed sneering face particularly repulsive since her nightmare of him. In the dream she and this new Murray Kaye she'd met through Sarah were being naughty—that was all, naughty—in Murray's back seat. Suddenly Murray changed into Gable, crushing her down, smothering her, with his fat hand unbearably clawing at the inside of her thigh. She'd fought her way out of sleep and had hardly slept that night for fear of dreaming again. Don't say dreams like that weren't Gable's fault. He had a high estimate of his irresistible charms—she could check his references, lucky girls by the dozen grateful to him for life. Fat pig. But smart enough to stop short of open insults, just as he'd been smart enough to police-proof his John P. McCarron deal that was costing her plenty, so much it was sickening. She still hadn't put pencil to paper to calculate the loss on the shipment poor Danny was breaking his back moving down to the van this very moment.

That this repulsive . . . slug had outsmarted her! He must have guessed she'd tuned herself up at last, with Reisel's help, to the pitch of letting him go. He was cunning—stupid, but cunning—and hadn't even had to be cunning after all the fair warning that he had gotten from her, depression or no depression. So three weeks ago the second he'd stepped into the shop she'd called him into the office, and afterward she'd been relieved that he'd spoken first!

"Happy days are here again."

The McCarron order had been enough to forgive him his past and his present too with his leer and insolent little proposition of the day—"Teach you how to celebrate tonight, free private lesson?"—so quiet you could think you'd imagined it. In fact she hadn't quite heard him say it. It had rippled back later, like an echo. She'd been preoccupied with the order sheet.

"Why," she'd innocently asked, "didn't you fill in prices and terms?"

"They have all that on the price list. Okay then for tonight?"

"Okay what for tonight?"

The sneer had been up already. "Okay G.A.," he'd rattled off one of his meaningless funny as a crutch taglines.

Danny and Leah had both commented, "No prices?" but they'd been overjoyed too. John P. McCarron hadn't given Quality Lamps an order like this since Jack Berger'd walked out on Naomi a good year and a half back. Danny hadn't hesitated to hustle out the items in stock, and when—unheard of—the McCarron check in full arrived ten days after partial delivery, Naomi'd simply assumed they'd decided on the quick payment discount this time. And even though there'd seemed no relation between the check and the actual bill, she'd lifted the telephone in all good faith—what a sap!—presuming that they'd made a mistake.

Those Gentile bastards, those thieves! If a poor person had stolen what they'd stolen he'd be caught by the shoulder, thrown into the Black Maria and driven to jail. But they'd set nothing on paper, only Gable had, privately, at Quality's expense, with a private payoff for Gable. No matter how much that guy claimed he was a bar mitzvah in his campaign to get her to bed with him, he wasn't! On the phone John P. McCarron's buyer, after the fake surprise, had given her his thin-nosed snot including the blacklist hint—and all so genteel, the genteel Gentiles, the way *they* know how to do it.

The swindle stood at the end in spite of what she unhappily agreed to pretend had been a misunderstanding. And now this nothing Gable—his good luck she wasn't a man: she would have sent him away black and blue—had the nerve to sit here and smirk!

"Whatsa matter honey? You wanted orders, and that deal wasn't so bad."

"Get your fat ass off my desk and out of this factory—and stay out!"

"Say," he bent so close she could feel his breath, "so you've evaluated my ass—ain't it nice? So roll down your desk top already and let's go where my ass can do you some good. . . ."

He was actually reaching to close her desk, but ducking her slap in the face he sat down on the floor with a thud that returned the spring, salt air and sunshine for Naomi. She tried not to but the giggle slipped out and swelled into uncontrollable laughing almost worth the expense of this cheap crook with the indignant rooster expression. She would not have guessed his agility jumping up though.

"You're all alike," Gable's voice sailed back from the exit, "you Jews."

"Drop dead," Naomi yelled, "you blubbery anti-Semite!"

Danny couldn't figure it out. "That guy was in *shul* in his glad rags last Yom Kippur. He's Jewish."

"And I'm Mayor John F. Hylan."

"What did you do to him," Leah was curious, "after you finished flirting with him? He looked all shriveled up."

"Flirting with him? I was firing him!"

Naomi broke the bad John P. McCarron's Sons news and Danny grew red as those stop signs you saw from the upper deck of the Fifth Avenue bus, except that with him it meant go—after Gable if she and Leah hadn't grabbed him, over to McCarron's with blood in his eye if they hadn't held on.

"Don't be so excited dear," Leah teased him, "it's only money."

Naomi—"What do you mean only? Don't you care we were robbed?"—gaped at Leah like crazy.

"Hush, children. I'll begin my seven days' mourning . . . tomorrow."

Danny said, "The Village sophisticate."

Leah let loose a yawn the equal of dawn's early bray when the alarm roused you to a day in the factory.

"You could damage your jaw," Naomi commented resentfully.

"You might at least praise my fillings. Henny does."

"Who's Henny?"

"A friend."

"Boy or girl?"

"Guess again kid. All man."

With just enough orphan boy mixed in for Leah's taste?

"My little Lower East Side mama," Henny had comfortably sighed their first time lying down. "No wonder Al with the *yarmulke* loved your apron strings."

All the while those blue eyes had been laughing, and did Henny look . . . not handsome, but rugged, attractive, without the perennial steel-rimmed spectacles on. Still, how much was truth and how much was poetry? As she'd explained to Henny, she was too old to believe in just leaping into the void and repeating your parents'—in Leah's case her mother's—mistakes.

"You mean," Henny'd said, "I, John Henry Lieber, Jr., remind you of your father the roué?"

To say yes would have been coarse, but could you be certain the correct answer was no? There'd been a piquancy to winning him away from that Bessie Gould crawler—effortlessly. Leah'd been only too happy to keep her nympho charms out of the in every sense airless back room of the Occult Arts Shop as she'd been ordered to by the proprietress. Henny'd therefore telephoned to ask why he didn't see Leah there and she'd referred him to Betsy for the reasons. Actually, he'd said, it was the seeing and not the reasons that counted with him. Leah'd needled him he'd still have to get Betsy's permission wouldn't he, and he'd just laughed no to that.

Leah'd thought did he take you for a moron without any memory? The way he'd catered to Bessie before Leah's own eyes!

So, "I'm really too busy," Leah'd said, "I'll see you in church."

"Not me you won't. You wouldn't tell me that even in jest if you'd sat through one-tenth of the hellfire sermons I had to as a boy, Leah. They still give me nightmares. Let's make it some other place."

"Variety is the spice of life, I suppose."

"I agree, Leah. But why do you say so?"

No man of thirty could be that innocent. He really belonged in the sales not the actuarial department of that insurance company or whatever it was he worked for.

She'd said, "Let's leave it at church."

But John Henry Lieber, Jr., kept turning up at The Teakettle for late breakfast Sundays, her friend Ivy's, Sicily Pete's, New School lectures that put Leah to sleep—as open to look at as a Catskill Mountain in sunlight. Before she'd known it she'd become half a pair by default. But was he really a Catskill or only a bunch of lighting effects? Take Papa. He'd known how to keep his lady friends underground. To this day Leah had never seen him with one. Until Danny's Secret Service reports had been capped by the knock-'em-down hearts and flowers episode any woman could tell you the impeccable Reisel might have prevented from taking place, Leah hadn't believed in her heart her father was a skirt-chaser. Nor did she believe Henny was. But are beliefs based on wishes? He easily explained the catering-to-Betsy incidents as common politeness. At her store she'd needed his help, and then that painter Krimsky shouldn't have called her a Philistine just because she was one.

Politeness—the enlightenment sparked out like the electric bulb over a character's head in the funnies—Leah'd hardly been aware of that concept till she'd met Henny. He was certainly the most polite person, outside of the devious Reisel, that she'd ever run across. And perhaps he was honest. You didn't hear him denying Betsy'd been his girl friend, maybe still was. "She's a very nice girl—" had Leah's ears been playing tricks?—"and it's true that I've been trying to improve her taste and her stock—"

"Don't unburden your eugenic ambitions to me, Henny. They're not the key to my heart."

"Oh, I love your remarks!" Henny'd pasted kisses all over her for that one. "The fact is, since the war, I have no eugenic ambitions. I was speaking of those horrible trinkets Betsy's amassed that the Occult Arts Shop is loaded with and nobody buys."

"Horrible?" Leah on the pillow beside him had tilted her brows. "I thought you thought that they're nice."

"That Victorian junk? I think she's picked most of it up to torture her father, poor man, since he pays the bills. I've advised her against that but she's been reading this Freud and she tends to blame her parents for everything. You have no idea how those showcases full of eyesores have made my eyes sore."

"And you let me go on believing . . ."

"I wouldn't disparage your taste, Leah. But you'll learn, while we're running the store."

He was serious. He felt that Betsy was getting bored with the shop and might want to sell out any day now.

"Do you still find these things out on Bessie's pillow?"

"Betsy's?" He'd raised his good thick white arm and solemnly sworn, "I do not, so help me Jesus," and, with a grin, again covered her with kisses. "But back to business, darling."

Which at that juncture even with business-minded Jack Berger would have been pleasure. But not Henny-boy—if she could only accept him at face value!—who always seemed to mean what he said. They'd marry and they'd buy Betsy's business or buy Betsy's business and marry, preferably the former since then he'd be lord and master from the outset and Leah would, in accordance with the marriage contract, give herself meekly to his guidance on Occult Arts Shop matters, not like stubborn Betsy. After each foreign raid Betsy'd spread out the booty hot off the steamship, greedily keep for herself the stuff that Henny approved of, and—"Do those Philistines who stroll in here from uptown imagine that I scour Europe for nothing?"—proceed to overprice the rest against all of his persuasions. Why shouldn't Leah and Henny rectify that, clear the dross at what it should sell for, build a stock of elegant not too costly pieces, and at the willing expense of their customers enjoy the Village, ocean breezes and Europe—when they'd own the business?

Leah'd yawned. "But I own part of a business already."

"I see your dentist goes in for platinum. Very becoming, Leah."

Now—the second yawn around she'd gazed at him gazing into her mouth—that's what you call love. Or was it?

"How," she'd suspiciously asked, "do we divide this imaginary investment? Your good taste, my money?"

"Oh no. Your taste isn't that bad, Leah. And I've saved enough money, when the time comes. You can use yours for the trousseau."

Was this angel an angel, or the sharpest fox alive?

11

NAOMI WENT OUT OF HER OFFICE TO DANNY AND SHE gritted her teeth against the deafening lathes. "Does Gable have a mother?" she shouted.

Danny let out a squawk, laughed and shook his head. "I'm losing my voice," he yelled. "Yeah, hard to believe ain't it? She was with him last Yom Kippur outside of *shul*."

"He just had the nerve to call me up for his final week's pay that he stole in advance. He says his mother has cancer and the Jewish so-called doctors are bleeding him dry with bills. Could you go to his house and find out? How can you stand this awful noise?" Naomi screamed. "I mean, ask a neighbor?"

"No. Why the detective work? Send him a check, if he's turning it into blood money."

Naomi began writing a check, but how many times was she supposed to be taken in by that actor? No rush, checks can always be written. She'd get Murray's opinion. Gee, the thought of Murray, the bumpy reddish-gold hair, the tickly mustache, the straight nose—her collar ad man—made her all hot and bothered! She and Murray could drive up to the Bronx where Gable claimed he lived and she could see for herself. Afterwards they'd park in one of those country streets where you kissed, your eyes fluttered, and the leaves fluttered over you. Murray wanted to be the Quality Lamps salesman, he'd dropped enough hints. Naomi hadn't let on that she'd caught them but actually that's what she wanted too. Murray was so handsome, ambitious, studying all his free nights at the Postgraduate Business School. How was it, she'd asked him, they hadn't met there before Sarah had introduced them? Murray'd given his sweet, slow heavy-lidded smile, her Chink she called him. "The heavens were being stingy with you," Murray'd said in his cute drawl. Had ever a girl fallen so much in love so fast? "With you, you mean," she'd kissed him. In the boy trades she'd certainly gotten the better of the bargain. One after another she'd shown Sarah Babe Lewenthal, Irving Jacobs and Morty Schneiderman, and one after another Sarah'd shrugged and said, "Oh, he's all right." Naomi didn't think they were anything to write home about either, but who could tell for somebody else? Finally in Naomi's house Sarah the kidder'd said, "I'll confess. My type would be a sincere tan-haired blue-eyed boy, about seventy inches tall, something like Danny, only intelligent." Danny'd been there on the spot, so Naomi'd asked him, "Do you hear that, Danny?"

"What?"

"Do you know somebody like you, only with brains, for Sarah?"

Danny'd laughed, "I don't even know me," and hurried out of the house.

"Where's he running to," Sarah had asked, "Reisel?"

Was that where Danny went all the time? You couldn't prove it by Naomi. "Reisel says they go to a concert occasionally." The next double date had been Sarah's turn, and her friend Joe had brought his friend Murray Kaye. Murray'd held out his hand and Naomi had been surprised, she'd told him later, how white it was, that a boy who had to do such rough work had such beautiful hands.

He'd shrugged. "A little hand lotion," and she'd suppressed a giggle. But it only showed how ambitious he was, keeping his hands nice for the future. What a shame a boy like Murray had to stand hawking vegetables weekends, sleep on chairs in a flat full of brothers and sisters so close to the Williamsburg Bridge that the traffic looked like it was in your front room, and wear out shoes searching for work when there wasn't any. Not that he was worried. In the Postgraduate School library after class he'd turn the *Wall Street Journal* pages and whisper to her about tariffs, rising investments and why business would be picking up soon. Where Murray pointed she'd squint and nod and try to avoid seeming dumb—but their elbows touched!

If business would only pick up already she'd start him even as shipping boy at Quality, with the understanding on the QT that soon he'd have her job and she'd have the mommy job with the babies. But after her Gable troubles, how could she make Murray salesman straight from a vegetable market? Not that he couldn't do it, she could train him. But still better, Murray should land a position in a big banking house. Then there'd be his salary and her share in Quality even though she was home with the kids. Except Murray said forget banking houses, even the Jewish ones wouldn't hire a Jew. What an outrage! Anti-Semites like that Ford—"Never buy one of his cars, Murray!"—blamed the Jews for everything including bad weather, and Jews wouldn't take other Jews?

"They take money, that's what they take and why not," Murray shrugged, "Jew or Gentile."

Besides the brokerage business was chicken feed, unless you owned the business. The real profits were in quick-gain investing. Murray's father hoarded candy store pennies to put in the bank for the 4 percent interest.

So there were your sixteen hours a day behind a counter and there was your 4 percent interest. Some prospect! Yet all his father wanted was money. The *Morning American* used to discount you maybe three cents a ton if you picked the papers up at their South Street plant. So how could Murray's father resist? He'd send down the oldest son—ten years old, yep, Murray, the kid in person—in the dark before school. Down was okay, you walked the mile and a half. But those trolleys back in the rush hour! Either you couldn't get on or you'd get pushed in so you couldn't get off. More than once Murray had gotten stuck—in the middle of the streetcar with tears in his eyes, idiot kid—five or ten blocks past his stop with that heavy bundle of newspapers. Then he'd have to rush with his arms falling off, untie the papers, pile them on the stand outside the store, wait while his father counted to make sure he wasn't holding back any change, and head for school double time.

Naomi'd hardly been able to speak. "You have a mean father."

"What can anybody expect from a man who sees life in pennies? Look—" At the library table Naomi'd followed his finger down the Stock Exchange columns. Murray had a letter from the vice-president of Hunt's Restaurants in reply to one he'd written Hunt's. See, at fourteen now. Their last dividend paid 7 percent, they had three new stores in the works. Murray had begged his father to buy a thousand dollars' worth and within six months, bet Murray's bottom dollar, sell at twenty-two for a 60 not a 4 percent gain, 120 percent to be accurate and prorate the time. What did his old man say?

"So bet your bottom dollar. Go gamble with your apples and oranges, not with my money."

How about Naomi? Did she have five hundred dollars? Naomi hemmed and hawed. Three hundred dollars profit was tempting, but . . . She didn't want to sound like his father, but suppose Hunt's didn't go up? Suppose Hunt's went down? Murray'd smiled and looked sorry for her. Hunt's had declined last year, leveled off, and now—he'd explained it before: in a bad year they were expanding with good profits—they had to rise.

The arched windows of the Postgraduate library faced a purple sunset between the New York skyscrapers; sweet air flowed in from Jersey. "Let's sit in the park awhile," Naomi gasped.

Love and kisses on a park bench distracted Murray, but he was back on his hobbyhorse for the walk home and Naomi promised to mull over Hunt's.

Naomi did have five hundred dollars and a lot more than five hundred dollars. But the bank's 4 percent suited her too, not to mention the satisfaction of reading the bankbooks. And even in a bad year Quality Lamps was averaging, according to her calculations, roughly 4⅝ percent on the up-to-date capital, nothing to be ashamed of though the word McCarron did make her slightly sick.

That lowlife Gable must have invented the cancer if not the mother.

Naomi certainly hoped so. Small as it was (let Gable say) she'd already deducted that forfeited pay from the McCarron loss. Every little bit helps! She'd been licking her lips even more over the savings from no salesman altogether these three and a half weeks, no commissions, no salary! Re-orders were coming in anyway and why shouldn't they? Giving Christmas presents to Quality Lamps customers, all right. But from Tiffany's, because Leah enjoyed playing big shot with her mink coat-collar back from her shoulders like a millionaire's wife while she drawled too bored for words at the clerk trotting out cut-glass bowls at an arm and a leg or silver vases that held one skinny flower? Maybe the presents did pay, as Leah claimed. Regardless, the reorders proved that a salesman should earn commissions on new accounts only. Danny said that was nuts, no salesman would work on that basis, not if you wanted him looking in on the old accounts too.

"When you're salesman," Naomi'd said, "I'll take that into consideration."

"You mean never?"

She'd meant so much the opposite that she could have bitten her blabbermouth tongue. What was the rush while they could get along the way they were and save money? Luckily—see how they left her all the headaches!—her brother and sister didn't ask what about a new salesman. But if the salesman wasn't expected to look in on old accounts, what was the salary for?

"So he'll always have fare," Leah had cracked, "to a Salvation Army soup kitchen."

Very funny, but who had to keep the business end solvent? Leah did her job taking care of the trimming department, but those boring boredom yawns all morning long with tears streaming out of her eyes not only got under your skin but were a fine example for the other workers. Comment, and more jokes. "You're right, sissy, either I give up the shop or wear out my handkerchiefs—there ain't room for both in this county." So she'd better get Leah a few handkerchiefs for her birthday. The older sister might be growing rapidly younger, but she wasn't crazy enough to quit the business.

Unless—

Unless Leah settled down and had babies with that Henny whatever he was. Say she did. The problem would be—even in daydreams no sense having pipe dreams—buy her out, or keep her as a smaller percent silent partner. The choice would be Leah's of course, she wasn't a stranger. But what a wrench if she chose the cash. Naomi hated so to go backwards! Still (you could be philosophical) they'd eventually make back that capital and have Leah's share of the profits, 16⅔ percent each, into the bargain. That was something to dream of! And with Danny salesman no commissions and salaries to outsiders, Reisel's pay—even increased—as shop forelady would be less than what Danny got now, and Reisel's replacement to trim lamps would be paid less than what Reisel got now. Naomi the efficiency expert!

But when Naomi let the scheme bubble over to Murray and waited for praise, he only commented. "Well you better do something, and soon. I never heard of a business without a salesman." As to driving uptown to verify Gable's story, Murray said, "Why waste gas? Surprising you hired a phony like him in the first place, you're so particular."

Poor boy, now he was sore at her on account of the job. But what could she do? Leah married and leaving still was a daydream. Friday Leah came for supper—"Wouldn't for the world miss your chicken soup, Mama"—and caught Ma in one of her blue moods.

"You manage to though," Ma said. "You could live here and have soup every night in this big empty apartment."

"Don't try to pull the wool over my eyes kiddo. It's empty because you're not here. How's your boy friend Mr. Rappaport in his wheelchair upstairs you do free housekeeping for? Are you still helping Mrs. Weisbart nurse her kids through the measles or are they up to chicken pox now? Does Mr. Blum the paintner still have his leg in a cask?"

"And I can also sit, brood over my older daughter, and grow old."

"Grow wise too, as befits growing old."

"Are you wise, with your friends? Married men?"

"Worse," Leah winked. "A Gentile."

"What about Henny?" Naomi challenged her.

"That's him," Leah said.

"A Gentile named Henny?" Ma said. "Please, Leah, your mother may be old but she isn't senile yet. You mean he's married."

So Leah concocted a man's name—John Henry Lieber, Jr.: that boiled down to Henny?—and a smiling cock-and-bull story about Lutheran orphanages (if such places existed) and Christian childhoods, with plenty of jokes sprinkled in, till she finally forced a smile and wave of the hand out of Ma.

If you were serious about a boy would you say that he was Gentile? One thing was sure, the Quality Lamps profits would be divided three ways for a long time to come, maybe forever. And on Tuesday Mr. Giffin of the America Hotel called up and asked nastily where was her salesman. Then Friday Humboldt Jones's Mothersill called and laughed in her ear, "Are you people still alive there?" Too bad, no more putting the salesman matter off.

Cheer up though. Danny sales, Leah forelady, Reisel with a five dollar raise in charge of the trimming department: a net cut of fifty, fifty-five dollars a week, and a lot more when business and commissions got back to normal.

Naomi did put it off one more day just to round out the week and banged on the partition glass to bring Leah into the office. "Congratulations, forelady," Naomi broke the news happily—and her sister looked at her like crazy.

"Do you think up these rattlebrain ideas alone, or is that what they teach you at the Postgraduate School? If you want to insult the customers why send them Danny when it's so simple to give them a Bronx cheer over the phone? And what made you imagine I'd be the forelady? I may not stay here at all."

You had to pinch yourself to make sure you were awake and bite your cheeks to keep from grinning!

"Why, where will you go Leah?"

"Time will tell—if I do go. Meantime, you just place an ad for a salesman and stop this foolishness."

An ad! That meant that for two dollars and thirty-eight cents she could drag out one more week of no salesman and by Leah's advice. And with Danny salesman or not, there was the 16⅔ percent to look forward to when Leah left!

Oh lucky day—and lucky week. From three lines of small print in *The World* a shabby mob of schlemiels jammed the two flights of stairs before the factory opened so you had to force your way up. Salary on top of commission? You felt they would work—at anything—for a roll and coffee, they were desperate. You had to be sorry for them, but underneath—jubilant. When Naomi saw what they had there, she insisted Leah sit in on the interviews. And Leah, after she found herself handing out half dollars then quarters as charity, excused herself and returned to the shop. So there was no way out except Danny. And the truth was, as long as Leah'd refused forelady, Naomi preferred Reisel—would Reisel be overjoyed!—and no yawns. You had to keep your fingers crossed though. If a real salesman in their line happened to apply you'd be obliged to hire him. But none did!

At closing Saturday Naomi whispered in Reisel's ear, "You're forelady," and boy did Reisel's eyes light!

"Then Daniel is salesman? I am happy for him."

Only, you couldn't say that Danny himself was that happy.

"The hell I am!" he burst out at Naomi, and absurdly noted that his voice had a nice tenor resonance with just the two of them in the loft. "I got to rush, Naomi." The afternoon was young, the sun shone like silver off the slate roof of the pier, though how he'd catch up to Reisel, or where, was beyond him. "You put that ad in again for next week."

"You just sit down and listen. You never know what's good for you. If not for me you wouldn't even be in the business."

No argument there, and with times slow he was still making money and hoped to make more. And also nine hours a day he was in the same place as Reisel, and—headaches, heartaches, what the hell. There was the joy too. Who was the only man who could honestly claim that if she needed a rat killed in Norfolk Street she'd call him? Grandma'd waved the *Forward* at that rat peeping up at her, which proved that even a socialist rag has its uses. But the scared one had been his Reisel. Danny'd shown up, he'd been scared too, she'd looked that pale and sick on a chair after she'd heard Grandma's yelp and run in just in time to see the rat's hairy ass wriggle back into the hole in the wall. The throwing up Reisel'd done before he got there. On Leah's advice—how she'd become a rat expert she wouldn't say: she swore she didn't have any at Bank Street—he'd spent a Sunday down at Reisel's fully equipped for the national pastime: catcher's mask, chest protector and shin guards that he'd borrowed from the Settlement House. By itself Reisel pointing at him in gales of laughter had been worth the trip. Then he'd shaken the poison bait outside the hole as Leah'd instructed, grabbed the baseball bat, also borrowed, and waited. You know something? That rat was game. You cornered him and he fought you, bat and all. Danny'd hated to slug him. With the rat knocked out of the box, Danny'd taken out carpenter tools and closed off those holes again all over the dump. Reisel had given him that pursed smile, "You're a saint," that could melt him at twenty below zero. He'd grinned, "St. George?" but dragon or no dragon, Reisel wouldn't give a Christian saint credit.

Gee he'd had fun that day!

Except for being with Reisel, the top of the Carnegie Hall top balcony, the gods she called it, wasn't such fun. There was something to hear in her pal Beethoven but he hadn't heard it yet. But he'd admitted that to Reisel and he'd heard something better. "Do not despair Daniel. Nothing good comes easily." Now if that wasn't a message about themselves, a promise practically, what was? It made three-handed rummy with his pals Gittel and Bookbinder a pleasure, while Reisel—what a girl!—would lift her eyes from her book for a fond smile at her two willing suckers, Danny with his headful of numbers even in a penny game and Bookbinder win or lose with a happy cigar.

And his sister at her desk here hoped to nag him into days without Reisel? Naomi was nuts. And him a salesman? Go smile for customers when he could barely smile for himself at vaudeville booking agents? Nix was the answer, no matter how smart Naomi was. And she was a smart kid, his sister, dangling the golden apples to set his mouth watering. Still, no Reisel all day? Nah. He just slumped to his spine—no chance now of catching up to Reisel before tonight anyway—and let Naomi rave on. But then she got too damn smart with her push that Reisel agreed with her, in fact that him as salesman had been Reisel's idea so (a giggle) Reisel could be forelady.

"That's a lie!" he hit the ceiling.

"Why a lie?" Naomi had the nerve to ask him surprised. "And if I'd listened to Reisel I'd've gotten rid of Gable before he had time to steal. Oh could I kick myself!"

"And Reisel wants to help tie up cartons, weld a frame here and there, putter with broken-down lathes to save on a repair man?"

"Sure, she says she can do all that." Naomi grinned. "Blame on genius."

And that was the shot that brought Danny down like a punctured balloon. Jesus Christ, what he'd selected to fall in love with. That she could use him like this, turn out this selfish—in cold blood. Sir Walter Raleigh ruined his three button model for the Queen, but Saint Danny's queen walked over the coat with you in it. If they coined gold medals for chumps he'd certainly earned one.

"Okay, I'll cut my throat. It's as easy as shaving."

"Hooray!"

And before you could say boo, Naomi had ledgers off shelves, order books out of cabinets, and memos and price lists jumping like grasshoppers from her piled-high desk.

"What's this?" Danny slowed her up.

"Sales dope past and present."

"To kill the rest of my dead afternoon? Excuse me, I'm only the future dope. So long sis."

Naomi opened her mouth to squawk, then laughed. "We'll be rich yet!" she grabbed his hands.

"You'll tell me when, and I'll start counting."

Meanwhile give him a word or two with his beloved. He'd skipped lunch so's to clear everything up for a fast getaway before the weekend, but the hell with lunch. On Norfolk Street the sun poured down yellow, the breeze licked up short skirts, the entire Lower East Side was selling, munching and shouting over the sidewalks. The little guy inside Danny's head gave the ol' vise one more twist and who could blame him with no food? So off the carts Danny fed him the best the season could offer, hot chestnuts in case he felt cold and hair oil ices in case he felt hot. The little guy in charge of the headache laughed sorry, not this junk, but Danny sure didn't intend to break bread with Reisel.

He didn't have to, she wasn't home. Grandma waved from the window, and two hours later opened the door. Poor Gitteleh, she was incommunicado with a coffin drape over her inside window and the space between the door and the floor stuffed with towels.

"It's a bad day for Gitteleh," Grandma shook her head. "Today she hears voices saying bad things."

So with the voices that Danny heard that made two of them. Grandma had her cane on one side, he gave her his arm on the other to lean her way back and resume her box seat at the Norfolk Street uproar.

"Ah, life is sweet, only it ages you, Danneleh."

"Today's proverbs day, huh Grandma?" He kissed that parchment cheek with the warts and peeled the fat off his hard Harding times bankroll. "Let's raise the rent that you pay Reisel. I understand she feels pinched for dough."

"You're a good boy, Danneleh. You and Reisel will make a fine couple."

"Couple of what?"

"What did you say, Danneleh?"

"I said I love ya. Where's your paper and pencil?"

He scribbled a short and sweet proposal of marriage—why not, between a saint and an angel both going up in the world?—and enter Reisel with

Bookbinder and a bag of delicatessen. "Here," Danny passed the offer to Reisel, "as long as it's written. Now you can turn me down, sue me for breach of promise and quit working altogether."

She read it and, "Listen Daniel," she touched his sleeve but he pulled it away from her, "thank you very much for this, but please visit Sarah."

"My cousin Sarah? Why?"

"She is in love with you."

"You're nuts, and even if she were," he heard himself bleat in this uncontrollable voice but hurtled on just the same, "don't find me girls, or jobs, or anything else. I'll do my own finding and you quit twisting my head—it hurts enough without help from you. And I can hardly wait to begin selling, angel, so I won't have you all day long to look at."

"Daniel, you will live to thank me."

"Why wait? Thanks."

He breezed with Bookbinder waving a knish for him to stay, have a snack, breezed back for goodbye to Grandma and had the knish waved to him again. If you have the mind of a knish—potato mushy inside a leatherhead—why eat one besides. And with that mind and that aching leatherhead no wonder that the feet started off in seven different directions. But wherever they took him no more mooning for Reisel. And only a fool would starve himself sick. In Ratner's Second Avenue at a table of desperate eaters he held his own with a set of potato dumplings—or, you might say, a kind of knish—swamped in sour cream followed by a mound of triple-tiered chocolate cake washed down by well-sugared coffee to satisfy that hunger. He didn't satisfy it, he only stuffed it, but all that food must have stunned the little guy at the vise because the headache slowed down. And so did Danny. With his belt let out he sat there like a man of sixty, picking his teeth.

And Jesus, outside with the Saturday night mobs strolling under the El and window-shopping like summer, Danny had to raise his topcoat collar and still he shivered. Ptomaine from that meal? He felt weak, the crowd spun him like a feather. With her he wouldn't have eaten like that. Then they could have gone to the pictures. They did go once, to a big Civil War Ku Klux Klan stinko. "For the mind of an eight years old child," Reisel had rung clearer than the piano hammering out bugle calls, flames and other mayhem, "a glorification of murderers!" Then had come the shushes, and now, out of him, still came this sick chuckle.

The hell with that. You don't need four eyes to see movies. He was near Fourteenth Street and, two eyes forward, began shoving the others around for a change. Under the Bijou marquee a girl laid a hand on him and he brushed her off without even looking at her.

"Heyyy," she whined, "yo'-all don't have to push—"

Then he looked. "I'm sorry."

"Change yo' luck, white boy?" White boy. She was a blonde dame with a flat Negro nose, red mouth and green flapper hat. "Change yo' luck?" with a pathetic hard times half-smile. She was not exactly the girl of his dreams, a good chunky thirty, but he went half-mast anyway and why not change his luck.

But, "How change my luck when we both have blue eyes?" he cracked on the way to her flat.

"Oh my mammy and pappy in Virginia," she assured him, "they black as sin!"

The tenement stank like Reisel's, but Reisel's flat of course wasn't smelly. Danny breathed through his mouth while the lucky black blonde began trooping infants—"Now you shut your mouth now Cleon! Quit that whimpering! And you Claude, bring me the basin"—three of them, different shades, different sizes, out of the bedroom. Then she vamped Danny in and Claude brought the basin and sulked out. She followed Danny's eye to a wall sooty and full of smears as if the plasterer had started and then thrown his hands up on the job. "I done them patches myself," she proudly said, took his buck, yanked her skirt belly high and spread herself out on a brass bed that looked like the battlefield in a World War movie, enough to kill the appetite of a goat.

"Let's make it another time," Danny said, "now that I know where—"

"Oh no, I run a honest business," she cut him off with this crazy glint, "I don't accept nothing for nothing. I charges my price and I gives good value!"

"The kids need their sleep—"

"Don't pay no mind to them. They always worrying me! Come here, pretty boy—"

So you couldn't go hurt her feelings.

But he'd told her, he was flabby as yesterday's soup greens, and Danny the wild horse of Tompkins Square took ten years to come.

"Mah mah," the lady was full of motherly concern, "I bet you-all drink too much black coffee."

"Nah, fifteen, twenty cups a day—is that too much?"

"Ver' bad for the health young man, ver' bad."

Finally he made it to the Bijou and lucky to find a seat in that mob of neckers. He stuck as long as he could with the dummy dressed in her underwear (desert princess) happy to be abducted by a sideburns dago (desert prince). Then between sweet popcorn and sour sweat, the piano clanking away and the midget inside his head playing a tom-toms accompaniment, he muttered "Horseshit" at the true love on the screen he usually dreamed by and beat it past an angry ripple of knees.

Home—in case his blood wasn't thumping enough—he opened the door to a Victrola blast of "Yes We Have No Bananas." Who Naomi fell in love with—she was shuffling cheek-to-cheek with sleepy-eyed Murray—was none of Danny's business, he had his own troubles. But with the drawl and curl of the lip, for hate at first sight a couple of months ago he'd found Murray perfect. And now the "Bananas." You could hate this guy any time! Did jolly Joe Seiden think Danny was hating *him*? Joe stood stranded in the middle of the floor like an overweight Maypole, staring as if Danny were a two-headed lemon, and Sarah on the sofa was suddenly too desperate for a view of the park by lamplight—if you could see it from across half the room—to give Danny a look, let alone a hello. So much for that blame on genius love theory. But what theory?—just words to get rid of him. The cleverness. Sarah was panting for him, so she was engaged to be married to Joe the fruitman. Jesus Christ, never seeing Reisel again would be one day too soon! The needle slid off the last groove and the racket suddenly hushed.

"Romantic," Danny commented.

Naomi—"You bet he is!"—squeezed her collar ad, and, "Meet our new salesman. He'd better be better than the old one," she got sly on Danny, "or you're next Murray."

Was that his sister's angle? Then she had another guess coming! "I meant the tune," Danny said.

"It's a smash hit," Naomi informed him.

"Yeah, it smashes the eardrums."

"Quoting Reisel!" Naomi became ecstatic. "Is she happy that she's forelady?"

"Who's Reisel? I have ears too. So was the movie I just walked out on in the middle a smash hit, but I'm not blind either."

"Get in on a pass?" Murray checked his Ingersoll watch to see if you could still catch the last show. "Have any more passes?"

"Yeah." Danny fished out a quarter. "Want one?"

Murray shrugged, gave in to cruel fortune and consoled himself with a newspaper. But Naomi, "Don't tempt him," plumped herself on his lap with a kiss.

"Hey," Murray said, "my crease—"

"He enjoys passes best," Naomi giggled, "all kinds," she gazed at him, a real find, "huh Tootsie?"

Tootsie shifted her slightly to get a cigarette out of his pocket. "I wish I'd fallen into your business, Daniel," he drawled and scraped a match, "to afford throwing away quarters, though by my calculations the economy should be picking up soon."

Danny said, "Our business—"

"Tootsie," Naomi clamped her lids tight, "you're blowing smoke in my face."

"Have one, then it won't bother you."

"Ugh!"

But accommodating Murray carefully flicked ash into a tray so as not to dirty the rug—neat he was—and held the cigarette out at arm's length.

"Our business can do—"

"Naturally it can do better," Murray blew some smoke Danny's way. "It's run by amateurs."

"So make room for a professional, Danny," Joe jumped in merrily. "Go ahead Murray, show him what you can do, like at the fruit store, don't be bashful. . . . Here y'are—" Joe yodeled, while Sarah flamed like fever. Go stop her Joe, even if Danny had had a quarrel with Reisel—"get your hard ripe to-ma-toes you only should live so long, blind po-ta-toes no eyes to see with. . . . Say, that see was high C—but you should hear Murray sing it on Essex Street!"

Sleepy Murray hoisted and dropped his eyebrows, dragged on his cigarette and let Naomi swatting smoke with both hands defend him too.

"Your boy friend is so funny, Sarah!"

"Who's that?" Sarah said.

"Murray is a financial wizard! Wait till he finishes school—he'll be making his million while you're still making jokes, Joe! Isn't that true, Murray?"

"My part is. About Joe I offer no unpaid prognostications."

"Unpaid prognostications?" Joe burbled. "I'll take an unpaid ride in Murray's tin lizzie! 'Five cents please, before stepping aboard.' "

No ruffling Murray, but Naomi was getting good and fed up with the humor. "If you want to be so generous with rides why don't you buy a secondhand wreck with half the running boards eaten away, patch it up from the junkyards the way Murray did and go down seven in the morning Sundays to make it shine? And gas isn't free either."

"Ha ha ha—not even to you. And if air wasn't free my buddy'd quit breathing—ha ha ha! But to have his own girl friend of six full weeks' standing cough up a nickel before she hops into his auto—ha ha ha!"

What was the answer to that?

Murray's golden mustache massaged Naomi's white throat, "Good discipline for you cutie, huh?" and Naomi's eyes swooned.

Ouch—the little guy upstairs landed Danny a right hook to the brain. Maybe with food . . . "Ma home?"

Naomi murmured with that guy still in her neck, "Family gathering at Uncle Frank's, he sent the car for her. You should see his Packard," Naomi giggled, "it's like a funeral."

"Eats gas," her swain muttered.

On the sofa jolly Joe decided to join in the fun too and moved in for close work with Sarah, so Danny—he had had to fall in love with a dodger—made himself scarce. In the kitchen the icebox was full, but he had no idea what he wanted.

But Sarah squirmed free of Joe and jumped up. "Joe, put something on the Victrola."

"You're standing."

Sarah sat down.

Joe laughed, "What I go through for love," and went to crank the machine.

"Here's a penny," Sarah told Murray, "gimme a cigarette."

Murray busy with Naomi waved the penny aside and passed Sarah the pack. She recklessly inhaled, but God was satisfied with a couple of coughs and didn't prevent the tobacco from going to her head instantly. Imagine the luck, so many times alone here and Danny running out or no Danny. Then bring Joe once out of despair—and despair!

"Danny—" she called drunkenly, and he came back from the kitchen. "Hello Danny."

She offered him her best heart-shaped smile, but—"You don't look well, Sarah"—he only noticed how flushed she was.

"Gee thanks, Danny."

"Sure you're not feverish?" he could sympathize, the way he himself felt.

"Yes, I have a fever, but it'll pass, or at least I think it'll pass. Or else I'll die—or live."

Ah care not
Like knights of old . . .

With the eyes pained and the fingers snapping Joe foxtrotted over to retrieve the girl friend.

Who gets rich . . . and piles up the gold,
Ah just wanna . . . get the girl and be
Ha–a–a–a–appy. . . .

Sarah was crushing her cigarette against an ashtray—"One puff," Murray took time out from petting, "and you're finished?"—for both hands free for fat boy, so how sick could she be? Danny beat it to give in to his headache, although once you gave in that little guy really pummeled you. The darkness was nice, and the cool pillow, but Jesus there was that old tune throbbing—bad as "Bananas"—he used to play on his uke.

"Reisel," he whispered, "my head hurts. . . ."

Sarah turning to dance with Danny bumped into Joe. What did you have to do with that dopey doll, nail him down? She knew she shouldn't, but she went after him this time.

"Hey," Joe called, "where you going?"

"Oh Joe, to the express to Brighton Beach."

Murray hee-hawed, for once the laugh was on Joe. But good simple Joe, you could hear him laughing loudest. Sarah felt her way through the dark hall, she poked her ashamed shameless head into unlighted rooms, and wouldn't she have followed Danny into his bedroom if the door hadn't been closed?

12

REISEL SAID, "DULL!" THE FORELADY IN TRAINING, WITH Danny her afternoon nose rag—so *she* thought. His sales mornings taking snot from customers were plenty for him. But his former beloved was chockful of complaints, all aimed at his solar plexus.

On top of which from his first day as salesman he'd been blessed with a beautiful cold. The whole day long his nose ran, he sniffled, and his head felt like somebody else's, a balloon anchored by mistake to his shoulders. To cap the disgust he had Abie and Mikey his stock clerk dummies. Nearness made their heart grow fonder. They packed cartons but their eyes followed the forelady like cats after a bird. Why not, the way she tossed that flame of hair off her forehead while she tucked straw around lamps she'd just crated? The face, the firm-muscled arms with sleeves up in June, the shirtwaist filling as she leaned—that camouflage drove the two schlemiels crazy. But this birdie was a hawk with sharp talons. She twisted a glare at them and their scared peepers popped back in what passed for their heads.

Still they were lucky. They'd never learn the way he'd learned.

Reisel hit Danny again with her "Dull!" as if she'd missed him the first time.

"You asked for id," he reminded her as coolly as you can when your nose is totally clogged.

"For what?"

"The job."

"The job? The lamps are dull, not the job. For my own home I should prefer a more decorative lamp, hand-painted, the shade at least. Last night I sketched a design. Would you like to see it?"

Danny stared at that businesslike face that turned you into a goose egg. "What's wrong with brass lamps? Shine 'em up and they're fine." The forelady de luxe muttered something. "Are you speakig to me?" Danny stood up to her. "I can't hear you."

"Never mind. I shall speak to Naomi. . . . Wrist-danglers!" she gave it to the goggle-eyed helpers. "Do you expect me to do all of your tasks?" She viciously hammered a box shut. And she was fast, three short weeks and she was twice as fast as those dimwits.

Reisel the forelady was good at her job.

As Danny the salesman was punk at his.

Frederick Stewart Inc., bastards all, had been that A.M.'s mouthful. The lamp buyer McLeod kept Danny cooling his feet in McLeodland—a carpety dusk spotted with lamplight, where sun and air were unknown. A pink and white doll, cute, flowery in a bright summer print—your heart reached out to her—must have been furnishing the honeymoon nest, clicking lamps on and off a few aisles away in the hush. With the help of Miss Rooney the sales clerk the girl stuck herself with a fancy brass lemon of cupids pawing down at some nippleless nymphs. Then Miss Rooney with the straw hair and the freckles came back and took care of the hush while Danny kept checking his timepiece.

"Mr. McLeod's a handsome one, isn't he?" Miss Rooney tittered. "A Galway boy, with that hair and jaw. Now you, O'Share, I'll bet your family's from County Kildare."

"Yeah," Danny worried his watch, "Kildare on the Dnieper."

Did that set her off giggling!

"Dnya, Dnya, dnya, didn'ya wha? Why didn't ya?" Full of sound—to quote his former beloved quoting her quotes—and signifying absolute nothing. "If somebody invited me to go stepping—"semi-hysteria—"not mentioning names . . . I might even say yes."

If it were just a job, say like Rapid Transit when he was a kid, he would have skedaddled fast—and Stewart's could keep their lamp department and carpets and whole goddam seven cavernous stories, elevators included. But being one third of Quality Lamps you stood there taking that nonsense. He actually forced himself, on the sly, to jot Miss Rooney's name in his notebook to flatter her with on his next call.

McLeod finally let him into the office, yeah, a broth of a boy that McLeod, the Galway sheik with the manly jaw and the pale eyes that looked in any direction but yours. Danny stared at the son of a bitch while McLeod accepted phone calls and reviewed Babe Ruth's yesterday's homers with a fellow clown who stuck in his noodle when Danny was talking (but just on business). Then McLeod jumped up and disappeared altogether. In the end McLeod gave the Quality Lamps literature a flick of the finger and lied he'd call in his order when ready. And Danny had to say thank you.

Between his cold and McLeod's stinking cigar, Danny stumbled not only blinded but choked into the sunlight and crowds. He couldn't breathe, he tried to swallow with a throat cut in half, he went cold in the heat. . . . In a lunch counter mirror the guy who looked the way Danny felt turned out to be Danny.

That was just the beginning.

His greasy spoon chop meat must have been peppered with glass. In Lewin's Lamps off Herald Square that unhealthy stuff ground around in his gizzard while he ground out his spiel to . . . Miss Lewin? with a face like a heavyweight pug and as tough. Danny turned Quality catalog pages and Miss Lewin kept one agate eye on who came in the door and the other on her salesman down front.

She gave Danny an order and he almost dropped dead.

And outside he almost was killed. Trolley cars clanged over the yellow-soaked cobblestones, trucks rumbled by and taxis barking *geruga.* Danny made a dash into that tumult and a spasm of pain through his crotch doubled him up in the path of a pair of nyaaing rearing truck horses. A red bulbous teamster with his fist clenched on his whip gave Danny plenty of hell.

How long Danny sat slumped on a bench beside old geezers and derelicts in the Herald Square traffic island, he didn't know. But at the factory, "Late," Reisel commented, "and therefore I could not find the Humboldt Jones invoices I had not been told of." Punchy Danny heard himself say he was sorry, but the forelady wasn't concerned with his sorrows. "You may do as you please after all since this is your business firm not mine. Still I should not bear the blame."

Home Danny flopped into bed, enjoyed a perfect night's sleep, and woke feeling as if he'd just run fifty miles. Had he caught a disease from the whores, with his heavy lids, bitter tongue and thighs like lead? Sure, in the looking glass, in his checked flannel suit, white collar, striped shirt and brown knitted tie you saw the picture of health, but what did that prove? They spruce up corpses too.

"Selling agrees with him," Naomi observed over breakfast. "Look at that suntan."

"He looks peaked to me," Ma had to go say. "Are you sure you're well?"

"Last legs, Ma."

So they thought he was kidding. The trolley rattled uptown through late spring sunshine. And he? He huddled at the window, cold and clammy as winter, watched gray slide by outside, and wished he never had to get off.

At Vandervaart's Fifth Avenue, Share the intruder smiled to the buyer in full war paint Miss Salisbury and opened his sales pitch with a yawn he'd never expected. Grab your kisser, apologize: no use—big insult, and she lost no time swinging the tomahawk to get even.

"Your line is so ugly!"

He delivered his textbook grin and tried to hold onto his temper, "You'll find that customers like them," but his goddam voice trembled.

She forced a yawn, wise guy. "Excuse me," she obnoxiously smiled, "it must be the hour."

With his blood banging he raged past counters.

"Hey dummy— Hello dummy—"

Danny felt for his fly—buttoned—and just flicked his eyeballs toward the unmentionable salesgirl in the unmentionables department with her looks and bare arms and charming Neanderthal humor. If you could screw her right there on the carpeting he would have shut her mouth for her gladly. As it was he gave another flick of the eyeballs for a floorwalker to report her to, but locate one of those when you want him. Danny flung forward to escape that sixth story cave.

"God are you fast and furious—"

Big girl blue in Vandervaart uniform, after him? He perked up. "Miss Salisbury change her mind?"

"Miss who? Do you deny that you're Danny Share?"

The electric light dawned—it couldn't be, but it was—on Carrie Baum, with the same satirical eye and the light brown hair still bobbed like a boy's but she'd stopped looking boyish. All of a sudden she'd developed a shape, slim, true, but with curves here and there, plus a rich smear of red where Carrie's lips always used to be pale and stretched thin for a wisecrack. He said her name, grabbed her hands and, since the tilt of her face seemed to suggest it, placed a kiss on those lips.

First she kissed, then she asked, "You are Danny Share? I haven't kissed you promiscuously? Ssh," she smirked, "don't laugh so loud," she looked over her shoulder, "if that floorwalker sees me it's curtains. I've got to get out of here, can you give me employment?"

"I—"

"Not this second, I have to run back. Tonight—write this down—lucky 7 Cornelia Street, apartment two B. And don't get ideas because I live in the Village."

"My sister lives in the Village."

"You noble youth, God dropped you down out of heaven. And you don't answer when called. I like that."

"Was that you calling me dummy?"

"Dummy? I called you Danny. Oy, that floorwalker's in Corsets already. Eight o'clock sharp."

She blew him a kiss and, though he reached after her, slipped away.

Jesus—in the flood of Fifth Avenue sunlight all his ailments were gone!

But three more morning calls and all his ailments were back. Sure you could blame the sore throat on wasted breath, but sick and tired don't vanish one minute and pop up the next if it's just a cold. You pay for your fun. Who needed a date tonight? With the disease he might have, he wasn't entitled to so much as a kiss.

Yet he wanted kisses, gee his heart ached for them. Such luck, God-sent you would suppose, to have run into Carrie. If only he didn't have . . .

whatever he had. All his life he'd loathed playboy stuff, he'd shunned it like poison—and this was the payoff?

Underneath he didn't really believe he was that sick. He took care and ordered what Childs' called the businessman's and he called the business-girl's sliced chicken platter for lunch. After the meal he was ready to eat, but at least he didn't have Cancer the Crab in his belly like yesterday. So all he had to do was keep the old legs in motion.

For that the no sales afternoon was an improvement on the no sales morning. The afternoon customers wouldn't bother to listen, and the last prospect Gorson of Gorson Brothers yawned in his face to give the day perfect balance.

This couldn't go on. At the shop Danny asked Reisel what about her hand-painted shades scheme.

The joy, the excitement! "Original imitations!" An outsider would have imagined the girl's prince had arrived.

Synagogue, Shakespeare and lampshades were her big moments. Compare Carrie with this, green valley with Death Valley. Had he been on the wrong railroad track! Jesus, only give him his health!

The forelady cleared the end of the shipping table nearest the miserly daylight seeping into the joint, and—"I did not show these to Naomi since you did not approve"—laid out illustrations. Chinese, Greek, Persian—variations were endless and no designer to pay since you copied the ancients! She admired red tulips, plum blossoms and green or blue waterfalls while he stared at her bent body and felt like giving her a tulip and waterfall she'd never forget. She turned, his face kept stony hard—and you think she cared? She saw her product. Too bad she wasn't born twins, she could have also picked up in sales where Jack Berger'd left off. Nor—"Though I happen to be an excellent artist, as you see," slight titter, "since I have drawn these myself"—were artists required, merely copyists, with her to direct them.

Twins? Triplets minimum.

"You mean we should send Leah out selling too?"

The forelady ever quick on the uptake reproached him, "Be proud of your work, Daniel," but sweeter than honey—since whatever she wanted she got.

Did this in Reisel seem ambitious? So what's wrong with ambition? Step on a face or so, no omelets without eggs, and Reisel was an honorable girl, a good loyal employee. Naomi, Reisel tittered, was very conservative, which was no more than wise—for the most part. (So much for I did not show these to Naomi because you did not approve. Still why not flatter the boss?) "But risk nothing gain nothing," the forelady said, "not that this is truly a risk."

Blame on genius okay.

Genius likewise knew how to keep mum, sitting in Naomi's office with modest eyes through Danny's intro that gave full credit where credit was due. Reisel spoke only when she was spoken to—self-effacing, catch on?—and let Danny and Leah do all the pushing. Naomi—sure thing—resisted, but Danny's yawn stories, Leah yawning "He's right," and the half-empty order book meant they had to do something. Tastes change. Maybe there'd been more to Gable the bust than the depression and Gable. Eventually Naomi gave in, they trooped out, and Reisel merrily discarded the modesty.

"Test me a little in the machine department, where your fine fumbling machinist Marshak tries to screen information from me which I learn anyway!" Limp rag Share hung for a second, and what do you know—she had the nerve to clamp her hand on his forehead. "You have a fever and must go home to bed. I am a doctor! . . . Golda—" she called, but luckily the grind and wheeze of fumbling Marshak's machine drowned her out.

Now Danny really felt like a hospital case, sweat iced his temples. If he only could have fired her on the spot, never seen her again! And the wizard, she stood there mind-reading, with her patented martyred pity in handcuffs expression. But business before displeasure. He aimed his thumb toward Marshak—"Ladies first"—over there at the lathe. Vase bores, chasings, finishes: Marshak had never been anyone's gem but had he always been this lousy without Danny noticing? Danny glared up at skinny Marshak and asked him. Marshak waved his arms, blustered and defended bad work.

"What, I'm on the outside breaking my back trying to sell and you in the shop here undermining me? You're fired!"

And instantly the drab sparrowy Mrs. Marshak and the innumerable small Marshaks in their lord and master's Rutgers Street castle rose to haunt Danny—never mind that Marshak's murderous look was for the forelady, not him.

But you couldn't beat the forelady. She suggested an opportunity for improvement and saved Marshak his job—not that Marshak loved her any the better for it. Danny certainly didn't for being saved from the consequences of his own bad temper. He was entitled to no Reisel on off hours, wasn't he? Where did it say his grandmother had to live in Reisel's house so he had to visit there? He left the forelady in full charge—exactly as planned by Reisel—and pointed his heavy breathing toward Norfolk Street. Summer sun, straw hats, the pavements booming, and no Grandma in the window? Gittel in a flapper print opened the door, rolled her eyes, stretched up and kissed him.

"I'm playing the secret agent pisha-paysha, join us."

The little old girl skipped back to Grandma's room where the cards and Grandma were on the bed. "Doesn't Gitteleh look nice today, Danneleh, in the new dress Reisel bought her?" Grandma said.

Aw, Christ, come on, how can you hate Reisel? So he played the two of them an hour of pisha-paysha. And now that he'd put his foot down on where Grandma lived, the next step was to find out whether he himself was dead or alive. Embarrassing though to ask a strange sawbones Do I have something liable to melt my brain even softer than it is normally. He hustled over to the library, pulled down Dr. Britannica and like a damn fool read up on symptoms. As you'd figure, the news was so-so, some symptoms he had and some he hadn't. But the minus gave you no comfort, and the plus—like this elephant weight you wished you could sleep off in . . . Carrie's loving arms and wake up cured from—scared you ten times as much as before.

Outside of a chronic broken leg his old man used to enjoy and for all Danny knew or cared maybe still did, the Share family didn't deal much with doctors. Danny ended in the East Side Dispensary in a crowd of infants in misery, their trumpet-lunged mothers, and old ones lucky the battle was nearly over but still in there struggling. Then he sat seething mad with the other cattle with medical histories, but surprised himself and stuck it out to the doctor. This guy could have been first cousin to the school doctor in Orange who rushed an aspirin to that kid who'd slipped off the elevated running track in the gym and been instantly killed. A glance at the shabby mustache consulting a watch and Danny knew he'd wasted his time. Burning red he spit out what bothered him, and on the third stab this medical man was lucky enough to strike blood for a test. Then he looked Danny over the way Danny looked over the funny papers and he murmured he didn't think that Danny had anything serious. Neither did Danny think he had anything serious, but he felt as if he was dying and he wanted to know! But why talk and let 'em hear your voice shake with anger. He kept quiet.

First Avenue and the rows of windowpanes shining in twilight were a relief after the babies, carbolic, old age and sickness, yet go try to enjoy it. At the same time—he was that hungry—he could have taken a bite out of one of those truck horses clomping by. Dying do you have any appetite?

Help!

He ducked into a candy store phone booth, searched for Carrie's number in each of the eleven pockets of his vest, pants and jacket, not to mention in his little address book, found it in the pocket he'd started with, and offered to treat her to his troubles and supper.

He didn't have to hunt for lucky 7 in the narrow wind of Cornelia Street in the dusk, Carrie was downstairs waiting.

"So tell Aunt Carrie, what kind of troubles, outside of heartbreak, loneliness and can't we sleep together tonight?—to which the answer is no."

"I feel better already," Danny laughed, and he did, "but that wasn't the question."

"Well you haven't changed," she tucked her arm under his, "and that's one welcome change."

There was a kind of big city wolf in kid gloves whose specialty was to strum on your heartstrings, Carrie explained, and a couple of years of them tended to put a country girl on the defensive. Danny said she didn't have to tell him, he happened to have one in the family by marriage. Then, Carrie went on, she'd made the mistake of setting up light housekeeping with Shirley Shine directly from graduation on the lawn of Orange High School. She should have known better, what with the sheep's eyes that wolverine Shirley used to cast upon Danny all over the place.

"All over what place?"

"You were a year ahead of us so I grant you maybe not in the classrooms. Only in the study hall, lunchroom and corridors."

"A quiet girl, a brunette, kind of plain?"

"Some quiet. She was only a chicken farmer's daughter, but she sure knew her onions and yeggs."

Sheep's eyes—how do you like that?—and even now Danny was dim about which one Shirley Shine used to be. But Carrie informed him that Shirley hadn't been dim at 7 Cornelia Street. There Shine had shone, like a red light in the window. Luckily Shirley beat it to Paris six months ago to trail down some Bolshevik lemon who was learning to his sorrow that free love wasn't necessarily free.

Danny grinned, "Jealous?"

"I Carrie Baum jealous of a long drink of water who rippled lies into your ear?"

"You mean she was tall?"

"He was tall, stupid. And I must admit, considering—lest you get too conceited—the assortment of crumbs and other stale bread I've come across in New York, it was a relief bumping into you this morning, even hurtling through lingerie with a face on you like a gorilla's."

"One of my regular expressions to maintain zero sales."

"Then I'd hate to see the other expressions."

"Or else," it seemed funny now, "I yawn at the buyer."

Walking along Carrie smiled up into this clean-jawed blue-eyed boy's smile. For the first time since the lousy night she'd caught that fucken Bolshevik her alleged boy friend Schiffstein in bed with her flatmate and alleged best friend Shirley Shine, the Village dusk with store lights going on glittered like a platinum bracelet.

"You smile at them that way, Danny, and they don't buy?"

"Actually," and in violation of Reisel's advice he made a face at the thought of his work, "I hoist my mouth higher."

"Hey watch out for your ears! What a salesman, no wonder—"

He assured Carrie he'd been kidding. But—depressing—maybe that was how he affected customers. On top of that, he was lost. But a splash of yellow among brownstones and he was found—only the red checked tablecloths suggested spaghetti and he'd had Rumanian shell steak in mind. Still, spaghetti, shell steak—food is food. So, "This is it," he lied.

Besides the spaghetti they featured illegal wine with service in teapots in honor of prohibition. The dago red curdled his throat but branched warmly into his chest and pleasantly rose to his head.

Carrie said, "Wine? Wine's dangerous." She sipped some. "Say," she challenged him, "you don't happen to be another city slicker? Started out in this joint before and had luck with the ladies?"

"Pot luck, but not here. My sister mentioned a place, but to tell you the truth Carrie, I couldn't locate it."

She beamed, "Honest John at my service," toasted, "Good luck to us, Danny," and poured the first refill into their teacups.

Danny's health improved by leaps and bounds, or maybe by gulps and swallows. Since Carrie wanted to know, through the happiest haze of her bare arms and throat, her firm chin, her red lips, her breasts in a beige knitted blouse, Danny told her all the trade secrets of lamps: proportion, color, design, durability—and they all took on double meanings. He had to chuckle over his first excitement talking shop. And he let this exciting . . . exciting girl whose oval face he wanted to place kisses on instruct him in business in a voice in the distance, though they were close enough across the small table for a musky armpit warmth of hers to work him up too. His sister's textbooks from the Postgraduate library? Forget them, just . . . Serious, he had to be a serious salesman, she was a serious saleslady. Woolly fuzz clung to the curve of her breasts and down the curve of her belly, so that as she asked him, and then that scent, asked him—

"—or even smiles, unless you're amused which is doubtful, if the creeps I have to deal with are any criterion . . . Danny," she patted him on the cheek, "are you listening? Be alert! Remember, you used to say that to me, coaching me in sines and cosines?"

"And you, and you, and you used to say what a . . . lousy teacher I was."

"Did I say that? I must have been sober. You taught me better than the math teacher. Remember him, that Mr. Copeland who always had us doing examples to his stopwatch? Well my father was happy to tell me that last winter the capitalist tool lost so much playing stocks he hanged himself in his own toilet!"

"Did he?" Danny eased a not so tasty twirl of spaghetti into his mouth and emptied his teacup again. "In the toilet, that . . . dignified Mr. Copeland?"

"Yeah, that typical dignified Orange New Jersey anti-Semite, who looked down on us grubby Jews. Money makes the world go round, kiddo."

"Sure, but . . . to hang yourself for it? He never hanged himself because he stank as a teacher—"

"Let him go hang," Carrie said, "it's your money that we're interested in."

"You a gold-digger, Carrie?"

"Yeah, that's why I had a boy friend a Communist, and what a mess he turned out to be—and all your fault too."

"My fault? If he was my fault, I'll make amends. Did I know him? He give me as reference?"

"No, you treasure. Your relations, even by consort—I mean your Uncle Willie's . . . friend, Anna—"

"My aunt."

"Yeah, your aunt. Let somebody ask her for your address and you'd think they were staging a raid on the Philadelphia mint. And then— The big town's full of rats but there are a few long-tail ones in the country also. Imagine, sending me, shy Carrie Baum, to stammer at some stranger's door in a pigsty in Hester Street! No wonder I was driven to desperation and that bum of a Bolshevik Schiffstein."

"Hello Carrie," he took her face in his hands, "that was my pigsty, we moved," and he didn't hurry the kiss. "I'm sure sorry I missed you the first time!"

Learn from your mistakes was her Carrie Baum's motto, and take it easy on love at first sight after Ted Schiffstein. But this Danny Share lapping up your sales tips along with the wine—he was a find she should never have lost! The weaker sex, she'd stupidly let Ted bowl her over at that Young Workers' League dance she and Shirley Shine the still waters kid had blundered into, real hicks, and she hadn't bothered to look Danny up till too late.

Notwithstanding, fair exchange is no robbery. At Union Square she'd run into Schiffstein's six feet of handsome with shiny dark hair and surface refinement and he'd run into her juicy size ten.

"Are you affiliated?" Ted Schiffstein had asked while they were dancing.

"With the farmer," she'd cracked. "I'm his daughter."

"How do you do?" He'd slid that athlete's size palm to lower down on her spine. "I'm the traveling salesman."

And that's all Schiffstein had been, the bullshit Bolshevik with his united front from below. But the effect he'd had on her epidermis she'd been careful to give him not one single inkling of, that glib reasoner fast with the hands. When the night school paid him for the eight hours a week he condescended to teach, he brought you to speakeasies to drown resistance en route to the pelvic regions while he told you what Marx really meant. You'd shoo him off, he'd gaze at you hurt and soulful.

She never let him into the house unless Shirley was home.

Plenty of laughs but, looking back, plenty of gut-grinding too and a year and a half thrown out of the window.

Short of a marriage proposal he'd tried everything on her. Yet she'd told him plainly enough. Any time he was ready to put the Revolution in mothballs, pass his exams and settle down as high school teacher of French, she was ready to settle down with him.

"And maybe," Schiffstein had finally sneered, "you want me to sprout a mustache like a comb, grow short, and change my name to Joe Silver?"

"Comrade Joe Silver you forgot to say, Comrade," she could work her twist in with a smile.

Because that little temper of his had represented pure jealousy. One of

Schiffstein's strategies aimed at whetting a young lady's appetite was to go underground now and then. Carrie's countermaneuver was don't let grass from underground grow under your feet, and among others she'd dated poor stumpy Joe the high school teacher of German with the thick black hair and mustache and hopeless eyes in between. But Joe at least was a genuine Bolshie, not like Ted and Daddy Moishe. They shot union workers in West Virginia, Joe's heart ached. Union workers shot a few scabs in Ohio, Joe couldn't eat. A black one got lynched in Georgia somewhere and Joe became sick. Not that Joe was a humanitarian, far from it. The only question for Joe—since obviously J.P. Morgan & Company, Standard Oil and Dupont weren't tranquilly awaiting another bomb explosion on Wall Street—was in which direction the guns should be pointed. But without warning one summer night in the park Joe grabbed her arms and proposed, so you could conclude that *Das Kapital* was not in conflict with marriage.

You turned down Joe, the sad eyes looked sadder. But Schiffstein schemed to get even. Complaints poured in by mail from Jersey about Daddy Moishe's latest tenth-rate do-nothing housekeeper—that she was also cut-rate that Bolshevik neglected to mention—so Carrie made a trip to the farm on a sunshiny Sunday to see what was what. How Daddy's face had brightened, as always, in triumph at the return of the prodigal—then fell: no suitcases. Still, you could have played tick-tack-toe on the furniture dust. Carrie fired that biddy while fearless Moishe hid himself out in the henhouses, after which Carrie had to squander most of the rest of the day off locating a Bridget in town at going prices—which weren't that high, as she didn't fail to point out to Moishe. Even so she got home too early—not that it mattered. Whatever the hour Schiffstein would have been sure to be there just as he was: bare-assed on top of her squirming flatmate Shirley Shine on the sofa. Why the sofa—Shine had had a bed—if impresario Schiffstein hadn't been staging a public performance?

Back from a week or two of dead silence Schiffstein used to smirk, "Party business," and Carrie'd never been sucker enough to ask how was business or which party. To her the female Union Square misfits you saw at the clubroom in their misfitting rags were in the same class as the prostitutes a block further east.

But this? He was hopeless.

She'd stood arms folded while Schiffstein put on clothes and dropped feeble sarcasms. Shine, even after he left, had simply kept sitting there with her breasts slightly sagging and her eyes on her toenails.

Disgusting!

"I can't help it, I love him."

What had that ineffectual supposed Carrie did, hate him?

What a catch a no-nonsense Ted would have been—a college man!—to rub Daddy's nose in. A daydream had been the weak grin Moishe'd produce at her happy news after the black years he'd prophesied for filial ingratitude! Imagine, walking out and inconveniencing Moishe, with so many marital prospects right there in Orange he had no fears she ever would marry. He'd actually chanted don't look for his sympathy the day she'd crawl back from the bums she was so anxious for in New York.

"Well," he'd asked, her first visit to Orange, "has Prince Charming emerged out of the sewers?"

"He's emerged and blood-red!" she'd enjoyed needling her Moishe.

And that Shirley Shine had the crust to whine about love! Lie down when they push and spread your legs far apart and that's love—yeh yeh. And men will respect you—sure sure. Flaming youth—horseshit! She Carrie Baum was flaming all right—and with proofs best known to herself. Meeting Danny again, that sweetheart with the American nose, beautiful blues and wavy hair, she flamed in Vandervaart's and she flamed over wine and spaghetti. But in contrast to Schiffstein the weasel whose one thought was squeeze into the coop, this straight from the shoulder kid hearkened to you as to a voice from Mt. Sinai.

What did Danny think, it was his fault they didn't snap at his product? Inventory reduction—and it had been going on for a year and a half! She'd gotten that straight from the horse's face she meant mouth, Miss Grime the lingerie buyer with the bounce of peppery hair and a mind equally fluffy. She Carrie Baum had clasped her hands in sheer admiration of that Gentile head: so *that* was why they'd been carrying only popular sizes and numbers! The customers who'd asked for unpopular sizes and walked away sore Carrie of course never referred to when Miss Grime was around. These buyers, see, they know all—like God—and they can't be mistaken: go talk to a wall.

Never inform 'em only remind 'em. Above all never correct 'em.

Get it?

But no cause to feel like a chicken tossed in the pond. Did Danny originate the depression? Why when hard times hit two years ago after the war didn't Cohen's boxes where Carrie was bookkeeper de luxe and sole office staff fold up like one of Cohen's boxes? Boy did they love her there, almost too much: especially Cohen. Just the same she'd been reduced to passing for Lutheran to peddle her talents to Vandervaart's where kosher is poison. Did her daddy crow over her, "Denying your faith, huh?" Moishe the atheistical hypocrite. "What do you mean?" she'd cracked right back at her Moishe. "I am a victim of the capitalist system just like you, ain't I? Except with me it's just temporary." What Daddy Moishe really wanted was for her to move back to Orange and take care of him. Obviously a little white lie didn't interfere with your faith. She was a Jew and proud of it!—and religiously Rosh Hashonah, Yom Kippur and the anniversary of Mother's death the first of December she lit a memorial candle. Even so, Vandervaart's had put her on for the Christmas rush only, and she would have been gone years ago if not for her immediate intelligent yeses that had made Miss Grime see what a bargain they had. Still and all, she Carrie Baum a mere saleslady?

She'd started by testing Danny, see, and he'd passed A-1. He really was an illuminations expert. All he had to do was be patient, remember her hints, and work his points in—minus the jawbreaking smiles. In fact smiling was frowned upon. "Your strong point's sincerity," she breathed in his face.

Sincerity did make life with the customers easier, but the customers sincerely gave him very few orders. And while the East Side Dispensary gang labeled him a picture of health, his body didn't fit into the picture. He consulted Dr. Britannica again more than once and rooted out wasting diseases, all that you wanted. Lungs trickled away, marrow dissolved, heart crusted up, and you croaked. Except—you half believed it half didn't—it was no gag. Yet asleep, or with Carrie, you forgot you were sick.

Go figure.

Business stank so anyway that he took a week off in August when Carrie took hers, woke well the first seconds after the alarm clock went off, and then health and business stretched him like dead in the heat the tan shade of the awnings didn't help much. Meanwhile milk wagon horses clopped by cheerfully and happy kids shouted downstairs in Tompkins Square Park. But at breakfast Ma didn't mention his health, so how far gone could he be?

And one foot out of the door—with the green shaggy trees, early mothers, half-naked toddlers, baby carriages, women with shopping bags, working stiffs crossing the park—health poured into him like the sun from the hot fuzzy sky! One of those dames on a bench glanced at him, he flipped her a wink and she blushed and smiled.

Killer Dan!

Near the kiosk blazing in sunlight at the Astor Place subway entrance with the press of bodies shuffling down to the hole waited his special body with her breasts mouth-wateringly molded in a black bathing suit underneath a white bare-armed blouse. A red band flamed in Carrie's sun-shot hair, and when she saw him she didn't move a muscle except for that faint come-hither smile. Her leisurely good-morning kiss stirred up dirty looks among the wilted already and sheet-white hard workers—too bad for them!

Danny transferred the picnic basket from her arm to his, bumped a few hard workers with it going downstairs and gathered a few more dirty looks. A hot sour trainful of protuberant bodies and offspring also on their way to the beach went crashing through Brooklyn. But at Nevins Street he and Carrie slid into seats, and arm in slippery arm with her, Danny pleasantly, hornily drowsy massaged Carrie's thigh screened by the basket and towels while now and then she'd tickle his ear lobe with a dart of her tongue. And in the green foam-flecked Brighton swells he caught Carrie at a distance from other swimmers and splashers and held her close chest-high in water. She reached down like in olden days at the farm and flicked that torpedo bumping her belly.

"Suffer," she twinkled at Danny, "till June 1923."

"And then?" he teased her.

"And then," she shoved him glubbing down underwater, "last one to the blanket's a rotten egg."

Carrie turned out a tuna sandwich on roll with cool as a cucumber slices that turned you into a wolf.

Too bad, Carrie dreamily munched, he hadn't happened to find her last April say. They could have been making the summer still hotter now. She gave Danny a tuna fish kiss in the oval of shade of the umbrella he'd rented and happily draped a towel over the sudden tent in his one piece bathing suit.

"Why wait?" Danny cracked.

"Oh from age thirteen I've taken June bride for granted."

"With a bum for a husband?"

"Bum?"

"As a businessman," he bit into his sandwich, "I'm a flop," cross his heart and hope to be contradicted, "in case I was the groom."

"Bull-oney!"

On flops she was an expert since her childhood with Moishe the flop—correct, her darling daddy! The last family affair Moishe had eaten crow at was the marriage of his niece her cousin Gladys to the doctor Gladys had lassoed with diamonds. Or, to make a short story long, like the sun and the ocean, Uncle Jesse, Daddy's brother, otherwise known as Bowery Diamonds—wholesale only, unless you were a relative, a friend, or brought money—had been celebrating the nuptials of his daughter Gladys and the condemned man Dr. Nate Barasch M.D. Don't forget the M.D.—as if you could. And remember the Dr.

Memory's tricky.

As kids Gladys and Carrie had lived on the same block up in Harlem, and many a sizzling day all the Baums—Mother, Jesse and Moishe, Aunt Milly, she and Gladys, even a big brother or two of Gladys's sometimes—loaded shopping bags full of food and took the Battery boat out to Coney. But of those picnic delights delicately sprinkled with beach sand, guess what made Gladys drool most?

Shoulder chuck.

From Carrie's—those days—thin shoulder. Did that little muttface dog of a cousin take a bite out of her!

What Carrie did in return modesty forbade going into.

But they knew each other, Gladys and Carrie, even better than . . . better than . . .

"Capulet knew Montague?" Danny suggested.

"Gangsters?"

"Yeah," Danny laughed, "gangsters from Shakespeare."

"Even better than—Firpo knew Dempsey!"

Did Danny ever go to the prizefights? Her former fighting Bolshevik used to take her, to the top tier in the Garden, on the theory that it would get her excited. Once it got her so excited she hauled off and gave Schiffstein a good left to the face. That's what she liked about Danny—he was a gent! She and Gladys also used to meet on neutral ground—funerals, weddings, bar mitzvahs—as years passed.

So granted Moishe's a flop—and so what, if you're Gladys and he's your uncle and you have any manners—but never between his varied careers of furrier and farmer had he been a glazier. Therefore at your wedding reception as Madam Physician, why look through Moishe's daughter—yes, her, Carrie Baum—as if she were window glass?

Carrie in such situations knew how to show the opposition her back which at this late date, while it still would be bitten, at least wouldn't have actual fillets removed. But oh Moishe, poor Daddy Moishe blurted, "Gladys, you know your cousin Carrie—?"

Gladys gave her face like sour cream standing too long an extra curdle, perked her bird head here and there and flew after juicier worms than Uncle Moishe with his stunned silly grin. . . . Danny with outraged fists wished he had Gladys here under the umbrella now. But naah, Carrie went on, Gladys never was that important. Carrie'd comforted Daddy Moishe with an hors d'oeuvre, a pat and a wink, and he'd puffed up as if nothing had happened, her pouter pigeon, and demanded why the commiseration.

Why not the commiseration? Worried-eyed Uncle Jesse had always had a single idea in that narrow shrewd Baumian skull of his: to get rich. And Uncle Jesse the watchmaker did get rich on others' joys, including Moishe's who'd bought Mother's engagement ring wholesale through Jesse. In those days Jesse only took a commission from dealers he knew, his steppingstones to his own diamond business. Gold sprang at his fingers. While Moishe—he himself said so and it was never denied—who used to match pelts and the fur coat seemed created not made, transformed himself to a Socialist and later a Bolshevik midwife for chickens. After the armistice the good wartime egg prices sank and Moishe complained.

"You want them to resume firing, pacifist," Carrie'd teased him, "so eggs'll go up?"

Moishe's growl had been (Carrie smiled), "The system is rotten!"

"Not so rotten for Jesse."

"If you believe in exploiting women and children!"

During the crashes of '03 and '07 Jesse the exploiter did ruthlessly tax his sons most of their pay and send Aunt Milly out sewing. In Carrie's little Baum group the Tomer side—meaning Mother—had all the guts. Mother sick as she was later on could reminisce with a smile about the man-sized hard times in 1903. She'd gone to the shop then, put Carrie to play on the floor with fox heads you could make snap at each other, fired Moishe's assistants because Moishe was too embarrassed to let them go, finished their work and refused to let Moishe give up. The '07 panic you could have put in your eye without blinking, it had been nothing, a light gust to blow away sparrows. But by then Mother hadn't had strength to help, or even to argue, and Moishe'd let himself fail. The pioneer, he'd moved them West—to Orange, New Jersey, and a farm of scared chickens—and he'd known who was to blame.

"Wall Street crooks, with their corners on copper!"

So much as Carrie loved Daddy Moishe, don't talk to her about flops. She knew a flop when she saw one, and she didn't see any under their beach umbrella!

But Jesus, Danny answered her, at Quality Lamps Naomi gloomily sat in the office shuffling papers and losses. Ma was there sewing shades only by courtesy of Leah, who said the old workhorse was happier working so don't dare fire her. Reisel was shipping boy and, with some help from Danny late afternoons, fumbling lathe man in place of Marshak they'd finally had to lay off anyway to save his pay. How much time Reisel had left for perfecting her mechanical skills there at West Street before total eclipse would be hard to say, but if Danny were a gambler outside of card games, believe him Carrie his bet would be sooner rather than later.

Carrie studied a motor launch dazzling the sea between the bright cottony horizon and a green-bearded pier where kids squealed distantly.

"Get me that for my birthday," she said.

"What with, cigarette coupons?"

"Listen, since you're in such a rush," she followed that silver spray, "how about bribing 'em?"

"Bribing who?"

"The department store buyers, who else?" she craftily smiled down at him. "Okay okay don't look so shocked. How do you think Persimmon Simmons from Apex Mills makes an occasional sale to Miss Unmentionable Grime? A twenty dollar bill here, a thirty dollar bill there—you slip it to 'em along with the price list. Ask Kathy Nudnick the secretary—her name is actually Nugent—she's seen them pull that unmentionable stuff when they think no one's looking."

"I just stopped knowing you."

Carrie let Danny have a backhand slap on that hard belly of his.

"But I haven't stopped knowing you, Honest John."

She meant she knew he liked kisses? She plastered him one with a chestful of herself pressing down—and she was right.

A week off only lasts seven days though, and on the seventh day Danny knew why God needed rest: to buck Himself up for blue Monday. Worst of all, after six days of good health Danny woke Sunday with a full day's vacation left, swung out of bed—and flopped right down again with the walls spinning around. In a room of thick August sun he felt himself trembling like winter.

Britannica says euphoria is a well-known TB symptom. And chill sweat, chest pains—he had them all. Yet he wasn't consumptive, he knew he wasn't. He sneaked in a thermometer reading.

Normal.

Jesus!

But TB is night fevers. In his white suit, chocolate tie matching the band on his tilted straw lid, and his face a healthy tan in the mirror he felt fine knock wood, temporarily, for the time being anyway. Ma exclaimed, "Lady killer!" and Naomi stuck with nothing to do for the day until the financial mastermind Murray was through hawking vegetables stared at her knockout of a brother.

In Cornelia Street, "A million dollars!" Carrie appraised him, and he could raise her a couple of million for her well filled out organdy print with huge tawny flowers and mantrapping tendrils wickedly twining around her. So up at the Polo Grounds to root for the Babe to hit one into the stands Danny figured what the hell since he and she added up to two million, blew himself to box seats and flipped the usher a quarter while the hoity-toi in the dugout section looked them over wondering who the celebrities were.

"Thought you were filing your petition of bankruptcy, big shot," Carrie said.

"We ain't begging bread just yet," Danny let her know who was boss.

But what an afternoon! High into the air perfumed with mown grass the Babe smacked one with two on—and did Danny and Carrie scream, did they hug one another, did they kiss—and the Yanks whipped the Boston Red Sox 5–2! Danny grabbed a cab afterward and treated Carrie to lobster on 125th Street at Faye's to celebrate.

"I like it," Carrie said, "but why the extravagance?"

"The doomed man enjoyed a hearty last supper."

He told her about his jack-in-the-box waking up act in the morning and she dismissed that symptom without skipping a bite. How many times did that happen, when a fast move confuses your blood stream so it can't tell heads from tails.

Jesus, that Carrie knew the right thing to say!

Then Danny suggested some Tchaikovsky over at Lewisohn Stadium, but Carrie cracked she'd had enough of those Bolsheviks. She chose the bus down Fifth Avenue instead, where she wouldn't have minded owning the Carnegie mansion one bit, though the Clark and Vanderbilt castles also were okay with her. Danny asked what about the Forty-second Street Library, she could get rid of the books. But she only laughed and planted those winding tendrils of hers closer against his white suit.

On a bench in Washington Square under a hot shaggy tree labeled *American Elm* Danny took off his jacket and resumed a good hold on Carrie. She'd thought up some sales tips for him—"Don't worry, these are legitimate"—since Monday at the beach. "Never mind business," Danny muttered alongside her ear, but she went right ahead with the sales conference.

Now, she sexily murmured hoarse from the baseball game, here's what he had to do. Buy a map of downtown—which she'd already picked up at a newsstand and happened to have in her purse—and *X* where the customers were. Sure dummy, she moved her lips along his grained cheek while he squeezed her waist, she knew he knew where the customers were. But you put it down on paper, eliminate targets you've been firing at without any hits, and circle new prospects. Then scout the new prospects before you go and swoop down on 'em. Note their price ranges she sighed while Danny's tongue flicked salt sweat off the curve of her throat, see what they carry. Then slug 'em—she smeared a kiss back and forth over his lips—yes slug 'em with the same style that they sell only different, yours has some extra twist that the others don't have. But—again a long kiss and strollers in the park or no strollers he moved in on that small exciting chest of hers—but, and get this: talk up the differences so your product seems new and at the same time doesn't scare 'em. What did he mean Quality Lamps weren't that different from everyone else's? You say they're different—and they become different!

Would you believe that the very next week sales began stirring? They didn't exactly bounce up and foxtrot, but they showed signs of life! Except while they showed signs of life, Danny felt signs of death—eyelids heavy as shingles, legs like pillars, the world's weight on his shoulders. But evenings with Carrie or his pals at the card game or even a visit once in a while to Grandma and he was himself again, pretty much. Terminal days and (knock wood) cured nights? This was a new one even on Dr. Britannica.

Carrie said, "Stick your tongue out," and diagnosed, "Summer cold."

"In September?"

"They hang on like glue. Come kiss me misery. If I also catch it then you'll have company."

She didn't catch it, but how could you accuse her of that?

Yet sales were turning into a joy!

Naomi was leery that this wouldn't keep up, but Danny the newborn confidence kid—no risks, no profits!—was so sure they would that single-handed he revived Reisel's painted shades scheme. Because Carrie said the hand-painted notion she liked, while reserving opinion about the ex-love of his life the concoctress until such time as she could personally cast orbs on this Raisin. P.S., he was positive, Carrie wanted to know, that it *was* the ex-love of his life? How do you like that Carrie dame? Had the surprising catch in his heart about Reisel come out in his voice? Of course he didn't let on and sternly asked did he ask whether that Bolshie was the ex-love of Carrie's life? Carrie said true, but you saw that she had doubts on the subject of Reisel—which kind of flattered him!

Yep, a full day's work fooling Carrie on any subject, though he no more wanted to fool her than himself. She was his girl all right, and they kept proving you can mix business with pleasure. Lunches if he could lug his carcass in time to Vandervaart's from where he happened to be, necking in movie theaters with the weather cooler and cooler, Village strolls: then he'd said, then they would kiss, then the customer'd said. . . .

offer the fat retail vendors exclusive franchise for Quality Lamps, within

Her advice always worked! How did he break into Gamble's? Carrie said a mile radius say—no, half a mile—and maybe they'll bite. The guy at Gamble's gobbled the proposition up hook, line and sinker! Carrie's Fifth Avenue mansions were a comedy routine, but wait. One of these days they'd see where Danny-o the sweet singer'd live! With that order under his belt he marched into Gamble's radio department and treated himself to a big Stromberg-Carlson complete with loudspeaker—forget crystal sets and earphones! The truckmen knocked at the door on Tompkins Square, Ma shook her head they had the wrong flat. That Ma, she was scared of the expensive mahogany sheen even after Danny told her it was hers and good Shabbos!

They turned it on and out poured sound rich as life: "Buy Fletcher's Castoria!" Naomi the anxious big sister even on his dough had to take three or four gulps, but she finally tuned in to "Yes We Have No Bananas" —who needed Victrola records?—and Danny fox-trotted her then one-stepped Ma around the living-room rug.

But the phone—that was more than poor Naomi could swallow. A Saturday afternoon—Naomi'd gone shopping from work—he and Ma watched them wire it up. "My big shot," Ma kissed him smack on the mouth, "with a telephone in the house!" Je-sus, was he proud!

Naomi was on the spot though to pick up the telephone when it rang at the end of his happy 1 A.M. trip home from a million good nights in Carrie's hallway, and to pass him a glance like ice along with the receiver.

But Carrie said, "Good night dear—" ah, sweet—to his hello. . . .

By the time he'd washed up and come humming out of the bathroom he'd forgotten his sister's hard look, only there she was with a dark one. "Watch out," she warned him, "for extravagant girl friends." Now wasn't that stupid, when Carrie was just the opposite? Naomi had never laid eyes on Carrie.

Business kept getting better, and the more it improved the more ideas Carrie had for grabbing more business. Tonight's had been print different price lists for different suckers, each with a hike for the particular item they were most likely to buy. Then suck 'em in with reductions to what looks like a bargain—psychological, see?

How did Carrie dream 'em all up?

Sometimes, she told him, she actually would be asleep and dreaming of Danny—"Never mind the plot, wise guy"—and the action would drift to practical matters, she literally did dream ideas. What did he think, she Carrie Baum used her noodle just for chewing her gum or selling unmentionables for good-for-nothings to drape themselves in who'd had the luck to be born into money or marry it? Know what she wished? She wished she'd been born a man—she'd give this old globe a spin on its axis! That was true, Danny agreed. She was the real salesman, he was nothing but the ventriloquist's dummy.

"Listen sonny boy," she'd wagged him a finger, "to me you can say anything, but never speak words like that to anyone else—even in fun. You are the salesman."

How was that for letting the other guy take the credit, in contrast to the holy act from Kadzyrnye! No, Carrie's status quo as woman was perfect with him, and Jesus whenever good sales and good health came into conjunction he was popping the question!

And his sister had the gall to be disparaging that one? The way Naomi stood poised at the bathroom ready to scrap he had it on the tip of his tongue to give her what's what. But Jesus, she looked so miserable—and he was so happy. He felt . . . sad for her. "What's dough for," he tried reasoning, "if not phones? And," he grinned, "Stromberg-Carlsons?"

But that only prompted a big-sister harangue. Never mind, don't let a sale or two go to your head, they had a phone in the shop, Murray wasn't too proud to call her up there in a pinch, and here in the pinch the candy store on the corner had one. "What I hate most is seeing . . . people . . . twist you around on their little finger."

"But you're nuts," he finally burst out, "and I'll prove it," he fondly patted that worried dollface, "you wait."

Meanwhile late as it was he was overflowing with energy. For before lights out reading in bed *Romeo and Juliet* should have suited his mood, but the dame on the fire escape kept looking more like Reisel than Carrie. So he yawned and quit—and boy could he have used Carrie right now instead of a book!

"So—Naomi's really a good kid—invite her for supper why don't you?" Danny told Carrie after he let her in on the extravagance gag. "And don't forget Murray if you want oil stock tips—from vegetable oils."

Carrie produced a chuckle for the benefit of her special audience and gave Central the number of that telltale telephone. Miss Hatchet Girl picked it up in a hurry considering she was so anti-phone—or was it just anti-Carrie? But the show must go on and a short sweet intro of dying to meet you (you should live so long) led naturally into how about supper here at Cornelia Street next Sunday? And oh was Carrie's Danny boy innocent if his idea of a good kid was this cagy sister who has to consult her brother before saying yes lest a yes . . . compromise him. However, a few more laughs at both ends of the line and it was a date. Flies with sugar not vinegar was Carrie's motto. The swatting takes place later on.

"Satisfied, master?" she plumped herself down on Danny's lap.

More than satisfied.

Naomi met Carrie and Naomi liked Carrie, exactly as Danny had predicted. Naomi liked the muslin curtains, the plants, the five-and-ten sunset over the couch—the whole cute little flat. She stood spellbound in front of the birdcage as if God had just created canaries, and she marveled at Carrie's bright shining kitchen. Carrie winked—"From my housemaid knees—" then amazed Danny's sister with boiled beef and horseradish that duplicated what they cooked at home!

"We're," Carrie assured her, "from the same school of thought."

Murray Canine, excuse Carrie, Kaye she meant, the collar ad dude with the light bumpy hair and oriental eyelids swallowed two free meals at one sitting, lit a cigarette and let them know the time's ripe to buy Western & Pacific—in the works was a Tacoma Beach line! He became slightly concerned when Danny suggested investing in a movie, but Carrie instantly pushed back the throw rugs and smoothed Murray's brow by putting on a Victrola record for dancing.

They danced, they necked, Murray told risqué jokes from his army days and made the girls giggle and blush, Carrie served coffee and strudel ("Of course home baked!")—and Naomi impulsively kissed Carrie goodbye!

Some Carrie, eh?

And whoever was to blame for the upsurge in sales, Quality Lamps turned into a Gehenna of machine noise and shouts again—too much so in fact for Leah's three Village boys labeled Artists they took on to paint shades. Naomi and Reisel quietly replaced the ninnies with nice plain thin girls who sat at a table, dipped their brushes and got the job done. In October Naomi hired more shipping clerks too.

"Let's have five," Leah the Liberal said, "why break backs?"

Danny snarled "What are backs for?" with his personal busted back well in mind.

He enjoyed the further satisfaction of the forelady Reisel's silent disapproval. But a week or two later—he still had more consideration for Reisel's back don't ask him why than she ever would have for his—he said okay, make it five shipping clerks.

And now, with snow caking the streets, they'd had to hire a second drill and lathe man for the first time in history. Heaven—if not for Danny's dreary nine to six plague that made him hate to sit down to sell, it was that damn hard getting up. The fever that he brought home the evenings he tested it was so low—too low to mention without sounding foolish—that if he hadn't felt lousy all day he'd never have known he had a fever.

Summer cold?

No cold at all, Carrie said. You work hard—what's the surprise?—you get tired. Even she Carrie Baum felt slightly knocked out these days with Christmas rush at the store.

Which made sense.

And to cap it all off, the merry eighth selling day before Christmas they loaded rush reorders on Danny such as Jack Berger himself had never brought in! Four P.M. Danny landed limp as a rag—with good reason, right?—in a taxicab and gazed half-dead yet elated at his order book. Wait till Carrie saw this!

"Where to Mac?"

The cabbie's voice was an unpleasant shock.

"Vandervaart's Fifth Avenue I told you."
"You told me nuttin'."
"You hear me the second time?"
"You mean the first time."
"Then get a move on."
Prick.
But Humboldt Jones alone: 125 Number 16s, 150 Number 9s, 24 Number 3s torch style, 250 Number 1 hand-painted Aladdins.
250 Number 1 hand-painted Aladdins!
Then the Bier order, Gamble's, Van Vecht & Co., Brown's . . .
And Reisel got her thrills reading Shakespeare?
On Vandervaart's fifth floor Danny barged straight in at that milling counter and for once in his life surprised Carrie.
"You?"
She stood there cradling underwear.
Danny pushed her the order pad—let the ritzy ones stare! Carrie gave it a look, and bubbled over. "So what are you doing here, dummy? Get them going on this at your factory!" As he happily winked and started away, "Hey—" she brought him back for a holiday kiss. "See you in Cornelia Street Danny-doll."
He half-aimed a leg toward Miss Salisbury's office in this acre of counters draped red and green and swarming with women. What a finisher that would be to the week, using these orders to ram an initial order down the throat of that special bitch! But slim asses in furs blocked the aisles, heaviness poured over his shoulders again, and he only wanted to get out in the air. He flipped two bits to the Vandervaart's doorman, dropped back into a cab, and kept rereading the order book the whole trip to West Street. And had to giggle, feeling this jolly and lousy at once.
Santa Share, the spirit of Christmas! A gander at that pad and Naomi's eyes widened like a silky blonde angel's who'd just gotten a good word from God. She jumped up from her desk, kissed Danny on the run—she and Carrie really were from the same school of thought—and in ten seconds flat had Leah and the forelady (with a victory smile for the triumph of her particular project) writing production tickets full speed along with herself. A light snow flickered again, over the piers and sheds and herring-gray water, the motor trucks, the wagons and horses, longshoremen unloading the platforms: just like the prehistoric afternoon that Jack Berger quit. Danny stood by in a glorious daze with his hands deep in his overcoat pockets—he, the sweet singer!—and the girls sat hunched working.
Had all this stuff really happened?
At Humboldt Jones a few hours ago Mothersill'd sternly pestered him, "That's a positive delivery date you've given me Share?" on a hopeful worried interrogative lilt. Now that had happened—hadn't it?—and there were the tickets for proof. The snow was real: you saw it fuzzing the cobbles. And the shop tumult rocking your brains was anything but imagi-

nary. So he really was making good! He'd buy Carrie a diamond ring that would blind 'em with jealousy both sides of her counter at Vandervaart's—not that she'd be there much longer. They'd drive around in a shiny black Dodge closed sedan and live uptown in Harlem!

But just as a lost-soul shriek "Don't put that here, you—" from Abie the head shipping clerk was submerged in a sputter and whine of machines, Leah said, "How's Grandma, Reisel?"

"Depressed," Reisel kept her eyes on her writing, "since her old friend Bertha Axelrod died of TB in Denver."

With that Danny's throat grabbed him, his chest turned to fire, his skin went clammy. Would he live to get married? His first impulse was to run home to bed.

Ridiculous.

A poor sick middle-aged woman with a musical bum of a son taking years off her life finally died, so that meant Danny—? Get a grip on yourself, Danny-o, check the stock to save Reisel the job, which is only fair since she's stuck here in the office. Just the same as he hung his hat and coat on the antler rack he knocked wood, softly so's not to be noticed but with all his heart in it. And when Louis the stockman asked was he okay, Danny could feel his own mouth pointing down as if he were at his own funeral.

"In the pink," Danny answered this jinx, "and I'll be even better if you shake your ass slightly while I call out these numbers."

Of course at quitting time he apologized to Louis even if he himself had done most of the ass-shaking dead as he was.

Then exactly how dead could he be?

But he couldn't face overtime writing tickets with the girls still at it augmented by Ma. Even from a distance the sight of his better than Shakespeare order books sickened him now—which brought the panicky sweat back.

Lifting his collar against skittering snow in the dark turbulent streets was like lifting the globe. At lamplit corners trucks bore down on you as if out of the smoldering sky. It was all you could do—bastards!—to cross from corner to corner alive. And near the Twenty-third Street pier where taxis were usually strung out like hot dogs wouldn't you see the last three snapped up under your nose in this weather? The lights of the streetcar he'd missed shone a cheery yellow a few blocks away in the eastbound traffic jam.

Walk home in this snow?

Walk or no walk, how dead could he be if such an idea had entered his mind?

He walked, pushed ahead rather, and if you were stopped in your tracks blame the east wind blasting snow in your face. In Tompkins Square the last game ragged leaves were clinging to white-fringed trees through this swirling storm. They were gamer than he was. He couldn't have done that walk over again. Or the two flights that he climbed, ready to drop yet starving. He warmed last night's pot of chicken and as he made steady traffic between the table and stove for refills he had to remind himself finally that this was supper for three not just him.

Could a corpse be this hungry? No sooner wondered than he began choking. Down the wrong pipe? But cough spasms that cut like a knife? TB'd gotten Bertha Axelrod.

But Dr. Britannica said TB has no appetite.

The throat closing first, or first the wrong pipe? He wasn't sure. He glanced toward the clock and without his seeing the time his heart sank. On top of all this he had to push himself over to Carrie's.

He had to lie down a second—and look how his hands shook unbuttoning his shirt. He stripped bare, and what for? It wasn't pajama hour. The hell with putting the underwear back on, he lay down that way. The sheets were nice and cool though, the radiator cozily gurgled, and—at death's door and this horny? Hey Carrie!

He tried swallowing, the throat wasn't that bad.

Two hundred and fifty Number 1 hand-painted Aladdins!—he deserved Carrie naked! . . . Tomorrow was Saturday, but if he hit Miss Salisbury early he might still get in his spiel, tickle 'er with today's order book. . . . And say, big sale in Vandervaart's Lamps, complete with Santa Claus ringing the bell and kisses under the mistletoe. So, Christmas spirit, Danny grabbed a slim-assed fur coat to have his kisses too. For come-hither smirks—he had to grin in her face—this curlyhead couldn't be beat. And she was surprisingly willing—a total stranger!—to let him unbutton her, raise her frock, pull her unmentionables down. That store dick Danny's age shaking his head? Then don't look if it bothers ya.

Danny plunged his shaft in, the bare-assed lady started off nicely, and . . . where was he? Alone in bed in the dark . . . and the throat bit him worse than ever.

13

UNLESS THEY WERE HAVING SUPPER TOGETHER DANNY'D show up at Cornelia Street eight o'clock, eight-fifteen the latest. So half-past eight and no Danny, especially after his struck gold in the Klondike stop at the store? Boy had those rich bitches' eyes popped at the sight of her Carrie Baum's property! Ever have hunches? She'd had this hunch at the time clock—only a hundred and forty-four more or less punches to her wedding the first Sunday in June which she believed fell on June first next year?—that at home there'd be another surprise, snow or no snow: Danny in the vestibule a full two hours early with a small diamond ring, two carats say.

What had she found? Some hunch. Angelo the janitor shoveling snow off the stoop. Just as well, she'd figured. Sonny boy must have been in the factory late with that windfall of orders. And why pay your neighborhood jeweler's rent, extravagant as Angel Food Cake who wouldn't melt in your mouth Naomi knew her future sister-in-law was. You can get just as engaged wholesale at Uncle Jesse's on the Bowery, with cousin Gladys's heartache thrown in free when Uncle Jesse broke her the news.

But this was the limit: no word and still no Danny. Hatchet girl disapproved of the phone, but for all the calls that Danny made you'd think that he didn't have one. So Carrie called him and got—who else?—Naomi, plus music and chatter in the background. "Carrie!" Miss Hypocrisy's voice brightened like sunshine. No—as if that hubbub didn't exist—she hadn't noticed when Danny left, she'd ask Ma. Wasn't that sweet?—they could be sisters already. Now these friendly Shares wouldn't be trying to pull a fast one on Carrie, a party perhaps, under Miss Kiss of Death's auspices, pathetically intended to place sonny boy in the arms of a more preferred candidate? To her dying day Carrie would never forget last month's welcomes into the family. First at Bank Street Leah Share had tilted that neat tan chin of hers like in society movies and tried tripping you up with her smiles about the advantages of a girl's living alone in the Village, freedom, new ideas, this that and the other thing to worm out of you that Cornelia Street was for screwing. Carrie had been able to fend Leah off without sounding like a prude, then—get this. When it was time to leave finally, the moral big sister's boy friend Henny had said good night to the visitors and stayed on the side of the door where the double bed was. Imagine that whore, cross-examining her! And there'd been the Tompkins Square supper, with Ma's mournful face attributed not to Naomi's fatty brisket of beef that you wouldn't wish on an alley cat but to poor Mr. Rappaport or his wheelchair upstairs, one of which had just broken down.

"Relatives?" Carrie'd been sympathetic.

"Only neighbors, poor things."

So you saw where the son's intended fit in, even with the girl to girl chat with Ma Carrie worked up on recipes. But the old girl came to the phone now with the Tompkins Square frolics suddenly hushed. "He left an hour ago Carrie," she wailed, "where could he be?"

A fine how do you do! Didn't the woman think Carrie knew how to worry, if there was something to worry about? "Oh you'd hear if anything happened," she cut Ma down to size, "they notify next of kin right away." Then she laughed, patted Ma back into shape with a few sweet probabilities and sat down plenty burned up to file her nails.

In Tompkins Square Golda hardly knew which tore at her most: what could have happened to Danny, or that his young woman didn't care about him. Poor boy—and what could you say to him that would alter matters? Naomi and her boy friend interrupted their embarrassing dancing to agree with Carrie's guess that Danny had gotten stuck in the snow. Oh God, let them be right. . . .

Then the phone rang nearly killing her with anxiety and as usual Naomi ran to it.

"Danny," Naomi came back laughing, "got stuck in the snow."

See, Golda told herself, typical mother, how you jump to conclusions just because you hate so to lose him? Well loser—a son, even if he married a saint, you're bound to lose him. The house was clean, the laundry drying, the Sabbath pot roast for tomorrow on the stove simmering, and the Stromberg-Carlson a mixed blessing that turned the living room into an indecent dance hall for two. Golda ran up a flight to chatter to Mr. Rappaport, poor man, whose speech was so slurred since his last stroke that about the only answer he was capable of was his eyes full of gratitude.

But for Golda, what solace?

Danny the dead dude phoned home as ordered and then collapsed to Carrie's couch.

"Why didn't you walk," Carrie tapped her foot in front of him, "when the trolley broke down?"

He shot her a smile so ghastly—"I broke down with it"—that she forgot about discipline.

"Are you sick?"

"Summer cold."

He tossed it off lightly, but he sat fully qualified as a terminal case by his symptoms, the hour and Dr. Britannica. He'd woken up from his nap ten times as dead as when he lay down, it was night, he was sure he had fever though he had been too panicked to see, and a deep breath would hurt his chest. He'd intended taking a cab, but a streetcar came first. Near Broadway it ran into snowdrifts and except for him and an old geezer also too feeble to move himself all the passengers got off. Danny'd sat huddled in a dim street of factories where hypnotic snow built up on window ledges to look like headstones. An hour dragged by before the snow tapered to a white race of wind and a track gang went at the drifts like a dream of gravediggers. Jesus, would he be around for next year's snow? Now in his fancy camel's hair coat he lacked the strength to peel off he sat like part of the sofa.

Carrie studied the scared blue eyes, the pink cheeks, that face of a born Casanova minus the conceit that those lightweights specialized in. She touched his temples and pulse and tested his lips with a kiss.

"You're not sick."

"I swear," some joke with that grin, "six months on and off."

So with just the teeniest scared twinge herself though she'd never show it Carrie got into her imitation tigerskin coat and pulled her hat on like a helmet. When she was a kid the first season in Orange a smart Yankee Doodle sold Moishe a wagonload of good healthy chickens without bothering to mention that if you move 'em they become homesick and die. So those chickens died to a chicken, and Moishe also lay down to die, of chickenitis. That was Moishe. But that wasn't Danny and why should it be with his chickens popping out golden eggs? But then there'd been Mother. She'd also felt tired out for six months and, God forbid, Hodgkin's disease, TB, pneumonia—what didn't she have at the end? Life knew how to play dirty tricks, from insignificant ones like Schiffstein, to . . . yeah . . . Mother. She Carrie Baum was taking no more of that stuff—no sir, nix, nothing doing!

"On your toes sonny boy."

So—Danny pushed himself up—she was the same as the rest of them. "Some good show playing?"

"Yeah, entitled Carrie's cousin by marriage the doctor."

What a relief! Now it was her responsibility, and her sawbones' whoever he was. Danny already felt so much better in the taxi bumping on snow chains to Harlem he wasn't sure there was any sense going. But Carrie insisted, and the old suck of fear drained him again. It was tough—"How come?"—sounding lighthearted.

"Because, sonny boy, your Aunt Carrie doesn't relish filing her nails while you lounge around on trolley cars playing sick."

Whew!

And on Mt. Morris Park West outside Dr. Nate Barasch M.D.'s chocolate house with white icing Danny's health didn't seem to be worrying his aunt Carrie a bit. A yellow dog sniffing at a garbage can in front of the stoop paused to bare fangs, snarl and actually snap at Carrie. And she paused to boot it one in the ribs—what a kick!—that sent it howling belly-deep into the drifts at the top of the park.

"That bitch can't be my cousin Gladys," she said so sedately that Danny had to give her a healthy kiss on those refreshingly cool lips, "because," she rang Gladys's bell, "she never greets me first."

Tonight though Gladys greeted her after the maid let them in. What was the alternative with cousin Carrie—"Cousin Gladys!"—sailing into the reception room behind a funny outstretched cousinly arm? Gladys looked like a death mask all right, which she hoisted a fraction on one side and said she'd see if the doctor could see them. Imagine Gladys's joy, and Danny's, when this Nate with thinning hair, a smile a yard wide and football shoulders that dwarfed his stick of a wife rushed out to kiss and hug Carrie.

"Hey," Carrie laughed, "I ain't the patient this time Nathan."

"I'm the patient," Nate winked with a hand out for the intro, "and Carrie's my tonic—the little I see of her. You still assert," he pointed at Carrie, "romance can't possibly run in the family?"

Sallow Gladys turned green and then a darkening blue. Danny only flushed a brick-red. Of all jokers he hated this type the worst.

But no horsing around on the job for Dr. Nate Barasch M.D. He listened to your troubles no smiles. He wound a tube on your arm, stethoscoped you, fluoroscoped you, jabbed you all over—and praised your insides organ by organ! "Been working hard, huh?"—a clairvoyant too!

What did Danny have? Mild red throat. Medicine? Gargle with salt water. Let his life saver Carrie laugh "Hypochondriac" at him, he was alive! He had his whole life ahead of him!

In a tiled ice cream parlor on 116th Street he and Carrie sealed their engagement with hot chocolates nice and creamy on top but thin underneath.

"What do you expect," Carrie said, "with the neighborhood running down and the Jews running away?"

"Yeah? I counted on moving here."

"Harlem's dead."

"Then where'll we live?"

"Leave it to Carrie."

"So hot chocolate's a Jewish dish."

And he looked so cute Carrie kissed him.

What a girl he was getting! Why wait till June to get married? How about say next week?

"Nix," Carrie said.

At her wedding she intended to have all and sundry, from her girlhood chum and viper in the bosom Shirley Shine, should that one be back from her siege of Paris, to Dr. Barasch's wife—"Think she'll remember me? Or maybe her bought and paid for if not quite owned hubby'll have to remind her."

"You like him a lot, huh?" Danny went exploring.

"Except medically, he's like fluff."

So Danny kissed her.

"Say," she said, "you're the jealous type," as if she had just made the discovery.

"The Moor of Venice, that's me."

She wrinkled her face unbecomingly—"Wha?"—as he wished she wouldn't, then went on with the wedding party, from the rich uncles Jesse (hers) and Frank (his), to the beauteous damsel in white chiffon, tiara and veil floating down the aisle on the nonplused arm of Daddy Moishe, and with this handsome guy in tails and striped pants beside her under the canopy—why the Orange New Jersey Jews were just going to drown in their own drool in the synagogue!

The way her eyes shone Danny couldn't help kissing her.

Which reminded Carrie, apropos of Jesse and Frank, she'd had a good tip from Miss O'Sullivan in Vandervaart's Lamps how to sell to Miss Salisbury. So—two minds in a single channel: Miss Salisbury headed his tomorrow's roster!—Danny had to lean forward and kiss her. Except that from there—according to O'Sullivan Miss Salisbury was a crook: but no bribes required—the channel diverged into two separate streams. Miss Salisbury liked a salesman to pad a bill and rebate the difference to . . . guess who?

Carrie twinkled, whereas it didn't strike Danny funny.

"We fired Gable for something like that."

"How do you think our uncles got rich?"

"That's not how my uncle got rich. He got rich through hard work."

"He's old-fashioned."

"Then I'm old-fashioned."

Carrie's eyes narrowed with the answer to that, then relaxed, and she gave Danny a kiss. "Okay, that makes three of us." So, workhorse, had he visited the management of the New Oriental Hotel they were building on East Thirty-ninth, shown 'em the Reisel originals yet? And how do you like that—Danny kissed her—they were swimming together again. He'd figured the New Oriental for his second call—make it first—in the morning!

And what a morning—crisp blue air in your healthy lungs, a trolley clang in the distance, auto horns going *geruga*, dazzling snow! At the ferry —Jesus, had that been yesterday when he was on his last legs?—taxis were merrily lined up in splashes of sunlight, shadow and slush. He hopped into a cab and had it wait meter ticking at Quality while he ran upstairs fishing for keys to go get a couple of demonstration models Reisel herself had painted.

The joint was already unlocked though, and by—who but? Reisel with that slim supple back in a white blouse and black skirt didn't see him, too busy setting up work for her shipping boys. In the olden days he used to bawl her out, his little pal, for getting in ahead of anyone else to hunch over shades. Reisel of course always had reasons. Weekdays she would simply come to work—where else could she go?—after early prayers in the Essex Street Synagogue. Saturday? Sabbath there were no early prayers true. Jews inoffensive to God did not find themselves nailed to a job on Sabbath, and prayers began later. But she woke at the same hour anyway, and where else could she go but here?

"I'm inoffensive to God," Danny would say, "and I work Saturdays."

"You," despondently, "are more an American."

Jesus, the way his heart went out to her now! He slipped off his butter yellow eight-bucks kidskin gloves, clasped her arms from behind, and for the first time in his life stole a kiss. And turning, was she beautiful with those waves of red hair, the white forehead, soft cheeks and quiet eyes.

"What," she cooled him off in a hurry, "was that for?"

So, "Wish me luck," he sourly grinned, "I'm engaged."

She softened, he softened. They shook hands and he stood there—why kid yourself?—longing for her, almost wishing . . .

What use is wishing? He grabbed a lamp in each fist, told his cabbie East Broadway, and became the earliest bird at the library—with the back of his hand to that quack Dr. Britannica! The librarian dug him up the Government pamphlets on Far Eastern trade. And though your stomach turned along with the pages of this stuff he flipped lucky and landed not only in tariffs but at the schedule for chinaware! Today was gonna be a gold mine, he knew it! He scribbled the dope down, studied the figures his ride uptown to the Forty-second Street office of New Oriental, and—keep smiling sunshine!—nabbed the owner, the general manager and the decorator in one fell swoop! They had an importer lined up for all the Oriental decor? That was just Danny's point: these lamps were pure U.S.A.—this much per piece savings on tariff, and shipping costs zero.

The decorator was the sugary hitch since there was more cut for him in the imports. He lithped—not so dumb either—it was rather unlikely that the lot would measure up to the samples, and usually that was a fact though of course Danny kept the fact to himself. Reisel's sample lamps had something extra, a finish that Sadie's, Annie's or Becky's did not. But the owner liked what he saw at that price, and Danny guaranteed the owner would like the whole shipment, not that Danny relished the shopwork overtime he'd have to put in to free Reisel to do finishing touches. But it was worth it, an order this size.

What a deal!

Except for a head throb so mild you hardly could notice it he burst out of that building like Hercules. The cab inched up Fifth Avenue in a welter of taxis, double-deck buses, snow wagons at corners, limousines, good-looking women with chauffeurs letting them out at the shops and bringing traffic to a standstill. But it was okay with Danny—this was his big parade! Himself, he got off at Vandervaart's rear entrance on Madison so he'd hit Miss Salisbury before he hit Carrie.

Salisbury was crooked all right. Sure, she granted his imitations were good, but, she frosted him lightly with that superior Gentile smile, Vandervaart's clientele didn't care to save money, they came to spend it. Danny—what did it cost him?—was full of yeses. "Not," Miss Salisbury graciously nodded, "that they'd recognize the difference between originals and copies if the trademark and price were the same. But in that case," she made her bid for a partner in crime, "why sell them copies?"

Actually this dame hadn't changed much except for her hat, which was brimless this season and clamped like blinders to her thoroughbred head. But Danny must have changed quite a bit. She gave no sign she'd ever met him before, let alone remembered his famous yawn. He remembered her yawn, but that shot he hadn't had something she wanted and at the right price: Reisel's lamps. Yeah, he'd changed okay. He could have laughed in her face, and for good measure spit down her long throat and sent no bill for the soda. But where's the profit in spit? No more than in yawns. So he played dumb to her pitch with another sure, she was right, yes yes yes—and those sarcastic yeses could have queered the act if he hadn't transposed keys to "Miss Salisbury, no doubt about that," while he heard himself like someone else talking, "but folks do like the good buys you give 'em at your late winter sales."

And it worked!

She tapped her pencil awhile on his price list to make him think she was thinking, then tried for a knot in his guts for face-saving purposes—two weeks' delivery or else. Nyaa to her—he was set for day and night in the factory anyway!

How was that for half a day's industry!

And you beat dawn to the punch mornings groggy but healthy, giving 'em a hand in machines, stock and shipping; a lunch sandwich in the loft with Reisel to look forward to like in the good old days; the rounds afternoons keeping the customers happy; back to the shop as acting forelady—Reisel's joke he wasn't so sure he liked; piling into a cab to Second Avenue with Ma, Reisel, Naomi and Leah for a supper at Ratner's or Rapoport's that met Reisel's strictly kosher specifications; and the shop again till nine, ten at night and even later for him, Naomi and Reisel, winding up dazed and happy with everything under control, giggling together under Naomi's one stingy bulb in the office at the rush of money into the books.

"This lady," Danny waggled his thumb at Reisel, "should be a partner too."

Reisel's eyes popped wide open, but Naomi tilted her cheeks as if she'd just tasted castor oil but see how brave she was. So Reisel said she had no wish to be partner: her needs were met as forelady. She thanked him for the compliment, but she was not as materialistic as he in her aspirations.

"Which are?"

"To become better."

"And what's wrong with me?"

"You're not bad—" dead serious. "But you should pray once in a while, or at least meditate. You should read, think, consider. You should listen more to Beethoven and never permit yourself to grow lax. Of course your fiancée, whom I look forward to meeting, will encourage you in these things."

If Naomi grinned at that joke no wonder Danny guffawed.

"Reisel dear," he drunkenly clasped both her hands and with Naomi as chaperone what choice did Reisel have except between a scene and swallowing *her* teaspoon of castor oil, "I bet your cousin here's let you know that Carrie's up-and-at-'em, do or die, the opposite of all that stuff."

"Then the encouragement," Reisel gave a tentative tug toward freeing herself, "will be up to you."

"No no no, Princess Logic. No one can do it by their own bootstraps. So there's just one solution, since I haven't ordered Carrie a ring yet. I marry you instead, as written."

Reisel's eyes danced, her lips trembled at the edge of a smile, "You are hopeless," and she pushed him away.

What laughs, what fun! He had never been happier!

Happy even to shiver into work under a white sky with black menacing clouds over a West Street so deathly still you could hear ice floes groaning against the black hulls of freighters at dock. Exciting before you ducked into the Quality building, the endless stretch of cobbles shining like silver, the boarded-up platforms, the silent wagons with their shafts empty, the early salt air refreshing you. Then you caught up to Naomi on the cold creaking brown stairway that smelled of damp.

"Where were you?"

"Ocean voyage," he cracked.

"You're a nut!" his sister giggled.

Then Reisel to smile at you while she scarcely took her eyes off the shade she was dabbing finishing touches to.

On the stroke of eight Leah yawned in.

"If this is success, success isn't for me kiddo."

"Shut up," Danny said, "and trim shades."

At ten Officer Kelly strolled in for some coffee Leah had made—Reisel brewed tea like a good Jewish girl—and to have his big red palm greased for not seeing them break the blue law against breaking your back on Sunday. Danny kept his back turned on that bum, and Naomi took care of the smiles and payoff. Now and then Danny would stop for a squint at the bamboo bridges, green twisted trees and pink flowers Reisel'd retouched after Annie or Becky or Sadie passed them along. "Blame on genius," he breathed on that white nape of hers he felt like kissing.

"Tell me something which I do not already know."

He couldn't believe, when Carrie breezed in flashing her engagement ring, that half his Sunday'd whizzed past so soon. At the art table where he was assembling vases and shades alongside Reisel and her squad of paintresses, Carrie—"Here to free the slaves"—bent for a kiss. "Or at least the slave. Two o'clock Sunday is where I draw the line."

Reisel said, "Let me admire your ring."

"Yes, I found it acceptable," Carrie winked at this Raisin.

Leah in a lumpy gray canvas apron condescended to saunter over and crack at her Carrie Baum, "It's more than acceptable. It's worth every ounce of his sweat."

"Lay off my sweat," Danny joined in the joke.

"I'd rather lay on it," Carrie smirked not at him but at her pair of antagonists, the flaming torch whom one of these days sooner or later she would douse for keeps with the slightest of efforts, and the mouse-brown but rhino-tough oldest sister, whose wagon would be by no means easy to fix.

But leave it to Carrie. What could be done she would do. She was happy believe her that at Uncle Jesse's her fighting spirit had prevailed over caution. She'd intended to wait a month or so with the ring, so Uncle Jesse wouldn't mistake her for the tag end of the Christmas rush. But when Danny phoned her elated to babble that since Raisin hadn't taken up his offer to jilt her Carrie Baum they might as well go buy the ring, she changed her mind in a hurry. She ordered her boy—and was pleased to note no signs of wriggling in the absence of Raisin—to excuse himself the very next day around noon, and off to Bowery Diamonds.

"Why not Tiffany's?" her spendthrift had said.

She'd been tempted, tempted to ram Tiffany's down the gagging throats of the ladies Share, Leah and Ma—with Naomi she was bosom pals—and incidentally of the lesbian Raisin. Why else would Raisin Buttinsky turn down Danny-boy who could have been as helplessly hers as he was helplessly Carrie's, while the same Raisin kept preaching to Naomi till Naomi'd gotten good and fed up that Naomi should get rid of the peerless Kaye? When Naomi all lit up with love and hot pants asked Carrie, "Well what do you think of my Murray?" Carrie'd laughed, "Only good if you marry him and only bad if you don't." "But isn't he nice?" "I love his carroty waves." If Naomi wanted to cut her own throat what business was it of Raisin's, unless Raisin was after making the little blonde Kewpie doll cousin her own business? Carrie may have moved into the Village by mistake, but she hadn't been living there deaf dumb and blind! That Raisin was a lesbian and the husbandy half if ever she'd seen one.

But—whither thou goest there I shall go, and whatever thou spendest that much out of my pocket—why cut your nose and so on, she'd said nix to Tiffany's and added, "Do you know, sonny boy, you have some of your father's worst tendencies?"

He'd thought she was kidding, and for her part—dumb to be smart at your own expense—she was relieved. She'd never met Danny's father though she was curious to at least have a look at the ogre who'd changed sonny boy with every attribute of a born lady-killer into the most moral young man on earth—and apparently without the boy's even knowing it!

A lot of stuff in this world is mental.

Even at Uncle Jesse's—funny little man in his grayish-white shirt blousing over baggy black pants held up by frayed suspenders, complaining that business had never been worse while he walked her and Danny through his buzzing establishment of diamond cutters at stones, setters bent with loupes in their eye, sales counters, customers—even there the feelings and opinions of others, specifically the gang she'd be marrying into, had been her first consideration. "Nothing ostentatious," she'd said, and had sort of meant it.

Ah, Uncle Jesse was crafty, trotting out dull stuff with his tweezers, flawed stuff, invisible stuff till you yawned. Then he hit you with a marquise, fancy cut, that made even his eyes glitter like the lights in the diamond.

And good lord, was she Carrie Baum nuts, hesitating in order to spare the likes of Leah Share from having her eyes crawl out of her head?

"I shouldn't," Carrie had actually said, "it'll make people jealous."

She'd been leaning toward Uncle Jesse and the jewel on the velvet and Danny's hand had come down on her hip. "Make 'em!" he'd said. And it was her hip, wasn't it?

"Uncle Jesse," she'd said straight-faced, "you won't tell my cousin Gladys the size of my diamond the second that you see her?"

"God forbid."

So here it was on the third finger left hand, the gorgeous glittering pointy oval flanked by small brilliant stones. Go blind, girls. At the same time, you have to keep the opposition off balance.

"Still it's true, seven days' work a week is extreme," she gave Leah her best pathos smile. "I wanted a tycoon, but now I'm thinking it over."

"No you're not," brown Leah sang.

It takes two to argue?

But Carrie comically hoisted her hands, "The game's up," so what could dear Leah do except call it quits? Meanwhile Danny switched from work clothes to glad rags including the small diamond stickpin Carrie'd bought him that famous afternoon at Uncle Jesse's though from their silence on the item the Hester Street penny pinchers didn't approve of that either. But you put your arm in this guy's and eyes popped wherever you went—like Carnegie Hall, to sit with the silver-haired parquet swells and hear the great Stokowski conduct the great Beethoven's great Fifth.

In the big mirror out in the vestibule her imitation tigerskin had looked pretty bleh next to her elegant doll in his blue-gray Homburg hat. The music became quieter and she reviewed possibilities. Raccoon? Too sporty. Sealskin? No, too bulky.

La, la la, la-la la-la . . .

A real problem. Maybe for the present a good fitted dark cloth with a fox collar say would be best . . . Look at Danny, fighting the world to music with little jerks of the jaw, fist and knee. Wasn't he cute? She could have eaten him up! . . . And for the future, she'd march in one fine day to order her mink from one of her father's furrier so-called associates, like Bellovsky, who'd clucked their tongues gloating when they heard Moishe'd failed. Wouldn't that turn them green!

For Danny New Year's Eve this year fell on the February Saturday night they wrapped up the New Oriental Hotel order to Reisel's, to his, to Ma's, to Leah's, to Naomi's, to the whole damn Quality Lamps' satisfaction! To celebrate he kept everyone on overtime pay this last day, not only the family and Becky, Annie and Sadie. "All right, all right," Naomi had laughed, "I'm too dizzy to argue." She was more drunk than dizzy, reeling with work like all of them. Leah brought in two jugs of home-fermented wine for a punch, but they were happy and punch-drunk to begin with. Herbie the truckman with the shipping boys' help lugged up the Victrola from Tompkins Square and everyone danced but Reisel.

"Why don't you dance, why don't you dance?" Danny pulled her by the hand.

"My role is observer in life."

But Reisel tittered, then giggled, then threw back her head and couldn't stop laughing. For the special occasion she had tasted some punch, unaccustomed as she was, and let Danny hold her fingers.

"Carrie loves Beethoven's Fifth," he said.

"You have told me that one million times."

They couldn't stop laughing. Whatever they said made them hysterical. Ma interrupted, "Dance with me, I'm a relative too," and doubled him up.

He and Ma hilariously stepped on each other's feet a while. Then Danny picked up his uke that he'd fished out of the closet this morning, dusted and strummed for the first time since Hector was a pup—and Hector was a big dog now—and brought to work for the festivities. He emptied another punch glass in a gulp, zig-zagged among flushed shouting happy folks back to Reisel, stuck his foot on a box, leaned toward her, and lo—the old troubadour!

Have a heart
Entirely at your . . . dis-po-sal,
Quite apart
From conventional . . . pro-po-sal . . .

He played a hundred choruses of that into Reisel's almost unwillingly smiling eyes while the rest of them danced to it. Then—"Dammit!"—a string snapped.

"And a good thing too," well-potted Leah with an arm on the shoulder of Louis the stockman told her brother, "since the mismatch you're insisting on against your pie-eyed sis's advice is no doubt pining away for you in Cornelia Street this very moment."

"No doubt. So?"

Leah waved a loose wrist toward Reisel.

"So you're engaged to be married to one and serenading another?"

"Serenading 'er, pie-eyed sis, not marrying her."

Quite apart
From—

Reisel yawned, "Excuse me, I must leave now and attend to my duties at home so long neglected."

"Midnight Saturday night?"

But she caught up her coat from the antler rack and was gone.

By then the party was pretty well petered out anyway, and on the trolley car with Ma and the girls Danny sat collar raised and hands deep in his pockets cozy and half asleep dreaming over the fun. At Avenue A Leah gave him a poke and a wink.

"Time to wake up kiddo."

He stood shivering alongside them under the lamppost with no trolley in sight down the long streets with here and there arm-in-arm couples winding up dates. Oy, Monday the rounds again full time, and with the old sinking heart? That was the trouble with selling, like playing cards. Once you knew all about it where was the fun in it?

Hey—the bucks. Can you beat that? He'd forgotten the bucks!

And besides there was Sunday.

So full of vim and vigor on a cold overcast Sunday that scraped your bones and made you wish for unholy matrimony under a feather bed, Danny all wrapped up coat scarf and gloves ran for the crosstown trolley to Carrie's at Avenue A and 4th and was almost knocked down by a flivver. To rub it in the guy yelled, "Whattsa matter daydreamer, y'in love?", and Danny strolled over with his fists doubled. But his pal Lefty Lefkowitz was the driver with a girl next to him, and—Roy and Gil Weinstein, Art Davis —half the card game in back.

Lefty cracked to the girl, "He's hooked, with his head in the sack, so he can't see traffic coming. Or else his hope is merciful suicide. Hop in," he told Danny, "you still have a few months to live."

"Can't play cards today," Danny said.

Was he an unconscious gagman? The bunch of 'em whinnied like Uncle Willie's Rosa the mare, only without her good nature. "You can play, dude," Lefty brayed. "Hannah'll let you play if I ask her to . . . nice? Huh Hannah?" But Hannah blushed and looked flustered like somebody's kid sister. Lefty nudged her. "Go ahead Hannah, let's see you vamp him. Can you vamp a guy, Hannah?"

Jesus, Lefkowitz looked ratty, mean, with his white teeth bunched together in that faceful of bones. And Danny called these his friends? "Why are you picking on the girl?" Danny said. "Leave her alone."

Lefkowitz poked his head out. "Tail—" he breathed, while Hannah slid out of the car. Jesus, with the bent nose, the build, and the light fuzz on her lip she sure did remind Danny of Carrie. "What's your name?" Hannah caught Danny's hand. "Come on Danny, I'll ride on your lap."

Don't think he wasn't tempted. But, "Promised to go shopping with a friend," he had to explain.

She said, bright-eyed as you'd want, "I'll go shopping."

"How about them?" Danny ducked the main issue.

"How about you?"

Cars began honking. Hannah suddenly thumbed her nose at Danny—Jesus, the image of Carrie!—slid back in the auto beside Lefty and the bunch drove off convulsed. Danny was still grinning and waving after that cute head when some son of a bitch and what the hell for oofed him slamming into a cobbled wall—where in Jesus did that come from?—and over a ledge. A brake screeched.

He lay head and shoulders across the curb, with the black nasty grin of a tire ready—"No"—to bite down on him. The last turn of the hub as he threw his arms up to shield himself gleamed PACKARD.

14

AT THE LIP OF THIS HEART-CURDLING CAVERN OF DISease and carbolic Carrie's blood boiled. And your blood had to boil: it was that hot here. Gray out but broad daylight, and inside under huge dusty panes and remote ceiling lights the gloom of a morgue. Her fiancé in a municipal ward of what looked like a double row of half-exposed cadavers? He had a leg hooked to the ceiling like pork in the Jefferson Market, and his face perfectly matched his ghastly pillowcase. The mother had a grip on her son like a drowner ready to sink the third time and drag him down with her, the sister Naomi smiled through the phony knot of concern on her forehead.

Carrie could have torn that detestable pair apart, putting him at the mercy of butchers. But it was cheap here, it was cheap.

The kid's scared-stiff eyes rolled up and he spoke like through hot potatoes. "Wha' th' doctor say, Carrie?"

"He said you'll be fine," the mother wailed like a mourner.

"Hear that, stupid?" Carrie flicked the tip of his nose. "What do you mean getting hit in the ass by an automobile when we're supposed to buy me a coat? Now I'm stuck with my fake tiger stripes until you're up." She stroked that pale cheek and touched his eyes shut. "You're okay, sleep, baby."

He managed to smile, to squeeze her fingertips. His lips parted faintingly and he dozed.

Carrie said quietly, "Why not just shoot him, like they do horses?" and you could see the guilt written over them.

Golda bad as things were was always ready for worse. "Did you speak to the doctor?" She wrung her hands. "Did he tell you something?"

Naomi felt Carrie'd read her mind. Yet she'd only thought . . . She hadn't done anything. The admitting clerk's condoling voice on the phone had shrunken her insides. In the taxi—what did money mean now?—to

East Side City Hospital she and Ma'd bumped along in a silence gray as the weather. Her little brother, and who knew what awful news? Then what a relief—no serious injuries aside from the fracture—and the possibilities this accident opened for Tootsie had blossomed out in her mind like a flower in sunshine. Right away she'd been ashamed of herself. To think of job opportunities for Murray when Danny was suffering.

But to the hospital doctor the word suffer was like an insult. He'd lectured Naomi that they'd been administering ether as an anesthetic since 1843 and opium alkaloids whatever they were as analgesics—"Pain killers?"—he'd shot her his sarcastic look—since the inception of medical history. Could she have done without that ridicule specialist with the dirty-blond hair, as young-looking as Danny though he must have been older. But maybe he was a good doctor. In the smelly ward Danny himself had groggily mumbled he felt as if he was dying but it didn't hurt much. In fact Ma had asked, "Can we take him home, Doctor?" And the doctor'd answered, "You could also shoot him," the same as Carrie. So that snotty doctor must have ratted on them to Carrie.

But Naomi and Ma had meant well, Danny would be better off if you could get him home safely. The doctor himself said there might be a hairline fracture besides the multiple the X-ray showed clearly, but ask him how come the doubt and you fell into his big mouth again. Once the leg was set, he sneered, it was set for the hairline break too if there was one. So why mention it then, just to show off? How could anyone trust a doctor like that, a Gentile named Harvey? You could only pray for Danny's leg to heal quickly in spite of the medical attention and for Tootsie to get settled. Tootsie's quitting the Postgraduate College of Business last month had made her just sick. Tootsie hadn't been completely honest either, about shifting to New York University. To transfer to a pay school for morons, when Postgraduate College was free? How Tootsie had reddened when she blurted that, how mad he'd become!

"Maybe you'd better find someone smarter if I'm such a moron."

Then he'd squinted at her over his cigarette smoke. Sure long ago guys like the Lehman brothers, Kuhn, Loeb and Bache may have squeezed themselves into the big money. Nowadays they didn't love Jews so on Wall Street that you can work your way to the top, or even slip in at the bottom, with a degree from a Bolsheviks' nest like the Postgraduate College.

Yet that wasn't like Tootsie, throwing dollars away. Naomi had been so worried that she'd asked Reisel's opinion, Reisel asked Bookbinder, Bookbinder asked Finn the Postgraduate Librarian he bound books for sometimes, and Finn asked the registrar. Poor Tootsie—those dirty rats at Postgraduate College had thrown him out on account of low grades! Didn't they make allowances for a boy slaving all hours, hustling to classes dead tired, with a family that bled him instead of helping him?

In the war he'd drawn a high draft number thank God, he hadn't been over there. He'd only tramped through Southern mud in the rain with a forty pound pack while cows sheltered in barns watched in amazement. Or else been dragged from three hours' sleep to crawl through homemade no man's lands with barbed wire spools and then bellywopped into the stuff they'd just finished stringing. Or enjoyed live mortar practice Naomi'd felt faint simply hearing of, with more than one defective gun muzzle exploding a platoon into nasty black blobs over the ground. Or nearly died with a case of the flu he'd caught in the epidemic from his darling buddies who called him Jewboy.

Guess what had worried his father?

With New York prices sky-high why hadn't Murray sent home more pay?

Oh Tootsie! Seventy, eighty hours a week in the Essex Street market, from dark to dark every day except Saturday—his boss was religious, some religion, the hypocrite! And loyal Tootsie stood up for him. Tootsie wanted the twenty a week, those were the conditions. And from that twenty to dish out a hundred dollars to New York University? Tootsie spoke of the fees as if he'd just lost his best friend, and Naomi's heart hurt too. The father meanwhile had bankbooks stashed away in various places because he suspected all persons including his wife, and certainly didn't trust any single bank with his pitiful hoard. Even that didn't bother Tootsie. What ate him was that the blood money his father'd transfused from the family over the years could have been earning a fortune in General Electric, American Steamships, Chrysler, Prudential stocks. Not that Tootsie'd have profited. His mother was sole beneficiary when the old man kicked off, provided she could outlast the candy store hours and the high blood pressure that his father also endowed her with. But out of obstinacy being a sucker for banks? Crummy Treasury notes pay higher returns!

Even if Naomi disagreed about banks, how she adored Tootsie when he was indignant! And how smart he was—that stupid Postgraduate College of Business! Money breeds money, Tootsie said, poverty breeds wishes. There were two ways of playing the stock market. One is foolproof: big solid cash-down investments. Would the U.S.A. ever skid back to gaslights and clipper ships? How many horses and buggies did you still see on the streets? Sure, he was no dreamer. Securities rise, they likewise can fall—though for the long run up up up was the tune. He'd begged his old man during the war to buy DuPont or Remington, and—"J.P. Morgan, can you break a nickel?"—been ridiculed for his pains. So instead—this was more the playing way of playing the market—you figure the odds and take a flyer on margin, which has the added drawback of costing you interest. And as might have been expected, his flyers so far hadn't flown, like Eagle Aircraft with federal contracts supposedly in the bag only the bag had a hole in the bottom. Ouch, had that soured him once and for all on airplanes!

Poor Tootsie, having to gamble and dream. Naomi loathed that father of his! God in heaven, when she'd have children what wouldn't she do for them! Only, the way things were going, when would she have children? Her kid brother was marrying in June, and Carrie had smirked that she intended to get working on kids right away, why wait, have 'em and get done with it was Carrie Baum's motto. Where would Naomi's kids come from, the Essex Street Fruit Market? Tootsie in Quality Lamps was the one solution. Then he could forget about stocks. So at the height of the rush she'd asked Reisel what sense it made, Reisel killing herself at two jobs and Danny the same, when they could get a real find like Murray to work for them. Imagine Naomi's feelings to have seen Reisel shrug doubtfully.

"So narrow, so pinched a soul? And he has already told you one lie."

"Where is he narrow, because he has a terrible job and no money? And one little white lie—to save his pride—about why he changed schools?"

"With who knows how many black ones behind it."

"I love Murray."

"More the reason for exercise of your normal caution."

Reisel the expert, with that Bookbinder always around at her house, a man of that age. Why the first few times Naomi saw him she had supposed he was there for Gittel not Reisel. And Reisel took it upon herself to advise Naomi on love? But Naomi had had the presence of mind not to express that thought. Otherwise Reisel would have come up with another clever depressing answer that certainly wouldn't have changed a wisp of Naomi's feelings for Tootsie. Instead she'd brought Reisel back to the subject and Reisel had agreed personalities aside they could use a capable man.

Naomi's little brother had let loose though when she tackled him on the trolley home. "Somebody maybe, but not Murray. Let him stick to bananas for my dough."

"Reisel agrees with me."

"Then you and Reisel better plan a new business. Over my dead body that guy."

See how a person gets punished for crazy talk? Not dead—God forbid! —but with that leg in a cast they absolutely needed Tootsie. Why he'd be doing them a favor coming to work for them now! And in her brother's best personal interests too. Remember how Danny'd fought tooth and nail against selling? He'd never wanted to sell to begin with!

So why should Carrie accuse them across the hospital bed?

"Carrie, what did we do wrong?"

"You ask me?" Carrie gave an angry twist of the head. "In this charnel house? I'm getting him out of here," and strode off.

"Carrie, the doctor said no—"

"Did he!"

In the corridor Carrie slammed the phone booth door so hard it bounced open again. And on the telephone cousin Gladys was pulling the cute act? "No, I wouldn't like to tell you. I'll tell your husband the doctor." And next Carrie was left tapping her foot while Nate and his mismate were having some kind of discussion? Nate finally came on and she told him, did she tell him! He wasn't the only one with marriage problems—and her still single. Her boy came from the thriftiest goddam family on earth!

"Whoa," Nate laughed, "who said I have problems?"
And might she drop dead in a phone booth if sight unseen he didn't defend her miserable in-laws to be. He wanted to know what their alternative had been.
"What was my alternative," Carrie answered him, "at the cost of a nickel?" They could have called a competent physician—or did she have the wrong number?—that had been their alternative. They could have turned thumbs down instantly to a charity pestilence hole where they couldn't possibly understand even how to paste plaster on.
"Bandages. With a multiple tibia he can't be in plaster. . . . Carrie, be fair. East Side City's the training school for Postgraduate College of Medicine. Rest assured, they've an excellent staff."
"Am I blind? Contrary Mary, what's gotten into you? Did you wake on the wrong side and see something bad the first thing this morning? If you'd like to be trained on by their excellent staff, just break a leg and run down here. Meanwhile I want your patient Daniel Share—remember him, your patient?—sprung from this Gehenna in fifteen minutes flat."
"You can't move a patient in traction, Carrie."
Don Juan with the thinning hair—Gladys must have been listening in over his shoulder—kept blahing his explanations into Carrie's ear, strictly the doctor of medicine. First chance he had he would run down, he knew a few fellas at East Side City, and look in on Danny.
Big heart!
The East Side City resident Harvey handed her the same dish of boloney but with pepper added—of course give and take. And she was fresh out of doctors, unless you included in the profession that nice dumpy Mincher who conducted poor Mother to the next world, or Gray, who'd recommended Mincher when they moved to New Jersey.
Was ever a woman frustrated so?
God help East Side City Hospital if anything further went wrong with her boy! In the corridor outside the emergency ward her pathetic couple of in-laws to be sat ejected and dejected on hard folding chairs. Blood from stones, silk from pigs' ears?—she almost felt sorry for them. "Forget my display please, I was shocked," galvanizing Naomi up, oy, for a hug.
Sure, have your own way and hugs come six for a nickel, far from an extravagance. Hugs or not, Danny's sentence was weeks in this dungeon, with nurses to shoo visitors away. You hardly had time to hear out his bad dream: he couldn't locate the lamp factory, roaming streets, climbing stairs —wrong places strange faces—with his heart and order book empty. A year of hustling accounts, a year of killing himself that had seemed more like ten years, and the fruits of that misery had been frittered away in an Avenue A gutter! Then a nurse allowed you ten seconds' grace for a murmur of cheer and a peck on the lips—and skiddoo.
Future in-laws, municipal hospitals, and the practice of medicine! In a fury Carrie tracked down an old Village date of hers, Jerry Belik the ambulance chaser. Could he be any good, packed into an office with five

other lawyers each with a swivel, desk and side chair and the legal diploma framed on the wall? Still the Woolworth Building was an impressive address and even facing an alley in perpetual twilight must have meant plenty in rent even divided six ways. But say was he hungry—and no matter how his bank account stood, when wouldn't Jerry be hungry?—and so much the better. How that six-and-a-half-foot-long paper tiger had pursued her on the basis of her wisecrack that her daddy owned an estate in New Jersey and that she worked for laughs and pin money! That had been a courtship of cheap moving pictures to elevate a girl's spirits in the intervals between Schiffstein. And when you considered those shameless cross-examinations over the ten-cent muffin and coffee in Oxford's in his bass voice that rattled up from the hollows of his big feet, his bloodhound pursuit of your financial rating since Dun and Bradstreet had happened to overlook Daddy Moishe, how could you doubt Jerry in a negligence case? Jerry'd finally excavated to Moishe's estate, not with her help—it had been too much fun watching him suffer. Probably her wet hen pal Shirley Shine had given away Daddy Moishe's chickens. And Carrie'd been rebuked by her ardent suitor with the skinny forefinger.

"You've fibbed."

And darned if Jerry hadn't rumbled some sort of rigmarole with much as he'd wish it otherwise his means just then prevented him from committing himself to the kind of layout a girl like her deserved. Nevertheless as a friend—no promises, did you get the kid's drift? and therefore no breach of promises—she should be certain he always would be at her disposal. "Jerry," she'd given him five, "if I ever get run over, you get the call," and most likely set up his prayers for the next month or two.

So now Carrie leaned toward that long crafty-sad face with the eyes twinkling dollar signs and unleashed him on whatever manslaughterer had sailed Danny into a chamber of horrors with his leg in a sling. Let the son of a bitch pay through the nose, wipe the bum out!

Jerry swung forward likewise, pen in hand.

"Witnesses?"

"Dozens," she improvised, she'd phone him their names.

To keep the lad drooling, she haggled over the contingency fee until Jer's normally greenish complexion glowed a nice healthy pink. Then—she Carrie Baum little as the likes of Jerry Belik would ever understand this was after justice not cash!—she gave in to a fifty–fifty split of whatever the case might realize.

At the station house to her joy Honest Abe Lincoln suddenly gazing out of a five dollar bill on the blotter of Officer Donovan's desk procured her two elderly Bolshevik witnesses with, Officer Johnny J. Donovan informed her poker-faced, a hatred of automobiles.

Fog, drizzle, damp crowds, the mobbed El she had to shove herself into next day after work going to Danny, she Carrie Baum did not give one little damn, she was that happy. You will learn, Mr. Archibald Swope, referred to as defendant herein, that in your wild haste to pick up the rents of your Lower East Side properties you do not knock down Carrie Baum's property nolle prosequi! She reached East Side City Hospital a half hour early: absolutely no admittance, they were feeding the animals. But surprise—a couple of skins tucked into the palm of Nurse Marion Dorn and what a help Danny-boy's fiancée could be with the tray!

The chief help that Danny-boy's fiancée could be with the tray of some brownish mess on a plate and a mugful of some murky liquid was to get it out of his sight. She hustled out to a delicatessen for a gala picnic supper for two—corned beef, pastrami, pickles, celery tonic—everything a boy needed to bring the roses back to his cheeks.

"But—" she fished up the legal papers from Jerry—"sign first, in your blood."

Himself, Danny hadn't thought of a lawsuit, but by now blood for blood he was ready for anything. He wrote his name down so hard he dislocated the weights on the trick apparatus up there and gritted his teeth at the shock. Carrie hurried to get the traction adjusted and when Nurse Adams on duty now made a surly comment on the feedbag, Carrie sweetened her up with a great big prune bun. Which only proved—though in the smelly twilight flotilla of beds this dragged just a weak smile out of the boy—that some nurses come cheaper than others. Danny ate, drank, lay back and breathed a long sigh. In every sense tenderly—"Baby sad?"—Carrie eased herself sidesaddle to the edge of the bed and . . . pressed that slim girlish hand of his.

"Not sad," Danny's face crinkled, "worried sick."

Who'd be peddling lamps while he was laid up, that's what he wanted to know. His old man—Danny also was wondering who'd sicked that guy on him—had flashed in for a visit in a beaver collar and bowler hat, like a King Lear from the Yiddish Art Theater. "A broken leg," his father had kept gloomily shaking the head, "I hope that you'll be spared the worst aftereffects." He'd sung crutches, limps, agonized sweat bullets to sell one lousy necktie. "Of course lamps aren't so hard, you can sit down if they let you while you expound the advantages. Still . . ." To shut him up and get rid of him Danny'd offered him the money in the side-table drawer. So Hymie had gotten on his high horse, returned a twenty he'd cadged before, and marched out insulted.

"Out of the goodness of his heart he showed up to needle me."

Carrie silently added the father to her Share shit list.

Ask Naomi, Danny went on, what she was doing about a salesman and she looked at you cockeyed. "Don't worry," she said . . . Danny tossed up his arms and let them plop. Don't worry. She had something in mind—he could read her like a book—such as hire nobody and save twenty-four cents. Even apart from drugged dreams, neighboring moans and groans—sometimes his own strangled groan would wake him—curtains pulled around beds and corpses wheeled to the morgue, he could hardly sleep nights. Sure, he loved his sisters. When he first opened his eyes here to Naomi then Leah they'd looked like he'd felt, so much so his heart had sunk that he'd reached the end of the line. But humoring him to pacify him? Leah lied sales applicants were breaking the doors down in West Street, the question sonny was which one not to beat off. Show him the ad? They'd called an agency. Yeah. But say they had. Where do you find a three months' salesman? Don't worry—despair. . . . He was almost desperate enough to grab Naomi's nickel-nurser the banana oil man, just for reorders till the bandages were removed. Yeah. Then he'd have to let Kid Languor stay on, a permanent fixture. Jesus Christ!

"Nix," Carrie said, "on that green banana. I wish I were a man. I'd do your selling myself and solve the whole problem. Of course," she twinkled at him, "you'd be stuck with me after the three months were up. Mind? Puckering up, eh? Listen—" she kissed him—"does your Aunt Carrie not rise to the occasion! Put your foot down, the good one, to Naomi. Let her latch onto a live wire, and when you're ready to put the other foot down, let him go sizzle the road." And wouldn't that honest blue-eyed mick of a face survey her suspiciously on behalf of some unknown unhired coolie.

"The road to where?"

"Cincinnati, Detroit, Hotzeplotz—we'll work it out. Quality Lamps Light the City, why not the Country? Why shouldn't *we* drive Packards around and run people over?"

Danny grinned, "You dog," with mansions and limousines brightening those baby-blues now.

Carrie slipped her icy hand under the sheet—"Get rich quick kiddo"—and gave that hot supple belly a good hard cold rub. Danny winced, the dumb pulleys pulled their act again, and Carrie had to run fetch nurse Adams. And who were there in Siberia but the three bears she meant Shares, the immigrant Raisin with a shawl on the head, and for a fifth between them still another female, some mouse with curls—the ladies-in-waiting on the corridor spine crackers. Carrie cheerfully flashed the marquise at them as she brought back the nurse—and did they look stunned! But merciful Carrie didn't keep them in suspense about the boy's condition that long once she'd seen them.

Just long enough for them to feel to the marrow who her boy'd be forsaking all others for.

For Leah's Friday night noodle soup and roast chicken visits Naomi always made sure to meet Murray elsewhere, at Sarah's, or—if Sarah was on one of her on and off outs with Joe Seiden God only knew why—at New York University after Tootsie's pitiful classes. Altogether no thanks to Leah, especially if the weather was cold and Naomi and Murray had to sit over coffee at some nasty drugstore counter below Washington Square with dirty looks from the counterman as if they were loitering. It was embarrassing. A boy had no money, so people branded him cheap!

But tonight, a Friday to Naomi's misfortune, she had a sick headache and here was Leah. Naomi knew she should pull herself together and go meet Tootsie—anything to keep Leah as long as possible from setting eyes on Tootsie. Jack Berger, manly as he'd been, hadn't suited Naomi's sister any more than Phil Stein had, rotten as he'd been. Why should Leah think any better of darling Tootsie? Or else, since Naomi gave in to the headache and lay down with a vinegar compress which was no good for the curse anyhow, she should have stayed in bed when Tootsie came. Then he would have given a sympathetic kiss to her and gone right home. Instead, at Tootsie's voice sick as she was she dressed and smeared lipstick on. So before she could say a word Tootsie complained, "What goes on? You just leave me standing there in the cold outside N.Y.U.?" Granted he thought she'd stood him up, he could have used a little more tact.

Naturally Ma shook her head and Leah had to butt in, "She was painting the town vinegar-white with her headache bandage."

And naturally Murray would suppose—"You can tell that just by looking"—that some stupid joke was on him. Naomi's stiff upper lip wilted and she had to lie down again, she couldn't cope with them all. Then Tootsie said, "You really are under the weather," and touched her sick cheek. What a darling!

But how much of a surprise was it in the factory next day to hear Leah's crack about his all-around thrift, even in displays of affection. What had Leah expected him to do, jump on top of Naomi in bed? My God, when Naomi and Murray were alone Naomi had all she could do to push him away he got her so hot and bothered. He too. He'd grin, "Next stop Allen Street." That meant prostitutes—though she'd made it clear she wasn't interested in such information. In spite of what her smart aleck sister said he showed almost too much emotion, not like that iceberg Stein, throwing you out of hotel rooms in a strange city at midnight. A lot Leah knew. Leah'd simply taken a hate on Murray because the two of them had left Tompkins Square together last night and he hadn't driven Leah home. Why should he have, for her sarcastic mouth? Then and there Naomi made up her mind that Murray was their new salesman—and with nobody's permission either needed or requested! Sunday she told Murray to come in Monday and get to know all about their lamps first so when he went out to sell he'd know what he was selling.

"I'm not that interested in selling," he said, "I'd prefer your job."

"Then what would I do?"

"You'll do my shirts, my socks—you'll have plenty to do."

He laid hands on her, so maybe he didn't go to the—ugh—prostitutes that often, though he said they were very reasonable, only seventy-five cents. She told him yes fine, that was her idea too, she didn't mind doing diapers and socks. Meanwhile, till Danny came back, Tootsie'd learn, then he'd sell. And that was okay with Tootsie.

Only the poor kid misunderstood how they worked at Quality Lamps and marched in his first day dressed like Astor's pet horse, with his blue pinstripe suit, a pink shirt and white collar, and a bright blue tie from the birthday lot she'd gotten him through Papa. Again as luck had it Leah saw him first and—that was how well she knew him after one meeting—mistook him for a customer.

"The bohemian girl," Leah supposedly made fun of herself to Ma later, "I trotted over and simpered, 'Sir, can I help?' Could I kick myself!"

Kick Tootsie she meant.

And what was so terrible if he'd thought his new job required a Sunday suit? Now that Reisel was in charge of lamp decoration and Leah who'd yawned at lamp decoration now yawned as forelady, you can bet that Naomi's big sister lost no time badgering Tootsie to lend a hand with those crates. Naomi saw. She was at her desk watching through the partition glass. Tootsie squinted against one of his cigarettes he smoked too many of, without a word took off his jacket, folded it neatly over a crate and pitched in with shipping boy work. Leah was offended because he talked back to her afterward. "Workers work, managers manage. Firms do better that way." And why not, even if not in their particular firm? That was what they taught you in college. But oh no, not for Leah. Murray could have used more time in the factory but Naomi had to send him out on the rounds right away to separate him from her sister.

One friend, Carrie—and the rest enemies. Between Danny's bad temper and his wrapped-up leg Naomi was scared to tell him Murray was the new salesman. What would she have done if not for Carrie, much as Carrie had scared her for a second with that fierce look. But then Carrie'd laughed, "Don't be alarmed, that's my expression cogitationally," and given Naomi a pat. "You can't skin a cat with spilt milk. Lie."

"Lie what?"

"Make up a salesman for Danny."

So Naomi had made up Kalman Morgan, Morgan for Murray and K equaled Kaye, with wholesale paper experience from Tootsie's stocks and bonds he was always talking about. Leah—"Why did you tell Danny Morgan, after J.P.?"—would not skip a trick. Tootsie'd once remarked to Naomi that with ten million Moishes on the Lower East Side known as Murray, when he received his degree he'd let himself be known legally as . . . Morgan Kaye, Jr.

"That should be Gentile enough for Wall Street, huh?"

She'd felt dizzy. "You mean you're converting?"

"Just the name, silly."

What a . . . cornered kid—how he tore at her heartstrings!

But that must have been how Morgan had popped into her head when Danny suddenly asked what the new guy's name was. Next her brother had wanted her to send him this Morgan to coach.

"And let him waste an hour and a half on the trolleys?" she'd been inspired. "Coach me and I'll tell him . . . I'll see if I remember my steno."

And no cracks from Carrie, more of a sister than her actual sister, about the great J.P. Morgan-Murray. On a convenient chicken soup Friday the actual sister let loose beginning with flattery to a sensible brainy silky-haired doll like Naomi. "Let him stay salesman. It doesn't matter to me—" Big favor! Murray mightn't have been a dynamo, but he still could persuade people. "—But him as your tootsie? Reason declares: stingy, opinionated, a herring on ice blowing cigarette smoke in your face. Come on blondie, come on baby doll," Leah had the nerve to reach for her hands, which she yanked away, "you deserve better than that."

"I got what I deserved, thanks to you."

"You did?"

"Yes, breaking up with Jack Berger, thanks to your jealousy."

"Mama," Leah turned to Golda full splash over the dishes, "did you hear your younger daughter?"

"Am I deaf?"

"Then don't just stand there like that sponge in your hand, Mama," Leah cried out. "Let's have your vote."

"I vote for my children, but will they vote for me?"

"What a help," Leah laughed. "But Naomi, you were wrong, baby. I ran into Kid Swagger, yes Jack, last Saturday on Fifth Avenue, with a carbuncle on his tie, a rock on his finger, a gold watch he kept flashing the size of a clock on Metropolitan Life, and an apartment on Riverside Drive he invited me to—not for the etchings alone, for his five G's as he put it worth of furnishings furnished by Sloane's, not to mention his river view as good as from the 1917 Hoboken liner steaming toward the Bay with that phony —he's even changed his name: Jack Berger, John Mount—on his way over to give the heinies their whipping."

"I hope you enjoyed the view."

"I didn't avail myself of it. Soon I may have a much better one," the woman of mystery added, "than any that candidate for the Big House could offer—and so should you baby, listen to me. Two wrongs don't make a Mr. Right."

Know-it-all Leah, even before she moved to the Village. What Leah didn't know and Naomi wasn't going to spoil again by telling her—bad enough Naomi had overflowed to killjoy Reisel and gotten Reisel's "You must take care not to confuse the dictates of the body with advice from the spirit"—was that sick with love for Jack as Naomi had been, when she met Tootsie it was as if Jack Berger had never existed.

So Naomi didn't need her sister constantly dredging up Jack.

Oh America, that all Hymie's life whiners sniveled about! How many years since his last virgin—what was her name: Madge, Mary, Maureen? —with the coal-heaver father out of a job? Meeting her you saw the bull of a papa and his cronies in caps—from a distance, thank God—lounging against stoops or ashcans in Paradise Alley. Who could keep track of the old-time panics with Hymie's own papa's snarls and abuse with sons to sweat and no work, but thanks to Hymie's little whatever her name was, the '93 panic was a panic he'd never forget. Even the contractors were crying that year—but not Hymie Share. He'd had his work cut out for him, the warm happy months of rides on the Elevated up to the woods at the edge of the fields in West Farms with what was her name, when suddenly from a cute Irish girl she was transformed like magic into a drab of missed periods and threats he must marry her. Did he pray to God just let him out of this and he should drop dead if he'd ever go near a virgin again. God listened, she turned out not to be pregnant, and—with the exception of Debbie Horowitz and you saw what happened: a plague on that witch!—Hymie'd stuck to his word: No more girls without husbands.

Still was he a brute? He had feelings. Principles absolutely—but heartlessness no. Do unto your neighbor as you would be done by. Hilda adored him from the moment he'd met her through that little nothing, his wife's cousin Sarah, in the Actors Café. With Hilda's amazement at small things like a cab up Fifth Avenue and a steak and bootleg glass of champagne in Delmonico's main dining room, with her eyes drinking him in while he spoke, her gratitude, what could he do but fall in love with her? And if his heart had gone out to a timid adoring girl, had that cost Madame Henriette Nadler a penny? Not one cent of the short rations she kept him on!

Since Horowitz with the tie sweatshop could elevate himself from a ground floor Baxter Street flat to a West Broadway loft and branch out wholesale, why shouldn't Hymie also benefit from prosperity by the sweat of his own brow? As to Horowitz's niece the witch Debbie, you peeked into that madhouse—stitchers pressers, snippers packers—and knock wood she was nowhere in sight. Horowitz, this little gray man at the edge of the bedlam, said to him, to him, Hymie Share, "You're still alive?" and Hymie had to throw his head back and laugh.

He swindled the swindler into letting him take out a line on commission—sure on a steady basis, what else? Hymie breezed like a whirlwind through hell-and-gone haberdasheries in God's country Brooklyn, undersold competition with Horowitz's junk labeled pure silk, fattened his wallet—and for the present resigned, leaving Horowitz to stare at him goggle-eyed.

Guess what the great thespian Nadler accused him of when he popped in with a posy of violets to tickle her under the chin with? That he did not fool her, running around every day with some woman.

False. He saw Hilda at night, and not even then if his ham actress was at liberty and dragged him cast as hopeless admirer to show off to her pals. But if you honestly said you'd been working, what did you say you did with the money?

So he kissed her and kidded her, "No woman like you."

"As you weel discover, if you do not watch your step."

What a difference, her and his Hilda: the fake and the real! One goes at your throat with little sharp teeth, the other defends you in a fury. That small piece of cheese his wife's cousin Sarah had dished out all kinds of poison about him to her friend Hilda: woman-chaser, bad old man, monster thrown out of the house—and had Hilda given it back to her! Hilda, fortunately, had heard the real truth from Hymie's own lips and fallen in love with him for it.

"Years don't make people old," words came tumbling from Hilda's mouth while you listened in pleased surprise. "Those . . . boys, at the Settlement dances, who look a person up and down and then . . . pass her by—they're old. Oh, they're so wise and cautious! You're young. Lucky me, to have met you. Last night I dreamt I was . . . searching for you through the whole city, and I couldn't find you. I woke up in despair, until . . . I remembered—"

Hilda had caught his fingers and kissed them in a café where he sat with her! So what had he been able to do except give in?

His cane in his hand, his Homburg at just the right angle—and from the bedroom door in the Broadway Central three pairs of stupefied eyes that had never seen such a thing as a man going out in the morning: his hennaed Madame's, her cat's and her slavering mutt's. Where was he going? Where he usually went, to Glantz in hope of business. He had to rehearse the same old story again, how Glantz was considering wholesaling, there could be something in it for Hymie. Well beezness, hard as it was to believe . . . "But eet had better be business."

Let her go to hell, eet had better be. Such a send-off could throw a wet blanket on a man's whole day if he let it. But one breath of March sunlight like spring and Hymie pushed that . . . landlady out of his mind.

What a darling, what an innocent Hilda! In the rush of the Commodore lobby, the new place he'd picked for his new bride, she hung back with a dear, funny anxiety. She'd lied for the millinery she and her mother both worked at that she was sick, and now she thought she'd better go in to work, they'd find out. Then, on account of the Chicago address tag Hymie had strung on a suitcase he'd brought to make the man and wife check-in look kosher, the bellhop had to be chummy and ask her how was yesterday's weather out West ma'am.

"Out . . . West?"

"Chicago was fine," Hymie flipped the man a fat half a dollar, "but here's even better."

Here could not have been any better. With their palatial bedroom over a big sunny court and Hilda's sweet frightened body he was so able to calm and excite, who could have been younger than Hymie? He brought her to such a pitch that when it must have hurt most she only gasped and squeezed harder!

She wouldn't go down for lunch, the darling, she had all that she wanted in this hushed, unbelievable room. Little by little the sun crept from their bed, reddened the top row of windows across the courtyard, then faded altogether. Finally, in the twilight, muffled honks from the rush hour city brought dinnertime and la Nadler closer. Hymie sat up in bed and laid his hand on Hilda's waist.

"Your mama won't miss you?"

"Miss me? She . . . despises me. But I'll show her. I'm taking my man home so she can see you."

Oy.

"Your married man?"

"What you are isn't married. Throwing you out." Hilda drew him down again fondly. "Catch me throwing you out."

So he and Glantz would have grabbed a bite in Flatbush. Old lady Nadler should award him a medal—with her corsets and varicose veins.

But Ida Klainvogel was another of those spiteful bloodsuckers, even worse than Hilda had said. Hilda dug up a picture of old Klainvogel, a skullcap and beard about fifty, and if the eyes had been that sad and the forehead that worried no wonder, he should rest in peace Klainvogel, with what he'd had for a wife. She was an up-to-date lady, this Ida Klainvogel, with a chopped wave of hair and a starvation figure. A wise glance toward him, toward her daughter and back, and, "You knew Jake?" she said. "Yes, Share, I remember. He looked up to you like an older brother, didn't he, when you were at Wolfe's?"

And at the Broadway Central all of a sudden Henrietta was living by farmers' hours, asleep eleven o'clock with the safety lock on while he pounded the door on one side and her hound bayed on the other. She was asleep like he was asleep. Fagged out he was from a day of exertion, but did he rattle that doorknob!

"Go," her revolting stage voice came floating out, "ah-way."

"Where," he yelped over that good for nothing yelping dog, "this time of night?"

"Wherevair you came from."

Automatically he gave the knob a couple of more shakes . . . but say, was that idea so bad? He had to plead for accommodations in the Broadway Central Hotel when he had a room in the Commodore till tomorrow? He lounged in a taxi to uptown, a cute waitress in the coffee shop at the hotel served him a glistening Danish with raisins, he soaked in a luxurious tub, he curled up glowing and drowsy between linen sheets still fragrant not of a lumpy old lady's vanishing cream but of the Narcisse des Bois he'd given Hilda, her first perfume, that she'd dabbed on to please him. He felt her lips taking kisses from his as he fell asleep with a smile, and he woke fresh, alive, set for a good hearty breakfast.

Quite a difference—he munched buttered toast from room service with his pinkie stuck up in the air—from the Bleecker Street bedbugs on the lockout before. Henrietta there always was. She could stew till whenever he wanted. Soon she'd have had her offended wife act up to the neck, the artiste. She was an artiste, and he wasn't an artiste? He was as good an artiste as she, better, let her ask Hilda. And he was supposed to play second fiddle day in and day out to the prima donna, her cat and her dog?

He distributed tips left and right, paid his bill, checked his valise in Grand Central Station underneath the hotel, then settled himself in the lobby with the *Morning American* till he'd surprise Hilda at noon. But who had patience with newspapers? He did not bet on racehorses except at the track, so what was so special if Rebuke won the Tia Juana Special? As to the front page love nest murder, with pictures of the deceased in her underwear and the figure didn't compare to his Hilda, he could never understand why people who can't get along don't just say goodbye and good luck instead of breaking out the artillery. So he deposited the *American* where it belonged, in a handy wastebasket and relished the number of ladies' eyes—and not all so ancient—that got entangled with his before he swung his walking stick past the doorman into swarming Forty-second Street sunshine. A shame—Madison Avenue was full of skinny ones hypnotized by shop window displays—his dear girl had to sew her poor fingers off for these ugly felt helmets that they were wearing.

He posted himself across from the millinery, and ah at last, modesty, there she was, with that healthy figure and her eyes fixed on the sidewalk! Hymie danced tiptoe through the crowds and caught her—and did she give a gasp!

"No lunch with Mama?"

"I've had enough of her insults. I'm moving out. Hymie, let's . . . look for an apartment?" She glanced at him worriedly. "Since you're in a rooming house anyhow?"

Hymie couldn't say the proposition was thrilling, for him to support an apartment after all he'd been through. "Theatrical management has its ups," he told her, "but this minute it's downs."

Hilda—they'd never discussed embarrassing topics like this before—blushed and pleaded, "That doesn't matter." She earned thirty a week, heavy weeks thirty-five.

Live right and God takes care of you! Drop dead Madame Nadler and your dog and your cat and your smelly two rooms in the Broadway Central—though of course he'd still have to sleep there tonight. He pressed Hilda's hands, "Practical lady," and they beamed at each other like children while lunch-goers jostled them and they didn't notice. "Bubbeleh, you have a few dollars? I'll treat you to Longchamps."

"She's," Hilda emptied her purse for him—it amounted to peanuts, with an apology—"always doled me out my own money."

"Woolworth's," he reassured the darling, "will do the trick too."

Just as well Woolworth's. At the five-and-ten lunch counter Hilda was so excited she could hardly swallow a bite. She wished they could find a glass house to live in and let people throw stones as long as everyone saw them together. She was so proud of him! And he proud of her. With a face alive like this, full of color, oh not to mention the body, a young girl, let the whole world see them, in particular Madame Henriette Nadler.

Hilda was going to waste no time. She'd take the afternoon off, they would apartment hunt right now. In fact she'd quit! She would not go on working hemmed in next to her mother. And the boss wasn't going to bully her out of the wages he owed her either, the way he did with some girls who left him. She happily laughed.

"You make me brave."

"Brave bubbeleh," Hymie laughed too but from the other side of the mouth, "only who'll pay the rent if you quit?"

"I can get a new job in a minute, I'm a good worker. Till I met you that's all I was good for."

Argue with love. But he wished he were as certain as she was about her new job. She marched into the old one a heroine, and—what?—she marched out with a red face and eyes down. So the boss had cheated her of her money. Hymie could have wrung the girl's foolish neck.

"I couldn't bring myself to saying I quit, he would have fired my mother out of spite. I said I still didn't feel well."

"Sure darling," Hymie breathed easy again, "why cut off your nose to spite your face?"

"No, it wasn't that. Suddenly she doesn't bother me any more." Hilda kissed him there in the street. "On account of you I'm a better person already."

Oh Cinderella—Hymie wished that he could give her a palace! Anyway, with him there wouldn't be the Stanton Street hole in the wall where an economical mother bloodsucks her own child to dress up in the latest style like a corpse with bony knees showing. Just off Canal Street, near the theaters and all the cafés, stood the new house they were building six or seven years ago when he broke his leg. As far as parks were concerned Hymie could take them or leave them, but the second that Hilda set foot in Essex Street she clapped together her hands at some trees with brown sticky branches. The apartment his family enjoyed—at his expense—faced a park. Why should Hilda have less?

And what a vacancy—big, airy, with a toilet and bathtub as fixtures. You opened the radiator, steam heat clanked out. You squinted into the gas stove no wildlife, you tapped your cane on the wall and the building still stood. His innocent bubbeleh was speechless with ecstasy in front of the gray little landlord.

And one month's concession.

Hymie was prepared to sign, and imagine, the scrawny cipher with the pot belly and the shirt rumpled under his coat—what good did he have of his riches?—demanded rent on the spot.

"But," Hymie reminded the creature, "the first month is free."

A shrug. "The last month is free."

Jolly along misery until doomsday, the one-track mind of a landlord was filled up with rent. Finally this specimen would go halfies: half a month now and at the end of a year a half a month free. But no down payment no lease. Hold the place till Saturday? Hymie and his daughter could look the landlord up Saturday, and if no one else beat them to it the place would be here. Hymie could have stepped on that roach, but, "We have no daughter," Hilda told him off for them both.

Still, Hymie's bubbeleh was so anxious for that flat—and she would have it, he guaranteed. Meanwhile she should go pack, he knew another hotel temporarily, not the Commodore—less expensive but nicer with a park underneath. Himself, at West Broadway he asked Horowitz for ties on credit, and did that Horowitz have a vile mouth! Hymie gave as good as he got, and next tried hocking his suitcaseful of clothing from Grand Central. On Sixth Avenue a pawnbroker, for a man's silk underwear, pima shirts and practically new three button worsted, offered four big smackaroos. Was that a way for a Jew to treat a Jew? Let that bloodsucker drop dead with his four dollars. Hymie checked in with the full suitcase at the Madison Square and smiled down at the people taking shortcuts through the park down there, dotting the sidewalks like ants, risking their lives between automobiles and trucks, hurrying in and out of high buildings that blocked off the late sunshine.

A bunch of poor fish!

There was time before his family would be home from work so he could borrow some money. He left a call with the operator and stretched out for a nice nap.

Golda honestly supposed that the young man with the Homburg and cane had rung the wrong bell before she saw it was Hymie. Then what tumult in her chest, the way her heart skittered. Should she—why else was he at her door finally—take him back? Both her ducks Naomi and Danny so they said wanted her after the weddings. However, the parties of the second part—Naomi's prince, Danny's princess—forced sickly grins if the subject came up. And the party of the third part, Golda herself, would as soon have ridden the express to the cemetery as be fifth wheel to either of those chilling prospective households-in-law. Her eldest Leah kept wisecracking, "Mama don't worry, when the hour strikes you'll turn into a Village flapper." But did Golda want this man, or was it just vanity, not to be the woman whose husband had left her?

Hymie smiled, "Should I stay in the hall?"

"No no—"

He'd forgotten by now what a nice flat it was, his children's that he'd raised to prosperity by the sweat of his brow: their overstuffed gold-brocade sofa he made himself at home on, an Oriental rug, the deep easy chairs, and of course on the tables fancy lamps from their factory. His son on crutches poked the royal nose in, nodded—thanks very much—and, with some tact for once, disappeared back into his bedroom. With his son an ex-tenant in June maybe Hymie'd been slightly too much in a hurry today committing himself. . . . Ah, but you thought of that loving girl, with her attributes, who'd be with you tonight and the regrets thinned out and disappeared like the clouds passing the moon now.

His wife—"You're flourishing, Hymie"—reminded him in her flat voice that she was there.

"The latest tan check!" he spread his jacket for her. But she hung like bad weather, not a smile not another sound from that long face with black marks under the eyes. A shame, a woman who'd soured so—he tried to brighten her up. "And under the El on Sixth Avenue they had the gall to offer two dollars for a beautiful garment like this. Yet it just goes to show, you can't tell a book by its cover."

"Some books are old stories. What do you want, Hymie?"

Be nice and they spit in your eye. But—"Twenty, twenty-five dollars a couple of weeks"—whatever he got in this place was more than owed him.

Naomi changing into her housecoat heard voices inside, her mother's and . . . it couldn't be. She tugged a comb a few times through her hair, peered into the living-room, and—"Pa!"—it was. Had he come back after all, now at the worst possible moment when she still hadn't told Danny that Murray was the salesman? "What are you doing here?" She clasped her chest.

Hymie was not aggrieved that his favorite who he'd brought up in unstinting love had without a word to the father engaged herself—and to a lemon, from his good information from Hilda through that snotty Sarah. But she was aggrieved because as his duty he'd reminded her look before you leap. Meanwhile his wife God bless her—"He's collecting for a good cause"—kept dropping cannonballs on him.

"Good cause?" Naomi was baffled.

"There he sits. What better cause to invest twenty dollars in?"

Him selfish? That was carrying it a little too far. "For ties!" he told them no more than the truth.

"For his ties," Golda nodded.

Poor Ma, she was bitter and who could blame her, but—"Let me get the money"—such a relief, Naomi could breathe again. And ties were much better than women, though the last time she'd seen Pa ties and women had seemed mixed up like batter. It had been a mistake, she'd sensed it beforehand, taking ties from her father for Tootsie's birthday last fall. In a way it was Murray's fault with his everlasting economy that was bound to be catching. Reisel told her she must fight these tendencies, and Reisel was right. Naomi hadn't been able to resist asking Pa for wholesale knowing he probably wouldn't charge her at all. So along with Pa's telephone number Danny had charmingly told her that their father was part of some white-powdered dame's animal club on lower Broadway. She'd hollered at her brother for that, but Pa insisted she pick up the ties there and it turned out to be as bad as Danny had said. Worse. She'd felt so ashamed of Pa, showing off the rooms as if they were his. With pink frills everywhere, a cat that ran under the bed and—you almost got scared to death—a drooling dog the size of a horse, in a glance you saw it was a woman's apartment. Naomi'd come close to blurting Why don't you come home Pa, Ma misses you. Only Pa'd always been one of Danny's various hates, and who wanted to fall into her brother's mouth? And if she pestered Danny into saying all right for Ma's sake, how would she ever persuade him to let Murray into the business. So she'd just stood like a sap with the expression she could never disguise when she felt unhappy. Of course Pa'd been offended and the free ties gave him the right to add his two cents to everyone else's about her engagement. Did she need the worry she was rushing into something she shouldn't? And Pa had been more offended when she answered him back. So she could at least make it up to him now. In June, after Danny was married, she'd make it up to Ma too. She'd bring her parents together again, which would be better for Ma besides than living with one of her children.

Naomi unpinned the money bag she kept attached to her step-ins, removed two tens, added a five which would pay for those ties she'd given Murray—more than pay for them—replaced the five, took it out again, tried a deep breath, and in the end with only slight pain brought in twenty-five dollars. So she got the big kiss and poor Ma got the wink.

Well! Downstairs Hymie gave himself a hearty smack on the wallet and for a second enjoyed the fresh loamy smell—a park could have its points! —from Tompkins Square Park across the way in the lamplight. He hailed a taxicab and kept it at Hilda's, where even out in the street you could hear the mother screaming. The parlor looked like a battlefield, with the mother red throwing clothes on the floor and the daughter white gathering them into a tired satchel. With the dignity of the man Ida Klainvogel's Jake used to regard as an older brother, Hymie tipped his Homburg, helped Hilda pack, and with his ears ringing from the mother's abuse wished her good health.

Then—what?—Hilda sat in the taxi like a stone, mute. You caressed her—like wood. At Essex Street you told her come watch him sign her first lease. She wouldn't. You had to go by yourself. And in their room at Madison Square she sat like doomed. You touched her, she stared.

"I'm sorry. You're stuck with a crazy girl. She's driven me crazy."

"She's crazy not you, bubbeleh. You don't have time to be crazy, we have to go down and eat supper."

"I have time till I die. I only hope that it's soon."

Oy, at five dollars a night with his vanishing bankroll it would have to be soon. Was this what he'd fallen into? But he drew over a chair, and while her limp hands were cold, under the short skirt her lap was warm and exciting. "How would I live then, bubbeleh?" he asked with moist lashes.

Hilda glanced at him. "No?"

What, tears now? She moved forward and threw herself at him.

"Thank you thank you thank you thank you."

Was Hymie an artiste, Madame Henriette Nadler, or was he not? They had bed first, then supper, then—better than dying, his Hilda said—he took her to Delancey Street to buy furniture on easy payments.

Surprise—he had forgotten his checkbook. So—the furniture man gave a smile only moderately nauseated ten at night after two hours of choosing and haggling—the first easy payment would have to wait till tomorrow. As to where it would come from, never, never would he ask his fine son the expulsion expert lounging around like a king at home. That was a last resort absolutely. But his daughter Leah the advanced woman—a father was entitled to be accommodated with a small loan from her!

You couldn't make the touch in their factory in front of Naomi after you'd just touched Naomi. So, next morning, he began by sneaking his wardrobe out of Fatty's suite in the Broadway Central through a nice tip to the porter. They tied his trunk to the top of a taxi and on Essex Street a few coins to the hookey players had the trunk hauled upstairs to the bare bedroom which fixed up, Madame Nadler, would make Hotel Broadway Central look like a dump by comparison. Quickly he changed to dapper gray sharkskin, only hoping to pop Henrietta's eyes out in the Actors Café. Sure enough she was present and did her eyes pop seeing that garment from her closet on him! A wave to his cronies and he let Madame Henriette straighten out her digestive system as best she could while he rushed uptown to hold hands at lunch with his Hilda.

And with the last purple of sunset staining the sky down the end of a long street he snapped his cane through the clear evening air in the Village where for his money the privates of industry beat the captains any day of the week, cuddly brown mice with their long legs and short coats, twitching up stoops. Then inviting lights flicked on in the houses. Ah, in—yes—Leah's block a real juicy one hurried past with her arms full, and her in particular he wouldn't have minded. . . . But, she maneuvered bundles, purse and a key on top of her stoop, and he could swear—had that been his daughter Leah passing him by? He pulled out the eyeglasses to stick on his nose, and, so help him—

Raise children—so they'll ignore you!

"Papa how sweet of you!"—and everything in that smile was false but the teeth—"You've come to wish me a happy birthday!"

"Many happy returns bubbeleh," and two could play at that game, "how old are you today, twenty-one?"

"Henny," Leah called toward the kitchen, "did you hear that? Is it any wonder my papa's a joy to the world?"

While Miss Black Hand dipped her knife into a father, from the kitchen emerged . . . her fairy prince, built like granite with a dainty green apron on and smiling eyeglasses (a straight Gentile haircomb by the name of Henny?), wiping his fingers on the apron to give Hymie a shake.

"Never mind what she says, Mr. Share, Leah will always be my baby too."

And this Gentile Jew or Jewish Gentile began belaboring him with engagements, birthdays and—what?—grand opening parties, and if a person parted his lips to change the subject a minute to something important, the daughter would chime in, "Isn't that wonderful? Aren't you thrilled, Papa?" Thank God the turtledove's nostrils finally hustled him back to his pot roast.

"Leah," Hymie talked while the talking was good, "I'm only mortified that what I wanted to bring for your birthday I couldn't. Temporarily I'm—"

"Oh Papa that doesn't matter, you brought yourself and good wishes. Now—you've never been here before, have you? Last year you must have forgotten my birthday the way I wish I could every year but so many people won't let me. So let me show you my lovely apartment."

The father had to grind his jaws under a smile and she showed him her lovely apartment, picture by picture, trinket by trinket, one flowerpot on top of another. "Isn't this bed lamp charming? Reisel painted the vase and shade. You remember Reisel?" If he caught his death of cold on the balcony for a squint in the dark at a backyard like a thicket, his daughter could take the credit. And she kept him out there. "My preview of Italy," she chirped at him.

"Italy?"

"Oh Papa, for our honeymoon, Henny just told you. Weren't you listening? Henny's given notice at Universal Assurance, I'm giving notice at Quality Lamps, and we've bought the lease to a nice curio shop. Aren't you pleased for us?" Inside the smart aleck sat him down on her sofa hard as a box and—"Well Papa!"—beamed in his face. Through teeth still knocking together he had to explain his Horowitz deal—better than commission: cash on the line like in the peddler days but to sell to retailers—without a sign of encouragement from the Village wise guy.

"So that's it," Leah said.

He shrugged, "For two weeks," and could see those eyes enjoying themselves at the expense of a father.

"The blink of an eyelash, eh Papa?"

And so help him God she left him flat—disappeared! An emergency maybe? No: voices, though she hadn't gone to the kitchen. Yet in this idiot apartment that's where the whispers were coming from and much as you strained you couldn't hear. Crane the neck, you saw Miss Henny's broad back with his pots and pans. A father proposes, but a stranger disposes. And the father?

He cooled his heels.

Where did his son and eldest daughter inherit those hard hearts? And people paid cash at the Civic to shed tears over a Yiddish *King Lear*!

With a father's heartfelt curse Hymie got into his overcoat. But dignity,

Father. She would not hear him complain. Then her bell rang as he was buttoning up and for this needless to say his daughter came rushing. Blood is thicker than water? You should have seen the welcome she handed some mutt with a mouthful of gums between a weather-stained fedora and a scarf like a shoeshine rag. At that it was the kitchen fairy, the rat that bit when your back was turned, who condescended to introduce you. And if this Waldstein or Baldstone was likewise new to the daughter, more shame to her while a father walked out ignored.

"Papa don't run— Here."

An I.O.U.? Very funny.

Exactly One Hundred Dollars, the check said, *Leah Share*. . . .

"Bubbeleh," Hymie smacked her a loving kiss, "you were the one I could always count on!"

"Take your coat off, Mr. Share," Henny said, "stay for the party."

"Certainly, Papa," his daughter couldn't resist, "is it so important you meet Glantz right away, I mean Horowitz?"

"Yes, Horowitz," Hymie let the child have her joke, and he even figured out an excuse for her young man. "Are you a cook—I mean by profession?" And if that was also a joke, they were hysterical laughing, let them enjoy themselves even at his expense. He kissed his daughter once more, gave the two nice young men a cordial goodbye and made tracks.

As the door closed behind Hymie, "Lively father you have, Leah," at the birthday party Julius Waldman wistfully exposed those protruding teeth. "Mine keeps out of the way, except to reach high shelves for my mother."

"Is she very short?" Leah asked.

"About the height of Napoleon."

So despite his looks—malocclusion, a round-shouldered stance, resembling Napoleon only in height, tie askew, the suit that seemed slept in—this Julius they'd invited to meet Naomi was far from being a dud. As Henny'd warned though, small possibility the meeting would come to anything. Too bad Naomi hadn't met Julius before she'd met Murray. But where could Naomi have met Julius? Not in the actuarial department of Universal Assurance Inc. where he and Henny worked. Not in the Bronx under the supervision of Mother Waldman. Certainly not here in Bank Street since Leah had never heard of Julius Waldman until a week ago.

In sweet April, one short month, the State of New York would certify Leah the happiest girl in the world, yet only because fast as she'd run from happiness happiness had been too fast for her. Still she'd never believed in the pursuit of sorrows either and had brought all sorts of nice girls over, from Ivy down, in the attempt to float Danny free of the vasty deep Carrie Baum. And what had that dumb kid brother of Leah's done? He'd used his pighead to ignore them. On the other hand her sister's odious Tootsie had remained hearsay until probably too late. When light dawned Leah'd rung up Al Greenfield to propose Naomi to him seriously, the way she should have done to begin with. "I'm engaged," Al had announced with the effervescence of a man who had a date with the gallows. What was there left to do but congratulate him on his Shifra the Essex Street rabbi's youngest. But Al had cut in he'd heard from a cousin of Leah's, Shifra's best friend, that Leah was still unattached.

Leah'd laughed, "Say semi-attached," not getting his drift.

To which the doleful voice'd answered, "I'd rather meet you than your sister."

What rotten luck for Naomi it all was! Yet the optimist Henny—who also considered Carrie Baum lots of fun and claimed he admired her panther figure—could assert that since by Leah's own testimony she'd messed up her sister's past and turned the good citizen Berger into a gangster, fate was kind in blocking her tackle at Naomi's future. To say Jack Berger'd been born a gangster had given Henny pause only to sip his occasional cocktail mixed with whiskey that Leah's bootlegger assured her was right off the boat and insist you mustn't arrange people's lives for them. Why, a miserable colleague of his at Universal, a Jewish guy as it happened, had nearly drowned himself in the Harlem River because his mother had nagged him into breaking his engagement to a girl that he really liked. The suicide leap would probably have worked too if the impulse hadn't come on the bridge to the Polo Grounds a nice day last summer with plenty of other pedestrians also on their way to the ballgame. So they'd dragged Julie Waldman back off the girders.

Why hadn't Henny ever suggested this lovelorner for Naomi? Because—hug John Henry Lieber, Jr., or strangle him?—her sister had a boy friend already, and one very likely okay despite his drawbacks.

Nevertheless Julius had been rounded up as forlorn hope for the birthday, engagement and pre-farewell party.

"A party on Thursday?" Naomi had asked suspiciously on the phone.

Leah'd cracked, "For a birthday on Thursday," with just bare plausibility, pretending Murray's classes had never occurred to her, let alone Carrie's working late Thursday nights in the department store. Both those two of course were invited for whatever the hour, so Julius would have to shine fast—if Naomi would let him.

Fat chance, with Naomi's scowl Leah's way at the sight of an extra man in the background. Julius was shy but far from stupid. A quick lift of the cheek and he turned his back on Her Small Highness with the crown of gold braids, told Mama how do you do, and immediately became Danny's best friend with a waiver of the handshake to take care of the crutches. Then the two self-effacers with Henny as third sipped Leah's best closet Chianti and philosophized about getting run over. Should Leah have provided a Julia for Danny rather than a Julius for her sullen sister?

Julius said that he was knocked down eight hours a day by Universal the statistical juggernaut, where Chief Actuary Condon their boss claimed to like nothing better than to curl up with a good set of figures—no joking, numbers he meant—and you never reached the top of Mount Paper.

Danny saw Julius's point. He himself felt that way about selling, good at it as he'd unfortunately turned out to be. So now on the road or should he say the Tompkins Square Park bench to recovery, he had two minds—or at least a mind and a half—about Quality Lamps Light the Planet. With a crutch under each arm and the uke on a strap, he'd become the Tiny Tots' Troubadour, ask any young mama down in the Square. The mamas crowded around him and swore that a nursery tune off his tonsils made Uncle Don who sang that stuff on the radio sound like a foghorn from the river. And did the kids go for Danny's repertory—unless that was flattery so he would let them draw pictures on his bandages.

Julius—Henny too—was impressed by the quantity of Danny's fans' hieroglyphics. You saw trolleys sketched, street cleaners, tenement houses; artists' signatures *Eddie, Sol, Ruthie*; trembly autographs *Rubin* and *Norma.* On the sophisticated side a naughty arrow darting from the thigh to a quivering heart labeled *Carrie*; Ma's *Be Happy*; Reisel's *Reflect* and Uncle Willie's *Eyes Open Kiddo.* Who were *Get well dear*, *Adele* and *Also from Molly*? He didn't know, just two plump mamas.

But even with a leg broken so the vacation wasn't your fault, Danny told Julius and Henny over Henny's pot roast that made the mouth water just from inhaling it, being boss made a difference. After all, he wasn't chained down to selling. Here in New York he'd done the dirty work, and his sister hadn't had trouble finding some guy to fill in. Now expansion was the ticket—Rochester, Syracuse, Albany, points west and south—with him in the office. "Stick around for mansions in season," he winked at Leah, "uptown, Lake George, Coral Gables. . . . " He began nagging Henny too. After all, Henny'd be a Quality Lamps partner by marriage. Curios was Henny's long-anticipated pleasure, how could he sell lamps? That was how. Who works at pleasures? Henny and Leah could keep the store going with working stiffs ten cents a dozen and drop in at their leisure. What did they mean, "But?" Danny strummed his uke nights, they'd strum their Curios. How about it?

They were saved by the bell, Sixth Avenue Jewelers, with a slender gilt-wrapped parcel.

"*Blood is still thicker than water*," Leah read out, "*A Happy Birthday from your Papa*!" She dangled a string of bloodshot green ovals. "Ain't my papa generous?"

Henny beamed, "Didn't I tell you that you'd never regret tonight's good deed?"

"And you were right, pureheart. Cast bread upon waters and it comes back French toast—if you supply eggs. Want a beautiful bracelet, Mama?"

"No," Golda said, "enjoy what good comes, and don't look from where."

"From a loan he cadged off you, Leah?" Danny was not impressed, and picked up where he'd left off, only switching to Julius. Julius himself had said he hated his job. Quit then, Danny could use dependable men. "And your boss can curdle up with his figures."

Julius said, "I'd still have a boss."

"But me," Danny pointed him who. The bust days were over—it was all boom from now on, never mind Uncle Willie's Socialist tracts he treated you to for your convalescence. Uncle Willie meant well, but the facts were against him. At Quality Lamps a guy with Julius's head was bound to work up to partners, instead of plugging bogged down in arithmetic tables.

Till Naomi more than had it up to the neck. Bad enough that out of resentment she'd spent twice as much as she'd wanted to on a nightgown for Leah. With her brother it was love at first sight for some passing stranger her sister had dragged up here to undermine Murray. And Naomi had to quake because Tootsie was their hardworking salesman? That doing the dirty work remark of her brother's, hadn't that sounded like a dig at Tootsie as salesman? Had Leah told Danny? Though on second thought no one had, there hadn't been any explosions. So Danny could sit here giving away partnerships while he shoveled in this disgusting meal Naomi was sure wasn't kosher, prepared by a man—some man, alias Henny the kitchen maid—she was sure wasn't Jewish.

Even Pa borrowed money from her and Leah, but only Leah got gifts.

Now Leah and Henny were edifying everybody with the H.M.S. *Berengaria* honeymoon and treasure hunt trip as they called it, to search out knickknacks in Europe to sell on Waverly Place. Did you hear Ma complain Henny wasn't good enough for her daughter, or Danny say—since Quality Lamps was financing Henny's Curios Shop—that Henny had already succeeded in his treasure hunt? Not a sound. Such comments were reserved strictly for Naomi's boy friends. After Leah's and Henny's effusions died down, Naomi announced her own wedding date, June fifteenth—she'd tell Tootsie tomorrow.

"Naturally," she said, "our honeymoon can't be any more than a week in the country—we'll both have to be back in the factory."

Didn't her brother suddenly bristle. "What factory?"

"Until your expansion there's only one that I know of, the one I'm running on West Street."

"I've already told you no Murray."

"Then I'd better tell you that he's been working for us all the time."

"What!"

Danny shot up to a streak of pain and instant despair and bounced forward palms against the table—beaten idiot warrior with bent head and clenched teeth—splashing coffee in laps and causing all-around consternation. He ended apologizing while they eased him back to his chair, phoned that deathly hospital, draped his coat on his shoulders and carted him like a comedy king chair and all to a cab. His mother got in with the men and took his hand but he pulled it away.

"You also keep secrets from me."

"Well, you see what happened."

She looked so ghastly that in spite of Tootsie and pain he had to grab her hand and comfort her.

"Okay," he said, "she wants him to sell? Let him sell. I'm through selling for good."

"Why not?" Golda gave him a kiss. "You're the boss."

Leah watched the cab disappear in the dark beyond the Bleecker Street triangle, carried the chair back upstairs and glared at her sister.

"Unspeakable."

"I could also say that," Naomi reminded her, "so it's best not to speak."

Leah cleared up the dud of a party—with all his innocence Henny'd been right, she shouldn't have had it, not like this anyway—and Naomi on her sister's green coffin-shaped couch waited in silence for Murray. She only hoped—he was so slow!—he'd get here in time for her to get out before Carrie came. Thank God he did, and she saved the explanations for outside in his automobile.

"That guy'll stop nowhere," Murray lazily smiled, "to extend a vacation."

Naomi gave Murray vacation so he'd never forget it. The smile faded fast, his face became swarthy red. And let him never forget he owed his livelihood to her brother's hard work.

Murray said, "All right, that's enough."

"I'll let you know when it's enough! In my family broken legs are not a subject for humor. If you disagree, we'd better think over getting married June fifteenth."

"June fifteenth? I didn't know I proposed."

"Oh didn't you? With a memory like that maybe Danny is right you shouldn't be working for us. And I'm perfectly willing to forget the date too."

For two cents Murray'd have booted this broad out of his car. But June fifteenth was fine with him and he kept his mouth shut. He'd get his in every sense then beginning June fifteenth—and he'd give her hers!

A knock on the window startled them. Carrie in her tigerskin coat was smiling in.

"Change of venue?"

Omitting the Murray part Naomi told her the news. "The cast must have slipped," she thought of saying.

"And he's back in that shambles? Let me into this auto."

This round Carrie made it in time—her boyo was still in a wheelchair in a dim corridor where a disinfectant reek choked your throat like true love in the movies. But he didn't want to be taken uptown to Dr. Nate and nice Morningside Hospital, he was in no mood for travel.

"But this slaughterhouse?"

"They're okay. I did the slaughtering."

He'd recover from the fracture, he told her, before he recovered from how stupid he'd been. Tootsie, no Tootsie—Naomi'd kissed Danny with tears in her eyes, Tootsie'd squeezed his paw with the proper hospital face—why the hell should that have been so important to him?

"But Naomi knew it was important to you, so why did she tell you tonight?"

"She had to tell me sooner or later."

"Why not later then, after your leg was healed?"

"Who knows? Something seemed to be eating her."

After all that plotting to keep Tootsie a secret? There had to be more to it than some petty grievance. Danny's temper wasn't a secret, explode him and there might be pieces. So Naomi set off the fuse—and why just when Leah was leaving?

Because with Leah gone, Naomi and Tootsie would have a free hand at the till—provided no Danny. The naïve little doll was some little schemer, eh? Quite a bunch, eh?

But if they were ten times as smart, she Carrie Baum could outsmart 'em all!

She Carrie Baum though had ever been a girl to face facts, no matter how unpleasant. Could it be that there was no one to outsmart? At the East Side City Hospital bedside conference the next evening Naomi all but got down on hands and knees for Leah to put off—not her marriage, gee, Naomi'd never ask that—but the *Berengaria*, the ocean voyage, just that, till Danny could come back to work. Why if the business suffered, Leah would too, as a partner. So how come Naomi's anxiety for her deadweight partner Leah to stay? To pin the blame on in case Naomi got caught stealing? But Naomi could just as easily—easier—pin the blame on Leah if Leah was away.

In any case laughing Leah and grinning Henny were catching that *Berengaria* to Le Havre, April showers or merry sunshine. So Carrie inhaled to offer the supreme sacrifice—quitting Vandervaart's and filling the breach at Quality Lamps like a good soldier who could find out exactly what was going on there—when Naomi began recruiting her.

Knock me down!

Naomi knocked Carrie down: higher pay plus a bonus for Share brides-to-be, self-respecting work, not waiting on Gentiles—

"Hey," Henny grinned, "I'm a Gentile and proud of it!"

"I thought so," Naomi told him, "but now that I'm getting to know you you're so nice that I forgot."

Thus a good time was had by all and a still better time by Naomi at Carrie's one condition for letting the arm be twisted: no bridely bonuses. She'd accept the same pay as any forelady-in-training—and not a cent less. Naomi vented her joy on their recumbent figure, and—ouch!—displaced Danny's leg from the trolley in her enthusiasm. So if the luckiest day Quality Lamps ever enjoyed dawned the blustery morn she Carrie Baum strolled in at West Street as a regular, the entry hadn't been that forced. And the first to admit to herself that her own evil mind had imagined a plotter in a Naomi as transparent as window glass was her Carrie Baum.

Far from playing footsie with Tootsie and the Quality books, Naomi only wanted to prove by the book how good a salesman her Murray was.

Murray wasn't that good, and Murray wasn't that bad. Business, the market, money—as he himself pointed out—were all streaking toward heaven and he was just managing to hold onto Danny's accounts. Trouble with Tootsie, he was in the wrong racket. For fun Carrie would jot down his Wall Street tips, and amazing how many winners he picked. Tootsie himself wasn't amazed. His heart only bled he hadn't the capital to play with. Actually he did purchase small blocks on margin, but—his tears flowed and Carrie had a sympathetic eye and a sharp ear—between commissions, interest charges and creeping profits, where was he? In Columbia Street. And where was he headed? Tompkins Square, two flights up from his mother-in-law. He expected to save a fortune on furniture by hauling Naomi's bedroom set upstairs, and if that broke his hump slightly he'd know where to repair it. And when Danny and Carrie would take the fatal step and the mother-in-law would make her move to the Hennys, Murray had first call on the rest of the furniture, free of charge naturally. So he and Naomi could put up a card table in the kitchen and leave the living room empty awhile, it was the playroom that counted, huh? But apart—he presumed—from the playroom his wife-to-be had a bit of learning to do. She didn't understand yet that investment and gambling are two different kettles of fish—but he'd learn her. As far as Carrie could see that was a mighty long learn he had ahead, and she wished him luck. But as a salesman he was costing her Carrie Baum money.

Should there come a time, Jerry Belik the shyster rumbled into Carrie's ear in his officeful of desks, attorneys and one thin stenographer, should there come a time that a jury considers awards in the present negligence suit, blessed are the poor as the Good Book says. Or to put it more clearly, if in consequence of culpable injury to plaintiff business profits diminished, then rose, after plaintiff—having suffered anguish both physical, mental and moral—resumed normal activities, loss owing to injury could reasonably be postulated at maximum. But if the books distinguish negligibly, or not at all, between plaintiff's absence and presence at his place of livelihood, the unavoidable inference is that business loss has been negligible.

So two left feet Tootsie, either sell with a roar for tidal wave profits, or flop for Carrie's lawsuit. But that's where you always found Tootsie: neither here nor there. So in effect Tootsie's sales gains were a loss, and to reflect the real picture the Quality ledgers should produce a curve down. Therefore to honor the spirit of the law a corrected set was imperative.

But how, where, when does a shop forelady help those books to show the right spirit? Sneaking into the closed plant Sundays seemed the only solution, until at Carrie's engagement party in April she caught little Naomi wistfully staring her way.

"My lipstick smeared?" Carrie asked.

"No, you're lovely. I'm ashamed to tell you what I was thinking."

"Go ahead, I'll owe you the penny."

How could Naomi have refused such an offer?

"You'll get all the presents."

"Why shouldn't I? It's my party."

"No, I mean the wedding presents Carrie, you and Danny marrying before me and Murray."

Eerie wasn't it—to wish and it happens? Leah the snows of yesteryear, Danny not back yet and Naomi about to absent herself, leaving nobody here but us chickens: Carrie and those ledgers!

"We'll both get the same presents. But why don't you marry first, Naomi? Marry in May then."

"I thought of that," the little louse glumly answered. "The Catskills could be freezing for a May honeymoon."

Carrie took a deep breath.

"Okay, sis. You marry on June first, I'll take the end of the month."

And like a fly to honey Naomi came at your neck with her single extravagance: love and kisses. And from Limpy came pure love when Carrie told him the date change, the whys and the wherefores. "I've got myself," he said, "a real angel." Because heaven took care of her?

Oh didn't it!

June the first bubbled like oil on a hot pan. The asphalt glare hurt your eyes, life slowed to a crawl. The Essex Street Synagogue was like a Turkish bath, the only two who looked cool up on that women's shelf were dear old Grandma in her brooch and white lace collar and Carrie in organdy. Downstairs the little bride entered the married estate wilted before she so much as had the good of it. Then, following a sweaty food orgy at Moskowitz & Lupowitz, Tootsie cranked up the flivver, crept in next to his worried mate, and off they vibrated to Swan Lake.

The next evening boss pro tem de luxe Carrie outwaited Raisin in the factory and negotiated half a bushel of ledgers down to a cab. For an extra quarter tacked to the tip the cabbie deposited the load upstairs at lucky 7 Cornelia, and for six nights till three in the morning she Carrie Baum rectified those books. And balancing off the rectifications was no easy task either! What a mess, and what a mess that lamp business was. What Leah'd taught Carrie during her first weeks at Quality you could have put in your eye. But with savvy, a strong back and Danny's offstage coaching, Carrie had soon had the machinists, stockmen and shipping boys on their toes and hopping in unison. What to do about Tootsie she hadn't figured out yet but have no fear.

And the twenty-ninth of June broke like a cool blue and green kiss, spring in summer, with Heaven Caterers strewing rose petals in Orange New Jersey for her Carrie Baum to walk down the aisle on. And you know, she'd never been what you call religious—Mother had not, and Daddy Moishe certainly not, the Bolshevik scoffer now in formal afternoon dress beside Carrie under the wedding canopy. But from the rabbi in baritone and the cantor in tenor through the wedding guests and your handsome cripple in his cutaway coat, it was elating to have every big gun of the Jewish religion at your disposal! On the reception line old Golda with the forced smile might have been the queen mother but she Carrie B. Share was queen—and Carrie found herself actually liking these kissing dummies, including her enemies like the flip Leah and the deep Raisin. God, even cousin Gladys recognized Carrie—and remembered her name! Then, with Grandma Share's warty hands one on Carrie's wrist one on Danny's, Carrie was absorbing the endless Yiddish benedictions with a sort of motherly pleasure, and out of nowhere the lunatic element, Raisin's mother —"Tombstone, don't hog the bride"—gave Grandma Share a push. And—could this be happening?—Carrie was toppling under an armful of Grandma with popping eyes and a wheeze like a bicycle pump, and they were going down to the floor slow motion together.

Tombstone no fooling—asphyxiation! The sisters-in-law's husbands got Carrie up, straight-haired Henny and bumpy-haired Tootsie with the cigarette dangling that could brand you for life, and between the disheveled bride—dammit, with a rent in the wedding gown—and his grandmother stretched out like a black setting sun, poor Limpy didn't know which way to limp. And damn Carrie if walk-on Gladys didn't upstage her, front and center alongside the husband the doctor who was bent over Grandma and unhappily testifying, "Expired. . . ."

Listen, if an old lady drops dead—though she could have held it in a few hours longer—you can't holler at her. But in the confusion old girl Gittel with her finger pointing your way—"Was she the murderer? Who sent you?"—pinning the rap on you?

And behind Gittel Raisin—"Excuse my mother, she's not well"—was a close second. So why did you bring her if she's not well? At Quality Carrie'd had to admit that, your future hubby's former heart throb or not, for lamp decoration the girl was Raisin. But everyone is replaceable.

In the postmortem the rabbi voted that the Jewish religion, with all due honor prescribed to the dead, affords life the precedence. Or in plain English her Carrie B. Share's wedding comes first. That, however, was not the way it worked out. Willie left, but after all it had been his old mother. Golda broke down in the rabbi's office—after all Grandma'd been her old enemy. The voice of God Leah the atheist suggested that the wedding music was quite out of place under the circumstances, and—"Sure," Carrie gave a wave of the hand, "send 'em away"—poor Daddy Moishe with a bleeding heart for the money sent away the paid-for musicians. Then Raisin had to stage Baba Rivka's funeral properly the next afternoon, so the honeymoon west in the new eight cylinder Franklin—"Sure, what's the rush?" Carrie told poor miserable Limpy—had to be put off a day.

Shares, you'll pay for this!

15

AND IN THE FIRST MAIL ONE FINE SUMMER MORNING Reisel received a postcard that her piano would be delivered on Saturday. Now, Rabbi Glushak, and Mrs. Glushak, see the proof that Reisel was not the holy person that, from a few weeks' acquaintance with her, you have taken her for. Reisel walked down the 128th Street hill from home and down the Convent Avenue steps past the milk bottling plant with its platforms, silver cans and blue-edged white puddles toward West Broadway and the synagogue in this benign endless sunlight that surged to the heavens like her own anything but benign pride. The old sexton turned his stubbled face from her when she left the bright street for the synagogue twilight of blue and red stained glass. Dark, unfortunate soul, he saw no place for a young woman there except in time of disaster or as an adjunct to a man on the High Holy Days. Rabbi Glushak though, on the way from his office to the dais, crinkled his smile of pleasure and welcome to her over the thick gray-threaded black beard so much like Papá's. Nevertheless the muttering sexton was right today, and Rabbi Glushak was wrong. Reisel took her seat in the rear of the women's side of the aisle, far apart from the few ancients up front and the quorum of men, and when the service began was hard put to concentrate even on the prayer for peace for Baba Rivka.

That postcard burned through Reisel's purse like a declaration of love. Why, hardly home from his honeymoon and Daniel had thought of her, and so lavishly. Poor young man, what this message spoke of his marriage. The gift of course, the piano, she would have to refuse. Propriety—God!—self-preservation demanded a refusal, often as he had promised a piano to her if she would leave Norfolk Street for where she would have room to put it. The Daniel of the promise had not been the husband of the malicious, hard woman whom he was married to. Already Carrie had paused behind Reisel's paintresses at Quality Lamps and asked in her mocking voice, "This painting can be done by machine also, huh?"

"One half of our lamps are decorated by machine, Carrie," Reisel had kept her voice level, "but in the hand-painted are sixty-five percent of the profits."

If tigers smiled, their eyes would have looked like Daniel's wife's. One could leave of course, Reisel did not fear for her living. But who wished the weariness of beginning again some place else? At home one was sufficiently weary. During the move from Norfolk Street Reisel had despaired of Mamá's sanity and gone cold at the prospect of a bedlam for her. Uptown how could Mamá be left alone to cower in a rear corner of a rear room as she had been in the empty apartment at Norfolk? Rubin Bookbinder had said, "Gitteleh come, we're driving you home to Kadzyrnye."

"Kadzyrnye in hell, you deputy assassin. Tell your masters I'm not deceived."

Bookbinder and Reisel had tried to seize Mamá's arms, Mamá had screamed, "Help, Jews—they're kidnapping a girl into white slavery!" And the strength—you could not budge her! Finally Reisel had calmed her by a ruse. Reisel had sent Rubin to find a taxi and taken her own turn screaming. "Mamá, cease whimpering and stand up this instant! He has given up since a woman of your virtue is of no use in white slavery! In any case, I am leaving. Goodbye!" And Mamá had quietly followed. St. Nicholas Heights, though Mamá with a crafty smile had asked, "Where are the pushcarts?" was an improvement, for Mamá ventured after her library romances as she used to in Tompkins Square, and she even played cards again with the white slaver Rubin. But of course lurking in these airy streets that climbed to the shouts of boys at ball-playing in St. Nicholas Park was the dark imminence awaiting its chance to crush Mamá for regicide. So Mamá stayed the idle patient and Reisel the white slave. And mutter over this as you will in solitude, heaven knows Reisel would not speak one word to derange further that poor, sad unbalanced mind.

Yet viewed in the light of this hard life, was Reisel to be intimidated by a virago into graceless rejection of an act of pure kindness? The piano—ehh! She could afford her own and planned shopping for one soon, when she was settled in her new flat, and were it to come from Rubin Bookbinder not a moment would be lost informing that Schirmer Company to spare themselves the trucking expense. But Rubin would not dare send such a gift. His largesse he was sensible enough to reserve for such as the "widow" and little boy who lived next door to him in the Chelsea graystone he was forever urging Reisel to come see. On Fourteenth Street on a Saturday afternoon however Reisel had run into him with the widow, who had been laden with parcels he had just paid for. While Bookbinder grinned the widow had told Reisel they were marrying as soon as her divorce became final. Her sweet little boy there too did not in the slightest resemble Bookbinder, so, supporting the pair of them, Rubin was in a way generous. Today, as usual, Reisel opened the shop and laid out work for her young women daubers. And as usual Lilith strolled in arm in arm with poor Daniel her willing possession, while Naomi preceded unwilling Murray with his disgruntled cigarette dangling. Sullenly Murray gathered the order books and catalogs he refused to keep in the house overnight, and after, as usual, a word with Carrie on their stocks gambling he sauntered out. Then as usual Carrie swung her provocative leg from the desk edge in the office and retouched her face while regaling eager yet flustered Naomi with (no doubt) the latest lusts of the bedroom. But Daniel's blue-eyed greeting conveyed no anticipatory gleams to Reisel, nothing but fond good nature.

So with the sunniest of hearts in a sultry overcast the next Saturday afternoon, Reisel enjoyed her new piano from the moment the truckmen wrapped it in quilts and ropes and hoisted it the three stories into her living-room window. The tuner would not come till Monday, but she at once sounded two thrilling chords. Then the truckers brought up the stool and a carton of music—Beethoven, Schubert, all the essentials. And—dear cousin—there was a card "For your new house, Danny & Carrie" in Daniel's boyish scrawl.

Well, thank you, dear Daniel—dared these unaccustomed fingers of hers attempt an easy sonata?—and thank you, dearest Carrie, whom he gives only diamond marquises.

And—Reisel perceived instantly when she thanked Carrie in person Monday, since Saturday night and Sunday (at least his wife busied him) one thousand trips to the corner drugstore did not reach them by phone—does not tell of pianos to Reisel! But doubly fortunate these thanks—"You are too kind to me, you and Daniel, you should not have done it"—where silence would have implied only complicity.

"Then," smirk of full armor, "we'll try not to repeat it."

So Daniel, thank God for him, was not yet totally subject to his wife's manipulations, his holiness still protected him. First, this morning, with a lamp vase in hand as if on business Reisel had waited till Daniel finished shouting instructions to his machinists out of sight of his spouse. Already the motor noises had screwed Reisel's nerves tight with the usual headache to come, but she had smiled in deep affection to him and poor Daniel had stood charmed.

"How could you send so extreme a gift to me? I am amazed."

"What?" His face had straightened into displeasure. "What's wrong with that glaze?"

"What glaze?" she had screamed. "I speak of a piano and he speaks of glaze."

"Piano?"

"My piano, which you should not have bought. Are you deaf?"

"In the right ear, slightly," he had shouted back. "I thought my watch stopped the other afternoon—it seemed it should have been later—so I held it to my ear and it was a while before I heard any tick. Then they delivered the piano? Do you like it?" Such happy eagerness! "How was the music? I told the salesman," he had grinned sheepishly, "your favorite tunesmiths and he made the picks."

Virtue, ah sadly misallied. For his coarse wife Reisel clarified, so as not to embarrass her, "Such a rich sound, almost the equal to our Bechstein in Kadzyrnye."

"Bechstein?" What the hell had Limpy given this dame, a cow? In spite of Carrie's boy's ability screwing your ass off—and with all those Share lemons she'd hit the peach: a real jackpot!—Carrie had wed an innocent. Hardly were the Rocky Mountain and Grand Canyon snapshots cool from the honeymoon than her little hubby was dishing out presents on the sly?

"My grand piano," Raisin said, "destroyed by barbarians."

Piano! Say, what went on here?

And that evening in the Franklin on the way home up the Grand Concourse Kid Profile at the wheel still kept mum on the subject. See how crafty Raisin had too much craft for her own good? Carrie's strong silent man had not even spoken to straighten out his lay of the land not to speak.

"Capital expenditures without consultation, Limpy, and all I get is unnegotiable credit from Raisin?"

"Cut out the Limpy. Reisel's housewarming gift you mean?"

"Grand pianos?"

"An upright, and I told you a million times, Pussy. That was her piano from long before I ever laid a glove on you, any day she'd ditch Norfolk Street. You always smiled approvingly too."

"Approvingly? Hear a joke and I smile. Exactly what is this Raisin to you anyhow?"

"My cousin. You know Pussy, you could use some more family feeling."

And in a flash—"Danny watch out!"—the Franklin veered, skinny maples lining the local lane rushed scraggly leaves toward them, and the driver was driving under her skirt at the wifely thigh. Who Limpy was lusting after was wearing his wedding ring, and no sooner inside their door than they were inside, around, all over each other, washed by the last tawny Grand Concourse sunlight through their living-room window.

"People," Carrie gasped, "can get babies from this—"

"Those babies are on their own," he gasped back. "Not so *fast*, Pussy—"

So the piano was upright okay, a deal between Kid Honesty's soft heart, their bankroll and Raisin's finesse. To know 'em work with 'em, and Raisin eight hours a day made a laugh out of the old Lesbian theory. High in the ranks of chippies whose specialty is raking in chips without any disbursement stood La Raisin. Back in Carrie's training days Raisin had once butted in at Leah's department. "This porcelain, Carrie, is especially fragile. . . . Do you hear that, young men? Take care, eh? We lost two broken last order." With a flash of her friendly teeth Raisin bothered to melt even lowly shipping boys for her easy kicks and send them flowing over the floor. True, shipping boys' eyes were very poppable and—these adolescents could make a girl's mouth water—Carrie herself had popped 'em once or twice with a wink or a nudge. But—boss is boss—the lash was best: keep the Israelites groaning. The Israelite she Carrie B. Share guaranteed would end up groaning the loudest was Raisin Leben—but no urgency, first things first. Down with the coupon clippers, as Daddy Moishe would growl—in this case Mrs. Leah S. Lieber.

For the Friday night chicken soup bacchanalias Carrie and Limpy parked the Franklin on Waverly Place where the sunset made gold dust of Curios' window, which got washed only by rain. "Like flowers," the good servant Ma Share kidded her son-in-law while she served the guests wine and crackers. So the customers wouldn't see in, look in, drop in. Who needed customers, or even the store itself? Sip wine, then lock up with a back in two hours sign. Silently, partnerly, Quality Lamps ground out the shekels for the remote control Share-Liebers. Later on Carrie told Limpy she was glad Leah, Henny and Ma didn't have to depend on that shabby store for a living. And what do you think the blinkers on kid answered her?

"They're doing fine there Pussy, Leah said so herself."

There was more than one way though to skin Leah the cat. You help Naomi with payroll a gloomy Friday, as for Naomi which Friday wasn't? Then you sunnily snap Leah's check to Naomi—"Easy come"—written out nice and neat in your strong clear penmanship.

And, "Hard go," Naomi came right through. Now was the sky, or was it not, the limit for Carrie! "Leah's my sister, I love her," Naomi thrashed in deeper, "but Italy, Rome—"

"Rome's in Italy."

"That's right. And apartments on Washington Place and stores on Waverly Place—"

"Leah says that they make good money there."

"That's what galls me."

"That she should keep her partnership here?"

"Yes."

"I don't know, Naomi. Didn't she give birth to this business?"

"Still I don't think it's fair."

"Buy her out then."

"And lose all that capital?"

"Then let her let you borrow back the capital as a sisterly four percent loan, same as the bank gives."

Did that child perk up! "Do you think she would, Carrie?"

"Sure. She loves you."

And did Leah just adore the suggestion at her own dinner table at Washington Place. "Naomi baby," she said, "if not for me that business wouldn't exist."

Limpy also looked at Naomi like crazy, and Tootsie snickered smoke at the roast beef as if a lose for the helpmeet was his win. But Henny—see how you can misjudge a sucker?—saved the day for little Mrs. Greed his sister-in-law.

"No special privileges Leah," Henny laughed. "They used to say that at the orphanage when they'd refuse a kid something extra. A silent partner's no partner, by the sweat of the brow thou shalt live, dear. Besides, the other income was fine for your hope chest, but now you have me darling so your hopes have been realized. See, Golda is smiling—that means I'm right. Why pile riches on riches, isn't that so Mama?"

"My cup, darling boy," Golda covered Henny's hand, "runneth over!"

So Leah gulped, shrugged and exited from Quality Lamps smiling, while silent partner Carrie watched with a smile. With a sister gone, could a cousin be far behind? And for a helping hand in the morning, Carrie felt queasy, no doubt from Leah's garlicky roast. Poor Limpy—he'd never had a sick wife before—was more upset than Carrie was. But she drew up her nightgown for him to kiss the dimple each side of her tummy to make it better and sent him down to the Franklin with a pierce arrow. The remedy worked too, and her health improved in no time. She phoned Limpy and he enthusiastically promised various follow-up treatments.

Her immediate follow-up was her two-piece gray twill with the maroon collar cut low enough to create interest but not so low as to provoke bestiality. From her secretary drawer she extracted a lamp design of Ming Toy Raisin's she'd happened to extract from the shop an afternoon she'd been last out, and—with a smile for her henhouse neighbors sunning their large open mouths and tiny offspring in front of the house—she was off. To exercise the mamas' eye muscles she hailed a taxi. But it was such a crisp fall day—a pleasure—that she let the guy go and strolled her foxy neckpiece chic as West End Avenue down the Mt. Eden slope of pathetic hardworking stores leading nowhere except to the El.

La Vine née Levine on Canal Street baked the vases for Quality Lamps, but why risk tattletales? In Orange you could cheer up Daddy Moishe by listening to his sighs about his lonely travail while daughters kept house for strangers namely their husband. And just the wrong side of the tracks near Orange station, where the laborers lived in row shacks near the canal, she'd drop in on old man Persons' pottery shack and get a line on how to fire a Raisin.

Lo! The pottery shack with its single measly kiln had become a whitewashed two-story factory gleaming in sunlight. What a transformation!—half the shacks had crept away to make room for this, and in the office crotchety Persons had metamorphosed into an oily Zuaracce not far in his thirties. Carrie's eye roll and obvious question tilted him back genially in his swivel chair.

"Why I bought out old man Persons, so he can enjoy his declining days without worry on the County Poor Farm."

"That was real sweet of you."

"I'm," he ogled her, "a sweet guy."

"Then," Carrie helped herself to a seat, crossed a fetching leg to warm the heart and lower the estimate, and whipped out Ming Toy's design, "sweets for the sweet. You couldn't mass-produce something like this?"

"When it comes to clay," the lovelight in the black eyes hardened to dollar signs and you saw the magician who'd put PERSONS in capital letters, "I can mass-produce anything." Zuaracce went to pencil and paper. "By the hundred?"

"Say by the thousand."

"Still better."

"Cheap, huh?"

"I meet any competing price within reason."

He frowned at pluses and minuses, he proposed highway robbery without the use of a gun as if he were offering charity, he noted Carrie's amusement, and he delivered his pitch. Sure, botch jobs cost less. But heat your molds to the minute so the form comes out perfect, don't skimp engraving your transfer designs, ink your etched plates with the best color oxides found on the market, and you have something different: a PERSONS product!

Could he be telling the truth? The price he quoted was high enough to buy you about two thousand vases' worth of Raisin, gum arabic, paint, glaze, the entire crew of Quality paintresses and countless banana splits. "For instance?" Carrie worriedly asked.

"Hey Miss Nixon—bring me two Sèvres pots from the glost storeroom."

While waiting, Zuaracce was charmed to find that Carrie originally hailed from the backwoods of Orange. Himself, he was from the city, he'd begun at his father's furnace on Mulberry Street. . . .

Miss Nixon returned cute as a cake of soap with cheerful blue vacant eyes and in each hand a pot that in the old days on the farm Carrie wouldn't even have kept under the bed for emergencies.

"What," Zuaracce demanded, "are those, Miss Nixon, if I may ask?"

Miss Nixon became flustered, "Jimmy . . . Mr. Ruane . . . said we were out of the Sevens."

"Sèvres, not Sevens. Take those back! . . . And my wife," he showed Valentino-white teeth to Carrie, "asks me where I get my gray hairs," while he greased his hand on his black ones.

The kid reappeared with the news—what a surprise—that the Sèvres had already been loaded and shipped. Oh slippery McGhee! Carrie tried him for fun on two-tone machine-finished pots like Quality Lamps' ready-made line from La Vine and you had to take your hat off to this high pressure boy's brass. If Limpy had half of it she'd be counting her millions!

"You're not," Carrie said, "pulling the wool over my eyes just because you're a big city man and I'm a little girl from the country?"

Did Zuaracce's face light up at ladybird Carrie he imagined he'd knock off with the same stone that brought in her business! "A discount," he actually licked his lips, "might be arranged. . . . Say, let's meet at five, they have a speak in town since you left. Maybe I can give you ideas."

"Thanks Mr. Zuaracce," Carrie outtoothed him, "but you couldn't give me any ideas I don't have already."

That got him so hot and bothered that he escorted her all the way to the sunny sidewalk, where their wedding rings flashed one at the other. Zuaracce was well-packed, with his sleeves rolled up his solid white tapering arms, this bubbly talent who probably could strip a chicken without making it cluck. Of course Carrie didn't pluck that easy; although—how? she wondered—he might have picked up an impression she did. Still he had confirmed what she had supposed: you can manufacture Raisin lamps by the thousand. So he wanted her name, he didn't know what to call her?

"You can call me Lucy Richardson," she mentioned a fellow alumna from Orange High and started away.

"But Lucy, where do you live?"

"West End Avenue, 501—"

He whistled impressed, he winked, he kept waving—she would be hearing from him!

At the station square from a tin lizzie or so and the hick horses and wagons of girlhood memory she extracted a taxi to Moishe's. And look, there was the high school shrinking back on its lawn in brick-red embarrassment that it had been Limpy and not any math teacher who had taught her proportions. Thus, after you reduced Zuaracce's ridiculous estimate proportionally to La Vine's lower prices, *X* equaled they were losing a fortune on Raisin. Now wasn't that bound to be intensely educational to little Naomi?

The taxi bumped along the dirt road past the W–W–Willie Sh–Share estate and Carrie called a "H–h–hiya W–Willie" at the trees stained a Socialist pink and at the same time showering gold—her daddy's sour grapes dream about life and cash. But poor Moishe, you have to be born a tree for that combo.

The cabbie tilted his profile. "This it?"

"Drive on," she said.

But Carrie's magic passes—Raisin, low cost machine Orientals—for sending Naomi into a tight-fisted ecstasy and making Raisin disappear only turned Naomi into a worm. To begin with, the saving of an ex-Raisin's pay never penetrated that silky-blond head. The opposite. Waste Reisel in the stitching department again? was an argument for staying deep in the rut. The more Carrie reasoned, the more yellow-hair squirmed. Sure Naomi didn't mind getting rich, but taking such chances? Suppose that machine-made Orientals didn't sell? Let her in on the secret that the fun of it is in taking a chance, advise her try a few hundred as a parallel item, laugh that the suckers buy whatever you sell if you handle 'em right—and she writhed as if you were whipping her . . . which Carrie wouldn't at all have minded doing. Finally Vice President Naomi of Quality Lamps wished she were home having babies instead of here with decisions.

"Then why don't you have babies and stay home with them?"

Primsie—"You think I'm not trying?"—blushed a beautiful scarlet.

Who'd asked God to dream up women anyway? With the same hocus-pocus He could have kept it entirely men. No wonder this Mussolini disciplined some dumb wops with castor oil! And to rub salt in wounds, if she Carrie B. Share happened to put in a Saturday afternoon shopping, Limpy was just as likely to be at Raisin's plunking out tunes on Carrie's piano or groping for the inside dope on the Beethoven that Raisin would knock out.

So, as a surprise to Limpy, to stop the music, and to show the world the difference between the pianos that she Carrie B. Share gave away and the pianos she kept, she had Steinway & Sons install a solid-mahogany grand in her living room. Limpy went gaga, you'd think you handed him the keys to a Cadillac. He dropped his coat on the sofa against all her instructions, flipped his hat up, and serenaded her—

Two four six eight
Who do I ap-pre-ci-ate,
I appre-ci-ate my loving ba-bee—

like Tin Pan Alley in the musicals.

And that lovey night, since Limpy saw the light best in the dark, she unfolded her gut-twister conference with his sister to him. But fair is fair, Carrie had Limpy naked, he was primed more for funny business than business. "Love her anyway Pussy," he grabbed ahold, "she never had a Borneo coat as a kid," and did he revise the agenda. The Borneo was the coat Moishe'd snipped Carrie from every leftover in the shop—weasel, Hudson seal, muskrat, skunk, with a fox collar with buttons for eyes and tiny sharp teeth to scare the other kids with. This particular night she wasn't that much in the mood but regardless she did her Wild Woman of Borneo act that drove Limpy crazy, and real business had to wait until the dawn's early light.

Just as well.

Orientals by hand and Orientals by machine would only compete with each other. Sure, Carrie was right, machine was cheaper—he knew that. And sure machine Orientals would sell, even with Tootsie's doing the selling. But the great Daniel Share who if not for her would never have taken his first baby steps didn't wanna. Calm too, while he gobbled bacon and eggs as if he hadn't had a square meal in years.

"I take pride in those lamps, they're real quality at the price. La Vine does a good job with the two-tones, but a live touch has . . . a distinction to it."

"Raisin say that?"

And Blue Eyes—"Not with me listening"—had the nerve to get tough with her!

But better keep quiet than say things you'll regret, especially with the grand climax physical due any day in the Limpy lawsuit.

"You might mention to your husband," Jerry the Belik had creaked out at his driest, "that it will be up to him to help the insurance company physician determine the full extent of suffering caused by the policyholder's negligence."

"He'll limp good, don't worry."

Jerry'd looked her straight in the eye. "I didn't say that." Jer was a fox all right!

By noon the stern lines cut deeper down Limpy's forehead. In the dim of a landing on their way out to lunch she gave his thigh a good clutch.

"Still sore at the only Pussy you have, huh?"

"It's my normal headache, who's sore?"

But you knew he was.

Carrie pressed close and kissed the headache all over, and Limpy softened, then he rousingly hardened. Mr. Jensen of Jensen's two-bit matchbox enterprise stepped out of his loft with an offended look at them from under his derby that embarrassed Limpy into letting her go.

"We're fully licensed," Carrie winked at her husband.

Limpy met the challenge and nothing headachy about the long one he kissed her, or the free massage that went with it. And in the autumn blue crisp as a new dollar bill over the piers, the masts and truck-filled West Street he was her boy again, minus the headache and all for hookey.

"Uh uh, business first—and it's going to be a pleasure, you'll hear."

At Fisherino's marbletop tables, cutlery clinked, dishes rattled, and Carrie outlined a hypothetical lamp business honey, where you had a hand-painted china and shades specialty of one lousy workbench. Did that mean you were stuck with seven grand a year plus a share of the profits, a mere Grand Concourse apartment, a measly Franklin automobile and a chinchilla coat your wifie just adored a north wind for and wore to the shop to drive the girls crazy? Hey—they weren't doing that badly, were they Limpy ol' kid ol' boy? But—she asked now that she had him grinning—could they do better? And she answered and how they could, with New York barely exploited and the sticks waiting out there like a sheep ready for fleecing. Give 'em plenty of brand-new antiques at low cost, from plenty of paintress dames at more of those benches!

Bright-eyed Limpy—"Genius, Pussy!"—suspended eating his chowder, then clouded. "Only where'll we put new paintresses, on the ceiling?"

"In our second-floor loft, the one that old Baldy Jensen is going to sell us his lease to."

"Genius!"

Some genius, caught between Raisin and the deep blue sea. You start out to cashier a petty officer and you wind up appointing her captain. Who else except Raisin did they have to boss a floorful of paintresses? But keep cogitating brain and don't worry. In the end Miss Shakespeare the pianiste will still be the girl overboard. First, Raisin unbeknownst to herself will be training her own replacement. Observe that Carrie's swain for once cagey did not utter the word Raisin. But then neither did Carrie. Limpy did say he didn't relish speaking to Jensen though.

"I'll speak."

"Would you Pussy? I hate bargaining."

"Some businessman. What would you do without me?"

"Same as before—fall apart."

Which gave you a funny feeling, didn't it, relative to your lord and master?

Jensen's heart if he had one was by no means worn on his sleeve, but lust is a mighty emotion and Carrie had seen it shine through many an eye before this. No doubt, marooned behind a rolltop desk in a half-empty one-machine loft, Roach Walk on the wainscoting not to mention Mouse Run for the underfed fellow Carrie alarmed as she came in, even a Jensen would daydream. The small hope and large unbelief on Mr. Jensen's pasty rectangular mug was that what should come of this call should be Carrie. Out of good nature she tried to jolly the beanbag, but when he heard what was what he turned off the jolly.

"I'm not accustomed to doing business with women." And he took a last stab. "Not this sort of business."

"Think of me," she kidded him, "as a man who'll pay your moving expenses" (his Grand Army of the Republic dodderers were gently prodding a carton in his dead factory) "to improved quarters."

Did he go dry with his lie "The quarters suit me"—sure, sure. It would take a lot more than moving expenses to make him think of moving. How much more? Say five thousand dollars more. Carrie's laughter, pardon her please, was merry, but of course Mr. Jensen had intended the joke. She offered five hundred on top of moving him and he guessed she wanted to make him laugh too, though he'd split the difference and let his lease go for forty-seven hundred and fifty. To be a sport Carrie upped the five hundred offer: three months' rent in his new location.

"Say listen, Miss . . . Mrs. . . . Shnare? What you people must understand is that I don't conduct business by bargaining."

"Sure. You just toss out different figures till you reach an agreement. We people too."

"Nothing of the sort. Changing my premises had never entered my mind. You walked in after my loft and I lowered my snap estimate of the cost to move, no more than that. You've heard my final price."

"I can only wish you continued good luck here then, Mr. Jensen."

You'll learn, you sour-faced tinhorn, what it is to tangle with Carrie B. Share. And she edified him with a slow stroll to the door so he could gnash his teeth in frustration tonight beside Mrs. Jensen. Beside Mr. Share that night Carrie announced they were going into the real estate business, yeah! They'd buy the whole damn building on West Street right from under Mr. Jensen. Jensen would dribble out like a dead tennis ball.

Did Limpy in every sense rise to the occasion! When Jack Berger and Leah picked West Street for the business—"Gee, remember?" Limpy babbled, "I was still Willie's sweet singer then"—the 1919 depression rent was dirt cheap. Now it was real aggravation though, running a local business and paying a landlord for long distance freightage facilities that Quality Lamps didn't use. Yet moving was such a bother that he'd stayed put. But if the business ballooned as per plan, West Street was perfect, in their own building rent would be cost, there'd be tax savings, and, most important of all, with Fisherino their street floor tenant you could say they'd be paid to eat lobster. Where did you find another love pot like his Pussy to . . . stew up these ideas?

But at the books by day in the office with Naomi scared stiff that her brother might insist on a small business risk, the shooting star more or less burned itself out. Okay, Limpy starchlessly pleaded with his sister, grant a smaller draw for themselves on account of mortgage and maintenance.

"Why grant that," Carrie tried to put Humpty Dumpty together again, "when there'll be five times the inventory turnover?"

And wrong-way Share, a Limpy all right, was suddenly carrying the ball toward his own goalpost. Pleasant dreams—the whiner—but they were still a small business. Where would a say twenty G's down payment for a building like this come from? Their puny reserve? Or put the business in hock? Which cued Naomi.

"And probably stay in hock the rest of our lives!"

"Well cheer up," Carrie could at least restore the little sister-in-law to full gloom, "Carrie'll think of a way."

And not merely think.

She looked up Jerry Belik in his new Fourth Avenue quarters and was given the grand tour though a glance covered the ground from the golden Belik LL.B ATTORNEY AT LAW on the frosted glass, past Miss Rabbit hunched at the typewriter, to Jerry's comical desk that filled half the room. The view was hardware stores, lunchrooms, a seedy corner hotel and an office tower that put Jerry in the dark. On the plus side he was just a few blocks south of Park Avenue and if Carrie knew her Jerry he would not be here long.

"And there isn't another lawyer in sight," she laughed, "not like downtown."

"Merely step one," came Jerry's proud rumble.

"What's step two?"

He sucked in his stomach, opened his drawer and produced a studio portrait.

"My fiancée."

The photo was recent and no wonder that he kept it hidden. The washed-out round-shouldered blonde looked faded, young as she was. And this long drink of water with tiny steel-framed eyeglasses perched on his fightless prizefighter's nose had once had the audacity to research a proposal to her Carrie Baum!

"The papa in real estate?" Carrie cracked.

"Yes, in Yonkers," Jerry eyed her suspiciously. "Have you met Pauline?"

"Just the picture, I don't get that far into the sticks. Why are you putting it back in the drawer, haven't you finished the credit check?"

Jerry laughed, "Well we're not married yet," but he turned professional the second she mentioned settling the Limpy lawsuit. Premature action would skim the cream off the settlement and that would be a shame—he told her straight-faced as an Indian—after the kind of pain that the doctor found so impressive the day he saw Mr. Share.

"That was real pain, conniver." And how it had hit Limpy that particular day had been a miracle. He had wanted to give up the lawsuit the night before, he couldn't be bothered, he'd been all better for months, he had work to do at the factory. He'd even dredged up that ridiculous business about his being to blame in the first place. Quite an evening her Limpy had given her, winding up with her turning her back on him in bed. But in the morning—"See!" she'd kissed him all over—Limpy had almost fallen down when he tried to stand up.

To keep Jerry on his toes though, Carrie gave him a Christmas deadline.

"Haste makes waste, Carrie."

"Okay Ben Franklin, but don't squander my time, because that's what life's made of."

And he wouldn't, that sharpster. Her time was his time. He'd milk the cow when the udder was full, according to best farming procedures. Meanwhile, the day they started handing out medals to wives, Carrie's should be at least eighteen carat gold. What other wife would stake her life's savings for the benefit of a hubby? She just happened to bump into Tootsie on his way out of the factory, and, as usual with her wishes, he volunteered the market tip before she could ask.

"Carrie, spare me a thousand for a few months?" the cigarette drooped wistfully. "Pay you seven percent?"

"Gladly, with no percent—if I had it. But I'd have to hock my chinchilla and you wouldn't want a frail girl like me exposed to the elements with winter near?"

Wouldn't he! For his part she could hock herself to the step-ins—or naked, for that matter. He had a sure thing, she should buy some herself. Out of his Quality Lamps briefcase came graphs, charts and correspondence with company executives to prove Miami Electric Power was ready to soar. Tootsie knew how to convince you, squinting under the poverty bulb in the loft door with his own cigarette smoke in his eye. For securities he was a go-getter. Land was moving a mile a minute in Florida, they were clearing it, paving it, building homes where there used to be maybe a shack raising pigs, and streets and houses would have to be lit. He had you ready to hock the chinchilla and toss in your fancy-cut engagement marquise baguettes and all. But with all said if not done, "I couldn't," she simpered girlishly, "Danny'd murder me."

Back went Tootsie's literature. "Two of a kind."

"Temperament, temperament."

"Not you. My wife and your husband I meant."

"Temperament, even more so. Do you have room for anything else in that briefcase, like say a Quality Lamps catalog?"

"I keep that," Tootsie made a face, "in my pocket."

Poor Tootsie, on the day of reckoning she would almost hate to give him the ax. But why wait for Miami Electric to spark your profits? Why not get title for quick resale to land they'll lay the cables through?

Then the evening arrived that Dr. Nate Barasch quit fishing around and, "Congratulations, Mother," confirmed—or did he?—her worst fears. Humor, she answered him, had its place like anything else and this wasn't it. Nate reprimanded her that she knew very well it was patient's health first with him and if a witticism followed Gladys was not permitted to include that in the bill. Congratulations or not, he wound up, she was pregnant kid. For a moment she considered sounding him out about an abortion. Quality Lamps Inc.—she'd had Jerry incorporate them with a wave of his typist—required her full-time attention and kids are a drag no matter how much you love 'em. But as long as spontaneous combustion had started her off, she might as well shoot the works—boy, girl and poodle—and get it over with. And her sister-in-law Naomi grinding for children! She Carrie B. Share would manage and better than manage. When you're destiny's tot, obstacles become stepping-stones!

It was a nuisance true that tender titties forbade sleep on your tummy, but deliciously maddening when you seduced Limpy into playing on those hard pregnant nipples. What is so rare as a Sunday in winter with rain on the windows fluttering waves of shadow across your royal bed like the shivers Limpy's delicate maneuvers for baby's sake sent through you. He was a born father, her Limpy. The indisposition she alleged if business away from business came up was harder on him than on her. So what if you felt a vague bellyache? She'd had worse, like when she devoured that bushel or so of corn on the cob as a child. Mother, actually, that week in the country that had given Moishe his accursed chicken raising idea, had been in bed with one of her sudden attacks, not that that had prevented Mother from cooking supper. But Moishe had dished it out, and while Daddy'd been reading his *The World Tomorrow* over his meal, had little Carrie taken it—until it took her at midnight. Sick as Mother had been had Moishe heard a word or two from his wife. What a mother, what an Eva—all Carrie's! Limpy stroked Carrie's belly and told her no rough stuff behind his back, they had to treat Russell nice.

"Russell?"

"Our son."

"I should be kicking, not him. Imagine that nothing, trying to slow down me Carrie B. Share! He'll find out. Who's Russell? Your father's father was honest Abe, wasn't he?"

"Some honest Abe. He used to cackle 'Beautiful little boy, what did you learn in Torah today?' while he pinched me black and blue. Uncle Willie said, 'Yeah, being a class victim soured your grandpa,' but I used to feel more like the victim. Russell sounds nice."

Was he playing dumb? He meant Reisel sounded nice—which was kinda raw, eh? But don't worry, Mother, poor Eva, poor kid, it's your baby, Ezra if it's a boy, otherwise Eva—and the reverse for the second child.

Yeah, pregnancy bothered Carrie as much as it had bothered Jenny the cow after Carrie and Moishe'd had Jenny serviced by Mr. Gallagher's bull. And a lot less. With the bull still busy, Jenny'd gotten bored and simply ambled over to where the grass was greener with the roaring idiot stuck and dragging after her. Far be it from Carrie to resort to such extreme wanderlust, but play sick, later phone Limpy you were much improved—and upward and onward.

Jerry Belik had set a wedding date with his Pauline, so her father must have owned Yonkers with deeds fully attested. The daddy's tentacles—oops, Jerry'd used the word interests—didn't reach down to Florida, and Jerry himself preferred Long Island to invest in rather than a sweltering climate three fourths underwater and subject to hurricanes. But if she insisted, he hurriedly added with the prospect of a commission split shining out of the eager set of his face, he could recommend Edelstein a former colleague now in real estate.

Oy did Jerry send her slumming to the East Bronx that raw forenoon where packed blocks of houses converged on a shopping street below the El. With her chinchilla clutched tight at the throat she picked her way among ladies pinching items on vegetable stands while their forlorn kiddies hung on looking cold. This was a center for shares in a subtropical paradise?

Edelstein's office was a store in a row of stores, between a marked down dry-goods irregulars and a grocery specializing in stinking cheese. And—Carrie peeked through his window—Edelstein was a busy man at his roll-top desk in the back pointing his corrugations and grandfatherly white hair frankly and earnestly at two ladies of the outside type only humble, like their shopping bags on the floor while they sat seeking their fortune.

Good Lord, to live lives like that, poor fish, gasping to be skinned in the underwater lots Jerry'd hinted about. And that bastard Jerry, sending her Carrie B. Share to a run-down con man for the sake of a few bucks commission! But if Jerry with every reason not to would thoroughly screw you even for peanuts, where do you go? To Henny Lieber, or the rabbi in Orange? Where do honest ones come to land speculators? And suppose Henny did happen to know from his insurance days, do you tell honesty mum's the word to your wife? Wasn't this a fine state of affairs, with no one in sight to trust! After some neck-stretching Carrie caught a cab that had wandered into the neighborhood and told the driver Wall Street. In a world of crooks why not start at the top?

At Guaranty Trust—now this was what Carrie called a store to do business with—she maneuvered her next with winks and a sunshiny face so her adviser was Mr. Freede a tycoon in the bud, almost as clean-cut as her

Limpy, cleaner in fact at the bald spot. And did that naughty young man set out to charm her with a flash of teeth and an offer of cigarettes in honor of the Carrie B. Share eyes and figure and the chinchilla fur coat that he helped her off with just the way Limpy always did, real gents the Gentiles. Then Freede showed off how much he knew about mortgages and waterfront industrial property, and he seemed to know quite a lot. What would she have done without him? She girlishly stuffed the data he gave her into her purse, and as she thanked him profusely he pulled his solid gold graduation watch from his vest, to his astonishment discovered that it was lunch hour and asked if she'd care to join him.

Now wouldn't she have loved to, if she hadn't been committed for lunch! But next time, when she'd be back with . . . what did he call it?—she giggled—her plans fully matured. Had he by the way ever heard of Edelstein Limited that dealt in Florida land?

"Edelstein?" The way Master Freede wrinkled his nose the smell from Westchester Avenue must have carried all the way down here to Wall Street. "Why would you want to get yourself mixed up with an Edelstein?" Master Freede would just jot down the names of a few reputable Florida agencies.

Carrie asked you, wasn't this Guaranty anti-Semite a darling? And her without even a midget account at Uncle Pierponteleh's he should rest in peace. As to Hendricks Realty Southern, which headed Master Freede's little list, Carrie right through the nose in a United Cigar Store phone booth played her own Puss-in-Boots with a call as Mrs. Share's secretary so the red carpet would be out when she arrived.

Meanwhile the wind lashed bone-deep down the canyons, piercing even chinchilla. Shivering toward 233 Broadway and hungry too she came upon Whyte's in Fulton Street. "Oh no, Whyte's is too steep for me," Jerry the sport Belik had shaken his head on their way to his favorite economy drugstore lunch counter from his Strivers' Row spot in the Woolworth Building last spring, "that's," with awe, "for executives, Carrie." So today she dropped in at Whyte's and cast her executive eye on—some bargain—a bunch of cigars in brown-paneled alcoves. But she relished the eyes cast, as usual, on her, all executives' a girl might presume. The nice lunch—she was ravenous over the lamb chops—didn't break you either, though you did miss out on the pleasurable sense of thrift Jerry enjoyed with an American cheese sandwich such as he hadn't been able to recommend highly enough at that drugstore of his.

Till she reached 233 Broadway it hadn't occurred to her that that was the Woolworth Building, Jerry's old stamping grounds. But no danger of finding her Guaranty Trust tip Hendricks Realty Southern—the directory said fifty-eighth floor—squashed into a two-by-four in the building innards like Jerry's old joint.

The elevator sucked itself up at the speed of light and her stomach got off at the fifth—so long Ezra!

You were at the top of the world, where was her parachute—though who wanted to use one? Exhilarating, in marble halls a mile drop to streets seething like a boxful of ants! Clouds shredded themselves on skyscrapers shooting up to salute you as if you were Duke Mussolini in the newsreels, the North River glinted with tiny steamers at dock you could pick up and play with. Brick, river, bridges: the view swept uptown. But itsy-bitsy Quality Lamps? Blocked out, you couldn't see it.

She Carrie Baum would drag it up by the bootstraps, this high and higher!

She owned the thousand that poor Tootsie was breathing hard for, and more than a thousand: her rainy day bundle courtesy three years in the Vandervaart galleys plus the hidden economies of a year's wedded bliss. And to build on sand in Miami so she could build on rock in New York she also stood ready—faint heart ne'er won fair factory—to pawn her marquise. And at Hendricks this Sigsbee who looked right off the Mayflower with the gray of his eyes, temples and sharkskin suit kept nodding yes total attention as she sketched him her plans. Then as if she hadn't spoken a word he proceeded with a sales talk for swampland. Ali Baba piled blueprint on brochure, and brochure on blueprint. Lots, golden sands, swaying palms and breezes cooled by the Gulf Stream were enough to turn lower Broadway into the Arabian Nights by daylight.

Couldn't downtrodden Israel under the El in the Bronx take lessons from Hendricks Realty Southern!

When the talking machine paused to rewind, Carrie set a few fresh breezes blowing herself. And, down from the magic carpet, Mr. Sigsbee could agree no need necessarily for long-term holdings, true. Though they paid best of course—Sigsbee could not help himself: he was off and running again—only yesterday Hendricks had accepted nine hundred thousand dollars for a Palm Beach strip they had acquired for a hundred and ninety thousand prewar.

Whoa, Dobbin!

With a 10 percent binder you could buy three nice dry seashore lots in Golden Beach just nine miles north of Miami. Hendricks Realty Southern would gladly resell on your behalf (a small commission per lot) before the next payment was due—although her best buy without question would be long-term hol—

Would she have swapped Tootsie for Sigsbee any day of the year to light up the U.S.A. with Quality Lamps!

She hocked the ring, and do you think Limpy noticed her half-naked hand though she flaunted it at him, on him, all over him? Her dreamer, with his popular tunes of the day, on the piano, bathtub vocals, even whistling in the afternoons after his headache would ease off at West Street. Who noticed the hand? Leah the hawk, "Where is your beautiful diamond?" at the weekly noodle soup debauch at Washington Place. Carrie said that she had hocked it, and everyone laughed.

Thirty days later her ring was back on her finger, plus 10 percent. So you could trust Guaranty Trust to pick you a winner. Still coconuts don't grow out of peanuts, not even in Florida. You couldn't fool Sigsbee, long term pays better: for you if you keep up the payments, for Hendricks Realty Southern of course whether you do or you don't. At this rate Ezra'd be an old man with whiskers by the time she owned West Street.

Maybe after all the solution was stocks? But with easy marks buying lots twenty, thirty, forty miles out of Miami like bargains on Rivington Street, why had Miami Electric Power stock dropped?

"Why ask me?" morose Tootsie said after supper at Leah's. He'd scraped together the usual few bucks, bought Miami Electric Power on the usual margin and been wiped out as usual. "Look at this," he jabbed toward his cigarette, "I can't so much as get a match to ignite."

"Here, gimme—" Carrie leaned her scent and equipment toward the impervious Tootsie and struck a fat steady flame. "Hey Murray—don't be so fierce, you're blowing smoke in the face of your benefactress."

"Sorry. I wasn't aiming at you."

But his target the little woman with her baby obsession busily discussing with Leah what the doctor she'd been to'd said, what she'd said—was out of range of her hubby's smoke and oblivious to his venomous look. In fact, ". . . I do if he refuses to go?" Naomi shot Tootsie a nasty glance of her own. Housewife Henny helping Mama Golda with the dishes inside laughingly called Limpy bloodthirsty because as far as Limpy was concerned too bad Lenin hadn't taken his whole crew of Bolshies with him the other day when his apoplexy—"good for the apoplexy"—finished him off. Henny the intellect wanted to give the Bolshies a chance, the Ku Kluxers here were what worried him.

In real life Tootsie said good and loud for his Naomi's benefit, "Don't be simple, Carrie. The market's manipulated, like everything else. No reason Miami Electric Power should have gone down if they hadn't been selling short damn my luck. Now it's ready to turn—and I can never buy outright!"

Naomi itemizing her different specimen tests for Leah made sure not to listen.

Carrie listened—and she bought outright. From Tootsie's lips to the Stock Exchange's ears. Miami Electric Power began going up and rose higher than where Tootsie had plunged in and scraped some more skin off his nose.

Oy Tootsie. At the end of the day he'd storm into the factory—from window-shopping at his broker's blackboard?—slap down his order book on his wife's desk and report the progress of Carrie's securities he didn't know Carrie owned. "Is this all?" Naomi would examine the book and look up at him cross-eyed. "Only reorders?" Leave it to Carrie, his days were numbered at Quality. But if Tootsie was a charity case, when it came to the stock market he blessedly gave.

"Here," Tootsie rattled his *Evening Sun* market reports pages at her and Naomi the day Miami Electric Power fell three-eighths of a point, "is where I would have taken my profits and bought myself New York Central and Radio . . . and," his desperate eye ran over the columns, "Automotive!"

Carrie took her profits, and bought herself New York Central and Radio and Automotive. While her stuff went up—eleven and a half juicy points for wonderful Radio, what was Tootsie doing with his ice cream soda allowance from the little woman? Taking a flyer on Wyoming Wildcat Aircraft. "But Tootsie," you laughed at him—because the mystery wasn't that mysterious once you began taking an interest—"you know how high the odds are against a new outfit."

"I got to get capital."

Carrie had capital, though not enough—her melon belly was rounding faster with Ezra swimming around in there. But—losers lose, winners win—she didn't take flyers. She calmly phoned her broker from home mornings when necessary and then waddled Ezra on and off a cab to the factory. Otherwise she drove down with Limpy against Limpy's protests.

"Our delivery room isn't for childbirth, Pussy—"

Naomi said, "That's pretty disgusting coming in with that belly."

Jealousy. But give the little girl credit, she would cater to Carrie. Naomi insisted—insisted!—that Carrie take the swivel chair and the desk while Naomi switched to a straight chair and small table. So Carrie was in the driver's seat, where she belonged. Too bad Ezra who'd put her there would put her out of there. But she'd contract, the factory would expand, and she'd be back and permanently. By Eva's turn to be born, Mommy would have the whole works under control. With expansion they'd need new salesmen, at least one for a start, and that start would be the beginning of Tootsie's end. Well, you couldn't get rid of Tootsie, even if Naomi's witch doctors produced her a child—an uphill job. How about sending them both out of town, settling them down in, say, Jericho, that desolation on the Great Lakes she and Limpy'd got lost in on their honeymoon when they were trying to drive back East via Chicago. Oil tanks, small dead or half-dead factories, working stiffs' cottages with pathetic gardens of scraggly green clumps in summer-baked clay: but railroad tracks, freight cars, unused sidings—perfect, she'd thought, with cheap rents and with out of work labor loafing on bottom porch steps, as a Midwest assembly and distribution depot for Quality Lamps. Sure, send Naomi and Tootsie there as high-titled stock clerks, with the salesmen working out of New York. The routine would be perfect for Naomi. Then home to their cottage frugal where Naomi would spur Tootsie on with wild dreams of motherhood.

Not that dreams can't be practical, provided you give 'em a hand.

By happy birthday George Washington Carrie had almost doubled her money, and she could not tell a lie: not Limpy or any other Share was ever going to hear about her stocks and real estate winnings. A girl likes to keep a finger on her own funds. Then for happy Passover came the word from Jerry to enter the Promised Land, the lawsuit was settled. Ten thousand big smackeroos for her (he didn't mention his ten but who cared?) in payment of Limpy! "And no more," Jerry couldn't stop pleading his case, "than that young man richly deserves for a permanent disability." The insurance company should have clocked Limpy's speed just now racing downstairs at West Street before the truck got away. To Carrie's "Hey we've struck gold" his voice sailed up that they'd forgotten to load part of the Hammerschlaft order. But if Carrie wrote Jerry a five thousand check to add to the settlement and he wrote her a check for the total, she could hand Limpy fifteen G's with no reference to Radio, Miami Electric Power or Golden Beach and still have a thousand of her own to play with. By the time Limpy panted into the office—"Just caught them. Where's the gold, my wheelbarrow's outside"—she had on her green flared Lane Bryant spring maternity special and she kissed him ta-ta, secret errand.

"No, I'm not about to give birth stupie, anyway not to Ezra."

Why certainly, Jerry said when Carrie sprang the request at him in his office, he'd be glad to oblige her with the larger check. For finagling at no cost to himself he was always your man.

"Come Jerry, I'll blow you to a roast beef on roll at the drugstore."

"Uh, why should you, Carrie? We'll go Dutch."

Whereas—one extreme to the other—she beat Limpy home and he smiled amazed at the news and, "It's yours," he handed the check back to her.

"Sure it's mine—it's our factory!"

She had to turn the Quality Lamps on in their living room, sit him down, and explain it to him. Add five thousand from the Quality treasury and they qualified for a mortgage for the Quality Building! Also, sonny boy, their cash contribution gave them majority interest in the business—they were the boss!

"Naomi and I are partners, Pussy. No need to change that."

"Who's changing what? We're incorporated, it's bookkeeping arithmetic. Unless Naomi matches your fifteen thousand."

"Using what?"

"And Ezra," she fiercely rubbed Limpy's apparatus, "calls himself the baby around here! Using her bank account from her twenty-five a month Lower East Side apartment full of furniture secondhand from you and your mother that didn't cost Naomi a nickel."

"Why should it have?" Danny got good leverage for the first kiss. "That's nice furniture, I bought it myself." He pushed her down on the couch belly and all with Aaron's rod ready to strike a geyser for Passover.

"We'll," Carrie drew up her step-ins to help him, "be late for the other Passsover ceremonies—"

"They'll think we're Elijah."

Danny at the maternity desk asked, "Seen the whites of his eyes yet?"

The nurse said, "Now you're laughing," and it was flattering, her kidding around with you, a tall nifty carrot-top.

Danny giggled. "Because I took your advice Brigid."

He'd sped Carrie a mile a minute to Morningside Hospital, and after she'd patted his cheek, told him don't worry and been swallowed up by Maternity, he'd wanted to know where was her cousin the doctor. Then the nurse had cracked that Dr. Barasch leaves strict instructions never to call him, evenings especially, till you see the whites of the child's eyes, and Danny had let that nurse have it so she'd had to explain the joke in unfunny detail. Then she'd added her don't worry and suggested a speakeasy for medicinal purposes a few blocks away on 125th Street, near Faye's Oyster House. "But isn't it a crime that with an Irish cleft jaw like yours you should have an honest prohibition-agent glint in your Erin blue eye?" "Me?" Danny'd said. "Sure and it's a *nechtiger tog*." "You know the Gaelic?" the nurse had laughed, and said, "Tell Jimmy Brigid sent you." Some fun, with his gizzard stuck to his spine. He'd hung around and hung around in the Lysol stink of the lobby, he'd kept asking Brigid but she'd lost interest and only shaken her head, he'd phoned Nate to find out what the hell was holding up the parade but Gladys answered that Nate was making a house call and there was no need to phone him as he was never late for obstetrics.

So Danny had marched out in a rage again, snapped "Brigid" at the speakeasy grille, and come sailing back on two martinis. Brigid's next advice was go home to bed, it would take a while yet.

"Can you make it?" she said. "How much of that stuff did you guzzle? I'd drive you," she shrugged, "but I'm not off until midnight."

"Oh I can make it," another giggle got through. "Everything seems far away, but I've got my Stutz."

"Use it well," Brigid said.

In the air, the mild country-sweet air at the park rising in lamp and shadow to G. Washington's little brick fort crowning the rocks, window lights here and there on Morningside Heights enticed him, but he didn't know anybody who lived up in those buildings. Jesus Christ, it was like starting west on his honeymoon with America spread out in front of him—plains, valley clefts, forests!

He drove slowly, with great care, through that . . . grassy perfume and the dark streets, almost empty, hardly anyone out this hour, the six blocks to Reisel's. Reisel in a robe with her hair in papers gazed in alarm at him.

"Has something . . . happened to Carrie?"

"She's left me, for some kid." Danny giggled at the auburn hair in the curlers. "*Et tu, Brute*—feminine wiles?"

"Ugh—smell that drunken breath."

"Where's Gittel?"

"Hiding, in terror of you."

"Get dressed," Danny heard himself say, "I'll take you for a ride."

"And like any gangster leave me dead at some wayside. Come in, someone must protect you from yourself. I shall prepare coffee." Danny aimed himself toward the piano, but Reisel pulled him away. "Will you wake up the whole house?" So Danny tried to slip her a kiss, but she pushed him away.

"Pull push." He dropped to a kitchen chair and hung his arms over the back of it. "You meant you'll protect yourself from me. When I fell in love with Carrie I was drunk, if my memory is correct. When I fell in love with you I was sober."

"You are as drunk as a peasant now or you would never believe that you fell in love with me."

"I fell."

"Mere logic," Reisel banged the coffeepot down on the stove—poor neighbors—"demonstrates that love is not changeable."

"I never was good at logic," Danny said. "But say, won't he be the lucky one—my son, with a brand new fresh start."

"And so can all of us make brand new fresh starts, if we have the courage."

"You know," Danny said, "much as I love you Reisel, you can be a wet blanket."

"Now," Reisel giggled, "I am a blanket."

Danny laughed—did he laugh! Nice, sipping coffee with a Reisel dressed in her nightgown. Better still, contrary to rumor coffee did not sober you up. He tried to kiss Reisel good night and of course she ducked in time, and downstairs again he breathed in this . . . luscious May night. The Convent Avenue drugstore was closed, he couldn't phone the hospital. So he drove back instead.

Then as he walked into the lobby he shivered. Suppose, while he'd been enjoying himself, Carrie had died? At the desk sat another Brigid on duty, long-faced, with doom written all over her. But she flicked through some cards, and . . . mother and infant both fine.

Yippee!

Halfway home it struck him—holy Jesus—he hadn't found out whether he was a father or mother!

16

AT LEAH AND HENNY'S FOR THE BIWEEKLY SUPPER WITH Ma Naomi tried to control herself, she lied that Tootsie hadn't come with her on account of a terrible cold, she even made herself smile. But with dinner on the table Ma kept toddling Carrie's baby all over the apartment. Ezra would plunge ahead, then—so cute!—stop and look back proud of himself with that wide gap-toothed grin.

"Mama," Leah scolded her, "this is your own chicken soup getting cold."

Ma exclaimed, "I can't help it, I'm infatuated with this young man!" and Carrie with her eight-months' stomach toward the next baby smirked proudly. And this awful winter what did Naomi have to show for going on two years of married life? Terrible scenes, slammed doors by her husband, and—a sniff came, she couldn't suppress it—red eyes. Danny was smiling at his son's antics, but he—"What's the matter?"—caught Naomi's hand.

"He called me a cheap bitch," and tears and everything else came out.

Love's old sweet song. Stocks rose, but not Tootsie's. The lemons he was pushed into because she starved him for money shriveled right on the tree. Henny suggested she stake Murray to some good oil or telephone stocks. Danny'd picked up a few shares on Henny's say-so and they'd done well so far.

"It's all gambling!" Naomi yelled at their brother-in-law as if he were to blame for Wall Street. "If only I could get him away from . . . these influences, if I could find him a job he likes. Why should he be a salesman? —he hates selling. Danny isn't a salesman."

Grant his sister's troubles, but did that get Danny-o's dander up! "You elected him salesman, kiddo, by single ballot."

"I did not!"

Then Carrie sprang a land of milk and honey on them, north of Chicago and south of Wisconsin on Lake Michigan, and appropriately named Jericho.

"Remember it Danny, from our honeymoon?"

But all Danny remembered, for a big laugh from all present, was the honeymoon.

In any case, Jericho had been a grain market for the East and Europe, but after the war it had gone sour. Carrie didn't know about the jetsam, but the flotsam was perfect: railroad facilities, low rent and cheap labor in your backyard. She even remembered a particular vacant factory—it shouldn't be difficult to track down in a two-bit town like Jericho—that would be just right as the assembling depot, Quality Lamps West. No new capital costs—New York does the production, like now, but for the first time at full plant capacity—and the savings on freightage from West Street to Jericho with compact parts shipment would give Quality that extra competitive edge out west. So if not California here we come, at least watch out Duluth—and Tootsie M. Kaye, Manager-in-Chief, Jericho!

Leah whistled to think that she'd started Quality Lamps and had considered herself a businesswoman, and Carrie winked at Leah, the professional at the amateur sent out to pasture. But Naomi was in an ecstasy.

"A whole factory for him to manage!"

"Not a whole," Carrie was honest with her. "West Street has all the machinery and skilled labor—but seventy percent of a factory."

"Percent, pershment—Murray'll be so happy, and I'll be so happy."

Except that Danny wasn't so happy. You're doing fine in the East, why chase to the West? And all of a sudden, he asked Naomi, risks didn't bother her? Between the noodle soup and the broiled chicken it was an accepted fact that the warehouse and shipping expenses wouldn't eat up the supposed Duluth profits? But Naomi cited their out-of-town salesman Jacobson—"Hatchet-face," she giggled drunk with hope, "our Jewish Indian, with the Florida tan from a sunlamp." Fred Jacobson had already staged winning campaigns as far south as Morgantown. And hadn't he said a million times, give him the word and expenses and he'd give them the golden West on a platter?

"Oh," Naomi leaned over to smack a kiss on her sister-in-law's cheek, "isn't Carrie a marvel with her ideas!"

So between the soup and the chicken Naomi's Jacobson tune had changed completely. A year or so ago when Carrie got them Jacobson, Naomi'd gagged at the price of the guy, and so had Danny. But Carrie'd cracked, "It's a steal," and what did they think, Carrie had laughed, you can build a business on greed alone? Naomi'd resented that, but Carrie'd pinched Danny's sister's china-doll cheek and kept laughing. "Don't feel guilty, I didn't mean you." She'd meant some Zuaracce who'd enlarged Persons' pottery in Orange from a shack to a castle. Persons? Zuaracce? "Why," Carrie had begun to lose patience, "I told you about that long ago, before we decided to expand the hand-painted line." Jacobson sold for

Zuaracce, that's who they were stealing him from. Naomi'd asked was it ethical to steal another firm's salesman, and Carrie—"We're not *kidnapping* him"—had really been tickled. Danny would have backed up his sister then though, if it had been the principle not the commission that had been bothering her.

Now Naomi couldn't wait for Danny to do the advance scouting, rent a Jericho factory—Carrie kept saying warehouse, Naomi kept saying factory—and a nice place not too expensive for her and Murray till they could buy their own home. Danny—"In a two-bit town like Jericho?"—kept fighting his rear guard action. But Naomi said that the smaller the bit town the better she'd like it. Every morning Murray would go to manage the factory, and she'd keep house with her baby, the way Carrie did!

That excited Ma. "You mean, darling—?"

But Naomi was only prophesying. How could she have children if Murray wore himself out all hours over those horrible magazines and stock market papers? Oh the wonderful day when they could escape the stock market!

"Naomi," Carrie tried to wise her up, "you'd need the Canadian Rockies for that. Everywhere else you're going to have stock markets."

But Naomi stayed just as anxious to go. "Jericho can't be one great big stock market like New York. And maybe my luck will change with a move."

With a move away from her husband her luck would change.

At West Eighty-fourth Street Danny undressed Ezra with plenty of kisses—could that very short crawler put Daddy and Grandma Share through their paces with everything from horsie to mountain-climbing up Leah's bookshelves—inserted him half-asleep into pajamas and nestled him face down in his crib. Then Carrie crossed her wrists behind Danny's neck with her pregnant belly poking his belt.

"Go West young man," she said to his happy kiss, "you promised your sister."

"Don't tag unpromised promises on me, Mama," he kissed her again. "Who would we sell to if the farmers are starving around Jericho?"

"Let the farmers fill up on their surplus wheat by the light of their silvery kerosene lamps," Carrie laughed. "Our hicks'll be in the cities."

"And this hick's staying in New York City."

But the seducer he shared his bed with knew how to prod you with dreams of glory: Share, the captain of industry—Park Avenue, yachts, country estates, the newsreel guys pleading for a smile for the camera. Sure you didn't believe it, but you liked it. Jesus, he was proud of his business! You reached West Street mornings—a tumult: trucks honking, bass serenades from freighters getting up steam, that salt smack from baskets of fish being lugged into Fisherino's, his tenant! There were these muscle men, the rank and file haulers—and this building belonged to him, Dan Q. Share, the entire three stories, every gray brick! A few years back who would have even conceived of owning the building? Carrie. And when he'd start, in the middle of the night, out of a graveyard nightmare and grab out from the dead to the live body—whose?—beside him, "I'll rescue you kiddo," Carrie'd mumble and groggily hang her hot thigh over his hip. That was how Eva originated—the girl on the way—an impromptu rescue. And what a good sport Carrie had been, pregnant again, with Ezra just about beginning to crawl. "Sharpshooter. Your brother-in-law Tootsie could take lessons from you," she'd smirked at Danny. Quite a girl Carrie, who saved you from your bad dreams and made your good ones come true.

Even so, he tapped that belly of hers. "Leave with Eva inside?"

"As a coming-out gift to Eva."

"You give birth here, and I'm in Chicago?"

"Jericho," she giggled. "You should see me give birth without you."

He nixed that scheme in a hurry. And in spite of Carrie's bright pictures of Limpy king of the jungle both Eastern and Western Divisions, and Naomi's reproachful looks as time passed, he kept stalling—his heart wasn't really in it—till Teddy's . . . "This brunette prefers gentlemen anyway," Carrie cracked when Eva turned out to be another boy . . . six month birthday. "You want your old burper close to the premises, don't you?" Danny twisted his head around to ask that sour milk bundle he held on his shoulder. Not only did old Blubber-face answer "Da—" but he smiled and rolled out a thunderclap.

"See, Pussy—what more can you ask for?" Danny squeezed his soft Teddy-o. "That meant yes."

"That meant gas," his tickler Pussy cracked. "Kiss the boys goodbye and start packing."

"Not so fast—" Danny fought it out as gamely as any rat you could corner. Who'd cover the shop and give Naomi a hand in the office if he went to Jericho for a month? Reisel—she never failed you in a matter of work—was perfectly willing. Only who wanted Reisel exhausting herself between downstairs with the paintresses and upstairs with production, shipping and salesmen? Unless you made the paintress Millie Zook queen for a day—temporary paintress forelady—and all that dame had to have was a little authority with her flat nasty voice tumbling over the harelip. Danny didn't hold physical defects against anybody—he himself limped—but what Reisel put up with "Just because," Reisel said, "you must feel sorry for Zook." Himself, he would have preferred to give Zook the gate and feel sorry for her at a distance. Why Carrie had hired her to begin with beat his comprehension. Carrie'd said, "We're not casting for the *Ziegfeld Follies*, kiddo. She knows her job. In an emergency la Zook could take over."

"What emergency?"

"Say Raisin gets married."

Of course anything's possible. For a lifetime the only art Ma had ever glanced at was on postcards or calendars. Now Henny had converted her to a museum and gallery fan who brought her grandsons art reproductions that Ezra improved on with crayons and that Teddy—given a chance—tore hunks off and ate. "I'm improving baby's taste, anyhow," Grandma would laugh, and each visit more pictures. So some day Reisel might marry, but Danny wasn't prepared to bet the family jewels on it.

As to Danny's last defense against Jericho, Carrie steamrollered him without the blink of an eyelash.

"Don't bother Raisin, and don't bother Millie. I Carrie B. Share will drop in at West Street and keep the machinery humming."

"With Ezra and Teddy humming in the machinery?"

"Those two gents will be home—or in the park holding their own against those ritzy housewives and their brats that I had a year and a day of—taking care of their caretaker."

"Those two gents want their mommy, not some dry needlenose."

"Who Carrie's picked you'll like." Next she hollered Rebecca the maid into the living room. "Mr. Share, meet Mrs. Ward, the new governess."

"And old maid?" Danny asked.

"Rebecca ain't no old maid, but the new maid is starting Monday."

"Miz Share," Becky swore, "you a caution," and immediately ran to earn her extra ten a week by snatching up Teddy with his fine pair of lungs from Ezra beating a tattoo—"Just," everyone's charmer, "pyaying dwum"—on his brother's belly.

When you saw what you'd actually known, that Becky was the boys' big brown playmate, you liked the idea of a governess. Carrie's legal eagle pal Belik who sometimes did work for Quality had a governess for his kid up in Yonkers, and of course Central Park West was loaded with German accents in white uniforms.

So the reservation was picked up for the Twentieth Century Limited, the bags were packed, the train boarded and Duluth here we come—or at least watch out Jericho!

Fate no sooner knocked on the door than Danny found himself falling asleep. He fought it, but Chicago's Concert Hall was too dim and warm. . . . Sound washed over him . . . like a summer seashore . . . with Ezra . . . patting sand castles together. Carrie forgive him, in the morning he'd rise to the occasion. The Twentieth Century to Jericho . . . but tomorrow. For now he gave up the battle and sighed snuggling against Carrie's shoulder.

He sailed down—oh Jesus, it really was happening this time—into his black, airless grave. . . . But his head snapped back to—thank God—life, light, a . . . stage? Uhh, he was in Chicago already, with a young girl on his left—not Carrie—dark, none too pleased. Had he jostled her? He sat up straight and did eyeball calisthenics. You couldn't trust yourself though to the conductor's lumbering shoulders and the baton. The unison strings, even the basses partnering high dancing stools, were just as hypnotic. Then the gleaming brass made you cross-eyed and the reeds undulated like snakes. He blinked, he bit his cheeks, he kept pinching himself. And Jesus Christ—still his eyes would roll—Beethoven was no help with his damn swelling country andante!

That happy piece of music appreciation sparked a snort, and again lightning flashed from the left. He was a boor, and she had intelligent eyes. He'd have to apologize to her and her husband.

At intermission she stayed but the husband and friends made tracks without an excuse me, so maybe she wasn't used to apologies that much. Danny begged her pardon regardless and the glance that had looked stern in faint light seemed scared under the grand chandeliers.

"I shouldn't have come to the concert after overnight from New York on a sleepless sleeper. The berth fit me like a coffin, perfect for nightmares. But my favorite tune, Beethoven's Fifth, and no Jericho for the evening—so I came."

The long lashes flicked up. "You have nightmares?"

The same one, since Ezra. After his first son was born and they'd let the nurse go—they hadn't been that hasty the next time around—Danny used to stagger out of bed for the 2 A.M. feeding, give the missus a break. Besides, he'd been a born mother the way his heart melted to that warm baby in the crook of his arm. The old soak would drink himself blind, take a pat on the back and a kiss or two and begin whimpering for his shut-eye. Danny would drop like a stone himself, then wake feeling buried.

The girl said, the young woman, she wore the wedding band but she did seem young to be married—more a schoolgirl who shot timid glances at you, "My nightmare's the opposite. I dream I go to the doctor because I have no children. Then he . . . Well, never mind what he does. He says it's cancer and he tells me the cure. But the cure is worse than the disease."

"Worse than cancer? What is the cure?"

"I never remember."

The warning bells chimed, but Danny began sketching the day for her that had put him to sleep before: Chicago rank as a butcher's; Jericho and the lake dotted with tanks that made your mouth taste of gas; a cabbie who steered you into the heart of a traffic jam to let the meter tick up; real estate agents—fast talkers who showed you cavernous warehouses going to seed, one warehouse had actual crabgrass bursting through at the door. What he hated worst was the—

But the house lights dimmed, the orchestra he hadn't heard tuning up became silent, and—Jesus, once you start babbling!—what did she care what he hated worst, though the husband and friends chatted even through the applause for the conductor bobbing out of the wings like an oversized Cupid. The husband had the same sort of good looks as she, long-lashed, narrow-faced, only her dark bob was straight and his hair looked marceled, with a soft girlish cheek to go with it. A brunette Tootsie: no wonder no kids.

But at Beethoven's heroic raps for attention Danny found himself wide awake and elated—the hell with that landlord Hubbell today and those real estate guys!—on horseback leading his wagon train of spoils home with women cheering as he cantered through towns. The second movement he was Hamlet Act Five, the four shoulder exit with anguished Reisel reaching after the stiff. By the scherzo though he was pooped, just as Beethoven was picking up steam. He'd promised Carrie a call noon tomorrow and nothing solid to tell her, he'd have to fight this crowd for a cab, and ahead of him were his headache and the grand Lysol special, Hotel Jericho Palace with a view of two trolley wires along a Broadway the boys down on the farm couldn't escape from quickly enough.

Even so the last crashing chords were a mercy.

The marcel-haired fellow's gang got up, except her. She timidly smiled, and Danny groping under the seat for his hat hoisted his cheek.

"You didn't say," she blurted, "what you hate worst."

You could have knocked him down with a feather!

"Oh that." He shrugged, he smiled. "Bargaining, making deals."

"Then why do you do it?"

"I don't. That is, I try not to, I state my maximum offer. Then they start trying to make a monkey out of me, I blow up, and they admire my style and keep bargaining." He watched marcel inching up the aisle without a look back for the missus. "Has your husband forgotten you?"

"Most likely—"was she a Midwest deadpan comedienne?—"he's very resourceful."

"Then," Danny pointed, "you better catch up."

Now she was surprised.

Which man was it in the milling aisles? She and Danny rose too. That one? A complete stranger. Her husband was a composer who—she told Danny as they joined the crowd—loved music so much that he could hardly bear listening to most of it. If it was Beethoven's last quartets, Art might go, and even then she'd have to be sure to get last row tickets. Art would keep shaking his head at the way Beethoven had destroyed structure and if there were people behind them, she'd found out long ago, there'd soon be hisses of "Sit still." So tonight Art was home, or at least not here. Yes, then she could have coffee with Danny, but what would they talk about?

"What we've been talking about."

She still wasn't sure, but . . . Her name was Sydelle Fields, or did he prefer Delphine? Art did, when he introduced her at faculty parties—more exotic, to keep them guessing.

"Guessing what?"

"Whether we're Jewish."

"Why keep anyone guessing? I'm Jewish and—"

"—and proud of it," Sydelle sang along in the mild night air of Michigan Avenue, and she allowed him a funny handclasp on that with the heel of her palm bunched up. So perhaps she should have said Sydelle Feldstein, as her wedding certificate did. Art had been Feldstein before they'd assumed their little Episcopalian incognito—with the court's blessing—for a university job. Had Art been quietly furious through the whole episode, though the idea had been his, doing it right he'd said, as long as his wife and the homosexuals were driving him out of New York.

"You . . . and homosexuals?"

"Separately. I deprived Art of sustenance by quitting my job, and the homosexuals are Art's conspiracy theory of the music world. Still there's no denying that he was neither published nor played—not counting the once we rented Aeolian Hall for a concert—until we came to Chicago."

"Could be that he was right. I'm an ex-smileless boy bard, and I never figured out what a guy had to do for a booking."

"You too, a frustrated artist?"

"Not in the bathtub I'm not. You ought to hear me."

"The bathtub," Sydelle shook her head, "isn't enough for a bard."

She entertained herself also, on viola and violin, hours of them, whenever Art was out of the house and she didn't have lessons to give or University Orchestra rehearsals. Professional orchestras, the Concert Hall Orchestra—perhaps Danny'd noticed—had no women except for the harpist. Art wrote a lot of duets for piano—his instrument—and violin or viola, and they played them at recitals. Art teased her that she'd picked the wrong man at the Conservatory. If she had said yes to the great Zeller of the New York Quartet—he was the Conservatory star—he might have propelled her across the musical heavens. Why hadn't she said yes? Because she'd been in love with Art Feldstein.

"Besides," Sydelle laughed, "Yasha Zeller's question was not 'Will you marry me?' "

So she'd married Art and dropped out of the Conservatory, she told Danny as they strolled. Art stayed for his degree and composed, and she'd been the breadwinner with children's lessons by day and medical secretarying evenings for a tooth and body team, the Jason Brothers. The diplomas on the waiting-room wall attested them doctor and dentist, but they specialized in selling cigars. They operated a chain of cigar stores up in Harlem, and collections came first, and patients came last. The dentist Jason was useless for cavities, he could only pull teeth. The doctor was better, he prescribed colored water on the theory that if it didn't cure it didn't kill either. And Sydelle as a former Conservatory student was the very one they were looking for to give injections and clean teeth. They said, "Sure, bring in your fiddle, feel free to practice." There never was time to practice anything except marginal medicine, and the work must have stunned her. Otherwise how could she have stayed three whole years? As it was, she might still have been reading blood pressure if Mrs. Posner hadn't come in for a second opinion about her overweight and in the absence of both the doctor and dentist nearly died under Sydelle's hands. What a night that had been, the poor obese woman gasping and turning a pale cast of blue on a clammy leatherette couch in a roomful of excited patients, with Sydelle administering nitroglycerin and telephoning cigar stores in Harlem. The police and an ambulance arrived first, and when Dr. Jason dropped in long afterward with his Boston bag full of money not medical instruments, he calmly called up the hospital and then praised Sydelle for her lifesaving resourcefulness, adding, "Bill that woman five dollars." Doctors Jason of Rivington Street. Yes, she had known Danny's old neighborhood all her life, and last but not least from Rivington corner Norfolk to Houston and Avenue A for the trolley to their Village attic, actually a Downing Street top floor—Art would not have anyone over him—where before going into the kitchen you stamped your feet in hope of frightening the roaches away. Then the Irish lady downstairs would bang up.

Houston Street, Downing? Danny stopped Sydelle in front of a hotel where a uniformed general kept the revolving doors moving. Why she and he were next thing to blood relatives! She'd taken the crosstown car three blocks from his house, and gotten off three blocks from his wife's before they were married. It was a miracle Sydelle and he hadn't ever run into each other!

"A lifesaving mira—"

Under the marquee a rusher to a cab sideswiped Sydelle so she would have gone sprawling if Danny hadn't caught hold. He turned a bellicose shoulder toward that punk and his dame, but Sydelle laughed like chimes and said no, an everyday occurrence, she was push prone, always in someone's way.

Danny smiled wonderingly. "You don't get sore?"

"Just bruised sometimes."

"Then we're a well-balanced pair. I fly right off the handle." He tapped the general on the double-breasted gold braid. "They have coffee in there?"

Sydelle held back. "Palmer House? The Loop isn't far."

"Not a respectable house?"

"Too respectable. For the Philistines, Art says."

"Then I qualify. You be my guest."

"I don't believe that you qualify."

"Why not? I know nothing, Sydelle."

"Modest too?"

What did she mean, too?

And it was only a nice coffee shop, white cloths on square tables, curlicue-backed cane chairs, and a wallpaper design of forget-me-nots that made you think of the blue climbing flowers alongside Uncle Willie's pond in the spring.

Danny ordered himself a parfait with his coffee but Sydelle didn't dare taste sweets much as she loved them.

"A slim girl like you?"

"A fat girl in disguise." She was always famished but discipline forbade more than coffee and melba toast.

He brought her back to the lifesaving miracle.

"You remembered," she sang, "what I was saying!"

Danny grinned. "Fair exchange is no robbery."

Sydelle didn't know what he meant.

The lifesaving miracle was simply his never having happened to visit the brothers Jason with a toothache or headache.

"If I'd visited with my headaches I'd have had to pay rent you'd have seen so much of me. I still would, though my tonight's headache—how do you like that?—it's disappeared."

"Why," Sydelle was concerned, "should you have headaches?"

"Carrie's cousin by marriage the Doctor says I'm too highly strung, like my old broken-down uke that I think I lost on our move from the Bronx to West Eighty-fourth Street. But I say Nate's nuts. I'm the Rock of Gibraltar, with the help of my aspirin."

"Are you sure that you're the Rock of Gibraltar? Aspirin can be habit forming."

"No, they're not habit forming Sydelle, I take 'em every day."

Then he heard what he'd said, he guffawed, a fine spray of coffee dotted the gray of Sydelle's frock, and he was patting her chest with a napkin. She kept saying it didn't matter, but was he embarrassed! He insisted that she go to the powder room and he slipped the dame there at the door a couple of bucks to do what she could with those stains.

Sydelle's curious glance at him watching helplessly after her was none too reassuring. What a clod, what an end to the evening that had dropped in his lap.

Ten minutes alone—his chair had its stupid back to the powder room—and he switched to her chair so he could watch for her without spraining his neck. But another crawling ten minutes, and she might already have come out—and walked out. Who'd blame her?

You couldn't ask the powder room woman if you'd been ditched. So call it quits. He turned to signal the waitress when suddenly down Sydelle plumped herself on what had been his seat and lit a cigarette in perfect good humor.

"Look what a job that lady did. She kept me trapped in my step-ins until she had the dress spotless, she was so pleased with what you gave her!"

And before he could warn Sydelle she sipped from his cold coffee cup.

From your pillow in the hotel you saw prairie moonlight swimming in the black of store windows and washing the clapboard buildings on Broadway Jericho with a stage set hush of adventure. The sidewalks had been pulled in long ago. Even in the cab to Cornell Street where Sydelle lived she'd held her wristwatch to the flickering blue of the street lamps and sung "Cinderella's a pumpkin again," and Danny'd apologized how the hours had flown.

Yet they'd stood in the entrance of her elegant courtyard with dimly lit paths around central hedges and gone right on talking.

She'd asked if he was going to the Mozart next week and when he said he didn't know if he'd be here next week and besides he didn't care that much for Mozart, she'd laughed "Yes you do."

"But I don't I tell you."

"You do. You just haven't found out yet."

And off he'd gone on his musical history, from the bar mitzvah ukulele from his sisters to the concert grand Carrie gave him for love. He knew he ought to like Mozart and those guys. So he'd bought himself a bunch of music at Schirmer's and worked his way down from Beethoven's *Moonlight Sonata* to Schubert's *Merry Melody*. Now and then at the factory he'd catch his cousin Reisel—she ran the hand painting on their second floor—for tips on arpeggios that he couldn't handle.

"You can't learn an instrument in the abstract," Sydelle said.

"That's what Reisel said."

So he'd asked Reisel to teach him, and Reisel had asked how could she teach him since she was not invited to his house and Carrie would not come to hers. Why that sudden fuss he would never understand—he'd always visited his two cousins but Carrie didn't and he couldn't blame her, with the Bolshie agents after the mother, Gittel, for murder.

Sydelle was shocked. "Murder!"

That brought you to cousin Elya the Reds wiped out, and to another of Danny's headaches. His cousin Reisel, the physician without a diploma, had decided that something more countrified—like the old country but without the old country folk—would assist her mother's health. All Danny had to do was find her a country home in the city. And when he'd find one, tricking Reisel into letting somebody defray the expense would be an even worse headache. Sydelle had gazed at him and said he was generous. "How?" he'd laughed. What's right's right.

So one evening he'd stuck his exercise book for five-year-olds under his arm and told Carrie he was heading over to Reisel's for a music lesson. "Head," Carrie'd shrugged, "though what you need music lessons for is beyond me." And it was true, he could knock out popular tunes of the day without any trouble, but with classical whenever he hit arpeggios you'd think his limp had tripped him up.

Sydelle had asked, "What limp?"

And he was sidetracked to the prehistoric date with Carrie he'd never arrived at because an automobile got him first. But he seemed completely recovered? Then, he laughed, Indian summer night air must agree with his bones.

Reisel had taught him Shakespeare, but you read Shakespeare and your clinkers are silent. At the piano his clinkers jangled loud and often, and every clinker Reisel would laugh. And if you knew his beautiful cousin Reisel who seldom laughed, you'd understand that when she laughed he laughed.

Plenty of laughs and next to no music.

He had a professional teacher now, a schlemiely Sol Schaeffer Carrie had found who taught the kids of some dame she'd met in the park, and every mistake got you a lecture on major and minor chords. Then Schaeffer set your hands at a hundred and eighty degrees to your wrists—and sing ho for the next wrong note and lecture. Not that Schaeffer—

"But God," Danny'd flicked his watch case open, "your husband'll want to murder me, keeping you out so late."

"In this particular instance," she'd laughed with every note perfect, "it's likelier to be ladies first."

That laugh . . .

In a moonlight like summer that patterned the big bed he had to himself at Hotel Jericho Palace, Danny drifted back to Palmer House where he'd given his third cup of coffee a whirl after the concert. "You make tempests," Sydelle had laughed. . . .

He drowsed off to a musical accompaniment, that laugh.

A week and Danny was slaphappy from looking at buildings. Either the rent was too high, or the place was too decrepit. Evenings he'd dig up musical events if he could, since that girl Sydelle had told him exposure's the trick. But culture didn't come any easier. Tuesday the University Quartet squeezed him dry in their Brahms wringer, four thin sounds grinding away and not a one of them his Concert Hall sleepytime gal although he was positive she had said she performed with some University outfit. Wednesday at the opera he at least enjoyed some of the Puccini tunes before he dozed off, and he didn't land on anyone's shoulder. She was nowhere in sight among the intermission crowds either. Friday was the Concert Hall Mozart, but a full day's palaver from two separate real estate hustlers had him so good and snappy that he'd hurt the second punk's feelings and of course then felt sorry. To make matters worse, to this moonface who'd sputtered about an honest reputation he'd apologized that he was a landlord himself, but—

Some landlord. One in a million, Carrie'd said at the time of the big Jensen-West Street fiasco, with no flattery implied. What landlord snarls it out with a tenant whose lease is up, and then without being asked sends the bum a charity check to cover moving expenses? "St. Daniel," Carrie'd been at the end of her tether. "With his windfall Jensen'll raise an altar to you and burn a stink bomb in front of it." Danny'd been the sputterer then that he didn't like Jensen any more than she did, that she herself had said Jensen was hanging on by low rent and the skin of his teeth to a business as near collapse as the crummy matchboxes he peddled, and that, for all the shouting, he'd given Jensen that extra push down. But Carrie'd been right. Even now three years later the thought of what a fool Jensen must have considered him made Danny's face burn.

And Jesus did Danny ache for his wife. He'd kept his promise—which didn't include bankruptcy for the sake of expansion. He phoned the Chicago terminal now and there was a 9 P.M. slow train that would hit New

York late tomorrow, yeah, a long drag, but better than an overnight wait for the Twentieth Century. He began tossing shirts into a suitcase, then stopped halfway through to ring Carrie, hear her voice on the phone, let her know.

But think of Carrie, and what kind of businessman did he call himself? Whatever he had he owed to Quality Lamps. His wife and kids were his refuge, so in appreciation he was supposed to rush back to them empty-handed and whining? The hell he was!

Only, another Jericho evening to kill. The thought of it, today's ruins palmed off as factories, the same dose tomorrow, screwed his nerves to high C. And for making your head throb the "pig woman" adultery they dished out as news or the latest tariff laws dim as the glass chandeliers in the Jericho Palace dining room went well with the slab of saddle riding as steak, the dead street curtained off, and the jolly traveling salesmen with their noise and cigar smoke at the next table. Concert Hall and a seat by seat search for the little girl who isn't there, like at the Brahms?

Screw Mozart!

At the Jericho Bijou Jack Mulhall gave dissipation and his snobby moneybags fiancée Bebe Daniels the brushoff, and a good loud pianist in the theater pit pounded out Canadian north wood chopping to go with Jack's new clean life and Danny's old throbbing skull.

An advantage of a blinding headache in Jericho is that when you file out of the movie house you're too sick to notice Broadway.

In the morning with warehouses, renovations, tools and office furniture like a stone on his heart, Danny called this sleek seal of an agent Berlin to go out with again. In the beginning of the week Danny'd felt like knocking the guy down with his take it or leave it, snot, and who needs you. But the asslickers were even more nauseating. And with fog slicking the cobblestones and shredding off on the dock piles, there Carrie's honeymoon souvenir stood in the gray, two brown brick stories, you couldn't mistake it!

The owner would adapt to suit on a three-year lease, the rent was just right!

Danny grinned "What's the hitch?" but Berlin wasn't a smiler and by noon back in Jericho had the lease and a fat Waterman's pen ready.

"You wouldn't want a customer," Danny stared at Berlin, "to sign blind?"

"I've got two other parties after that property."

But Danny must have been turning into a real businessman. He kept his temper. And in the Trade Center that afternoon Belik the lawyer's Chicago counterpart Dove okayed the lease. "But the rent," Dove's admiration was genuine as he slipped Danny's twenty-five dollars down south, "even if conditions are slightly depressed in the Wisconsin vicinity. Did you pull a pistol on him?"

Was Danny flattered!

Only how come the wisp of worry? The depressed conditions were the very reason he'd headed for Jericho!

In the Trade Center lobby starving Danny gobbled a chocolate bar, phoned Carrie at West Street, and from the strange voice that answered found out that—oh, that Carrie—he was now boss of a private secretary! And Carrie? "Oh Mrs. Share goes home at three-thirty sharp, Mr. Share—" the titter was at least pleasant—"she says to be with her monsters." What a Carrie!

At home Becky answered—damn Indian summer!—4 P.M. in November and his gang was out in the park.

"Any message, Mr. Share?"

"Yeah, tell her her husband's a hero, Becky."

"Why ever'body," plenty of high-pitched yuks, "knows that, Mr. Share."

Some hero.

Hadn't he smelled fish half a continent from Fisherino's, the way that that Berlin had hovered impatiently while Danny'd inspected the building? Danny hadn't let the punk rush him. What had to be noted—pull down walls here, put up walls there, repairs, outlets, voltage—he'd taken good care to note. He'd even asked how about the freight rates, and that annoyed crook had shrugged they'd be the same of course as for anywhere in the area.

With the lease signed and delivered Danny phoned Illinois Northern for a time schedule and discovered he'd rented a warehouse on a branch line the railroad had stopped service on since late '21!

Then he played idiot at Berstoff Realtors—ranting about contract cancellation to the faint curl of Robert Berlin's well-shaven cheek.

"You read the lease," Berlin cut him short. "You received no misinformation from us."

If Danny were half the marvel at business that he was at hitting the ceiling he'd have been the Henry Ford of the lamps racket by now. Back went his fist and Berlin would have had it in the smooth smart aleck kisser if Rostoff the partner plus the office boy and the blonde Bertha secretary hadn't all jumped in out of nowhere.

And for the best. Bad enough conned, let alone jail for this . . . prime beef on the hoof. Or was Berlin a stuffed sack with a nasty expression on top, something that would bleed sawdust like the bayonet practice dummies that had disgusted Henny so in behind the lines training during the war? "Then imagine," Henny'd say, "ripping into a live man. I couldn't do it." With a peach like this to aim at, Danny could have done it.

In the hotel he glared at the wing chair with the fading slipcover roses still on to remind you—and hadn't he warned Carrie they were looking for trouble!—of the happy season before Jericho. Then he sat down with the small print of the lease. Footage seemed to include the railroad siding, but nowhere were railroads mentioned. They were clever, the Berstoff Realtors. You couldn't as much as sublet. You paid through the nose for vacating *prior to said date specified herein* and you kept paying *until such time as*—fat chance!—they hooked a new sucker.

Rostoff the chummy half of the firm had confided on Danny's way out, "If I were you," and Danny's hand had mechanically folded into a fist, "I would negotiate some special deal with Illinois Northern to reopen the branch line. So your customers'll pay a dollar extra a lamp." And if the bulb had lit up over Danny's thick skull then that lit up now—a branch line running at no cost to Berstoff Realtors could double the rents of their property there—he would have used that fist on Rostoff and gone back for Berlin, jail would have been worth it.

There had to be some way out—he'd sue!

With his word against Berstoff Realtors? And he could also complain to the Chamber of Commerce—or God. Or let them sue him? Humiliating as it was, he phoned Dove the lawyer—and they could, they had the contract, if it was worth it for them to go to New York and they did sound like a pretty tough outfit. They could assert, even as to intention, ignorance of the lessee's operational procedures.

And now let Carrie in on his business coup? Danny tossed himself to the ugly brass bed and tried to think. His only thought though was the minute satisfaction derivable from his shoe marks on the wash-worn spread. Then —there absolutely had to be a solution—he sprang up.

Jericho was bad enough with the sun out. For complete depression it was unbeatable now with the long flat sky clouded over near twilight. With his teeth on edge he weaved and ducked along Broadway between slow-moving hicks and hicks at a standstill. Scarecrow types around a store front employment agency seemed to have mislaid their shaving gear. Carriage cows wheeled shopping bags and tow-headed kids. His two guys peek-a-boo Ezra and big-eyed Teddy the Prince of Drool were working their act at 20 West Eighty-fourth Street, and he was enjoying the sights in Jericho. Teddy's mother—if Carrie could only forget Quality Lamps for a second—would ask Teddy what redheaded monkey up in the old family tree he took after, and the father's son (the silky red was the same auburn as Reisel's) would miss his mouth with his thumb. And still Danny's baby was like a blaze against overcast beside these flat-faced children with their thumb in their mouth but too dumb to suck it.

Indian summer was as played out as Danny felt he was. Black-edged clouds were moving ahead of a damp wind from the Great Lakes. He ignored the first drops and he kept pumping while he tried to wring juice out of a dry brain. But the chill finally got him. Die of pneumonia in Jericho? Or—he pulled his famous death-defying stunt known as crossing the street, this time from behind a parked vegetable wagon so a truck almost nipped him—get run over here?

In the Jericho Palace lobby you could order a seven bucks pint from a bellhop shriveled down to tough wrinkled leather. Upstairs Danny pulled his wet shoes off and sat himself wrapped in a blanket at the window the way Grandma used to in winter sometimes except that she'd never felt obliged to gulp rotgut to help solve her woes.

The stuff did oil the brain though, and with luck you might not even go blind.

But how could Bustoff Realtors claim ignorance of your operational intent? Quality Lamps. By what do you ship lamps if not by railroad? Kiddy car?

Trucks.

Holy Jesus Christ, what in the hell was the matter with him? Sure, Carrie had said the railroad, but that's all they used was trucks. A few days outta town and had he become a . . . an amnesiac? In New York City Quality trucks delivered. Then Carrie and Jacobson had knocked heads together and come up with a winner—trucks on longer hauls where the roads were okay, south especially, trucks beat railroads silly. Cheaper, yeah, and actually faster—considering the time your freight stands on a siding while those bums who shut down branch lines make up a train.

Gee, Pussy . . .

Relaxed, Jesus was he relaxed, but another gulp anyway it felt so . . . nice . . . and relaxed. He raised the green flask—he hadn't drunk that much—to the happy raindrops drumming the black windowpane. But Carrie was so damn clever with her cheap business head, go to Jericho for cheap labor, cheap this and cheap that. Where was the cheap, ship to Chicago, then to Jericho, then back to Chicago? Naw, the trucks drive straight here—and up Bustoff's with branch lines! Took him to figure that out—the born tycoon! He lurched for the telephone to break Pussy the news and that he'd see her the day after tomorrow—and the phone went off in his hand.

A girl's voice next-to-whispered, "Mr. Share?"—the Bustoff Bertha! So Bust, or Off, must have had second thoughts about the raw deal and screw them. But she went on, a million miles away, "Sydelle Fields, you probably don't remember me, from Beethoven?," then sounded closer, "I've a very good piano teacher for you in New York, my friend Genevieve I went to Conservatory with, except," there was that laugh, the chimes, "she received her diploma . . ."

"I'll," he scribbled down the name and address, "be rattling off Mozart next trip then."

"Were you at the Mozart last night?"

"I went lowbrow—heavy business."

"I just went. But I'm glad you didn't. They played the G minor symphony and you would have seen me cry."

"That bad?"

"Oh, you need to be educated. That unbearably beautiful."

So Danny wrote down "Mozart G Minor" under "Genevieve Chessman" and almost wished—almost, but not quite—he weren't catching the mother's milk train home tomorrow after he found Naomi somewhere to live.

As soon as Central could put the call through Danny was blowing his cross-country bugle to Pussy how guts, native talent and firewater had again won the West. She smacked him big juicy kisses but nixed a trip home before he'd have Quality Lamps West all set up.

And no matter how much long distance love you made to your wife, no furloughs permitted.

No need to hang up if a man answered still it would be odd asking a guy you'd never met to tout you on concerts. But Sydelle picked up the phone, with happy surprise. She said just a second she'd go look in the paper and went before he could tell her don't bother, he stupidly hadn't thought of the paper. Meanwhile she'd remembered—though the Concert Hall had a pleasant program: Brahms and Mendelssohn—"If you can stand some quavering Sibelius beforehand, you can hear . . . us. Art actually, I'll be submerged." Art was conducting the University strings in his *Concerto Rococo.*

"Also quavering?"

"At their dire peril, when Art conducts."

So the kid was putting Danny through college, in the University Great Hall with stained glass to the rafters of hanging banners: Leipzig, Leiden, Cambridge, Pisa. Maybe he should have stuck it out, gone to college at night, become a lawyer—or better still a music professor. He'd always liked music. So the crowd was a flop, two or three hundred scattered along a brown chairs vista, who cared? You'd be chatting like these profs with the students, the famous Prof Share, expert on . . . ignorance. Be famous, know famous people, sit around, exchange witty remarks with 'em with nary a Berlin or Rostoff on the horizon. On the stage the orchestra was right up his alley with their tune-up clinkers, and Sydelle in a white satin blouse made him even more at home catching his wave and throwing it back. Then chandeliers dimmed the length of Great Hall, relatives, friends and faculty clapped, and out marched the husband.

Jesus, what in hell had possessed her to marry a gray-haired ramrod? She and that guy had been students together at the Conservatory? Or had Danny gotten it wrong, ramrod had been her teacher? No, a student she'd said—and must he have been left back plenty! Why the guy could have been her father. Was she some kind of sick one?

And while Art jerked his arms—or were they pistons with sleeves?—the music trembled and sagged just the way Sydelle had predicted. And she'd sounded proud of her husband too! So okay, love is blind, but why the hell had she dragged Danny here? And worse ahead—ramrod modern. At their dire peril when Art conducts? Holy Jesus—at your dire peril! Long before the lousy symphony blared to a halt Danny's aching ass on the brown leather board felt like midnight.

And what kind of shit did he have in his blood, that he couldn't grab his hat and coat too and join the posthaste rush to the exits? Hymie Share never would have considered himself stuck. Gut-grinding out of politeness to a dame, a stranger at that? But Hymie's son eased his trousers from his sore behind, and there Sydelle sailed—out of the wings, down off the stage, and up the aisle toward him—smiling yet!

"Weren't we awful—and Dr. Brick stands waving his baton in time to the orchestra. And I," Sydelle cheerfully added, "forced you to come."

"That wasn't Art?"

"Don't let Art hear you. Didn't you look in the program? See, here it is. If you thought that was Art, what must you have been thinking about me?"

"What a mind reader you are and what an idiot I am," Danny rapped himself on the noggin. "I couldn't figure it out."

"There you are. We've only met twice, and I've made you suffer already."

"We've only met twice?" Sydelle just smiled, so he counted. Twice was correct. "Seemed more."

"Oh look Danny, Art's strings are wandering on, I'd better run, I'm concertmaster for the *Concerto*. . . . Oh and afterwards the greenroom is just behind stage right—I want you and Art to meet."

At the stage steps Sydelle turned, smiled and fluttered her fingers to him. And waved again after she had brought out her violin. Nice friendly kid, bending with a smile to an old Graycloud—they sure grew mature students in this racket—with his cello. The geezer must have returned a good one because Sydelle threw back her head and laughed—and Danny found himself grinning along from shallow left field.

Graceful too, sounding an A to the strings.

For ramrod Brick—go figure appearances—they'd played like a soggy banana. And here Art Fields merely ambled out like a slugger to home plate—broad-shouldered with that muscular droop of the neck—and every last violin viola cello and bass of 'em sat up at the edge of the chair, including the missus, who gazed dead serious at hubby on the podium.

Why in God's name couldn't Danny's pal Julius Waldman have married a girl like this so you could talk to her once in a while? Instead Julius had sprung a juicy Lena on them, with a set of horse teeth and lots of laughs. After a few double dates, "What do you think of her, Danny?" Julius'd asked.

"When I don't see her, I don't think of her."

"Well you'll be seeing more of her. We're engaged."

"You in love with her?"

"That's what she wanted to know."

"And what did you say?"

"I took a chance, I said yes."

"She like what you like—good concerts and rotten movies?"

"No movie," Julius had grinned, "is too rotten for Lena. And another point in her favor—my mother loathes her. As for concerts, she's willing to learn."

Lena was a good-natured slob, Carrie got along fine with her, better than with Julius—Carrie'd never cared for what she called his negative humor. But Lena would never learn. After *Moby Dick* at the Rivoli the book was mentioned and Lena jumped in to giggle, "I didn't even know there was such a dick."

Julius had orated, " 'O time, strength, cash and patience,' " and treated his wife to a belly rub in the middle of the Great White Way Saturday night.

So Julius might have been happily married, but not for Danny's dough. Danny hadn't heard of *Moby Dick* either till the movie came out—it happened his book tout Reisel didn't like sea stories. Besides nowadays how often did he have a moment with Reisel? Still, people should want to read books, not just make off-color jokes of 'em.

And they should want to hear music, even by Arthur Fields.

Fields—if he looked like a hitter he led like an umpire—should have named the thing "Baseball Concerto." He pointed for strikes and shrugged off balls. Over the shoulder for an out, and he stooped with his paws spread flat for safe at home! Sydelle stayed submerged, as she'd predicted. Fields called a strike and you saw the slim twist of the torso as Mrs. Fields went into action. But the other violins stabbed up or down too and all you heard were the different sections yelping and growling to one another. This goddam hurricane needled you cold one movement, whimpered at you the next in minor key clinkers that you finally caught on were intentional, and wound up thundering loud enough—who'd have guessed you could perpetrate that with strings alone?—to fracture an eardrum. But as Sydelle had predicted, the Sibelius stumblebums went at it like heroes so the stuff at least moved along.

In the greenroom with Fields fans all around them Sydelle—God!—was a midget next to her husband. Hey, and there was Dr. Brick, a good sport, pumping Fields' hand and smiling out words of wisdom while Fields listened and put his two cents in with a smile, not like dog eat dog in the lamp business. But strain an ear and Dr. Brick's ". . . had quite a few nice details" sounded like dirty banana oil. "I did envy you that lot of professional musicians, Arthur, that you brought in to bolster our amateurs."

Art smiled, "You mean those four friends of mine?"

"Yes, they might have been utilized to better effect in Sibelius."

"I doubt," Art's big baseball pan was sugar all over, "that they could have improved the special quality you get out of an orchestra, Nelson."

That's where Sydelle touched Art's arm to stop him from getting run over. But she could have saved her energy.

"Takes experience," Dr. Brick said, and when Art said, "Then I can only keep plugging and hope," ol' Dr. Nelson Brick said "That's right, never say die," stiff-armed Art a teammate jab to the ribs and eased away happy. Sydelle's wandering eyes lit on Danny, widened—and she left hubby and came to the surface.

"Did you hear those insults?" she asked. "I was afraid any second Art would have his wish and be out of a job—Dr. Brick's very influential on the faculty—and I'd be back," she could laugh, "taking pulses. Teaching my little chubbies and skinnies violin doesn't pay very well."

She looked at Danny, but could he say that Art's piece had hit him like West Street at full blast?

She asked, "Was the concerto too much for you?" So he nodded. She gazed at him like a hick at the Woolworth Building. "You're so honest! Have you ever told a lie?" She pealed out that laugh. "Look, he has to think for the answer. Come, have fruit punch—" At a sideboard with clumps of talkers she poured him a cup. "You've earned it for honesty."

"Who isn't honest, outside of Washington—D.C. I mean. You're honest."

"One question at a time," Sydelle laughed, and she sang, popping up fingers, "Dr. Jason, M.D., Dr. Jason, D.D.S., Dr. Brick, Mus. D. and various assorted professors—"

"All doctors," Danny was tickled. "Oh yeah, and except my real estate agents. Oh, and I mustn't forget my father. With him honesty isn't even a policy."

"Mine has principles, and that's just as bad, if not worse, if you're a poor sour pickles man corner Delancey and Essex."

"Another block that I lived on—and I never saw you!"

"Because I had to leave home, never darken my father's door again. It was good for my little sister Rhea though—he let her go to high school. But afterwards—my corrupting influence—she married Lee Sung, the sweetest most lovable boy in the world. She met Lee—he was in the School of Architecture—at the Claremont Avenue apartment I shared with a girl . . . Genevieve, I told you about her. So since Lee is Chinese, Rhea too must never darken my father's door again."

"And he didn't like Art I bet!"

"The least of Papa's concerns was art, although Papa had been a bugler in the Czar's army—there's a photograph of him with the bugle bell pressing against his stomach—before he escaped to America. He wanted me to go to business when I finished eighth grade, so I had to leave home."

"At fourteen? God! Lucky your old man isn't here, I'd tear him apart!"

"Stop," she just touched Danny's cuff and took her finger away, "you'll make me cry," and her eyes really were moist, "after all of those tears then. I was thirteen," she added shyly, "I skipped twice in school."

"Thirteen! Worse yet. Where did you go?"

"My Aunt Rosie took me. She was very unusual, she honestly loved me. If she hadn't died I would have been obliged to get my Bachelor of Music. Miss Farmer my viola teacher at the settlement house told Aunt Rosie that I was a sort of Mischa Elman in skirts—I was a settlement house prodigy—"

"Which settlement house?"

"Henry Street."

"I almost never went to the Henry Street Settlement. At least I didn't miss my chance there."

"Chance?"

"Of running into you."

The way she stared he took a whisk at his fly: buttoned.

"Thank you, Danny."

"You're welcome. But for what?" And still she scrutinized him. "What's going on?" he grinned, but Sydelle shook her head. "Then how about your Aunt Rosie?"

"Aunt Rosie said to Miss Farmer, 'Do you need to tell me? Throwing a gifted child like this out of the house! Go tell my—' and she made an unflattering reference to my father."

"A bum, she called him a bum, right? because that's what he was! But where was your mother? My bum of a father had the same effect though the throw was reversed—I threw him out and I've never regretted it—but I wish you could meet my mother! . . . Sydelle, what's wrong? Why are you looking at me like that? I go overboard on the subject of my father, that's what's wrong, huh?"

"There's nothing wrong. Look, I was just wringing my hands, exactly like my mother. That's what she did through the whole thing. . . . I do wish you could have met Art. You know, he does have a marvelous gift for any instrument. He brings out all their possibilities."

"Why can't I meet him? He's standing there with those people."

"Because his music was too much for you. He's very sensitive."

"I could lie," Danny cracked, "I could say it had quite a few nice details. But no kidding, Sydelle, now that I think back—"

"Honestly?"

And they were both helplessly laughing.

"Come then," Sydelle led him, "while he's with his patrons."

The big guy seemed to be having a real chat now—snappy remarks, good humor, hands way in the pockets, baseball shoulders relaxed—with the patrons costumed in character: soup-and-fish on the skinny gent, the dame with silvery hair shingled short and a black knee-length evening gown with a low *V* back and front—Danny'd have to find one of those, bring it home—that was scrawny on her but wouldn't be scrawny on Carrie.

Sydelle—"Here's a new convert to my husband's music"—mentioned the couple's eminent name, but if Danny'd ever heard it before, trying to figure how the hell he was going to get out of this he missed it now.

"Converted?" Art's big face diabolically curled. "From what?"

"From Sibelius and a foot in the grave. Your stuff really woke me up."

"What composer," the paw lifted out of the pocket and up in the air, "could, I ask you—" Art turned his pleasantest face yet to the richies, and back to Danny—"ask for more than a wide-awake audience?"

Could Weber and Fields playing the Palace top Share and Fields at the greenroom? They wowed 'em. Mr. Gotrocks guffawed.

And was Sydelle happy and proud—and there was this feeling you and she were the twosome!

Geruga!

Seven A.M. Joe the garageman outraged Eighty-fourth Street honking the horn. And if business kept up, and it would, Carrie'd soon have him calling for her around the corner and outraging Central Park West. She gave the monsters a holler, a squeeze, a tickle and kiss see you later, at Columbus Avenue dropped Joe at the garage, and by half-past seven kid cavalry, nostrils flared, was braking on West Street with the horse laugh for an intemperate truck driver or two she'd cut off.

Quality was vacant in early light, with those exciting smells of oil, glue and rich sawdust. My whole goddam building, Mother, and another in Jericho! What do you think of your baby Carrie? I'll have factories over the whole goddam U.S.A.! Yes, I, Carrie B. Share.

Where would Quality Lamps be without Carrie?

The years Carrie's uncalled for sons had been calling, Naomi'd suddenly begun hoarding prehistoric orders and memos up to the ceiling, bills of lading in quadruplicate, indecipherable receipts given and taken—every scrap in some unlikely spot, like the bones Daddy Moishe's dog Mitzi she should rest in peace used to bury back of the farmhouse.

"I know where everything is!" Naomi wailed.

"Then," Carrie laughed, "start talking kiddo," and no wonder Quality had been missing delivery dates.

The North River through this office or better still vice versa, would be the best cleanser. And what about Quality Lamps West? With Naomi let loose in Jericho—a mixed blessing, you saw now: she'd always been geared to running a corner candy store—they'd have to buy Limpy a commutation ticket to keep tabs on her.

But Carrie would straighten it all out.

While the front office girl saved confetti, who was handling orders first come first served like seats Saturday night in the neighborhood movie? That Raisin that Carrie absolutely had to separate from the pudding, who'd had the gall yet, our proud beauty, to try worming her way upstairs with Naomi's exit to Deadwood Gulch as pretext. Carrie'd squashed that worm, and she had a couple of other ideas as to Raisin. Raisin's expression when Millie Zook answered that they were painting the Wanamaker vases ahead of Vandervaart's because Mrs. Share wanted the Wanamaker order shipped first was an angry step in the right direction. Had there been some mistake, Raisin bit and snottily wondered to Carrie? Well if an employee had to be told that Vandervaart's you had but Wanamaker's you'd just landed and wanted to keep, there was no point telling her.

"No mistake Reisel," Carrie flipped her a wink, "don't worry about it."

The red blotches on Raisin's cheeks meant live boil taking place.

"Actually," Carrie confided, "if not for those ridiculous tariffs—enough to make a girl switch to the Democrats almost—we could get our cheap decorated china from Hong Kong and dispose of the whole painting department."

Then Carrie had Miss Ray Most in the office put in a few hours typing copies of a letter—to Honorable Senator Reed Smoot, Honorable Representative Willis C. Hawley, and the Honorable Asshole in the White House —for the suspicious Jews in the factory to sign. Free enterprise. Competitive market in lamps. Amendment of the outdated Fordney-McCumber Act. Ray whined—but cheerfully, cheerfully—"Must it say Honorable on all these letters?"

"Sure," Carrie winked, "be a hypocrite."

The peons all signed including the paintresses—when Carrie asks you you sign—except Raisin.

"Dot law," the hundred percent greenhorn went shrill, "protects American workers."

There'd never blown so red the Raisin.

And nary a word from her since that was not on strictest business!

Carrie B. Share, expert steamer and presser!

In spite of cries of pain from Naomi—"Who needs a secretary?"—Carrie hired a secretary, Mrs. Minnie Hertz, a widow the opposite of merry with a reproachful smile on one scrawny cheek.

"Remember, Naomi, Danny lacks your experience," Carrie said straight-faced, "Mrs. Hertz'll be worth every penny."

The ambitious Miss Most size nine sat stonily typing.

Mid-afternoons as soon as Carrie could make it she was off and running again in the Stutz. On West Eighty-fourth the eager progeny—skinny on foot fatty in the go-cart—would be waiting with Becky for the pleasure jaunt down the block to the garage. Peek-a-boo Joe their pal the garage-man jumped in for the whiz back to the house and what fun! Mommy at the wheel with Teddy pulling her boyish bob from behind gave doggy howls for mercy, and Ezra from the prize seat next to Mommy slew 'em with his giggle around to his year-minus brother, "Act your age, Teddy."

Becky would vanish to get that slow Emma started with supper, and in the playground nice days Carrie would swing the whooping monsters hi–i–igh as the sun up in the treetops. Or with bundled up Teddy figuring out withered leaves on the ground, she'd put on the scared stiff act for daredevil Ezra grinning at her from the top of that steep rock over the path, the snub-nosed image of his handsome daddy. Then the athlete would slide down on his fannyless fanny for a lift and a hug, doing his mackinaw plenty of dirt for Becky to play amazed about afterward.

And in the long late-autumn evenings Carrie would snuggle up with her

Forbes, her *Financial World* or her *Barron's,* like any good wifie while hubby's away.

Half the activity in Chicago half in Jericho so what the hell—let the better half win. Danny opened up the *Chicago Tribune* to the Hyde Park classified and what do you know, a Hotel Wellington at Fifty-third and Park. What could be handier when your piano teacher lived on Cornell? And would Sydelle be surprised. He'd remarked he must be forgetting everything he'd learned on the piano, and she'd said, "I'll give you lessons if you want as long as you're staying awhile." Hubby Art had treated her to a look as if she'd offered Danny her far from substantial pelt for a Jericho orgy. But to Art's sharp question was Danny studying violin or viola, piano seemed to have been if not the best answer at least an acceptable one. "My wife's third instrument," Art had considered it, "but she could be helpful." Then Art fired question two point-blank at Danny. "You sure you're a businessman?"

"My wife has her doubts sometimes."

"Well she might. Business and music are a contradiction in terms."

Sydelle pointed out that her husband's patrons the Stairs were in business, and—she'd shivered—the slaughtering business at that.

"That's different," Art stuck to his guns, "Mr. Stairs is only the son."

So Danny'd cracked, "I'm only the father," which got a grin from Samson scourge of the Philistines and allowed Danny to bring out a diapers snapshot of his pair of future Presidents of the U.S.A. if they hadn't gone and let themselves be circumcised.

But Art couldn't have been more wide of the mark. This businessman was rewarding himself with the piano lessons. Never had Danny gotten so much done in so short a time. He'd driven Geary the truck rental guy in Cicero to divulge that outright purchase beats renting. He'd speeded up the landlord's repairmen and electricians with the most modest of incentive bonuses. He'd found a local potter Grove who could supply ready-made vases with a wiring hole in the base. He'd jollied Hearn the surly Jericho carpenter into extra crew to hurry the warehouse shelves and partitions. Yes, jollied, terrible-tempered Share—and what had come over him? A friendly chat uncovered perfectly decent secondhand office furniture you could buy from Danny's night watchman's brother-in-law on the South Side on Langley Street, and, to top everything, exposed the night watchman Giles—Giles fully confessed it—as the best banjo who'd ever handled a pick.

Giles told Danny enemies had pushed him out of regular banjo jobs in the city. These cats'd bring in kid country cousins from down by the levee and an experienced Chicago hand could go look for grub money where he could find it. And if he found it nowhere, he had to go find it somewhere. Giles nightwatched, you get in your sleep—though of course not this particular job, boss. What didn't Giles play on that banjo by a tin barrel fire just the two of them outside the warehouse one evening with a frosty dark blue sky of stars flung over the lake! The excitement—black empty factories looming, rust flashing off unused railroad tracks, and Giles croaking some kind of hoarse chant, skinny and gray-faced with the gray kinky hair.

If you lose . . . your money,
Don't you go and lose . . . your mind . . .
If you tired of your woman,
Don' come messin' roun' . . . with mine . . .

The flames licked up, Danny took a try at the banjo, and Giles told him he played like a pro, boss, could use practice, but like a pro.

"But if I wasn't boss not like a pro."

"Pro boss or no boss," Giles said.

On Giles's night off this week he had a job on Calumet, he gave the address to Danny. "If those speakeasy cats look cockeye at you, don't blink. John Giles is the password."

So Danny passed Sydelle the password and invited her and Art come be his guests.

"Oh, the reasons that Art wouldn't," Sydelle rewarded him with her laugh. "To begin with, Art doesn't drink. His first attachment is to his consciousness."

"Then he never bumps into walls."

"He always does, but mostly the walls apologize and give way. Then, Art doesn't like jazz. Art says . . ." they both had to smile . . . "Art says that jazz would put him to sleep if not for the noise. He says it's a syrupy flow devoid of the slightest understanding of modern harmonics."

"Harmonics is Greek to me, but you should hear Giles on the banjo."

She said she'd like to, she might, she'd see.

Did she mean Artless? While Danny tried to figure that out, Sydelle couldn't get over Hotel Wellington with its view of Greece in the park below: a museum dome and columns set in a shriveling wreath of treetops. Then there was his suite of period furniture—elegant curves and blue velour covering. And the romantic baby grand piano with the afternoon light glancing off its dark polish.

"But," Danny kept on being surprised, "you have all this around the corner."

"Of course. Well, not exactly all this, Danny. You saw the good front we put up, our front room, but even that's dim John M. Smyth modern facing the courtyard, and the rest of the apartment is dark. See? Art is right, I'll never be satisfied. Did I tell you how we lived in the Village? Besides Art's used upright piano, there was a table we made out of a door and some bricks, and a few boards to sit on. Art used to smack his hands after we'd have visitors and say, 'Think they took home their quota of splinters?' In

Greenwich Village I complained about the mice running over my legs—at first we had a mattress on the floor to sleep on—"

"But that was nuts."

"The idea seemed like fun, *La Bohème,* but I complained. Now we do have possessions—for the faculty socializing if you want your contract renewed—and all I dream of," she waved at the crisp blue and gold outdoors, "is Greece, or Paris, or anywhere but where I am."

"Why not go? Art has summers off."

"We need whatever we make, for his career. That's why I charge you so much—charge you at all, Danny—for lessons."

This nutty joy that she liked him!

"Charge more—I can pay."

Sydelle turned from the window with another of her mysterious gazes. "I know you can. . . . But," you'd think she'd lost her last friend, "I don't know why you should, considering how little you get from me."

"Little I get from you? Listen."

He sat down to his minuet and she stroked and sat down on a blue velour chair behind him. Not that he was less expert in clinkers—though even they had improved since he'd been giving the eighty-eights the time here he hadn't been giving them at the practice studio you rented by the hour on Michigan Avenue. But at least his fingers had stopped itching for "Sleepy Time Gal" after three minutes of Bach. Remembering to lay off the pedal was easy when Sydelle had wised you up that Bach never laid foot on a pedal unless playing the organ—in which case he laid two feet. But Danny even remembered to keep the left-hand accompaniment toned down in the minuet and the left hand theme louder in the little fugue.

He finished, and "Hear that?" whipped around with his victory cry.

Sydelle was so happy her eyes were moist.

"If you were one of my chubbies, I'd kiss you."

Suddenly, out of the blue, Carrie had to deal with some fielder in Jericho and piano lessons—Carrie's own fault, encouraging Kid Fumble Fingers to begin with—coffeeklatches, houses for Naomi!

Limpy couldn't praise this dame Field enough. If not for her, so his story went, there'd still be nowhere for Naomi to live in Jericho. From the real estate crooks he'd been offered model homes featuring masonry cracks, broken sashes, Great Lakes in the cellar, bats in the attic, ladder stairs or a location two blocks from Jericho's Harlem. But how often had Carrie told Limpy that realty is a business like any other? They drive their bargain, you drive yours—and make sure your drive gets the most mileage. Not with the Field broad—could Carrie have plowed that Field under!—instigating him with her "They're so obviously dishonest."

Whereas the rental ads that this Field steered Limpy to are honest?

What a setup he wound up taking, one house away from the lake! If it only had been in New York perfect for Gittel—all sky and water! Sydelle—Carrie's retarded youth Limpy old enough to know better laughed over the telephone—shivered on the porch in front of a display of storm clouds and whitecaps and wondered through chattering teeth how Naomi would tear herself from the place to go to business. For the missus—the dreamer didn't say which missus he had in mind—a big kitchen facing the lake, and for cuddling a cozy living-room fireplace. With a downstairs guest room and bath you could have friends there for a weekend conversation. Upstairs you had the big bedroom plus two rooms for the kids. Jesus, Galahad wound up, you had to envy Naomi the setup.

Any other husband Carrie would have treated to a long-distance rap on the rump. But you let sleeping gay dogs lie.

Everything else though that a girl could do long distance she did. Mournful Freddy Jacobson found himself hustled West to settle the sales routes. The second that Naomi could get herself ready Carrie and the Stutz deposited her with Tootsie and the rest of the baggage at Grand Central Station to press parting tears to Grandma Share's cheeks. Carrie even treated Naomi to the difference between the Twentieth Century and the regular run to Chicago (slower trip lower fare), and placed a kiss on her lips, gardenias on her shoulder and a box of Schrafft's bittersweet chocolates ("Carrie—" eyes wet—"I'm going to miss you!") in her grateful hands.

With the babble, dancers, smoke and confusion, the first horrible blast from Giles and his four bandstand buddies would ordinarily have blown Danny out of the speakeasy right back onto the sidewalk. But Sydelle wasn't his wife to grumble at like when some movie stinko outstandingly stank. Then, to lie to Giles that his bunch was the biggest event since Columbus discovered America, buy him a bottle and learn from his own lips that he invented jazz and what year, you had to edge around the bandstand and dig him up in a steamy kitchen and service bar where waiters nudged you aside.

"What the hell are you doing in here?" Danny asked him.

Giles turned to grin at the trombone with the sunken chest and light coffee complexion and that guy let loose a very unpleasant bray. "We guests," Giles winked at the cook, who looked jet-black between his white apron and his white hat, "of the short-order man."

At their table again, "Disgusting," Sydelle said to Danny.

"Me too," he grabbed at the chance, "let's go."

But just then the band struck up, Sydelle motioned wait, and he was stuck—for God knows how long the way she was overjoyed by the racket up front. Since it still wasn't his wife—some joke—no point grousing. And since he was stuck, and those dark bright glances kept saying listen, he loosened his shoulders and tried to open his ears.

And what do you know—with Art Fields' concerto, Bach beginners' edition and bootleg gin under the belt, little by little the blare shaped into melody—he was liking it!

Liking it? This well-packed brown guy moistened his lips, placed the cornet between them, capped it with a goddam toilet plunger rubber to mute it and ecstatically blew, the clarinet ribboned around, the trombone gently smeared, a girl on the piano and Giles plucked out the rhythm, and they dug into you like Beethoven's Fifth.

So Danny-o could learn after all! "My mother in music!" he congratulated . . . Sydelle? . . . himself? over the babel.

"And your daughter—" she shyly raised him a toast—"in Orange Blossoms."

"Let's dance!"

And Sydelle nodded yes!

But the touch of that slender back was so exciting he had to lead rear end out like Sambo in vaudeville. And on that dime-sized floor where you more shuffled than danced and more swayed than shuffled, she must have noticed his stupid . . . manifestation.

In the middle of the number, "I'd better sit down," she said.

Was his face red as he followed her, and what could he say, pardon my hard-on? He pulled the chair back for her and said he was sorry.

"That I became dizzy?" Sydelle laughed. "And until we stood up I was such a sophisticated drinker."

That's all it was! Danny breathed easy again. "I'll order coffee, but why do you drink then? You don't need to be drunk."

"You mean I'm frivolous enough in my sober state."

Danny shrugged. "Just the opposite. You can't be improved on sober—and you're sober. You sound sober."

"I am in full possession of my amazed senses."

Why amazed? As usual she wasn't a squealer.

Amazed senses notwithstanding she was not in possession, as she said, of her amazed limbs and had to lean on him leaving the joint. Calumet was a cool midnight blue, with Saturday-nighters drifting through showers of lamplight. "Fresh air help?" he bent to her.

"As long as you keep a good grip on me."

But it was himself he had to keep a good grip on, with the press of her arm and body. So to change the subject he said, "Still you've got to admire Giles, taking that kitchen crap just to play the banjo."

"I admire," her whole weight was on him, "Danny Share."

He grinned "How come?" at that nice surprise. But—go talk to the Sphinx—he'd given up waiting for answers and flagged a taxi.

"Danny, I can't go home in my present condition. Art will stop speaking to me. Though—" those bells she laughed with were right in tune—"that might be preferable to what he'll say."

So, in a soda parlor, coffee was prescribed anyhow.

"But you said Art was busy composing."

"What I didn't say," she stirred her cup not too happily, "is he likes me to be there when he's composing."

"What for?"

"Afterward."

"You're the pretty little attendant, huh?"

"Well, he is the artist, and an outstanding one."

"How about you? You saved him the price of a first violin when he hired those professionals to give his concerto a lift."

"Ssh, Dr. Brick might be here disguised as a lemon fizz, he thinks they donated their services." Sydelle laughed, then didn't laugh. "What will I do when you take all of your kind words back to New York with you tomorrow?"

"What's so kind about stating the facts?"

"Will you be back?"

Danny shrugged. "It's a shame you ever left New York, I could have dozed off on your shoulder just as easily at Carnegie Hall as here. Last week Fred Jacobson and I carved out the sales routes from Duluth to Albuquerque, and at the Jericho warehouse today my brother-in-law Murray swore to me that he's sick of the stock market, he's strictly a lamp executive now. So it doesn't look as if I'll be needed."

"You'll be needed."

"You think Quality'll flop in the West?"

"As soon as you leave."

"Not on that count. Naomi can handle it in spite of all Carrie's belittling."

"Then I'll have to go East and visit. My family's there. I'll become reconciled with my father."

"He doesn't deserve it."

"Yes, I seem to be growing in generosity by leaps and bounds. Your influence."

Was he proud!—and before he knew what his dumb hand was doing it pulled a Hymie reaching for hers that was sloshing muddy coffee around in the cup. You'd think she'd been bitten, for a second he was sure he'd spoiled everything. But—what a relief—Sydelle resumed moodily tipping her coffee cup the same as before. She didn't seem sore at all! All the way to her doorstep Danny couldn't stop talking. He was the world's worst correspondent—"The second worst," Sydelle mournfully put in, "I'm the worst"—but he swore that he'd write, he'd have to: about *Moby Dick* and those other books in her bon voyage package; how much he'd disgrace her as her friend Genevieve Chessman's pupil; whether he ever caught up to Mozart's G Minor Symphony.

"Well," she said, "it'll be better than nothing."

His walk back those elated couple of blocks from her house to the Hotel Wellington he kept feeling the pressure of her funny little bunched up goodbye handshake, as though she still were touching him. In the Wellington he actually plumped himself at the writing desk to get a jump on the correspondence he'd promised her, but he couldn't sit. And when he got up his feet went every which way. Black windowpanes of the museum in the park, Sydelle's Greek temple, gleamed like a lake. If you craned, there were stars.

What a clear night, what a trip this had been and he'd been dead set against it, what a girl that Sydelle was! Jesus, did he wish Carrie were handy, would he Carrie her—boy! Say, what about buying Carrie a Pierce-Arrow tomorrow right out of a showroom, drive it home to New York!

Would she be surprised!

The man Carrie'd whipped out to Jericho and barely restrained there to do what had to be done was due back Tuesday and he phones he'll be back Thursday instead—with a surprise! How come (need wifie ask) the delay? His answer—"What's your favorite color?"—was guessing games.

"Not green, but don't make me see red."

"I'll—" gleeful yet—"make you see red!"

So in two no doubt brimming days Carrie's AWOL knight errant could be expected with armor slightly tarnished around the fly and, her couturier, some red rag for appeasement purposes?

Freddy Jacobson popped his sad Indian head into the office.

"Danny back?"

"No, poor me," she heard herself merrily exclaim, "I'm still footloose."

And that same night what on earth could have brought Freddy on an emergency call to West Eighty-fourth Street? Urgent thoughts since this morning. Considering costs, didn't Independence on the Southwest route make sense as a boundary, then go further if conditions proved favorable?

"Could conditions," Carrie smiled—hubby playing the Field, Becky gone for the day, the monsters tucked in and snoring—"ever prove any more favorable than they are right now?"

Freddy looked wistful. "Of course I'd like to hope so."

How would this dark wiry bundle of muscles be on top of a girl? If he pushed, would she push him away? After Ezra, and again after Teddy, she'd sworn off screwing for life. But each time, before the end of the month's layoff her cousin the doctor had prescribed, she'd been wild to lay on. The noble Share of course had stuck strictly to doctor's orders, and she'd found herself casting a lustful eye even in the direction of her husband's bookworm pal—with emphasis on the worm—Julius Waldman. But even then she Carrie Baum had not felt more hot and bothered than she did this minute.

Jacobson didn't push, the round-the-clock salesman. The odd part was that selling merchandise—that was what attracted her when he was with Zuaracce's—he was all confidence, brisk, and no words wasted. Let the fruit tremble and Freddy Jacobson was there under the tree. But in love look at the naggy schlemiel who couldn't quit talking, persuading, with his same old Victorian hints have pity on me. Carrie calmed down surprised at herself, a married lady, and finally mothered him away to his spotless Helen at home and his boy and girl in scrubbed clothes.

Christmas Day the Twentieth Century Limited arrived and cooled off —Carrie called up Grand Central Station—and no sign of the former Galahad. But just when Daddy Moishe her guest was far enough into the turkey to take time to gloat over the bust she had married, that very bust blew in like a gale and somehow pumped Daddy Moishe's hand first. Next came love, kisses and gifts: toys for the monsters, handkerchiefs for Rebecca, cash for Emma he was meeting for the first time, and yeah—the dog—a slinky gown black not red for the dumb little woman. But before Carrie could crack who'd modeled that number for him, with a masterly arm around her waist he ran her—"Hey—" to the window and he pulled it up to that wind that made you gasp and sent the drapes flying.

"Like your new car?"

And down there herding the tame row of brownstones in the darkening street of swirling newspaper stood her flaming tapering Pierce-Arrow that flared to frog's eyes out of the fenders, ready for a long panther spring!

Carrie kissed the guy slow and plenty to the tugs—"Ma . . . Mommy"— of those jealous monsters and to the sickly grin of Daddy Moishe.

Orgasms? After the first forty or fifty ripples who counts? Chicago to New York's say nine hundred, a thousand miles including heading south instead of east at St. Mary, Pennsylvania, and almost ending up in a coal mine, with stops in Cleveland and Allentown plus stops to eat. So even bowling along in Carrie's new magic carpet Kid Galahad couldn't have gotten home one second faster.

Then in a lull he said, "What a great month that was, Pussy!"

So the first guess had been right? "Almost two months and it went that quickly, eh?" She braced herself for his true confession.

"Yeah, I like being boss. I never felt like one till I went out there."

Her conquering hero—so that was all it had been—nipped at her arched throat, put his hand on her breast, and showed her who's boss in the way she liked to be shown.

And in the morning even after she'd shouted to Joe the garageman and all Eighty-fourth Street that he could bring the Stutz back to the garage she was driving her Pierce today, the boss—"Hey boss, time to get up boss!"— still lay half dead on his pillow with Ezra punching that tasty curve of his father's shoulder and asking him what he was doing in Mommy's bed.

17

WITH THE BIGGEST BOY LIMPY AS USUAL THE GREEDIEST, Carrie's boys demolished the devil's-food cake she'd baked them. Then Limpy galoshed the other two boys, wrapped their bright shining faces up to the nose with red scarves, and took them and the sled into the gray flickering Saturday for a haul through the park in the snow.

And on the kitchen counter—"Hello stranger"—a letter to mail Limpy'd forgotten.

Hmm, *Mrs. Sydelle Fields, 61 Cornell St, Chic, Ill*, in his inimitable scrawl which Carrie could imitate and—for business purposes if he wasn't around and you needed his Daniel L. Share in a hurry—sometimes did. The lightweight envelope told you that there wasn't much in it, but that the noncorrespondent Limpy had written at all was something to ponder.

Detective story villains occasionally steam open mail, but all Carrie got holding Limpy's envelope over a boiling pot was scalded fingertips. She calmly turned off the gas jet and opened the letter in the regular way—just in time, as skinny Emma with snow on her Uncle Tom's hat staggered in under big bundles from shopping.

Where more appropriate to read the master's masterpiece than the master's own den suddenly littered with books the couple of weeks he'd been back from Jericho. Funny Limpy, "You going to read all this stuff Limpy?" she'd flustered him, but if buying books was his meat far be it from her. Herself, she liked brain-teasers, and for that, nothing, nothing on earth more rewarding day in day out than the old *Wall Street Journal*. Mother, do you hear me in heaven? Your little girl's secret portfolio passed sixty-five thousand—yours and mine, Mother, nobody else's—by this morning's quotations!

Why hadn't she lived, the naughty woman, to squeeze hands with Carrie moments like that? And wouldn't it have been nice—Carrie interestedly settled herself with the letter on Limpy's Morris chair alongside the snow frosted window with a cozy view of white chimney pots—to have someone to sigh with over what we girls endure from our lords and masters. Would Mother have been tickled silly at Daddy Moishe the lady-killer in Orange on market days flirting a mile a minute with neighbors' wives—of course only the young ones. If one ever bit—Carrie could just hear Mother say it—you wouldn't see him for dust.

So what did Limpy have on his mind?

Oops—out fell . . . last summer's Far Rockaway snapshot of her and the monsters under a beach umbrella all smiles and you had to laugh out loud at the bubble on big-eyed Teddy's delighted mouth. *That's*—oy, some vagabond lover—*what my gang looks like.* Next more old stuff in the lad's eighth grade scribble, this Genevieve Carrie'd heard all about who'd turned out to be a teacher only of the viola. Any time Limpy wanted to switch instruments Genny stood ready if the position she no doubt had in mind—was another ever as innocent as Carrie's Limpy?—could be referred to as standing. Yeah, and Genevieve's piano teaching lead Tallarico Limpy was going to call and arrange lessons with, a mister—you didn't catch Genny referring a prospect to female competition.

So how come Sydelle had referred Limpy to Genny and with a letter of reference yet? So he'd be grateful? He was grateful. But he would have been just as grateful if the original steer had been to some Mr. Tallarico instead of Miss Chessman. Was it possible that out of a hundred and twenty million connivers in the great big U.S.A. two pure souls had bumped into each other in Chicago? That couldn't be. There had to be something more to it.

Thanks for this, thanks for that, thanks for the books Sydelle had started him off with. That Freed had something there Limpy wrote, but Limpy wasn't sure what.

Freed?

In a second Carrie was on her knees on her sister-in-law Leah's housewarming contribution for the move three years ago, a Fereghan Leah'd told her with pride. But to Carrie it looked like an old rug with the crap beaten out of it and she'd hidden it in here. Where Limpy had hidden the Freed book though was anyone's guess: book piles, books in cartons, miscellaneous books on half-empty shelves—what a mess! She supposed she'd have to straighten it out for him, he never would for himself. And he was so neat in the office. He'd actually grabbed his hair when he saw what Naomi had left, even with the mess weeded out and filed neatly in folders by Minnie Hertz. Carrie hoisted half an armful of books from the floor to a shelf, then remembered the letter.

In the snowy yard back of the brownstones the three trees looked rather nice in ermine—she'd have to try that, with the non-melting variety.

Sayyy, look at this in the letter. . . .

. . . For instance, Limpy had had this dream. His overnight stop in Cleveland he'd dreamed he was in Chicago searching in the dark under the

El for some guy who could steer him to a vague other guy, both total strangers. The second guy he never did locate, but the first hung out in the Palmer House coffee shop. This gent only would mutter. Half you missed, and what you'd thought you understood you forgot by the time you were outside under that web of El tracks again. So you were nowhere and a worry weighed down on you about being lost and no station in Jericho. A train began pulling out but your legs were like stones, you heavyheartedly missed it. Then, there on that platform with fuzzy lights all along it stood —guess who? Yes, Sydelle, and she waved and called. Then it seemed that he'd been looking for her all the while—what do you think of this dreamer, getting himself lost and found by strange women—and boy did he wake up happy!

At least he had the decency to wake up.

Or had he? After the waking up, half a page to his dream girl was scratched out with impenetrable penmanship slashes and ovals. Then his big question was: *Where do you find those two guys in Freed?* And he signed off *Yours sincerely* like a message from West Street.

Well, he liked her all right, but she was in Chicago, he was in New York, and an ounce of prevention—Carrie reduced the billet-doux into neat little squares which she flushed down the toilet—is worth a pound of cure. The snapshot she saved, you don't tear up you and yours. And to keep on the safe side, Monday better forestall any return trips to Jericho by Limpy. To the moment Naomi went West that shrewd little dummy never had hinted sales had leveled off. Of course a hustler like Tootsie would take no interest in competitive lines at Macy's and Gimbels—imitation imitations from fly-by-nights with fancy names like Majestic Lamps and Oriental Originals aiming to beat Quality at Quality's own game underselling—and not only at Macy's and Gimbels, but at Quality outlets like Bier's and Proctor's. But Fred Jacobson had warned Naomi that the same thing was happening out of town—at Bamberger's in Newark, Filene's, Rittenhouse's. So why hadn't Fred said something to Carrie? Oh—Fred put on the holy face he used on the customers if they wanted too big a discount—he'd assumed that Naomi had told Carrie. Bullshit he'd assumed. He wanted your ass and you didn't tumble, so that's how he got even. Too bad he was so good a salesman, otherwise Carrie'd have sent him packing and fast. When she and Limpy realized what was what, apart from obvious remedies here they had agreed on an even stricter control over Jericho. They'd already received Tootsie's first weekly business traffic report, but weekly wasn't often enough. With that pair of fifth wheels you had to get on the phone long distance and check them daily. And who had the time? She herself was too busy keeping the salesmen whipped up to a rich creamy froth. So let Limpy do it—two birds with one stone—and nip Jericho crises in the bud.

With that settled Carrie roused dreamy Emma—she was afraid she'd just have to fire that girl—with a helping hand toward the hollandaise sauce for the flounder.

The three boys burst in like country air—"Hey fellas!"—tracking snow into Carrie's elegant living room. She didn't have to trail Limpy to know that he was hunting through the apartment while she corralled the monsters in the foyer and roughhoused kissed conversed with and unpeeled them there.

"I can't remember whether I mailed a letter I wrote."

"A letter? Who to?"

He dared shoot her his blue-eyed managerial stare. "To Sydelle."

"Aha, and what did it say may a little wifie inquire?"

He shrugged. "It said thanks."

"So you have reasons for gratitude, eh sonny boy?"

"Yeah they're in the den, dig into them. I'll be overjoyed to discuss them with you."

"Well if that's all it is—"

"And what else would it be?"

"—let me finish with this fellow," she pinned down Teddy crawling away while Ezra went into convulsions over the word fellow, "and I'll help you look."

"No, don't bother. I'm pretty sure that I mailed it."

And never mentioned the dream, that funny double-crossing louse Limpy!

18

"NOTHING THAT I TELL YOU," AND SINCE REISEL WAS SO damn set on getting out Danny wished that she would get the hell out and the faster the better, "can induce you to stay, huh?"

"Oh then you are the offended one. Please do not inconvenience yourself further with these formalities, for the delectation," Reisel barely moving her lips threw a glance toward Minnie Hertz and Riva Wartels listening as hard as they could under pretense of making love to their work, "of the legion of envious. The second floor—my part of it—will be left in good order this evening."

Reisel walked out of the office with that . . . Amazon swing that still excited you after all these years, and Danny sat ready to explode out of his swivel chair from the heat and oppression. The awnings were down, but the sun pulsed in off the river like capital punishment. In the shop in Epstein's department someone kept starting and stopping a lathe till you could crawl out of your skin. Were they trying to bust the motor? Danny hollered "Hey Epstein!" over the partition but the machine went steadily now and drowned him out. During his trip West last year his wife had practically had the office torn down and reconstructed. Why in hell couldn't she have had them raise the wall to the ceiling? Then he'd just have to contend with the machine-gun typewriters of the two gargoyles she'd hired.

He had to smile though. Ezra'd heard that complaint once and called Hertz and Wartels Mommy's gargles. But damned if Danny'd known what he was falling into when he took full charge of the office. Delinquent accounts he'd pared down, screwed up books he was still struggling with. On a six hour basis his whirlwind wife couldn't quite manage production plus the sales managing job she'd invented, so what spilled over landed on him, plus responsibility for Naomi in Jericho. Give his wife credit: salesmen, husbands, she kept you hustling. Meeting the impossible delivery dates the sales hustlers saddled you with was your problem. Back from Jericho—right is right—he'd sided with Reisel. She was the painting forelady and painting orders were supposed to go to her not Millie Zook.

"Listen Limpy, I haven't the time to be that finicky. You handle the painting orders however you like."

Another job brushed off on him.

An outward-bound liner blasted a bass hoot that shook you down to the marrow with your head pounding to the vibrations.

No one who cared for him would ever have pulled all this stuff on him. The honeymoon sure was over. But Jesus—he slapped his pencil on Carrie's memo of new numbers he mustn't forget to add to the catalog—Reisel was nuts!

Minnie Hertz hovered with still another goddam cup of coffee from her bottomless pot.

"No thanks," he squeezed out a smile and a joke, "heat like this is unconstitutional."

"Oh but Mr. Share," these women never let bad enough alone, "a cup of tea is refreshing, especially under trying circumstances."

"Trying circumstances?" He fixed blue eyes like winter on her. "What circumstances are those?"

Pink splotched her cheeks and the tip of her thin shiny nose as she humbly gave him her I beg your pardon. They racked and roasted him and they were the martyrs for him to feel lousy about. Reisel too.

Reisel especially!

If Carrie'd been wrong about paint orders in December, Carrie'd been right about reduced costs in May. What the hell if you saved on color? Their shades and vases were still tops for the dough—in fact Oriental and Majestic already had thrown in the towel at Bier's and were selling as loss leaders at Proctor's. And even with business in general lousy this year, Carrie's mighty midget Gnopf the salesman a wisecracker exactly her style had a broad shoulder in the door at Saks 34th Street.

And what had been so wrong about making Millie Zook assistant forelady? As Carrie said, maybe Reisel was slightly jealous of her own prerogatives. For chrissakes she should have thanked him for relieving her of the new squad of paintresses they'd put on to stock Jericho.

"Botchwork is no relief!"

Four P.M. every day you could expect Reisel upstairs with the evidence. Look—smudges! Give him a microscope and he'd look. So Zook wasn't the retouch artist that Reisel was—that was why she was only assistant forelady. But the orders were filled and they were okay with the buyers.

"I do not believe in cheating the ignorant."

"Jesus Christ, Reisel—"

"Do not Jesus Christ me, I have nothing to do—thank God—with Jesus Christ."

"It's just an expression."

"I beg to differ with you it is not just an expression. It is mean greed, with profit as holy."

"That's what they say about the Jews, Reisel."

"Naturally, to shift the blame from themselves. That is elementary psychology, for which you do not have to read your detestable Freud."

"Where's Freud detestable? He says I love my mother."

But you couldn't laugh Reisel off. And today, earlier than usual, right after Carrie had gone home to the kids, Reisel strode in cradling a vase in each arm like a pair of infants. You had to feel sorry for her with her obsessions. She belonged in a plush apartment bringing up kids for a lucky father to come home to instead of throwing her life away on a lousy factory.

"Shoddy!"

She planted the pair of vases on his desk. But they weren't a pair. She'd dismantled an old Quality lamp she'd had at home and brought in the vase to show up the latest rush order. Could you argue? Next to home talent with its rich healthy glow, the flash special looked poverty-stricken, a poor relation jaundiced and mottled pink like Minnie Hertz with a grievance. Amazing, the work they used to do when they had the time. But now time was of the essence, and damn it, Reisel knew that.

"What do you want from me, Reisel?"

"I want nothing from you, not the hideous work of your Zook, not your salary, and not your job."

Abject apologies for wrong choice of words, the competition rehash, what Moe Giskin the accountant said, raise offers: all breath wasted.

Danny trotted downstairs to Reisel in the middle of those benches of rank female sweat sharpened with the paint odor. "Reisel—"

"Nothing to discuss."

In Zook's section he picked up a piece of ware that had dried. "You call this decoration?"

"You want thpeed," with her nathty harelip.

At closing Reisel returned him the envelope that he'd had Wartels prepare. "There is some mistake."

Danny handed it back. "There is no mistake."

"I do not accept charity."

"Reisel, what are you doing, where are you going, how will you live?"

"I should like my week's salary please, less the half-day for tomorrow."

"Reisel don't quit, I need you here," he made himself lie.

"You are well served for your purposes and you do not need me."

Could he have exploded a granite fist in that granite face.

So she left with her salary, less the half-day for Saturday. And now what, back to blousemaking at thirty-five a week after the pay she earned here? And could you force money on her? Trick her into letting you help her out? Oh Jesus Christ, he'd had his dose of that, trying to find her a nice house to live in.

During that search he'd lied to Carrie about Sunday morning piano lessons from a guy Tallarico that he'd never set eyes on and that—the way life was at Quality Lamps if you called his after hours headache to a drone of hot air from an alleged cooling device living—he wasn't likely to. One lie breeds another just as they say, so he had to abuse the Steinway at home because who studies piano without practicing? West Street drove him nuts days, and at night Mozart did the trick. Danny'd figured that as long as he'd fallen into this trap and the Philharmonic never played the G minor Symphony at his convenience, he'd buy a piano reduction at Schirmer's and try to qualify as the Mozart fan Sydelle said you ought to be. Possibly in the key of C without sharps or flats he might have been as good as her word—although since she'd never answered his letter it hardly mattered, did it? But they kept slipping in the black notes and accidentals on him and the more flats the more accidents. Wise guy Ezra took a cue from his mommy: "Daddy, my eardwums!" So the only fan Danny proved himself to be was the fan he'd been from the start, an Ezra fan, with a feint to the midsection and two kisses to his giggler for flinching.

And Sunday mornings he'd walk his feet off and without a Sydelle to convert the house-hunt grind to fun. He might still have been walking, if not for Jerry Belik who droned you hot air in all seasons. Well, as Carrie said, unless you wanted Jerry your enemy and you didn't want that—as Quality Lamps shyster he did his job—it was hard to exclude him from your gatherings of people that you'd met in his living room. And what the hell, Danny took as much pride as Carrie in hobnobbing with guys whose names you read in the paper. So while husky Liela the maid was passing the predinner gin fizzes around at one of their parties, Jerry was wagging his drink and peddling real estate in the tickled direction of Rob Ward the alderman.

"Too bad, eh Jerry, that your pa-in-law couldn't persuade the Metropolitan Commission to run the trolley line a bit closer to the river?"

"We didn't want them to, Rob. Country surroundings in the city is our main selling point. Your missus would like it."

"She might at that—kids, dogs, a romp through the woods, a neighborly chat about the price of potatoes. But then Simone likes wherever I put her—almost. Now," Alderman Ward's foxy face worked, "if you and your pa-in-law appealed to our sinning tendencies so rampant today and hinted that your secluded surroundings are ideal for a love nest, you might very well have an even stronger selling point."

"Oh no, Kingsbridge is a very respectable neighborhood."

"Jerry, you're an expert on real estate," Rob winked at Danny, "but you've got something to learn about love nests."

So Eureka—on a slope over Spuyten Duyvil half a mile from the Belik love nest sites you avoided like the scene of a crime, there it stood, a hideous green frame job but that could be painted white. And it was perfect inside, not fancy enough to arouse Reisel's suspicions but not uncomfortable either. The Harlem River below crawled between the slopes of the Bronx and Manhattan to the icy Hudson with light blowing across it. Through woods in back bare of course when Danny was there after New Year's you could see the clumpy snow-dusted Palisades in New Jersey. Goats had even been nibbling beside a shack between the near shore and the railroad tracks. And if the property was out of the way so was Kadzyrnye and here there were no apartment house windows for Gittel's secret police to post themselves at.

Next you simply cashed in your telephone stock. Then to handle the closing you got yourself a lawyer whose name wasn't Belik. After that you cast Julius Waldman—who else was there?—as landlord.

Julius had twirled a make-believe mustache, but the brown eyes and wrinkled tweeds hadn't looked half as shrewd as Teddy-o going Boo.

"You must pay the rent, my proud beauty. I hope she's at least a beauty."

"She's a beauty, but don't let that fool you."

"Joking aside Dan, what do I say?"

"Whatever you want, as long as you don't say a word to Lena."

"My own wife, with whom I share every thought?"

"I can imagine. This special thought she'd run straight to Carrie, Carrie wouldn't miss giving Reisel a dig first chance she'd get and there goes the whole act. What a royal pain in the ass it all is."

And you mustn't forget that Reisel knew that landlords give nothing away. Rock bottom rent had to be rock bottom for a six room Kingsbridge house or she'd still smell something fishy. So with apologies, praise and detailed lies about the increase in business, you force a pay raise on her. Carrie naturally wanted to know what was the idea all of a sudden. You barked, "She deserves it is the idea!"

"Limpy, such vehemence! You're not still carrying the torch for cousin Raisin?"

Up his ass he was carrying the torch.

You were now ready to place a for rent ad in the *New York Post.*

"Hey Reisel, look at this—country surroundings!"

The day they'd moved in Gittel had stood at the window watching the sun bleed into the river while Reisel's blood had gone into such a fury of opening boxes and flinging pots out of barrels that Danny'd wondered why he'd knocked himself out coming to help, the same old story.

"Well Mamá," at supper Reisel hadn't been able to keep quiet any longer, "dare I ask how you enjoy the beautiful view just like Kadzyrnye?"

"This afternoon they dropped the Czar murder charge against me. The Bolsheviks confessed."

"Mamá, I am glad to hear this sign of good health. You understand there never was any Czar murder charge against you?"

"I always knew it was crazy."

Easy as pie.

And now the new twist to his throbbing brain was how to get Reisel to take money outright? A rich uncle in Kadzyrnye died and willed her the chamber pot crammed with kopecks? Crazy as this heat in September, but what else could it be but something like that? Only, excuse me Reisel, not just this minute. You quit, but I still have to work here.

Easier said than done with everyone else gone, the lights out in the factory, the ceiling fan gasping like midsummer and traffic squawks rising muffled like out of his childhood, only then it had been horses and wagons. Danny actually dozed off a second, three years old in Essex Street, put to bed with a kiss from Ma in the last orange blaze of daylight. The catnap refreshed him, till he remembered for what: Carrie's sales orders, the production schedule, the instructions to Naomi he'd been putting off the whole day. His brother-in-law Murray was resentful, he hadn't been appointed captain of industry so he'd resigned from answering the phone. At this hour Danny would have to call his sister at home where she'd have plenty of time to bring him up to date about her miseries since Wednesday—and would that be a pleasure. Recently Giskin the accountant congratulated Carrie and him. Under the new regime they were in the black, every month blacker and blacker.

Carrie'd cracked, "So I can move to Central Park South, Giskie?"

"South no, but you can keep your lease West."

That was the Buryton lease, the Berries for Carrie and him too for that matter, the move to Central Park West the end of the month. Funny how around the corner made all the difference! So, big shot, to have that you do this.

Yet he had this up to the gullet.

Okay, skip Naomi this once, but at least check the order books and do next week's planning.

He couldn't. Production schedule—he was the goddam schedule. Without Reisel to curb her who knew how Millie Zook would run wild? Not only would he chase around holding the machines floor together, but now he'd have the second floor too. And floor or no floor, how would he take care of Reisel? He saw his Labor Day weekend draining away. Instead of a bathing suit and a few Orange Blossoms on the Sandy Point patio as Alderman Rob Ward's welcome guest, there'd be Kingsbridge and pleading with Reisel while she ignored you. "I must do my housework, I do not have maids." And even the return for my sake—it really was life and death—would have to be sneaked in. You wouldn't want Gittel to hear and be upset. In the end Reisel would agree—he knew his Reisel—but not before she had put him through the wringer and hung him to flap on the line.

Say, unless he ran up from here tonight. Before Carrie'd left he'd told her not in the sweetest of tones why didn't she forget the tycoonery for twenty-four hours, take the car and drive the kids to Rob and Simone Ward's now instead of tomorrow so they could cool off and play. He'd seen her winding up for the strikeout, but to his surprise she'd changed her mind and laughed, "Okay master, since you demand it. We'll cool off and play." So he was in the clear, he could just ring Reisel's bell: Help, a bite for a starving man? She ties your intestines in knots but she insists that you eat, the hospitality girl. That approach might get a smile—shortcut the torture and save him his Saturday afternoon. Only what a drag, a solid two hours' round trip with that hike from the El. Hard to believe time was when no distance would have been too long to travel to Reisel.

The sun slithering under the awning formed—Danny shuddered—a loathsome pulsating caterpillar of light on Minnie Hertz's attached sales summary. He swiveled to lower the shade and blot that thing out when a second ship blast rattled his skull. The *Nieuw Amsterdam* with a pin-cushion prow and two chesty tugs alongside cut through splinters of sun-light toward the Bay. At the white rails above a black shining hull the dolls leaning were people—and Jesus, wouldn't he have liked to be on a sundeck sipping his coffee and reading his Dickens with a goddam blue ocean around him! Move over Sydelle, make room for another escapist. As a kid he'd sat in the kitchen through those silences—or worse, through lively chatter from Leah—when his old man had been having too much fun to show up for supper. Danny'd daydreamed himself out of the house, the boy bard of the Palace, always with a beloved shining at him from the first row. He'd gotten married and thought he'd outgrown that stuff, Carrie had been all the girl he'd needed. But nothing like a production schedule for bringing it back.

"Art says," Sydelle had said as they'd strolled into Marshall Field's last November, "why pay Marshall Field prices when Carson's sells the same thing for less."

"Then," Danny had laughed, "how come you're taking me to Marshall Field?"

"See what a friend you've made? I love luxury even to look at."

"We're birds of a feather. My feelings don't get hurt by luxury either."

And that smile, as if she'd come into a million bucks. The farewell present he did force on her was the Libido perfume—"What a name, but," she'd breathed the scent in, she'd closed her eyes, "so sweet!"—that she herself had picked as his wife's gift. But Danny had already gotten some-thing for Carrie. And Sydelle had given him a six bar intro to Freud when he asked if Libido was the name of the Italian who manufactured the stuff.

"Libido," Sydelle had laughed—God, he'd certainly gotten in a lot of laughing with her and not too much since—"is what you dream but the superego won't let you. That's your conscience, but more so. I don't believe most of us are that unconscious—maybe you."

"Hey that sounds like an insult."

"Well it isn't, it's praise. You have no ignoble motives."

"Such as?"

"Don't be so willing to learn!"

And they'd laughed.

But in the coffee shop later on Sydelle said, "He says that life is a wish. But why should it be?"

"Art says?"

"There you are, Art acts what he wants. No, Freud says."

And Sydelle claimed that for the coffeeklatscher before Danny's eyes Freud's book was her biography. "Why," Sydelle brimmed with self-incriminating evidence, "look at the gifts I helped you choose!" She'd raised each box with a graceful arch of the wrist. Scotch scarves to brighten his mother's throat winter days on her gallery tours, Wedgwood to charm his sister Leah and her artistic Henny, Ezra's black lacquered Japanese magic box and Teddy's pink miniature French telephone rattle, Becky's hankies from Ireland, matching sweaters from Italy to warm lovebirds like Naomi and Tootsie when the northwesters blew over the lake at their house—

"Helped choose? You chose 'em. If not for you I'd—"

"Danny, that's what I'm saying. And last but not least (you shouldn't have) Istanbul attar of roses. Do you see what all of them have in common?" He was lucky if he could see his nose in front of his face, so she'd had to tell him. They were all from abroad!

"A coincidence, so what? I liked them too."

"Escape, escape, escape—" she'd sung out.

And maybe—though what did she have to escape from?—she had had something there.

On the way East a quick glance at the *Plain Dealer* the Cleveland Hilton left free at your door—Ford's Model A car due out in rainbow colors but for a pot of gold you pay extra, Jimmy Dundee by a knockout over Kowalik in six—and he'd torn open his own last but not least, Sydelle's farewell books package. Lo and behold—and even now nine months later he still was smiling—her biography was on top: *An Outline of Psychoanalysis,* with her maiden name Sydelle Binder on the flyleaf in that lilting handwriting just like her voice.

Hey, interesting what you pull without realizing. He fell asleep reading, and he'd never forget that dream he'd had that he'd written her, first despair hunting for you didn't know what, and then—God, the joy—Sydelle on the El platform asking what had taken him so long, with that voice, with that smile!

Half awake, in what city were you? Furniture—but whose?—shaped itself in the dark. And—was he nuts?—he had smelled attar of roses. He'd imagined that Sydelle was in bed beside him and had lumpishly reached for her.

He'd written that to her too. But it had seemed rotten taste, the bed stuff, as if screwing were what you had on your mind and it wasn't. It was the walks and the talk, the music, the laughs, above all the simply being together. So he had scratched out the perfume part—and what had been left? A dry thank you note.

Jesus and the way for months he'd burned at no answer. He distinctly saw himself dropping that letter into the mailbox on the corner. But say the letter had been lost. Would she have been prosecuted for writing him anyhow? But the volcano you used as a hatrack simmered down and you recognized how stupid you were. He himself could be busy—driven—up to the ears, and not her? She'd wanted kids though Art was against them, hostages to fortune he called them, deadly to a career. Maybe she'd had one. Besides in a way she'd been first to write. Practically as soon as he'd gotten back to New York he'd phoned Genevieve Chessman with regards from Sydelle to sign up for lessons—and Genevieve had shot regards from Sydelle right back at him. Genevieve had told him he must be the phenomenon that Sydelle said he was to have made Sydelle take pen to paper. So—birds of a feather again—Sydelle also wasn't a writer, but she'd gone to the trouble!

Danny'd laughed wrong notes phenomenon but Genevieve wouldn't believe that, any more than she'd believe (she'd asked his age for pedagogical purposes) he was not far from thirty—not with his boyish tenor. He'd have to show her, she was from Missouri, she really was. Friend Sydelle had drilled Genevieve's backwoods accent out of her when they were roomies near Grant's Tomb, which compared to Marshfield on the James River where she hailed from was like a flag-waving curtain in a George M. Cohan show. Danny, she had trusted, had never been bogged down in Marshfield Mo.?

"That must have been the one town I didn't lose time in, coming home from Chicago."

"Lucky man!"

She did want to meet him, she loved to gossip. How, for instance, was poor Art Feldstein?—Fields she meant. She'd witnessed that grim chase of his after Sydelle until Sydelle rather unwillingly had let him catch up to her at City Hall. Danny'd been surprised, he'd supposed Art had always been a few lengths ahead in that match.

"But quick tell," Genevieve had urged him, "what makes you think so? But wait—look at the hour."

Genevieve had had to be running, to a small party. Unless he'd like to join her? Sure he would have liked, but he couldn't. He and Carrie were scheduled at his mother's that particular Friday. But about the lessons—

About the lessons—wasn't it hell?—she'd stopped giving piano since her student days, only viola when she wasn't fiddling around in an all-girl's band at the Jimmy Rooney Café. Would Danny like to take up viola? What a pity. Then Vittorio Tallarico from Parma she'd found in Paris last year who still seemed to lurk on the margins ought to be a good teacher, he was so polite even under extreme provocation—not that he could help himself. The Parmigiani are famous for their cheese, music school and politeness.

Genevieve sure had been fun on the phone, and he'd kept intending to invite her and her find Tallarico over, just as he'd kept intending to call Tallarico for lessons and give himself an excuse to write Sydelle again and tell her about what he'd done. He hated to put down he'd done nothing.

Pure idiocy. He wasn't a musician, he was a businessman. He pushed aside the sales books and summary, pulled out a clean sheet of paper, and began making up for lost time.

Surprise!—remember the old coffeeklatscher? Believe it or not still alive and kicking, I've become aces at kicking and composing you letters just before falling asleep and then falling asleep. I mean I should have written again long ago but I was ashamed to, no music. Even the dreams, no more happy endings, just searching in the dark under the El and if I do catch a glimpse of you, you have a sad face. How come? Nothing to celebrate anyway.

Are you a ma now? You ought to be, you know your kids. Remember the escape presents you picked out for mine? They made a big hit. Then of course Ezra built up blocks with your magic box as a penthouse and Teddy made a big hit, he knocked the house down. After the crying, Ezra said, "Daddy, I don't have much hope for my brother." Teddy's grandma though prophesies that Teddy will be a great scholar because he races into the den when I sit down to read and drags every book he can reach out of the bookcases. I hope she's right but she's proud of me too so as you and Freud say it may all be wishes.

I read your Freud. As I wrote you shouldn't have given me your own girlhood copy though I value it all the more for that reason. I've done so much reading since you sparked me off that I've hardly opened my Shakespeare, just Romeo or so kicking about no news from Verona. Brentano's had a complete set of Melville and I read him till a cold sweat broke out on my forehead. *Moby Dick*'s still best, the guy who bobs up to the surface at the end reminds me of me except that I haven't bobbed yet. But those South Seas stories, if I'd have made that getaway I'd never have come back. And where's your *Madame Bovary* supposed to remind me of you? Was I eager to get at information about you but you were kidding. No resources? What resources are you short of outside of pen and ink? That's right, I'm talking about the little letter that isn't there.

Better still, how about New York? What do you say, you make up with your father I make up with mine, keeping in mind my headaches now are your fault? I've got brain fever with reading and no one to tell it to. Before you my pal Julius was a big event even with Lena along, he was the heavy thinker. Now either he's become lighter or I've become heavier. So could I use a sociable cup of coffee Palmer House style, in fact for a while I had a dumb wish

Look—the sun perched on the Hoboken housetops had slanted that crappy caterpillar back on the desk and in red, which was even more disgusting. Pull the shade down any more you're left in the dark. He piled up an order books barricade instead . . . and it worked.

a dumb wish

He'd forgotten the dumb wish.

Not for the phone to ring, that was sure. But it began ringing.

Pick up the receiver and have Carrie nag him that what, he hadn't called Naomi yet? He blew his long sigh and he picked up the receiver.

"Danny? This is Sydelle, Sydelle Fields?"

"I was just this second writing to you!"

She laughed—and those chimes were in tune always! "And to think you've been my personification of honesty."

"I swear!"

"I believe you!"

This was her third call to him. The first had been from the Astor Hotel when she finally wobbled off the bus with her enormous suitcase. The second had been from the drugstore corner Essex and Rivington before she went upstairs and exchanged hugs and tears with her mother and downstairs again to the corner of Delancey where her father cried too, right into the pickles, and with an iron grip on Sydelle's arm announced to the pickle buyers that his daughter was home. Her scheme for the third call had been to make it just after five, in the hope the workers would be gone and the owner would not. But after lunch and dishes and reassurances to her mother about herself and her likewise flown-away sister, she had lain down for a nap and sunken into a five hour stupor on a dream bus with no stops and no destination. She'd probably still be imprisoned there if her mother hadn't waked her to go remind Papa that it was Shabbos, he should shut the stall, supper was ready. Papa gave a yell, "Ladies, pickles—new, half-sour, sour that a bite and you'll cry like they picked your pocketbook!," and with really no hope she'd pretended she had a lady's errand at the drugstore—and here Danny was!

"And here I've been all day long, where seldom is heard an encouraging word. Tell me which dummy did you speak to?"

"The first time you were out of the office, and the second the dummy was at my end of the line. I was ashamed to ask the same voice the same question."

"You shoulda asked. Hey I'll meet you—I'll tell you my troubles over blintzes in Ratner's!"

The laughter chimed. "What a memory. I'd like to Danny, but if Papa ever closes the stall I have to listen to his troubles over pot roast at Binder's."

"Hey I've just smacked my stupid head and no headache. And the caterpillar is gone too." He told her about it. "Nothing left but order books in the dark—nice."

Sydelle laughed at the order books shield but she supposed the sun caterpillar had something to do with sexuality—she was sure an outspoken girl—like snakes or mice. Danny couldn't see that. As a kid working in Orange he'd been kind of fascinated by snakes and he loved brown-and-white country mice—they were cute. He thought she was mulling over the problem when, "Could you," she changed the subject shyly, "drop down afterward, for a very short while?"

The weird part was that suddenly the production schedule began humming like Uncle Willie's beehives in May. When Sydelle was in Chicago again maybe Quality would get better returns from long distance calls to her instead of Naomi. Danny finished the schedule, put in the Jericho call—and was luck with him tonight!

"Your par-tee does not answer."

In the future he could keep a change of clothes in the locker, he occasionally met Carrie to step out straight from work. But if the Brooks Brothers summer blue was at home, the Weber & Heilbroner lightweight gray sharkskin he wore to the office was no disgrace. He plumped out his tie, buttoned his jacket, gave the straw lid a Hizzoner the Mayor Jimmy Walker tilt over the eye and himself a wink in the mirror.

You felt sorry for the Lower East Side crawling along in shirtsleeves and suspenders, panting on boxes outside the tenements, big bare-armed mamas fanning themselves. The heat muffled sounds, even kids seemed to move in a trance—and Danny smiled.

Three times she'd phoned him!

And in Ratner's the few scattered souls among rows of long white-topped tables poked at their food as if they'd been sentenced to eating. Except—old home night!—for the cool customer who from time immemorial had always had his Sunday best handy. Yes, Old Boy Blue, his old man, yet not so old either in the varsity masquerade, Danny's laughable enemy with a plain slightly overweight girl he was bewitching.

Danny smiled down at them.

"Fish good?"

The girl looked to her mentor, but no one ever fazed Hymie Share.

"Sturgeon straight from the Hudson, a man couldn't do better. Sit down, the treat is on me."

Tonight—"Hit it rich?"—who wouldn't Danny like?

"Friendship, health, happiness," his father orated to the adoring girl friend, "these are my riches. In my life I've been sweated, I've been crossed, I've been cheated. For perfidy, Hilda, you've heard the name Frank Trachtenberg over and over again, a man—and we were relatives then—who robbed millions out of a poor man's pocket, and here is my son who can bear me out. But now, Hilda, I also am an entrepreneur, so—one of these days—you'll come with me, we'll look up Trachtenberg, and we'll laugh at Trachtenberg and his riches! And who gets all the credit, and," he winked at the girl, "most of the cash? Hilda here. Hilda, say hello to the famous Danny."

But Hilda's round-jawed face with a wisp of hair the weather stuck to her forehead shone only for Hymie. "I have to force money on you."

"Could a man," Hymie lifted his hands, "ask higher praise in America?"

"Or," Hilda said, "be more praiseworthy."

They were Hilda Modiste, Millinery De Luxe, Broadway across from the old Herald Building. Danny should send his missus down and Hymie would fit her compliments Hilda's with fashions direct from Paris.

"Better than Paris!" Hilda corrected him.

"She means," Hymie admitted modestly, "I'm the designer."

"And salesman."

"And let me tell you," Hymie sighed, "those pampered ladies are difficult. But who has to worry," he brightened, "if you have Hilda in the back!"

Damned if Hilda didn't explode a victory smile at the famous Danny. "And your cousin," she burst out, "was my best friend."

"What cousin?"

"You should remember, you broke her heart. Sarah."

"You've heard that old story too?" Danny laughed her off. "Don't believe it. We were friends."

"That's why she made Joe transfer to California, because you were friends."

"What are you proving, Hilda, that I'm a chip—some sort of louse? Is Sarah happy? . . . She has children? . . . Joe's doing okay in the Post Office? . . . Then I'm happy too, for Sarah. I like Sarah."

But to hear this from everywhere? It made you feel stupid. He'd have to consult Freud and Sydelle on Sarah, because either everybody was nuts or he was a walking example of the unconscious.

Nine-thirty though on Sydelle's favorite corner plenty of drugstore cowboys and cowgirls shouting and jostling, but no Sydelle. By ten between the heat, shovers begrudging you an inch on earth and the kid with a short skin-tight dress and curves like a pretzel who kept giving you the haw-haw from among the green types she shooed off like flies, he'd had old home night to the ears. Art was in Chicago, at least so Danny assumed. What excuse could Sydelle have? Or was it a gag? His letter never had reached her. Was this to get even maybe? Who could tell? Maybe she had changed her mind and of course he'd been in transit—Dan the boob? Gittel seemed to have graduated, but there was no population shortage in cuckooland. Ten-fifteen and Danny-o did a little of his own pushing along the sidewalk and up a stoop jammed like Saturday night at the movies. You had to strike a match, no vestibule light—but the address hadn't been part of the joke: Binder was on a letter box. They were a flight up through the old reek of cat piss and hall toilets, so the evening wasn't a total loss. He'd gone a long way since this and he should have gone even further. But don't worry—he gave their bell key so hard a twist that dammit it bit him—he wouldn't be back. He sucked the scratch on his finger, heard voices—let 'em try getting snotty—scuffling, and . . .

This beautiful? Or was it her lip rouge he'd never seen on that dark intelligent face before, and the black bang of hair with gray glints over the cool exciting white frock? God, he had this . . . pang of loss. She crossed her lips, came out to him on the landing, and even then spoke in all but a whisper.

". . . I said thank you Danny, you waited! Rhea joined the reunion, my sister, and no matter what escape I could devise Rhea said she'd come with me. I want her to meet you, but not now, Lee had to give up his job in Hawaii, their baby is dying—"

"Oh Christ! Listen, go in—I wanted to see you, I've seen you."

"Oh Danny, you are— Do you know what my father asked me just now? Did I still have that hobby, referring to the viola. . . . I'll phone you. Wait," her eyes laughed under those lashes, "where's my letter? . . . You mean," she slanted the "Dear Sydelle" then the broken off wish toward the dim fuzzy electric bulb on the ceiling, "you really were writing one! . . . Thank you Danny— Good night, I'll phone you. . . . Danny— We're moving," Sydelle whispered, "back to New York!"

Rain streamed along the panes at Alderman Rob Ward's, lashed the roof and splashed down off the drainpipes. In the dark, beach and water tumbled into each other, and from the windows over the porch the house was like a liner hissing through the Atlantic. The monsters had been put to bed half naked in the heat and now that the temperature'd dropped (but not Carrie's temperature) she kissed the snub noses of those two knocked-out athletes and drew sheets up to their chins without their moving a muscle except the snore muscle. In the next room Iona and Rochelle Ward—especially that Rochelle who'd thought she'd like a bite out of Teddy but instead got Ezra's billygoat butt in the backside, which, two in one blow, had inadvertently sent Teddy bawling as well—were their mother's responsibility. But good-natured Simone Ward—what other mother would have scolded her own bawling progeny that Shelly had had what she deserved for being so naughty?—had given a yelp with the first rain globs and rushed off shutting windows. So what the hell, Carrie also covered Simone's pair—perfect angels asleep.

Simone hurrying in almost ran into her with the usual eek and they affectionately caught each other. Simone peeked past Carrie's shoulder into the nursery, kissed her—"You're the best friend I've ever had!"—yawned in her face, and laughed. "It isn't the company, it's the hour—"

"You mean ten P.M.?"

"I get so sleepy!"

"You prefer your five mile swim in the morning to a late cozy chat with the best friend you ever had."

"But I don't," Carrie's wholesome Indian-brown pal assured her with a grip on the arm that could make you yell Uncle, "it's just that I— Go on, you're teasing me—" Simone yawned into a laugh. "See, my eyes are open with toothpicks." Another kiss. Then, "Oh! But Rob's downstairs—he'd love a chat, he always complains I lack conversation—and you know how he likes to stay up all hours. . . ." Still Simone yawned. "I love falling asleep when it rains, the rain is so lulling. . . ."

You'd think it would be the other way around, the mature husband yawning and the young wife bursting with ha-cha. But in his study the distinguished alderman who'd reached pepper-and-salt at the temples was impatiently flipping a new white page of a book. And—exciting!—with rain washing the windows, flickers of lightning and the couch lamplight dimming as power wavered, the room seemed far away from the rest of the house. You felt as free as today's sunset dip in the raw with Rob risking eyestrain on the porch to decide whether seeing's believing.

The nerve of that Share! If not for her Carrie Baum he'd have been back on the farm long ago raising chickens—and as thanks, tycoonery sneers? Whereas present company was overjoyed at her presence! Even before she finished getting the words out, "Good book?" the reading matter was tabled.

"Trash, Carrie."

"Then I have a message for you—two messages. Simone says we should talk, and Danny says we should play."

Rob reached for her hand and this time she left it in his. "Let's—" and how do you like that, he'd gone husky over her!—"do both Carrie. . . ." Was she in love with the guy? Looks he had, from the thin patrician nose to the dapper turn of the ankle. Carrie sat down but apart from the I love you's he muttered, he mainly talked with his hands. Aroused a girl may be, but there still is self-respect.

"Rob," she slowed him up, "suppose I lack conversation?"

He stared stupefied, then astonished Carrie with an apology. "I was rude, and in Gadsville Arizona where I was raised, you were expected to address a young lady with gallantry. Trouble is, since I left Gadsville and the gallant three hundred, the ladies I've met have very seldom been ladies."

"Aw Rob, you met Simone."

"Simone was a surprise—and, not her fault, not quite all she seemed."

"Flatter me. What do I seem?"

"Beautiful, with a wise mind and a live heart."

"Say Rob, you're an expert!"

And damn her if he didn't unhand her and look reproachful. "I love you, Carrie. I was afraid I'd been too blatant about it, but apparently I haven't been blatant enough."

He was so expert it defied credibility, but at least the amenities had been taken care of. "Then you really do care," she kidded him, and let him grab. But how come all the thank you's in her neck? Was he serious, possibly, or just thorough? With her back buttons he was not expert, she had to lend a hand. Then his arm got stuck in the sleeve of his own jacket—another incompetent?—and she had to help with that too. And in the accommodating storm that splashed, crashed and howled as if it would go on for hours, Rob struck like lightning.

A flash or two, and . . . *phut* . . . finished.

For this we drive ahead of time to Long Island? And for this women sigh, cry, drown themselves, drink iodine, jump out of high buildings? Limpy, sure, was down at the end of round one—but far from out. Whereas Rob lay dead on her chest.

"Rob—"

He came back if not to life at least to motion and shifted alongside her. "You're the first real woman I've ever known," he deigned to pay her a compliment which she didn't deign to return. But poor Rob—he really did care—was in raptures without compliments. "A man can love you, share his joys with you, everything! Now keep this under your hat Carrie. I'll bet you'll never guess who your lover is!"

"Thor?"

Rob guffawed "You're a caution, Carrie," and bestowed a kiss and squeeze on her. "If only a man's life were his own in politics," he suddenly brooded. "Oh Carrie, I love you more every second— Divorce is impossible," he was muttering to himself again, "even the Mayor—with his constituency—doesn't dare to risk a divorce. . . . But Carrie, listen—"

In the last election Rob had cleaned up the Fifteenth District with 80 percent of the vote. But in the Sixteenth, where the club ran young Sidney Kalman because his dad was a heavy contributor, Sidney not only lost—but to a Republican *woman*! So the high muck-a-mucks were having Sidney move to Rob's district and Rob resign from the Board of Aldermen.

"The louses!"

"No no Carrie—oh, you're loyal!"

The rest of the deal, after the Board elects Sidney to fill Rob's vacancy, is that old man Kalman's joy's expressed by another whopping contribution —and Carrie's lover, her adorer, is appointed to the Supreme Court of New York State! His Honor Judge Ward! What would they say about that back in old Gadsville!

The gallant Gadsville three hundred would have to speak for theirself. But if this—Carrie gave the pathetic little fellow of his downstairs with the *goyisher* cap on a flip that Rob took for love and kissed her for—was His Honor Judge Ward then she could have been President of the whole goddam U.S.A. And any sweet young thing she would have happened to lay would have had herself a lay to remember!

Five minutes past closing time sharp the sparkling day after the downpour Danny answered the phone and a strange voice laughed "How's business?" Luckily—it was Carrie—he hadn't jumped into conversation with Sydelle.

"I only have good and bad news."

Carrie—"Spill me the bad, we'll save the good for in bed"—couldn't have been in better humor.

Naomi and Reisel, the bad were. Yeah, neither did he understand why Reisel had picked right now to quit. Naomi, he'd asked her a cheery

"Inventory and orders up-to-date?" and had she leaped down his throat. What did he want, praise? his sister had asked. All right, she'd praise him. The system he had laid out in Jericho must have been foolproof, otherwise the warehouse would be upside down, like her crazy head. He kept continual tabs on her for the telephone company's benefit, but yesterday (she'd sobbed) at her wit's end and without a soul to turn to in this town he hadn't called. Or if he had last night it must have been in the middle of the tumult. Either she'd been screaming and hadn't heard or else Murray was in the garage trying to kill himself.

"And," Carrie cracked, "of course failing."

Murray'd borrowed three thousand dollars and dropped the whole wad inside a few weeks. Naomi had been bound to find out, they'd put a lien on his pay.

Danny had exclaimed, "Christ, how could he be that stupid, Naomi?"

"He isn't stupid! You know that business only began picking up the last month or so. Is it his fault everything goes wrong and the market doesn't know when to collapse? If not for the money— Maybe I should give him money. What good are bank accounts if he shuts himself in the coupé and runs the motor to commit suicide."

"Give him your share of the business too while you're at it."

"I'm sick of the business. He just stayed in bed this morning with his back to me and he didn't move, I was afraid he was dead. I had to shake him before he pushed me away thank God. He said go tick marks in my warehouse, I didn't have to worry, he wouldn't cost me fifty cents worth of gas killing himself, I was doing the job for him without gas. Can you tell me what I left New York for?"

"Would you want to come back?"

"How can I come back," she'd wailed, "who would take my place?"

Danny hadn't said. But this morning he'd given Millie Zook a smile, an executive session him and her and a pat on the shoulder, and he hadn't left the painting department before Millie was telling one of the botchers—straight through the nose but not unkindly—"Not like that, hand me the brush and I'll show you"! So his idea was Reisel in Jericho, Naomi here in the office and himself in the shop again.

Carrie's praise was a groan. "That's as lousy an idea as I ever heard sonny boy. You'll have Reisel retouching Jericho, Naomi papering West Street and customers canceling left and right."

"I can trust Reisel and keep an eye on Naomi."

Dead silence.

Then, "Well good luck to you," dry and snappy. "When will you be here?"

Marching orders? He hung up boiling and without promises, and—second thoughts?—the phone rang right back. His "Yeah?" instead of hello was this round's stopper.

Then that . . . unique voice asked, "Danny, is something wrong?"—Sydelle, unmistakable, and he apologized.

"You got tuned in on business as usual."

"And I was about to ask you if you'd come on my business."

"Your business? That's pleasure!"

The chimes laughed what did he mean by that, but he meant, of course he meant . . . a pleasure for him. . . .

They met in the silver shadows the El ties dropped under the 125th Street Broadway station and, walking through the gold breeze that kept Sydelle smilingly brushing back her hair, he wanted to know what she thought of his Naomi solution. Poor Naomi, she said, marrying a man and discovering he was going to spend his life being unfaithful to you with the stock market. Yet people became bound to each other. . . . But she thought Danny's solution fine, very generous, since to make sure Naomi didn't get lost again in her paper-burrowing proclivities he'd still be concerned with the office work he didn't care for.

"But not as much, and there'll be more of the manual stuff. There's a lot of satisfaction in seeing the actual production run right."

"It isn't easy being a steel-jawed industrialist."

"No, especially when I'm shaving."

But hey—he was with her and he'd completely lost track of where he was! They'd reached Morningside Heights, below the park was the hospital room—in that tier of blazing sunlight—where Ezra was born. Danny hadn't been in the neighborhood since. Just before the Mount Morris Park section went Negro—did she know Mount Morris Park, a little southeast? —Dr. Nate the doctor sold his house and moved to near Yankee Stadium, the ritziest part of the Grand Concourse. He'd switched to a Bronx hospital too, the Eden, in time for Teddy. God, all that seemed like a different century! Now Ezra with Teddy close behind had a turtle that would plow full speed down the sand into the ocean while Ezra would giggle, "We must prevent him from swimming to Europe."

Why was Sydelle smiling at him like that?

But hey—hadn't they better go about her business? Oy and Kingsbridge to Reisel's. By the time they got to the picnic lunch Sydelle had brought—Danny grabbed at his watch—it would have turned into supper! But Sydelle caught his wrist and said not to worry. When she was with him—hadn't he noticed?—she became very quick and efficient, like in finding a house for poor Naomi . . . or in buying escape gifts. Yet with Art just the opposite: purchases were folly invariably and flats she chose were too expensive. Only that Art was on the last pages of his *Fantasia El Dorado* at the Stairs' Highland Park estate with the velvet-green lawn sloping to the lake, and the days were short to the new Conservatory term, or he would never have entrusted her with serious tasks like finding an apartment.

First though she must deliver to Professor Kulnikoff, Art's friend and esteemed teacher at the Conservatory, her precious passport from exile that Danny'd gallantly seized from under her arm and had tucked under his, Art's *Pontiac* Symphony rescored for octet. No, the octet was for strings, not General Motors and the Pontiac automobile horn. In fact Professor

Kulnikoff's Pontiac—he'd suggested the theme to Art—was a courageous Indian who led a war against the ancestors of the automobile manufacturers and of course lost, and lost his life. Oh wait until Danny heard the piece! Even by the University Orchestra under Dr. Brick, with each individual string entering on a different note from the others and in varying pitch, like the death of the fugue, that lovely music emerged—Danny would love it, just wait! The faintly dissonant final bars had brought tears to her eyes as she'd plucked the viola.

And how had Art arrived at his true métier, landscape music in the American vein? Dragged, fighting, against his will. First the Concert Hall Orchestra had had to bring Art's enemy and unesteemed teacher Chalmers Wakefield, the great syrup purveyor Art called him, to lead the première of his own latest concoction, *Roundup*. The mere advertisement for Chalmers two winters ago had made Art so furious that he had sat down, secondarily to compose, primarily to prove the world was against him. They wanted goo, he would pour goo down their throats and let them choke on it. Wakefield and his friends were the musical Mussolinis of the Academy with the Prix de Rome at their disposal, Art was going to get himself recommended for the Prix de Rome if for no other reason than to embarrass those . . . Art had used one of his words. And just as Art had been fighting his guiding star, Sydelle had fought hers and attempted to dissuade him by saying that such people were unembarrassable. Luckily Art was too strong-minded to have listened to her.

At first Art had sneered that you could turn out this American stuff by the yard, and she never had seen him work so fast. Or rather, not seen him. Soon he only loomed dazed late at night with rumpled hair in his studio doorway. Or, early in the morning he'd try out passages on her on the piano. "Corny, huh?" he'd challenge her. But his new music was wonderful, from the strings' treble calling the tribes to purify themselves to the bass forest creakings when Pontiac lay dead.

Art had sent the *Pontiac* score not only to Professor Kulnikoff, with a penciled note "Will this win me a Prix de Rome?" but to Professor Chalmers Wakefield with what Art referred to as claptrap letter number one—congratulations on recent successes etcetera etcetera, leading to hopes of Chalmers' good offices on Art's behalf. Chalmers had lost no time replying from London where the letter had been forwarded—he was conducting the London Symphony in a work of his own—that the important news was not of his successes but that Art was composing again. Unfortunately (one is so pressed after a series of major public performances—Chalmers' correspondence was overwhelming) Chalmers would not be able to get to Art's score right now. As for the Prix de Rome, he believed that the next one was falling to an intensely interesting young Boston composer named Steinert. Perhaps Art might pep up his work for future consideration. Meanwhile best of luck and all credit to Art for perseverance.

Art gave Chalmers all credit too. "No wonder he's chairman, huh, of the

Composition Department at the Conservatory, he's clever, that . . ." Art had used that three-letter word meaning homosexual. "But if my revered teacher Kulnikoff's reply is silence, what could I expect from this guy?"

Danny stopped Sydelle in front of the sunny red brick Conservatory across from the green hushed weekend slope of Riverside Drive.

"But you said Art never expected anything to begin with. Why should he cry?"

"You *know*, Danny, one doesn't expect yet one does."

When Professor Kulnikoff's no longer expected answer did finally arrive, no tears—pure joy and amazement, with Sydelle the amazed. Professor Kulnikoff had the keenest ear in the world, so the praise with minor correctable reservations gratified but didn't surprise. Nor did it seem such a big surprise that after a fifteen-year reign by Chalmers Wakefield the Composition Department faculty with a little fresh blood transfused should have overthrown him and elected a very decent man, Carl Svendsen, as chairman. Professor Kulnikoff's advice forget the Prix de Rome—some scion of a New England family of musical patrons had the next one wrapped up anyway—had been no news. The amazing part was Professsor Kulnikoff's insistence that the Conservatory needed a man like Art on the faculty, and that Art needed New York where, at worst, if his performances had to be student performances—although with works like the *Pontiac* Symphony Professor Kulnikoff guaranteed that brighter days lay ahead—at least the students might as well be students of music, not cost accounting.

Sydelle had tremblingly looked up from the letter. In Chicago the University Appointments Committee had met and Dr. Brick had gripped Art's hand—"Congratulations, you're permanent faculty, bub"—to make, as Art said, the best of bad medicine. Such security was what Sydelle had thought that she wanted. Once she had it she could not have been more depressed, condemned to Chicago for life. One day her desperate intuition had told her so strongly Danny was back that she'd phoned Jericho and hardly had been able to speak when a man answered. Murray then? He'd been very nice. She'd pretended to be a Winnetka lamp store and Murray'd said he could transmit her order or she could send it directly to Mr. Share in New York.

She gazed with shining eyes at Danny, "Dear Mr. Share," and he didn't know what to do, he felt like grabbing her.

You should have heard Art berate the telephone company for the short long distance call to Jericho they were charged with that Sydelle had lied she'd known nothing about. What a furor! Yet she would have phoned West Street from Cornell Street if it hadn't seemed so hopeless. Imagine what Art would have said then. She shoulda, Danny said, she should have called and reversed the charges. Or called from a booth, she sang out—no bill! Odd, she thought, that that hadn't occurred to her.

As to the rest, she laughed, though Art loathed New York and all of its facts and artifacts from Klein's basement where he used to buy irregular suits to Broadway and the music publishers, he'd stated without hesitation that if Professor Kulnikoff's offer was not a mirage she'd better get ready to pack!

"Since then," Sydelle said—"in reply to your letter—I've been conversing with you every day Danny, though of course you had no means of knowing."

"And ignorance is bliss?"

She raised inquisitive lashes to him. "What's bliss?"

"Why those conversations I lost out on!"

And the Conservatory corridors—he felt like a kid again in the country in a shower of music, only in Orange it used to be birds and here Bach, Debussy, clangy modern on piano, a sweet soprano voice in a long-haired love song.

"My peace is gone," Sydelle said, *"my heart is sore—* Don't look so alarmed," she laughed, "that's the Schubert she's singing. And I feel like a student again, with every room taken—" But ah, here was a piano room vacant, would he mind waiting there a very short while, he could practice? Professor Kulnikoff had asked for the *Pontiac* scored for octet to recommend to a music publisher friend. . . . "Danny, would you rather I put him off? You look so stern—"

"Stern? That song got me."

Sydelle—"Be back soon"—gratefully waved him goodbye.

You shut the door and from an arched sunny cloister the helter-skelter counterpoint poured through the windows—with robin trills in the intervals!

Man alive!

You wanted to sing like a bird—and Danny did, he aimed all the old torch songs at Mr. Red Robin down there under a tree. After the fourth go-around of being asked not to laugh when he heard Danny sigh, Red Robin hopped along the grass, cocked his head and indignantly cheeped. So Danny ignored his own instructions and laughed.

And Sydelle in wonder—"You really are a troubadour"—was framed in the doorway.

"Sure as heaven's above," he sang her that line.

"You should follow the sun, and make those happy who hear you."

"With you accompanying me?"

She moved toward him with so pained a smile he thought she was sick, and, "Yes," she touched his cheek, "I'd accompany you—"

So—he knew he shouldn't but knowing wasn't a help—he pressed that palm to his lips. And from there where do you go, a married man with a, yeah, loving wife and two adoring children as they say in the obits? Up the arm to the shoulder and down, like the comedians at the National Burlesque, or like his father? Yet—he let her hand go and smiled up at her the way she smiled down at him—he could understand that smile now: joy, tears, the whole works . . . and what more could you ask?

"What you must think of me," Sydelle said.

"What, how often—I must have been fighting it, but I'm licked."

"Oh God, still he says these things! What am I going to do about you, my dear boy that I'm corrupting?"

"Cheer up!" he tapped her under the chin. "First you'll let me help you find an apartment, then you'll feed me your picnic lunch—you bring pickles sour that I'll cry my eyes out?—then you'll ride me to Reisel's. . . ." Sydelle sighed deeply and widened her eyes in front of her pocket mirror to dab away moisture with her powder puff, and whatever she did you could have kissed her. "So"—*Ridi Pagliaccio*—Danny asked his friend whose grace left him breathless as they stepped back into the sunshine, "where's the corruption?"

In Rubin Bookbinder's factory smocked girls pasted and cut from high stools at tables and aproned men worked machines. Books were stacked everywhere, some bare to the spine, some luxurious in leather. How among the brutal towers of lower New York Bookbinder had discovered a loft full of windows and sunshine Reisel could not imagine.

"Seek," Rubin grinned, and he tapped cigar ash to the floor, "and you shall find." A blonde menial of his practically bursting out of her smock cast a conspirator's smile upon her happy employer, who did not hesitate to wink at the slut. "Daniel's a good boy," Rubin said. "His wife is too much for him."

"I endured a year's persecution," Reisel said, "from that horrible woman."

"Yes, very difficult, and you couldn't say that to him. I won't hear complaints about you from anyone either."

"Where is the comparison? What is my job here supposed to be? Your workers are assiduous, your bindings are excellent."

"The best. Bibliophiles all over America send me their work."

"You advertise?"

"Not a nickel's worth. They tell one another—collectors, millionaires' agents, store buyers. There are thousands of bookbinders, but only one Bookbinder."

"With his disgusting cigars."

"I'll give up smoking after the wedding."

"Which one are you marrying?"

"Why you, Reiseleh—and your mama of course. Who else?"

"You have a large loft for a small bookbinder."

"Ten thousand feet! See this machine? All by itself it interleafs the pages with transparent paper until the glue dries. My invention—did you know that I was so talented? I've invented other machines too—come I'll show you. Nobody else has such machines. That's why I can afford Havana cigars. Robert here is tooling the leather. See this gold leaf? One hundred and fifty dollars a ream! Feel that, the best calf. You see what a catch I am? That's why I brought you here in your desperation, to show you."

"Do not trifle with me."

"Ah Reiseleh, you're the trifler, not me. It's true that the help wanted is for my poor heart—"

"You are despicable." Reisel thrust her pocketbook under her arm. "Goodbye."

"Reisel—my God!" Rubin grabbed at his Homburg on a hatrack. "Come with me."

"Where?"

"Not to a rabbi, or a hotel either, don't worry."

In an empty store you had to squeeze through crowds corner Nassau and Fulton to get into, carpenters were sawing planks and hammering bookshelves together. Sunlight rose from sawdust and teemed over unopened crates. A letterer—BOOKBINDER'S FINE EDI . . . —was working on the window.

"Like it? It's your bookshop to run."

"At what pay?" Reisel joked in her pleasure as if pay mattered. "I have already been offered a factory managership elsewhere."

"All right, whatever it is, I meet the offer—only leave me enough to buy a cigar now and then. Elsewhere where? Who offered?"

"Daniel, to run Jericho."

"Ah Reiseleh, but you wouldn't go, you didn't want to break a Bookbinder's heart."

"I was tempted, but," Reisel made a face, "it would not have worked. The evil of that woman is too far-reaching."

"Well my fine Reiseleh, don't think that I'm an easy mark either. You just try reading here, or yawning, or especially flirting with rich old customers, and you'll be fired so fast your beautiful head won't even have time to spin. I warn you, I may smile with a cigar, but my workers tremble when I so much as pass by."

"Yes, I saw them trembling. Thank you, Bookbinder, you are a good man, Rubin."

"But not good enough for you, hah?"

"Perhaps I am not good enough."

And Rubin pleased her with a sincere laugh.

19

OH LORD, ON THE LOWER EAST SIDE THURSDAY NIGHTS after Sydelle's mother fed her boiled flanken, horseradish and tears and her father fed her an insult or two, she and Danny would meet outside the drugstore like kids and stroll through this endless Indian summer to the Stanton Street recreation pier they should have gone to with each other as kids.

You found space at the ledge, and if a rat dashed along the planks below, Sydelle would fold her legs up in a hurry and—bonus—catch your arm. Everyone who used to be there would be there—chess players, kibitzers, shuffleboarders, girl chasers boy chasers, husbands and wives on benches—plus snappy up-to-date Charlestoners to a banjo. God, tugs would slip by like shadows, from the Brooklyn side lights would sink gold ropes in the river, and love, sympathy, flowed out of you, touched every edge of your life like the dark current that lapped the bridge and the pier. And lunch hours, if you could make it, you met her somewhere uncentrally located.

After a lunch with Sydelle, Danny ran into Golda in of all places the sunny bustle of West Street.

"So Ma you finally couldn't resist, you're here to see how big a shot your boy has become."

But Golda eyed the boy's blue pinstripe suit, the white petaled handkerchief, the rakish Homburg, the maroon-and-gold tie. "You're surely dressed like a big shot. The only other man I ever saw looking so elegant during business hours was . . . your father."

"Everyone's always told me I'm a chip off the old block."

"God forbid, even in jest. He didn't take a book to lunch with him."

"This? Maybe it's camouflage."

"Are you serious?"

"Would I use persiflage on my mother?"

"Camouflage, persiflage, you certainly are happy today, aren't you? But I hope it is persiflage. If not, be careful. People are human, but even Indian summer comes to an end. I have bad news. Your sister's husband is dying."

In the Ritz-Carlton restaurant (because Sydelle once said she liked luxury) Sydelle's smile as Danny read from Sam Weller's adventures had kept him rattling merrily on, and in the end her "See, and I'd never cared for Dickens, soon I'll have grown too light for you, like your friend Julius Waldman," had been worth a million cheese rarebits getting so cold you couldn't eat 'em! Now all of a sudden the joy dried up, the insides shrank, his legs tottered. Just this past Friday night Henny had been explaining modern art—the swing of a line, the rhythm of color—to him and Carrie down in the store. Besides the curios, Henny had decided to show four or five pictures by painters he knew. The girl who'd owned the store before them used to, Henny had said, though more for social reasons than art's sake. "So that's art?" Carrie'd said. "It won't make you rich." "But no life without it," Henny'd given them that straightforward smile. And now, "Henny dying?" Danny heard himself rasp.

"God forbid! Murray—"

Oh Christ, that poor jerk . . . And to have even botched up the gas pipe. Jesus, and imagine Naomi opening the door on that scene. . . . Golda had been phoning West Street for an hour after Naomi had called. Carrie had been out also.

"Don't you and Carrie," his mother had a suspicion, "have lunch together?"

"Carrie ate with our live wire salesman and a buyer, and I ate with . . ." oh it was sweet to dwell on . . . "my book."

Golda had Leah's orders bring Danny back with his suitcase. The three of them were due on the Twentieth Century Limited by 5:31.

He sighed, "Yeah," and there went tonight's piano lesson just as he was beginning to regain the classical feel and legitimately, at New York prices.

Saturday afternoons Sydelle and he had been sneaking up to a piano practice loft on 125th Street where he'd paid by the hour to commit—music. Then one twilight Sydelle with supper prepared had been at home daydreaming by her window when in walked Art from his composition seminar. He'd shocked her with lights and, in the dazzle, stared across the room to say, "I don't suppose you ever thought of looking up that businessman pianist you gave lessons to in Chicago?" Sydelle's head had spun, her legs had been like water, she'd been sure she'd been found out. But Art had only asked, "Why the gloom? You couldn't stop raving how good a learner he was, and his money was certainly good." How wonderful, if asked, simply to be able to say she was going to Danny Share, Danny Share, Danny Share! But already she accepted Danny's Ritz-Carlton lunches with no more shame than those half-naked ladies showed who supported the ceiling in back of the fiddler, the pianist and "Tales from the Vienna Woods" in that dining-room she loved full of flowers, mirrors and arches, accepted cabs uptown to her after-lunch pupils, accepted recitals by his grandmother's poor protegée's heartless son Ilya Axelrod who played Schubert and Beethoven like an angel, heartbreakingly. And in return she was to charge him for lessons again? So she'd said, "But Art, we don't need the money now." But Art did need the money. Did she suppose the Conservatory had bought him for life? To begin with it was next summer in Paris for him, that's where the real music was not counting his own—Boulanger, Stravinsky—and that would cost him a bundle, not to mention the extra for her. "Oh I'd gladly stay home!" she'd blurted and Art had said, "Don't be ridiculous. You just ask that Sheer or Shore or whatever his name was. He studies piano and you're a trained music teacher."

So Danny had remarked, "It beats me why he won't visit the pickle stand with you. He and your father ought to get along fine. You're this that and the other thing to them both—except what you are."

"I don't understand, Danny. What am I?"

"A slow learner, teacher. But I'll tell you again. You're a musician—one of the best."

"Though it's not much use, is it? But," those dark eyes that saw so much had never seen that, "Art and my father are similar in that one respect. I'd never thought of it—"

"Well start thinking. Meanwhile what's fair is fair. I'll pay for the lessons."

"Because," she had teased him, "you want to send me to Paris."

"Same as I want to jump off this pier and drown."

And the same, now, as he wanted to send himself to Jericho. But, "Okay Ma," he blew another sigh, he'd have to phone Sydelle from the station and with this luck—damn that poor idiot Murray—probably wind up speaking to Art. "Soon as Carrie comes in."

Golda leaned forward from the new mahogany side chair she'd noticed only to sit down on in the new office he'd been raving about that she hadn't noticed at all and pressed his fingers.

"Darling boy. You're very refreshing, I can tell you after a treat I had of selfishness in all its old glory."

She had stopped first in the old neighborhood at Murray's father's candy store on Columbia Street and in front of a storeful of engrossed schoolchildren with mouths sucking candy Mr. Dave Kaye had shouted at her so vehemently that his eyes bulged and his two tufts of hair stood on end. He should shut his place of business and go hold Murray's hand? On the money that Murray had enriched him with maybe, the good son? Upstairs the mother, grant her this, did shed tears—though whether for Murray or for her husband or for herself it would have been hard to say. Dave had had two heart attacks, not just one like Murray—

"Heart attack?" Danny broke in.

"Yes, heart attack."

"Not suicide?"

"You know they were reconciled. I showed you her letter—they were like doves, she was hoping to become pregnant."

Some doves, though Danny must have skipped the doves section in the interminable letters Ma got from Naomi. He only recalled Naomi's bribing Murray with five hundred dollars from malingering in bed to malingering at a La Salle broker's ticker. Then Murray would drive home—he took the coupé and let his wife support him by trolley—with a sheet of beautiful arithmetic proving what twenty-five thousand dollars' worth of stocks would have paid and what the five hundred dollars' worth had paid. So Naomi got sneered at for her money. Danny'd never wished death on Murray but his sister would be a lot better off without him once she recovered. Of course you didn't say this, just as you didn't say about 85 percent of what you had on your mind, except to Sydelle.

Murray's mother couldn't have been that concerned either. What had concerned her was who would take care of Dave, even if she could afford the fare to . . . wherever Murray was. Golda offered her the fare, but the mother only kept on sniffing her thank-you thank-you's how could she go, and finally listed the addresses of Murray's brothers and sisters though how could they go? Her sons worked and her daughters—the grandmother had suddenly beamed—had young children, such babies you could eat them alive! Then Mrs. Kaye remembered why Golda was there, and her face had puckered again. . . .

Carrie strolled in—"Ma! Or are you a mirage?"—from a heady two cocktail and thousand item transaction with Dorman's chain stores, but Golda's news sat her down fast.

You always made fun of Tootsie but Carrie'd liked him, she'd had a soft spot in her heart for that schlemiel. So Tootsie was finished, at his last gasp in some hick hospital while his beloved stock market that had only done dirt to him was in an orgy of gains. Life never slows down for you, you've got to grab it on the run.

Even look at herself as to hapless Tootsie. You're appalled for a second, then other considerations pop up. Such is life.

Such is life that it took death to bring her mother-in-law to their lately poshed headquarters—carpets, soundproofing for Limpy's sensitive ears, with a showroom between gala executive offices (finally!) his and hers instead of a former lumber room with file cases squeezed in. Jerry Belik's latest climb to what he self-effacingly called his aerie—our American eagle soaring above a metropolis of negligence cases—on the new Graybar building thirtieth floor had been Carrie's inspiration for this. So Golda the scream in her usual funeral garb, the black coat silk for the crazy weather we're having and a black felt comically perched over a gray shingle cut by the born hairdresser Leah, told her sad tale with no pause for side issues. Daddy Moishe in contrast had been nosing around here to the tune of the last carpet tacks being hammered. With the sickliest grin a loving daughter could hope for, "While the proletariat breaks its back and its eardrums," he'd commented.

"The best-paid proletariat in New York, Moishe. Though," Carrie had laughed, "for the sake of the Revolution I should give 'em less pay and more knout."

"Never mind," her daddy'd warned her with his wall to wall envy, "their day will dawn—the surplus-value morons!"

And whenever their day dawned, apart from her magic lamps East Coast to Phoenix she had the wherewithal—lucky Moishe, wasn't ignorance bliss—to throw them quite a party. In this bull market—yet study your *Journal of Finance* or your *Barron's* or even *The New York Times* every day and at 9 percent call money rates and stocks selling at fifty times earnings how long could it last?—her quarter of a million nest egg was hatching quietly to three hundred grand! And believe you Carrie B. Share incubation took place on the wing. Between West Street, business lunches, two eager monsters swarming all over you when you got home afternoons, a social life where with one little finger you kept Rob Ward balanced on his high-tension wire while you used the other hand to shake Hizzoner the Mayor's who Rob introduced you to, the opera in your gold lamé wrap and your personal Limpy in evening dress (and this damn Indian summer had better vanish like those Americans it was named after—then out breaks the ermine!), the theater to roll off your seat in hysterics in at *Animal Crackers* or to catch your eight hours' sleep in through *Strange Interlude*, how much time was left for your stock market picks? An hour or so before beddy depending on how engrossed Limpy was in whatever he happened to be reading, because when he lay down you wanted to be right there underneath him. Or an occasional free evening when you nixed Limpy's kind offer for a romantic stroll in the rain, or on Limpy's piano lesson nights, or when Town Hall tonight was featuring more heavy piano stuff Limpy wouldn't miss and she Carrie B. Share wouldn't do anything else but, by her grandmother-in-law of sainted memory's world-famous former prodigy Izzie pardon me Ilya Axelrod who kept you yawning in a half-empty house of dilapidated longhairs.

So how come she was the big winner, and Tootsie who lived ate breathed stock quotations was the twentieth century flop? He had crap in his blood—that was why. The Jericho anti-Semites had killed him? Phooey! Dead of night operators, smearing paint on garage doors for Hallowe'en.

K	K	K
i	r	i
l	o	k
l	o	e
	k	s
	e	
	d	

WHICH POLLUTE CHRISTIAN WOMEN

No wonder they wore sheets on their head. Otherwise they might find themselves face to face with a Limpy, who tilted forward and clutched both arms of his executive chair as if to dismantle it when Golda reached this little episode.

Tootsie'd thrown a stone at the saying, spluttered a few choice words on Christian women, yelled at Naomi that they were through with Jericho, they were packing right now, flown to the porch two steps at a time and crashed down so hard Naomi had thought that the next door anti-Semite had shot him.

All her fault, all her fault, Naomi had kept repeating to her mother at long distance rates so you knew it was really curtains for Tootsie. Naomi was the alleged Christian woman. The dirty old man next door, a fifty year old Swede four times her size with a loose solemn face like a piece of meat hanging too long, had been insisting the year she and Tootsie had been in Jericho that she couldn't fool him, she wasn't Jewish.

"I'm Jewish. My mother is Jewish, my father is Jewish, all my grandparents were Jewish."

"No," Mr. Larsen had said, "I'm an expert on race. You're not Jewish." At the same time he was very broad-minded. "My old lady's a Catholic." He'd meant his wife, and he'd tried to date Naomi on the grounds that they Christians should share more than trolley rides while Moses—he called Murray that—pretty cushy, drove off in an automobile. Naomi'd given him a Moses he'd never forget. Maybe last night, Hallowe'en, he had gotten even. Or maybe not. He'd been leaving for the gasworks when Murray collapsed and he was the one who drove them in their coupé all the way to the hospital in Highland Park.

But if not him some kindred spirit, that craven son of a bitch. "And Naomi is to blame," Carrie shrugged, "if Murray also lacked guts? Don't look so surprised. You want to be a Lehman, a Bache, a kosher J.P. Morgan, you push in and do it: brokerage clerk, price poster, runner, anything for a foot in the door. You don't try to wring it out of Naomi and throw heart attacks if she doesn't let you." Limpy and Golda had to admit that Carrie had a point there. As for Carrie herself, which she kept to herself, she was champing at the bit to get out to Jericho. The Jericho foreman Milosh Radic or Radish for short Limpy hired as laborer last year and promoted after Tootsie altogether quit toddling into the warehouse was the only kind of Bohemian she could stand—one from Bohemia—and a whiz into the bargain. So retire Naomi and Radish should fit right into the groove. Only whose whiz would Radish be from a distance, yours or his own? But she'd decide this on the spot. Then a vacation from poor Rob's mercy pleas would be refreshing. Above all she hadn't quenched that Field broad in Chicago just to ship Limpy into the sunset right back to her. So Carrie surprised Limpy and her mother-in-law again with she'd go, West Street—yeh yeh—could spare her better than it could spare Danny. And was her stick-in-the-mud pleased. "Thanks Pussy," he put up an objection for form's sake, "but it's my sister—"

"And my best friend. In this kind of trouble girls are more comfort, huh Ma?"

Golda said, "You'll do, dear."
What else could Golda say?

Danny's first piano lesson night with Carrie away Ezra decided to behave like a four-year-old child. With Becky sitting by to stay late, Teddy the little devil fell asleep like a cheer-up halfway through Daddy's Pied Piper of Essex Street who played kids to the land of Nod with a banjo like Daddy's, and Ezra was in the clear to pucker up—"Where's Mommy?"—with those large damp blue eyes.

"Didn't Mommy hug you like this . . . and kiss you like . . . that and say she'd talk to you on the telephone?"

Mournfully Ezra nodded.

"And didn't you giggle that you'd take care of Daddy?"

"Sure. I tried to be brave, but my bravery's used up."

So Danny sent Becky home and with the pajamas kid cuddled on his lap he phoned the teacher. Was there another girl like Sydelle? At his hello the chimes sang, "I know—the lesson is canceled, Teddy misses his mommy."

"Ezra."

"Lucky poor Ezra, to have a Danny when he misses his mommy. Kiss him on the nose for me, and give him the lesson."

"He can barely keep his eyes open enough to make sure I'm here. . . . Now he's jabbing me, I've embarrassed the bum."

"Shut up, Daddy!"

"Hear that?"

"I wish he were mine. . . ."

For his wish Danny had a flash of himself in a strange town on a leafy spring morning far from November, with a captivated knot of listeners tossing coins into a straw lid for the bard of Essex Street and his . . . beloved accompanist . . .

Another elbow poke—"I said Daddy!"—brought him back.

"And I say what?"

"And I say what was your piano teacher Mr. Tallarico saying about me?"

"Mr. Tallarico eh? That I should teach you the piano. Then if I want to go for a lesson instead of you groaning 'Where's Mommy?' "—the groaner giggled—"you'll say, 'Sure go ahead, Daddy,' and you'll sit down and get busy practicing yourself."

Ezra's eyes opened wide. He slid off Danny's knee, ran on pajama feet to the piano, climbed on the bench and delicately struck a black note.

"Well come on Daddy and start teaching me!"

A blast hello from Teddy long distance and for all Carrie's questions did he play blocks, color his coloring book, kiss his friend Teddy bear for his mommy, his end of the conversation was over. Then with background squabbling "Let go!" and "Mommy listen—" Ezra was on the wire and off. Next distant tinkling—a record on the Victrola?—clanks—the plumbing just gave?—Ezra's usual "Hey!," shouts, and the healthy bawling of Teddy. "Did you hear me play, Mommy?" Ezra came on again. "I'm studying piano!"

"Mr. Tallarico your teacher?"

"Mr. Share. Daddy says I'm a prodigy!"

But when she kiddingly bitched to the prodigy's discoverer that Tootsie ought to have the decency either to recover or die, her hubby lost no time volunteering to take her place. Big surprise, with Fields Arthur 61 Cornell sure enough large as life in the Chicago directory. She told Limpy no, now that Ezra had finally gotten started no sense throwing a monkey wrench into his career with the guy pushing five.

So they let it go at that and a friendly long distance kiss.

No wonder a year in Jericho had Tootsie half dead. Two weeks and a day and Carrie was ready to crawl out of her skin. Which beat Leah. Leah hadn't lasted a week before she packed it in. Who could blame her? Why break your back on a hard cot of Naomi's when Henny could break it for you so much more comfortably in New York? As for her Carrie B. Share for the first time since leaving the farm in Orange New Jersey she'd found out that a busy day isn't necessarily a full one. Naomi had never learned to drive. Even as a back-seat driver she found every tree along the road a hazard and all other automobiles dangerous adversaries. So Carrie was the hospital chauffeur, pick up and deliver, for her sister- and mother-in-law. In the hospital you jollied the patient, gave him man to man talk, or even pleaded "Chin up fella!" with nothing to show for it but that irritating death mask of his. The crafty bastard, he could speak if he wanted to. Carrie'd gone back for a glove once and seen him smiling pretty as you please at the corn-fed night nurse. Maybe stylish stout was his preference. For his near and dear he'd progressed from cream cheese white to Muenster cheese yellow—cheesy. Yet the tests showed improvement, even the doctor was stymied.

From the hospital the first week or so Carrie had rushed to hold the warehouse together—but what was there to hold? A dozen Polacks, Hunkies and Swedes unpacked lamp sections, joined them packed them and shipped them, under the quick but careful eye of Milosh Radish who was something like his name—long and stringy with a sting to him. The small raise Carrie gave him to keep him sharp Radish accepted as a matter of course. On speculation she could have broken him into the office routine, simple as that was—Limpy may have been a born cripple at salesmanship, but at paring work to the core he was tops—a perpetual inventory of orders and parts. Then suppose that Tootsie gathered his wits and decided life was worth living? Naomi'd resume the job of stretching a half day's work to a full day's and a good foreman like Radish would be soured by the promotion that never took place.

By ten this disgusting Jericho Saturday morning with a rain curling the lake and flinging itself at gas tanks and dead factories a lot blacker than the typewriter ribbon Naomi'd saved the firm a fortune on not changing it the year she'd been here, Carrie'd checked the shipments with Radish, answered the mail and returned Naomi's desk to the spick-and-span order to which it was totally unaccustomed. So till closing Carrie could watch the railroad tracks rusting away in the downpour and inhale a tincture of gasoline with the fish stink from the lake. Or she could jump into her vicuña, rattle Tootsie's toy coupé into the city and see if Elizabeth Arden's had some nice slinky step-ins for her New York unveiling for Limpy once dumb Tootsie made his move.

But if her sister-in-law had been along on this underwater drive they wouldn't have had to wait for the demise of Tootsie, Naomi would have dropped dead from terror. Carrie, she merely squinted through the streaming windshield and squeezed good loud *gerugas* out of the horn at the near misses. Weather or no weather—make way Chicago!

Chicago made way, but where the hell did they hide Michigan Avenue? She yelled the inquiry at a beefy traffic cop with rain sliding off his black slicker and he was only too glad to lean into the auto close enough for a kiss if she hadn't leaned back. The clearest of the directions he crooned was—a show in himself—the hour he went off duty and he could show her around, he was a guest of honor at some very classy speakeasies. Romeo also did say turn left so she turned left to nowhere, labeled Jackson Boulevard, and look—Jones & Co. Brokers, New York and Chicago, the only sharers of her Carrie Baum's three and a half G's worth of secret! She'd been in their Wall Street office just the once she'd opened her account with that snotty John Ashley who did you a favor taking your Jewish three thousand dollars and she'd handled her John business thereafter by remote control. Apparently though as your bundle grows bigger it's automatically converted to Christianity because John Ashley was very polite nowadays and friendly enough for a stab at first name terms—which she'd squelched in a hurry. Yet in this hick town that gilt-edged glass front struck her like home sweet home and she parked and went in.

In the row below the board and the ticker a Kid Lewis type from her "Murder the bum, Kid!" Madison Square Garden balcony days lounged like king of the roost between the only two empty seats, our tapering welterweight in a gray rumpled suit, with his derby and overcoat on one chair and the newspaper listings he was studying on another.

"May I, Mr. Lewis?"

"Pray do," he cheerfully pointed a Roamin' nose from Jerusalem her way, and with brown thinning hair and a light cowhide complexion his age was anyone's guess, "although the name's Sam'l Quinn, not Lewis."

She translated her little joke and was he sore—like Hercules when the Amazon handed over her step-ins.

"I do keep in condition," Sam'l bragged, "the pool every day and handball on Sundays." He flexed her his biceps. "Feel this."

"An iron man!"

He laughed, "Not quite—"

She smirked straight ahead and already she was receiving her luncheon invitation RSVP. "Ssh," Carrie nodded up toward the board, "mustn't interfere with my studies."

"In for much?"

"Three hundred and twenty-five thousand?"

Did Sam'l Quinn think that was hilarious! But watching shares jump a point a minute sometimes was no joke after the freight cars like hearses molding on side tracks in the Jericho slop. Jewish rye masquerading as Viennese sold for a dime a loaf at a bakery Naomi'd found only an eleven blocks' walk from her house—fine for Naomi's figure and tight purse, but what do depressed prices like that mean for the market? And after the whole world's bought a radio what'll they do, throw it out and keep buying? Carrie'd dumped that Radio stock—she hated it—at the June break, then with some qualms rebought at fifty points lower. If you asked Carrie, Naomi was right that Tootsie was right. Only, between desperation and greed his timing was off, the poor sap. Now he should have been selling short and what was he doing?—wasting his energy dying. But look at her. In spite of your better judgment you had this millionaire complex. Since she'd sat down her paper profits were nudging four hundred grand. Cash in, cash in. . . .

The sky was the limit, let it ride one more day.

Sam'l Quinn woke her up. "You look happy."

"I shouldn't, with an impending death in the family."

"Look sad, I'll console you."

"I'll keep that in mind."

"Who's dying?"

She sketched him the Tootsie saga.

"Nothing to worry about. My wife's been dying of heart trouble for years and she'll still be dying of it long after I'm gone."

"Then why aren't you gone?"

"My daughter'd be shocked."

"Small child?"

"Thanks girlie—I'll have to see a lot more of you. I'm a year old grandpapa with one of the most eminent urologists in the U.S.A.—young as he is—as a son-in-law."

"And the money that bought such a son-in-law can't take care of your wife from a distance?"

"I couldn't afford to buy my son-in-law a catheter. He and Pearl married for love. The President of the United States is a patient of his."

"Incoming or outgoing?"

"It's a professional secret but I think Coolidge's trouble is outgoing."

"I'll hit ya."

"And I'll hit back, remember Kid Lewis."

A thin-noser on the platform announced closing time.

Carrie said, "So long, Sam'l."
"I'll buy you that lunch now, if you don't eat too much."
"Uh uh. I'm expected."
He tapped her wedding ring. "By that?"
"You just leave that out of it."
"What's your name? Where can I look you up."
"Tillie the Toiler," Carrie was into the aisle. "I'll look you up if I want."
"Where?"
"Here."
With Tootsie's relapse to blue cheese going green, her stoking coal in Naomi's cellar to prevent her sister-in-law's tears from freezing to icicles, and a big shipment from Limpy, Carrie practically forgot Sam'l Quinn the physical culture kid except for a risqué dream or so and even there he was mixed up with some complete stranger. But late the next Thursday when she detoured for a glance at that magic Jones & Co. board before fetching the girls home from the hospital, there he grinned between his coat and his paper.
"Your fault if I'm fired, Tillie. I'm here on company time."
"I hope," she smirked, "you at least picked up . . . a few dollars."
"That's automatic, so where's the fun."
"When the market breaks you'll have fun."
"I bet you were one of those Alfred E. Smith Bolsheviks Tillie."
"That bet you win. I voted for Alfred E. Smith for President. What do I owe you?"
"Dinner—I'll pay."
"Say, you're a sport, Sam'l. Another time maybe."
"No pity on my poor heart?"
"Your son-in-law certifies you have one of those too?"
"A full set of organs Tillie as you'll see for yourself."

With his two mourners beside him no wonder this guy lay there as ghastly as the night light over his hospital bed. Carrie threw the bright switch, winked at Naomi and Golda with their pallbearers' faces and pinched Tootsie's cheek.
"Lay off," he twisted away.
"He breathes, he speaks! Good news buster, you're in on a quick killing."
"I'm a quick kill you mean. Give me a cigarette."
"Just what the doctor ordered eh? Cheer up—"
She delved in her purse and Golda stretched a hand nay.
"Carrie—he mustn't smoke."
"Smoke?" Carrie laughed. "This is a hair of the dog that bit him."
She tickled his nose with an envelope until "Okay okay," he whined in danger of smiling, "what's in there already?"
"Your thousand dollar short sell for Radio to flop within thirty days."

"Mine?"

"It was too good to pass up, even for somebody else such as a lunkhead like you, you lunkhead."

He pulled the contract out and—what do you think of that?—gave his tear-dazzled helpmeet a grunt "Raise the bed, will ya?" As Tootsie read roses snaked back in his cheeks. "Radio won't flop, not with my luck."

" 'Attaboy, don't tempt fate with good cheer. It flopped before, it'll nosedive again. Look at this—I bought another thousand for Teddy."

"You think so, huh?" He pushed himself higher. "Anyone have a paper?"

Naomi kept hugging Carrie that night and happily sniffling. She even asked were they warm enough, there was plenty of coal in the cellar! In the morning they stopped at the bank for Naomi to get a form for the joint account that she'd promised Tootsie and all he'd have to contribute was health, she swore she'd never so much as take a peek at the bankbook.

And damned if the patient himself wasn't out of bed next to the window enjoying his new lease on life and the hazy day sweet as summer by burying himself in a *Wall Street Journal* that he'd borrowed from one of the residents.

The haze cleared by forenoon with Carrie's work at the warehouse, and asking Limpy on the phone if he was still bearing up set her seething deliciously as that sparkling blue lake. His "Just barely" didn't quell a girl's spirits either. She reported her Tootsie rescue and "What a Carrie!" Limpy breathed into the static.

He should know half of it!

A jolly so-long to Radish and the rest of the boys, and a crank to the old coupé that started it groaning and shivering, and Carrie was off to—what? Chicago anyway. At the sunshiny curb at Jackson she wasted no time locking up—who would steal this panting jalopy? But in the plush den of Jones & Co. the addicts were conspicuous for the absence of Sam'l Kid Lewis Quinn.

Well then, in the midst of that pop-eyed greed ranged under the board the question was how rich is rich? What do you say Mother? Better a modest wheelbarrowful or a millionaire broke?

A Gentile in blue serge with a desk plate Mr. Dice had the crust to criticize her sell orders. Of many of the shares she held—and he could recommend others—the possibilities were unlimited. Why their scarcity alone put them at a premium. Far from wise, surrendering your position in a good stock. She stared at Mr. Dice, sank the whole pile in good old United States government bonds and at twelve below par into the bargain, and watched Mr. Dice do his paperwork.

Mother, you and me kid—we're rich, and with nobody's permission!

Now be there Kid Lewis. . . .

In the main room on two of his three chairs—the coat had stayed home—there he waited, Sam'l in person, with his chunky legs sprawled.

"Today," Sam'l noted, "you look ecstatic!"
"And feel like . . . half a million!"
"Heartless Tillie, while people die."
"My brother-in-law? I've restored him to life."
"The Messiah in skirts! And how about me? Ready to restore languishing Sam'l to life?"
"Do you need restoration?"
In a jiffy with his newspaper folded and his derby in place—"Refurbishing say, at the edges"—he offered her his arm.
Outside Sam'l the conqueror took charge of Tootsie's junk heap. "Sensible car," he said. "I run a Model T myself home in Pittsburgh, though a relative of mine by marriage would prefer her Rolls-Royce, her chauffeur, her repairs and her upkeep."
And with restaurants wherever you turn on the Loop, Sam'l drove her across a bridge and a brown soupy river with chicken-fat glints, all the soup she ever saw that lunchtime. In a four or five table cupboard in a hotel on old mother Hubbard Street put in the dark by skyscrapers, merry Sam'l advised you to skip soup it's too filling, fill up on the soda crackers before they bring you the omelet. Carrie said that they could wash down the crackers with water and run, and Sam'l laughed, he couldn't get over her. He seriously added though that it was the best value in town for white tablecloths and a bottomless coffee cup.
"This hotel is where I always stay in Chicago, and a cheerful little place for the money it is."
Upstairs his faithful overcoat and change of old suit hung humbly in the closet, and a miraculous slice of sunshine across the chair, dresser and bed through an airshaft wide as a yawn did brighten the tiny room. But who had time for scenery? This Kid didn't spar. He peeled you and piled on you with a quick pair of hands, stunned you with uppercuts, and—my God, Limpy primed with honeymoonshine never used to do better—at the bell stayed right in there slugging away at the risk of his health. . . .
"Grandpapa—"
"Shut up Tillie—"
In a calmer moment though, "Let me tell you Tillie," he said, "you actually are a Messiah. I hadn't done that in years."
She fingered the coarse curls of that he-man chest expansion. "Funny, the light makes the white hairs look dark."
"Then if I stick to afternoon hours I can stop dyeing my chest."
"You mean that you get paid for this? You're lucky that I'm not your boss."
"Tillie I'll tell you, I'm my own boss."
"Why you nickel-nurser, I might have known. Of what?"
"Frugal's the word Tillie, don't be unkind. High tension insulation."
"Who'd want," Carrie flicked his wisp of a pecker, "their high tension insulated?"

"Tillie I'm already in love with you!" He pulled her down breasts to hard chest, smoothed her behind, spilled into her lips "Here McCormick's, Willys-Overland in Toledo, Victrola in Camden New Jersey, in my home town U.S. Steel—they want my special processing all over. . . . But Tillie Tillie Tillie—"

A flurry of hooks and jabs by Carrie and with the Kid limp on the canvas, "Nice knowing you sonny boy," she reached toward her wristwatch on the chair. But that guy had mitts like a vise.

"Name and address first girlie. I look forward to a long happy life with you, off and on."

"Thanks boss, but the on's about over, so you'd better get used to the off."

"That's what I like about you! Lays are a dime a dozen—"

"That's wholesale of course?"

"Oh you Tillie! But the little chitchat in between," he clamped you down kind of excitingly with his mighty right arm while he went through your handbag, "*that* . . . Carrie B. Share," he read off her Jones & Co. account card, "Two hundred one Central Park West . . . *that* doesn't come by the carload."

One more dreamer.

How the old Danny would have raged these weeks Carrie was away, with his junior whirlwinds at home, and production, shipping, the office and Carrie's salesmen all on his head in West Street. Instead, Daddy and boss, he was the most good-humored man in the world, which proves that good humor is catching. He caught his from Sydelle at the forty minute lunch hours in the Royal Cafeteria on Twenty-third Street—hurry there hurry back—where all love needs for sustenance is warm talk and a bite of food that always seemed to be cold. Sydelle ran down there from practicing —Danny'd reminded her that she was a musician and nowadays she practiced incessantly—housekeeping, lesson giving, concertmistressing Art's *El Dorado* rehearsals at the Conservatory, solo visits to her parents Thursdays and duets to Art's mother Fridays, learning the viola part of the new *Serious* Quartet Art had composed to show that he retained his integrity, flirting her old flame-thrower Zeller into playing the cello part of the *Serious* with Professor Kulnikoff and a young Art enthusiast named Chuck Siegel as violins, and biting back yawns on the wifely fringe of faculty socials.

"And still you smile," Danny would imbecilically grin at her.

"At the prospect before me," she would smile.

And this morning just as he was about ready to grab hat coat and scarf and race through the cold to their steamy Eden her call came she couldn't make it, and of course he was disappointed. Was she okay though?

"Lunchtime snatches—" and her deep gloom, this despondence, was an entirely new voice to him—"are hardly satisfactory anyway, are they?"

He had to laugh. "I told you, to me they're wonderful." And he'd thought to her too, so where do you stand on anything if you can't tell even how . . . this one feels? "Sydelle, I'll phone Becky now to stay overnight, even a daddy's entitled to an evening off, and we'll have dinner at the Ritz-Carlton instead of lunch at the Royal Cafeteria."

"Tonight I'm scheduled to help smile Dr. Koussevitzky into doing Art's *Pontiac* Symphony with the Boston Symphony Orchestra, though if I were to stop smiling forever he'll still do it, or if he won't someone else will."

"Stop smiling forever? Sydelle, what's wrong? Are you sick?"

"No, not exactly . . . No, it's nothing, nothing. Goodbye."

She'd called from a booth, you couldn't call back. He just sat at his desk through the empty lunch hour watching phantom freighters slip past the Jersey shore in a film of mist while his cheese on rye curled at the edges. And phoning her from home later while Becky was feeding the kids he got Art, who supposed his wife had missed a scheduled lesson.

"I'm afraid she's doldrumming. Didn't she at least let you know?"

Sydelle was sick and the great Fields was put out! For Sydelle naturally Art's word was scripture. "As Art wittily says, just look at other women—it isn't the condition that's the curse, I am." She'd mope, she'd offend Art by the sight of her and still more by shutting herself into the bedroom like a martyr to womanhood. And the false pregnancies she made Art suffer through! Danny'd listen with fists to that stuff.

Yet you heard the Conservatory orchestra play Fields' *Pontiac* Symphony and while the music was going on you could have kissed the bastard for writing it, it was so beautiful. How do you explain that? To do the job right you had to hoard your feelings, let 'em pour into the tune? But that's what troubadour Danny'd done as a kid and everyone had said smile. . . .

"What would you do with a wife like me?" Sydelle had asked gaily.

Danny'd shrugged, "Hold your hand and be grateful," and she had gazed at him with that love.

But that had been last month. Last month sick as she'd been she'd come to the telephone. Now no. He blundered more dead than alive into the kitchen.

Ezra raised his eyes over the spoon. "What's wrong, Daddy?"

"What's wrong, Daddy?" Teddy spooned in another mouthful.

Even Becky looked anxious.

"You eat and I starve," he sat down with them, "is what's wrong."

But Danny himself could sense how ghastly his good cheer was, and his bedtime story afterwards was such a flop with his losing the thread of which bear said what about Goldilocks that the boys began pummeling each other, and him, with their pillows.

He couldn't telephone her again, he'd get Art. In the den he brought out letter paper but what was there to say, kiddo, if you're miserable I'm miserable? Trees near the lamplights down in the park stretched gray branches toward blobs of darkness.

Bell ring? The Buryton didn't let your own mother up unannounced, so Carrie must have made a fast getaway from Jericho, she wasn't due back until tomorrow. And he wished he didn't have to face her right now.

He opened the door, and "I must seem respectable," Sydelle gave a half-sick laugh, "no one stopped me downstairs."

She was haggard—he drew her into the foyer and touched her face—she had black marks under the eyes. "You shouldna." But he held her tight, that cold overcoat like fresh air.

She whispered, "We've never been so close, have we?"

"Hardly room for the buttons."

Then—he was bubbling over—he wanted Sydelle to see this elegant joint of his: the parquet floors, the grand piano, the best imitation Chippendale that money can buy! But Sydelle wouldn't let go, she only could stay for a moment. She'd all but promised Art sick as she was—yes, she still was sick, now Danny was really beginning to know her, wasn't he?—that she'd meet him at the Conservatory reception for Dr. Koussevitzky. Fortunately it was being held downtown here in a trustee's mansion on the other side of the park. With that she took her coat off and sat down on the couch with Danny to touch him, loll against him, kiss his lips.

"What if your children come in?" she murmured.

"I'll say Daddy's dreaming."

"It's like a dream," she couldn't stop kissing him, "isn't it?" Then she jumped up. "How could I have spoken to you that way this morning, regardless of what day of the month? Besides, I think that I'm better now." She glanced at her watch. "Danny, I must run—"

But she walked did not run to the nearest exit, which wasn't the door she'd come in by but Danny's liquor closet. She laughed and got out the second try. Winter or no winter Danny threw the window up and in the dark below with Central Park lamplights a blue haze of precious stones she left the building and still she walked slowly, paused, waved to him across the nine stories, walked, looked up and waved, and a third time, before—slowly—she walked on toward the bus stop.

Danny had hardly ever cried in his life, even as a kid when his father would take a swipe at him. Yet here were tears blinding him—and he never hoped to feel happier!

The small seducer Ezra twinkled at Carrie, "Mommy may I play the piano?" and won his hug.

"But don't fire," Carrie sent him into hysteria, "till you see the whites of its keys."

"Now sit down and listen—"

"You mean come down!" Teddy flew up in the air and landed in a fury on the heads of the Ansbachers downstairs who by now had stopped dropping up to complain about the monsters, you just got a call from the management. So as Schubert's *Merry Melody* began—nice tune—Carrie caught her redheaded bandit by the arm, perched him on her lap on the couch, pointed at the living-room windows and asked him if he saw that stuff splashing along like a river.

"That's rain, dum-dum," Teddy said.

"And what's pushing it?"

"March winds."

"And who goes out in rain and March winds except for mailmen and idiots?"

"You can send him out and good riddance," Ezra chimed in with lyrics to go with the music, "he's an idiot all right."

So Teddy broke loose to thunder the bass and pipe his own treble when his brother piled on him. Referee Carrie broke up the clinch and the telephone rang on schedule. Becky looked in holding a bitten cinnamon bun with her pinkie classily extended.

"Swedlow the manager I suppose," Carrie said. "Just tell him okay, the bout's over."

"It ain't Swedlow this time. Liela says Sam'l?"

"Sam'l who?"

"Sam'l who?" Becky called.

"Quinn he claim," Liela called back.

"He claim . . . claims . . . Quinn."

"Never heard of him. Who needs salesmen by telephone when you've had your own duds all day. Come on General," she gave Teddy a tug, "let's start another invasion."

Teddy raced to the nursery—thank God that four year old kids can't keep their mind on the same subject too long—to set up the toy soldiers as Liela trumpeted again: "Now he say alias Kid Lewis."

Carrie picked the bedroom extension up, changed her mind, and "My my," took the call in the living room with Ezra's musical background, "so you're still alive."

"Just about, Tillie, though forlorn and forgotten."

"You sound pretty cheerful, considering what's happening to Quinn & Co. I see your common stock dropped twelve and a half points."

"I'll buy all the Quinn stock you have to sell."

"How did you lose your Willys-Overland account, a hard driver like you?"

"Oh those guys. They're heading for bankruptcy so they decided to do their own insulation worse for less money and let the customers take care of repairs later on. But lose a carp—" big shot, he swaggered—"hook yourself a few herring and more than make up for it. If there's an aircraft manufacturer in the New York area I haven't just signed, he ain't sprouted wings yet. So you've been following my adventures, huh girlie?"

"Only the ones they print in the paper."

"Tillie, you're the spice of life! Hop in a cab—me and my other suit eagerly await you at the Imperial."

"You, at the Imperial?"

"Yes, four dollars a day, and all I've had out of it so far are a few nights' sleep and more baths than I need. Nevertheless it's a legitimate business expense, except that it's galling having to put on a show for a crew of petty mechanics like Forbes, Haitek and the rest of that bunch. So I'll expect you in say thirty minutes."

"Isn't that kind of short notice for a girl?"

"A businessman is always willing to meet a situation halfway. Make it three-quarters of an hour."

"The truth is fella, I'm entertaining a couple of guys right here this minute, and one of them," she lowered her voice, "is looking very resentful, so I'd better sign off."

"Hubby?"

"Uh uh."

"Then I'll hop the cab and make it a trio—I eat up competition."

"Not this competiton you won't."

"Don't worry—and I'll wash 'em down from my own flask."

"Into which you've dipped deep already."

"Wide-awake Tillie! I have been celebrating those aircraft contracts a little—but the best is yet to come!"

And wasn't he eager! She was still setting up troops for Teddy to knock down again with bang-bangs that submerged the easy Bach from Ezra's piano inside when Liela dubiously announced Mr. Lewis. Carrie said, "Sure, send him in," and kept on with the tin soldiers.

Quinn got the picture, the rumpled captain of industry with thin graying hair and with damp cuffs from the rain. But just because Teddy stuck his jaw out and said "Go 'way—can't you see that we're playing?" did Quinn have to cock forefingers and thumbs and frighten the child out of his wits with machine-gun fire and mean eyes?

Teddy stared, screwed up his face, held his arms out to his mother, and bawled. In the living room Ezra went on with Bach.

"Do you also haunt houses?" Carrie said.

"Just when asked, as I presumed that I was. . . . Don't cry little boy, I was only trying to get a game."

"Well come inside, let me give you a drink, not that you need it."

Quinn made short shrift of the drink, of the introduction to Ezra, and of another drink. He'd been down to Camden with a couple of his vice-presidents to solve some renewal problem with the Victrola people, a back-breaking day and a half but he'd solved the problem—he had, not those high-priced chumps on his payroll. Now he wouldn't go so far as to say the eighty-five sooty miles north on the Jersey Central had been solely to see her, but the fact that she was there—he was in obvious form again—had inspired him to canvass the New York area.

And there she sat telling him she was busy tonight?

"Yes, it's *Carmen* tonight—I mean at the opera."

"On the level? That sounds like home. Very well. I'm not leaving till Friday morning. We'll round out your cultural activities tomorrow night then?"

"Uh uh, we're invited to an important party tomorrow. The governor of New York will be there."

"You mean you eat with Democrats?"

"It isn't the eats, it's the little chitchat in between."

Quinn took in the framed portrait next to hers on the piano.

"Another one of your guys?"

"Limpy? Yes, he lives here too."

"Limpy eh?"

"Don't make a mountain out of a pet name. He has a slight limp from an old automobile accident."

"With you driving?"

"I never have accidents."

"Quite a dog."

"Yes, Daniel is easy on the eyes if I say so myself about my own husband."

"I wasn't referring to him," Old Baldpate took a cut at her.

Carrie smiled.

20

A WINDY MARCH DAY WHEN TOOTSIE SHOULDN'T HAVE been outdoors he astonished Naomi by strolling into the warehouse. "Tootsie!" And—Radic was in conference with her in the office—she immediately blushed on account of the pet name.

Tootsie hung up his coat—"Building's still here I see"—and she had a flash of delirious happiness. He'd sold those nerve-racking stocks, put the money in the bank and come back to work! In such excitement that Radic looked at her (but she didn't care!) she told the foreman that they'd finish the scheduling after lunch. But Tootsie—"Speak to New York today yet?" —had simply come to discuss something by long distance with Carrie, it would be stocks of course. Naomi shivered in her pants, he'd never done this before. What must have happened . . . She put in the New York call, reported to Danny, and then Murray and Carrie spoke. Naomi hummed to herself, rattled papers, scratched her pen on her pad—anything not to overhear the worst.

Later that week she asked Carrie whether Murray—Naomi didn't dare express her real fears because if you did they might come true—had made some bad trades. Carrie laughed to beat the band not that she'd heard of, in fact he'd saved a fortune on that phone call alone. But Carrie did warn that Murray had better get out of the market while the getting was good.

So much for doctors. It was perfectly all right for a man who'd had a coronary to have intercourse with his wife within reason, so there was nothing to prevent Naomi from having children. That's what the doctor said. All she had to do was relax.

How could you relax?

The craziest thing Naomi'd ever done was give her husband the bankbooks. In the hospital Murray had looked at them in surprise, and, "You won't regret it kid," squeezed her hand. Had her heart been full, had she seen herself on the verge of a new life: a loving Tootsie, babies, the works.

A week home and his one word had been "Up." Not himself, he hadn't been up, though in the hospital he'd already been walking. The Polanski woman she'd hired to take care of him he'd chase out three times a day to buy the papers and he'd stay in bed. From bed he'd finally thrown a whole financial section at Mrs. Polanski, who'd given on the spot notice. Naomi had asked him to apologize and he'd asked her for what. He had aimed that paper at the radio and Mrs. Polanski'd happened to pass. Besides, the paper had been as dumb as the stock market, it hadn't hit anything.

The market had been up and that crummy Radio had been up.

Furthermore he'd had that town of Jew-haters, sickbeds and stale information up to his neck. He didn't know about her he'd said, but he was kissing Jericho goodbye. The closer he'd live to La Salle Street and the market the better. So no need to dish out any more good money for Mrs. Polanski.

He'd had the heart attack but Naomi was also human. Live in Chicago with a two hours' one-way trip to the warehouse? Where did he get his nerve?

Oh God, from the bankbooks.

While he'd been in the bathtub—now instead of smoking to calm his nerves he would soak with his stock reports that made her sick and he'd stay in so long she'd be scared he'd drowned—she'd peeked in the chifforobe to see if the bankbooks were there.

They'd been intact and she had felt awful for distrusting the poor kid. She'd been crazy about the house with all those rooms, nurseries, but if you'd almost died in a town where they burned crosses on front lawns and smeared filthy sayings on your garage you'd want to move too.

That's what she'd replied to Ma's letter full of moral support like consider getting up before daybreak in winter for trolleys and buses, putting in a full business day, then buses and trolleys back to shopping and housekeeping. Naomi's brother'd thought he was privileged to fly off the handle long distance: was she trying to kill herself for that guy, meaning Tootsie? She'd given a guy to Danny! Of course Danny had meant well, they had made up right away. Besides, the rent you saved in Chicago, six rooms for fifty dollars a month!

Danny had laughed, "Where, on their Hester Street?"

"No," she'd blurted, "it's more like Orchard Street."

"That's my sister," Danny'd laughed harder.

"Well I am your sister."

So she had moved with high hopes. Mornings she would kiss sleeping Tootsie on the ear and tiptoe out in the first streaks of light to catch forty winks on the Chicago Avenue trolley, the Intercity bus and the Jericho North End trolley. The Chicago West Side did happily remind her of the New York East Side full of Jews and small stores. Even the funny two-story houses with high back steps like stilts were strung together with laundry lines like her childhood backyards. Best of all Tootsie had been elated to be within walking distance of La Salle Street—why waste gas?—and his, oy, broker's office. But after a few days she'd come home dead tired, and Murray would say, "Up."

Carrie could joke money is indispensable providing you know how to dispense it, and merrily make her way back to New York. Naomi owed Carrie Murray's life, she'd never forget that. She'd still have nightmares of him dead—terrible. But before she had at least had her bankbooks.

Then a Saturday afternoon she'd stepped off the Chicago Avenue trolley from business into an east wind that had blown her right in front of an automobile. Brakes had screeched, people had turned—it had been a wonder that she hadn't been run down the way Danny had been years ago. In the vestibule on Kedzie Avenue her hands had been so numb that she hadn't been able to unlock the door. And who'd wanted to ring the bell and hear the word Up before you'd gotten into the house even?

Would it have been so bad if the car had hit her a little, to be taken care of for a while in a nice warm hospital?

She'd breathed on her fingertips, managed the unlocking—and there in the sun parlor had sat Murray behind his card table with a smirk she would have very well been able to do without.

But he'd drawled, "Down," and waved her over. Naomi'd looked at where he'd pointed but he had had so many figures written down that you could get cross-eyed. "I merely chalked up five thousand dollars today."

"Fi—" Naomi hadn't believed her own ears but Tootsie's smile had been contagious. "That was Carrie's—"

"Carrie's my foot. Where did she get the idea except from me? C'm'ere."

He'd craftily slipped his arm around Naomi blue coat and all and gone to work on the buttons. She'd kissed his curly blond hair, his ears, eyes, nose. "But isn't it too soon?" she had giggled. "The doctor said—"

"Don't get too excited he said." He'd yanked her arms free of her coatsleeves and he'd unbuttoned her dress. "Who's excited?"

"Tootsie—they'll see us!"

Half naked she'd led him to the bedroom. "Down!" she'd giggled.

Tootsie really hadn't become carried away, he always was . . . methodical, though now that was just what the doctor had ordered. But she, she'd never felt such thrills and had had all she could do for the sake of Tootsie's health not to cry out, scratch, bite, fling herself. If ever Richard—she'd named the baby-to-be for Grandma Rivka—should have gotten himself started, it had been that gray December afternoon she'd been too hot even to think about pregnancy let alone to be anxious that she was being too anxious. But the darned market had gone down one week too late, the next day she'd had her period.

Lucky in stocks unlucky in love.

She could brag in letters to Ma that instead of her bus and trolleys and dragging bundles home knocking her out, she was so peppy she was afraid she was sick. Ma hoped that she at least closed her eyes on the bus coming home. Naomi did, but eyes closed or open, Kedzie Avenue in Chicago or Front Street Jericho, preparing tomorrow's supper for Tootsie or the order tickets for Milosh Radic, her mind was a tumult with Tootsie's stocks: Anaconda, U.S. Steel, Standard Oil of New Jersey.

Who'd ever dreamed Naomi Share would read newspapers, the business section especially! When it was time to go home she barely could choke out good nights to the men, her heart would pound so. Then you didn't find a newsboy within miles of that godforsaken edge of Jericho near the lake. It was thirty minutes' torture to Intercity Terminal and a kiosk. On the Chicago bus her trembling fingers picked out the closing quotations.

The crazy stocks couldn't stop going up even though—Tootsie scared her silly—business wasn't that wonderful. In Naomi's own company the new orders that Danny phoned were nowhere near what they used to be. Sizzling Saturdays last summer Murray would drive to the beach while she put in overtime. Now she could have actually laid off a couple of men—and Carrie agreed—but Danny insisted on carrying them till business would pick up.

"In a pig's eye it'll pick up," Tootsie curled his lip, "and what's happening in that two-bit enterprise is happening everywhere."

But Tootsie said if the suckers wanted to push what should have been a bear market over the moon, he'd go along for the ride—only *he* knew how to get off! He didn't care what the stock was—Telephone or Moe's Belly-buttons—a point and half drop and he sold. Still, Naomi couldn't forget, people lost. Tootsie patted the little woman on the behind.

"Losers weepers finders keepers."

But how could you be sure?

Day after day, week after week, month after month, she came home in trepidation from Jericho—sure, so far, to Tootsie's happy expression at the card table in the sun parlor. But till you opened the door you nearly dropped dead from heart failure yourself. They had become rich with his trades. Naomi's pen ran away with her in the letters to Ma. Knock wood when she had the baby she'd give, sell she meant, Danny her share of the business. Murray and she (oh God, they only shouldn't lose it all: this she kept to herself with crossed fingers) were set for the rest of their lives. Ma's theme song was don't be hasty. Sick at heart as Naomi was, did that make her sicker!

She trusted in the card table fortune the same way Ma did.

A lot of nights, across the space between the twin beds she'd given in to Tootsie about after his attack and bought with a sinking heart, he'd shake her awake. "Groaning again," he'd scold her. America was wild about the installment plan. Don't own anything, just make easy payments and fatten the bankers. Not Naomi and Tootsie. They paid cash on the line. Yet she'd dream that these burly movers were in her house—always Tompkins Square where she didn't belong because she was married already—repossessing her furniture. In despair she'd plead, "But—" But had she forgotten to make a payment? Jack Berger would grin, "They left you one of your beds." One was all you needed. But when she went to lie down with her heart thumping for Jack to follow, there'd be no bed. So Jack would shrug "See you in church" and he'd be gone too. Then in the terrible misery that she had lost everything, she'd groan.

Did you need a psychologist to explain such a dream? Her first thought when Tootsie'd wake her would be of slipping into his bed. But Tootsie had to have his rest, so she'd struggle to control herself, and most often succeed. If not, there was the anxiety that you shouldn't have disturbed him.

Even if you made love before breakfast Sunday and holidays the way the marriage manual recommended, in the back of your mind you were worrying that this time next week you might be penniless.

So almost like clockwork every four weeks her hopes were washed out. Wasn't she crazy, when Tootsie's trades did nothing but win?

None of her pretty folders from Michigan and Wisconsin resorts—the expense would have been worth it even though their friends Nat and Lucy from the synagogue Tootsie went to kidded her that she must think babies grow on trees—could induce Tootsie to leave La Salle Street and his brokers for a vacation. But you could still look down at your handsome sleepyhead at the Oak Street Beach summer Sundays, tap his bow lips with your lips and feel in your bones you'd been pregnant for three hours already! Or else you'd take his hand for a Saturday afternoon stroll alongside of the lagoon a few blocks from the house, interrupt the happy analysis of his morning's trades to point at the lucky mothers with their perambulators and try to give fate a nudge with "That's me next year." But men—her funny Tootsie only showed interest if the mother was young with a trim figure. Or he'd laugh at you while you wiggled your finger at the monkeys in the Lincoln Park Zoo—they were so cute that you just wanted to hug them!

At least you were rich until tomorrow.

Then home from business the day after Labor Day she unlocked the door and . . . no Tootsie, no card table even. Did she feel faint, did her insides shrink. Not a sound in that gloomy apartment where all the rooms between the sun parlor in front and the kitchen in back were hemmed in by the houses on either side. She switched on a living room lamp, no Tootsie. Light trickled into the bedroom though, where—"Oh God help me!" she gasped—his body was stretched out on the bed.

His voice—"What's eating you?"—almost frightened her out of her wits.

She bent over him and touched him—"Oh Tootsie"—with such affection, but he brushed her away.

"Don't be hysterical."

"Now I know that something bad happened."

"Nothing bad happened till you got here."

"You've lost everything."

He stuck his head up. "I've lost nothing!" Even in the shadows she thought his eyes would pop out.

She shut up, God forbid that her first fear stepping into the room should come true. Yet she felt practically as sick as if it had. She knew her Murray. He'd lost, he'd lost everything. But how? In the evening paper the market had closed higher again: Telephone, Anaconda, Quinn & Co. If he held those stocks now. He never mentioned the bad trades, only the good ones.

Or—Naomi went cold—had he switched to down?

With a twilight like midsummer muffling sounds she heard radio music like from the grave,

How could I . . . doubt you,
I'm lost with . . . out you . . .

Her yesterday's wash as limp as she was still hung in the airless backyard, the kitchen steamed with chicken reheating that she'd cooked last night for today, and her fingers numbly shelling peas were like ice. *Lost* stuck out of those lyrics and made her sick. He'd switched to down and she could bust, she couldn't say anything on account of his health. She tried to compose her face, look less gloomy when he sat down to supper. But how could she?

"In mourning?" he grunted.

"You switched to down."

He sailed his plate, peas chicken and all, crashing against the kitchen sink. At the door—see? you couldn't say anything—he turned with actual flecks of foam on his mouth.

"Be happy you lump, you drag, you miserly bitch—I cashed in my stocks!"

"Where's the money then?"

"None of your goddam business!"

So he hadn't cashed in, or why was he angry? Wiped out he meant. If only he had cashed in, a hundred and ninety thousand dollars.

Dream money anyway, she'd never believed in it. But—she felt sicker yet—her real money was gone too. He'd shut himself in the bedroom in this heat that was bad for him, so she couldn't look in the chifforobe, not that she supposed the bankbooks would be there. And just last spring he'd had the bankbooks on the card table to show her that night. He'd redeposited all her money he'd been so far ahead! He'd said, "Be happy," the identical words, except that time she'd been happy, she hadn't realized how happy. He'd started the lovemaking the way he did on such days sometimes and she'd thought what rotten luck she was having her period. Never satisfied, so you're punished.

She cleaned the mess off the floor, a perfectly good plate broken so you couldn't paste it together. She herself had no appetite but Murray shouldn't go hungry, it was bad for his health.

"Tootsie," she leaned into the darkness, "come eat, I've finished."

Not a stir, not a murmur. She went closer and, thank God, "Scram," he said.

From the sun parlor she absently stared at passers-by through street shadows and lamplight. What had she done wrong? A young man glanced up a second and gave her the once-over, and how do you like that—she still blushed! She was thirty-one barely and, except for Ma, looking young ran in the family, men did stare at her with her silky blonde hair and china doll complexion and did make her blush. So how come she felt old?

She heard Murray's footsteps after they had stopped, like an echo, then a clinking of cutlery.

The bankbooks—not that she had the least hope. She sneaked into the bedroom, turned the light on and opened the chifforobe.

There . . . and all there, not a penny added, not a penny taken away!

You hated to admit it but sometimes she'd felt she'd made a mistake marrying Tootsie, he only thought of himself. Now see how wrong that feeling was, the poor kid. He'd lost everything, but saved hers! How her heart went out to him sitting there in the kitchen with his sad *Financial Chronicle* propped between the sugar bowl and his plate of chicken bones he'd picked clean. His poor sallow cheeks had never gotten their color back since he'd been sick. She gave him a baked apple from the icebox.

"Tootsie, I'm sorry—"

"I'm sorry. I—" He made a face. "I hate to be a fall guy for imbeciles who keep buying. But Ainsley here though," he brightened up, "says this market can't last."

Maybe he would win on down? But—"You're what I care about, not the market"—Naomi virtuously restrained herself.

"Yeah," Tootsie moodily dug into the apple, "the market's only what I care about."

So she'd said the wrong thing anyway.

But Wednesday night the market was lower and sure enough Tootsie, the card table and the notebooks were in the sun parlor again.

"You won on down!"

"What a mind." But he wasn't upset, thank God. "Get a drill and I'll engrave it on you that I sold out. . . . Hah, still she doesn't believe me." He left her standing with her armful of bundles—could it be true, could she bank on this happiness?—and brought in his portfolio. He smirked, "Paralysis set in?" laid her groceries on the sofa and waved a receipt. "The average was off eight points today—with Kaye in U.S. government bonds!"

Did Naomi plaster kisses on Tootsie till he laughed "Okay okay—" What a wonderful evening it became, with them facing each other across the table long after supper was over, reveling in the details of Tootsie's moves yesterday. Any sap could sell when the market was slipping. He'd sold on the upswing! The laws of business and credit hadn't yet been repealed! Loan on demand to every damn fool in America and what can your credit structure do but disintegrate? Of course eight points was like spit in the ocean, but it would grease the toboggan he'd bet his bottom dollar.

Naomi—"Don't bet your bottom dollar"—was exhilarated enough for a joke.

"Don't worry kid," Tootsie nipped her cheek.

Her luck to be having her period!

And by the time her period ended stocks were climbing and Tootsie was so bad-tempered you couldn't go near him. He muttered, "Maybe I got out prematurely," words like ice on Naomi's heart. Don't ask her whether he had gotten back in, she wrote to Ma. He was so rumpled, waxen, that you feared for his life let alone questioned him. Sundays he stayed in his pajamas all day poring over his investment magazines and newspapers. So far he had left the bankbooks alone, but— Still when Ma advised her to quietly put the bankbooks in a safe place, she let Ma know that the way Murray looked she was not taking back bankbooks and please stop nagging her! The stock market went down, up, down—who knew where it went? Naomi only knew that the market was her hell on earth. Pregnancy? It would have to be like the Gentiles and Virgin Mary. The one good thing she could say about the stocks was that they made her so miserable she hardly cared business at the warehouse was falling off sickeningly.

She quit buying the evening paper. Why throw out three cents a day, fifteen cents a week, sixty-five cents a month to torture yourself? You couldn't help sneaking glimpses on the bus and the trolleys, and the chilly October night she caught this tag end of a headline **WALL STREET!** her teeth began chattering and her legs went so weak she was sure she must have contracted pneumonia and wouldn't reach home alive. And before, half dead, she could slip her key in the lock, Tootsie threw the door open with a grin of pain that shocked her out of her stupor.

"Tootsie, what's the matter?—"

"Haven't you heard? The Wall Street wizards are all kaput!" He shook those headlines like a person gone crazy, so it wasn't pain, it was the other extreme. "A sixteen million share crash—" he kissed her, he would have kissed anyone then. "Tell me, did I call it? Did I unload just about at the peak last month after all? When it took guts to unload? Did I murder 'em? My big shot broker jumped out of an eleventh story window today—ha ha!"

He rolled his eyes and even crumpled himself up on the floor imitating the broker God forbid. But who could rejoice any more? Tomorrow you might not get a word out of him. It had her empty, his Wall Street. And he was supposed to avoid overexcitement.

"Oh Tootsie, what's the good of it, that's only today. . . . Oh stand up Tootsie—"

He kept staring along the green and tan carpet swirls.

"Tootsie!"

His hand was like lead.
"Tootsie Tootsie Tootsie—breathe Tootsie, breathe darling!"

With Naomi in a state of collapse a Lucy somebody telephoned Golda long distance and Leah telephoned Limpy. A glance at her husband's drop-jawed expression and Carrie signed on over the bedroom extension. Lucy's husband had gotten Tootsie to the undertakers', but— His name was Murray? Very well brother—Murray, who'd led their sister through six years of hell and finished by pauperizing her, Leah would be pardoned for saying. Henny and she must have been pikers among yesterday's losers in comparison to . . . Murray. Don't ask her how much Henny and she had lost, Henny'd spared telling her. But if death excused everything, fine, Murray was excused. Naomi was her concern. The poor kid was beyond deciding even what to do with the body. The funeral service was tomorrow in the synagogue Murray'd been attending since the first heart attack. But should Naomi bury him in Chicago or send him back to New York? If possible a Jew should be buried the day after he dies, that's what Naomi sobbed Murray would have wanted. Only how could Naomi leave him at the ends of the earth? Who'd visit him? Obviously she'd send him back. It did seem cruel to be put away in a strange place and forgotten, in spite of Mr. Dave Kaye's shouting at their mother over the phone, "She could murder my boy there, she can bury him here!" As it was Leah and Golda hated the idea of Naomi alone two more days till they could reach her. Kind as this Lucy was she was only a friendly acquaintance, Naomi had never mentioned her in the letters. Henny whose only regret was having but one life to lose for the family stood ready to hop an overnight plane to the kid, but a widow at a time was enough as far as Leah was concerned.

So—three or four birds to the stone—as soon as they hung up daredevil Carrie volunteered to pack a bag pronto and fly to Chicago.

Limpy gave her a look. "You also tired of living?"

"Why tired of living? Lindbergh flew the Atlantic and I can't handle the Appalachians with a chauffeur?"

With sales slow as they were, Carrie Lamps Inc. had to—and would—cut costs and not by layoffs alone. Carrie had made up her mind to install some kilns at West Street and Front Street and bake her own vases. The drag was that Limpy, she was beginning to fear, did not have a real business head. It would take him months before he'd come around to a jump like that. Who wanted, he argued, to get into the pottery mess? The eventual savings never would pay for the initial cost. What a crusher that would be to La Vine the potter from his main customer. And the papers forecast business improvement by spring anyway, etcetera etcetera. And till you nagged Limpy into self-preservation—maybe business would improve and maybe it wouldn't, and Levine was their worry?—you couldn't budge.

Poor woebegone Tootsie, she wouldn't be able to bring him back alive this time. Yet who ever heard of throwing an actual hemorrhage because your trades played a dirty trick and cleaned you out? Even Daddy Moishe the quitter for all his ranting against so-called fate and the capitalist system never ranted his blood pressure higher than a light whiny pink. However, she could keep Limpy away from his Chicago playmate. By long distance —she knew her Limpy—she could trim the fat and install kilns in Jericho to begin with. And in her spare time she could haul little Naomi out of the slough of despond a lot faster than that trip ordinarily takes.

The only flying she did that night though was underneath Limpy. It must have been the death in the family that affected him this way: desperate kisses, clingings, love mumblings. He might not be a Kid Lewis in business but he sure was a Manassa Mauler at pleasure!

Such a night and—since the lord and master must put his foot down and go—you had to concern yourself about ancient history girl friends? She Carrie B. Share would have her kilns in due course, Limpy would at least pass out pink slips in Jericho, and, after all, Naomi was his bereaved sister. Herself, she wouldn't grow bored where she was, even apart from West Street. Nowadays a girl read the market reports mainly for entertainment value, but what you studied was the political news, those dry subway and highway items. After bridge at Hizzoner Rob Ward's or the Mr. and Mrs. Alderman Salomons' or right in your own living room on Central Park West, Justice Ward would corner you to plead his lost cause and, if questioned, would impatiently toss off little tips that could give you the edge in a juicy real estate deal. The faithful dog Rob also sprouted complimentary boxes—how did he come upon them you wondered—for the *Follies*, the *Scandals*, the fights, and Simone Ward would invite her and Limpy (why do you suppose the Shares were so privileged?) or her alone if Limpy was at a lesson or concert. With Limpy in town the last thing Carrie needed was follies, scandals and fights as a threesome with Rob the man in the middle. With Limpy out of town it was different, should she happen to be at loose ends after sending the monsters to the land of Nod full of giggles over her tough Little Red Riding Hood whose favorite repast was wolf soufflé.

Carrie only envied Limpy the ride in that elongated tin lizzie with wings taking off into a smeary sky above Newark Airport.

In the end, as Danny told Sydelle long distance from Midway Airport, he could have let Carrie go. Noise and shaking aside the trip was no worse than a country road in an automobile. But what should he have done, stayed home to wait for news of a plane crash?

"Still—" Sydelle said.

You barely could hear her through the static. What, "Breath's pollution?"

"I said death," she sang out, "could be a solution."

"You mean for us, suicide?"

She did not mean suicide. In Chicago, where Danny was now and she wished she were or he weren't, Art and Professor Brick had gone with the University Orchestra to give a concert in Springfield during a Christmas vacation and the bus ran off the road in a snowstorm. That news had kept Sydelle frantic until she'd heard there had been no injuries. But now—

"The hell with that," Danny said.

Not that he didn't understand even actual spouse murderers. Sure you could always leave—except that you couldn't. As it was his thoughts were rotten enough. Was it Carrie's fault that he'd married too soon? Jesus Christ, she'd made him, she'd made the business, and no two kids had ever drawn a better mother than Carrie.

Danny shipped Murray home on the first freight east. He'd suggested sending the coffin by air but Naomi'd given a desolate shrug. "How can I? He was afraid of heights." And nutty as that remark had seemed, Danny'd been somehow deeply touched by it. Thursday he picked up Leah at Union Station, and in Jericho that afternoon he laid off half the crew, very pleasant. But it had to be done, and—again Carrie'd been right—should have been done months ago. The same day he negotiated a new lease for six months at 15 percent lower rent from those Berstoff bastards by threatening to close the warehouse altogether and Berlin's acceptance with a few face-saving threats of his own did Danny's heart good. Then a quick factory management course for Radic the foreman, get Naomi's furniture on the interstate van, and no reason to stay in Chicago. Certainly Danny was only too damn eager to board that Twentieth Century with his sisters on Saturday.

Instead he wasted a week running down every wheels, kilns and pottery supplies outfit in the metropolitan area. Nights he didn't spend at Concert Hall missing Sydelle he put in at his hotel over teeth-gritting estimates of labor, material and operational costs. Usually he was the fastest pencil alive at this sort of work, but now arithmetic mistakes constantly had him clutching his head and backtracking. Carrie was always right, but this time she was wrong.

But Danny still didn't pack his bag. It took a full day conferring and rechecking numbers, but Radic who was nobody's fool agreed in the end that tacking on a pottery operation with business in a slump was tantamount to cutting your throat.

Then for Danny's trouble—go figure women—in New York Carrie gave him a queer look and said, "All that bother," as if he'd been away playing hooky!

21

NEVER UNDERESTIMATE THE HONESTY OF A LIMPY. BEcause Carrie did she had this back-breaker she'd wished on herself, shutting down Jericho. Yet how could a girl have believed that his lonely hours out here last November really had been spent doping out kilns, even if confirmed by her manager Radic? So she'd dragged herself to Chicago by train— And there too, Limpy'd said absolutely no to flying. Was that the lighthearted playboy attitude?

From Union Station Carrie'd checked into the Drake, glanced at the view of the beach and Lake Michigan (very nice if you hadn't just left your own private seashore), checked the Chicago directory and . . . no Arthur Fields! In such times with a hubby a schoolteacher Limpy's little mistress of scales moves to the suburbs? What goes on? Carrie phoned the University and Arthur didn't teach there any more, hadn't taught last term either. So what do you know, there hadn't been any mistress, scaly or otherwise, and all Carrie had to do was what she'd talked Limpy out of: put in time in Chicago and Jericho with a sad-faced crew to be laid off, merchandise and fixtures to be disposed of, machines to be sold or sent east by truck.

With Front Street emptied for the rats both long-tailed and named Berstoff Realty—might the latter also fold up and soon—Radic thought he'd try auto repairs, folks were sticking to old cars nowadays, if they could afford gas. The pair of Hunky laborers Carrie'd kept on to help close shop were pretty down in the mouth though, even with the two weeks' bonus she passed to all hands. Cheer up, she told the poor guys, something was bound to come along. Anyhow you couldn't beat weather like this. The lake frisked under little clouds drifting across a perfect blue outside of a smudge here and there.

But the sky was clear because most of the refineries to the north were shut down. Last night in her cab back to the Drake from her dinner with Dove the lawyer and his bright-eyed canary of a little woman, she'd seen men huddled asleep under some drive near the river like bundles of old clothes—and in a bone-gnawing drizzle that made you glad you'd brought your raincoat along even though it was summer.

Now, from the trolley regular guy Carrie hopped with Radic and the two new out-of-work working stiffs, you had the full benefit of a crawl past closed factories, gravel piles with a steam shovel sometimes dug in askew to stand rusting, and hovels in sharp sunlight with an occasional back-country type staring or chewing a toothpick.

What could possibly come along with that incompetent in the White House if you lived to be pushed around? Selling apples on corners?

Recently La Vine the potter asked for a quarter of an hour of their time at West Street and he was in such bad shape he announced himself to Riva Wartels as Levine. Then he offered them a drowning man's proposition. Advance him cash for the next three months' orders and he'd make them vases at an 18 percent discount. Carrie, Limpy and Naomi had glanced at each other. They'd already cut their sales staff to Gnopf and Jacobson, gotten rid of most of the paintresses, brought the rest upstairs to where they used to be and put the second floor up for rent with no takers, sold trucks at a loss, and, with Naomi's cute little nose back at the grindstone you couldn't see for her papers—that kid's desk never heard of depressions—kept Ezra's gargle Wartels and let the other girls go. In February Gnopf and Freddy had whipped up a small froth of orders and you could almost take stock in the Washington prosperity bulletins. But the froth subsided to a simmer, and now the pot was barely lukewarm. What little profit could still be sucked out of the West was being eaten up by the Jericho plant, simple economy told you ship direct from New York. Yet with all the economy who could guarantee a next order? As to La Vine's, it couldn't be shakier.

Limpy'd said, "Harvey, if we had cash to spare I'd lend it to you."

Levine had given a sick nod. "That's what the banks say."

"Move your ovens downstairs here," Carrie'd joked, "we'll put you on the payroll."

Levine's old baby face'd sagged still more dejected. "I wouldn't wish them on you."

For Carrie with her half a million in bonds, her thirty grand interest on bonds, her property along the route of the proposed Bronx subway extension, and Homestake Mining she'd bought big in lately because with bankruptcies wherever you turned and low costs and low prices what was as good as gold if not gold, the thrill was gone in the lamp business. She'd even advised Limpy let nature take its course right down the drain, buy up some good cigar stores instead, or combined drug and cigar. People smoked themselves silly and got themselves sick depression or no depression. The scholar'd paused in his reading to shoot her his iron glance. He'd thought she was kidding and you had to take care what you said to him about the business situation these days. Once he actually went so far as to blow off steam to her Carrie B. Share about the infallible Raisin! Raisin the aristocrat, when he was visiting her and her mother, had said never mind the five million who did not work while she could sell her beautiful bindings to the elite and since you produce shoddy goods why surprise if at last they are not wanted. Whereas, Limpy foamed, works of art were in the highest demand?

You hated to admit it, but Raisin might have something there: no depression for Cadillacs.

At the Intercity Bus Terminal Radic—that guy had spine—simply said "Goodbye missus," but the two hopeless ones wished Carrie luck.

Yet the same sun that lighted misery shone on plush suburbs on the way to Chicago, mansions from modest ten room to palace, with pink columbine and white iris to match the cheeks of well-fed kiddies racing up well-trimmed lawns. These were the citizens our President the great engineer engineered a chicken in every pot and two cars in every garage for. They bought whatever they wanted, not only six rolls with seeds for a nickel. Limpy the milk wagon horse knew when to go and when to stand still but his blinders screened the sad fact that in lamps cheap was dead. The market was this invisible type in there somewhere behind the hedges and elms, the luxury trade and the higher the price the better they liked it. Maybe she actually would give Harvey Levine a warm home at West Street for himself and his ovens, provided he could bake a fine porcelain. For the hand details she'd hire a real artist or two, no Raisin amateurs. The quality outlets she already had, like Vandervaart's, Van Vecht, Bier. So let's make Limpy a genius and try 'em with quality instead of alleged loss leaders. And if he flopped, let him at least flop in style.

How was that for an idle hour's achievement?

At the La Salle Street terminal she phoned Midway Airport and reserved a place on a Transcontinental night flight, and at 5 A.M. in the pale green of dawn she was bucking over beautiful sleepy patchwork America.

Ride 'im cowgirl!

Waiting for the Messiah is an old Jewish custom, but when you get stood up don't cry too loud.

Still Danny waited for Sydelle and sweated in the Conservatory entranceway in a night like a steam box. Steady rain past the lamplights brought no relief from the heat, and of the fewer and fewer music students straying up the black shining street not a one came close enough to that goddam grace to be mistaken for her even from a distance. At the top of the hill when he turned, idiot, to gape for her in the other direction, mist thick as his wits curled along Riverside Drive and wiped out Grant's Tomb. From thirteen on he never could figure out women. Why try at thirty?

Art had insulted her, and finally, finally, she'd felt . . . not insulted, but slightly resentful. Koussevitzky commissioned Art to write a twenty minute piece to show off the Boston Symphony strings under the stars this summer. Danny had listened almost in despair at Sydelle's pride when she told him this. The Boston Symphony! Koussevitzky! Had Carrie ever expressed pride in her husband? Yeah in his looks, how he dressed and matters of equal import. Sydelle couldn't get over how crazy Dr. Koussevitzky was about the excerpt that Art played him on the piano. And much as Sydelle hated to leave Danny that long, she'd supposed there'd be no way out of her being with Art in Boston the week of his first major triumph. To her astonishment when the time came—"See, Danny, you've taught me to value myself a little"—Art supposed nothing of the sort. With hotel expense there and lesson fees here Art supposed she might as well stay in New York and take care of her three or four summer pupils since he'd be engaged in rehearsals mornings and consultation with Dr. Koussevitzky evenings about the next day's work, which would leave her at loose ends anyway. Then, Art supposed, she could come up Wednesday for the concert, Kulnikoff was driving, and would drive them back after the party in the summer house near Great Barrington.

That had been when Sydelle supposed that she couldn't come for the concert either, since she met her fifth pupil Wednesdays, Danny Share. "Oh he'll excuse you," to Art that had been a laughing matter and he'd disappeared to his studio. Well, she'd shown Art, or at least gotten a start on showing him, with Share the Boob—stood up Danny saw now—as pro tem beneficiary. Carrie and the kids were in Sandy Point for the summer, so Danny'd been in the city and free for Sydelle last Thursday and Friday. God had she been loving, giving him duet practice lessons at the Conservatory both nights, perspiring, wiping palms, laughing in the heat. Afterward on a Riverside Drive bench the kissing started that obliterated the park, people and the thick dark nap of the sky and river. Before it stopped he'd asked so as not to be a ninny, though—how was that?—yes was the last answer he'd wanted, if they should go to his house, or hers, or a hotel? "No dear," she'd said, "that would spoil my relationship with Art." Her "dear" though! The exaltation had stayed with him through the whole Sandy Point weekend. But Monday night Sydelle had been full of gloom, she didn't want to go downtown to eat, or to the Claremont Inn garden. She'd picked some dump near Columbia more a lunchroom than a restaurant and she smoked more than ate there. Wouldn't you guess, there'd been a call from Art long distance from Boston. When it came to stingy he matched Danny's sister Naomi so you knew he must have had something to get off his chest. Dr. Koussevitzky was chopping Art's score to mincemeat, and if not for Art's career he would have told the mighty conductor to . . . and Art had used an obscene expression. Then he'd asked her what time she and Kulnikoff were starting for Boston the next day and his silence had been grim after she said she had not made any arrangements with Professor Kulnikoff. In that case, Art had wanted to know what bus she was taking. Again she'd reminded him she was meeting Danny Share Wednesday. He'd told her never mind Danny Share, it was her damn wifely duty to be present in Boston when he premièred. Or—Art had suddenly had a non-musical inspiration—was there more to this than a lesson?

She'd felt her life turning upside down like in a nightmare. She didn't know who she wanted, what she wanted. She'd dropped into a muteness that she was famous for in her marriage. Then Art had taken back that remark, finished, "You be here," and added, "Speak, damn you." So she'd said goodbye, and put away her viola that she'd been practicing.

And after supper she'd said goodbye to Danny also, she had a headache, he needn't have bothered to bring along his music. She'd even told him he needn't walk her home, but he'd walked her, walked home gloom in a sultry gloom, and taken his own gloom home and tried to read but couldn't, in the heaviness of cretonned chairs and limp festooned curtains.

Then at West Street yesterday with Naomi studiously bent over invoices and twice as studiously eavesdropping, Sydelle phoned with the marching orders. Her father had bought an acre of cucumbers and borrowed a small truck that she was picking them up in, she'd call for Danny about noon. Yes, she drove. She'd driven Art and those precious satchelfuls of manuscript to Chicago in a 1916 Whippet which Art immediately sold there and she'd driven them back in a 1913 Model T Ford which Art sold here. Danny hadn't known that? Well he knew it now.

"But in this rain? You won't see."

"All the better. But if you don't want to—"

With Carrie away how could he? This depression had set him back ten years and what was he but a small family business again? But while there wasn't enough work to keep two bosses busy there was plenty for one, and he still never had a minute to catch a breath in. However, Sydelle had Art for refusals. Danny muttered okay and with no explanations to his sister—should he have said that was Glantz calling?—went back to pitch in ten times harder with Kreps at the lathes.

Very nice too later on saying so long for the day to Naomi, also without explanations. She just nodded embarrassed—and why shouldn't she be? Like father like brother. Yet a look at the truck driver in a beige party frock full of pleats between a black oilskin hat and galoshes with flaps open and your whole heart was here in the cab of her battered groaning prewar Reo truck.

"The dress?" Sydelle kept her eye on the splashing cobbles and city traffic ahead. "I put it on for you, even if I can't hope to compete with your usual driver."

But there was no competition: no Carrie, no boys, no Quality Lamps. Get away Honest John and you were perfectly comfortable.

In the wet dusk of the auto deck on the ferry Sydelle said suddenly, "That was your sister I spoke to, wasn't it? Is she still in mourning?"

"That's," Danny grinned, "what she told Abe Goldman."

His mother and Naomi were living together now a flight up from Leah on Washington Place, and Ma'd gotten Naomi down to meet this candidate in Leah's apartment. Abe was an insurance salesman from Henny's actuarial days, a good egg, steady, perfect for Naomi. He was nobody's Apollo but at the sight of her his face had lit up like the Fourth of July. Unfortunately the effect hadn't been mutual. He wore seventy-five-dollar suits but he was a bulky fellow with flat feet the army had made even flatter and his clothes never lay right.

"So she relapsed into grief," Sydelle commented.

"Yeah, she thought he was a gargle. And he called her up quite a few times after that too."

"Don't fear for Naomi—a new suit, a new suitor."

"Why not, after Tootsie?"

"And you?"

"My case isn't exactly the same."

"So?"

So what could you do but shrug, and—past dismal towns, marshes, fiery smokestacks with their sulphur stink, a sodden landscape where you reached out to wipe off the windshield when it became impenetrable—watch that dark intent profile as if every second were the last you were going to see of her. Besides everything else she was a good driver, without that touch of recklessness Carrie had—into Newark with frame houses, machine shops and rain-black gas tanks, and out into the country again to a truck farm west of the Oranges. The proud ex-farm boy dude took off his jacket and helped the farmer load bushel baskets of cucumbers to the open truck in a steady drizzle while the knockout in the party dress waited under the shed. "Bad weather for wives," the farmer deadpanned him, and Sydelle did look sort of somber.

Bumping away in the loaded Reo Danny twanged, "Bad weather for wives?" But she wasn't smiling. "Anything wrong, Sydelle?" And whatever was wrong—maybe that she hadn't gotten in her viola hours today?—she wasn't talking either. Let Art be offended. But she turned left at Route 17.

"The Holland Tunnel is straight ahead Sydelle."

"But your house, or my house, to lie down in," like an offer of medicine, "is to the north. I'm treating you—now you see how it is—like a husband, so you should be privileged like a husband."

"I'm privileged."

But he didn't feel privileged, he felt drained, limp, overwhelmed by this girl.

"Isn't it time," she said, "that we found out what our relationship means?"

"I thought," he tried to make light of it, but his voice came out a croak, "I knew what it meant."

"I've shocked you," she glanced at him.

"Sydelle watch out!"

Green leaves, white sky, slick black highway and a yellow Stutz roadster with dead aim on them careened, tires screeched, boughs splattered the windshield . . . and the Reo righted itself, shuddered and died next to the road that still had a cucumber or two rolling across it. The Stutz with a fist waving—"dumb bi–i–i–itch—" receded into the gray.

"You all right?"

Sydelle nodded.

"Sure?" Danny insisted.

Her eyes were moist, loving again, and again she nodded.

"Then I'll crank up?"

But the Reo was beyond cranking. In a pelting rain Danny puttered under the hood, where the water hose had burst in the excitement of being in the wrong lane and the gears seemed to be stripped. He looked up and there was Sydelle's tragic face behind him, tears mixed with rain. His hands were filthy but he touched a white handkerchief to that . . . God . . . beloved face and those tears. "Don't cry, we'll have it fixed. And," he winked, "there are still enough future sour pickles left to bring tears to the eyes and burn to the heart a lifetime."

"I almost killed you."

"A miss," filthy or not he caught her fingers, "is as good as a mile," and with a moan she collapsed against him.

He was holding her as excited as hell, comforting her, bringing her back to the cab, when a leer passing blared, "Why'n'ya get married and pull down the shade!"

Vermin with sayings.

The rest of the afternoon went watching rain splash in the mud in front of a cavernous garage in Millburn where the Reo was hauled and overhauled, and falling deeper in love if that were possible. In New York—what the hell, since they'd had the trip part of their honeymoon—he told her that there was still his house or her house, after she'd get rid of the truck. But Sydelle had said no and she'd apologized for her whole day's behavior, she didn't know what had gotten into her.

That though had been way back yesterday, more than twenty-four hours ago. Meanwhile, no doubt, she'd found out what had gotten into her, and the answer had not been Danny Share. She had an Art to insult her, not only to step on her but to kick her, and she was his doormat so naturally she would crumple up, in this case trundle along to Boston for the première.

Now the last students had wandered away from the Conservatory, the long wet hill was empty, and Danny's head hadn't been this sick since the good old Reisel days. The entrance lights of the Conservatory went out, apartment windows along the block were black with a yellow patch here and there. Plain enough, this was Wednesday okay, she'd changed her plans. In Boston the concert was surely over, Art was in the greenroom with the famous maestro, the fans and the decorative little woman. And dull Danny-o stared out from the edge of the rain. But Jesus if he'd had an appointment with her and dropped dead he'd have had his goddam corpse carried by so she wouldn't stand like an idiot waiting!

He separated himself from the building and, with his umbrella closed, tilted his throbbing forehead to the spray of rain. Art was a musician, Sydelle could be one whenever she wanted, Carrie—

Who'd hired La Vine at sixty a week and taken an oven off his hands for better than the bid La Vine would have gotten at his bankruptcy auction? Why La Vine practically kissed Carrie's skirts, his salvation he called her. And she'd found Iz Schwartz, pleased to the hilt as that guy was with himself his oily ringlets and his dark manly jaw, to paint the luxury line that she'd thought up. Schwartz was chockful of modern designs coarse enough for rich taste, plus a design on Naomi. Whenever he could he parked himself on her desk with, as Carrie said, a tape measure in one eye and an adding machine in the other. But as Carrie also said even Naomi wouldn't fall for a phony like that. Meanwhile Jacobson and Gnopf were already beginning to write high-priced orders for the phony's productions, despite the fact that cubes by Picasso himself, let alone by Iz Schwartz, were not to the impeccable Reisel's taste and that in his heart Danny agreed with his former paintress-in-chief.

Carrie was the real businessman.

And the ex-boy bard, what was he? A manual dexterity executive with a briefcase full of piano music the way Murray's used to be full of stock prospectuses.

Who'd expect to find a cab in the rain, especially up here in nowhere. But on his way to the subway damned if his imbecile feet didn't turn off at 123rd Street straight toward Sydelle's.

It couldn't be—but it was—Sydelle coming uphill in the black oilskin hat and raincoat, slowly with her head bent. Did his heart fill! She sensed someone and her lashes flicked up alarmed.

"You!"

She ran the few steps to him, kissed his lips, laid her hand on his chest.

"I tried to reach you, Janet died, Rhea's baby, my sister's, all of a sudden, she was so well after the last transfusion . . . I told you that. But you'd gone. . . . "

Your eyes welled, you thought of your own kids. But he drew her tight, held on to her even upstairs while she was unlocking the door, held her close in the apartment that he'd only seen empty and really didn't see now. She told him dear to take his damp things off but when he did she stopped him with "Not everything!" and came into bed wearing her step-ins. Yet she wanted the light on that he switched off and, when he said the light hurt his eyes, reached lithely across him anyway to switch it on.

"A headache, those poor eyes?" she leaned to kiss them. "From waiting for me . . . " And she was up to bring him aspirin and a compress, and water to drink. She lay down again, darkened the room, and took his head to her breast. "Sleep dear—"

"Some lover."

"Oh never a better!"

And never a girl like this that you could do no wrong for, that you woke up to with her slim willing body in the dark—though as far as that went no one had ever beat Carrie—with her kissing you and crooning "My marriage in heaven" when you made love to her, as often as you made love to her, "My marriage in heaven. . . . "

And she'd been worried she wouldn't suit him, a virgin all over again, the way she had been with Art. Slept with him before they were married? She laughed that pure laugh, like bells. You might say that she hadn't exactly slept with him in that sense for a year after they were married, which was what really had endeared Art to her. He was so determined on all of his rights, she'd never imagined he could have been so patient and understanding about her stupid incompetence with that one. Perhaps her difficulty had been physiological, but she'd been too shy to bring such a complaint to a doctor, especially not Dr. Jason she worked for then when the less spent the better and an employment incentive had been the free medical care—which meant that Dr. Jason prescribed aspirins free if you had a cold but you bought your own aspirins. Finally after a year of her stupid trying, Art had had a wife in more than name only.

Danny couldn't believe it.

22

THIRTY-TWO YEARS OLD, FULL OF LOVE, AND NAOMI HAD no one to give it to. Instead of babies a strap on a trolley through cold morning sunshine over the same Seventh Avenue stores, the same tenements, and for good measure some freak rubbing against you. If you told them stop it as Naomi foolishly had before she became accustomed to New York again, you got a "Hoity-toi, the riffraff's disturbing 'er," and ground against harder while the rest stared straight ahead. At least in Jericho you had a seat on the trolley and that anti-Semitic wolf Larsen from next door who sat next to you never actually touched you.

Ma, a great help, would say, "Take a taxi, I'll pay."

They thought God knows what, that Naomi was penniless. But how could she have shamed Tootsie he should rest in peace by telling the truth, that he died out of pure spite that everyone else lost and he won? Leah and Henny'd lost in the market, Danny said he'd lost, Carrie didn't say but she must have lost, while Naomi had this hundred and ninety-six thousand five hundred and forty-two dollars in the vault in bonds mostly, her joy and anxiety, with banks failing left and right.

The rubbing kept up and no matter how much you shifted he shifted with you. At . . . Twelfth Street—six blocks, and it felt like hours already—the trolley lurched and accidentally on purpose Naomi instead of his five cent thrills gave him her handbag rim in the stomach and before he could catch his breath a sugar water smile and an excuse me. So he stopped rubbing.

Depressing though, jabbing people, you felt ashamed for them and—God knows why—even more ashamed for yourself.

Iz Schwartz's next proposal, she was accepting.

There, she'd taken the leap—and why not? Only, did he love her for herself? Not even Ma knew about the bonds, so how could Iz? But Naomi was a partner drawing a hundred and fifty a week, and Iz's thirty-seven high as it was—too high she'd said when they hired him but her brother and Carrie insisted that you get what you pay for—was not much in comparison, so it could be the money. Still from the moment Carrie introduced them with an office wisecrack "If Mrs. Kaye says something you jump, she's in charge of your pay," Iz hadn't been able to take his eyes off Naomi, and he'd thought, he told her later, she was just the bookkeeper. And even if he hadn't thought that, matrimony had been anything but his object.

The . . . excitement . . . that made her gasp when he touched her breast and kissed her that first date in Crotona Park last summer she'd only experienced before with Jack Berger. Tootsie never had had such an effect on her. And right away Iz had sensed it and tried to drag her into the bushes. Naturally she hadn't let him. Then the dark eyes she'd only seen laughing had actually flashed under the arc lamp.

"Why did you insist on the Bronx, my neighborhood? Why the secrecy?"

"I'll tell you some other time."

"Never mind some other time. Where did you tell your husband you went—a kaffeeklatsch with the girls?"

"My husband's dead almost a year."

Iz had been stunned. He'd apologized he'd misunderstood. But she could take comfort that the altered circumstances had hardly changed his approach. "Then," the rugged face with the handsome dimpled jaw looked so cute and eager, "come—" he'd laid his jacket out on the grass in the shadows—"sit down here for a minute, as long as you're a widow."

"I'm not a merry one."

He'd grinned, "I'll teach you."

"I'm too old to learn."

"You'll never see twenty-one again?"

"Or twenty-two either."

"So you're twenty-three." He'd stood in front of her and tilted her chin. "Perfect. I'm twenty-six."

"Perfect for what?"

"I'll tell you some other time."

But a woman in her thirties doesn't need every word spelled out. He'd meant perfect for marriage. So shouldn't it have been reassuring that he'd followed up with a seduction campaign? One night he'd gone so far as to rent a room in the Concourse Plaza Hotel to take her to, he'd shown her the key.

"I beg of you, Cutie. That's the cream of three weeks' hard labor I've got invested there!"

You thought of Iz and you smiled.

Finally on a lower deck bus date with waves of rain blowing up Fifth Avenue and plastering dead leaves over the sidewalks, Iz had sat so moodily next to her in his broad-shouldered Saturday night overcoat with his arms crossed on his chest that she was sure—not that she could have helped it—that she'd said no once too often. He said, "Okay, I give up," and did her heart sink. She missed him already.

Then he'd said, "So let's get married."

"Why?" she'd heard herself say.

"Why! Because I've tried everything—cards, dames and horses— and all I can concentrate on is our goddam secret dates. That's why."

She'd felt so wonderful she'd just smiled between the white mansions slipping by on the right and the dark park on the left.

"Next week," Iz had gone on as if somebody were dragging it out of him, "you'll come up to Vyse Avenue and eat my mother's pot roast—she might as well face the worst."

"Worst? You have some nerve, not that I'm coming."

"Yes worst, the loss of her meal ticket, her sonny boy—and to a strange woman yet. But at least the cloud'll have a small silver lining. She'll brag to her friends her Izzie, that smart boy, married into a business."

"Dream on. And if there wasn't a business?"

"What do you think I am, a gold-digger with muscles? You'd dance to here comes the groom anyway. But there is a business, so what should I do Cutie, drag you upstairs in the rain and throw you off the top of the bus to get rid of you?"

Still he'd said that, marrying into the business, and she wished that he hadn't. If only you could discuss it with someone.

She and Ma had Reisel and Gittel to Washington Place for supper, with Gittel all rouge and powder—Ma called her a real American lady—bragging how she was being chased by a retired Post Office official, a widower who owned a house near her in Kingsbridge. Reisel—"Mamá, sometimes I think you were more sensible when you were crazy"—was very annoyed and, with Gittel and Ma in the living room, during the dishwashing Reisel commented that if that widower was not careful he might find himself with a second wife, a true romance based on aged lust. Who wanted to hear that sour stuff? So Naomi'd kept her mouth shut about her own romance based on— She didn't know what it was based on.

Whatever it was based on it went without saying that the family would detest any boy she found appealing—David, Phil, Jack, whoever it was. Iz brought up some vases to Saul Kreps in machines, looked in at the office, saw Carrie, winked to Naomi—he hadn't found out yet Carrie had eyes in the back of her head—and disappeared. So, "He's good at what I hired him for," Carrie had said, "but if I were you I'd steer clear of that four-flusher."

But that hulk Goldman of Leah's who still hadn't stopped pestering Naomi was a paragon, with his crazy droning about pure mathematics that he'd studied but loved too much to spoil by making a living at it, his bargain suits that bunched at the shoulders, and the wonderful insurance he sold for a secure future and a happy present with banks closing and people losing their money? Or Reisel's introduction Max Moskowitz would have suited them better with his beak and bald head and two grown-up children of ten and twelve and his morose expression except when his eyes lit up and he bored you about his collection of leather books and his chain of shoestores. Carrie herself had introduced Naomi to one of her lawyer friends, a Sidney Bellsey with nice dark eyes. But his craziness was to quiz you on current events—Bolshevik treason trials, German fascists—as if you were in seventh grade. Naomi had stopped buying the papers because she couldn't bear to read about bank failures, so she'd failed.

Such marvels, and she should steer clear of Iz? Instead she kept him a secret. There was a . . . naughty pleasure in addressing Iz with a business face during business hours, while he called her Mrs. Kaye. Luckily Carrie came less and less to the office, not that she was needed. For Naomi business was fine, better than with out-of-town factories that you escaped from by the skin of your teeth, even if you did draw less now. With a cook and a governess—Naomi's kids wouldn't have any governesses, not for a second—what could Carrie be doing with her free time? Leah'd asked and got a joke in reply: real estate and securities. What real estate, what securities? The stock market insanity was over, thank God. Did Carrie mean the half-empty West Street loft next to the factory and the bargain tenement in the Bronx she'd bought after the crash? But think of Danny and his mysterious early departures from work. Some mystery, he was running to that woman who was brazenly chasing him. At the office you trembled to pick up the phone she called so often. Embarrassing, but let Riva Wartels answer and the calls would be the talk of the factory. And Danny's stone face instead of an explanation, if only a lie. But why should he explain, if Carrie was up to the same kind of monkey business?

Some advisers!

But look—the identical Seventh Avenue beanery with a poverty menu in enormous black letters filling the window—the trolley car hadn't moved an inch all this time. Ahead all you saw were straphangers stretching to see. The man next to her shrugged.

"Another bank closed or something."

Naomi went cold in spite of her winter coat and the steamy car full of bodies. There were half a dozen banks at Fourteenth Street, but she knew in her bones hers was the failed one. She squirmed, she wriggled, she pushed herself off that trolley car and ran the two blocks as fast as these damn long skirts would let her.

Oh no no no no no.

It was her bank on the corner that the milling fedoras herded by cops were tilted to, overflowing the sidewalk and tying up honking clanging traffic. Naomi wormed her way through the crowd, and a shrivel-faced man with his mouth twisted said to her, "They can't, my life's savings—" What could his life savings have been with a frayed collar ear-high in the cold? Her hundred and ninety-six thousand plus years of premiums were in that building, thanks to her sister-in-law Carrie.

Why had Naomi let herself be talked into going along to Carrie's—oh did it hurt, she had an actual pain in her chest—only a week ago? Why hadn't she made up her mind then to marry Iz and gone to his mother's instead? Why? Henny with his sweet smile—he'd had his arm across Leah's shoulders after eight years of marriage—had opened his overcoat and told Naomi sure, get ready, they'd wait. Why wasn't it her luck ever to meet someone like Henny only single? Plain as he was you forgot the plainness. He was handsome, even with glasses, when he smiled like that.

At her brother's the visit had turned out completely senseless. As usual Ezra giggled, ran away from Naomi and the quarter she held out, and hid God knows where. Teddy joined in, cut off Naomi at the playroom, raised his chubby palm and ordered her, "Gimme money Auntie." He was cute with his red hair, freckles and mischievous expression, and of course she loved him too. But Ezra seemed frailer, your arms ached to squeeze him—if you could catch him. She felt cheated giving Teddy a whole quarter—a nickel would have been plenty for him—and more so when he blared out a laugh and also ran away when she tried to gather him up. He came back though, rattled his piggy bank with her lost quarter in it, and dragged her by the finger into the playroom to show her how he kicked Ezra's electric trains off the tracks.

"Train wreck!" he announced.

But she had him playing nicely with that warm little hand in hers so she could press his forefinger on the right buttons to work the track switches, when she heard Carrie inside " . . . in savings banks?"

Naomi immediately stood up—"Hey where do you think you're going!" Teddy wailed and gave the trains a good kick—and she rushed into the living room in time to hear " . . . fail too," from Henny.

"Sooner or later," Carrie smirked, "everything fails. The idea is to be elsewhere when it happens."

Naomi had cried out, "Savings banks fail?"

Carrie had laughed. They'd been discussing high grade utilities, not savings banks. For Naomi's quarters Carrie assured her savings banks beat piggy banks any day. And what hadn't Carrie known about savings banks' coulds and couldn'ts: insured and uninsured mortgages, common stocks, corporate senior securities. What a relief! Naomi had hardly minded Ezra cuddled on Ma's lap reading Ma about Hugh Matson from some baseball book while Ma kept exclaiming "You don't say!" Who needed Ezra? Naomi'd have her own babies to cuddle. Then she'd forgotten herself and worried out loud about her vault in the Chase National Bank. Everyone stared, she was supposed to be broke.

"Vault?" Leah said.

"For Grandma's diamond earrings," thank God she'd had that much presence of mind, "that Reisel gave me. I've never had my ears pierced."

Did they laugh. "Don't rush your virgin ears," Carrie'd said. "Even if Mr. Rockefeller's bank fails, his vault won't fail without dynamite."

If.

She'd been so eaten up by Carrie's "if" that she hadn't slept that night. In the morning she'd worn her shabbiest clothes and a kerchief the way she always did to the bank so robbers wouldn't get ideas seeing her. First she stopped at the Italian's to buy a nickel's worth of soupgreens. Then at Chase National on Carrie's say-so she'd stuffed her shopping bag and, with the soupgreens on top for camouflage, she'd trudged like an old lady to . . . Fourteenth Street, oh God, to here, and with silly superstitious confidence on account of the name Bank of the United States though she'd known it was just a name, she'd rented a large box for her United States bonds and Grandma's earrings. Why couldn't they have kept her out last week instead of today, when cops guarded the pillars and bronze doors and didn't know anything about vaults?

She glimpsed traffic moving again.

But she couldn't stand another streetcar, she'd lost one nickel already, she'd lost everything, and she didn't feel well besides. She pulled herself back to Washington Place through sick cold sunlight that cut into you like a surgical knife, and if Ma's face was a reflection of hers—who knows?—this might be the end of Naomi. And who cares? Now she could understand Tootsie in the hospital—why live?

"Go down to Leah, phone Danny I won't be in, Ma." Dully she told Ma what had happened. " . . . So I threw away . . . Grandma's earrings."

"Earrings so what?" Ma held her close. "There'll be weddings and funerals without them."

Ma was so good, always had been, Naomi was tempted to tell her the real trouble. But how could she? Chase hadn't failed. Tootsie's shame had become her shame entirely, and the price Tootsie had paid she was about to pay.

Ma put her to bed, Ma soothed her forehead, Ma gave her messages not to worry about earrings, Danny said her earrings were as safe as the gold in Fort Leavenworth. Furthermore Carrie's friend Ed E-square Evans was on the State Senate Banking Committee and Danny would ask Carrie to speak to him. Carrie'd let loose this catastrophe on Naomi. She might well speak to him. Only, if you had to speak to Banking Committees, what chance was there?

Just the same Danny was a good kid too, he meant well.

But it was all over with his sister Naomi, she knew these symptoms: chest pains, weakness, a catch in your breath—Tootsie had had all of them.

Count on Carrie. At the Wards no sooner was the dinner party adjourned to the living room than she was surrounded by her politicians and lawyers: Rob Ward himself, that Sid Bellsey Danny'd liked enough to pressure Carrie into introducing to Naomi, with—as Carrie'd predicted—no takers, and Ed E-square Evans. And Carrie knew how to gradually concentrate her fire until the group melted down to her and E-square alone.

"Don't be alarmed Daniel." Sophie Evans who never drank materialized with a cocktail in hand. "Carrie knows Ed would make love to a snake if it stood still long enough. . . . Why the wonder," she smiled up like a withered blonde child, "in your beautiful blue eyes? My disloyalty, in violation of the division of labor in the E-square family, Ed complaining and I listening laceratedly? That's changed, Daniel, since the divorce proceedings."

"Divorce!"

Sophie patted the drawn skin of her throat. "Isn't it time, dear?"

He supposed it was, in spite of their children who were his fellows' playmates. Only just before at the table E-square's compliment to Simone Ward on the meal had been that his wife as Simone knew couldn't prepare food like this even for company, and the senatorial resonance had been very loud in a silence that fell before Simone gave her cook the credit. To which E-square had imperturbably insisted, "Nevertheless." Rich as he was he wouldn't hire Sophie a cleaning woman let alone a cook but of course that hadn't been mentioned.

"For myself I can't see divorce," Danny said.

"And why should you?"

"That's right," he lied. "But I must say I can't blame you."

"I'm blameless, Daniel. Ed wants the divorce."

"Ed!"

Ed with a career of humiliating his wife was helping himself to a divorce while Danny took Sydelle to hotel rooms? In the Madison Square Hotel lobby after Danny'd signed the register Sydelle had touched his arm. "Don't be angry, we don't have to go up—" Whatever he'd been he hadn't been angry, or if he had been, at himself not her. But he hated those check-in clerks, he hated the Chicago addresses he put in the book to make the stop look legitimate, though—don't ask him why—he always wrote his own name, he hated the luggage he bought and threw away later because what do you do with it, take it home? Also, since he couldn't face staring down the same room clerk twice, were there enough hotels in New York for a lifetime of adultery?

Still more detestable, upstairs with her in his arms he never wanted to leave.

Then in his own bed Carrie'd pull her nightgown up to the armpits, lay that hot voluptuous body against him, and if he hesitated grabbing her the stopwatch hadn't yet been invented to measure so short an interval. Meanwhile Sydelle once went weeks with all sorts of subterfuges before she gave in to Art. "How faithful," she'd despondently smiled at Danny, "can a faithless woman be?" And faithful to him she'd meant, not to her husband, Danny's hotel hopper, his coffee consumer, his shiverer in the cold on winter nights when there were no concerts and the movies were so rank you hesitated to go in even for warmth.

So Danny didn't believe Sophie.

"That's why," he challenged her, "you're here together tonight?"

"I have to cleave to him especially now, or with his legal abilities he might prove desertion and save himself the support of the boys too. He has every other justification for divorce."

"Oh come on, stop it Sophie!"

"Daniel," she pressed his hand, "I never dreamed you sympathized so. . . . But it's common knowledge. A bad housekeeper, censurable cooking, a squanderer, if I had to support myself I couldn't qualify as a servant . . . and Charles and Ed Jr. keep getting left back in school."

Danny glanced with disgust—"Also your fault?"—across the room of talkers and laughers toward E-square with the charm turned on full blast for Carrie.

"Haven't you been told that my narrow pelvis squeezed their wits out at birth?"

"But they're bright. I've played with them."

"As Ed has not. Well, that he can't help, with six months in Albany, political functions, guest speeches on behalf of the underdog."

"Hypocrisy."

"No dear, he's sincere in those speeches. He won my heart with one of them at Vassar chapel before the war. Odd one's doom. Drenched with Poughkeepsie idealism as I was, I felt lazy that day, I didn't want to go to the chapel but my roommate nagged me to—and there was young Assemblyman Evans, the ex-football hero, fair, husky, a perfect Jew for an advanced-thinking Episcopalian young lady like myself: he looked Gentile and proved that Jews are like anyone else. Not that that fact impressed my father. Father took the estrangement with him to the grave. Anyway Edward—he hadn't yet multiplied his initials to become honest E-square on the square—appeared at Vassar, sincerely and winningly, almost just as you see him. He's not that much heavier, between golf and tennis. He lectured us rotten money, clothing and beau snobs about the promise of America, what we owed the unfortunate, privileges we had to renounce so every single person in this beautiful land would have a chance—no guarantees—just a chance. He brought tears to my eyes," she smiled wistfully up at Danny, she emptied her glass, "not for the last time I assure you. Even then, I wasn't among the radicals who ran down front to gush over him. I was shy, I hung back. He started the conversation—I was his type, and I'm still his type. He's dropping me for a reasonable facsimile ten years younger, Daniel. You know Dorothy Vincent."

"His secretary? For chrissakes. Does he think she'll take his guff?"

"I hope that she won't, but he has her converting to Judaism already. . . . Whew!" Sophie swiped at her pale hair. "The lifelong Sunday school girl—a drink and I'm drunk. Look at them tête-à-tête," Sophie craned raffishly toward the hubbub, "your wife and my pro tem husband. Daniel, do you suppose four can play at that game?"

"What game?" Danny showed her his stony blue stare. "Carrie's asking him for a favor for me."

Carrie said, "For the tenth time Ed, don't be a stinker. And how about your career?"

"Career, when I was the man three years ago and Farley and the boys put that mediocrity Roosevelt in the Governor's Mansion? Career, when the upstate Republicans swamped my direct unemployment relief bill, or when my bill for a hundred percent on the dollar to unemployed wiped out by failed banks isn't reported out of committee? I don't know whether I'll run next time round. Evans & Evans Attorneys-at-Law has more business than I know what to do with."

"And what'll you do with your abuse? Dorothy won't be a Sophie."

"Exactly—praise heavens. You've seen the shipshape office Dorothy keeps me, while that one over there no doubt slandering me to your husband ruined half of my twenty thousand dollars' worth of living-room furniture by the simple device of leaving the shades up every day to suntan the brocade and dry out the wood."

"That old junk? Maybe your great-grandmother ruined it."

"My great-grandmother was a frugal industrious immigrant woman—a Lower East Side pioneer you might say—who sent my grandfather to Columbia College in the teeth of the Gentiles and set him up in the law."

"So, a perfectly nice woman like Sophie, she gave up family and money —and even converted to Judaism for you— and you're ditching her because a few crow's feet've set in due to you."

"Let her be grateful to me until her dying day. Judaism's the only sane faith—good works while you're alive."

"Like you, huh?"

"Why not like me? She loathed that father of hers, virtually pulled me into bed with her just to spite him. The great James Margeson Jr., chairman of the board. His Peerless Motors was one bankruptcy I enjoyed reading about even if it was posthumous, James Peerless Margeson Jr.! Not a penny did I see out of that marriage. Maybe if I dared now the way I dared then I would be in the Governor's Mansion. I've suffered more than the Talmud demands with that—" His eyes flicked: Limpy was chatting with Simone Ward—"that . . . wherever she is."

"Ed, you're marked for Gehenna, you and your doxies together."

"Well if they end up there too," Ed lumped his cheek, "it won't be Gehenna."

"But I'm your redeemer."

"Svelte brunettes aren't exactly my type, but I'm willing to have a go at it to please you Carrie."

"The supreme sacrifice I would never ask. This is a small good deed Ed."

"Deep down so I feared."

Carrie presented the saga of her sister-in-law in bed three days dying of the late husband's heart disease and a Bank of the United States vault. "We asked the big New York banks to save the Bank of the United States," E-square was still burned up over it, "but the Bank of the United States is known as a Jewish outfit, so they decided to let it fold. Nice, eh? However, your sister-in-law will be able to go to her vault without favors as soon as the dust settles."

"By that time it may settle on her. Already in her weakened condition she's engaged herself to a frisky type like you Ed but minus the brains."

"What's she got in the vault?"

"Grandma's earrings."

"I see." E-square did not smile as he scribbled himself a memo. "She'll have them tomorrow."

So at the wheel crosstown Carrie could claim that she'd saved Naomi for a fate worse than death—lover boy Iz. Had Carrie ever mentioned that Iz had made his play for her when she hired him, with an "I guarantee satisfaction" that had sparkled with meanings? Yeah, pretty depressing to Danny's mind and the more so after the seven long years of Murray.

"On the bright side however," Carrie went on, "hard as I tried to dissuade Ed from divorce, Sophie is as good as rid of him."

"Ed can pull that," Danny said, "and sleep nights?"

Carrie laughed. "And not alone either."

Even after Naomi transferred her bonds and Grandma's earrings back to Chase National from that rotten Bank of the United States, she let Iz go on thinking she'd lost her whole savings small as they were and he twinkled at her keep smiling—she had him. Then at the Vyse Avenue interrogation by Mother Schwartz Naomi simpered she was just a forty-five a week courtesy partner in Quality Lamps, and Iz passed that test too. He reached Naomi a "Shake partner!" across the dining table spread of garlicky chicken in a tiny room cluttered up with a sofa, carved chairs, a cut-glass cabinet and immense shiny plants that looked as if they could eat you alive. "I'm a courtesy partner too. My ex-boss to be," he pinched a grudging smile out of his mother's hard little cheek—that Iz could soften a stone—"scoops up fifteen of my twenty-five every Friday before I can so much as yell help." So if he was a gold-digger it didn't take much gold to satisfy him.

On the subway down to Washington Place Naomi reminded him that he'd told a lie about his pay.

"A white lie's okay, Cutie. If my ma knew my real pay either she'd be nagging me to death for more money—she used to wring poor Papa dry, he should rest in peace—or else," he kissed Naomi with a flick of the tongue and she wished that they were married already and on the way home to bed, "I wouldn't even have the price of a Merry Widow."

"Me you mean?"

"For you, none other."

He spoke so nicely too! You could tell he'd been to college and forget Leah's the School of Design wasn't a college, Leah was forever defending Henny's bachelor's degree though Henny himself made fun of it. Leah must have found plenty of satisfaction in Tootsie's finally giving up school.

At the end of Naomi's first day back at business from her United States Bank sickness Iz had hustled her downtown and for all her coaxing he wouldn't say where—a Nassau Street jeweler's office. She'd been pleased, yet what about the expense? She did have an engagement ring.

"Where?" Iz had been so funny examining her hand. "Light must be bad, I can't see it."

He'd been reluctant—not that she'd listened to him—even to let her trade in her half-carat diamond that he called Tootsie's splinter. Was she going to the other extreme and marrying a spendthrift? But the stone he chose wasn't that extravagant and this time she didn't have to hide her finger from people, like with Tootsie.

So—"That's a material improvement already"—Leah had to be smart.

"What do you mean material?"

"Why simply that it's twice the size of poor Tootsie's—that's a very good sign."

"Who needs signs?" Henny said. "Iz is a nice guy."

But that was nice Henny saying so, no wonder Naomi still had half a crush on him. You should have heard her brother and Carrie when they got her alone upstairs with Ma—"Have you thought twice kid? Are you sure?" —until Ma stuck her two cents in.

"She's sure, leave her alone, she'll manage him."

"Manage him at what?" Naomi said.

"Never mind, he's a likable boy. He just reminds me of someone."

You didn't have to ask who. Ma meant Papa. Why? Because when they told the family the wedding date—the third night of Chanukkah, Christmas Eve actually—Iz teased her that Judas Maccabeus freed the Jews and Isidore Schwartz was putting his head in the noose to celebrate? Or because at the factory he understood a smile got more out of the paintresses than a frown? A lot the family knew about him and the new wedding band he'd insisted on, engraved *Cutie Love Iz.* Naomi'd always loved Pa—she still felt sorry for him in spite of the touches (you paid with interest for a few cost-price hats) and the rest of it, stuck with a dumpy Bronx millinery since the downtown store failed and an ugly woman Papa had been silly enough to show her a picture of. But never would Naomi forget the humiliation, while Pa was squandering money, of her threadbare green winter coat when she was a girl. Pa was selfish, the exact opposite of Iz! Would she mind, Iz asked, since there was her forty-five a week and his forty and his ma's practical nursing paid only two or three dollars a day when she was lucky enough to get work, if he went on giving the old girl the premarital fifteen? The thought of supporting that hateful woman didn't fill Naomi with ecstasy, but where was the resemblance between Pa and Iz? That they were both good-looking men you couldn't help liking?

In three weeks she'd be safe in the West Bronx with nobody but her husband in the apartment and was she glad. To think that at first she hadn't wanted to live that distance from Ma, and in the same borough as her mother-in-law besides. The three rooms were cute with arched windows that gave Iz an inspiration for Spanish decor, and Hope Street was right off the Grand Concourse, classy, Iz said, God's country, fresh air, you could inhale not like downtown. His friends swore by the Bronx too, nice boys his age, and Ma Schwartz—Iz did make you laugh—would be thirty-five guaranteed minutes away by bumpy crosstown trolley car. But what had really decided Naomi, apart from the rent—less than she was paying even adding the third she'd chip in with Danny and Leah so Ma could keep the Washington Place apartment as to everyone's surprise and Naomi's relief Ma wanted to—was that you only had to go across the way to give birth in Eden Hospital, and that down the hill was Claremont Park with a playground right at the entrance.

To give Danny credit though, he said that Atlantic City on a four day honeymoon was ridiculous, she'd waste half of it traveling, she should take a week, two weeks. And he forced a check on her—separate and distinct, he said, from a wedding gift—for a good hotel on the ocean down there, not some boardinghouse. But—though Iz made her blush joking that on four days the blushing bride wouldn't see much of the boardwalk—Naomi said no, the office was still her responsibility and she'd picked Christmas Eve for the wedding just because then, with the holiday, she'd be away from business only a day and a half. She wouldn't tempt fate by saying it but after Richard would be born she'd be on a honeymoon for the rest of her life. And darn it, she was worrying already—suppose she didn't become pregnant on a full week's honeymoon, let alone two weeks? She'd have no excuse. Four days were plenty.

So was she embarrassed, phoning New York Sunday afternoon from their enormous room of bay windows at Haddon Hall auspices of Danny, over the glinting gray scary ocean that kept you snuggling into Iz's exciting arms, where she was. Iz—she mouthed Iz stop but she couldn't help smiling—tickled her armpit and stroked her stomach while she tittered to her brother that between bundled-up strolls, feeding the pigeons and souvenir shopping on the boardwalk, a string trio at luncheon—Haddon Hall served luncheon, not lunch: was Danny satisfied?—and dancing at night, she'd decided to stay a week extra after all. Danny said amen and stay longer. And Naomi heard herself giving in, without even a struggle, that she'd stay two full weeks.

Experienced as she'd taken for granted she was, she'd never imagined marriage could be like this. Iz made love to you and who thought about pregnancy, oh did you have other things on your mind! And in the quiet, with the ocean swishing like cars at Washington Place, Iz dozed off and she glowed. She was positive she was pregnant already, she could sense Richard there.

And Richard was there! In March Dr. Vogel called it official. And Iz? He gaped as if she'd sentenced him to the electric chair.

"But I thought you were at the controls Cutie!"

Did Naomi give him a look. She may have kept a few things to herself before they were married, but Richard was the one thing she'd made clear.

"I mean," Iz was flustered, "nobody said right off the bat—" He laughed. "I mean—"

"For me this isn't right off the bat."

"For chrissakes Cutie, who counts the other guy?"

"Do you want a divorce?"

"Aw Cutie—" the comedian tried to draw her to his lap in their streamlined living room with crazy abstract pictures he'd bought cheap at Henny's to match the kaleidoscope twill of the upholstery—"after all the trouble I went to furnishing and decorating?"

"And I gave up a houseful of furniture to my mother and let you. But this is no laughing matter Iz. If you have doubts—"

He knew where the door was, he'd covered it with a flaming red bullfight poster. She wasn't going to have any aggravation during her pregnancy.

"Who's the joker in the family," he caught her chin and smiled himself down to give her a kiss on the stomach, "me, you or this Johnny-come-lately? But tell me, will your courtesy partnership be courteous enough to send you the forty-five for watching a baby, or will Don Isidore have to quit the brother-in-law—much as I love Danny boy—and get a job that pays what I'm worth?"

"The forty-five should be your biggest worry."

"In that case Cutie, or should I say Mama—we better find a four room apartment. I don't believe in sleeping with kids under the age of eighteen."

Then just when she could feel Richard moving around, the bleeding began. Sparrows merrily chirped in the trees that shaded a playgroundful of tots and mothers and she crossed to the hospital not to have her baby but lose it. Iz—he wasn't so bright sometimes—tried to console her: Dr. Vogel said it would have been a girl anyhow.

Wouldn't she have loved a little girl anyhow? She would have called her Roslyn and loved her.

That was her May Day.

The second miscarriage was her Happy New Year, and she woke in Eden to Iz and his sullen profile against a sky iron as her heart. He stared out the window with his mouth creased and he breathed a long martyred sigh. After the operating room the night before had she forgotten to smile appreciatively for his consolation identical with last year's, that Dr. Vogel said it would only have been a girl? Or was she interfering with his Saturday afternoon card game? Either way she hated him, and a hospital had this advantage: shut your eyes and he wasn't there. Maybe Vogel was right and the girl had been lucky not to be born. Honestly, Naomi was so weak and heartsick, would bleeding to death have been so bad?

High heels clacked in. Carrie in mink reaching Iz a backhand slap on the stomach was veiled by Naomi's lashes. "What's the matter with you, Iz," Carrie said, "two in a row. You'd better start taking vitamins."

"Take? I can give and to spare. You want an injection?"

"Behave yourself in front of the poor girl's very ears."

Remind him and his voice went down to a whisper. "She's asleep."

"Like fun she is. . . . Don't hide from me, kiddo."

Naomi felt herself lovingly kissed and threw her arms around Carrie's neck and burst into tears.

"Why?" her sister-in-law rubbed noses with her. "Many a sleepless night you'll spend over Richard one of these days. What did your quack say?"

"That it's better to have a miscarriage than an abnormal child."

"And he's still your doctor?"

"Henny says that Vogel is very good."

"Henny finds excuses even for President Hoover. You have changed physicians as of the next pregnancy to Nate Barasch, my cousin the doctor."

"I don't want a next pregnancy."

"Not tonight," Carrie winked at Iz, "but wait a few days," and pointed at the sky of massy gray clouds. "Richard's up there wanting his mommy to get him, which you will, as soon as we feed this clown," she jiggled a thumb toward Iz on the other side of the bed, "some monkey glands."

"Still at it huh?" Iz said. "You'd thank your lucky stars for a monkey with glands like mine."

With Naomi convalescing and Carrie dabbling in Bronx landladyship nowadays with even a little office up on the Hub with the Third Avenue El snaking around outside her window, Danny was here there and everywhere at Quality besides trying to beat Wartels to the phone in case Sydelle called. But West Street also became a built-in alibi for meeting Sydelle straight from work. You could claim overtime—here he was alone in the place and actually at it—a quick meal at Fisherino's, and a concert. All true, that was the crazy part—except of course when you found yourself in a hotel with her. Then you came home all hers, with that . . . fragrance . . . in your nostrils for hours afterward.

It really was Town Hall tonight though, and again, to Danny's relief, Carrie had not been interested. Paderewski or Fritz Kreisler she'd go, the glamour boys, but Szigeti or Ilya Axelrod no.

"Not to hear your son's new teacher?"

"Keep Axelrod and that dry stuff," Carrie'd squeezed grinning Ezra, "I have the pupil!"

So now Danny wrapped up the advertising copy and sales charts, went to the washroom, and began changing to his Brooks Brothers glen plaid.

The pupil was one more reason why Danny was a fan of that cold man's impassioned Beethoven: Axelrod—and he was nobody's flatterer—saying that your kid was remarkable! He'd grudgingly auditioned Ezra and certainly wouldn't have at all if Danny had done the asking. Sydelle had had to miss an Axelrod Beethoven recital, Carrie as usual had said nix, so Danny had taken Reisel. After the last otherworldly notes of Opus 109 had died away, "He plays holy music," Reisel had said. "Let us afford him the opportunity to be holy in his life as well."

Apart from Axelrod's following of young men the greenroom hadn't been that crowded and Axelrod's quick eye had picked out Reisel immediately. "This lady," he satirically addressed the ebony-haired boy he'd been talking to, "on March fifteenth—no, tenth, it was a very raw Saturday—nineteen twenty-one at Eddie Stuart's on Central Park South, scolded me to be good to my mother. . . . And now?" He'd elevated the sufficiently high brow while the boy friend smirked, so that Danny could have pasted the two of them. "You know that she died, so I can't be good to her any more."

"God in his abundance provides others whom you can be good to."

And Reisel had informed Axelrod that this young man whose grandmother had been Axelrod's mother's friend and protector now had a son, a prodigy of the piano. But no go, Axelrod didn't listen to children.

"You will not be listening to a child," Reisel had said. "In memory of your sainted mother you will be listening to a musician."

So, in his Fifty-fifth Street rooms of *japonaiseries* and elegant Louis-Seize furniture that Reisel supposed (considering the empty seats at his Town Hall concert) he must have inherited from his ancient Central Park South patron, Axelrod listened. Then—"No eavesdropping, a conceited little boy would be the last pupil I'd take"—he'd called to Ezra at the far end of the palatial room, where Ezra had been squashing the ears of a friendly wire-haired terrier which had also been listening. Finally Axelrod had notified Ezra he'd see him Thursdays four o'clock sharp. "At four-one you'll find nobody home, is that clear?" Ezra'd nodded, impressed. But in the hallway Master Conceited had inquired blandly, "Why did he say I shouldn't be treated as a child prodigy? I'm a child prodigy," and had gotten a loving punch from his father and a kiss from his Aunt Reisel.

Danny with his overcoat on his arm and his fedora and gloves in hand smiled all the way down to Fisherino's, remembering.

Standing—where else?—under the arc light just outside the building with his hand on a girl's shoulder was—who else?—his brother-in-law Iz. Their eyes met and they nodded, the girl too—she was a paintress, Cynthia Arons, no beauty but likable, a sympathetic type as was now being demonstrated. What did the big boss and good brother do? He sat down in sparsely occupied Fisherino's with his back to the window and ordered fillet of flounder.

What was he supposed to do, considering what he was doing tonight and what he easily might have done following the audition if it had been Reisel with a difference. He'd dropped Ezra off—"When Mother comes home, prodigy, tell her I drove Aunt Reisel back"—and he and Reisel had glided happily uptown in the Pierce over cobbles that shone in fading sunlight.

Unfortunately at Kingsbridge in the dark they'd just missed missing Gittel, freshly waved and peroxided with rouged rumpled cheeks, thin legs and silk stockings. Reisel made herself scarce to rattle pans in the kitchen while Gittel waiting for her beau showed off by asking Danny whether she should succumb to holy matrimony.

"Do you love this Brody?"

"Oh," she laughed, "love! Danny, are you still in your cradle? Every widow in the neighborhood is after Simeon Brody—and he's mine for the taking! Wait until you see him, you'd think he was a magnate, not a retired official. The only question is, Danneleh, do I want a man in my bed?" Then the bell rang and Gittel introduced Brody—long, lean, gray, well-groomed, just as she'd said, a velvet collar—and giggled, "Should I?"

Brody grinned, Danny too. Brody wanted her? Let him take her off Reisel's hands, what a relief that would be for Reisel. "Absolutely," Danny gave the lovebirds his blessing. And with the coast clear Reisel strode out of the kitchen.

"Does she want a man in her bed! Not a question but the last vestige of shame. Selfish! She will marry however, leaving me alone in the wilderness. But let her go, since I cannot stop her. I shall marry too."

And Jesus Christ, that dejection made you want to embrace her, kiss her, and—yes, muddlehead, after all these years and Sydelle too—love her. Thirty-five and she looked like next spring, and so damn wretched—amazing, to lose Gittel?—that simultaneously you found yourself with tears in your eyes and a hard-on.

"If you mean it Reisel, be careful who."

Did she brighten! "You still do care about me Daniel!"

And—"Of course I care"—he'd stupidly reached for her. Thank God she'd dodged him as adroitly as at twenty-three—and with the same roguish smile.

"Very well. I shall not marry without your consent."

And he had muttered "Fine," the sickening idiot—just the man to play the heavy with his brother-in-law, that Iz bastard who'd killed his taste for dinner, for the concert, and for meeting Sydelle.

But early as Danny reached Town Hall so Sydelle wouldn't have to wait she was there already under the marquee in the gnawing cold, and to see her face take on life, those dark loving eyes when she caught sight of him—oh God, was he privileged! The grace, the small erect figure in the fox-trimmed blue coat that he'd insisted on last fall at Bonwit Teller in spite of her self-depreciatory smile "Blue to go with my depressed character?," the intelligence, were . . . not beautiful—Reisel was beautiful, with the lustrous red hair and milky skin—but . . . elegant, admirable. He took her hands and said so to her. And going into the lobby he asked her, "Does

Cynthia look admirable to Iz?" He bought tickets and when they sat down he told her the story.

"If Cynthia does," she said, "I feel sorry for her."

"Why sorry?"

"That she met him second."

The lights dimmed, Ilya Axelrod—tall, unbending—walked quickly out of the wings, gave the audience an ironic nod, adjusted the piano stool and pitched in. Torrents of music flooded you in the *Tempest* Sonata, and you clung desperately hand in hand with Sydelle. Yet with Axelrod you heard every note. At intermission, after the *Waldstein*, Sydelle turned to Danny with full eyes.

"Anything is possible in life," she sang, "isn't it?"

And to his surprise she led the way to the cloakroom. He spread his palms. "Leave before the *Hammerklavier*?"

"Can I stand Beethoven banging against stone walls," Sydelle laughed, "with my own stone walls to bang against?"

"What stone walls?"

"I'll tell you at coffee."

"But first the *Hammerklavier*."

So they stayed, but Sydelle had been right, they shouldn't have. The *Hammerklavier* was hardly a theme song for happiness ahead, and going around the corner to the Algonquin for coffee she laughed, "There's always suicide," from the other side of her mouth.

While she'd spent yesterday afternoon at Huntington Epp's New Year's Day party in Tarrytown missing Danny, Professor Kulnikoff with Carl Svendsen as a chorus of affirmation and with Art smiling modestly in the background had ganged up on Mr. Epp himself, the master of the Culture Foundation money. What could Mr. Epp do but agree that he could scarcely conceive of a stronger applicant for a music fellowship than Arthur Fields.

And what would she do if she had to watch New York drift away in September with Danny on it and her in tow behind Art to Europe? It would be like dying.

There was a courageous answer to that if you had guts, but all Share had was a quick tongue. Two giddy dames on the alert for celebrities brought Danny back to the Algonquin around him with a request for his autograph. Wasn't he George O'Brien the actor?

"No, Moishe O'Brien the sword swallower."

"I told you he looked too young!"

To Sydelle he dredged up wisdom like slips between cups and lips and not crossing bridges you hadn't come to.

Only, at home last night, Art had been bubbling he had this plum in the bag. Disregard the music itself—that was the last concern of dispensers of Culture fellowships. Dr. Koussevitzky'd performed Fields, Matkowsky had performed Fields, in Chicago Guerin had played him, not to speak of those stumblebums in New Orleans and Minneapolis. Concert Artists was a prestige management and they already had a feeler for him from RKO Pictures he could tack on to his trophies list. And not only did he have his patron Stairs and Kulnikoff and Svendsen in his corner, but as acknowledged minority leader at the American Composers Society, Fields versus fags, he had his own disciples whose stuff he'd gotten performed by the Empire State Chamber bunch.

Did pusillanimity Share growl the hell with him, the hell with it all, let him sail to Europe, we'll see America first, I'll work up a new lamp business on the West Coast somewhere?

Right away.

Just last week Carrie and he had driven to Orange where a few years back Moishe the Communist—the same Moishe who'd cheered while Uncle Joe Stalin starved kulaks in the Workers' Paradise—had been salestalked into dreams of glory and the latest chicken incubators and brooders, right in time for the crash. Now between rock-bottom egg and poultry prices and the Orange National Bank's foreclosure threats Carrie'd joked she'd better bail Daddy Moishe out with her little landladying profits before he consumed his capital down to the last squawk. But what if you had no one to bail you out? In Times Square every night losers were lined up for free soup, and Danny would start over from scratch? The thought alone—not so much the starving as the starting—was like a mound on your chest. Then, Art had aimed at the Prix de Rome once and the closest he'd come to Rome was his occasional plate of spaghetti—inexpensive, filling and a treat for the missus—in Little Italy on the Lower East Side. So with luck it might all come out in the wash.

"At worst," Danny said, "it'll be for just a year."

"Just a year!"

That was Sydelle's first sharp glance at him, and he had to try talking her around. The queer truth was—no doubt he wanted too little—that for him knowing she loved him was enough even when they were apart.

Sydelle said, "I'm of a lower species."

23

AND ART'S CULTURE FOUNDATION FELLOWSHIP HAD BEEN in the bag all right. Epp tipped off Kulnikoff from the Foundation and Kulnikoff burst in on Art's composition seminar to clap him on the back—special delivery: Art didn't have to wait for a letter. Immediately he called the French Line and came home jubilant: it was Ile de France tourist for them in June—twenty-five dollars down and balance a month before sailing! He'd been primed for an on-the-spot celebration, but she'd pretended—not that it was much of a pretense—that she didn't feel well. With March sleet drumming West Street like a judgment from heaven, icing piers and glazing the cobbles, Danny sat at his desk at the telephone and what could he say? They were supposed to meet in a few hours, Schnabel was playing at Town Hall, but, Danny said, maybe she'd better not in such weather.

"I'll meet you," Sydelle said, "if I die for it."

From the uptown trolley and that cavernous El structure he'd hardly sloshed his way into the glinting side street when she was coming toward him, his Sydelle, always there first. But she was not interested in recitals tonight. "Take me somewhere," she told him with her tragic face.

So he had to let her wait in the Town Hall lobby while he raced around like a madman, looking up a hotel they'd never been to that he could arrive at by cab—he took a chance on the Seville a half mile downtown—finding a Times Square luggage store for a suitcase, packing his overcoat in it so it shouldn't feel empty. In a pneumonia sweat with winter rain needling him he waved at cabs in wet clogged Broadway at the height of the pre-theater rush. Then his taxi crawling around the block to pick up Sydelle was stalled in traffic so long he slammed his hat down on the seat and actually tore at his hair. The Seville was steamy as midsummer, and the bellman—"Plenty of heat"—turned up still another radiator for them. From a bay window you saw trees and a country church in a glistening dimness, the Little

Church Around the Corner the bellman said, where the actors get married. Yeah, they brought the girl they loved there and not to a hotel and married her.

The bellman left with his coin and Sydelle threw herself crying on Danny's neck. They were an hour in the room fully dressed with her missing him in advance and him kissing tears away before she could compose herself enough to go mournfully downstairs for coffee. And how could he lose her for a year? Tonight she was beautiful with her sorrows, the narrow face pale and downcast, the frame of black hair, the two-sweater suit she was wearing, a creamy white over red on that slight elegant figure. Between the elevator and the hotel coffee shop three separate men stared at her pop-eyed, but where did he have the right to be proud?

"The coward," he said over the coffee he didn't touch and she only stirred. "I can't bring myself simply to say to her 'I'm leaving,' and leave."

"You have children."

"They're no excuse."

"After your father?"

Danny said nothing. Feeling in the wrong toward Carrie didn't help either.

"And am I any different? If you asked me to run away with you I'd be obliged to, but I wouldn't want to." Sydelle kept stirring her cup. "Maybe something will happen."

"The melancholy Dan's lifelong philosophy!"

And he got a smile out of her at last, weak, but the first of the evening.

Nevertheless things didn't happen unless you made them happen, like Ed E-square Evans and other scum of the earth, such as your brother-in-law.

With Naomi in retirement deploying all of her forces to the latest pregnancy campaign, striking—Carrie kidded her and she blushed and didn't deny it—when the iron is hot, why would jolly Iz want to walk out on a virtual partnership at West Street? For a measly five a week more and speculation at Ajax Advertising? Those agencies went in and out of business so fast that a blink and you'd miss them. Just the same Don Isidore strolled into the office one gloomy day, charitably pinched Riva Wartels on the cheek and told her, "Go powder your nose dear, private conference."

At least the whole world isn't nuts. Riva became so angry that that sharp nose in question visibly twitched.

"When you're boss I'll go a lot further away than that, but till then don't give me orders."

Iz laughed, parked his can on your desk, leaned close enough to tempt you to spit down his throat, and out of the side of his mouth confidentially spilled the good news: assistant art director at Ajax now and director as soon as his compasses point was securely planted between the present incumbent's shoulders.

"Don't mention it to Naomi yet Dan, I want to surprise her with the first fifty buck pay in our family history."

"I'll have to mention it to her. She's part of the business."

Water off a duck's back. "I'd appreciate it," lovable flipped Danny a wink, with one for Riva, and strolled out happily.

Why not? He must have had his fill of Cynthia Arons. The kid had headed Iz's list for post-Christmas layoffs in the painting department. Danny'd called Iz upstairs then and wanted to be told what the idea was firing a girl who was their best assistant and there the longest.

Iz had grinned, "And paid the most. First in first out, you save on the payroll, boss."

"Not on my payroll."

For that private conference Danny had contrived an errand for Riva, after which she glanced at the revised list and muttered, "And he would have blamed it on you also."

Out of duty Danny called up his sister—it was her husband after all—and asked how about meeting the Ajax Advertising fifty and keeping Iz. Ha, Iz had known he had no concerns in that direction. You could virtually hear the arithmetic clicking at the Bronx end of the wire. For Naomi Ajax equaled an extra two hundred and fifty a year. Then add a hundred and twenty-five, your half of the cost if you gave Iz the raise here. And at that Danny was loose in the figuring.

Naomi said, "A new foreman would only be thirty-five dollars a week, or even thirty for a good one. . . . "

So now Iz had the play of the field during working hours with no Cynthia and no family spies. Of course Cynthia's cheeks looked sunken, she'd lost her girlish complexion, and she slouched at the workbench like a zombie, but small items like that don't sickly o'er men of action with the pale cast of thought.

Then in the middle of dinner on the first day of spring Liela called Danny to the phone, and it was Sydelle, and something had happened.

Professor Ullman—he was first violin in the Riverside Quartet—had collared Art in the office at the Conservatory. Their violist van Landingham was selling out for glamour, the Bucharest Quartet. Would Art's wife be interested in replacing him?

"And he—" Danny still couldn't bring himself to name names with Carrie and the boys an earshot away in the dining room—"vouched that you wouldn't."

That was exactly what Art had vouched. He'd given Ullman the brush-off she'd be in Paris soon, no point knocking herself out with the Riverside repertoire for half a dozen performances. Ullman according to Art had managed his ghastly smile and hoped she'd consider it anyway. Wise guy, Art told her, dying for Art to pull strings and find him a concert bureau since they'd be related by music—that was what was behind his kind-hearted offer.

Danny's blood churned. "Kindhearted! And who cares what was behind the offer?"

Sydelle had tremblingly asked the same question and had been told to calm down and be logical. The Riverside couldn't get a concert management on their merits, Ullman could have asked her directly if he really was after her, and with a plethora of unemployed violists why turn to a woman except for some ulterior motive? She'd been speechless, probably livid. So Art had shrugged that if she was that anxious for a couple of months of slave labor with some milksop musicians—that was why van Landingham gave them the air: you can't graft spine on worms—she was a citizen and free to dangle her wrists to Ullman and coo she'd love to. But if she thought Art intended to waive his integrity and praise the Riverside Quartet to Concert Artists with her or without her she had another think coming. All right, Sydelle had answered him in a shaking voice, she would exercise her citizenship, and perhaps for more than a couple of months of work—pardon her, slave labor.

But the medallion sunset blaze over Grant's Tomb had startled her when she came out of the house, on the way down to Amsterdam Avenue the nippy March air had cooled her off, and in the candy store she was calling from the proprietor was leaning over a paper spread on the counter and rocking his head at she didn't know what ominous news. And now she was . . . she wouldn't depress Danny with the word. Why hadn't she called Ullman? She didn't know, she'd walked right out. She supposed she must have wanted comfort from Danny first.

If you asked me to run away with you I'd feel obliged to, but I wouldn't want to. The same for him, in spades. With all the longing, they couldn't imagine themselves free for each other. Yet suppose Art were in Paris and she stayed here on Danny's say-so. Then Danny would be obliged to ask her: no way out. He took his life in his hands—who knew where it would end?—and said, "Phone him."

"Are you sure?"

"Daddy," the megaphone treble was out of Teddy, but the message was Carrie's, "I'm eating your French fries!"

Danny said into the phone, "I'm telling you."

"All right," none too happily, "if you're sure. . . . "

So could it be, could it be—wrong as it would be—that life was carrying him where his dreams with unhappy endings never did, to Sydelle for good? He slowly placed the receiver on the hook and stood in a half-believing trance at the telephone table. Night had fallen, past the grand piano with the newlywed photos of him and Carrie the park stretched like black spangled velvet to a choir of lights on the far side. My God, to be the one-man claque at Sydelle's recitals, to beam later on in greenrooms with people congratulating her, his Sydelle, his marriage from heaven to talk Shakespeare with the rest of your life! God, he even had the honeymoon home, he owned it outright, with the view of the Hudson River from

Kingsbridge. Gittel'd tittered at him, "Why shouldn't I be a June bride, like any other American girl?" and with her permanent, her peroxide straw hair and heavy makeup she could pass for a girl in her fifties if the light wasn't too strong. "You should see those cats when they have to smile at me and Brody!" Come June, Reisel would never stay in that house alone. And—Danny knew himself—he would never leave this house he was standing in right now. But it only takes one to leave. . . .

In the dining room Ezra said, "Don't worry Daddy, Ted didn't touch your French fries. Liela took them back to keep them warm." Teddy stuck his tongue full of chewed steak out at Ezra and Ezra merrily reached his knife and fork over. "Lean closer Teddy, I'll have some tongue." The tongue popped in and Teddy ran around the table to mix it up with his laughing brother till their mother chimed a knife on a waterglass.

"End of round nine," Carrie announced and Teddy scooted back to his chair. "Raisin problems?"

"Some ears." Danny's heart pounded. "Sydelle problems."

"A paintress?"

"A musician, you know that."

"How would I know?"

"Because I told you, years ago."

"I forgot. Tell me again."

"She's my piano teacher."

"Named Tallarico?"

"Named Fields."

Then it hit Carrie: the Windy City kid! So—best laid plans—this was where that one had disappeared to, and at parties and so forth Carrie'd been keeping her sharp eye on vulturesses her Galahad here never showed the slightest interest in. She'd even hesitated at saving herself the time downtown when Limpy volunteered to pick a replacement for Iz. Why let in new Raisins? But business was roaring along a mile a minute up in the Bronx, though not exactly with the couple of tenementsful of rent cripples that Limpy supposed she ran a real estate office for.

There was the Queens land she was acquiring including three solid acres in Ed E-square Evans' name for the tip on the Jamaica subway extension planned for within two years at most Ed said, so call it four. The Bronx line that had been one of Rob Ward's sweet nothings for nothing before he'd lost hope with her was just reaching an explosive climax two years late—and she still wouldn't have believed it if she hadn't taken the Cadillac for a spin to the top of the Grand Concourse and looked at the holes. Now wily Levy & Son Developers had stopped the silly offers and settled down to talk business about her Bedford Park lots they wanted to build on. To do the rising son Prince James Levy justice he knew how wily he was: enough to ogle her free of charge during the wrangling sessions and make his futile tries for a date afterwards behind Papa's back. But old man Levy with the nasty smile and wise eyes was such a shrewd bargainer that her anticipated thousand percent realization would be a special pleasure at his expense. Then her manager Arthur Mulloy—the silver-haired warrior of the soft tongue who'd taught her how to use the savings of the timid in one bank to buy good property dirt-cheap from another—couldn't seem to get that Central Park South hotel that the slump had halted construction on off his mind. "For thrills?" she'd laugh at Arthur, and the idea of her Carrie B. Share a three quarters of a million dollar mortgagee did titillate the spine. Arthur kept purring no, not for thrills, for profits. Even if the populace made Mr. Hoover—always respectful, Arthur, of the rich—our second living ex-President, the Democratic successor whoever he might turn out to be wouldn't do better and probably a lot worse. Did Carrie remember the condition that our idealistic Democratic President Wilson left the economy in while slaughtering our young men for the sake of the British? But, Arthur purred, he didn't mean to repine. What he was saying was, we could count on a nice long depression no matter who was elected. Provident millionaires would continue boarding up mansions, cutting staff and moving to hotel accommodations, especially to new ones with the latest facilities, like the Central Park South edifice in question. Then again if by some miracle the economy were to improve, so much the better: hotel space would be restored to its old premium status. As to money, the Corn Exchange Bank—he'd inquired—stood ready with corn, and why should it not? Was Mrs. Share cognizant of the fact that she'd passed her first million? She Carrie Baum was cognizant. Between municipal improvements and selling short it was not her depression. But hotel speculations? . . .

With all this on her mind she'd stayed uptown and let Limpy pick a new painting foreman. And you should see his willowy young choice, Lou Sorella—"So what," Limpy said, "he knows his stuff"—a girl could go for herself if sweet Lou were an out-and-out boy.

So who'd foreseen a So-dull she meant Sydelle revival—and what a revival! If Honest John hadn't kept So-dull a secret the piano lessons just could have been nothing but piano lessons. After the goings on in his little wifie's modern Chippendale bed what could Limpy have left for outside except finger exercises, and his piano playing had improved to the point where you could concentrate on your *Barron's* without clinkers jolting you out of your skin every few seconds. But dinnertime telephone calls and sudden hard-faced communiqués? Why that little bitch whoever she was must have been figuring the fish was hooked, just reel him in.

Which only proved the girlie didn't know much about Mrs. Carrie B. Share. "What's her problem?" Carrie asked sociably.

They were almost comical, the six waiting eyes Danny glanced at, Carrie's two brown, Ezra's two blue, and two more brown Teddy's. Me, I'm her problem, a man would have answered—but which man? You make the effort, you dare her to knock the chip off your shoulder, and for your pains a good-humored inquiry.

When it came to put up or shut up, which might never, which probably would never happen, there was always the note that you could leave and sneak away to—it still made your heart sink—California.

He shrugged, "A job," to his meat and potatoes.

See Limpy's steam fizzle out!

Which also proved there's more than one way to skin a kitten on the keys. Ideally a teacher switch would be best, but you wouldn't catch her Carrie B. Share making a mountain out of a contender's molehill. Yeah, she had been neglecting Limpy between dawn and beddy-by. Her more or less business parties weren't that much a pleasure to him, and she'd been too rushed lately even for the fights and the opera. That would be corrected however, and furthermore if he wanted to listen to chamber music she'd be right along with him in the chamber. And what did he work at when he worked late? Ill as she could afford the time she'd have to resume a maternal eye on Limpy in West Street, at least an hour or so every day. She'd smothered this Field before, an annoyance but she'd do it again.

So she finally got down to an Izzie Axelrod pardon her Ilya concert and when you gave Axelrod the benefit of being the appreciative teacher of Ezra Share, you had to admit that for a guy who came out like an undertaker he could really tickle the keys. But what really tickled you was Limpy's docility—not a sigh, not a long face the whole evening. Of course you had to do your part too: attentive, no yawns, no program reading. At intermission she cracked "That Mozart could turn out a good tune now and then," and Limpy laughed on cue for the longhairs popping their eyes the same as anyone else at gorgeous you in black net trim with your handsome escort. And in the Russian Tea Room he handsomely followed her and the dining-room captain between more glances, more turning heads. But was he ravenous, devouring blintzes and gulping coffee as if she hadn't fed him a full-course chicken Maryland dinner at home with bacon strips, candied sweets, the whole works. Herself she toyed with a fresh fruit salad and brought him up to date on family matters. Ezra had given Grandma—Limpy's mother answered the phone nowadays at Naomi's—a half-hour report on fourth grade, but Teddy'd said, "I can't speak to you Grandma, too busy playing." Naomi was snug in bed and so was Richard—what was his alternative since he wasn't due till late fall? Yeah, she was fine and why not, under the care of Carrie's cousin by marriage the doctor?

But to hear Naomi quoted that without Ma as chief cook and bottle washer at Hope Street she'd be lost, especially since Iz's new place needed him for even more overtime than he'd had to put in at West Street—that stopped Danny in the middle of a bite.

"What overtime did he ever put in at West Street?"

Carrie winked. "Get it?"

Iz's shenanigans seemed such a big joke to her that Danny wasn't sure he did get it. Anything goes but keep your wife in the dark? Was she offering him that as a consolation prize?

The worst was it was tempting.

Share didn't altogether fold up though. At home he searched through some more Plato for the authorization he hadn't found yet to ditch your wife in pursuit of the good. But Plato still didn't cooperate, and neither did Carrie. In bed the breasts and arched belly—you could laugh at her calisthenics to radio but she kept in condition—were tempting also.

And count on Share to give in.

. . . Good boy, Limpy.

And not only was Limpy suddenly having dinner in every night, but Saturday afternoon add travel time to a one-hour lesson and he was back in his Morris chair in the den with his nose in a book!

Women trying to meddle with her Carrie B. Share's private property!

Eventually those draggy fine points in the Levy & Son Bedford Park Road negotiations were settled to Mr. Levy's satisfaction—meaning to Carrie's. The lawyers smiled and lit up in her tiny office already so filled with smoke that the El cars just outside shaking you to the uterus rolled past like fog. Some day, as the silver-haired Arthur entreated her for the sake of still greater income, she'd have to move Tomer Realty to a queen's suite downtown befitting an enterprise named for Mother. Meanwhile the once Limpy dropped in with the monsters to call for her the Cinderella surroundings had suggested anything but golden slippers to him—which was the idea. Why lie unless necessary? Mr. Levy didn't notice the El train or the roar, he was busy buttoning the bill of sale into his briefcase while Arthur at his desk puffed a pipe and smoothed Levy & Son's check in happy reflection. Then the Levy contingent trooped out with an undertone promise from Prince James Levy he'd call her soon. Idiot, if he'd decided to wait downstairs with his shoulders, black shellac hair and gangster-olive complexion she just might have gone somewhere with him, she felt so exhilarated. As it was he'd better save his nickels for Bedford Park—he'd need 'em. She pinched Arthur's wreathed pink cheek, blew him to corned beef and cabbage in the Hub, and drove herself down to Quality in the first sprinklings of an April shower that smelled excitingly sweet though probably not to those poor Harlem bastards vacantly slouching in doorways.

And still our Great Engineer in the White House fiddled around with Reconstruction Financers and Home Loan Bankers. And apart from bankers who was financed? Levy & Son, to throw up high-priced rentals for allrightniks so the construction workers can buy plenty of ice-cream sodas and save the candy store men of America.

The one thing that she despised was ineptitude!

A foot in rain-glum West Street and she galvanized the joint upstairs and down—everywhere but behind Limpy's desk. A fresh eye on the product and not bad though she said so about a brainchild of her own, modern zigzags across semiporcelain vases and silk shades that she'd started Iz Schwartz on back then and that sweet Lou Sorella still fussed at with the paintresses. And Gnopf her mighty midget—"Carrie light of my life, where you been!"—dropped in with a fair order book. But streamlined wood was the trend, as Gnopf agreed. "How about investigating machinery for that?" she pushed Limpy. Space they had, the second floor was half empty and in a pinch she could get rid of the sea boots and pea jackets tenant in her building next door. They could expand to lamp tables too, and possibly Venetian blinds: *Quality—For Your Home!*

Limpy? He made light of it. Leave him alone, he was busy selling luxury hand-painted lamps as someone—who was it again?—had once advised him to.

And good advice that had been once. But God in heaven, he didn't simply want to sit here and stagnate, did he, with the same twenty-five thousand tops every year?—and don't forget you had to split that with the pregnant pensioner on Hope Street.

"Naomi'll probably move away from Hope Street," big joke, "after Richard is born."

Was he aggravating! What kind of businessman was that? Just watch, some other outfit would capitalize on streamlined wood to the music of her Carrie B. Share grinding her teeth. Meanwhile considering how rotten times were he was busy enough in his mulish way and with Kid Pregnancy gone his overtime wasn't of the Iz Schwartz variety. But never pat yourself on the back. At her half-past two kiss and so long she'd be beating the monsters home, he casually remarked he'd be eating out.

"Yeah? What's playing?"

"The Busch-Serkin Trio."

"Town Hall? That's for me, the tops in Schubert. I'll meet you there."

Nonplused? He was stupefied. She Carrie B. Share could name you half the empty lots in the Bronx and all the gilt-edged stocks on the board and not keep up with culture in her *Herald-Tribune*? What could be easier? Poor Limpy, he flip-flopped for an out via the monsters.

"Can Liela sleep in tonight?"

"She'll get paid for it, don't worry."

"I know she'll get paid for it, but on such short notice?"

"A whole afternoon? And it'll ease her conscience while she's padding our grocery bills."

And she left Limpy to break his date with that dame while she breezed home in the Cadillac through streets with hardly a puddle in them under a crackling blue sky that had cleared exactly as forecast.

But shit-in-his-blood Share called Sydelle at the last minute with a lie: base spinner broke down, looked like an all-hours repair job. And she said, "Don't sound so disheartened!" and that loving laugh chimed out for him. She said—could he believe his ears?—"I would have slept on your shoulder in Town Hall. . . ."

What with days working up Ullman's Brahms program and nights with pupils she still taught, here it was bright spring and she felt like winter. Of course Danny'd been right, she should have eliminated the pupils altogether. But between the ones that she'd given up and the Riverside Quartet, Art was so displeased that he was avoiding her as it was. She did live here, how could she bring in nothing? Generous Danny, she could not let him make good the whole loss. Perhaps she should have said no to the Riverside. She'd tell Danny now, mornings she had to leave the house—Art was composing—and hope she'd find a studio free at the Conservatory. In yesterday's April shower her viola had come out dry though a string broke in tuning—and three replacement strings comically broke one after the other—but she'd come out soaked. At the end of each hour she'd had to gather her damp belongings and clear out for students who had those particular rooms reserved. Luckily she had found another room free each time. But what if there should be no room? And Brahms alone wore her out, the string pieces were so sterile that relearning them was as bad as giving lessons. To think that at sixteen those quartets and quintets had been her favorites, emptiness that you flooded with your soupy yearnings and that led nowhere.

Like Danny—she must have meant him all right. He barely found voice to say she was a professional, she could play anyone. Her silence this round was lethal, and he deserved it.

Then, "What would I be Danny, if not for you? And here I've been complaining to you."

He sat beside Carrie later at the Schubert trios, but his full heart was with Sydelle. And the all-hours repair job that night took place in the den by lamplight in a hum of quiet with the clock turned to the wall so you wouldn't worry about how little sleep you'd have for next day in the factory. This Spaniard that he was reading wrote that all life was a struggle to be itself. When were you yourself—did the question have to be asked? With her you were yourself. Socrates bragged how few things there were that he needed. And you needed things? You needed a Persian carpet, libraries didn't have books? And over the bookcases Loftis's oil on wrapping paper landscapes with their leaps and flashes of color that you'd had to have. The tenth time Henny'd gladly shown them the paintings in the back room of Curios Carrie'd laughed, "Go ahead, get 'em, since you can't do without them. You can hang 'em in the den and I'll warn Liela to look the other way when she's dusting." Share, he hadn't had to be warned to look the other way. The good is that which has not been attained, he'd stopped looking at them quite a while past. Sydelle however was not a good to be attained but to be lived with, a mutual society not a possession. What was all this stuff but a subterfuge for what you were missing?

At the window a dark sky sparkled over roofs so dark that the buildings massed beyond the back yard seemed insubstantial. His heart caught, caught the way it had that day four murderous years ago—but he wouldn't have canceled an instant of those years—the sunny afternoon when he'd helped Sydelle find her apartment. "There's a snatch of the river," she'd sung stretched far out of the window, "if you're willing to risk a five-story fall"—while a square-jawed landlady, whose lace curtain lilt sounded amazingly like Reisel's Gymnasium English accent, assured him it was a bright bit of a nest for newlyweds like themselves. Hadn't he wished it!

But he was through with sickly wishing. Let come what may, he was as calm as the night, hopeful, and ready for anything.

Thursday Carrie shanghaied him to an interminable *Madama Butterfly* at the Metropolitan Opera and Friday Sydelle took her turn as captive at her mother-in-law's in Brooklyn. Still, Friday night Danny again was up reading until only a light here and there specked the brownstone and tenement rears that cubed the late shadows. Just like Plato, his Spaniard—wouldn't you have guessed it?—staged a full-scale retreat under the banner of responsibility. This shot though—you're responsible to yourself also, hey Joe, as you said in the beginning?—Danny wasn't falling for that so easily.

Gonna hitch myself . . . to that fast train roll–in' by . . .

Diamond stars at night, diamond light in the morning.

Trucks a clean shiny black wheezed by under the window in West Street, shed roofs shone orange, the Hudson glittered, the Jersey side was like yellow bouquets. A truck backfired, a horn blew, longshoremen at the pier alongside a freighter shouted to one another in the sun-cleansed light, each voice clear like a song—why not?—by Art Fields. The eyes smarted a bit from not much sleep but the fingers itched for three o'clock and those—after the *grave* intro—skittering Corelli duet allegros with Sydelle that flattered even Danny's retarded fingers, the piano parts were so easy! You sensed her beside you, the twist of her body as her bow bore down on the strings, her resonances dazzling the practice room, hurtling you down the page—my God, you were Ilya Axelrod himself—as if the page weren't there!

It took a couple of hard blinks to wrench the eyes back to the production schedule spread on the desk, but he could handle that too.

At quitting time the phone rang and Riva Wartels with her lips tucked over her teeth and her compact raised gave the boss a pleading glance, so Danny answered and sang out, "Quality—"

"Poor," Sydelle's voice said.

She was sick. She supposed she hadn't felt just right since the middle of the week, but now she felt all wrong. She'd waited till the last minute, she explained, but—

"I can hear your teeth chattering," Danny interrupted her. "Is Art there?"

Art was there, the doctor would be there.

Danny hustled up too, with daffodils Art laid wrapped on a table. "She's allergic to flowers," Art said.

Danny said, "I didn't know that."

"How would you?" the composer was jovial. But he pinned the blame for the grippe on her, running around in the rain, exhausting herself rehearsing with that crummy quartet she'd joined. And then took care of her, helped the poor haggard kid sit up in bed for aspirin and some dark medicine she apologetically swallowed. He put his hand on her forehead—"Burning," he commented to Danny—while fifth-wheel Share stood there looking serious.

And Art's virtue was rewarded. Her grippe dragged on for weeks and even then, with May sunshine fluttering her bedroom curtains, she felt heavy and dull. Certainly Ullman assured her she was his regular violist. For the April Brahms he had found a substitute—a man of course, Art pointed out—but two end-of-season programs still lay ahead. Only to date she hadn't been able to lift a finger to learn them. So the Riverside Quartet was turning into a will-o'-the-wisp.

Yet she didn't look sick Danny's third visit, pale from indoors sure but beautiful with those dark troubled eyes and long lashes. Art asked if Danny could stay awhile and left for his publisher's downtown. And Danny, as proof she was well, held her close and kissed her.

"Without fear of infection," he smiled into her face.

Sydelle threw her arms around him, took him to bed—and hurried him.

"What would you do," she asked him while he was dressing, "if Art were suddenly to come back?"

Danny snorted. "I wouldn't have such luck."

"Luck?"

But he was ashamed to admit that at this late date he'd still need a volcano to move him. And he foresaw no tremors.

At home Carrie cracked, "Triple piano lesson today?"

"Visiting a sick friend," he looked her in the eye.

"Sydelle sick?"

He nodded, and her innocent "Nothing serious I hope?" was her only objection, if you could call it that.

And finally the regular violist of the Riverside Quartet rose one morning, was deferred to by Art who generously left her the apartment to practice in though he told her that he couldn't see her practicing in her state of health—and, she said in depths of gloom to Danny over the telephone, she had lost her touch, her tone, everything.

"That's just mental," he said.

"It's real nevertheless."

To cheer her up he financed cabs—his and hers—to Central Park and brought all sorts of fruit and sandwiches from a Tenth Avenue delicatessen near Quality. They sat, they ate or rather he did—she hadn't much appetite, he held her worrisomely cold hand, he guaranteed that with green air, cheerful lunch-hourers strolling alongside the lagoon, full sunny benches, swans as white as if they just came back from the laundry, ducks quacking, she'd be better than ever. Her lost touch—she'd had colds before, it had happened before?

"But this time it's like doom."

Poor kid, she yawned, and Danny glanced at his wristwatch. His desk was loaded with the fall advertising and sales campaigns . . . and Carrie must have been at West Street an hour now. But how could you run from this one? Sydelle abruptly stood up. "It hasn't been so wonderful, today's outing, has it?" And he couldn't argue though he did.

Sydelle's lost touch stayed lost, and she resigned from the Riverside Quartet. Occasionally if the weather was good she'd drag herself out lunch-time to meet Danny at a bench on Riverside Drive. The Hudson sparkled, Sydelle yawned. And Saturday afternoons at the Conservatory Danny played what he had been practicing during the week and Sydelle yawned phrasing and time values corrections to earn her pay, her sole justification for existence. So your sublime joy became your abysmal misery. Finally a yawn swung Danny around on the piano stool.

"This can't go on," he told Sydelle sternly.

"So Art says too," she laughed yawning, "but it does."

"It's time you heard what a good doctor says."

"But—" a yawn, laughter, a shake of the head—"I have heard." If Danny, Sydelle said, thought he had reason to complain, which he had, think of her husband. Poor Art was confronted day and night with her moping, usually at full sickly length on the couch. She yawned over Charlotte Brontë's romantic governesses even while she lost herself in them, and mealtimes she hardly touched the food she herself had prepared. No wonder Art had his uncle the doctor see her again. So the lecture she received after Dr. Udall took her pulse and had her say "Ah"—that she was well, completely cured of the grippe, nothing wrong with her, and that she should stop this self-indulgence and go about her business—she was sure that she deserved, but she felt sick. "Danny," she touched his face in full view of the door glass and corridor-passers but he didn't give a damn, "don't be so angry—it doesn't matter." And she yawned.

"Is that what you pay him for?"

"The point is we don't, that was why he was so angry. He doesn't charge us."

"Then let's have an opinion from my wife's cousin the doctor by marriage who does charge—and plenty."

And laughing and yawning she let herself be put into a cab, where she more or less collapsed against him. He called out the sights—the Gothic of City College he'd been a born student of but never went to, the Polo Grounds he used to go to a lot, McCombs Dam Bridge over the Harlem River where he used to drive his first car that nice eight cylinder Franklin job—and Sydelle flicked a mere glance at each and raised her lips to be kissed. Last—but why rub it in, he didn't mention it—came the famous Grand Boulevard and Concourse, his honeymoon street. What did he used to think of then? He and Carrie went to the '23 World Series, where the Yanks whipped the Giants and sent him home happy from Yankee Stadium a few blocks down from where Nate's office was now.

Doctor's hours were over today, the maid said. But the word Share and there was Nate with the big grin and athletic handshake. While Gladys the Angel of Death with the malicious glint in the eye—so cousin Carrie's in the same boat I am—wrote up the new patient, Nate cracked to Danny, "I needn't ask how you're doing."

"Never mind how I'm doing. Just tell her how she's doing."

Nate turned serious. "Possible pregnancy?"

"Jesus Nate, can that one track of yours be called a mind?"

But Nate took Sydelle inside like a doctor and Gladys inspected the surfaces of the waiting room for dust, brushed off a speck, shot Danny a sour look and left him with the *Literary Digest* and the *Herald-Tribune.* In the paper—that poor baby, how could a father go on living?—the son of a bitch Lindbergh killer was still loose, Jews who could afford it were hot-footing it out of Germany in front of those Nazi sons of bitches, and on the music page another son of a bitch let you know you really hadn't liked Ilya Axelrod's Mozart—the pianism was too rough and unpolished that dumb you the other night thought you'd die in an agony of bliss of.

Danny even reached the business section: General Motors hits record low . . . and who cares! Nate was thorough, that was the reason you went to him. But—all this time?—Danny broke into a sick sweat. Something must have been wrong.

Waiting for a cab in the long shadows of the Grand Concourse Sydelle said yes, the cousin the doctor was thorough to the point of despair. All of her suspect chemistry had been left up there in vials, plus X-rays of her inner self such as it was. So perhaps she'd die in Danny's arms yet instead of going to Europe in one week, six days and twenty-one and three-quarter hours. Danny told her cut out that talk. Nate had said she seemed all right but since it had begun with the flu no point in guesswork. But in the taxi Sydelle laid her head against the cushion as if she had already consigned herself to some other world.

June came in hot and lowering, rain fell on some muggy days. If they met at their bench in Riverside Park Sydelle would sit as listless as the haze blurring the Jersey shore and the slate-gray river.

"Don't you feel," she said, "life is suspended? Maybe the sailing date will never come."

But Danny hadn't been thinking of the sailing date, only of the lab reports you had to wait an endless week for with her feeling no better. Saturday, to give superstition an assist, the outlook continued gray. But Danny went whistling by the graveyard with his music to West Street anyhow for the final lesson that afternoon. When bright and early Sydelle called from the candy store: cured! Danny's cousin the doctor had just joked that she must have been suffering from seasickness—which was no joke, she said to Danny, just an obvious statement of fact.

"I won't sail, I'll stay here. You won't have to do anything, dear, you have a family, I haven't—so your life will simply be enlarged, and so will mine!"

"Ridiculous," he said. "What do you think I am? But," he burbled, "didn't I tell you a month ago that you were okay? And I'll bet you have your touch back—have you tried?"

"No."

"Well what are you waiting for! And bring your violin later, all right? . . . Gee," he whispered into the mouthpiece behind Wartel's alert back, "am I happy!"

But later she phoned that they'd better cancel the lesson, she didn't seem used to the idea yet of being well, and it was raining. Sure, Danny understood, a natural letdown. The next week though—the last week—much as he exhorted Sydelle over the phone to trust her witch doctor Nate, she still felt the same and only wished she were in a deck chair already with a lulling ocean around her. All she wanted to do was sleep.

Not very flattering of her, jumping the gun on the year away. And the shipboard farewell ahead—yokel Businessman Dan submerged with a fake pleasant expression, his dumb champagne and flowers, and his hope of a sorrowful smile from her among the musical shots who all knew one another—roused the same eager anticipation as one of Carrie's political gatherings in his own living room.

Then the fatal day dawned—or had it? A familiar-looking child in pajamas (Ezra?)—"It's a hit, it's a hit"—half woke him from a store window full of official baseballs? bats? a home run? a strikeout? to early shadows and a scent of green that returned him, a kid himself, to a summer's day kitchen cot in Essex Street. "Teddy's sick," Ezra kept tugging, "Teddy's sick," and Carrie'd swung up from the bed to feel for her slippers.

But Ezra on the phone to West Street afterward saying the bags were packed Daddy come rescue him before the quarantine sticker was posted couldn't have sounded more pleased. A boiled live lobster, that's what Dr. Nate said Teddy was turning into. Naturally Teddy began crying till Dr. Nate folded the stethoscope into the little black bag and told him nothing to worry about, Teddy would only grow a new skin and don't bother saving the old one, Dr. Nate was not interested in secondhand skins. Baby Teddy never let go of Mommy's hand and his eyes were like marbles at the idea of a new skin. So— "So," suddenly Ezra's voice got lost in a giggle and his mother came on, "enough of your tedious narration, sport. So this monster encouraged the patient with 'Always knew my brother was a snake . . . in the grass.' " "And the crybaby," Ezra shouted in the background, "resumed wahing."

Nate had also said it was complications you had to worry about and, of course, in case Ezra wasn't infected the sooner you got him out of the house the better. Where to? Daddy Moishe's, where else, with Grandma in the Bronx guarding Aunt Naomi's belly and Aunt Leah and Uncle Henny scavenging for knickknacks in Mexico?

"There's my Uncle Willie's," Danny reminded her.

"Sure, with his lush of a consort."

Good, keep it up missus.

"My aunt is neither a lush nor a consort. She's my uncle's legally married wife."

"Since when?"

"Last fall."

"You were there?"

"In the judge's chambers."

"No kidding! How did she get rid of the other guy?"

"What other guy?"

"Why her husband."

"That poor man died in the crazy house with my uncle Willie at his bedside."

"My my, have you been growing secretive with your little wifie. But," Carrie knew how to laugh off the whole business, "let's give Grandpa a workout anyway. Moishe'll cry, but he'll love it."

Stop at Pier 57 with Ezra on the way to New Jersey? Who wanted to let Carrie know that Sydelle was leaving? Danny still had a vague scheme to keep his wife supposing the opposite—nights out by himself little as he relished that, and piano lessons with somebody else. And today of all days was not the time to parade his family affiliations in front of Sydelle. Which brought him to another one of his idiot phone calls, though scarlet fever at least beat lying. But before he could get the words out of his mouth Sydelle said she'd been about to phone him not to come to the cabin. She herself wouldn't be there till sailing time.

Then she asked, "What made you call now?"

And—"To hear how you are"—a lie popped out just the same.

"I'm not quite sure—busy."

"You'll write as soon as you're settled?"

"How can I promise? You know what kind of correspondent I am."

"Who wants correspondence?" he tried to joke. "An Eiffel Tower picture postcard with your address and I'll take it from there. . . . Oh, tell me a piano teacher—"

Hurriedly she mentioned a Ricky Paine from the Conservatory and said, "I really can't talk."

"Art there?"

"Yes."

So . . . That explained it, but didn't improve it. He sat stunned.

24

A COUPLE OF WEEKS OKAY, THOUGH EVEN THEN IT LEFT a naggy ache in the chest, to claw over whatever West Street mail deliveries you could beat Wartels to and find nothing but checks and orders. And across the doorsill of Danny's apartment with the quarantine notice posted he'd glance at Carrie—as if you could tell from that friendly face—and wonder might she be holding back the postcard from Sydelle? His wife was crafty, she knew how to out-muscle you, the way she'd done with that Busch-Serkin concert where your alternative to two's company would have been three's a crowd with Sydelle and her both. But shortstop his mail? Let her try. She wouldn't see him for dust.

If Sydelle were the world's best correspondent she'd still had to cross an ocean hadn't she, locate an apartment, get her bearings in a strange country? You want to worry, pick up the paper, now that you had plenty of time for it: more unemployed, more banks folding, more businessmen going down like the wooden ducks in the Palisades Park shooting gallery he and Ezra passed on the way to the merry-go-round Sunday. Or the Battle of Washington where the Great Engineer shooed those poor Bonus Army stiffs off the grass with only two vets shot dead.

"So far," the Communist Moishe muttered.

Uncle Willie was worried sick, really sick, over Storm Troopers unleashed on the German Socialists. Anna said, "He hardly eats," and at supper there with Ezra you saw this was so.

Moishe also present chimed in, "Good for those pinks."

"How about Hitler?" Uncle Willie astounded at the Party line looked at Moishe.

"A crackpot," Moishe made a face, "here today and gone tomorrow." Grandpa Moishe squeezed Ezra until the child yelled "Hey!" with his eyes nearly popping out. "You'll grow up to a better world," Moishe promised him.

In this world the checks Carrie sent her Daddy Moishe always came back endorsed and deposited, so Moishe was all right as long as Quality Lamps kept showing a profit, small as it was and growing smaller. To keep his mind off the invisible postcard Danny was looking into used wood-tooling machinery, not that he had Carrie's enthusiasm for a wooden lamp line but it might be a good hedge to the porcelain if you could hold down the overhead.

The trouble was the invisible postcard. In the back of the paper the Paris weather was in the balmy seventies, like here. So you brought Ezra into the city and outside the house to wave to his mommy nine stories up. Next you tossed a baseball around the Central Park grass and took him to the museum. What would they have there but a French art show where you stood in front of a *Pont-Neuf* with the same porcelain-blue sky and white clouds as here, homesick for Sydelle's Paris. You quit indulging yourself and looked down at Ezra . . . and Ezra was looking up at that painting, absently pounding his baseball into his fielder's glove, lost to the world. So Danny had to kiss him, and Ezra—"I love you Daddy"—hung the hand with the ball around Danny's neck. That sweetness should have been enough, shouldn't it? Yet no Sydelle and something was missing.

Then wedding anniversaries.

Last year Carrie's delighted eyes had glittered right back at the sparklers in the wristwatch he'd chosen not for the anniversary but for Sydelle, then bought two of. About hers Sydelle had worriedly asked how she could display so gorgeous a watch and Danny had shrugged that she should say it was gold plate and rhinestones. And he could take great pride in how he'd been rewarded with love—the best each had to offer—from both women. This year's gift was still easier: no shopping required. He hadn't been able to slip Sydelle the farewell brooch—a small peacock fan of rubies and emeralds set off by the usual diamond chips—because . . . how could he have let it happen no matter what? . . . he'd kept not seeing her at the end. So June twenty-ninth Carrie just had to go into the den, open the secretary drawer and untie the parcel. Worse, she improved the occasion with a diamond stud and cuff links for him—and before witnesses, Teddy in pajamas in the arms of cute Nurse Roth calling happy anniversaries from the back of the nice foyer ruddied in the last streaks of sunset. So—you can't be a boor—on your dusky ninth floor Buryton landing you beamed that it was just what you'd wanted, and followed up with comedy crossed eyes that drew a pitifully feeble laugh from Teddy hugging the new toy derrick from Daddy the way Daddy would have liked to hug him!

And with your wife in quarantine—broken only by a quick tongue-flicking thank you for the brooch kiss and a surreptitious crank of your starter which needless to say instantly engaged—how could you celebrate your wedding anniversary better than by giving the bride away at Gittel's wedding? Kingsbridge the week before had seen royal fireworks with Reisel screaming at her mother "Find your own synagogue for your unholy act!"

and Gittel calmly stating that marriage was ordained by Reisel's sacred Talmud that Gittel would not give two cents for. Reisel shouted do not cite Talmud to her, marriage was never ordained for old women's vanity, and Gittel informed her that better than that it was ordained by Gittel's own papa. In her dream Strool-liebe had called her into the warehouse where he was working on the books, raised his head which she'd been scared to face because she knew he was dead, and clearly said, "Marry Brody."

"What was ordained was that two decrepit fools meet!"

A curtain had billowed out, caught on a bush under the window, so Danny the peacemaker had given a comic boom, "Strool-liebe spe–e–eaks," and—"Trifle with life and death at your peril!" "Who, me?" he'd said—Reisel had mowed him down too.

The bare quorum of dodderers in the synagogue Danny had dug up for Gittel—whether they were depressed by the ungodly hour of morning, or being marooned at the in every sense end of the line in Irish Inwood, or contempt of the flesh, or lust for it—couldn't have contributed more morose amens. Gittel stood a waved, blue-tinted femme fatale with her chic little blue hat on the bias, but during the short and not so sweet marriage prayers you could always catch one set or other of gloomy eyes plastered on the bride's tightly armored hips, and Simeon Brody with his wide American nose and natty blue patch-pockets suit if looks could kill would have been at his funeral instead of his wedding. Then the rabbi asked did she Gittel Leben take this man, and, "I don't know," Gittel glanced up at Brody without much appetite, "he's so old. . . ." Furor in the quorum, and Brody's grown son and daughter eyed each other alarmed. Gittel though made a face, and shrugged. "All right, as long as we're here. . . ."

The couple of blocks to the wedding breakfast on Dyckman Street Gittel —"Lose a daughter . . . some loss . . . and gain two children"—kept up a lively three abreast conversation with her new son and daughter while Danny and the pensive groom followed in the bright early shadow of Vermilyea Avenue.

"Your wife," Danny said, "has made a hit with her stepchildren."

"That's natural," Mr. Brody's laugh said the joke was on him. "My daughter is elated I'm leaving her and my son is elated he's safe from taking me in. To tell the truth, I never expected to remarry. Your aunt and I were holding hands in the movies, so, going home, to say the obligatory I asked her. But," he grinned helplessly, "who anticipated she'd say yes? For a moment back there in *shul* I thought that I was getting a last minute reprieve but fate ruled otherwise. My anxiety now is can two really live as cheaply as one? My first wife took care of the financial affairs, I just handed over the pay envelope. I hope my pension suffices. I'd hate to have to go to the Republican Club looking for a job as a runner on Wall Street. I don't run so good any more. Though according to your aunt her daughter is an excellent housekeeper?"

"Gittel told you that Reisel would keep house?"

Mr. Brody—"Won't she?"—looked ready to run in the opposite direction.

Poor Brody. With the happy pair off in the bus to Swan Lake Danny shook hands with the even happier young Brodys and hopped in the Cadillac to go console the betrayed and deserted Reisel. And what did he see but her door wide open and Bookbinder with the smile and cigar crossing the lawn. Bookbinder laid an armful of dresses in the back of his sporty maroon open Marmon already piled high with cartons.

"The getaway vehicle," he waved.

Danny felt stunned. "With you?"

The cigar see-sawed with Rubin's merriment. "Wouldn't that be the day, Daniel! With her pots and pans. Reiseleh—" she came up the walk and tossed six or eight hatboxes in the front seat for Rubin to dispose of—"your cousin thinks we're eloping. What do you say?"

"I say be still if you value my friendship as my cousin evidently does not."

"Sure Daniel values your friendship. He'll take these hatboxes and what's left in the house in his automobile. But don't touch the piano Daniel," Rubin kept bubbling over, "we wouldn't want to dent your shiny Cadillac with the piano, my men'll pick up the piano tomorrow."

"Where to?"

"To a nunnery—look how she goes away with her tiger stride, she'll devour us yet, and we her benefactors!"

Downtown at the Martha Washington Hotel for women her benefactors were allowed in with her belongings only as far as the elevator in a dim green chintzy lobby. There she let the benefactors sit for an hour under the surveillance of two women desk clerks. And Martha Washington herself, Bookbinder chuckled, probably had an eye on them also from behind a curtain in that Mount Vernon mural to make sure they didn't sneak up the marble staircase. Finally a message from Reisel came that she'd meet them on the street. So like a couple of fools they stood in the shade of the portico for another five minutes before they heard her "Psst!" but saw no Reisel.

"Stupids! Up here!"

They went into the sun and craned their necks up at Juliet redheaded, creamily full-bloused and beautiful leaning over a wrought-iron balcony.

"Nice eh?" those perfect teeth smiled down. "Better than with ungrateful relatives. As soon as I find a rich husband I shall move catty-cornered to that pretty Hotel Seville over there."

"I'm not rich enough," Rubin Bookbinder laughed up, "with my twelve thousand square feet of factory, my own graystone a hop skip and jump from here, my convertible polished like new, and my own outlet bookstore run by a lovely manageress?"

For his qualifications Bookbinder got her heartbreaking smile. "You are not my type," she sweetly called.

Didn't you want to speed crosstown to your scarlet fever room in the Chelsea Hotel—though actually the next stop was Ezra in Orange—and write all this to Sydelle! Oh God, you could just hear that silver laugh of hers as she'd read it. And the Seville across the way, Sydelle and he had been there. Wasn't that the time when . . . But he couldn't place it, he'd hardly ever seen those hotels by daylight. It was an omen though, finding yourself back at a place where you had been together. There'd be a letter from her at West Street tomorrow—you just knew it!

Maybe if mail had come he would have stuck to his guns, phoned this guy Ricky Paine for piano lessons and sweltered in Central Park West under pretense of painting the town red. As it was, the Prince of Lethargy hadn't the heart. Last summer with a superior smile for the masses he used to lilt his way to Sydelle. This year Carrie did all the lilting. These Jewish pioneers to the Promised Land—an apartment in the Bronx—didn't leave Tomer Realty a breathing spell and how, Carrie'd ask, could she close the door on her public? So the easy way was for Danny to knock off at four as Carrie said and let her pick him up for the drive to Sandy Point every day. Out there in water fights with your giggling screeching sons you could forget your chronic disorder. Or you dozed on the sand between the lapping tide and the shadows, and later master-chefed steaks on your flagstone terrace grill. Some sufferer, grappling half asleep at daybreak with a naked woman you reached for as Sydelle and caught as your provocative wife, and yawning to a cool dawn across the horizon. The sky ignited and flamed, another hot day gasped in from the ocean while you had breakfast. Then you tiptoed to the garage leaving the boys and Liela still at their beauty nap, and with Carrie at the wheel you dozed along hot damp main streets toward the city. By the way, Carrie's voice made him start, had he seen yesterday's *Tribune*? Wurffler's Lamps may their tribe increase who'd tried the wood line Carrie blushed to recall she'd recommended in the spring had trailed even in the bankruptcy column.

She teased him, "Your glacial speed can be the ticket Limpy sometimes," and fondly pressed his cheek. "Especially in bed." Afterward she asked what did he think of those Yankees, they never lost a baseball game!

Was it his wife's fault he'd run into a girl who'd waked him up to more than indoor and outdoor sports? Or maybe—the best milk comes from contented cows—he'd been better off sleeping?

But no, my God, the excitement—they call it feverish and it is: your palms cold, forehead tight, throat parched—to be fingering through the first mail at the factory in the hush with no workers in yet. The instant hangover, true. But there'd be another mail. . . .

The one consolation was . . . what a consolation. She must have been either sick—though he'd never known a wrong diagnosis by Nate—or unhappy. You're having wonderful time, you drop the postcard. But with Art? She was his convenience. And France? At Sandy Point parties you were full of Sydelle and asked political wives who'd been to Paris what it was like. "Beautiful!" Which turned out to mean gowns and perfume. In the Paris paper *Le Temps* that he idiotically went out of his way to buy and ransack with the aid of a dictionary for some word of Fields in the music section, he'd deciphered that the French were anti-American on account of war debts. The U.S. had the nerve to want some of our money back. But speak to these dames and you didn't need war debts to hate Americans.

He should have kept her here by main force. If he could just write her, console her, cheer her up. Only where? Make believe you're a bill collector and bully the address out of her mother? He'd met Rhea the sister once, Sydelle had shown them off to each other and reported that Rhea said, "He's nice, you can marry him." Still how could he ask her, even if he hadn't stupidly forgotten her married name. And a tart voice on the phone at the Conservatory said that they did not give out professors' addresses. In desperation he called up the compact dynamo Kulnikoff Sydelle had once pointed out from a distance. Luck was with Danny. Kulnikoff was gone for the summer so you didn't have to trot out your cock-and-bull story just yet.

And after Labor Day when the weather broke and the city was comfortable again, the luck continued. Danny dropped up to the Conservatory and Kulnikoff had just left. And on the October first Auditorium Concert program on the bulletin board was *Poem for Piano: 1932 . . . Fields*. So you could defer the Kulnikoff bout—he'd certainly be in the audience—and if God really smiled down on you you'd have a postcard of hers long before then.

Limpy was such a good boy all summer—the only playing he'd possibly had time for had been her and the Sandy Point rented piano he shared with Ezra—that another year's supervision of his concert life hardly seemed indicated. Yet—as Carrie'd told Arthur Mulloy when she nixed that Central Park South hotel deal—why gamble? The first tunefest Danny went to—*The Sounds of Our Time*—near Grant's Tomb but from the handful they drew you'd think you were in Grant's Tomb, she let him go and followed him there no tickets required take any seat.

Behold the name Fields!

Then Limpy'd come to pay his respects and either this tunesmith Fields was an idiot or Limpy actually was a friend of the family after she Carrie B. Share'd invested a spring in these longhair brawls. Wherever the Fields were Limpy was sitting alone further down—amazing how handsome he was, her collar ad man—and completely impervious to the cute unboyed student types drinking in that wavy-haired Irish mug.

As soon as a violinist dug into catgut you understood the free admission. Another number machine-gunned you with drums and whined at you through saxophones. One guy even beat the crap out of a grunting celesta in three rounds poking it mercilessly in the teeth and while it was groggy dancing around it like Barney Ross at Madison Square Garden to jab it in the kidneys and make it groan foul. And instead of grabbing the next train out of town till the heat was off, each composer of *The Sounds of Our Time* shamelessly stood up to mitt his father and mother: who else could have clapped? But for *Poem for Piano: 1932 . . . Fields* a willowy bunny-toothed young man came on, tripped on his way to the piano but arrived there, and surprised Carrie with a nice dreamy tune, not Puccini by any means but head and shoulders over that other junk. Then bunny-tooth took a couple of bows . . . and—house lights—no Fields!

Limpy headed backstage as who didn't, and why was he limping so—it made you worry—with a crisp fall night outside? But—whither thou goest, let's keep an eye out—the relatives swallowed up in the auditorium were a capacity crowd in the greenroom, very convenient. From the edge of the bustle Carrie watched Limpy wait his turn—you could sense his jaws grinding—around a short bald stocky man of a thousand faces: pop-eyed surprise, smug smilery, wreath-cheeked joy, high-browed disagreement. So if that was Fields and who else could it have been, the guy did display energy. But he looked slightly small and brown next to Limpy. No wonder Mrs. Fields had set her sights higher. And what could Limpy have told him to elicit that evil grin and a comment obviously to match? Limpy went red, furious, to the back of his neck, and said something else that Fields answered poker-faced. Say, Carrie'd bet you a dollar that Fields' little woman was the discussion topic, not *Poem for Piano*. Then Limpy did a Bronko Nagurski to the end zone and out, and Carrie a broken-field slither to the enemy line. She winked at a sweet young thing gushing at Fields and as the kid paused trying to recognize the unknown she barged in: "Don't let her flatter you too much Mr. Fields, even though you deserve it."

"Fields?"—a pitying curl of the lip—"I'm Kulnikoff."

"An impostor! Where's Fields?"

"Fields is abroad, luckily."

"Sydelle too?"

"Another one? Young lady, the information counter is to the left of the entrance—or, to put it a better way in this case, to the right of the exit."

Carrie winked at Kulnikoff and let him enjoy the last word. And next, for congratulating the willowy bunny-toothed young pianist she enjoyed bunny's last words, which were that Sydelle was abroad too!

Poor Limpy.

Between spasms of her mangled insides Naomi supposed that she was dying and just as well. Depending on a baby for everything was only her last mistake. Other women could marry people they love but not she with her hard luck. She told her husband go out and eat and while she screamed her life's strength away on a hospital bed he went. And the doctor—she really was dying!—her sister-in-law's great cousin Barasch, where was he?

Barasch condescended to drop in finally, Naomi screaming sensed him there with his hands in his pockets. Then he touched her in different places and smiled—it was such a good joke—"False alarm, come back next month."

Her body whipped her around. "False alarm?" she screamed.

But, as he predicted, by midnight the pains began to subside. Ma kissed her—"Poor baby, you I mean"—and wiped her drenched face and chest.

Naomi couldn't deny it, she felt so weak and had such a foreboding. They'd be charging hubby for the night anyway the nurse suggested, so why not sleep it off here? The girl meant well but Naomi shuddered.

"God forbid under false pretenses."

When she could she dressed, and she and Ma sat awhile in the deathly still lobby faintly lit by the reception desk. An orderly started swishing a mop with some horrible disinfectant. "Ma—" Naomi croaked, and Golda murmured should she phone Iz to bring a cab?

"No, he might come and crack a joke," Naomi managed to say. "You find one."

But as soon as Ma found one and helped her outside to the lamplit stoop, if not for her stomach it was as though she'd given birth already and returned to life. The gutters were full of leaves from the park, the air was like cool water, and clouds like dark feathers hung under a bent silly moon. She leaned on Golda and giggled hoarsely, "Will Iz be surprised—"

Upstairs Golda was making up the couch to stay overnight when the bedroom door opened again with Iz's desperate "Cutie!" and Naomi was back in the living room dropping into a chair.

Golda caught her own throat. "What?"

"I'm all right, Ma. He has two women inside." She stood. "Get them out, him too. I'll wait in the kitchen."

It didn't take long. The girls, with the assistance of angry hisses from Iz, got themselves out—pretty too, you wouldn't believe it if you didn't know, the black-haired girl ashamed, the blonde shameless.

"Short furlough you had, wasn't it, Isidore?" the blonde laughed.

"Dottie!" black-hair exclaimed.

"Yetta!" the blonde made fun of her.

"Come on, come on Trouble," Golda's tousled son-in-law herded the blonde, "you weren't sent for—now beat it!" He shut the door on her raucous laugh and clutched his head with both hands.

And for the likes of them, those nothings, raucous or demure, the best years of Golda's life had been turned into a misery . . . and—now she was marveling—she'd put up with it! "One bumakeh wasn't enough," she addressed her son-in-law dryly. "You needed two?"

"Who needed her?" Iz flung his arms up. "She kept tagging along because in high school . . . and so forth. I couldn't get rid of her, Ma—"

"So as to the second your innocence is impeccable. And the other?"

"For chrissakes Ma—" Golda shushed the poor fool, he lowered his voice. "—Wasn't I pacing that hospital floor all afternoon like a comic strip? Didn't you with your own lips bring me Cutie's message I should go out and eat, I should go to the movies? And didn't I obey orders—and if you want to see two stinking pictures I recommend you the bill at Loew's Paradise—only at the Chinks' I ran into the Pish sisters and they also went to the Paradise and we wound up here. Did I expect Cutie back in the middle of the night any more than you did or she did? So I'm sorry, it was an honest mistake, it'll never happen again—what do you want from me?"

"Long ago I spoke for myself and spoke badly. I can't speak for my daughter."

Iz grabbed his hair. "Then let her speak for herself." He threw open the kitchen on Naomi's calm back. Her coat was neatly folded over a chair and she sipped tea. "Have a heart Cutie! You want me on my knees? Okay . . . I'm on my knees."

"I don't want you on your knees, and I don't want you in my bed either."

"For chrissakes, haven't I been as good as out of your bed for the past eight months?"

"Good?" Finally she looked at him. "I thought that was for the baby's sake. Or did the baby slip your mind in all the excitement? Either way, God forbid I should forget the baby, Iz, so no matter how long you pester me, I'm not going to let you upset me. But if you have a spark of decency left, shut that faucet off, it's dripping, and go now. I'm very tired."

"Go where?" Iz stood up and pleaded. "This is the place I live, remember?"

"Not any more, or at least not for the present. Go to your mother's, you've paid your room and board there in advance."

"You agreed—and after two years you're throwing that up to me also?"

But Naomi went to tighten the faucet valve and Golda—"Dress warm, it's nippy"—steered Iz toward the bedroom.

"What did I fall into, Ma?" he cried out. "It's a mantrap!"

"What trap? It's the opposite."

"I tell you I'm trapped!"

He refused to pack extra clothes though. He smoothed the rim of his hat in front of the mirror, kissed Golda's cheek with some difficulty with his hat in the way and said huskily, "Take care of my Cutie until tomorrow."

Golda had to smile at that stale act, and kept smiling while she raised the back window to fresh night air and stripped her daughter's bed by the faint glow of sky and street lamp. That clown! Good for Naomi! What did women need men for after all? Golda gingerly dropped a sheet to the floor. Filth and heartache?

"In the dark, Ma?"

"The best way for dirty laundry."

"Yes, repulsive!"

And bright and early Monday—"Are you efficient!" Golda said it with such enthusiasm that both women smiled—Naomi had the locks changed.

Right off the bat before Danny even met her the piano teacher was insulted. Sue him, he'd called up thinking Ricky was a man, asked for Mr. Paine and got Mrs. Paine in the ass.

She said, "Try Rockland State Hospital if you want John."

"I want Ricky."

"Then why did you ask for John?"

So in the writhing entrails the augury was war or in plain English hang up on this nut. Carrie nowadays was as concerned about his comings and goings as about what happened in *Hamlet*. The music that you hadn't been able to keep her away from in May hardly got a tumble from her in October: *Carmen* or *Mimi* for display of an evening gown, that was the sum of it. Could be she hadn't been playing watchdog. His Sydelle try might just have inspired her to try also—share hubby's hobby, the best of wives.

At that she'd tried, in contrast to his beloved. Secretaries, Kulnikoffs and humiliation for him, from Sydelle . . . silence. Then Danny's lie—that he owed Mrs. Fields for a piano lesson—that had flopped with Kulnikoff, clicked with the secretary of Art's business representatives Concert Artists. The secretary of course couldn't give Fields' address but she could forward Idiocy's letter and payment. But suppose the secretary censored the letter? So with his discreet note he had enclosed a check and maybe that had offended Sydelle, though love doesn't take offense that easy.

But poor as the prospects were for a life with Sydelle even when they'd be together again, you owed it to yourself to go through the motions. He made an appointment with Mrs. Paine and on a gorgeous blue and gold Indian summer Saturday afternoon he'd sooner have spent tossing a football around with Ezra and Teddy he strolled through Central Park past the down-and-outers' shanties—but each man has his own tears—to this guy, girl rather, at Carnegie Hall. But in the burst of light at her tower studio when the door opened—my God—Sydelle, back and staging this wonderful heart-stopping surprise for him. Then his eyes saw what was there, and with all Ricky Paine's pretty face and good figure he'd let himself in for a battle-ax. A few bars on the piano and she was no no no-ing, brushing his arms aside, and demonstrating with hard white hawkish hands.

"Do you know about baseball?" she asked deadpan.

"I played left field for the East Side Settlement House Thackeray Society when I was ten."

"We needn't delve into niceties. Pretend there's a baseball in each palm and rest your fingertips on the keyboard."

"Like claws, you mean?"

"For your information I studied in Vienna under Kepetsky, who was formerly a preparer for Leschetitzky."

"Were you ever in Paris?" You'd think he'd just unbuttoned his fly.
"Why that remark?"
"I'd like to go there next spring."
"Well I can't do you guidebook service. I was too busy in Paris unsuccessfully attempting to persuade my former husband that the radiators were not running around the room and that the voices were all in his head. Would you like to assume the proper hand position now?"
Yet she had waves of black hair to the shoulder, white skin, bow lips though pressed tight, a straight nose, a firm chin, a slender body that presumably men held though it beat him how it could happen. When she'd techniqued him into a cramp, he ventured that maybe for an amateur like him Sydelle's way would be more natural.
"If you prefer her way you're certainly free to return to her. As I recall she was never a pianist. Is she still in music?"
"Didn't she tell you she was with the Riverside Quartet before she . . ."
"I've only run into her twice since the Conservatory, and oddly—yes, first with Mel, then Arnold Korkus was with me—both times in the same week last spring and under the most deplorable circumstances."
"She stole your cab?"
"Why bring up cabs? She was simply there, with that nosy concerned expression nobody asked for. But let's not squander more of your time and money on that dismal subject."
Instead she squandered his time and money penciling his music full of expression marks—crescendos, diminuendos, pianissimos, don't ask him whatimos—so you could hardly pick out the notes. He could feel his neck redden while she busily defaced the *Appassionata* Sonata.
"Is that necessary? Technique okay, but I have expression."
"You're paying me five dollars an hour to improve both."
He would have paid her ten dollars an hour to improve neither. He already limped if the weather was wrong. Was he supposed to cripple himself hand and foot with her finger exercises? "Sydelle," he'd said a happy day six months ago in a practice room at the Conservatory, "my chords sound muddy." "Your ear," she'd looked at him, "belongs to a real musician." "Named Sydelle Binder." "Why my maiden name?" she'd shrugged. "Daniel Share, anyway." She'd told him harder on the top note and easier on the pedal—and did those chords sparkle like the spring sunlight!
Still sucker Share felt sorry for this edgy Paine dame with her mouth corners perpetually down. He swore each session would be the last, but he'd cool off—also the lessons kept you regularly practicing at least—and go one more time.
Then at the circumcision of, at last, his sister Naomi's bawling Richard with the worried little forehead—could you blame Richard for looking worried with the Jew-baiters here and the Nazis there?—Danny indignantly asked where was the father and Naomi's answer was come up with the car Saturday and help her move back to Ma's.

"You're shocked, huh?" she smiled.

He was, and why should he have been that she was leaving that punk? Later he wondered about this to Carrie and she said, "You're a conservative, Limpy, like the lame duck in the White House. You detest change."

"The hell I do!"

But Saturday—holy Jesus—he'd completely forgotten about the piano lesson! So he phoned Ricky. But before he could say that he was mailing her the check just the same of course, she lashed into his apologies with a two-pronged attack—commitment to music and cavalier disposal of others' valuable time . . . and he kept apologizing! And not merely apologizing, but humbly asking if next Saturday usual hour would be okay. She wasn't sure how okay it would be, he'd better phone during the week when his mind and her schedule were . . . a bit clearer. And he agreed to that too!

What kind of cripple was he? If la Paine wasn't divorceable, who was? He sent the bastard a check with no explanation and tracked down that other piano-teaching lead of Sydelle's from long ago Vittorio Tallarico in some dump on Jones Street. After all these years it was like taking piano lessons from a character out of *Classic Myths*, though Vittorio was just a nice small neat guy with black hair, a smile and an Italian accent that sounded more like France than like Little Italy. And—a good omen—Vittorio knew all about Paris for Danny!

The shipping clerks, the two Cohen kids related in name only, stuck their heads into the office where the hard-working entrepreneur who knew nothing of holidays looked up from his love letter to Sydelle.

"A happy New Year boss!"

"Happy New Year boys—"

The smiling faces vanished and in the quiet—you still heard the all afternoon scrape of snow shoveling—Irving Cohen the short gave Judah Cohen the tall the long and short of it. "Tonight's the night to get your end wet kiddo."

"Except that I have the unfuckenest prick in Williamsburg."

In the flaky air pressing the piers and the windows snow chains on trucks swung by muffled. The big door creaked to, the Cohen kids left the boss alone in the joint.

Danny's check for the concluding non-lesson from Ricky Paine had come through canceled, but the check to Sydelle naturally hadn't. By the time he finished crossing out that and other complaints, plus the maudlin, all that stood was the Gittel honeymoon anecdote like an island in a pond of penmanship ovals and slashes.

During the summer the new Gittel had unloaded herself on him here when he was his busiest hustling the fall shipments off the tables and on to the trucks.

"It took me hours to find you," Gittel holding Macy's bags to her bosom had yelled over the lathes, "the ignoramuses downtown can't understand clear Yiddish. So look pleased and kiss your cousin."

While Louis the stockman, the two Cohens and the driver Baliber looked pleased, Danny'd had to peck at her rumpled cheek and show her to the office instead of to the door. Brody let her wander around like this?

"Oh him, he's in Wall Street, wherever that is, where he works. He has pull at a political club so they found him a job. A blessing. Who needs him underfoot all day long—" She'd glanced at Riva Wartels's attentive back and roguishly whispered, "You know what he tried in the mountains? To get into my bed!"

"Didn't you let him?"

"My bed is sacred to the memory of my first husband."

"What did your second husband say about that?"

"He said," she'd held Danny's wrist, she'd giggled, "he guessed he's stuck."

Good joke, but Brody wasn't the only one who was stuck. Danny tore up the sheet and started over.

The hell with jokes, and the hell with diplomacy. Tell the secretary at Concert Artists if she read before forwarding, tell Fields, tell the world. January a year ago Sydelle had given him a T.S. Eliot inscribed "Happy birthday, young man." He hadn't said so then but he'd been disappointed—that genteel anti-Semite and his swan songs. Now with a Sydelle-less birthday coming up her correspondent felt at his last gasp also. Blunt Share could only put it in crude black and white—he loved her, there was no one like her.

Without rereading the note he wrote her name on an envelope and pasted that into another he hurriedly addressed to Concert Artists for forwarding. He locked up Quality Lamps for horrible 1932 and—Carrie was throwing tonight's shindig in their house—he could go home and get ready for the big celebration. Last year at E-square and Dorothy Evans' he'd happily toasted in 1932 because he and Sydelle had celebrated New Year's Eve in advance. Sydelle called the Turquoise Club wonderland whenever they went there for the jazz. One minute you were ringing a townhouse doorbell and looking into the looking-glass while taxis honked through the dark of West Fifty-fifth and the doorman was giving you the once-over from inside the speakeasy. Then the city would evaporate in smoke, chandelier light and a hot splash of music that made you smile to each other and made Danny sure he should have stuck to that old banjo no matter what instead of becoming a glass-jawed sergeant of industry.

But the last afternoon of 1931 a pianist had come up on the bandstand and above the talk of the not too many drinkers begun . . . a Chopin prelude! A stooped seamed New York waiter had already been standing by for the order, but Sydelle had pressed Danny's hand, "Chopin too! What won't wonderland provide given half a chance?" and she'd shut her eyes and brought his palm to her cheek. Then those long lashes rose, saw how angry the waiter was, and, "Excuse me," she'd tinkled a laugh off deaf ears, "but this young man makes my life magical."

So what had happened in six months? He was the same man wasn't he?

Heading for the Turquoise Club now to long for her was the flabbiest self-indulgence. But ankle-deep slush, a driving rain that blew his umbrella inside out and snapped two of the ribs, then straps on a couple of crowded steamy El cars, and he was set for a drink.

When, through the looking-glass—Jesus Christ, head-on, no chance of ducking—Ricky Paine! She stopped him dead in the vestibule and played naughty eyes on him while a stocky gangster type overtook her, paused, passed her, and stood presenting his case to heaven, which had blank-faced Cupids at the corners of a white enameled ceiling here as surrogates.

"I—" she swayed slightly—"owe you a lesson Danny Share."

"No no, that's okay, we're square."

"Square? I'm all precarious angles. Let me lean on you—" For that guy's glare she jiggled her fingers at him, "Ta ta—" and did he exit quick! "Ta ta," she echoed herself with a creamy curl of the cheek and rested on Danny. "Home James."

Jesus, like history repeating itself, almost. Could you fall in love with a Ricky Paine?

A buck, and the doorman flagged them a cab. But at the top of the stoop in that gale—"Invigorating!"—Ricky threw out her chest and did deep breathing exercises just long enough to get soaked before she collapsed against Danny. He half-carried her down and—"For three blocks?" she laughed—helped her in. The driver stepped on the gas and made a five yard plunge into a traffic jam. Water streamed off the windows.

"Cozy, no?" Ricky murmured. "We're in a submarine. You have beautiful hands," she smoothed one with hers, "but you must be taught how to use them."

"Who was your annoyed friend?"

"Vonce?"

"That's Yiddish for bedbug."

"I'm both, née Freiberg. But Vince the *vonce*, our professor of calisthenics—no, honestly, he is that, at New York University, not to speak of elsewhere. Can you imagine that man imagining I'm at his disposal Danny Share?"

"I loathe those guys. And he got you drunk too."

She tilted her lashes to him—Jesus Christ—just like Sydelle!

"My mind is perfectly clear. It's just that—" he felt her full weight—"I found it difficult standing."

Unlike his lovelorn pecker.

"Danny Share," Ricky shook herself, "I'm in love."

"With Vince?"

"Are you joking? Alan. That's why I drank those two Cuba Libres. But . . ." she pressed heavily against Danny again, "there's an age problem . . ."

"He's too old?"

"Now I will a round unvarnished tale deliver. I am."

"Where did you hear that expression," Danny was delighted, "unvarnished tale?"

"Simple arithmetic. He's still—"

"Forget him."

"Don't I try. *Otello*, by Verdi—"

But Sydelle exactly!—who would have guessed?

"—don't you," she cuddled closer, "know Shakespeare?"

So he kissed her, but with her mouth gaping she almost gobbled him down. And upstairs—

Sydelle would slip into bed in her underthings. This one brought him straight to her frilly bedroom—"Don't let go for a second or I'll be a fallen woman beforehand Danny Share"—and with his arm as a handrail performed her lean gymnastics until she was naked. And in bed she clutched you down there while she wrung out what she wanted so you couldn't move till too late.

Shakespeare? She'd been reading love excerpts on account of her student Alan who was too young to marry her. Concerts, opera even? Not this baby. She had enough music all week long. In her spare time she preferred tennis. Many a day the mighty Vonce squashed her on the courts, but today he got his squashing in a speakeasy.

And women like this were his father's full-time career?

"That's an erection?" she played with Danny's unwilling tool.

"So you found Sydelle Fields unpleasant, huh?"

"Sydelle who? Oh her—I should say so! Ugh, what memories! Having her stop me once on Park Avenue was bad enough, with her prying how was I. I was knocked up, that's how I was—the noble Mel knocked me up—and I was on my way to the doctor with Mel persecuting me every step that I should have the baby—as if he'd have supported it. Then Arnold took me a few days later for the actual abortion, and again Sydelle . . . What did Sydelle have to do with it? She was there—that was sufficient." Ricky gave a flick to his shriveled thing. "You're hopeless my boy." She yawned, she turned over, she cozied her palms under her cheek.

Danny dressed—sorry, Sydelle, and if there were other sins known or unknown that he'd committed, forgive him for those too. And he went home.

25

"THE BRONX," TEDDY WROTE IN HIS HOMEWORK, "IS NOT known anywhere," which Miss Clarke corrected in red to "everywhere." Teddy'd made the mistake because he'd been in a hurry to run out and shoot marbles at the edge of the green park, but he took a try anyhow at one of the teacher's gold stars for excellence he usually brought home to show off to Ma every day. He raised his hand and with innocent brown eyes assured Miss Clarke he knew all about the Bronx okay, his mother's office was there. He'd meant those fellows—Larry Israel, Fred Goodrich, Jimmy Wilson—who were so smart and kept claiming *they* never heard of it. Miss Clarke said that wasn't very nice blaming his classmates and Daddy agreed with her, but Ma laughed he'd been robbed.

Now at dinner, with the windows open and the curtains tied back to let in the last tawny sunlight, his mother—"Additional information for Miss Clarke"—passed him an envelope. It was just a letter to Ma's office in funny handwriting, but look at the postage stamp—the lady wearing a helmet: *France*. "What information?" He immediately began peeling off the stamp with his tongue working.

Ezra peered, "That it's from Paris, stupid, so the Bronx *is* known everywhere and you and Miss Clarke were both wrong," then calmly resumed eating.

"Show Daddy," Carrie said.

So when what you'd given up hope of finally arrived your guilty pulse hammered. But—let showdowns be showdowns—the hell with guilt. Only what was this? A foreign hand, not Sydelle's lilt. Danny's heart reared: Art, in disguise, and sent to Carrie at her Tomer Industries so the denounced villain Share couldn't possibly intercept it. And what trouble the great Fields must have gone to locating that address—Danny himself didn't know it offhand.

"It'll bite you," Carrie said sadly, "but read it anyway."

He gave her a hard stare. Then on the back of the envelope the writer's name was also Tomer—no Sydelle in question—the same as Carrie's mother's maiden name, and in the letter this woman, a Meta Tomer, gave news about Germany.

Just last Saturday you saw the Germans in action in the *March of Time* newsreel: Schicklgruber in a stadium May Day shouting horrible hausfraus —good-lookers too—into a shiny-lipped swoon as if they had God in a pulpit. And street scenes, Jews, middle-aged men with Stars of David pinned on, sweeping glass splinters, mopping sidewalks, while the fans jeered. And the Nollendorfplatz station, Berlin, the last refugee train out. Reisel said now there then here. She might be right. He and the boys hiked to the Palisades and KILL THE JEWS swastikas had already sprouted on the George Washington Bridge. Teddy had gotten scared.

"What will we do if they kill us, Daddy?"

"Kill them back."

And damned if he'd run. Was life that sweet? He'd stand still—they sell guns here, if not in Germany—and take a few home-grown beauties with him, Silver Shirts, Christian Fronters.

Big thoughts, but the letter from Meta Tomer bit him all right, her father slapped, kicked, punched by S.A. men, her mother kicked, both dragged out God knows where. In what she used to think of as her Breslau they were loading Jews into cattle vans. By some chance—good or bad she could hardly say, yet you struggle God knows why to stay alive—she'd been overnight at a friend's and then a Gentile neighbor risked arrest, not a large risk but how many took it, getting her to a train to the border. But in Europe who wanted Jews? She trembled at the sight of the police. All over they were sending Jews back, maybe from Paris too. At the American consulate they give a visa if a guarantee of support (she'd enclosed the form) is signed by an American, a relation, they shrug. Pardon her, you learn to think quickly. She told them she hadn't the New York cousins' address and they pointed at their telephone books. Please, Mr. Tomer, whether they were related she didn't know. She wrote down names in case, virtually a small family tree. But in Breslau before the Nazis she'd earned a living as a dressmaker. In America, if she should reach there, she would not be a burden. . . .

So this was the Europe Sydelle couldn't spare a second from to drop you a note? You read this and the grand passion dwindled.

Carrie, she'd closed shop early and headed for the Immigration Disservice in the Subtreasury Building, a simple citizeness, Tomer Industries. And with the Father of Our Country looming larger than life on the steps in front of the portal, a great-grandson of Our Country Mr. Francis J. Appleby lounges smaller than life in his swivel chair with his high-toned fingers pressed under his chin and his ice-in-the-eyes reserved for Jews only. The Hitler government, Mr. Apppleby sucked his fancy fingertips, has assured us of the safety of German Jews for one thing, for another this candidate for application for a visa is safe in France in any case. Then the sponsor, as well as the candidate, requires the most careful scrutiny. Mr. Appleby—why hadn't *Mr.* Tomer signed?—snapped a patrician finger at the affidavit. How could an old man like her grandpa sign, especially after all these years in the cemetery?

"Easy monsters," Carrie took a bow to her helpless thrashing sons, "a laugh's a laugh but if you spray like that I'll have to move you around the table to keep the walls the same color."

Downtown she hadn't mentioned her grandfather he should rest in peace. She'd explained that Tomer Industries was just little her, thanked Mr. Crappleby ("Easy boys—") for his valuable time and help and gone home to call her pal Senator Wagner for a bit of his slightly more valuable time and help. Luckily the Senator happened to be in town, and two hours later Jack Delaney gave her a ring from Wagner's office. He'd spoken long distance to the State Department and the message was consider the affidavit approved, allow Mr. Francis J. etcetera a week to arrange his face, and then jab him about progress.

Good luck to you Meta. Sure it might happen here, with Presbyterian churchmen at their New Jersey clambakes voting down sympathy—sympathy!—for kikes in Germany, but meanwhile Carrie didn't just clench fists like the hot-blooded Share. A Jew cried help and she helped! And escape was his cherished daydream, like in his boyhood when Ma didn't want him on her side against his father and Danny would sit wishing himself away with Jeanne, Edith, Maxine, Pearl—whichever it happened to be at the time? What kind of bastard was he?

A kind whose reform movement dissolved over transatlantic shipping schedules in the first heat of June.

The *Paris, Leviathan* and *Berengaria* were due in from Le Havre the anniversary of Sydelle's sailing. Why shouldn't she be on one of them? Lucky for his sons you couldn't simultaneously spread yourself over Piers 57, 62 and 54, so under a dull sky in Central Park that muggy Sunday he was their pride and joy fancy-Dannying short flies and topped grounders that they and their pals batted. That night Carrie had people over and Danny knew all the scores: baseball (if the Yankees didn't stop losing one ex-fan would be Carrie B. Share); Roosevelt's Blue Eagle (the Eagle's screams improving business a bit but no news at his well-paid factory); Hitler (what did they mean crackpot? German chancellor! And beware of the dogs in our front yard Huey Long, Joe McWilliams, Gerald L. K. Smith!) Yeah, glib Share noise of the party, drunk without drinks because he was sure Sydelle was back, probably he'd hear her voice tomorrow! Some Irma with an all-year-round suntan in a low-cut flowered dress, whose kosher restaurants tycoon husband sat across the room and never removed his smiling but worried eye from her, asked Danny if he had a brother for a sister she knew.

"Sorry," he told her, "only sisters."

"Then," she wreathed her nut-brown cheeks, "you'll have to do."

"Do what?"

"Need you ask?"

"Tell your sister thanks, I'm a happily married man."

Irma flipped her juicy behind, "Tell her yourself," and left him delighted, overjoyed!

In West Street in the morning he didn't wait for his freight elevator—too slow. Suppose Sydelle sneaked out of the house and called early? He raced up the three flights, fumbled the lock open with eager fingers, and—ring phone!

The phone rang only on business, and you couldn't keep beating Riva Wartels to the hello. A week of that and "Expecting good news, Mr. Share?" she gave him her horsy titter.

A look shut that one up fast, but it was embarrassing having to flash her the look, just as it was embarrassing asking Information every day was there an Arthur Fields listed. Worse, suppose Information quit being sorry and answered yes? The way Sydelle had hated going to Europe that she'd stay longer didn't make sense. Of course you could find out for sure from the Conservatory, but a full year not to write—did you want to? If she could read those letters of his maybe over a cigarette, why assume she'd pick up a phone?

By the end of the month though he'd reached his limit. You were half dead, fagged, anyway. Carrie noticed that and pitched in with the heart-warming advice why not go see Nate for a checkup—thanks kid—so you wondered whether by a happy coincidence some fatal disease hadn't caught up to you finally. Just the same he didn't see Nate. He dialled the Conservatory for his death sentence.

Holy Jesus—the secretary said that Professor Fields was still in Europe! Sydelle hadn't telephoned because she wasn't here!

Courtesy Hitler to show that you're still Jews, Ezra and Teddy were at a strictly kosher Maine camp where the sun rose and set to the Hebrew national anthem *Hatikvah.* So Danny was in the clear at Sandy Point the glorious Fourth to make glorious love, in pajama tops at breakfast with Carrie crooning next to his ear in time to the ocean, on the settee after lunch with bands of light swelling and narrowing on their rattan floor-mats, and—at the end of company, fireworks on the beach and good nights—naked for fireworks in their moon-flooded bed. And the whole day long crazy Danny was celebrating Sydelle.

But the inglorious Fifth—Professor Fields was back but not in—crazier Danny sat in the empty factory by the silent phone and went through work motions while he outbled the sunset.

Clouds over the river darkened to purple.

She must have been busy, just off the boat. Her furniture had been put in storage, Art didn't trust sublets. True, when she hit New York five years ago she phoned straight from the bus, but that time Art wasn't with her. You couldn't always run to a phone. Only, that time, she did. . . .

Think Danny-o called it quits?

On Eighth Avenue Danny-o bought a nice postcard with the Empire State Building needling a blue sky and a few innocent clouds and wrote her care of Art at the Conservatory: "Welcome to the big town, resuming lessons? Best to Art."

Once you sent that off—and no reply it went without saying—if you had a scintilla of shame left you couldn't call the Conservatory any more. So the Friday Quality Lamps closed for vacation Danny-o saw his happy workers to the door with a cheery goodbye and with a falsetto voice he called the Conservatory.

"Professor Fields," a man answered, "has deserted to Hollywood."

"Mrs. Fields as well?" Danielle caroled.

The man . . . couldn't say . . . about Mrs. Fields—but the split-second break meant he could if he wanted to. Only how do you beat down a stone wall—not just this guy, the whole year of wrong numbers? You're on the ropes Danny-o—so what's the use. He threw in the towel, he signed off.

Sharp-eyed Carrie—"What hit you, Limpy?"—stopped by to take him to Sandy Point and he could sense his own punch-drunk grin.

"Spring fever in August." He moved an invoice toward her. "I over-ordered nine thousand yards of silk tape."

Carrie patted his cheek. "You did good. Tape and everything else'll be going up with the dollar going down. Put some Quality catalogs in your briefcase, when I have a minute tomorrow we'll give your prices a face-lift."

But—he caught that supple waist—right now he didn't care about prices. He pulled her close and pressed his lips on target against those neat sturdy breasts.

"You won't have a minute."

"Anthony Adverse is molasses next to you Limpy."

He laughed, "Are you reading that?"

"Simone thought it was hot stuff poor thing—which," Carrie straddled his lap and kissed him at her leisure, "doesn't say much for Rob, does it?"

They were a pretty disheveled pair of industrialists leaving West Street and it wasn't till Danny woke up the next morning that he remembered that he'd forgotten Sydelle. Then why should his heart weigh like a lump in his chest? On the other side of the water Germans were hounding Jews through the streets. Here there was an enormous blue and white sky today to soak up sunshine under, waves slowly heaved in from the pale curve of the horizon to a white hiss of foam at the foot of his canvas chair. Carrie stood laughing thigh-deep in surf that muffled Rob Ward's shouts and the women's shrieks around a big glistening beach ball. It made you smile just to look at them in the sunlight and sparkle: his Venus in blue twisting for the ball; Simone Ward a tank suit peach with her brown shoulders raised and ready; E-square's buttercup number two Dorothy Evans with determined little palms slanted back; and Bernice Cash—lady languor in the presence of hubby Joe the laundry tycoon who was always burping, clutching his side and feeding pills to his ulcers—now without him a smiling flame-thrower at Justice Rob the willing catcher gray at the temples but green in the trunks.

A dame decided to give you the pink slip without even the courtesy of the slip and you were supposed to pull the shade down on life?

Danny exploded into the surf, he herded together shrieking Bernice, Dorothy and Simone, and he had a beach ball bounced off his noggin. Next he was knocked down—Carrie—and thrashing underwater. He pulled her down and they came up wrestling. Bernice distantly yelled "I'm next at him—" "I'll go you a round, Bernice," Rob volunteered. But Bernice—"Scared of Simone?"—kept her eye on Danny.

What a day, what a Carrie!

So she'd never been more than three inches into anyone's Five Foot Shelf of Classics. Neither had he before the leads from Reisel and then from . . . yeah. Was courting your wife with Antony, Cleopatra and Anna Karenina against the law?

Ta ta Sydelle—you were a good lay while you lasted.

Except that Carrie didn't court so easy along those lines. Her couple of stupid tenements filled up her days, and then there were social functions, shows, give or take parties. Sure, fall came and she put on her sable stole and went to the St. James Theater with him to see the *Hamlet* the papers hadn't been able to rave over enough. The outraged Danny could tear it apart as much as he wanted in Dave's Blue Room later and on the way home—the title character climbing the scenery as if he was trying to escape from his own performance, and who could blame him!—Carrie got a kick out of an actor with pep.

Danny ran for the text while Carrie was getting into her nightgown and she yawned and laughed "Shakespeare Breakspeare—no forced feeding," and went to sleep.

Bed had its uses to her, but reading wasn't among them. Crazy Danny felt so frustrated that he bought two more tickets and sent Reisel to that *Hamlet* to let him know if he really was crazy. Reisel—"Sufficient that you wasted your money, was I to waste my precious time?"—let him know she walked out on Act I dragging her friend Shifra past offended playgoers whose intellects were in their knees.

So what, Daniel wise man in Israel? With a lift from Carrie Meta Tomer was set up and at work in the garment district, not as sewer—"If you don't make big money fast," Carrie'd grinned to the girl she still had to fend off from kissing her hands, "my name is mud at the Labor Department"—but assistant designer. And since Meta—the word spread yell help to the Bronx—Carrie had been vouching for refugees, bringing them over and guarding them like a mother hen until the angel Carrie was a byword on Washington

Heights. Him? Other drunks drank, he read. And what was the great music lover looking for at the concerts he haunted, the Messiah in octaves?

Nah, just Sydelle.

The State Building conference room in back alley twilight where the Refugee Resettlement Committee that Carrie chaired met once a month was a perfect backdrop for that set of minds. They'd meet and, with some reluctance from Mr. Falconer of the New York Bank who stood for the taxpayers and Mr. Ryan Deputy Controller who stood for 1,358,486 workless Americans in the State of New York, they'd slice the legislature-allotted bacon among the assistance and educational organizations that made up a majority of the Committee. Then, without so much as one refugee resettled as a result of their splendid efforts, they'd congenially disperse while Hitler continued turning the Jews upside down. But study those assistance and education reports as Carrie did, compare expenditures with services rendered, and you saw that the folks she, the governor's wife, Simone Ward and the rest had vouched for weren't refugees—they were goddam pioneers, like Carrie's noncousin but sister under the skin Meta Tomer. Could that young lady make a bolt of material stand up and do tricks, and was she beginning to rake in shekels the good old American way! Sure some lost souls haunted Washington Heights with ghostly sighs, one took the gas pipe: survival of the fittest unfortunately. But why were the charity agencies on the Committee tax exempt if not to handle such cases without looting the Committee?

So after the November meeting she caught Dave Whitehill the governor's gloomy chief of operations who adorned each session with his lips clamped together and didn't unclamp 'em now. She talked and he put his coat on, the bastard, and to boot had the effrontery to say, "What would you do with the money, invest it less commission in real estate?"

But—elementary child psychology: another big wheel acting up because Eva Tomer's little girl Carrie could run rings around him and never feel winded—she kept her poise. The dogs manning our consulates growled "Means test—we don't admit public charges" if you asked why the immigration quotas stayed unfilled. She'd sink the Committee's appropriation skimpy as it was into Treasury bills as collateral for sneaking a few more homeless and tempest-tossed—did he ever have kids to take to read that poem at the base of the Statue of Liberty?—past the golden door.

Whitehill's ramrod back, slate-gray stare, angry jaw and gray proconsul fringe around the bald leathery dome convinced her—he had a brother named Weisberg, E-square Evans said—she'd run into another of those crummy Jewish anti-Semites. But stoneface went sunny.

"You really are out to help the people my boss has in mind."

"So why all those scowls, Pops?"

Now he could not quit grinning.

"Shocked."

"Shocked!"

"In the course of time," he took off his coat, sat down again at the conference table, and patted the chair next to him for her to sit on, "I've lost my hair, my wife, my son, my daughter, and most of my faith in humanity."

"But not your bite."

And she had him laughing out loud.

"Be careful, Carrie. That's how I fell in love with my wife. She was sassy too, nobody scared her."

"Till you married her and taught her the meaning of fright."

"I never did." The slanty-eyed Kalmuck smile became desperate. "That was the worst day of my life, the day Gertie died."

"Oh poor guy! Recently, huh?"

"Not that recently, but it sticks in my chest."

"Don't give in, Whitehill. You've got to live."

"Give in? I remarried, Carrie, an overripe banana."

Now it was Carrie who laughed out loud the way she drew these aging welterweights. This specimen had the chest and shoulders all right in his sharp pinstripe suit. Getting used to the leathery skinhead and gray hairs might take a while though, perhaps forever.

"Eight to five you're a misunderstood husband."

"Pick up the marbles—but past tense. What did she think she married, gray hairs what's left of them, a five acre Loudonville house and a bankroll? Any Shloime or his cousin in the suburbs of Albany my second and ex-wife fell for, and it was love every time."

"Was that her defense in court?"

"She didn't go to court, Carrie. I had the pictures."

"Why you sneaky bastard!"

"What do you mean?" he laughed.

Then he switched to politics—and some guys talked love like this with the eyes boring into you. Don't spend what the legislature allots you and no more funds from the legislature. Also if you don't spread the money around, what do the charity outfits need you for? And without their support what votes will you have when your enemies on the Committee raise a stink that a state unit is circumventing federal policy? His colleague Ryan was controllable only because they had a Jewish governor. And before the meeting Mr. Falconer man-to-manned Whitehill that conditions in Germany must be exaggerated. Falconer had it on good authority babies were being conceived by the concentration camp inmates.

"He told me that—with six hundred thousand marked out for destruction!"

Carrie, "You're a true bar mitzvah Whitehill," clapped those hard as steel biceps.

"You can call me Dave, from Rivington Street. But even if I weren't—that son of a bitch!" He looked at a watch tied on to his ditchdigger wrist by a thick black strap. "I have a lunch appointment with Ryan, but there must be some way around our blood money problem. You'll hear from me, Carrie. It's been a pleasure meeting the real you."

He should live so long, with two weeks of silence following. So up in the office she let Arthur Mulloy in on the subtleties of refugee financing and Arthur's blue larcenous eye twinkled instant light on the subject. Possibly a little bookkeeping hocus-pocus—nothing indictable, deferring payments to the charities of the funds the Committee voted them occurred to Arthur—might meet the requirements?

"Arthur, I could kiss you."

"Don't Carrie. My sister would disapprove of me kissing the boss."

Finally—sent for you yesterday and here you are today—Alibi Ike phoned just in from Albany. She'd been on Whitehill's mind a lot—thanks pal—but he'd been ears deep in patronage sessions since the day after the election. Could she come downtown for lunch? She was committed to her spaghetti and clam sauce at Mario's on Arthur Avenue but there was the Third Avenue El and he was welcome to join her.

"I have no time for Third Avenue Els, Carrie, I'm ears deep with the mayor today. Hop a cab to the Ritz-Carlton, I'll pay the fare."

"Sorry sport, I'm ears deep in real estate."

Who needed him? She worked out the next step for herself: escrow credits the agencies could administer as collateral for life and death visa cases and take title to at the end of the fiscal year. Then with the governor's okay there'd be a renewed budget allotment and fresh money for more collateral for refugees! Arthur approvingly puffed his pipe She hopped her Cadillac downtown to the governor's New York mansion and the governor's wife thought Carrie's was a wonderful idea, drop in the bucket though both women agreed it was. Then Carrie arranged a Ritz-Carlton luncheon but no Whitehill present. Sub rosa she invited her prospective majority vote in the Committee: Miss Gershon the fire-eater from Jewish Assistance, Mr. Larkin from the Protestants, the Catholics' Mr. Delaney and the nonsectarian fundraiser Mr. Graves who didn't care of what persuasion your money was. People are human, could be lives were in danger, the governor wanted this and in the end the dough would pass over to their organizations with interest anyway. They packed in the eats on her, they listened, and they approved.

Would Whitehill scowl in the next full Committee when this was voted official!

At that meeting Mr. Butler the eminent educator scowled. "We are a resettlement committee, not an underground railroad." He stood for eminently educating legal immigrants on arrival. Mr. Falconer and Mr. Ryan glumly agreed. But Whitehill came in with a big bright hello to Carrie and hung around after the meeting to clamp his manly grip on her arm—"You went over my head, Carrie"—and make her feel ready for anything as they stood grin to grin.

First the two of them took a cab through the gray cold to Fulton Street —he paid the fare—and in Whyte's Restaurant he glared down the same fat cigars she'd magnetized passing between the oak-paneled booths ten years ago at the outset of her merry career. The sport ordered her steak, good food for a scrapper.

"Thinking of managing me?" she cracked.

"I'm seriously considering it, Carrie. But no taking dives for punks."

His boyhood dream had been welterweight champ, he'd actually fought a few six-rounders billed as Whitehill. That was how he got the name, Weisberg translated to American, at St. Nicholas Arena at the turn of the century. Win? Did he look like a loser? He'd bowed out when the racketeers who booked fights expected him to throw one for fifty bucks.

"Whereas," Carrie said, "you wanted a hundred."

"You're darn tootin' I wanted a hundred. So I quit boxing for an honest game—politics."

Zoom—he was back to the late Gertie and if ever a woman was sincerely lamented Gertrude was. The Democratic Club was where he'd met her. He'd put himself through New York Law School and in 1906 Mr. Charles Francis Murphy made him the youngest district leader the Tenth Ward ever had. Why? For his talents ringing doorbells, working favor nights at the clubhouse—a citizen comes in looking for help, you do him a favor—and if necessary protecting the Jewish vote against the reform element. Gertie was teaching business subjects at Washington Irving High then and you should have seen her: slim, good-looking—but tough, with real character, a face that had meaning in it, not just a dummy with rouge and lipstick. In the course of the '07 panic she brought young girls in on favor nights, former pupils of hers for him to find jobs for. One okay, two okay, three okay. The fourth his suspicious nature overcame him and he asked was Gert drawing an agent's fee. Those magic words opened quite a trapdoor. Gert sent the girl out of his office and he got washed away by a deluge. She'd had some esteem for him, and he was worse than her husband—

"Husband!" Carrie exclaimed.

"Yes," Whitehill said complacently, "Gert was Mrs. Shiff when we met."

"And Shiff was on ogre."

"Why he was God's gift to woman, Carrie, blond, even better looking than yours, with a string of dress shops."

"And you sit here and tell me she fell for a shyster with a mug like yours?"

"Bald already too Carrie," he fixed those eyes on her. "And she still couldn't help herself."

Gert though gave it to him good with his agent's fee. We men—she meant him and Shiff—made her sick! Her husband resented her wasting her time on those kids when there were better things to do—wasting time, she bawled out Dave as if he'd said it, with Jewish children in the juvenile courts for prostitution! But to suggest a profit motive! Then—Gertrude had been an uptown girl, from Teachers College—she let him in on how these kids grew up, him, Dave Whitehill, whose mother enrolled him in a church school as a child for the clothing handouts and free lunch. You had brick fights with the public school kids and every now and then you saw the gutter swing up and hit you, not to mention the shiners and bloody noses you traded with your own classmates if a discussion of Judaism happened to arise. Two of his Rivington Street boyhood pals Gyp the Blood and Lefty Louie graduated to the electric chair in Sing Sing. But Gert—he shook his head smiling as if Gert were right there in front of him—swarmed over him with so much the worse if his experience had taught him nothing—he should be ashamed of himself!

He hadn't been ashamed of himself, but he'd been impressed.

Now Dave's daughter was married happily to a born Jim Perry, an engineer whose hard work—and in these times Jim was lucky to have gotten it—was in Leadville Colorado. Dave's son had been thrown out of Brown University for picketing the college president with an anti-ROTC sign PREXY IS A WARMONGER, and he was holed up on relief in a cold water flat on Sullivan Street—he wanted no part of the old man's tainted assistance. That left the ten room house in Loudonville for Dave to rattle around in, the house he and Gert had built and raised their kids in.

"Often I go to sleep praying let me dream of her, and I don't know which is worse, Carrie, when I do dream of her or I don't."

"Poor fella, you're lonely."

He laid his prizefighter paw over Carrie's hand on the table and she was sure the next stop would be his Ritz-Carlton bed. But what he had up his sleeve was that big black-strapped watch again. He sighed, patted her hand, and had to catch the 3 P.M. Albany Special for an evening conference!

But the clincher was his coming up to the Bronx to go clam digging with her in a bowl of spaghetti at Mario's and regaling her with homage to Gert in the form of teary eyes, a red nose and trumpet sneezes.

Snowed all last night in Loudonville, he told Carrie. He'd been finishing his section of the boss's budget message and past midnight the lawns, sheds and fir trees had looked so nice and white from the kitchen window that he had sipped his nightcap with half a mind—if not for the hour—to phone Carrie long distance and wish her an advance Merry Christmas. Upstairs no sooner had he dropped off to sleep to the crash of the wind circling the house than he'd waked with a start. Gert had been getting up—and at the same time it hadn't been Gert, it had been Carrie. Carrie had suddenly become his housekeeper instead of Mrs. Healy though only a little while ago he'd driven one of them home to Watervliet—Carrie, Adele Healy?—right after dinner on account of the snowstorm. But when he'd mumbled a question it had been Gert who told him hush, she was going out to brush the snow off the evergreens, otherwise the branches would break. Then he'd dozed a minute, jumped up, and gone after her turning on lights as far as the cellar before he'd gotten his bearings. And Carrie, had he felt desolate, and guilty too that the snow had been weighing down Gert's evergreens. He'd thrown a coat over his pajamas, picked up a rake and flashlight and gone into the snow ankle deep dusting off trees like a sleepwalker. The worst was that when he'd waked up entirely with his teeth knocking together, asked himself what he was doing out there, and quit, he'd felt as bad as when he began.

"That's . . . ap*choo* . . . how I caught a cold. Don't your heart bleed for Dave?"

And horny Carrie had left Mulloy a note that she might be gone for the day!

She yawned, "I told you already. You need a wife," and smirked, "not just a housekeeper."

"My . . . ap*choo*, excuse me," he grinned, "opinion exactly. How about someone like you, Carrie?"

She bowed to the compliment though he had a tough case. Carrie Baums do not grow on evergreens. But even a watered-down version would be a big improvement. E-square Evans had met the first wife Gert the dried prune with gardening gloves and a spade in her hand, and the second wife Millie a replica of the first to the identical perpetually pursed lips. "Might change your luck," Carrie granted him.

"Think aboud it."

"Offhand I can't think of anyone."

"Go home and look in the mirror, Carrie."

"Are you serious?"

"Am I ever frivolous?"

"Who would have guessed—" Carrie laughed—"the chief of state operations a dreamer!"

And he laughed too, full of confidence.

So in the cab back to the Hub she asked if he'd heard anything new about a highway on the Manhattan West Side where she had some property, and he was pretty sure . . . ap*choo* . . . that that ought to be aboud reaching a live boil, he'd let her know.

Make hay while the sun shines.

But the evening came when Danny stamped snow off his shoes in Town Hall, checked his hat and coat, marched grimly up to his box and wondered why he was there. A glance at the lonely souls in the balcony above and at the cluster in the orchestra below showed Sydelle wasn't. He could have shut himself in his den and . . . read. The boys had plenty of homework and the girl he'd married until death would them part hadn't been speaking to him for three days.

The Saturday after New Year's he'd gotten home, had lunch and, dull as he'd been from the party the night before, just sat down at the piano when his older boy politely invited him for a bellywop in the snow.

"Because you got in your practice," he'd caught beaming Ezra between his knees, "while I spent my morning manufacturing lamps."

Teddy'd dashed in, "What do you say!," backhanded a hit and run slap at Ezra's behind—"The sleds are getting warm—" and dashed out green scarf flying with Daddy's boy Ezra's cheerful fist a close second.

Put in your hours a day at the piano kid and don't grow up needing drinks at gatherings of the usual political pals with the usual talk and the usual slick dolled up women that you had to explain your remarks to. Time was, an invite from the governor of New York even for a second string party would have been heady enough without whiskey chasers. But now, "Introduce me to him once more tonight," Danny'd warned Carrie, "I about-face and leave." Carrie'd laughed, "He's always polite." And sure enough, the little king of the mountain had flicked Danny off with a smile while squeezing "Carrie dear—" by the wrist. Why not?—she was invaluable to his Refugee Committee and he had to thank her again. So here was a cultivated gent with an art collection on the walls from Rembrandt to Feininger—though you never saw the pictures for the heads intervening—and his preference was Carrie. Then Dave Whitehill—what had been eating him?—had popped up and stuck his gray-fringed mug in Danny's face with "How's the lamp business, Share?" as if the lamp business was an insult. And the noise, the crowds. Legal liquor notwithstanding, even his longing for Sydelle had come out dry.

Saturday too, for all of his Beethoven on the piano. Nothing, he'd felt nothing, and it was worse than suffering.

Then the door had slammed—Carrie—and he'd jumped as if he had been caught in the act. And she had stridden in pulling her gloves off.

"Prepare for moving day fella."

"Your East Side scheme?" Carrie wanted to crash the anti-Semitic Park Avenue barrier for a great view of traffic and drab gray buildings and he should do the applying—they'd never take Limpy Share for a Jew until too late. "That no still goes."

"Scheme eh? This isn't us, it's you."

Odd the jolt those seconds that he'd thought she was packing him in. Had Carrie—this had never entered his mind—found someone else?

"Wun Long Pan," she'd stuck her jaw out to mimic him. "Too bad, boy, resign yourself. You have no alternative."

His head had pounded. Did he want to leave, now that it was too late? But this scheme—shouldn't you know that Carrie slept dreamt and lived business—was to sell West Street and move Quality Lamps to twenty thousand bargain square feet in the Bronx, ridiculous. He'd shrugged and resumed fingering the piano. And suppose, she'd asked, that a waterfront project—highway, parks, the works—closed him up anyway? He hadn't heard of any waterfront project.

"Well your little wifie has, last night at the party. There's been a conjunction of the governor, the mayor and Moses the tour leader."

"Then," he'd faced her, "who'd want to buy?"

"How do you like your little wifie," she'd slapped his shoulder, "landing you a customer overnight!"

She'd landed Jablow a plumbing specialist so eager for that West Street access she'd had to skip lunch and drive him straight down, they'd just missed Limpy. The building she owned next door to Limpy's hadn't been big enough for big shot Jablow and his toiletries, he had to have the Quality Building also and break down walls!

"But I don't understand," Danny had said. "If he knows that the—"

"Who knows what he knows?"

"In short a sucker," Danny had swung back to the piano. "Nothing doing."

"Limpy—"

Carrie had tossed her coat to the couch, drawn up a chair and taken him by both hands to stop the music. Business is run on information. Weren't his salesmen always searching out new dealers? Wasn't he continually devising machinery and work improvements? Why, if not for an edge on the competititon? So she invested all sorts of time and energy farming these tips. If not her somebody else. And does Macy's tell Gimbels? She was putting it over on no one. Tips could turn sour, the wreckers might never go near the West Street buildings—the whole proposal could fall through.

"Get your customer to agree to that and I'll gladly talk business with him."

Carrie'd stared, then grabbed up her furs and stridden . . . not out of the house he'd been relieved, but to the bedroom. Then she'd come back.

"What about the sale I lose on my building?"

Danny had plunked out notes. "I'll buy your building."

"Thanks, hero. I could buy and sell you and your building . . . a hundred times over."

He'd taken it, he'd taken that nonsense—and it had been worth it, oh had that gush of missing Sydelle run through him again!

Well, so— That was really what he'd come to Town Hall tonight for, the Schubert quintet with two cellos with the adagio. But to get the good of it he'd have to sleep through an hour of Brahms. That wouldn't be difficult in the drowsy heat here after a day when not one but two of his trucks broke down in the snow, in Boston and outside of New Brunswick—not to mention the wear and tear of dinner at home where no matter who the leading lady addressed she had not addressed the alleged villain. But maybe the Brahms that'd stunk when the Budapest Quartet ran it off would improve this listening—the eternal optimist—with an unknown bunch the Lenkowskis? But hey, a Sydelle at last, Lenkowski, and their violist at that, she went with Ignatius Lenkowski, cello. Was this an omen? He yawned. He should have gotten in a snooze at home and arrived here at intermission. . . .

As it was he dozed off till a chair clonk on the knee woke him up. To add insult to injury the willowy figure of gray wisdom who'd just sat down was talking music to a young apple-cheeked pal.

" . . . and *Schna*bel," the older of the two guys was saying, "he positively ought to be strung up by the thumbs—preferred his own rancid cadenzas to Beethoven's in the Mozart concerto!"

Danny skipped for an empty box on the right, and once he was on his feet kept going down to the checkroom and out of the building. The air, the crunch of the snow, the crowds, light from restaurants and marquees woke him up. Was the Philharmonic performing? Suppose she happened to be at Carnegie Hall? Stupid sure and not for the first time—but tonight beyond all nights he had this feeling that he was going to see her! At Fifty-fifth he even detoured through the Hotel Wellington—musicians stayed there she'd told him. All that did though was warm his frozen ears for a moment, and on Fifty-seventh Street Carnegie Hall was dark. The bookstore a few doors away used to be their meeting place sometimes, but she wasn't there either. He piled himself up a complete Brontë sisters though and felt slightly better.

So he'd have to settle for the Lenkowski Sydelle, Mrs. Lenkowski the secret of whose success in contrast to his poor girl—some his—was that this one apparently didn't mind playing Brahms. His evening would be complete if they ruined the Schubert C Major.

But no one could ruin that.

Folks, smoke and talk filled Town Hall lobby, so with a leftover shiver from the freezing wind he rechecked his overcoat and ducked upstairs with his bag of books.

> *Of late years, an abundant shower of curates has fallen upon the north of England. . . .*

Boy!

He forgot where he was till the lights dimmed and the Lenkowski Quartet augmented came out to applause. He rattled *Shirley* back into the bag, hitched his trousers, folded his arms and sat ready.

The violist—his heart caught—was a version of Sydelle. She had the same slim back bending with some concern to the stern-faced Lenkowski, the same serious headshake when his lips moved. Was it her?

No, Mrs. Lenkowski had hair pulled back tight under a ribbon and she was taller, sort of elongated in a black flounced evening gown.

. . . Jesus, those tragic opening notes . . .

And how could Sydelle be married to a frowning runt with eyeglasses and a scraggly mustache? What would she see in him? And to have divorced Art and remarried in a year and a half? Danny'd known her—known her? been with her, loved her, adored her—five years and nothing had happened.

Yet every gesture—

Nah—they all moved like that. His Sydelle beat this one a mile. But not, you had to admit, when it came to playing. No wonder Lenkowski let his missus into the quartet, her viola silkenly weaved that gorgeous sound there with the others. And whoever she was, severe, minus a Danny to choose elegant gowns for her, Danny was in love with her through the whole devastating performance.

Then during the bows she smiled straight at him twice. Was it her, God forbid, or just the boxes and balcony smile all five—even Lenkowski with a lip lift like a glimmer of arctic sunlight—answered the thunderclaps and bravos with? Heavyhearted—whichever Sydelle she was it was embarrassing and pointless, but you couldn't be a ninny, you had to find out—he trudged himself to the greenroom on the boxes level and he waited.

And waited—and no musicians. He went back to the balcony and his question amazed the usherette turning up seats. Hadn't he heard the intermission announcement? She sent him backstage, where the musicians outnumbered the fans by now. Danny took his deep breath and plunged in for a block by Lenkowski who—with the grayhair alongside him that'd demanded capital punishment for Schnabel's thumbs—was laying fullback to tackle any late praisers. So Danny congratulated him that he'd never heard the Schubert done better.

"Only that?" the eyeglasses bulged askance.

"As good as the Budapest ain't bad."

"Well," the bass voice gargled like a version of Art Fields, "all right, thanks." He stretched a glance past Danny's shoulder for better odds but the horizon was empty, so he led his graying friend to the dressing room with a deep "Syd—" over his shoulder.

She was with the other cellist, the second violin, grayhair's young buddy, and a rumpled little middle-aged lady who stood by looking scared. Lenkowski's Syd answered, "In a minute," and it was her okay, polished hard in the tight hair with the black ribbon pinning her ears down, more like . . . other women, but oh her voice. "Hello Danny." The rumpled lady tried to hang back, but Sydelle drew her along. "Mama, this is Mr. Share, a former pupil of mine, not that I taught him very well." And she allowed Danny no time for contradictions. "This is my intrepid mother, who defied her spouse and the weather to hear me play—and with a new, Gentile husband to boot."

Her mother gave her a worried nudge—"Sydelle"—in case the father happened to be in the wings listening. Oy Mama, if the mama would only disappear through the ceiling. But Danny couldn't wish bad on her, he saw she wanted to. And he also saw her daughter's smile shiny as steel plate.

"You were worth coming for," he said. "You made me suffer, die—"

"But we restored you to life in the allegretto I hope."

But at least go down fighting, Danny-o. "I'm not sure yet. Since the last lesson you taught me I . . ." why not, nothing with nothing . . . "I could do better. Where do I get in touch with you?"

"You don't. I'm once more a Westerner, we teach at the Cleveland Institute. Have you tried that Ricky Paine? She seemed available."

Didn't the Westerner—how Danny's heart hurt—mow him down with those bullets. Then she wrinkled her nose to mimic him with a squint of comedy pain (was that how he looked?) and gave him a fast second of hope. "Sydelle, maybe for lunch while you're here, so I can tell you?" But already she'd shut him out again.

"Syd—"

Backstage quivered with the bass rumble from under the shining eyeglasses and sandy mustache at the dressing-room door.

"Oh," she kept smiling, "we have a dozen different things to do before the bus back tomorrow."

"Syd!"

"Yes, Nate." The door shut hard and Sydelle laughed her old heartbreaking chimes, but for the other guy. "Ignatius hates it when I call him Nate. . . . But I really must run—come, Mama." She gathered her skirt up, caught the mama by the hand and laughed, "If you want to keep up with me nowadays, speed is of the essence— Nice to have seen you, Danny." And she actually did run the giggling mama—"Sydelle, I can't"—into the dressing room.

Of course, this was what he'd wanted for her, to play music, live her own life. But without him? And all the important questions—what had he done, why should she torture him, how does the ox get home from the slaughterhouse?—he hadn't asked.

Carrie simply answered Dave Whitehill's question did she unload her West Street properties and Whitehill laid a forkful of lasagna back on his plate at Mario's as if he was about to jump out of the blue herringbone he wore like armor.

"The horse's ass!"

"Don't be extreme, Dave," Carrie smiled placidly. "So I happened to hitch my star to a milk wagon."

He sprayed out "Unhitch!" with such vehemence that she was glad—why raise the poor man's hopes in that direction—that she hadn't given in to the furious impulse last week after the tête-à-tête with her husband to phone Loudonville and ask Dave what he thought of her home-blown bottleneck.

Instead a few days of silence and sleeping alone and she'd calmed down, though that Share was beginning to be a big disappointment. How could she have been so mistaken twelve years ago when she picked that guy? She'd thought he was a man, that there was something to him, the sky the limit—which proved that even she Carrie Baum couldn't pick all winners. Tuesday night he'd made it back from his alleged concert looking as shattered as if his worry Mr. Huey P. Long had taken over America. Hubby hadn't known how close he'd come to being sent back where he came from—and not by Huey Long either. But while the music lover brushed his teeth she'd fished in his suit and fortunately for him brought up one—not two—one virtuous ticket stub. A little while later he'd dragged in from where his bed was made up, and for a second she'd thought that he was going to burst into tears. And—she must have been his woman trouble after all—he had grabbed her.

In that respect—no use talking—he was still a convenience.

So a phone call to the Board of Assessors had brought a schlemiel to Tomer Industries who Carrie assessed as needing, to say the least, a new pair of shoes. He had caught on right away, the soft-cheeked man. "So could baby, so could the wife and the aged parent. But our reform mayor says no, give 'em a pay cut, let 'em go barefoot."

"That's a shame," she passed him an envelope. "How can you perform your duties if the city won't pay you?"

The dog had counted the money before he'd put the bribe in his pocket. "Overassessed huh, like everyone else?"

"Under."

The assessor's watery brown eyes looked up unsurprised. "Oh, selling."

With such heads—just smart enough to be dumb—no wonder they fall into the civil service rut. "You think that higher taxes make sales? I want an honest assessment."

"Upping a valuation is easy—nobody objects except, as a rule, the landlord."

"I'm also interested in the West Street building next door to mine."

"It's also a shame I have to shiver in this threadbare overcoat with snow on the ground."

So another bill for the overcoat and that cat had seemed to be skinned, till Honest John with the limp came home with the news that some zealot with bags under the eyes and at the knees had wasted a good part of his morning over the Quality books and wound up hitting him with a crazy inflated assessment. Finally—oh crap with this fool!—he'd told the guy for chrissakes this valuation would cost the city double in restitution if the West Side improvement went through.

"And what did he say?" she'd asked.

"He said restitution wasn't his job."

As was not unexpected the assessor had had the nerve to show up at her office again, lay his filthy weather-stained hat on her desk and confide that the recommendations were ready in his portfolio but, as she saw, after he and the missus bought a few things for the kids he still didn't have enough for a new pair of shoes.

Carrie'd put her hand on the phone. "Buster, how would you like me to ring up your chairman that I requested an assessment review and you traveled all the way to the Bronx twice to blackmail me with a raise?"

He'd taken his hat—"Don't eat me lady, it was just a suggestion"—and gotten out fast.

Worms wearing pants.

This time he'd filed his report and the cat remained skinned.

More husbands she needed? She Carrie B. Share calmly ate her lasagna, sipped her dago red and laughed off Dave. "If I ever unhitch, I'll stay unhitched."

And what do you think of this he-man, clamping her wrist and splattering wine which luckily for him missed her brand-new Bergdorf Goodman creation. But Dave was why this dress combining businesslike blue with white lacy trimmings was having its virgin outing today, and the wine and his hold made her feel all over like trying a few more holds with him.

"I'm," he was snarling, "proposing marriage to you!"

"Why be," she smirked, "so drastic, Dave?"

"Carrie," he sat back, "you disappoint me."

"I intended," she shrugged and smiled around another mouthful, "the opposite."

But oy was this egg addled. In spite of her nothing doings he argued till she became as cold as his lasagna. And what prospects he offered: Loudonville, with her the girl with the hoe. He stood up for that kind of life for a woman. What was wrong with it? Having kids—sure he had that in mind—was a lot more important than real estate. What did she need real estate for? His net worth was three hundred grand!

"My my!" Carrie couldn't help grinning, and on the ride back to her office she was treated to a sulk like Teddy's last year when he was refused a two-wheeler.

And this one helped elect governors? Pathetic. She patted him, "Cheer up," but it was like knocking wood. Next Rosh Hashonah in *shul* she'd have to ask God who gave Him the dumb idea of wasting manhood on men.

Damn him, with a deskful of work he'd left her all unsettled. Her eye kept following the arctic curve of the El to the platform where the waiters for the Messiah stood hunched in the cold. Down in the street trolleys and trucks hypnotically lumbered between the El pillars and the last week's snow that had hardened to grimy paste at the curbs. Absurd—who needed these aging welterweights?

"Arthur—"

Mulloy poked his head in at her door.

"Put on your Homburg, we're gonna find a new office, befitting our . . . station."

They twinkled at one another.

"The Empire State Building," he said, "has space."

"High up?"

"Where else?"

26

SO FAR SINCE QUALITY LAMPS LANDED IN THE BRONX Danny would pounce on the annual Lenkowski Quartet ad in the papers with all the ferocity a good insult could give him. He was supposed to rush buy a ticket so that after the bravos Mrs. Sydelle Lenkowski could enjoy a cozy laugh with her second husband about Share the clown?

Unfortunately the Mott Haven railroad yard under his office—the acres of freight cars, tracks and switches from his loading platform to the edge of the water—was a constant reminder of Jericho. But a businessman doesn't indulge himself in mooning at views, and Danny didn't. He sat with his back to the window same as at West Street and turned around only in moments of the most sheer desperation, such as when the heating system broke down on and off for three winter weeks and his shivering workers filled orders by the bloodshot glow of electric heaters, or when the second floor began buckling under the weight of the ovens and it took him and two of his foremen a thrilling couple of days to devise a steel reinforcement below, or when he lost his temper with his salesman Gnopf. The idiot city—in the end they put up their downtown highway section without touching the buildings they'd boarded up—had lashed Danny out of West Street with a golden whip, waterfront compensation rates exactly as he'd warned that moron assessor. On that windfall—he had no interest in stocks—he'd paid off the old Quality Building mortgage though Carrie'd said don't, invest the bank's money in U.S. Steel with a war coming in Europe, to his joy and astonishment cleared sixty grand after Naomi's share and fallen into access Carrie had found for him here in Mott Haven that made West Street look sick. From your parking lot here you swung up to Eastern Boulevard and clear New England sailing once your truckers got out of the Whitlock Avenue traffic jams. The Willis Avenue bridge brought you into Manhattan, the new Triborough opened and there was Long Island. But

Gnopf didn't want the Island, he called it chickenfeed: small stores and small orders. And when Danny told him to cover the Island nevertheless, Gnopf came back from a perfunctory rattle through Queens—he'd quit at the city line—with a big eight lamp order to drive home his point. So after ten years together Danny heard himself shouting at Gnopf to get his ass out to Hicksville and bring in a list of the stops. Gnopf went and you were ashamed of yourself. In advance you knew he was right, the time and effort would be better spent coddling the big buyers. So thanks again Carrie. Every respectable voter still had one occupation, she'd said, even the eight million unemployed. The stork kept ensuing, and where do you stuff them all? Nassau County was the land of the future. And against his judgment, since she'd been so put out that he hadn't taken her mortgage suggestion, Danny'd listened. The land of the present Nassau was not. But why blame her because he'd gotten abusive to Gnopf? As usual the apology came on top of the outburst. He even blurted to Gnopf that there'd been other things on his mind.

Then he stood enjoying that special pain, Jericho out the window to the scrubby shore of cranes, coal chutes and barges—what he once had without realizing it. You had to squint away Harlem though on the other side of the river, the huddle of tenements fading to a cold sunlit haze of spires in lower Manhattan, the Empire State Building where Carrie was willing to blow what must have been her whole business income for the thrill of a streamlined setup up in the clouds. She could have it, it didn't thrill him. So the narrow green Harlem River hardly held that . . . oceanic promise of the Lake Michigan days. What did?

Not the stale old parties and gatherings of small talk that he went to or hosted with Carrie, not the paintresses downstairs and the machine whines and screams he'd soundproofed his office and showrooms against, certainly not Yankee Stadium summer Sundays with Carrie and the boys where Danny the second childhood baseball fan let loose his own whines and screams. At the Stadium last May Carrie'd let off a sarcastic "Irresistible" and he'd noticed a chorus girl type in the adjoining box behind the Yankee dugout, a player's wife probably, goggling at him. So what? Or his foreman Sorella hired a paintress—black-haired, bright-looking, a narrow face with that wondering smile when you talked to her—a rough version of what filled up Danny's jigsaw heart. The kid was bright all right, Letty Russo, but a few words let you know that bright as Letty was she could have been brighter. Now whenever Danny dropped downstairs she would smile expectantly—easy mark Letty—while the rest of the female proletarians in their exuberant smocks lumped cheeks at her. Couldn't Hymie Share have had himself a field day with such a harem.

Hymie's son would pass by with a nod and discuss drypoint and gold leaf lampshades with Sorella and Harvey La Vine for Vandervaart's medieval sales festival. Then Hymie's son would be at his desk late with everyone else gone, and to his disgust would catch himself fixed on the flick of lights in the night train to Cleveland, where . . . Lenkowski's wife lived.

The day he read along with the other good news in the papers—Nazis march into Rhineland and no one stopped 'em! Fascists bomb Addis Ababa—that the Lenkowskis would be playing at Town Hall, he decided he'd show her that the dying swan was not quite in extremis. He phoned Reisel to go with him—and he picked up another no for his collection!

"It is like dates."

Bookbinder on the blessed departure of his latest woman teased Reisel that instead of marrying him Reisel preferred men married already. What men? His friend Daniel. She gave it to Bookbinder hot and heavy. Perhaps she should attend night clubs with Bookbinder to watch women of the streets wriggle half naked rather than concerts should she choose—which she seldom did—with her cousin. Now Bookbinder—shameless—always was at the Martha Washington having her rung by the desk clerk (Reisel of course did not come down) or leaving humorous messages (she of course did not respond).

She said to Danny, "Why do you not take your wife?," his wise guy cousin—she knew why—displaying superiority.

Yet in a sense he didn't know why himself. For his purpose, to show Sydelle a knockout on his arm, Carrie would have done very well. Why didn't he want Carrie?

"In my nonage," he was inspired to say, "the violist used to be the love of my life."

And without asking what the program was, not that he himself had bothered to notice, Reisel changed her mind tittering and agreed.

On the concert night she sailed smiling out of the elevator, and Danny in a chintz armchair in the Martha Washington lobby could understand Rubin Bookbinder's endless marriage campaign. Reisel pushing forty? There must have been a mistake on the birth certificate. People took Danny for younger than his age in spite of the early gray at the temples—in that one respect he was his father's son. But Reisel in a snip of a hat on that crown of deep auburn curls and in a white Persian paw coat that on her beat Carrie's ermine for elegance struck you as fresh, as breathtaking, as the day she'd stepped off the boat at Ellis Island. Under the coat, when they checked it at Town Hall, she had a slender white jacket on with a fluffy blue schoolgirlish tie.

"You like my costume? I chose it for the love of your life."

"You're the love of my life. Marry me—I'll divorce Carrie."

"I do not," Reisel enjoyed that, "marry secondhand men."

And another big risk he'd taken.

The quartet had drawn so good a crowd that the granite Lenkowski actually beamed in the entrance bow. But that the shockingly pregnant Sydelle saw Danny and his companion there could be no doubt. From a front row box Reisel slumped back in hilarity with her hand on her mouth

—"My first Beethoven quartets for five players"—and pointed down at that grotesque belly.

And if that stage spectacle didn't cure him he was a hopeless case.

Danny's wife was a big committeewoman—Hadassah, Resettlement, Women for Jewish Palestine. Himself, Danny would have preferred bombing Berlin.

"Exterminate the Jews! Judah perish!"

That was the Gauleiter of Franconia while the President of the U.S.A., Carrie's idol—"He's working behind the scenes, his stand is well-known . . . and you're just the one who's entitled to criticize"—had no comment.

As it was, Tomer Industries spun the Cadillac down to the Federal Building to vouch for her immigrants, Quality Lamps tooled the silver-gray Packard Speedster down to vouch for his. Danny also joined Businessmen Against German Imports. If you sold drugs you were for boycotting wood pulp, if you published a paper you were for boycotting coal tar dyes—not to mention (speak of real cowardice!) the delegates still scared stiff of reciprocal boycott. His shouts in those battles of indignation and hot air restored him his youth of full-bloom headaches. But what was a headache when German imports fell off the graph, when Hitler's balls hurt! And in Mott Haven even with the mechanical crises eliminated you kept busy.

Time dragged, yet funneled away and you didn't know where years disappeared so quickly. Roosevelt's recovery petered out and you had costs to cut, workers to fire all over again—depressing, that's what a depression was—hard sales drives to plan. Then there were the boys, already high-schoolers, Ezra the front-running sophomore to swell you with pride and laughing Teddy the freshman in the middle of the pack to drive you crazy. Impresario Carrie sometimes trotted out the piano virtuoso Ezra for her company, and Ezra would always insist on at least one number by the four-hands team Son & Father. Danny himself enjoyed the sessions with Ezra a lot more in private but he was proud to play with him in front of those glum characters. Concert-going? You concentrated on listening to patterns and the hell with emotion. If that killed off most of the pleasure it also killed off the pain.

The bright spring morning arrived—CZECHOSLOVAKIAN POLICE DEPORT AUSTRIAN JEWS TO NAZI VIENNA—when he read a Lenkowski Quartet announcement and realized that the Ides of March, Sydelle's birthday, had slipped by and he still was enjoying his corn flakes and bananas.

Three cheers—he really was cured.

Like his limp: you forgot it until it ached.

Her child must have been two years old already.

All of a sudden Danny found himself at the main telephone office looking up Cleveland. Next he had F.A.O. Schwarz on Fifth Avenue send a cute Teddy bear to Baby Lenkowski. What the hell, it was her child, and her birthday too.

Mr. and Mrs. Ignatius Lenkowski replied with a readymade thank you card on behalf of Master Ignatius Anton to Mr. and Mrs. Daniel Share. Carrie opened it, so what: a baby gift for some music acquaintances. Sydelle hadn't even bothered to sign the card. And if a trace of the old Sydelle showed in a middle name after Chekhov for Ignatius Anton—though Anton also could have been simply from a Polish grandpapa—Ignatius came first.

Desperate Dan the worm, he was at least cured of ever writing to her again.

Danny was in and out of the cottage at Sandy Point all afternoon to get at the radio and the latest war bulletins. At last, at last—wait till France poured over the Siegfried Line into Germany! It made him wish he were French. Cross your fingers—maybe soon no more Hitler!

His guests sipping drinks outside on beach chairs quickly applied the wet blanket.

But had the French attacked, Professor George Ronzino wanted to know. The radio hadn't said? Then the professor feared that France wasn't ready. Ed E-square Evans to the exasperation of his wives past and present was in happy unanimity with George. Hitler'd moved into the Saar and France had done nothing, into Austria and France had done nothing, into Czechoslovakia and France had done nothing. All right. Now he bombs Warsaw and he has Poland reeling. What does France do? They make an announcement—a state of war exists.

Who'd sent for this crowd, the people that Danny didn't know why he was with?

George was E-square's first wife's second husband. Sophie Margeson Evans Ronzino, who Danny'd felt so sorry for when E-square ditched her way back, had dropped by without warning from the Lido Beach Club to show off her recent catch the Professor of History at Fordham, and by a lucky stroke she'd caught Dottie and E-square Evans visiting. Also present was Carrie's latest find Gordon Ross, Deputy Commissioner of Public Works and Commissioner of State Defense Industry: two in one blow. With Ross's six-and-a-half foot-long carcass, his tapering fingers, perpetual cigarette and long ironic face went his lacquered little wife Libby.

"Are you sisters?" Libby Ross studied E-square's wives. "You look just like twins."

Sophie wasn't upset. She seemed younger each time you saw her, while Dottie Evans had developed a leathery tinge to the cheek and lost her youth edge long ago. "Not sisters exactly," Sophie said. "You could say we went to the same school—but I graduated." No-nonsense Dottie explained the relationship between herself and the woman whose husband she'd picked off in days of yore and she counterattacked by bringing Sophie up to date on Edward's latest maneuvers—yes, she did mean political: for the United States Senate next year.

But E-square sacrificed his present wife with a friendly murmur to George, "Woman talk," which softened the professor's habitual tight-mouthed grin that looked ready to bite you. Then with a victory glance toward his ex-wife E-square drew the professor out on Mediterranean geography and the war just beginning. In the last war Suez guarding one end of the Mediterranean Sea and Gibraltar the other guaranteed that Italy would not oppose what we might call—the professor bared those white teeth—the good guys? But since the . . . good guys? . . . had permitted a Fascist state to establish itself at the Strait of Gibraltar, the prospect was ah somewhat different.

Ezra wide in the shoulders and skinny in the legs led two pals and Teddy in a dash out of the water after three girls they chased up the beach with sand flying. Teddy plump as he was was fast and overtook the girls and one of them in particular, a bursting little blonde of thirteen. He took a good hold on her—"Warm me up, Edith"—which she didn't seem to mind, but with people watching she broke away with a shriek "Teddy!" They all threw themselves blue with cold to a big blanket nearby and began pulling on sweat shirts. "Room in the icebox, Dad?" Ezra called across sociably through chattering teeth. "Teddy's ready to hi-hi-hibernate—"

But E-square Evans and the professor cheerfully finished off Europe along with their drinks and Danny—"I'd better enlist then"—was fighting mad, he barely tossed off a smile to his son.

Gordon Ross thought that that was funny. He lounged squinting at you with his satirical eye and sucking his cigarette while Libby Ross asked, "We're not in the war yet, are we?"

"At least not until after next year's election dear," Gordon Ross said. "But Canada is."

And Danny's satirical wife said, "Just who Canada needs," which decided Danny that on Tuesday he'd definitely hop a plane to Ottawa and volunteer for the Canadian air force. With this premature fall weather—sun and shadow kept chasing over a bright seething blue flecked with whitecaps—he'd have to walk slow to cover the stupid limp, but it could be done.

Meanwhile Libby Ross gave him a preliminary exam. "Oh the Canadians wouldn't take a grayhead anyway."

Ross drawled, "He could dye his hair." But Ross's wink was to Carrie, Carrie broke into a smile—and suddenly all this seemed to have happened before, but Danny couldn't place where.

The hell with them all.

At dinner, though, he heard Carrie ask Ezra was he having Pearl trouble, and the kid did look preoccupied. Teddy eating a chicken leg out of his hand mumbled that he wished he had Edith eating out of his hand the way his brother had Pearl eating out of *his* hand, so Danny asked Ezra was he okay and got a nod. But afterwards Ezra told Teddy to quit bothering him—"You're always bragging you're a bar mitzvah plus three when you're really a bar mitzvah plus one, so you're big enough for the girls and the boardwalk without me, if you're that anxious." So Teddy said sure he was that anxious and left, but Ezra outstayed the company and caught his father alone on the porch in front of the dark pounding ocean.

"Dad, don't go to Canada. That'd ruin our duets."

Danny turned—and the worry his bronzed handsome kid was playing straight-faced! The father fought tears he felt such love, and laid his arm along Ezra's shoulders.

"Think that they might stand a chance without me?"

"Not that you wouldn't be a help—" Ezra blurted.

They staggered around the porch, they laughed till they gasped, they waved at each other, they grabbed each other's fingers but couldn't hold on.

So Tuesday the old man went to Mott Haven as usual, not Canada, and apparently the Allies dawdling in France the whole winter could spare him. But in spring when fighting broke out in earnest he regretted his promise. "Don't worry, Dad," Ezra was cheerful, "our side'll murder 'em," but that wasn't how it looked in the papers Danny stayed up all hours searching through for scraps of good news. In *The Nation* some happy expert outlined Hitler's U.S.A. conquest scheme—northwards through South America. Like hell Hitler would, but you couldn't just sit up in the Bronx manufacturing lamps, raking in 1929 money again at the expense of people being slaughtered in Europe. How did you go about being a help, short of . . . Harvey La Vine down at the ovens liked the idea of converting to war matériel but what kind search Harvey. Gordon Ross probably knew through his Defense Industry board, but Danny hated to leave himself open to one of Ross's . . . remarks, or Carrie's. He settled for calling Ross's office in a disguised voice, as if the Commissioner himself would be picking up calls from small-time citizens. The guy Danny did speak to was another big help. You make your proposal and the board matches it up with contractors' requirements. What proposal? Why that's up to you, you're the businessman.

Danny finally took a deep breath and asked Carrie anyhow. "Pathetic," she shook her head at him, and he was quick with his "Forget it." But she didn't. Not a week later with the park a chartreuse billow she asked him between scalding spoonfuls of mushroom soup, "Well fire-eater, still ready to bomb Berlin?"

"Readier than the English and French seem to be."

"What do you expect, in a war run by men? Meanwhile, Laser Electronics on the Island is accepting bids for bombsight assemblies contracts—Gordon said. But you have to have soldering equipment, spray booths with ventilators and baking ovens."

"You know I have all that stuff."

"Say," more and more she sniped with her straight-faced contempt, "that's true."

Next day he, Harv La Vine and Sorella were at it nearly till midnight over the Laser Electronics specifications. Danny submitted a bid and with his pull got a quick answer: abuse from his wife.

"Incredible! The second time you've embarassed me—first Whitehill, now Ross!"

He'd bid too low.

"But the money is secondary and I thought that low bid—"

"Grow *up*! You make me sick!"

And he'd thrown Sydelle away.

That night he didn't stay in with the newspapers. They were nauseating anyway, Paris an open city. Jesus Christ, to save what? Even rats fight. The park, soft air, kids necking on benches, the lamp globes lighting leaves like a stage set: the whole works seemed unreal. His feet happened to aim downtown and he kept walking, through Times Square full of unbelievable lights, marquees and crowds, past the desolate clothing district, and to Thirty-fourth Street, empty with the department stores closed.

The open city.

Jesus he missed—who? He knew who he missed, but . . .

Whoever he missed, he turned crosstown toward the Martha Washington and dropped fagged out into a lobby chair while they called Reisel down. She was alarmed seeing him.

"Are you ill?"

Either undoubtedly against management rules you kiss her—all that concern gazing down at you—or you laugh.

He laughed. "I'd better not be ill if I want to drop bombs on Berlin."

It was no laughing matter to Reisel. She sat down and drank him in. He was flying to Ottawa to enlist tomorrow or at the latest—he had to get his hair dyed to lower his age—the day after.

"You do not require hair dye. You are young—and brave!"

"And a joke—since you never stop looking beautiful—made by God in heaven."

"I do not understand the joke."

Let a woman stay puzzled for once instead of him, he didn't explain the joke, just stayed stuck with his useless qualities. The question was, was *she* brave?

"I am a lion!"

"I know, from way back."

But was she lion enough to quit Bookbinder's Fine Editions and manage Quality in his place? For that she was a mouse. "I cannot, do not be angry with me." She would fight Nazis if she could, but she feared Carrie.

Who was angry? He hadn't expected her to say yes. In fact his heart went out to her in her invisible prison, he wanted to comfort her. "It's okay," he patted her cheek—and see, she flinched. "I'll put Harvey in charge, he'll handle it—though," he was quick to cheer her up with a compliment, "not the way you would."

But late in the sultry morning at North Beach Airport after the stop at the barber's to have his hair dyed he only phoned Harvey that he'd be away for today, and possibly tomorrow. The Canadians would surely allow a week to wind up personal business. The barber had been proud of the dye job and assured him he could pass for half his age but he'd be conservative, he'd say twenty-eight at the recruiting station. The leg (he tried it again) had been stiff when he got up but it had come around. Carrie and the boys he'd break the news to after it was official. Ezra was a year older, he was sixteen and he read the papers. Why those son of a bitches want to wipe us out, he'd see his father's point now. And Teddy—well, it was hard to admit to yourself that you had a fifteen year old son an opportunist, but maybe he'd change as time passed. Danny himself had certainly changed from what he was as a kid, though he could hardly say for the better. But a clever boy like his son Teddy shouldn't go signing Oxford pacifist pledges in school because the schoolmate canvasser was a girl he thought he could get to fellow-travel with that way. "Just a leaf from their book, Ez—" Teddy'd said when Ezra had challenged him—"boring from within." "But justice prevailed," Ezra had said. "You were boring and she was bored." "I withdrew my signature, didn't I," Teddy had defended himself, "when I saw that she was hopeless?" Interchanges like that would put their ma in stitches, but—Danny fought the feeling yet it was there—those Teddy stunts left a bad taste.

As to the wife, the less Danny told her, the fewer sneers.

Even so, how come he could fly away from his family now without the slightest compunction, whereas with Sydelle . . . But of course this trip wasn't to happiness, so it was okay. The engines roared, the plane rolled down the runway, gathered speed—and there was a haze of trees and houses receding. Where he sat the wing vibrated as if it was about to fall off. Didn't bother him.

Maybe he had been born to be a hero.

27

THE MORNING AFTER THE JAPS BOMBED PEARL HARBOR Teddy was fast asleep and, from the light under the den door, Dad just about up as Ezra was tiptoeing out of the house in the dark. Downtown, three fast steps at a time from the South Ferry subway station, and Nazis, Japs—let him at them! In the bay a pair of destroyers camouflaged with tough zigzags followed a convoy past Governor's Island in a thin pink light full of gulls gliding and made him feel halfway to the war already. Dad would understand—in Canada last year Dad himself had tried enlisting and it hadn't been his fault they hadn't taken him. What a great father Ezra had. And if Mom's highly irregular and uncalled for fishing expedition for where Dad had been those three days hadn't come up with a plane ticket from one of Dad's pockets, no one would even have known!

Mom though would be a different kettle of fish. At the first Pearl Harbor news flashes, Ezra's mother had started scheming up a safety zone for him far from combat, Carnegie Hall preferably. Her friend the governor's wife was a Carnegie Trustee and also a friend of Judson's who ran a concert bureau. The important thing was to establish Mom's precious boy as a professional musician. Then—and there was no rush—he could do his special part in the war playing for the troops. Ezra had kept quiet though till Mom's totally out of place stab at Dad that had it been up to her Ezra would have been on the concert stage years ago, never mind the sour grapes anti-prodigy advice of that third-rate pianist Izzie Axelrod. Then Ezra had told her flatly, "There happens to be no better pianist alive than my teacher Ilya Axelrod, and too bad for the benighted who don't appreciate him." But Ezra hadn't told her that he was joining the air force—sufficient unto the day.

At 7 A.M. not too many zealots were milling outside the army building though the line was long before the NCO's started letting them in. Filling out forms Ezra, white lie, added only a year to his age seventeen to qualify, and the physical exam went along swimmingly till, of all places, the room with the reeking waterfall where you handed in urine samples. Between a yawn and an apology Ezra almost dropped his specimen giving it to the sergeant, glanced back—and on the line stood his kid brother the con artist gazing cherubically into the distance.

Ezra clamped a big hand on Teddy's shoulder muscular for all its rotundity, yanked him off that line and didn't swallow one bit of his brother's surprise act.

"What's the idea of following me down here?" Ezra flashed.

"Who's following you? I'm joining the air force."

"I'll take care of the air force."

"There's room for two. You wipe out Berlin, I wipe out Tokyo."

"You just go home, sport, and wipe out your nose."

"Think I'd mind? But my sad tail's rendered it otherwise, Ez, my ex-girl friend. She says that I made her pregnant, and adds—I can't explain such vindictiveness—that statutory rape is good for ten years in New York even if the man is sixteen, which she pretends not to believe I am just because I'd told her I'm nineteen so she wouldn't feel she was going out with a fellow a year younger than she was. And she's right about the statutory rape, I looked it up," Teddy really looked worried, "in the law library."

"Who did you knock up, that poor little Jehovah's Witness you were driving wacky?"

"No, that bitchy Barnard girl Francine who picked me up in South Library, and me assiduously studying. That's my reward for promising Dad I'd be an A man in college. And she volunteered to be in charge of non-propagation of species—I didn't ask her to."

"How could you be so stupid? That was a two condoms one over the other for safety's sake job."

"What other kind is there, Ez?"

"Decent girls, sport, that a guy lays off. Tell Mom about your little contretemps. She'll get you out of it."

"And Dad'll give me that baffled look of his that makes me feel as if I'm in the wrong."

"*As if?* After you've knocked a girl up? They ought to drop you on Tokyo—scram."

"Ez quit shoving—you're not your brother's keeper."

"I'm not, but Mom is. It's bad enough I'm volunteering. Don't you think of anyone but yourself?"

"Hey you're one to talk."

"Those Fascists make me see red."

"And jail makes me feel blue. One side Ez, you're blocking these patriots who want to get to the pissery."

But Ezra clamped a waistlock on him, Teddy the classy five-nine hundred-and-fifty-five-pound freshman collegiate wrestler replied with a quick pivot and scissors, and they were on the damp pimply floor with a three-striped referee breaking up the catch-as-catch-can. Ezra lost no time revealing his brother's age, and—what would you expect—that egoist Teddy let the sergeant know that Ezra was underage too for that matter. The sergeant corrected Ezra's age in red on the form and sent him on, but Teddy laughably naked with even his folder taken away kept trying to reason with the man. Ezra—"See you in Sing Sing, sport"—bade his brother the good cheer that he deserved. Three hours later however, Ezra was back in the cold again on Whitehall Street, fighting mad and out of it for five months at least, till he was eighteen. What had he accomplished? His damn brother!

He stood there angry and hungry, wondering which way to head for a bite in this terra incognita of Els and ferries, soldiers coming and going, would-be volunteers still shuffling slowly in twos into the lobby, pigeons pecking and high gray buildings with windows like pigeonholes. Then someone whirled him around and so help him he was ready to give his comedian brother a poke to remember—and instead faced . . . "Dad!" That Teddy really stank, sicking their father down here on him.

Danny though, same as in Canada last year, had come to volunteer and some orthopedist had taken a look at the scars under the knee and paraded him into a solid rejection for combat duty. Next they'd offered restricted service and he'd said nix, he was on restricted service already with the war contracts he'd learned how to bid high enough for. So he'd hobbled out of the building and to cap the usual sweet despondency he'd run into this. He said to his son, "You were in there, weren't you?," and the answer was only too sickeningly obvious. "Do you have to chase the war, you dumb kid?" he was next to frantic. "Won't it come to you soon enough?"

"How about you?" it suddenly dawned on Ezra. "Weren't you in there too?"

"Where do I compare with you?"

That really got Ezra, he put his hand on his father's shoulder. "Aw Dad—those Fascists make me see red."

"So what? And you had to lie about your age—I'm taking care of that enlistment of yours right now. You did enlist, didn't you?"

"I didn't lie about my age, Dad. I started to, but it didn't work out. I'm a Flying Cadet candidate—" yet he couldn't help sounding proud of it—"as of my next birthday."

"You stupid—I don't know what to call you. And how about your mother?"

"What do you say we don't tell her, Dad?"

"You mean next May you'll just vanish?"

"I'll tell her before I go. Gee Dad, I—"

"Smart as you are you're stupid. Don't talk to me, I don't want to hear any more." Danny started away and, with Ezra keeping up, stopped wet-eyed and threw his arm around his son. "No way to reverse it?"

Ezra shrugged painfully. "I'm sorry, Dad. Now I feel bad too."

His father let go of him. "Good."

And if Ezra felt bad then, that was nothing to how he felt a few months later when he found out that Mom had gone to talk sense to Ilya. Worse, Ilya agreed that under the circumstances the time had come for Ezra's debut, and one exceptionally warm day in March Ilya sprang a full program, estimable but not grandiose, on him to work up for the fall: a Bach Italian concerto for solo piano, a Haydn D major sonata, the Schubert little A major—"For the so-called music critics be humble in your initial aspirations," Ilya said, "as I was not in my own career"—and the Prokofiev *Visions fugitives* to dazzle them to their typewriters.

"Only I won't be here in the fall most likely, Ilya, I'll be in the air force."

"How is that," the pianist's ironic eyes kept their twinkle, "when you haven't drawn a draft number yet?" And when Ezra told how it was, Ilya astonished him by closing the keyboard on today's lesson. "Too bad," Ilya remarked. "All my years of work with you wasted."

"Why wasted?" Ezra choked out. "I'll resume after the war."

"Who knows what, if anything, you'll have left then. Good luck to you, Ezra."

And his teacher, his friend he'd thought, dismissed him—just like that. Ezra stamped off from Fifty-fifth Street so furious that only at home did it occur to him he hadn't asked Axelrod to at least not spill the beans to Mom. But the request proved unnecessary. Mom brought home the good news that he should phone Mr. Judson's secretary at Columbia Concerts tomorrow to arrange an audition. Ezra and Dad glanced at each other, and no one could say Dad hadn't done his part since their inopportune meeting back in December in Whitehall Street. Great is great, and that was his father, with the usual piano duets, the jokes and the discussions—only not on the war news any more, as usual mostly bad—void of reproaches or even sighs or similar hints of displeasure.

So, with his brother and father watching, Ezra sat Mom down and himself in front of her and took her by the hands. "Carrie," he said man to man, "there's no point in my auditioning just now because I'll be busy dropping bombs on Berlin in the near future." And he held on and told her.

Carrie stared at her handsome, skinny, broad-shouldered boy, snotnose, baby . . . opened her mouth to let him have it—but the governor's older son had just pulled the same stunt, with a mother equally overjoyed, and what could you do?—and said nothing. Then she smiled and pressed his hands hard.

"Well soldier, now they can't win and we can't lose, Luzon and the Java Sea notwithstanding."

Ezra broke into a big grin and smacked his mother a kiss. "If you and my father over there ever require a testimonial, call on me."

But in their room after dinner his brother accused him of idiocy for giving up a Columbia Concerts audition when the simplest thing in the world was to bring your birth certificate down to the Adjutant's Office at Whitehall Street, show 'em you'd falsified your dossier up from age sixteen, and, with a wait of no more than five vindictive hours, obtain your release. How had he discovered all this? By the surest pedagogical method on earth: experience. What did Ezra think, Teddy'd given up by the waters of Whitehall Street last December? When the sarge went out to lunch Teddy'd simply started over again and the low declining sun had seen him a happy Flying Cadet candidate on inactive duty, same as Ez. Teddy had added only a year to his age to get in last term's straight A's and still qualify for active service somewhere as far from New York as possible about now, when that Francine's belly would have reached criminal proportions. Then lo—the Vital Force that watched over him ordained this week's unseasonable hot spell, and the other day on campus on the Low Library steps who'd sat coatless sporting her flat winter belly under a skirt but Francine—not the slightest bit pregnant! What did Ezra make of that little bitch? So, with a stop here to pick up the birth certificate, in a fast hour Teddy had been down at the Adjutant's Office. "A lieutenant bawls you out for obstructing the war effort, that's about it." Now Teddy would gladly advance Ezra's birth certificate a year to 1925, a simple job of overpainting and relettering such as Teddy'd learned at his Art Institute evening class.

But for thanks all Teddy got was his brother's, "That's okay—with you plugging the home front, sport, I'm not needed here," and a superfluous ethics lecture which in general Teddy agreed with but which was totally inapplicable to his brother's particular case.

Through dinner Danny'd been overjoyed, he'd expected all kinds of fireworks at the kid's depressing announcement. But that was Carrie. She might live in one world with her Gordon Rosses, E-squares and other assorted power boys while you lived in another, some of her comments might drive you to monastic resolutions she turned upside down hardly trying—yet count on her in a pinch! First chance alone with her, coasting in the Cadillac across the park for drinks at the Rosses', he started to tell her so.

"You're okay Carrie, I—"

"You and your half-assed crippled volunteering—" her glare straight out over the wheel changed sweet night air to stone—"that's sending that boy away needlessly." Just let her kid get safe and sound through the war that this incompetent had pushed him into—because she wasn't going to send Ezra off upset when the time came—and this bastard wouldn't see her for dust. She shifted her angry eyes to him. "Save your famous stare for the mirror, hero with others' lives—if I'd been born a man, I'd be in now, not Ezra—and just keep your mouth shut."

It was a mother talking no doubt, and—theory's theory but your own is your own—what could she say to make him sicker than he already felt over Ez? So he kept his mouth shut. But staying out of her bed from now on should be simple—even for him.

28

A FEW LIMPS OF DANNY'S AWAY FROM THE MARTHA Washington Hotel for women Reisel stood still. "Thank you very much for the kind invitation but you are going home to bed and not to a concert."

"Alone in bed is the worst thing for my case."

"Then take the train to your wife."

"That's half a dozen of the other. Come on, it's only a broken back. Up at Lewisohn Stadium when they see me with you the envy the solid citizens stuck with their wives'll radiate will work out my kinks like an ultraviolet lamp."

"Do not be ironical at my expense."

"No no, the treat's on me."

That pacified Reisel, "Poor Daniel," and the three of them—his ersatz girl friend, his sciatica and him—strolled through the mild August twilight of downtown streets empty for the weekend to a subway still thick with the midweek heat wave. Once he melted into that again he wished he'd gone home straight from the factory to a naked tub and a drowsy page or so of *Persuasion*, which he used to read for lost love recaptured and read now for the captains home safe and rich from whipping Napoleon. Already, counting changes of line, he'd been on three subways twice today, rushing home on his lunchless two o'clock lunch hour for a possible letter from Ez in the final delivery, finding an empty box—not even the bogus thrill of bills, junk or mail for Carrie—and rushing back to Mott Haven. But at Mott Haven there'd been three separate messages for him to call *Mr.* Wiggin of Laser Inc., a man who knew where he stood: with a big foot on your neck. You phoned him and after *Mr.* Wiggin's secretary screened you: "Yes? This is Mr. Wiggin . . . Say, Share, where's our order X-2859? There's a war on you know. . . ." Danny knew, Danny knew there was a war on.

July 18th, '43

Dear Folks,

. . . Now you may expand your chests. Your road delegate did us Shares proud in the European Circus under the big tent, U.S.O. sponsorship. My act was the Bach Italian concerto for solo piano (Mr. I. Axelrod, sit up and take notice) and the men were respectful. But, as you would anticipate, my popular tunes of the day had them cheering. In your absence Dad, I croaked vocals into the public address system and they still clapped. Missions have been a lark, like the nice safe reinforced concrete subterranean munitions works target that bombs bounce off like mosquitos so the Nazis don't even bother defending it. Between missions I've availed myself of a Bechstein—what do you think of that! The piano belongs to a scrap dealer named Mr. Wolfe the U.S.O. sent me to. He has a mansion on the outskirts immediately beyond the agricultural section and he proudly showed me "about the four rooms centrally heated in winter." Then he introduced me to his sixteen year old daughter, Clarissa, his real hope being that she'll pick up some pointers from me (on the piano, Teddy old sport). Clarissa's a cute beanpole though not, she admits, deeply int'r'st'd in her father's piano. I like Clarissa though. We sit side by side at the piano and whenever I explain something there she is smiling down at me. . . .

Plus a line of grown-up advice to his brother from Danny's smiling lieutenant.

. . . Regardless of the draft number, buzzie boy, don't jump the gun. Army life is routine once you're in, even for an idealist. . . .

Some kid, some man huh? Only what next—after a week of no mail?

But Danny's voice had hardly shaken reminding Mr. Wiggin that if Laser was late with the synchronization mirrors Quality had to be late delivering the bombsight mountings.

"I don't have time to piddle around with you Share. Ship tomorrow the latest or begin thinking about breach of contract."

The old boy bard felt like hitting *Mr.* Wiggin with a complete change of tune because what was the hurry? At that conference a few weeks ago Mr. Wiggin confidentially recommended Laser common stock to Danny in order to brag that he, Calvin Wiggin, would be rich for life if the war lasted two more years! But return to lamp making now? Not to mention the wife's tongue for an ex-war industrialist. No. In time of war just double up calmly with a slight case of stomach knots.

So downstairs Danny'd had Harv La Vine set up more spray booths and tables and arrange to keep half of the day girls on overtime. Then upstairs he'd sat down with Riva Wartels who'd been near tears at the latest orders from her enemy the new payroll withholding tax. Danny'd helped work it out and even joked that she didn't really want the Internal Revenue Service minds that dreamed up these forms fired because then we'd have unemployment back and more taxes and more forms dreamed up.

"Mr. Share," Riva'd turned her hollow admiring eyes on him, "I wish I had your equanimity."

"Equanimity! You use four-syllable words to your boss?"

Riva'd giggled hysterically, "Five," while Danny'd tried to keep the equanimity from hardening into a death's-head grin at the prospect of the Foster Electronics contract he still had to work out a bid for.

But it was true that the good old splitting headaches of youth Sydelle had cured were gone forever—his present equanimity seemed closer to cancer and he'd been ready for anything except the usual twelve- or fourteen-hour day, even Carrie. Carrie had taken off for Sandy Point early though, so he'd called Reisel and after the standard interrogation on the whereabouts of his wife, she'd agreed to the Stadium all-Tchaikovsky tonight. As per schedule in the same old hard-chaired amphitheater—why couldn't it be Sydelle he was with—under a dappled sky of stars and droning planes the same old lust simmered up in the audience from middle-aged eyes with plenty of know-how that evidently didn't know how to get next to a Reisel with these shoulders, this auburn hair and this profile. Even Danny, whose briefcase full of homework on his lap weighed him down with every year of his forty-one, found it hard to believe she was three years older than he and caught himself at all kinds of arithmetic confirming that well-known fact. If she'd aged at all it was to at the outside twenty-eight. Yet what had she done with her years, any more than he'd done with his?

Then the boys on the band shell broke into *Romeo and Juliet*, and still that music killed him with longing. Was senility setting in, or did this mean still hope? Sure he hoped, idiot. Only where would he find her, his somebody like Sydelle? Not at Central Park West in Carrie's crowd, not on Eastern Parkway in his—Julius Waldman, jolly lumpy Lena and their three kids—not at Quality Lamps Light Fools the Way to Dusty Death out out . . . Table 403 Riva, see, enter on time sheet column 7. . . . Give in, at home he had *Romeo and Juliet* on records with Art Fields' pal Koussevitzky. He let himself doze off, Sydelle was always willing to lend . . . ah . . . a dear shoulder. Waves pulsed in the distance, Danny reached for the nymph lying beside him at Sandy Point—and a skyscraper wave jolted him high and dry. . . .

Maestro Barbirolli was raising the orchestra to bravos, and Reisel—"I trust that you were asleep"—was considering Danny with extreme suspicion.

Danny grinned. "Did I make the most of it?" And at intermission, after the Fourth Symphony killed him even more, he heard his delinquent tongue off and running. "I once wound up asleep on a girl's shoulder to Tchaikovsky and we fell in love."

Reisel's eyes opened wide and darned if omitting names and dates he wasn't rattling away about Sydelle as if she were still his girl, until Reisel—"Not that little violinist ten years ago in the advanced stages of pregnancy?"—took the wind out of his sails.

"Violist. That," but even the first note sounded false, "was a different one. And it was more like eight years ago."

"Mm. And so she left her husband for an inferior, while you—"

"While I?"

"Nothing."

"Now you've summed me up lady."

But in spite of his smile when he said that, pardner, Reisel—"Poor Daniel"—was full of sympathy you couldn't cash in on. The boys—no Sydelles in this orchestra—began warming up: violins, a viola, a French horn call to the open road, a despairing bass note. Suddenly Reisel stood. "Come—you will accompany me to Rubin Bookbinder's birthday party."

"How about the *Pathétique* Symphony?"

"Lugubrious."

"Reisel you're nuts!"

He argued it all the way downtown on a double-decker to Chelsea, but Reisel held out for Beethoven.

"I prefer courage to naked longing."

So she'd seen through his Sydelle lie. "Even though," he tried to make light of her uncomfortable message, "he was a German?"

"Yes the everyday German, just as Judas Maccabeus was the everyday Jew."

"Turning Zionist, an orthodox woman like you?"

"Who will help us if we do not help ourselves?"

"Okay, quit rubbing it in already. So she half wanted me to take her away and I suffer from guts shortage."

"You still harp on that eh? Well we are there, I think. . . ." Under leaves pale green in lamplight she peered at the number on a graystone wafting light and chatter from long street floor windows. . . . "So," she pressed the bell, "eat drink and be merry." The door opened on a burst of heat and alcohol and a tall lean brunette not glad to see them stared out.

That one asked, "Who are you?"

"I know who we are," Reisel answered her, "but what do you do in Rubin Bookbinder's house?"

But Rubin himself sailed so astounded into the vestibule that the brunette's dagger look at Rubin as she passed back in never came near the mark. "Do I behold Reiseleh?" The happy warrior—and couldn't you almost envy him, silver hair, pink cheeks, cigar, light heart, light mind and all?—dug humorous knuckles into his eyes, then tugged Danny in. "I've been trying for ten years to show off my home to my appointed bride, and ten years she would never—"

"Save your uncalled for speeches," Reisel broke in, "and introduce us to your guests."

"Reiseleh, if I only knew half of them. All I can tell you—" Rubin made a good catch of his cigar ash—"is that for expert diagnosis of what ails you you're at the right party. . . . Okay, okay . . . Sheila—" he called to the brunette now busy with a full-lipped young man while aiming her dagger specialty at Reisel.

"Never mind Sheila. We have already met your concubine as you saw."

"Reiseleh let me live, they're her friends. You know I'm rotten on names."

"And not only on names . . . What are those hideous objects in the back?"

"You don't think my brown leather chairs are nice, Reiseleh, that match my cases of Bookbinder's Fine Editions? Then tomorrow they'll be out on the sidewalk, rest assured."

"I am amazed—a guest is pulling out one of your books. Are the pages cut?"

A very ripe girl in black lace-edged décolletage who'd separated herself from the babble had the same immediate appeal with her sad owlish face as Bookbinder's pitted and overblown garden Venus holding a lamplight beyond the French doors. But, Danny made himself think, you can't tell a book from its cover, and the girl not only peered—okay, gloomily—at the spine of a Bookbinder's Fine Edition, but opened it!

"Of course not. Would you want people to get their finger marks on the paper, Reiseleh?"

"One more word from you—" Danny heard Reisel's warning to Rubin, and Rubin's cheerful, "But I appreciate flowers. Come into the garden—" "Maud." "Who wants Maud?" "An English song from my happy girlhood." "You miss England? I'll discuss London with you." "Like I miss . . ."

Danny excused himself and edged through smoke and conversation.

" . . . pale man simply left a batch of death certificates on my desk. I didn't see him come in, and when I looked again he wasn't . . ."

". . . mmm, this caviar? Juicy black beads, must be the real . . ."

". . . necrosis, kraurosis—a complete mess."

"Arteriosclerotic?"

"The works, she . . ."

". . . a day with you and do . . ."

Near the garden threshold of Rubin's library, Danny asked this . . . Beverly, Betty . . . Beverly, "Good reading?"

"Camouflage," she brightened up, "against slights and insults from the medical profession. Where did Sheila get you from, the faculty?"

"I'm from the Bookbinder side of the birthday, if there's a Sheila side."

"If there's a Sheila side?" Beverly tossed the Bookbinder Fine Edition *Vanity Fair* to a brown leather love seat where it landed—ouch—on its ear. "Ain't it her birthday party, the louse? I could swear she said so the lunchtime I muscled the invitation out of her in the hospital cafeteria. And

I brought her toilet water and scanty thanks I received! I know, I'll switch the gift to Grandpa there before I take leave. Men use toilet water, my husband did—and may still if one of those screaming meanies hasn't hit him since the last V-mail from Sicily."

"Say, you miss the fella don't you?"

Beverly shrugged. "I miss him, but I don't let it worry me. I hardly know him."

"Do you know what color hair he has?"

She gave Danny a friendly poke in the arm. "Risqué, aren't you? I've heard that joke. Yes, he removed his hat before we became intimate. Jeff has red hair, like the dame you came in with. What's this garden bench maneuver she's making with Grandpa, trying to get herself put through medical school like Sheila? Care for a laugh? Look at Sheila's eagle eye on her from the table there. Instead of false pretenses toilet water, Sheila is gonna end up with a heart attack—and it's all she deserves for this creepy party. Anybody who left their dictionary and easy guidebook for medical secretaries in the office where it belongs like I did could just as well have gone to the movies. Maybe I should have, the baby's with his adoring grandparents anyway. . . . Yeah, Jeff left me a momento. You got kids? Well I hope you're not waiting for grandchildren before you decide to like children. Still I'm lucky Robin reduces my parents to drooling moronicy, otherwise I'd be stuck. In Jeff's family—after all, my father-in-law's a G-man, he sells postage stamps in Queens—I'm the black sheep by marriage. What does that make me, a ewe? Are ewes inferior animals?"

"I've never met a ewe, just a cow or so in my youth, and a few chickens."

"Am I a cow or a chicken?" Beverly laughed. "You don't have to answer that question. Say Stan . . . is that your name? . . . Dan, what say we lose this party?"

"Bookbinder's feelings might be hurt, Beverly. I practically just got here."

"Bookbinder's feelings, huh?"

"Do you like your work at the hospital?"

Beverly shot him an impatient glance, craned her neck toward the talkers, drinkers and eaters, and walked away. So why did he feel to blame on account of that nothing and pick up, as camouflage, the *Vanity Fair* she had thrown down? The pages were uncut. Suddenly he was ravenous. He eased between backs to the table, found himself face to face with Sheila, complimented her on the spread and had himself some cold shoulder along with the caviar canapés he bolted and washed down with a Veuve Cliquot '36 as effective as water.

In the cab crosstown Reisel asked him, "Why didn't you accompany that young lady home?"

"I didn't want to wake up her baby."

"Naturally," Reisel considered it, "that kind would run, sensing virtue."

Danny stared. Was she serious?

Some virtue, the fruitless search type. Or else there was his ring-the-bell virtue with Hotel Dixie whores when the discipline absolutely gave way.

And in Central Park West no magic had placed a letter from Ezra in the mailbox.

In Sandy Point the stupid doorbell cut through the croon and sigh of the surf, and upstairs Carrie's real estate captain Sonny Levy—"Carrie, who's that?"—hung fire in the middle of their lovemaking. Her answer was a ten-fingered pinch at this fat-assed hero. But again the doorbell and, "Your husband?" from the warrior up on his forearm now, the wolf dwindling to mouse. Carrie knew who it was, and it was not her husband. That extinct volcano didn't encumber her weekends any more.

But—"So what, soldier?"—what if it had been.

Levy muttered "A war at a time, lady," and in two shakes of a lamb's tail, while the bell got nervier every ring, he pulled on undershorts and shirt and the uniform they issue practically anyone nowadays. His commando trot pattered down the stairs, and the back door softly closed. Carrie peeped past the blackout curtain in the dark house and, sure enough—elongated, stooped, rumpled as she had never seen the Commissioner of War Industries before—Gordon Ross was the one at the front door down there with his finger glued to the bell.

All afternoon Carrie had been expecting Ross, and all afternoon she'd been on the phone instead receiving bulletins from him on the antics of Libby his little woman. Too bad, because the V-letter—Carrie's man-o'-war Ezra had bombed Berlin!—that Carrie had snatched out of the mail room in Central Park West today before she'd driven to the Island the long way around had put her in a celebratory mood, very tingly below the midriff. And too bad for Gordon. His alibis were legitimate, but Carrie was finding herself less and less interested in them.

While he was packing his overnight bag for Sandy Point he'd been considerate enough (he'd exercised his wit over the phone to Carrie when he should have been here already) to lie to Libby that he had business in Albany. And without the slightest evidence that it wasn't so apart from his refusal to ask Libby along which he never did when it was so, Libby had screamed her unreasonable disbelief loud enough to send their two boys just home from summer camp running out of the house in embarrassment.

"So why stay with her," Carrie had needled him, "since the kids bear the brunt of it anyway?"

Gordon on his high horse had informed her Libby'd shrieked she'd reached her limit with his nonsense and he'd kept his angina pains to himself and told Libby she was free to take steps. Steps. He knew that leave it to Libby and she'd cling till death—probably his—did them part. Early lust had hooked him to that small bundle and he was stuck. His boss the governor, a good family man, would not tolerate divorce by an appointee. "If a man can't manage his private life," the governor once said earnestly to Carrie, "how can he manage his public life?" To Carrie those were two separate things, but all Gordon ever did was talk. Since a small heart attack he'd had last year he'd been blustering that one of these days he was going to have himself a Reno vacation, unload Libby in the course of it, and to hell with public life. He could if he wanted to. He always had Roxxoil the Ross family oil corporation to fall back on. So one day Carrie'd lost patience and challenged him to do it, get the divorce, and not wait to be fired. He was a somebody in the Democratic Party. "Resign," she'd told him, "and angle for something bigger."

"Will you marry me if I do it?"

"No."

"Then," he'd said brightly, "where's my incentive?"

Cute chatter. Press these guys, the biggest of 'em—the best, she'd almost thought, but there was no best, not even in the White House—and watch 'em fold. No matter how many nitroglycerin pellets Gordon melted under his tongue during a day's work, he loved the title State Commissioner of War Industries and his name in the papers. Since heart attacks were a possibility, he dreamed, and tried to palm it off as a joke, why shouldn't Nelson chairman of the War Production Board have a heart attack and Gordon be invited to Washington to take over? And when Carrie started with this guy a few years ago she'd mistaken him for a man.

A tiff with Libby and—it only made sense—he'd had to lie down awhile with his fluttering heart. His next call, while the maid and the chauffeur had been carting Libby down to the limousine, had announced Libby's sharp turn of the back on him that had left her crumpled on the living-room floor and moaning her leg was broken. The third call had come from the doctor's office on Park Avenue, and the fourth—"There are no doctors around or if there are they're tied up with sick people, and this . . . lump," he'd meant his spouse, "will have me stuck here all night. I'm sorry Carrie. . . ." Carrie'd told him sure sure, not to worry about it.

Who needed that bargain?

But hadn't it left a girl frustrated! Clean-living Carrie, she'd bounced down the sand in the stark nude—years since she'd done this—and tried to work the excitement off swimming beyond the breakers in the late sunlight. But the warm insinuating currents had been too sexy, and she'd showered and dressed still at loose ends, famished, yet for something spicier than the tenderloin steaks she'd brought from New York at the cost of all those ration points. She'd spun her Cadillac to the village, emerged from the delicatessen with a mouth-watering bagful of everything from pastrami to pickles and been saluted so crudely, "Long time no see," by an army captain in summer tans that she'd felt slightly tickled though she'd kept moving. And the guy had moved with her.

"You don't remember me, huh Carrie?" he'd added gloomily.

"The face does seem familiar but I can't place the shoulder bars."

"Sonny Levy, Levy & Sons Developers, the Bedford Park deal?"

And from the mists of girlhood (almost) in her old Bronx Hub office under the El, Sonny had bloomed slightly thick around the midsection but not too much the worse for wear: nose coming at you, hair still freshly varnished and moody gleam in the eye.

"Why Sonny indeed! Hard campaigning, Captain?"

"Yeah, the Palm Beach Hotel Florida and Milford Crest in Connecticut. I was in on the surrenders. Now we're wearing down the Sandy Point Beach Club."

"Next you'll be dropping a foreclosure on Hitler by registered mail while my son bombs Berlin."

"You have a son old enough?"

"Don't dangle my kid on your line Sonny boy."

"What line? Is it my fault I joined up and—"

"—kept out of the infantry in spite of your low draft number?"

"I also wanted to escape from real estate, Carrie. So the Einsteins read my data and it's training centers procurement. 'Then better draft my father,' I tell 'em, 'I'm the bottoms at real estate.' 'Okay, I'll put you down for a transfer,' the major says, 'but I need you right now to fill out the complement.' It's been right now ever since. You still Tomer Industries?"

"On cloud seventy-two, Empire State Building. Right now we're busy buying up West Thirtieth Street. Arthur Mulloy keeps shaking his head, but once I tear down the furriers' joints including the one my daddy went broke in and build Tomer Palace for the fur industry it'll make a nice memorial to my mother."

"I wouldn't believe it looking at you Carrie." And had Levy looked!

"Hungry?" she'd kidded him.

"Always."

"For delicatessen," she'd tapped her bagful, "for delicatessen."

But he hadn't been able to make it just then for delicatessen. His major had one of those business conference dinners on at the Beach Club. But later . . . So she'd sent him away happy with a promise to save him a knish for say nine o'clock.

And just about nine o'clock who'd called up but—who else?—Ross, indignant. Libby hadn't fractured anything but his evening. Now, finally, he was on his way.

"No," Carrie'd told him, "it's too late Gordon," and meant it in every sense.

"Nonsense," he'd he-manned her. "See you soon."

She had called out, "I'm telling you," but he had hung up.

She'd rung back, gotten Libby's exasperated hellos, and quietly hung up herself. She'd done her part, and even if she hadn't she Carrie Baum was at nobody's disposal, including this one's. Yet seeing him outside now she almost felt sorry for him with his fagged, desperate swipe at his hair while he craned his neck up at the black windows. She didn't want the guy dropping dead on her doorstep, or anywhere else for that matter. She put on a man's voice and phoned the all-night taxi at the railroad station to pick her up—that is, him—and waited beside the blackout curtain till the cab came. Ross was puzzled and he bent to say something to the driver. But—smart boy—he swung the overnight bag to the back seat, angled himself in, and receded down the silent hedged street. On the beach side a jeep roared distantly, no doubt her other he-man making his getaway.

She showered away what's-his-name's traces, made herself decent in a nightgown and lay down with her billets-doux from her own private bombagator. To start from the beginning she turned her shoe box of letters upside down. Then she slipped the top one out of its envelope, kissed it and curled up next to the bed lamp for some good reading.

> . . . imagine the audacity, herding us virtual civilians through the rain from Atlantic City Station to the former Seaside Arms Hotel and me without my umbrella. Along the boardwalk though we passed squads of Flying Cadets marching like merry sunshine, so I can hardly wait to be weatherproofed like those chappies. . . .

And Carrie's mother—Eva had been blessed with a husband too—had not lived to be the grandma of a boy like this. Carrie ruffled through basic training to highlights from the University of West Virginia last year. Sure, the dormitories were where they lived and the classrooms were where they slept, and power-drunk shavetails burned him up, he was young yet, the justice kid. But when aviation students lost their Saturday off for being behind in the work or from shavetails' demerits, you didn't find her Carrie Baum's Ezra among them.

> . . . Soldier Share stood guard duty last night, so I slept all morning and am getting out of inspection and review this afternoon. I'm sergeant of the guard and my mock of stern command is enough to make any man tremble —laughing. . . .

But the guard moved and quick-step at those commands, Carrie knew without being told, you betcha. And most of this correspondence from her knight errant had to be read between the lines.

> . . . Yes Mom, nobody can fool you. It is true that to learn to fly a chappy must go up in the air. For me that took place just after I was promoted to the final class at the Morgantown filbert foundry. But mostly we're grounded, and as a matter of fact if you or Dad or Teddy could spare a #5 shoe ration coupon an extra pair of shoes would go well with my assortment of shoeshine kits. . . .

Or,

> . . . But what was there to mention about the flying, Mom, interested as I know you are in my many-faceted military achievements? It was just in a

little pipa cub to make certain we wouldn't become airsick and soil a large expensive airplane. . . .

Carrie reached graduation day and a bit of anarchist in her smiled already, in spite of that bastard of a major.

Victorville Army Air Field, Victorville California
announces the graduation of Class 33–7 Bombardiers
Saturday April twenty-four 1943

. . . Mom asks why I am ranked Flight Officer instead of 2nd Lieutenant. It only goes to show, as Dr. Kalakian taught us in Philosophy 1, that there is sometimes a difference between appearance and reality. Waiving the regulation that a Cadet must not gamble, to celebrate graduation eve Swift and I organized a crap game outside the recreation hall shower room. A fellow cadet we thought with only a towel around the midsection came out of the shower room, quietly watched the action a while and went to dress. When he reappeared dressed his shoulders had sprouted gold leaves. He ordered us to report ourselves, and that was how airman Share got demoted before being promoted. But I've been getting in piano practice a flight down in the same recreation hall, and I came out eighty dollars ahead in that crap game! . . .

Read this kid with his laugh a line to avoid worry for mother and you'd think war was a pinball game where whenever you please you press a lever and watch the board light up.

. . . No, we're not still after that nice safe underground munitions factory the Germans didn't defend. While we were celebrating Independence Day at the U.S.O., the RAF took revenge on us for the loss of the colonies by loading a 20,000 pounder so huge that they could barely get the plane off the ground. Then (see enclosed bragging Manchester Guardian clipping) they blew our German munitions works wide open. Ain't that awful, Mabel? Our flights now are routine. . . .

And for a nightcap, here came today's letter, yesterday's now.

. . . I know, Mom, as you write, that as a good Jewish mother you'd like to be alongside me or, next best, to picture yourself alongside me going *nyaa* to the Nazis, but there isn't that much to tell about combat flying. On the way to target, unless you're lead plane, the pilot simply stays in formation and the bombardier-navigator doesn't have much to do. . . .

Yeah, she skimmed over the next part—warming his father's bombsight up should you be on lead, or first, second or third behind lead. That ineffectual father of his never would have come near assembling a bombsight if not for her.

> . . . My friend Swift sleeps on the flight over. As an artist, naturally, I'm too highly strung for that, so I use the trip to get some reading done. . . .

And this books business for the father was skippable. Yeah, yeah . . . Ahh . . .

> . . . we always leave with a fighter escort and you know that we carry our own gunners. Antiaircraft fire is extremely remote, black bursts aimed at somebody else. Enemy planes (see, you asked for it and you're getting it, Mom), should there be any, fly by so fast there's no time to worry. So you approach target, take last-minute readings if you're on lead, electronically release the bombs for the squadron, navigate back to base and report for your air medal. That was the sequence a couple of weeks ago when our flying manhole cover happened to be on the lead and hit—*London Observer* photo modestly enclosed—Berlin! . . .

Hear that, Nazis? Her Carrie Baum's bar mitzvah Ezra pressed the button on that squadron's worth of explosions and sky-high master race smoke!

And her other—was that a Teddy! Eighteen and a half, and, in his spare time from the Ivy League where the only grade the profs knew how to give him was A, he managed a full-fledged cooperative art gallery on West Fifty-sixth Street, Group Shows, and actually sold the stuff—and not just to her collector friends like the governor—that his smearers turned out.

If you want real men—grow 'em yourself!

Here it was February, soon the war would be over, and still that L.J. Allen held out with his three condemnable Thirtieth Street lofts after Carrie had bought up the rest of the block to clear for Tomer Palace! The prophet of doom Mulloy harangued her, "Carrie, L.J. is an unwitting messenger from heaven. Forget Tomer Palace. Unload while the unloading's good: ten million prewar unemployed, ten million in the armed services, you draw the postwar economic conclusion." So the depression-stung Thirtieth Street landlords who'd been delighted to unload at Carrie's fair price had reasoned too. But that wasn't the way she Carrie Baum saw it. She saw an extra ten million back eager to spend and nothing to buy and an expanded industry with no choice but production unless they were willing to write off their wartime plant capacity—and what big American boys would want to do that? And what little American girl worthy of the name would want to live without her very own Persian lamb coat? No more of the furriers' sitting on their ass twenty-six weeks a year that had originally enticed Daddy Moishe into the fur business. Tomer Palace would be humming from sunny salesrooms on top to air-conditioned vaults on the bottom, and if the fur trade didn't happen to fill the joint the hell with 'em—she could always let in a blouse-maker or two. "Yes ma'am," Arthur'd muttered. "How much more should L.J. Allen be tickled with?" Tickled? For two cents she'd flatten L.J. like the Berlin job her kid started last summer. Trying to bleed her Carrie Baum. All she had to do was sic Jim Dillon at the Housing and Buildings Department on him. A dozen or so violations a day slapped on those firetraps endangering her property would bring L.J. around quite rapidly to her point of view.

But . . .

Maybe she was becoming superstitious in her old age. With Ezra in England in the middle of rockets bursting she didn't feel like forcing any deals. Since last fall the sneaky kid'd been stringing her along with tales of strategy changes and bad weather interfering with his getting in the required missions. But his crew—now he'd told her—had been stateside long ago for rest and retraining, except for Carrie's Captain Courageous. He'd volunteered for a second tour of combat duty because—some management: just what you'd expect—his group had found itself short of experienced airmen. He'd completed the second tour thank God, he was due and overdue to be sent back, and the same diddlers hadn't yet scraped together the nine other crew and ten ground personnel for a flight to the U.S.A. Her cheerful Charlie wrote though that as to buzz bombs, don't worry.

> . . . I take no chances. In town yesterday the sirens went off and me too—with the civilians to the nearest airraid shelter. Whitman with me yelled "Where you running?" and I replied "Home to Mother!" / At the local music school where I practice I've met a girl, a student there, Jane Cowley, who is an utter contradiction in terms: intelligent, beautiful and a coloratura soprano. We're working up some swell lieder sessions together. . . .

So he wasn't in such a big rush home to Mother. But enjoy yourself kiddo while it lasts, and don't let the grass grow under your feet. And who could ask for better for Teddy, in language school now in Chapel Hill with basic training behind him? Yeah, to date, keep all the fingers crossed, she'd been lucky with both her boys. So—fair exchange is no robbery and why tempt heaven by the demolition of a mere L.J. Allen?—she inclined toward a take it or leave it offer. If L.J. stayed too big for his breeches, his choking on 'em would be his own doing. Her Thirtieth Street properties with a good rent hike could keep very nicely for a postwar rise, and a block or so south Tomer Palace'd still go up in all its glory! The question was, what should her final figure be for L.J.? In the back of her cab home she pulled the sheaf labeled 30TH ST. out of her briefcase. But even on war daylight saving time the rainy twilight the nine-to-fivers with raised overcoat collars were pumping through along Fifth toward the subways was too dim to read by. So she gave it up for a snatch, between bodies and umbrellas, of Russek's window and what they were wearing. Were those white draperies evening gowns, show-nothing nighties, or shrouds? A green double-deck bus slid up to block her view . . . and—what was this?—her Cadillac ration-starved in the garage and she stockstill in a traffic jam?

She told the lump at the wheel, "Try Broadway," and got the kind of heavy-shouldered shrug that she just adored. And a saying.

"Rush hour lady, it ain't no better on Broadway."

"Try it," she was the milk of human kindness anyway, "what do you care?" And, "See?" she eased him down cheerfully when he steered into Broadway and traffic there was smacking briskly along the rain-black gutter up the Great Browned-out Way.

At Central Park West there was no mail in the box. Of course the father—could that empty barrel have been the father?—might have pirated it out on his lunch hour. Upstairs though under the table lamp in the foyer waited what was no doubt another of Teddy's merry Western Union war bulletins. Already, slipping her gloves off, she was smiling. His first telegram had read:

> Outfitted by Quartermaster's T/3 Myron the shipping clerk from Uncle Trachtenberg's Famous Men's Clothes stop Myron measures by eye stop You cant stop him stop Comic snapshot of Private T Share to follow.

And last week's:

> Ascertained fluent in French and German stop Therefore assigned to Officer Candidate School U North Carolina for Japanese studies stop Vital Force proposes Army disposes.

So she tore this one open, walked it smiling into her bedroom and—*War Department regrets to advise*—for the first time in her life felt weak in the knees. Midges rained in front of her eyes, she actually had to support herself against the bedpost. No more Ezra? Ridiculous . . .

But easy girlie. The same incompetents who ran short of airmen, the same who couldn't gather a crew to send home men who'd completed their combat tour—they were wiping out her son and she was believing it? In an accident, it said there. Accident her ass. Six months shot at and no accidents, and now maybe he'd walked in front of a plane against a red light? Who was this air force joker? She got on the phone long distance and after fourteen switches wound up with a shavetail who had the gall to console her that details from the English air base would undoubtedly follow. Undoubtedly, huh? She told him to put his superior officer on the wire, waited . . . and got cut off! She began again—then stopped. Who had time for toy soldiers? At Gordon Ross's she used to run into some finance major general, what was his name? Something Bauer, though what good could that brass-buttoned accountant do her? . . . Herman, right—Herm Bauer. She tried him at Whitehall Street, and no wonder kids were getting killed needlessly in this war—the general was gone for the day!

Look—she was dead on her feet, and standing. These bums drained you. She sat down. Who else was there? The only army men that she knew worth talking to—army men? men!—were Ezra and Teddy Share. She stared at her wristwatch: six-twelve . . . thirteen. . . .

Mulloy must have reached his Great Neck hacienda by now if he hadn't pulled a bar and grill stop on her. She waited another minute to get past the unlucky number and had the operator ring him. Kitty the sister answered with the usual syrup for the brother's boss, and—you could still count on miracles—yes, Arthur was home, and Kitty put him on.

"Arthur," Carrie told him "another word with these guys and I'm liable to say something unladylike. Track this nonsense down and call me right back." But as soon as he heard that stupid telegram—good God damn, from him too: oh for chrissakeses, heartfelt meows! "You can that crap," she said, "and start phoning. Goodbye."

"But Carrie—"

"Will you for once do what I say without a discussion!"

"Yes ma'am," Mulloy said.

The office phone used to ring and Danny would pounce on it—to live if it was Sydelle, otherwise die. Now the thing whined—who'd be calling him?—and he switched off the dictaphone to keep the noise off the record while he waited for whoever it was to give up. In the electric gloom of desks without people he stared past the parked trucks below toward the murk that blotted out the river. What was he, the switchboard for his four to midnight production floor? When the ringing stopped he resumed dictating for Wartels to transcribe tomorrow. He was laying it on the line to official murkdom, the Office of Price Administration. Directive 783254.67 to save gas in seventeen eastern states ruled out delivery traffic of less than 80 percent vehicle capacity. The OPA minds could congratulate themselves that with Quality compliance—easy on the sarcasm, Riva'd have to revise—the war planes they were saving the gas for wouldn't get finished. Should he also give them credit for aiding and abetting extortionists? His truckmen had to be sent out with bribe money because the police stopped partial-load bombsight shipments now on the pretext of a nonessential-driving-in-wartime violation. His plant manager Harvey jollied him why raise the blood pressure over New York's finest? "We have the cost-plus contracts, Dan, they have the ambition." "Ambition as what, cops or robbers?" "Hey, you're looking for liberty and justice for all!" That's what he was looking for, but no use mentioning it. Better stick to the point and let the hackles remain quietly risen. "Deliveries are scheduled on the basis of War Production Board code number . . ."

Where the hell was the memo that had that number?

During his guts-grinding search through a blotterful of papers that craftily glided to the bottom when you were after them the phone started again. Who'd want him—if him—that badly? Not his wife. Maybe Reisel, with an invigorating report of Brody's condition? Gittel's complaint at the very hospital bed Brody'd landed in with his stroke had been not what was she going to do, but what was she going to do with him? She'd dredged up ancient history, her father's houseful of servants. She had not remarried to become an old man's practical nurse! Brody luckily had been in some other world, moaning for water. Danny was paying the nurses practical and impractical, but Reisel was running to Brody nights and weekends like the angel of mercy she really was, fending her mother off, refusing to let Brody lose interest in his football, basketball or hockey results she read him from the papers, raising a superior smile on the good side of his face with philosophical sports questions like, "Brody, precisely what is their goal?" Eh, Danny picked the phone up—and it stopped. . . . Holy Jesus, this was a wise old WPB order and he wasn't going to find it. . . . He clutched his hair, once more the phone went off, and he answered fast.

Mulloy Carrie's factotum slung pebbles of sound—home . . . needed . . . telegram?—from a million miles away, then let loose a boulder—"Your boy's been in an accident, exactly what, I'm not clear on"—that sent Danny's brains spinning.

"Which boy?" Danny croaked.

"Ezra, I understand—"

Danny said stupidly, "Ezra hurt?"

"So I understand . . ."

Then why hadn't Carrie . . . Danny called home and she said, "Arthur?" "No, Danny, he—" And—"Get off the line!"—she hung up on him.

With a flash of Ezra home swathed in bandages or else why wouldn't she talk, he grabbed his coat and hat. In waves of heat from the ovens on his production floor with spray guns hissing and tools clanking he shuffled his feet while his night foreman Joe Landowne went for a pickup truck key. His head began banging like in the good old days, but outside in the rain pattering the parking lot the throbbing eased off. Only how had they shipped Ez home all of a sudden? Still, only hurt—and soon he'd be with that kidder, drinking in the wide smile, getting the lowdown on the coloratura duets this guy had been lucky enough to run into at the age of not even twenty. But the windshield fogged, you had to go at a crawl along dark streaming streets. Then at the Third Avenue bridge a red light stopped him, and damned if a cop didn't poke a big nose around and spin out the essential driving ban line! Danny was about to tell him emergency, but that beefy poker face—discuss Ezra, with this?—changed his mind. The cop went through the license and registration cards case as if the Messiah was hiding out in the folds disguised as a five dollar bill.

"Plenty of money in lamps now, huh," the lips moved and made sounds, "with a war on?"

"That's right, wheelbarrowsful to the bank. Give me the ticket, I've got to go somewhere."

"Big rush to the Ration Board for four new tires," the cop took his time writing, "Abie, I mean Danny?"

Danny said, "Izzie for Israel, Pat," tossed the ticket on the seat and stepped on the gas hard enough to take a year out of the transmission. He reached Central Park West though without any more of New York's finest to light up the future for him.

But Clarence the elevator man said good evening with no mention of Ez, so how could Ez be here? Oh idiot Danny, with a wish as a horse the brains were away galloping. Where would an accident have happened except in England? So his wife's nastiness this time—*Get off the line*—that as always embarrassed him for her had at least had a reason, you would want the line to be clear for more information. Lights were on in the foyer, the kitchen, the living room, but the apartment was deathly quiet. In her bedroom with the chandelier and all the lamps blazing she was in a trim light-gray dress with blue piping and held a hatpin between her teeth at the mirror while she adjusted a chic little blue felt. If she was setting herself to paint the town red, could things be that bad?

Just the same his "What's going on?" came out hollow.

She pushed a telegram at him and said through clamped teeth, "Read it, you've earned it—if it were true, God forbid."

> *. . . War Department regrets . . . death . . . aircraft accident . . .*

Danny sank to the edge of the bed and stared at those words. Captain Ezra Share, that was correct, and that was his serial number. But, *1 February 1944 . . . ?*

Then his wife snatched back the telegram. He started to say wait, but her high heels clattered, the hall door slammed.

The kid was due to fly back home, how could he have been in an aircraft accident February first? Danny's wife didn't believe that, and whatever else you might say about her she was a very smart woman.

Unless . . .

Unless . . . on the flight back . . . Aw no no no—on the flight back. Danny pounded his thigh, he ripped his jacket, he hit his head till it ached. On the flight back . . . He paced around, "No no no," then caught sight of the piano. He flung up the cover, and stupidly—he knew it while he was doing it, but who needed pianos, who'd ever needed them—he took it out on the keyboard with both fists till the blood made it too slippery. He ran for a broomstick then and his demolition job was going well when the telephone rang through the strings clanging.

Be Carrie, he prayed, and that telegram a mistake.

It was Ansbacher from the apartment downstairs, outraged at the disturbance. Danny swung the receiver down three times before it caught in the cradle, and he looked around panting.

But what was there to do?

At the Ross Park Avenue duplex Carrie showed Gordon the telegram and he put in hours cutting through channels for a call to somewhere in England. Meanwhile Libby the little woman kept complaining she was too sick for all this turmoil. Luckily Libby gave up and went to sleep just before England rang, so the only static Carrie had to deal with while she listened to what passed as a commanding officer was transatlantic. A plane that had flown twenty-eight combat missions had exploded in clear skies over Scotland on the way back to the States? Why? The incompetent couldn't say why, maybe a leak in the gas line, a ground personnel passenger who didn't know better lighting a cigarette— "Didn't know better!" Carrie let the bum have it. "Didn't you tell them not to light a cigarette, Major?"

But in the end hang up on him and what did he care, going his merry way. "My kid's really dead," she bared her teeth at Gordon, "he's really dead."

Ross shook his head, he clasped her hands in spite of the last summer's brush-off that had made him swear that he'd never speak to her again. God, to lose a kid—he also had two sons, difficult as they were he knew how he'd feel, how much love he'd need then. "Stay here tonight Carrie," he said, "the hell with Libby," and her look alone proved how foolish it was to lower your guard ever—with anyone.

"What's the matter with you," she twisted her face up. "Thanks for the phone call, but what's the matter with you!" And she walked out on him, the hard-on Samaritan. But her least concern was that weakling. Ezra had never had to be in the air force, and he had never had to be on that plane. In a cab crosstown through the park as black bleak and empty as her heart was, she set her thoughts on home. She was going to fix that killer's wagon, her mate pro tem's. She'd wipe that bastard Share out the way he'd wiped out her darling son, her funny, gifted kid she was never going to see any more. There were ways, maybe things she could do about his factory contracts. Only how? . . .

Nah, 3 A.M., she felt played out now. But just give her time.

Danny heard Carrie's key and, tousled as he was, stubbled, in his torn shirt, hope against hope he looked into her face when she came in and he got a glare back like murder. He swung his den door shut on her just as hard as she swung her bedroom door shut on him, but she was right. Fearless Fosdick out of the comic strips, with his big talk and asinine sorties to Canada and Whitehall Street, he'd shown the kid who'd followed the old man's lead in everything from piano to Yankee Stadium the way straight to the graveyard. Danny flopped on the studio couch in the dark and yanked at his hair. Why was it now? he moaned. Why couldn't you push back time, make a deal with God like in the olden days: Bring back Ezra, take me. . . .

He kept repeating that till the sounds were meaningless. Then he thrashed himself around till he reached the goddam lamp, and he picked up the *Anna Karenina* he was halfway through, serious consolatory reading he'd been able to do because Ez'd been safe, had been coming home. Now he looked at words, but he saw a patch of bare ground, and underneath, in a box, Ezra. Not so good, huh Ez, the old man gave you a bum steer, huh? . . .

Dawn lighted the Morris chair, the bookcases, the whole empty paraphernalia. He was renewing the offer . . . Bring back Ezra, take me . . . when the doorbell—what could it be but a telegram superseding the other one?—shocked him off the bed and into the foyer.

His wife had already let in Rabbi Mort Edelman from Ben Zion Synagogue down the block, God's dapper semipro with the gray mustache, at this hour gray in the face too and slightly peevish. He was reporting, Edelman said, for whatever the mysterious duty was that Carrie (a pillar of the synagogue with her donations he didn't say, but that went without saying or else he wouldn't have been here, not this early anyway) had called him about.

So Danny made it a quick round trip back to the studio couch. Harvey his plant manager gently tapped later, but a bark through the door from Danny reminded that guy what he was paid for and he went away. Other voices—Danny's wife's, Mulloy's, a new maid Carrie was breaking in, Carrie told Mulloy the old one could leave a telegram on the table a whole afternoon without letting you know but couldn't take a tongue lashing for it, Edelman again, this time with Mrs. Edelman—kept Danny on edge that somebody else might try to burst in on him. Nobody did though—he himself hadn't told anyone about Ezra—and he tossed there in leaden misery for most of two days, not eating, not sleeping, but at least alone. Then—Ma had seen an obituary in the *Times* for Ezra and collapsed: that was her worry—his sisters came, and Reisel. Leah leaned over him to press her damp cheek against him. He lay inert with his back to her. Naomi he jerked his hand away from and muttered, "Go home, you have a son to take care of, haven't you?"

"So do you," Leah said to him, "have a son."

That stood him up shaky as he was. "Get out of here, beat it!" He actually shoved her. Reisel touched him and he turned on her. "What are you here for, to read me the sports, or the funnies maybe? Get out, go read them to Brody if he's still breathing."

But they hovered, hectored him with their lousy kindness, drove him, finally, to tears. Then the inevitable, the big sister was feeding him from a dish of chicken soup.

The next day the slow army let Teddy up from Chapel Hill and—serious, no wisecracks—he threw his arms around his father. So you couldn't sit unwashed and unshaven as if you had only had one son. Teddy's persuasions that he attend Carrie's memorial service for Ezra at B'Nai Zion Danny couldn't give in to though, he had no stomach for heartfelt handclasps from his wife's notables. And then Uncle Willie showed up after a three night bus trip from Micanopy Florida where he farmed vegetables now, a seventy-five year old man with thinning white hair, broad-shouldered and chunky as he still was, and he'd lost Anna two years ago. You couldn't snap at him when he told you that impossible as it seemed, this misery passes. So Danny just shrugged.

"How can it pass?"

"If only it d–didn't," Willie said.

Meaning what? Misery by rote is still misery.

All in all, the end of the mourning week and back to Mott Haven was a relief. Harvey and Riva had done what they could while Danny was away, but before he knew it this first day back the dull-gray river had turned satin-black with blue glints from Harlem and he'd hardly dented his backlog. Fine. Keep busy, with too dulled to think as a bonus on the subway return trip.

At Central Park West under the canopy the doorman gave the usual salute but Clarence the elevator man peered through his eyeglasses with a hello as if to the prodigal son home for lamb chops. "Good you looked in, Mr. Share," Clarence incomprehensibly told him, "there is one letter," and fetched it off the elevator grille with no explanation of how it had jumped out of the mailbox. Overseas mail it was, no escaping, but at least the return address was *Col. Thomas Fabricant, C.O.*, not Ezra. Danny'd already suffered a take-off-any-day-now note full of good cheer from Ez—Danny's wife had made sure to thrust that on him—that had followed the death notice.

This letter Danny stuck in his pocket unopened, and—the elevator was still grounded—raised his eyebrows to Clarence. "I believe that's all there is, Mr. Share, but if you want to make double sure—" And—hadn't a tenner been enough of a Christmas tip?—at your floor say good night and the guy looks at you cockeyed.

Only no top lock: a blank hole. Had the place been broken into? Was that it? Inside it was dark, and . . . ? He flicked the foyer switch and no light, except—he actually pinched himself, but he wasn't dreaming—moonlight through bare windows, room after room . . . and not a stick in them.

He stood stunned at the edge of the vacant front room.

She'd moved out on him, planned this—it had to be planned—without the courtesy of a So long stupid?

Yet the sinking feeling was loss—for, crazy as it seemed, the end of the marriage not the furniture. . . .

But the den too—a clean sweep? He flung open the closet there, and—Jesus Christ, that son of a bitch—even his clothes and music! Leaving he kept his face straight for the hired help, but in a cigar store phone booth on Columbus his voice shook telling his lawyer Bernstein to get him his stuff back and fast. And he wasn't falling into her trap either, some squalid fleabag to grind his teeth in tonight. And hey, he must have been getting lucky. In spite of the hotel squeeze he found himself a nice high room in the St. Andrew facing the park a couple of blocks north. In the St. Andrew restaurant he forced some food down his throat, pumped past empty benches awhile in the bare moonlit park to walk off the heartburn and back at his room at the hotel felt for the key and found the commanding officer's letter too.

Danny sat down to read it, yeah, this, that, on target . . . Air Medal . . . guts. . . .

> . . . a real airman. At the beginning of his first tour of combat duty he did some U.S.O. singing for our men. As a result of that a Special Services officer requested a release for him to detached duty to perform for troops elsewhere. I was strapped for personnel at that time but called your son in anyway to get a line on him, and I remember his answer in welcome contrast to groans I've gotten at briefings when the map is rolled down to a risky target: "No sir, that's not what I'm here for. . . ."

Didn't that have Danny tearing his hair again. Oh you dumb stupid kid! Even your stupid old man was never that dumb!

Only, Danny was sure, he had been—and more than once. But don't look into it, unless you want to give the bereaved mother the satisfaction of a ten story leap out of the window.

A couple of days later the suitcases and cartons arrived via the Salvation Army—no thanks to Mrs. Share Bernstein said, her man Mulloy had had to worm her amusing donation stunt out of her. Now where the hell was Danny supposed to put all this stuff till they had a suite for him here?

No sooner did Mr. Hutchins commence droning down at the lectern about fields of force than up in the classroom tiers there echoed a gentle purr beside Teddy: Air Cadet Purvis snoring. The slump of khaki shoulders in seats below, the professor's voice, the fact that Teddy had taken this course before—at Columbia—the siren spring vagrantly wafting in from the green campus, the apathetic Rockies off to the west, all beckoned toward slumberland. But tomorrow began final exams in the crash program that Teddy was crashing through meteorically. Only Saturday off—the eagerly awaited 5 P.M. to 1 A.M. next go at free-of-charge immorality named Peggy Dunne—stood between him and the month of flight training, the change of address to, most likely, Lowry Field, and the unavoidable end of his kindly deception of his parents. Therefore instead of succumbing Teddy popped open his eyeballs, deftly applied a hotfoot to Purvis's far shoe and before the burning match turned snore into roar was studiously bent over his notebook breaking the news to Mother that he was no longer in Japanese studies and in fact for his six weeks now in Denver had been an aviation student.

> . . . For one thing, accident or no accident I hold the Germans, likewise the Japs, responsible for killing my brother. What a void they left, and I'm going to teach them. I liked Ez, needling and all. I was proud of him. I was the art man, he was the music man. I was the wrestler, he was the swimmer. What fields of endeavor didn't we encompass between us. When he played the Schumann concerto at the Conservatory I not only let everyone for rows around know that that was my brother but also you'll recall

brought Esther the Sabbath observer in honor of the occasion, a pure music lover and all orthodox Jewish elbows defending her virtue against a fellow, as I was aware. That's why I'm sacrificing sweet sleep at this Physics lecture to let you know that when I returned to Chapel Hill after Ez's memorial service I applied for this transfer, and, with a small bribe to a personnel sergeant, expedited the okay. But before you start endangering the morale of an air cadet with remonstrances—and remember that such was not your procedure with Ez when he enlisted—consider that

1. the war may be over before I've finished training, though my war aim is as stated;
2. fellows here from overseas for retraining bring word that skies over Europe are practically void of enemy aircraft; likewise the Pacific; and
3. I'm great at playing the odds.

So no emergency phone calls, telegrams or letters with dirty words like "dumb kid" or "snotnose," as case may be. I'll be as okay as if I'd finished Chapel Hill, which to tell the truth I couldn't have stood much longer anyway, it was so tedious. Already I'd been asking myself why Ez should have all the fun, and besides, dropping bombs on Japs is just another way of speaking to them in their own language. So don't worry, sayonara—see, my education is never wasted—and send me one of your perfumed letters with all the latest, preferably that whom God had joined together are no longer asunder, and that the approved wreckers are raising exhilarating clouds of dust for Tomer Palace on 30th Street . . .

Omit, let's see, bribing that sergeant, Chapel Hill tedious and bombing the Japs, and he could pretty much copy off the same thing to Dad. But odd how those few changes, plus substituting the Quality factory and bombsight mountings for the glorious battlefield where Mom's overmatched foe L.J. Allen had fled in confusion and where Tomer Palace would rise from the rubble, drained all the juice from Dad's version. Heigh-ho, he'd always been more at ease with Mother. Face it, Ez had been Dad's boy.

All the more reason that out of consideration for her loving Teddy—though certainly he loved Dad too—Mother should not have separated from Dad, much less blamed Ez's death on him. Ez had always been overboard on rectitude, from girls to politics, he'd known what he was doing when he joined up. Now it unsettled a fellow, Ez gone and they apart. A family should stick together.

If Mr. Hutchins could drone as fast as Teddy could correspond, the course would have been over long ago. Next Teddy found carbon paper and a sheet inscribed "Group Shows Inc., Teddy Share, Manager," but on second thought discarded that for a United States Air Force letterhead. In a dignified hand he addressed Mr. Gilbert Whitman, curator of the Yale Museum of Art, on behalf of Millie Cole the nude nipple specialist of Group Shows. In bed with Millie Teddy's furlough before the last, he had promised her a career, to proceed through Ivy League college art shows, small out of town museum shows, donations of paintings by Millie to museums and hospitals, and an artist in residency contract, to, grand climax, the big-name gallery New York show armored in credits. Out of bed Teddy was not so sure that Millie's was the worthiest of art for such a campaign, but if for no other than business reasons—people must trust you—his word was his bond. His short and sweet note to Whitman waved the flag, waved his mother's friend the governor-emeritus of New York at whose house Teddy had met Whitman, and gently waved Millie's work that Whitman had professed to admire in the governor's collection. Enclosed would be Millie's color slides, and if the show materialized—as why should it not?—there would be the first three steps of Millie's career in one blow. The other two, if circumstances still warranted, could wait till after V-day.

He sealed Mom's letter and Dad's, yawned, and glanced at his watch. There was still time for a little nap. But he cleverly slipped his shoes off first so that no retaliatory hotfoot would heat his foot.

On Park Avenue Carrie calmed down finally—what do you do with a kid like this?—and reread her letter from Teddy. She kissed the torn-out notebook sheet kindergarten-jagged for all of her son's savvy lingo that caught at your heart and left you laughing with tears in your eyes. Then she scribbled herself a memo to double her contributions to B'Nai Zion, the United Jewish Appeal, and Hadassah. For their sake God had better take care of him!

And on Central Park West Danny read his and he had this good fortune—gray as his hair was, there was plenty left to pull. But oh Jesus Christ had he underestimated this kid—feelings, loyalty, consideration—did he still have a son he could be thankful for! In synagogue from the next morning on before the prayer for the dead he said his prayer for the living: God, let this kid be luckier.

29

IN CARRIE'S PARK AVENUE BATTLEMENTS SHE ASSURED her son Teddy the property owner, gallery manager, war veteran and senior classman at Columbia in the handsome red pencil mustache and gray flannel suit that under rent control it would be next to impossible for him to occupy the entire East Eighty-eighth Street brownstone he'd just bought.

"Consider yourself lucky," she said, "if those Rent Office creeps allow you to move into your empty attic there."

"But Mother, I'll need the entire premises for my own admittedly small but burgeoning household, which would be legal my lawyer tells me."

Carrie sat up straight. "What's going on? Did you get yourself into something in England during the war?"

"Now and then, nothing worth speaking of."

The point was, he explained pacing his mother's vast living room that had everything Central Park West had had except poor Dad, that Teddy liked the idea of home life: affectionate greetings, home-cooked meals, sympathy, a bouncing baby or two to name after Ez. Settling down was at the head of his agenda, handy chart drawn up and all. Vertically you list the eligible entries, all tried and true—Carol, Millie, Pauline, Roberta, Judith—and horizontally their attributes, to which you assign weights. Fill in the boxes and the high score's the pick. Mom laughed so hard he had to run bring her water, it couldn't wait for the maid. "Are you picking a wife," Mom whinnied, "or a horse?"

"That the method finds winners at Empire City racecourse old girl is no case against it."

"And losers," Mom waxed maternal. "What's wrong with some of the winners you've met right here—Myron Laches's daughter Claudia for example, or Milt Diamond's Maxine? Their pas have too many millions?"

"The money doesn't disqualify them Mother, but they don't remind me of you."

"Don't sell me that," but Mom didn't like him any the less for trying, "and don't do anything dumb. Better let me look over whoever your chart works out to before you plunge on a marriage license. That," Mother preened her hair, "believe ancient wisdom, could be the worst two dollar bet you'll ever make. Marrying," she waved off his incipient protest at the allusion to Dad and gurgled again, "to gain possession of a brow-how-hownstone," and another tumbler of water became imperative while Teddy smiled along. Because Mom understood it wasn't for that sort of thing alone you get married, it was for the novelty that spiced life—though in a pinch one could always give one's gutsy Palestine coreligionists a hand fighting Arabs instead.

The chart in fact ultimately failed just because the field was so tried and true. Score on girls but marry virgins was the stodgy class of '48's motto—and oh pioneer what more zestful should the virgin you wed prove to have zest. Should she not however, like some virgins he had initiated without benefit of clergy, for grim opposition in a wrestling match give him a gym, not his future bedroom on East Eighty-eighth. And this was not to consider the avoidable bother of the annulment proceedings that must inevitably follow so wearisome a shortcoming on the part of a bride. No, postulating a candidate's beauty, wit, passion and the kinship in spirit to appreciate, among other things, Teddy's almost unique Tucker Torpedo automobile, minor deficiencies like lack of a maidenhead could be taken under advisement.

Only where do the dream girls grow?

Their shortage was never more acutely felt when, pure bluff, he dropped in the bleak night after Thanksgiving for the first time on his brownstone tenants in Yorkville with the friendly announcement that he was the new owner and, nothing personal, that the eviction notice, a mere formality, was on its way. The lower floors' Herrenvolk stood ready with the hammer of Thor, every remedy from the Rent Control Office to the courts that the erstwhile rotten democracy could afford. But what a shock, the top floor Koch who materialized. This fair slender silky-haired Jewess (she smiled yes to his *"Bist a Yid shayneleh?"* and even chanced a handclasp with a prospective landlord) gazed unperturbed at him through his apologetic ukase and rebutted him with sweet reason.

"But that's impossible, you can't evict me from my nice little apartment. Where would I go in this housing shortage?"

Teddy volunteered gallantly, "Help you look," and raised an elfin curve to her deliciously tinted lips.

"Are you really in such a debased line of business?" she asked.

"Why shouldn't I be?"

"Well for several reasons, and you're not chewing a fat cigar."

"My mother's in real estate and she doesn't chew."

"Ah, then she's the landlord."

"She's not, nor am I by vocation, so in a sense you're right." He glanced past her fetching shoulder to the living room cozy under lamplight with studio couch, books and records. "May I explain within?"

She hesitated, then, "All right, but don't take off your overcoat." Wasn't this Marsha Koch a joy—his possible destined bride even! He sat down in his coat but in a trice shifted the explanations to her.

She'd left home, she told him, a year ago in San Francisco. Freedom was a blessed relief—the alternative would have been bondsmaid to a father who made a very good impression on outsiders but was very wearing on insiders—yet she often felt too rushed to enjoy it. She worked hard as a technical copy editor at the tiniest of publishing firms to put herself through New York University night classes to teach—she was not entirely enthusiastic about this—English. The lack of enthusiasm, Teddy breathed, would be a number of good books spoiled for her by analysis? Marsha's eyes widened. "Exactly." Then a glance and, delightfully, as if it had been his indoors eccentricity, "Why don't you take off that heavy coat?" Teddy was also pleased to observe that when they discussed some of the books in question she didn't pell-mell cater to his opinions as most nubile young ladies did upon first acquaintance. On the other hand most nubile young ladies, such as Myron Laches's daughter Claudia or Milt Diamond's Maxine, were handicapped unlike Marsha by knowledge of Mom's Tomer Industries glittering in the background. But the engaging Marsha could accept him as a Columbia art history student and even as Group Shows paid manager—and not a step further. The sauerbraten trust downstairs wouldn't believe that at his age he had a family to settle in this building. Marsha wouldn't believe that a boy, as she put it, of his age was in a position to have made eleven cooperative artists on West Fifty-sixth Street unhappy with his notice to find themselves a new manager since henceforth he would be dealing for himself at his new Vanguards Gallery on East Seventy-fourth that a G.I. mortgage had also obtained for him. Much less did she believe ("Come on, Teddy!" as if they'd gone to Hebrew school together, so she was charmed as well as charming) that all but one of the Group Show-ers had defected to him so that his former employers now comprised his stable.

Putting all his cards on the table for Marsha was the opposite of his present purpose, and he did not do it. But just as his tonight's gesture at taking possession of this house was a preview of coming attractions, his life in art as far as he had described it to her was a current feature. Not that money mattered except symbolically but his anachronistic managerial post on salary plus 10 percent of sales rather than in full charge of those splashers' destinies had gone against the grain of nature itself. The single deserter when he made his move had been Millie Cole and unbeknownst to Millie he had left her not she him. The turn of century avant-garde excitement in art was perchance gone forever. But an impresario on the grand scale, with whatever materials no matter how long on dazzle and short on form, could create an avant-garde illusion so that not this or that artist but the impresario himself, the great prestidigitator, is in effect the great master. Such was the role that Teddy meant to impress on the world of art till Vanguards would mean Share. Toward this end Millie Cole had grown so superfluous with her nipples actual and figurative that he had persuaded George Pentzakis of the Gruen Gallery who could smack his lips over both to offer Millie the big one-man show Teddy'd promised her in a moment of frenzy long ago. So Millie had happily disappeared, and Teddy could think of two or three others he might get rid of after he'd clinch negotiations to spirit the supreme carpentry sculptress Ida Radin and the fluorescent tubing wizard Don Hunt away from the Antrim Gallery.

"But Marsha," Teddy did say, "what better recourse did those painters have? As an acknowledged authority on American art from V-J Day on—and what other significant new work is there? —I'm indispensable to them. Where I go, art follows."

Marsha gave him an amused wave away. "Then follow in here—"

To her bedroom? Miss Koch's destined bride stock fell several points. But she calmly brushed aside the hand that he laid on her hip and she pointed down to the backyard where two shadowy trees laced a dim patch of litter. "Can't you do something about that? It's a shame your predecessor let the garden run down."

What a find!

And Marsha held up in the trial period. "I have to care, Teddy," this extraordinary creature would fend him off.

How long did it take a fellow such as he to make a girl care? Not long. At the movies Saturday nights his choral comments turned the worst stinkos into comedy hits for her. Teddy with his A average Marsha could marvel seemed always free, but she was swamped with college homework. This he helped her dispose of so winter Sundays could go to jolly countryside spins into Connecticut in the Tucker Torpedo. He introduced the underprivileged chit to ballet and her eyes moistened to bemused Orpheus who didn't know when not to look back, and to the journeyman prince who lost his swan princess to a third-rate magician. And there came the evening in the crush out of Carnegie Hall where the accommodating Mozart had done Teddy's wooing for him that sweet Marsh lowered her eyes and confessed unsolicited that this couple of months must have been the happiest of her whole twenty-two years. Carpe diem, Teddy taxied her with love and kisses straight back to Eighty-eighth Street. In her bedroom overlooking the as yet wintry but now trim little rear garden in moonlight—he'd had Nature Processing Associates over to plot better things for spring—Marsh was an eager joy to make love to.

Then, linked loosely together still, he teased her, "You've cared before."

Her lids flicked up. "That's not true—and if it were? So have you cared before."

"Marsh haven't you heard of the double standard?"

"We're off it," the blue eyes looked ominous, "in this precinct."

That—whence this déjà vu?—sent Teddy up on his elbow. The determined lips, the heart-shaped face not the least bit girlsy at this moment, the spill of gold hair on the pillow brought back nothing. . . . Yet . . . Plato says knowledge is recollection, but Teddy could not recollect. "You remind me of someone—I just can't . . ."

"Thank you—and what vast archives you have to ransack."

"Better and better," he stroked that suspicious cheek. "Whoever it was, why didn't I ask her to marry me?"

"Are you proposing, Teddy?"

"And if I were?"

And she softened alackaday—so after all marriage had been her humdrum objective same as many another's—and tapped the pillow for him to lie down on again. But—what had the Vital Force and the Rent Control Law sent his way!—"Isn't it nice dear," she asked, "just like this?" And his appreciative student suddenly turned into a lecturer on the marriage blight.

Marsha's mother to the day she died had scarcely addressed Marsha's father except in scorn, and he'd scarcely replied except in anger, the Russian-employed cargo clerk at the West Coast branch of Amsovko Trading Company and the Russian-educated lady pharmacist. Shopping, cooking, cleaning, penny-pinching, nagging and regrets that as a young woman she had ever gotten herself into this fix: that had been her mother's career. Against Marsha's exhortations Karen, Marsha's sister older but hardly wiser, had married herself to an uneventful escape from home named Monroe Bergman and was busily renewing the cycle. And after the exhortations Marsha herself had come close to doing the same. She—but never mind that. She could say literally that any marriage she'd ever heard of was cause to shudder. Her best friends Julia and Irene, to multiply instances— But look at Teddy's own divorced parents!

Who she reminded him of was at the tip of his tongue . . . when Marsh embraced him.

"I've lectured you, haven't I? But now you know—you mustn't start me off on that hobbyhorse. . . ."

What a bride-to-be! Perhaps they'd get married on graduation day, if he could fit in City Hall just before or after commencement. Otherwise full-scale June would have the advantage of lovely Marsh in white for a panting crowd of his friends and enemies. Either way his lawyer would somehow have to get these premises vacated by May 1st for renovation. Meanwhile—Teddy kissed, he touched Marsha everywhere—a snappy pregnancy would clinch all: marriage, East Eighty-eighth occupancy, a little Ez. But what fellow would make capital of dear Marsh's body?

Not he.

An April showery eve Teddy dashed home from the college library just a bit tardily through the downpour to his Riverside Drive digs where he had promised Marsh a dinner. Happily it seemed he'd preceded her anyway, and he whipped up cocktails and a still life of a salad rivaling Cézanne, set onion cross-sections and mushrooms simmering and laid out filet mignon. Still she didn't arrive, so he assumed her stuck at the office and jumped back to his honors paper in Art. In the bright blue Mediterranean year 455 with civilization tumbling down who sailed along to catch it without a bounce—or maybe a bounce or two that an honest day's rapine will take—but the Vandals and their impresario Gaiseric, a much maligned lot. Up the welcoming Tiber those hearties roared with their classic knees showing and, with the treasures of Rome, down again toward the murmurous palm-lined Carthaginian boulevards. En route stormy weather, just like tonight's, caused them to hit a snag and down went a shipload of prime objects. Nice try though, and they made good headway with the rest . . .

His own headway, finally, suggested Marsh simply wasn't arriving. A call to Medical Publications where she worked brought no response, so rapid transit delay was his next guess. But—his Marsh was great for the costume juste—on the possibility she'd gone home to change he dialed East Eighty-eighth. Seven rings and he was about to hang up when she answered, and did she answer!

"How can you be so totally irresponsible?"

"I—Phi Beta Kappa, Summa Cum Laude, mortgagee on easy payments—irresponsible? Eureka—you were here on the dot and I wasn't. Damozel, I was carried away by the Vandals."

"While I was shivering drenched in your lobby for twenty minutes, but that's the least of it. To have gotten me pregnant! And the humiliation . . ." By phone that day, the doctor—news to Teddy—had begun, "The test was positive, Mrs. Koch." So she'd corrected him "Miss" and—evidently he disapproved of pregnant misses—in reply to a simple question he'd coldly informed her that abortions are against the law. As it happened, she'd just changed her mind about having an abortion—but the exposure to that man's . . . arrogance! " . . . Thanks to you, I must say."

Shades and curses of that little Francine bitch of his nonage whose pregnancy—fake it happened—had sent him fleeing to the army at sixteen, though this time to his honor extricating himself was the most fleeting of thoughts. Still it was quite a letdown, his disinterested witty auditor he'd seen as elegant hostess of his forthcoming salon and affectionate mother of his say . . . two . . . forthcoming sons with her present apartment as nursery, enceinting a fellow after all the bachelor girl farrago of hers. Elementary ballistics labeled that blast standard bore wedding shotgun.

"Good," his return was understandably a bit sulfuric. "Then you've decided to be a law abiding missus and give birth to a legitimate seven-months' term infant."

"Save your sarcasm, I've decided nothing of the kind. The baby and I will be very happy together—without your assistance!"

She hung up on him and his collector's instinct told him she wasn't kidding. Oh providential acid test that his Marsh emerged from pure gold —and now she met the requirements even of the Office of Rent Control! He popped a few succulent mushrooms into his mouth to keep body and soul together, threw on his raincoat and without bothering with the elevator burst down the stairs. Luckily before he so much as sprang his umbrella open a taxi drew up along the black shining street to his building and discharged a hunched and sodden middle-aged pair wretched enough to illustrate his bride's marriage theories. So he hopped in dry and enjoyed a drive east through Central Park where torrential shafts sexily bent new buds in yellow-green lamplight. At First Avenue nevertheless he paid off the cabbie. His umbrella at once blown inside out he tossed smilingly into the gutter and for two leisurely blocks he availed himself of the exhilarating commotion that rained down on him. In the brownstone after Marsh buzzed back he rose streaming, like a sea god named Proteus, before her incredulous eyes. With a bitten slice of toast heaped with cottage cheese in her fingers, her forehead under a towel pulled back tight and her provocative person in a blue kimono white jasmine trimmed she stood in her doorway watching him ascend. And—Amor, who finds his own eloquence! —on the landing he dropped to one knee and imprinted a solicitous kiss on her blue tummy.

"Swam as fast as I could to beg forgiveness of both my dear ones."

She half laughed half sobbed. "Oh damn you Teddy," she pulled him by the sopping hair, "come in and take those wet things off!" And once she'd put him into her charming if snug at the shoulders lemon kimono with cherry blossoms and served him toast and cottage cheese in the kitchen, winning her concession that a devoted hubby and pa beats any amount of free-lance copy editing was easy.

He could hardly wait to pit her against his mother and show her off to his father!

Danny hadn't gone to the opening of Teddy's Vanguards Gallery a few months ago—who needed loud crowds and drinks?—but had dropped in the first Saturday afterward. A buzz by a decorative receptionist and Teddy'd emerged through a draped doorway behind a period desk, shaken hands and jockeyed him upstairs to the nice enough offices and a busy enough staff of three more: two other girls—a secretary and an administrative assistant in charge of records—on the order of the receptionist, and a burly bookkeeper, a man. Downstairs again Teddy had given him a brief but distressing tour of the thick-carpeted elegantly corniced rooms hung with canvases split down the middle by a groove making two panels painted in one solid color. Danny'd glanced at his son and Teddy had said that those Estalellas would soon be highly valued. In the rear room where the desk was, they'd paused in front of leg trap collages by some woman and slingshot carvings by some man. Then Teddy'd merrily waved at the chromium chairs around a coffee table with art magazines on it.

"Twenty-two fifty takes any one of these chairs away, Dad."

"Why sell stuff like this," Danny'd nodded back to the wall objects, "if that's what you think of it?"

Teddy had shrugged good-humoredly. "Anybody can sell Rembrandts."

Just then through the same drapery Teddy had come out of this girl had materialized, slender, brunette, chic to the minute, as good-looking as the others, and—you didn't need a Reisel to pin them down: Danny himself had been meeting plenty of them of all ages the last few years—a dime a dozen no matter how much they cost, like the artwork there. This one had looked put out and had murmured something to Teddy. Teddy in full charge had murmured something back to her and she hadn't liked it, but she'd lumped it and left.

So Danny'd been glad that Teddy was doing well, but what did that have to do with himself? Nothing, he'd thought.

Yet this evening he was so heavyhearted driving the Cadillac from his factory down to the Village and Leah's dinner for his son and his son's just announced fiancée. Some prospect, whatever girl it was, whatever interchangeable part, who'd be putting the official seal to all his disappointment in Teddy.

He found a garage to park in, he reluctantly made his way through a flushed April sunset that he felt dead to, and upstairs in Washington Place he was introduced to . . . Marsha Koch, blonde, delicate, and as much like the usual article as gold coin to counterfeit dollar bills. Leah's chummy "First Marsha tell us how you managed to capture this free spirit" made you groan, but Marsha's eyes laughed and she only let Teddy breathe, "Auntie how much the reverse it was you'd never imagine." And when you spoke with Marsha—about her studies, then the Brontës, then Ezra's wonderful Mozart rondo recording Teddy'd played for her that Ezra had cut at the Conservatory, or where she lived and where she had grown up—she was serious though the eyes smiled, quiet, deep even. Later from across the room Danny watched her chatting with Leah, and good old Leah couldn't resist her for the love looks that Marsha sometimes dropped on Leah's favorite nephew Teddy. And with Marsha's intelligence that adoration surely must have been justified! Danny's son was brilliant, warm, generous, funny, and at twenty-three a top-notch earner. What more could a father ask?

Marsha pleased them all, why not?—Golda for Danny's reasons; Naomi and Danny's clever little nephew Richard through Marsha's shop talk with Richard about high school; and Henny . . . you could deserve it a lot less than Marsha and Henny would still like you, but Henny humorously explained to her that Teddy had two fathers of whom he was the second, and that she was rounding out Henny's family beautifully. As the senior father Danny pressed Marsha's hand as the party was breaking up and gave her fair warning.

"I'm liable to wear out my welcome with you after you're married."

"I can't see," Marsha pressed back, "how that can possibly happen."

Danny wished he could drive somebody home but Marsha and Teddy had come in the Tucker Torpedo and everyone else lived in the building. So Danny strolled alone toward the parking garage, and now in the night sky Venus—or was it the light of an airliner?—hung at the horn of the moon and under a street lamp new leaves fluttered. Danny—"I'm privileged!"—breathed the spring air in. Of course, Ezra should have been here tonight to meet this new admirer, poor old Ez—Danny's tongue clicked and his face twisted: oh Jesus—in the ground there, in England . . . .

Still—"I'm privileged"—he stuck to it.

30

GRATITUDE? IN THE ROTTEN YEAR 1950?

While Hymie's darling, his Hilda, stayed on earth, the likes of his dear friends Mrs. Bonnie Green and Madam Ada Lewis could not have enough of him. Now all at once no Hilda and him alone in the world, and he hadn't been entitled to turn to those two? Why Bonnie's own words had been that no other man had done the things for her that he'd done, from the first cup of coffee last spring at the cafeteria.

Then, last spring, out of the corner of his eye he'd spotted a plump little mamaleh beside him at the counter, but she'd been the one to swing around with a tray and a shopping bag and splash coffee over him. Naturally he'd been the gentleman, refusing her the blame with a flick of his breast pocket handkerchief along the damp trousers and charging a fresh cup of coffee for her to his check. Such treatment had been a novelty for Mrs. Bonnie Green. At a table in the middle of cab drivers and loafers she had kept up the apologies—she shouldn't have been there in the first place, she ate too much, she felt like a mental case. She'd even gone to a doctor in a panic that she had some fatal disease that would leave her two children orphans. The doctor had given her a clean bill of health, but, she'd anxiously asked Hymie, could she believe him? It did seem abnormal, didn't it, at three in the afternoon, not to be able to hold out for her own refrigerator a few blocks away?

Hymie had reassured her, "Eat—on you it looks good," and she'd blushed! Oy Hilda, as lately as that God had been sending him married virgins with schoolchildren. Bonnie's bargain of a husband had been a Bert the sport, whose foolish face under a part in the hair smiled at you from the framed wedding pose on Bonnie's chiffonier. In that picture Bonnie had been thin, underweight. Many a time Hymie'd thought thank you Bert for the delicious hard ripe tomato you made out of her. That whole spring and the first week of summer opposite her windows down Gerard Avenue —pick-pock pick-pock—idiots pocked on the tennis courts opposite that Bert couldn't get close enough to, and you pocked in her sunny bedroom. From 7 A.M. till three in the afternoon Bert exercised his calves delivering the United States mail, from four to six he gave the biceps a chance with a tennis racket. Then he ate Bonnie's heaped-up cooking, watched their new TV, and slept. And to add to Bert she'd had the two whirlwind sons seven and nine fast with the banged knees and slow with the homework, with a little measles thrown in, mumps, whooping cough.

After Bonnie's union with Hymie had been consecrated, she'd asked, "How old are you Hy?"

"Guess."

"Fifty-nine, sixt—no, fifty-nine?"

So could he have provided her with such bad service for a youngster historically eighty years old? A hot tub in the morning for the bum pin that was his lifetime memento from a hardhearted family, and—with sensible conservation of energy—he was as good a man almost as he had ever been! Only—an ungrateful woman cuts like a serpent's tooth—that had been last spring, not now. The days he'd visit Bonnie he'd tell Hilda that he was going to the racetrack and he'd relieve her in the millinery for early lunch. Noon sharp Hilda would be back with a good luck kiss for . . . her eternal lover (she used to call him that, oy, Hilda) and tell him hurry he'd miss the limousine to Jamaica. He'd say, "Ah, I changed my mind. I'll sit here with the hats and feast my eyes on you," and—fifty years old—his darling would also blush.

"Get out," she'd give him a love poke. Once, "Wait . . ." she'd dug up two dollars. "If something runs like red . . . or flame, like my face, bet on it for me."

"Win place or show?"

"Win win win, pick winners winner—"

She'd push him into the lunch hour crowds from the Bronx County Courthouse. Those happy days he'd pass the movies, the cafeteria and the cigar store under the El, and in the shade of Yankee Stadium the track limousine would wait with its pilgrims deep in the Talmud according to Clocker Lawton and Flasher Frank. Hymie for his part remembered nodding with his Alpine hat with the tiny red feather to Lou the bookmaker next to the newsstand.

"Lou, save an old man's failing eyesight. A hunch with flame, or blush, or red-in-the-face . . . the Last of the Mohicans maybe . . . is going at Jamaica this lovely May day?"

Lou had daintily picked his cigar stub from between those moist blooming lips. "Not to my ability, Hymie."

"Then my wife's saved two dollars. God send you plungers, Lou."

On the way back from Bonnie's Hymie'd bought Hilda roses—and how she'd loved him for that! And the flowers he had brought Bonnie—had *she* loved him for that! Before him the last flower that Bonnie had seen man and boy had been her high school prom corsage.

"And your wedding bouquet," Hymie'd reminded her.

"Just a white rose on a Bible," Bonnie'd said sadly, "and my father bought that."

Maybe he had harped too much on her marriage. But the way things had been—him with a wife, her with a husband, a girl thirty-three years old—who had wanted to encourage funny ideas? He had kept no secrets from Bonnie, he could have gone on for years and years with such a girl. And when suddenly Columbus discovered Korea to send soldiers to—the forty-ninth state—couldn't you bet that muscleman Bert would be in the Army reserves so after the parting tears for the husband Hymie would have Mrs. Green all to himself? It had looked like his America! But for that the Almighty would have had to give blubbering Bonnie a teaspoonful of character. Right from the beginning Bonnie and the Korean War were both a big bust.

"I'm his wife, Hy. How can I be unfaithful with his life in danger again?"

Bonnie's "again" had referred to Bert's World War II tour of service in New Guinea, and that war—for the duration Hymie had been faster than all of them spotting planes and ringing doorbells where they didn't have blackout curtains, three score and ten with his airraid warden helmet snappily tilted—a Jew had had to fight. But Bert, if you stick yourself in the reserves for three weeks' pin money a year don't cry if you're stuck.

At the end of June though, why argue with Bonnie? July Hymie would close the millinery anyhow and blow Hilda to a month in Far Rockaway where the seashore did his leg wonders, and Bonnie and the kids likewise had been due for the mountains. So he'd praised Bonnie for her good spirit, consoled her it would all come out in the wash (though between you him and the lamppost if ever there had breathed a sure loser, Bert was the man) . . . and September the minute school opened he'd strolled down Gerard Avenue across the street from the tennis courts to start the new term off right.

At her door the bursting object who'd taken in his astonishment had said, "I really put on weight this time Hy, didn't I?"

Put on weight! Hilda had had a belly too, but that at least had been the fibroid. This one had burrowed herself into an enormous slab of suntanned jelly, if you went by what showed. "In two months," he'd reached for what didn't show, "it's a miracle!" But she'd shied off, and when he was convinced she'd meant it he'd respected her principles. He'd asked how Bert was—still in California thank God last she'd heard—and this and that, and goodbye. For a look at the fat lady there was always the circus. But nobody could say that in her time of need he hadn't presented himself.

Then—what a contrast!

He'd left Hilda in the hospital, happy, well, he'd kissed her good night, the doctor had signed her out for tomorrow. And no sooner had he reached

Sheridan Avenue and stepped into his apartment than the phone rang from the hospital to come back. And fast as he had gone back, in a cab, it had been too slow. His Hilda had been under a sheet. They'd let him stand a minute with full eyes while he brushed that foam from the corner of her dear mouth, and even in death she had seemed to be thinking of him, with a little smile. Would she have wanted him to go back to that lonely apartment tonight? So he'd stayed on the train another station to Bonnie's.

Both miniature Berts had looked up and the nine year old curse had given him a wise "Who are you?" that Hymie could have wiped over the big shot's face. Bonnie, she had done her part, "Oh my God, I hope not Bert too—" Where had Bert entered into the picture, superstitious woman! She'd been so upset she'd automatically cut two black dripping wedges of chocolate cake, and had had to add two more for her whining offspring. Then she'd sat stuffing herself and matching him trouble for trouble.

His Hilda had gone for a hysterectomy and died of a heart attack? Her Bert had been in the advance to the Yalu River, home by Christmas General MacArthur had promised. But now that the Chinese had joined in, where was Bert? Some comparison! Hilda was dead, the undertakers had stuffed her in a bag and he'd had to watch them drag her away. He himself was half dead. And how was he going to sleep alone there on Sheridan Avenue, without Hilda? Her too, the dummy'd come back at him. She also never got a night's sleep any more, in spite of the pills she'd wheedled out of a doctor. Her heart palpitated, she couldn't breathe. The doctor said she didn't need sleeping pills she needed a diet, but—she licked chocolate off her fingertips—what could she do?

Hymie'd felt like choking that fat neck, but he'd kept his temper till she'd put the loudmouths to bed. Then he'd reduced himself to a beggar, thrown himself at her feet—and found out who the snotnoses took after: she'd gone snotty on him.

"Remarry if you're that desperate."

Leaving—"Let me outlast Methuselah, not to you sweetheart"—he'd slammed the door, and fine if the brats woke up!

But what a night in the dead of winter. On his way home even the Concourse Plaza Hotel whore had been off duty. From a lobby booth he'd phoned Mrs. Ada Romance pardon him Lewis—things were that bad—in her shining tower 888 Grand Concourse with her dog and her husband. The husband, his girlie magazines, his bankbooks and his insurance policies she used to be dying to give the air to for Hymie Share. Remember how she'd asked the famous question "How old are you Hyman?"

Why lie—"Eighty"—when the truth has the same effect?

"Never give a straight answer, will you? But I don't care, you've brought back my youth—that elation, I thought I'd never experience it again. . . . Hyman, take me away."

"Ada, I'm only a simple actor, and with what the Yiddish theater has come to how could I support you?"

"I was thinking we could scrape by on the social security, if you were sixty-five. But don't mind me," she'd stretched that soft pampered body up against him, "I'm just dreaming out loud. . . . "

That had been then, his other cafeteria special—who also had looked for him there, not him for her. In a September sun shower he'd ducked into the cafeteria where she'd sat with her tilted nose, shingled New Look haircut and tasty worsted. But crowded as the place had been he wouldn't have parked his hat under a chair at her table if he'd noticed her idiot little black dog first, latched on down there with its muzzle up while you tried to eat. Did that animal end up fixing him pretty! But the introductory lunch hour he hadn't even had time to scratch the mutt's head before the lady invited him with a glance to eavesdrop on four young—historically speaking—courthouse Talmudists at the next table. One droned, three attentively listened.

" . . . percent of the single women interviewed admitted to premarital intercourse. My percentage is better than eighteen but exclude the personality factor. That means you date a girl against four to one odds that she won't deliver. Notwithstanding, the average man keeps trying with the same girl three, four . . . as many as six months possibly. In a similar period, with due attention to my legal duties at Carlson & Neilsen, a weekly visit to my parents and similar business and social obligations, I can see fifty girls if necessary. I lay it on the line to them, and of fifty I statistically have to make out with . . . "

Mrs. Ada Lewis though, who'd named her Scotch terrieress Iris and her rotten kid of a daughter Danielle because the names were romantic, hadn't been able to hold it in any longer.

"Isn't that the limit?"

Hymie'd then popped a morsel of chicken pie into his mouth, stooped to pat her dog and—ugh—gotten his palm damp from nasty drizzled-on hair.

"Where does the 1950 generation come to romance?" he'd smiled at Ada anyway.

And she'd answered sadly, "Does romance exist any more?"

How could such a call not stir a man's sympathies? From home he would pass golden age row in Joyce Kilmer Park, where worn-out faces swung like rags to the Grand Concourse traffic with the healthful gas fumes, a fascinating pursuit they'd interrupt to gape at his smiling eye, tan cheek, black and gray tattersall plaid jacket with a maroon or blue ascot at the throat, Oxford gray slacks perfectly pressed by his Hilda, and lustrous black moccasins on the way to the youth sector. For a leisurely month in violation of the tenets of their young statistical cafeteria friend he'd courted Ada and Iris on the Walton Avenue side of the park facing a row of prewar six story palaces. Raw youth his lady friend was not, but plump and eager she was, waiting for more episodes (under his stage name Hyman Janowsky) of life in the Civic Theater down on Canal Street. Some of the reminiscences were comic, like the attempt—which failed!—of his leading lady Madame Henriette Nadler to upstage him in *The Evil Eye*. Others were tragic, after all these years he told them with a choked throat, like the death of his beloved leading lady Dora Kirschner, which had made Ada touch a tear too and . . . step by step . . . graduated him to the master bedroom of 888 Grand Concourse. Ada loved her husband Bernie, but that elation . . . how it had evaporated. High up, with the Empire State Building tickling a filmy sky way downtown, she philosophized in Hymie's arms on disappointments: family life, children, even success, money, and for her to hear Hymie agree—he'd give his own examples—was like hearing her own voice.

Why not? Whatever he said, whatever he did, he said and did for Ada. Hilda'd finally had to have the fibroid removed, he'd arranged for her to enter the hospital Thanksgiving Eve because with Danielle in from college for the weekend poor longing Ada would not have been free to see him then anyway.

Had that brought him thanks!

On the Wednesday he'd stayed with Hilda long beyond visiting hours. "Sorry," a wise guy nurse had cracked, "you can't sleep here." "Don't I wish he could," his darling Hilda had said. But he'd promised to be back next afternoon right after the Thanksgiving Day parade, with a Mickey Mouse balloon . . . or something nicer . . . for his darling—and had Hilda kissed him!

What sin he'd committed God only knew, to have gotten stuck with that Danielle Lewis Thanksgiving morning. He'd strolled carefree up from Sheridan through the gray day toward the subway downtown to the parade, with the surprise opal bracelet in the Tiffany box already in his pocket for Hilda. She'd know it was from Wilensky's on the Bowery, not Tiffany's, but she'd hug him, and she'd show off her gift to the women in the solarium. Oy Hilda Hilda Hilda Hilda . . . was she really gone?

Then at the park what had bounced across the brown landscape at him, but . . .

"Iris—come back here!"

And on the hill across from the courthouse this flame in woolens—hat, scarf, sweaters, stockings—kept yelling "Iris—" but a lot Iris cared. So what could Hymie do but slip his eyeglasses into his pocket, pick up disgusting Iris that even lapped at his face, and accommodate Danielle the famous Vassar drinker, course failer and contraceptives flaunter he'd heard so much crying about but had never seen. And at first sight she looked as juicy a specimen as you could wish for.

"A girl?" he'd scratched the stupid mutt's head for show.

"A bitch," the bitch had smiled, "like her owner."

"Ah, you should be more modest," he'd cracked—see, you dumb Ada?—"a young lady like you." But go insult 1950.

"I am too modest to make that claim for myself," Danielle'd twinkled at him. "It's my mother's dog."

"But to raise children," he'd stuck—and for what?—to Ada's guns, "is no cinch either."

"Says who?" Danielle had challenged him with her chest. "They simply strangle you with the purse strings!"

"They do that?" he'd laughed. "Then what's right is right, I'm on your side, don't hit me—"

"If you're on my side," the sexy cheeks had bunched up and she'd pushed an experienced palm at him with the thumb in the air and the four fingers together, "welcome stranger."

They serve a man spring chicken Thanksgiving and he shouldn't be thankful? He'd shaken with Danielle on that.

And from such a good start, once Danielle had disposed of Iris—"Did my mother yell bloody murder," she'd announced happily, "to hear I'm having something better than turkey"—it had been a hop skip and jump in a cab to the McAlpin Hotel where, two birds with one stone, he took a room over the parade on Broadway. Only, with those nice floats, girls, marching bands, giant balloons, before you could say Mickey Mouse Danielle had peeled herself bare, proving that the cafeteria counselor a couple of months before hadn't been so wrong—and might that counselor derive the pleasure from *his* 18 percent that Hymie'd derived from Danielle! Speak of misrepresentation! Minus the woolens it was chicken plucked—bony, with folds—to sicken the appetite. And a slob—a sweater dropped here, the skirt there, panties over the bedlamp—he'd pitied Ada, he'd made up his mind to be even nicer to her, with such a daughter! Danielle's final touch had been to toss herself on the bed with the skinny thighs up already, worse than a whore.

"Cover yourself," he'd said, "you'll catch cold."

"Cold? I'm steaming!"

So was the steam pipe—with the same sex appeal. So there should be no mistaken idea that he couldn't he'd laid her, then hurried back to the window to watch the parade. If he'd tell her come quick look, the giant Mickey Mouse was down there, she'd light a cigarette all exposed and crack, "I'd rather have it up here." Then she'd blown smoke rings. "At least I'm not being stuffed silly and lectured for dessert at my mother's Thanksgiving dinner."

"Don't worry. You'll be home in plenty of time for the first course."

"That's what you think, papa."

Ah—there came the dinosaur, rolling comical eyes practically into the bedroom. "Grandpapa," he'd murmured, and that had prompted the one sensible remark he'd heard out of the Vassar woman.

"Are you serious?"

"Why not?" The dinosaur had wobbled in the gray canyon and the sidewalk mob had screamed but Hymie'd known it would hold up. A rope pull and the balloon had been righted. "I'm sixty years old."

"Let's see your driver's license."

"I don't believe in automobiles, officer. . . . What's . . . that . . . you've . . . got . . . in . . . your . . . hand. You put that bracelet back in that box and that box back in that pocket."

"Uh uh. This is my Thanksgiving present. So kind of you."

"Or I'll break your head."

"Go on," she'd stuck her skinny arm under her back and her tongue out at him, "break my head."

He'd flipped her over and let her have two good shrieking whacks on the backside while he'd given that bracelet a twist out of her hand so she'd really had something to yell about. Then he'd gotten her out of there.

Outside in the crowd beginning to break up he'd bought her a Mickey Mouse balloon—"Here's what you wanted," and she'd suddenly exploded it next to his ear, some joke. Ada with all her hair-tearing about Danielle had made her own bed to sleep in, bringing up a daughter who didn't know the meaning of the word respect!

And at the subway—"Home? Not me"—Miss underfed Santa Claus in red had given him a Bronx cheer and wiggled off elsewhere. Wiggle, who cared? He'd done his part with the pickup, even better that delivery'd been refused. As it was, he'd reached Eden Hospital just on the visiting dot—and you didn't catch Hilda busting *her* Mickey Mouse!

The whole day Thanksgiving he'd stayed with her, and the next morning at cold dawn he'd beaten the surgeon there. All the way to the operating room he'd walked alongside the stretcher and held her hand.

"Hymie," she'd looked up, "your hand is so cold. Did you have breakfast?"

Oy Hilda, his aching heart . . .

Only later in the hospital cafeteria had he bolted some juice and coffee, bacon and eggs with cereal and bananas and a few slices of toast, and upstairs he'd been on tenterhooks passing time with the roommate—the hospital robe had brought out a nice broad pair of shoulders, she was a gym teacher, single too . . . but who'd had a mind for that?—until they'd brought Hilda down. Hilda's lids, eventually, had fluttered open on him and she'd moaned that she was parched, uncomfortable, in pain, sorry she was complaining. He'd moistened her lips with a cool cloth, he'd joked that's what she was there for, to complain.

"You've got a good husband," the roommate had told her.

Hoarsely Hilda'd confirmed, "The best."

But not good enough for that spoiled Lewis he'd taken every trouble for?

Just so's he shouldn't embarrass that . . . ungrateful woman by running into her and her bargain of a daughter, he'd dragged himself blocks out of the way and climbed such a mountain of steps up Claremont Park to the hospital his bad leg still was numb! Monday the holiday had been over, pisspot Danielle you could place in Poughkeepsie again, and Hilda had recovered enough to worry that the store would lose business. So, Hilda'd been sick, against his better judgment he'd humored her, he'd opened the store. Very necessary. Since the war who bought hats? The youth movement would twitch by with a rag on the head, or a wool sock like the Vassar collegian, or bareheaded altogether. Long ago he'd advised Hilda sell out, switch to a yarn store, let them knit their own hats. Would she listen?

Now he was the sufferer.

What a boring day that had been—cold, gray, hemmed in with hats. Once an hour something worthwhile might pump by to the bakery or the cafeteria, or down the block to the El. Occasionally between his yawns an antique would wander in and drive him crazy bringing out stock to show her.

Then—he hadn't believed his happy eyes—outside the window display who'd stood with her cute squint, the bitch, but Ada. His generous, his open heart! She hadn't seen him, he could have let her pass. But not him—he valued friendship! He'd had to tap on the glass to her and she'd looked up, surprised. Then next to her another one—young but nothing special: sallow with the usual kerchief—also had looked surprised. Who'd known she and Ada had been together? Only with the exultation, the pointing, the antics from that monkey in heat, the eyes bright and the skinny finger stabbing away while the lips poured toads in the mother's ear had he realized it was that curse Danielle. Student—didn't they teach you Sunday finishes a weekend and you go back to school?

Ada'd given him a glance and he'd lifted his shoulders and turned his palms up. How had he been supposed to recognize one more tube in a coat? And Ada had simply shrugged off the viper's venom, sensible woman he'd thought, as she had walked down the hill with that daughter. Yet he'd phoned Ada the next day to find out that he was the lowest and to get hung up on! Twice more and the same result.

But in the hour of a man's need Madam Romance, have a heart, show a drop of feeling for a fellow human desperate, his wife just died, or rest assured he could dispense with a dozen like you. Even in the hospital that terrible night, doctors, nurses—killers they really were—had offered him sympathy, pills to take. So he'd given Ada a last chance.

"Ada," he'd told, so far as he knew, a white lie, "I've lost my son—"

"I thought you hadn't seen him for twenty years. But I'm sorry about that, I really am. Please accept my condolences, if it isn't another lie. Goodbye."

And again that click! The crust of her, as if he'd ever told her a single word she hadn't wanted to hear! . . .

Then the hell with you Mrs. Ada Lewis you son of a bitch—like daughter like mother—and the hell with you Mrs. Bonnie Green! He had friends—plenty without them. Lou Berenson would tell him my God come right over, but who could stand that nutty Bella Berenson. Moe Gross likewise, with his terror of a wife Charlotte for all her good looks. So Hymie ended up on Clay Avenue at his pinochle pal Barney Frankel's with Barney's wife Esther and the two daughters making a fuss over him in a living room just as sunken as Ada Lewis's, maybe more so! And there were no accusations either. They listened with pity to what he'd gone through tonight with, he sobbed, his dear Hilda. Esther Berenson sobbed; Barney's big dependable face was crinkled up; the kid Ann—good-looking with brains, not a Danielle!—asked if she could bring Hymie something; and the older daughter Thelma, the big one, plain, but she'd always reminded him . . . oy . . . of his Hilda at that age—without even asking, Thelma brought him a schnapps to drink. And accommodations—the best, all frills—the married daughter's, Diane's, vacated room. Esther once more wiped her eyes to remember he and Hilda had attended Diane's wedding three winters ago. . . .

Maybe on account of sleeping in Diane's bed Hymie dreamt of the old days, the young days, with Hilda whispering to him about some movie they'd seen and no matter how many times she told him he couldn't make out the leading man's name. *What?* he kept saying, till he had her young body against him tight and she said right in his face, *Hyman Janowsky.* Suddenly he had to go and reeled to the toilet anxious to return to her fast. But oy how long it took, and he woke up meanwhile to his whole affliction. Eventually he dragged himself through the foyer again with its hum and shadows, opened the bedroom door . . . he'd closed it? . . . fell into bed and—the dead can come back?—was scared stiff bumping against her.

A thick voice "Lenny?" though and he half knew what was what. Still he missed Hilda so much he couldn't help it, he kept quiet—and she gathered him in. Which one it was, Ann or Thelma, he wasn't sure, so he let it be Ann. But in the first gray of morning she nudged him, "Better get back," and it was Thelma—just as well, the younger one might have raised a rumpus. He buried his head between those substantial bubbies, "I'm so blue, Thelma—" "Yeah, I know," she comforted him. So he said, "I'll see you again like this, darling?" "No I'm sorry Hymie, no repeats. But you'll be okay, people get used to losses . . . more or less. . . ."

Later, Barney answered him without enthusiasm that Thelma was going with some kind of fellow. Hymie asked, "By the name of Lenny?" "No," Barney said, "Nate. Lenny's my son-in-law." Then she was two-timing the family beauty her married sister Diane?

Oy Hilda, it was a world upside down where plain ones stole men from knockouts, strangers were like flesh and blood, and flesh and blood were like strangers. Barney, not one of Hymie's children, took time off and made the funeral arrangements Hymie was not able to face. At the chapel though, Hymie was shocked to see Golda coming toward him, gray but altogether rejuvenated. Maybe, if she wanted, he'd move back with her? But she said, "Papa, you're looking wonderful in spite of everything," and he realized that it was his daughter Leah. The other two—he looked around—had not condescended to pay respects to a bereaved father.

"Thank you. Naomi is well, and Danny?"

"Oh Papa, you weren't sure that it was me, would you know them if you saw them?" And Hilda, would you believe while he ached with his loss, his daughter sat beside him and piled Naomi with a boy of sixteen on him, and Danny with a grown son a successful businessman and hooray a war hero who'd already made Hymie—charming!—a great-grandfather, and a grandson lost in the war, a beautiful gifted boy? And his daughter wiped her tear not for today but for ancient history! For today she kept needling him in his woe, "How long were you with this . . . wife, Papa?"

"How long? All my life!" Then he saw her staring him in the eye, so he shrugged, "Twenty-five, thirty years, since my family got rid of me."

"Papa, I never got rid of you."

"You weren't there?"

"Where?"

No? He could have sworn she'd been a member in good standing of the Essex Street vipers' club. "Never mind, I forgive you, I forgive them. The question is, with Hilda gone, how will I manage?"

"It hurts now," his daughter touched his sleeve, "but it eases," smart aleck, changing the subject!

"The rent doesn't ease, the grocery bill doesn't ease."

"Papa," she laughed in his face, "you'll never age—you're the same boy you always were! How have you been paying your rent and groceries?"

You know, maybe God had done him a favor, having his children ignore him all these years? One minute with one of them and he could feel the blood pressure shoot up. "From hard work in a store," he informed Miss Wise Guy.

"Well," she had the audacity to grin, "do you still have the store?"

Oy Hilda, you went and what kind of specimens were left on earth? He would have let his clever daughter have it only the rabbi was ready to pray for dear Hilda and to praise her—as if anyone could give that sweet, loving girl, that loyal woman, a thousandth of her due. So who had the heart or the time for arguments? At the end of the service his daughter handed him another pat, "Don't worry Papa, you won't starve," and he pricked up his ears. But "Danny sends his condolences," she fizzled out, "and so does Henny." Henny? "Henny's the man I married, Papa, remember?" And she ran!

Let the father sit cooped up in a millinery! And the apartment, already a pigsty without Hilda? The seven days' mourning ended and Barney Frankel's Esther stopped dropping around to help out. Who'd cook, who'd clean? For a week Hymie advertised shop for sale, and who came? Old pots thinking maybe a job. If only Hilda had listened, why didn't you listen, Hilda? With a yarn store he could have found some nice young lady to run it and take care of everything. This way, he still owed Barney for the funeral extras the Burial Society didn't cover, though never would Hymie begrudge his darling that beautiful carved casket in light oak, like a cheerful piece of furniture not a coffin, just as he had never begrudged her the taxis, the best shows front and center or the dinners at Lindy's—all those things that she'd loved him for and to the end of her life never gotten used to. And now he should end up on charity while his children that he'd sweated in factories to raise lived off the fat of the land? Other daughters would have said Papa, come down, live with us. Or, they'd ignored him this long, he wouldn't want to impose on them with his first wife hovering around like the Angel of Death God forbid. He would have said why go to the bother, on top of the expense. Chip in a small annuity, seventy, seventy-five dollars a week, he wouldn't trouble them further. Not them, they kept mum. Shift for yourself Papa!

So he shifted.

First he ran himself ragged getting rid of that white elephant store—lock to the landlord, stock to R. Price & Co. that sold hats to the farmers' wives, and barrel to A. Zinamen Store Fixtures Bought Sold Rented. With those hard-earned dollars he could pay Barney off and not wear out his welcome. He met his obligations, now let his children meet theirs. Next stop, early Saturday, was Washington Place in a desolation of rain that decent children would not allow a father to step out in, with slush from yesterday's snow pouring into the sewers! At Leah's door—he leaned his good ear against it—he could have sworn he heard shuffling . . . and no matter how many rings no answer. At your convenience sweetheart. Meanwhile he took his daughters' fancy elevator (he lived two flights up in a walk-up!) another floor to Naomi's where an old cleaning woman with wild wisps of hair said, "What do you want, old man?"

Some nerve. But that intonation . . . Golda! Had she deteriorated!

"Golda, don't you know me?"

"Like you know me, I know you." And she walked away.

Naomi—if Leah was so smart—he recognized right away, even graying and with tight disfiguring lips. She avoided his eyes, embarrassed as well she was entitled to be, until he said gently, "Not even a condolence card?"

"Papa," she had the crust to face him then, "what was she to me?"

"And I?"

That she could not answer, his heart's darling that used to be, and let him stand with his coat on while she made it plain that her son came first, her mother came second, she herself of course came third, and the father—he finished so far up the track he was not worthy of mention. The lamp business? She was lucky if what she drew from Quality Lamps would pay her pride and joy's expenses beginning next fall at the Massachusetts Institute of Technology. For the father the long and short of it was a go speak to Danny and, when the father stared at her, a ten spot. Back at the other daughter's her Henny, a square head and round eyeglasses bargain Hymie had absolutely no recollection of, was kind enough to open the door this time and invite him to breakfast. But breakfast, a big twentier, and a long sermon about his good kind generous son, Leah would tell Danny the father had been here, was all he got. Yet in the Civic Theater years gone by

King Lear cried a full week with two matinees that he had thankless daughters. As to the good kind generous son, a father could speak for himself John, and with a dripping umbrella in a cigar store phone booth that steamed your glasses so you had to wipe them ten times to see where to dial he called up Prince Generosity.

And, "Mis-tah Shahr residence," reached the Chinese embassy? But it was Mr. Shahr valet speaking and the password father pinned down Mr. Shahr out visiting son.

Mr. Shahr visiting son, then Mr. Shahr senior likewise would visit son. And senior, they would learn, never stinted when it came to his family. He bought a stuffed toy for the infant, a pretty necklace—and be sure not at his daughter's store!—for the infant's mother, and for the successful businessman, the grandson, a beautiful big pink Waterman's fountain pen. Let the son take an example from the father! And let . . . oy . . . human nature take an example from nature. In the course of the taxi trip uptown to the grandson's swanky neighborhood the sky cleared and on East Eighty-eighth Hymie with his umbrella and the large bag for the baby stepped into winter sunlight glinting off glass and mica, a pleasure after the wet. But in the brownstone vestibule a touch on the bell—and barking, to eat you up alive. He was expected?

He was not expected. Teddy was only too glad to race his Afghan down the flight of stairs from the master bedroom and his wife's chastity ultimatum. He had never had any intention of rubbing Marsha's nose in his necessary frolics, but neither did he intend to acquiesce in a repeal of the rights of man. For goodness' sakes, what was a fellow supposed to do, philosophize for her? Where heavy industry fills up the national day what remained for the national evening but light industry? Teddy stood for adventure—she'd heard his war stories while they were courting, even been terrified for his sake retrospectively by some of them. If for some reason—thickening weather or a radar man's miscalculation—the squadron he piloted the lead plane in during the war overran the target, his next target, the target of choice, would not be an unopposed crossroads with a truck convoy to dump the bombs on. He would always choose—and if the navigator complained Teddy'd remind him that that was their job—a rerun over the original target with the antiaircraft fire neatly, so the Germans thought, zeroed in on them. Art dealing he had begun at sixteen with a stable of one, his painting teacher at the Art Institute, and Uncle Henny's Curios shop as gallery. That made nine years in the art game, including his four by V-mail to Group Shows, Inc. from the 44th Bombardment Group in Bentwaters, England. From nine-to-five slob to the highest eminences (if his mother's political bigwigs were any measure), America the wonderland was scooped out, bored silly. The slobs alas he could only refer to their favorite corner bar with the TV set. That he could entertain, shock, even momentarily galvanize the eminences with his wares was fine for the eminences and fine for the wares but by now unfortunately all but routine for him. Certainly his dear Marsha would not deny him the play of life that was his stock in trade?

So at the gallery she had stumbled upon him with the painter Nelly Morison the evening Nelly had been displaying next to ultimate appreciation for having just been admitted to the Vanguards stable. But precisely such small contretemps made life piquant. The issue between him and Marsha was of will not fidelity. Marsh had no competition, his little blonde bride and superb mother of their ineffable going-on-three Mathilda. He had let Marsh have her way about naming their first after Marsh's mother, furious as Teddy's mother had been that they hadn't called the child Eva after the grandma that Ez and Tomer Palace had been named for. But Marsha had to accept that as to other domestic conditions Teddy did not bargain, any more than he bargained with clients or Vanguards artists. He did not find it entertaining to be told—and told illogically, just like a woman—that instead of accompanying him tomorrow on his business trip he might just find her flying with Mathilda in the opposite direction.

And so the opportune doorbell had curtailed that wild talk and returned Marsh to packing.

Teddy opened the door and Hymie saw a well filled out sport with red hair and a mustache to match who thank God looped two fingers around the bark's collar.

"Custom made?" Hymie appraised the young man's fawn-colored suit.

"By our neighborhood tailor, Brooks Brothers."

"Nice, but," Hymie sighed insincerely, "beggars can't be choosers." He tapped the umbrella at his own—but why brag—just as natty karakul hat and fur-collared cheviot and that set off the mutt again. "The best I can do," Hymie had to shout with a tense eye on the slavering jaws, "is Weber and Heilbroner's."

"Shut up, Veblen. Don't let him bother you—if he bites bite him back."

"A German dog in shaggy pajamas?"

"Veblen is a Norwegian name . . . and who art thou ancient mariner?"

"Mariner? The rain stopped. If you're my grandson, I'm your grandfather."

"And vice versa . . . Come down a moment, dear," the grandson yelled up the staircase, "Grandpa Share's dropped in," and took Hymie's things to put away. "Marsha—? Can't tear herself away from the wifely duties. We and baby fly to Europe tomorrow."

"Europe? What's wrong with America?"

"In a word, you mean? For you Pops nothing—or for me either. It's Europe that's gasping for a—" the grandson waved at his foyer walls full of loud squiggles and caricatures in frames—"sort of Marshall Plan of the spirit. I'm opening a Vanguards art gallery in Munich—the Germans seem to go for this stuff."

The grandfather said tactfully, "You didn't paint all those yourself?"

"Not a one. Dropped the manual end early—no challenge."

"And this," but these eyesores told you impossible, "is how you make a living?"

"With an occasional meat dish that Conchita our old retainer is out shopping for at this very moment, yes Pops."

"Then I must say you're a genius."

"Such is the consensus."

And Teddy led the way with his Veblen—Hymie made sure to keep the grandson in the middle—to a living room with not a single piece of soft furniture for a man to sit down on, and— Hallelujah, there was the kind generous Danny, not that old-looking either—in this respect he took after the father—in fact in his second childhood with his legs folded under him on the floor at a toy table with a dishes set, a doll and a bossy infant. Teddy caught up his daughter, which allowed the overaged playmate to stand and give a father he hadn't seen all these years a limp handshake.

"Ask your venerable ancestor, Mattie," Teddy gave the offspring a hint there was a visitor, "what's in the great big bag he's holding," but, brilliant child, it hid its face in its father's neck.

So Hymie, "Happy birthday, belated," pulled out the stuffed toy.

"Daddy," smart as a whip whined, "what's bow-wow's name?"

"Panda," Danny the grandfather old enough to know better encouraged her yet, "is bow-wow's name," and not a thank you from smart as a whip either, even with Daddy's prompting. Then smart as a whip had to go on all fours with the underpants sticking out—keep it up girlie, some day they'll let you in Vassar—to yap the panda at Veblen with his moron chin on his paws. And Veblen didn't bark at her either. Next she drafted her imbecile grandfather again to feed bow-wow Panda while the company could twiddle its thumbs. But Hymie—let his son observe between bow-wow's spoonfuls and take an example—gave the grandson the pendant for the grandson's wife who lacked courtesy to come downstairs with a hello for a husband's grandparent!

Teddy said, "Charming, Marsh will love this," and passed the pendant down to the boy playing house. "Dad, imperative gallery appointments, I'm behind schedule already. Would you give this to Marsh and tell her don't keep dinner waiting for me?"

That, not a father in need, worried Hymie's son. "Aren't you and Marsha on speaking terms?" Danny asked.

"Lovers' tiff, she'll come around."

"Why don't *you* make it simple, Teddy, and come around, whatever it is?"

"Discipline," Teddy laughed, "must be maintained. . . . See you Dad, Grandpa." He rubbed noses with smart as a whip and would have been off—but "Hey," Hymie stopped him—without the fountain pen Hymie'd brought.

"Gramps—for my bar mitzvah!" the comedian said, but immediately shook hands, a good firm handshake not like Hymie's son, "Don't be a stranger, Grandpa," and ran out to fool the public.

A nice boy!

While generous Daniel, "No present for me, Papa?," gave the father a left-handed smile.

"For you my boy, I'm sorry to say, I only had left my poverty."

"All right, Papa," sarcastic pulled out a checkbook, "what can I do to qualify for a door prize?"

The big shot wanted humble? The father was willing to throw in humble at no extra charge. "My boy, nothing. I'd be only too—"

"Of course. And meanwhile?"

"Ah Danny, I'm afraid I'm not the man I used to be."

"Sure you are, Papa."

"Well, maybe, who knows. I still had to give the millinery away, that used to net ninety, a hundred a week."

And if he'd added on a few dollars, who knew how much the kind generous son would discount the father? On trust Hymie thanked his son to hear that the bookkeeper would mail a check every Friday so it ought to come Mondays. God should only guide that generous pen to at least the number fifty. Then, with the social security and a nickel on the subway to Leah every once in a while, a father could struggle and make ends meet. So, the son finished, and . . .

One O O!

"Danny," a father's heart overflowed, "you're a kind generous man! Blood is thicker than water, hah? That reminds me, I was sorry to hear about your other boy—"

And for the condolence—"Then you're set now," stone face stood up with a dismissal, "I'll get you your coat"—he was practically shoved out of the house by that maniac. Crazy as a loon, but don't argue, the lunatic could change his mind yet. Hymie put the coat on, pleasantly sent his regards to the nut's missus and got out in such a hurry—with a farewell bark from the dog also—he forgot his umbrella even.

But who cared, let them keep it for a rainy day. Him, with the bright sunshine and that hundred dollar annuity warming him up, he toddled along East Eighty-eighth toward York for a cab. And look—he gave a happy slap to one of those skinny trees with a gold spray of branches—it was like spring!

In his Cadillac to the Museum Danny told Reisel how his heart's delight Mattie's miniature chair half on half off a carpet had turned over and Mattie had bumped to the floor this morning. Grandpa Danny'd righted the stool, told her okay she could sit down now and Mattie'd said, "Sit down, sit down—but who's going to fall down!" Was it a wonder he was infatuated with a two and a half year old child? "And I may lose her yet too, Reisel. Marsha told me she'd put Teddy on notice that he toes the mark or she's taking the baby and trying California again. And my son quotes to me that discipline must be maintained." Then there was the great Hymie heist

—not that the heist itself bothered Danny, he'd asked for it. What he couldn't get over was his father's . . . complete self-absorption.

"Me, the memory of Ezra—he didn't care. Anything that happened to fall into his mouth fell out. So for the second time in my life I ejected him, and he was only worried I might rip up the check. And he was right: I came close."

"What would you expect from your father," Reisel flared all-out for Danny, "since he is commonplace, and consequently thinks there can be nothing better than commonplace, while you are exceptional, rare."

"Rare?" Danny laughed. "Practically extinct."

"Do not say such things even in jest. You must have courage."

And he almost could have fallen in love again with this chic burning spirit, his angel-faced partisan the wrong side of fifty and the auburn hair just barely gray-tinged. In a world of Hymies galore both male and female, how many Reisels? And, life's jokes, she'd choose Danny for the special occasions. Finally she'd induced Rubin Bookbinder to sell her the bookshop she'd been managing so many years, Bookbinder's Fine Editions. So tonight's celebration, Reisel had insisted, was her treat.

"My mother the same," Reisel went on moodily as Danny steered between iron-bare trees from the Fifth Avenue shadows into a burst of parking lot floodlights. "All day long, telephone calls what a bad daughter I am not moving her in with me. And even Rubin Bookbinder sells me the store in anger only after I taunted him with his twenty years' shameful hope of manipulating me into marriage by means of it. He muttered I have never appreciated what he has done for me—jealous old man!"

"Jealous?" They strolled through the Archaic corridor toward the Museum cafeteria. "Of who?"

Reisel giggled, "Of you," and Danny smiled along with the statues at that old joke.

Then at the Museum auditorium after they ate damned if another will-o'-the-wisp didn't go off in his hand!

LENKOWSKI STRING QUARTET
with
ALBERT TRAYNOR, VIOLA

New York City pulsing with music and she brought him to the Lenkowskis that he'd been dodging all these years because what was the use. But had canny Reisel set him up purposely—he'd blabbered to her about Sydelle long ago—the sort of push in the right direction, poor lonely man, that he was a continual beneficiary of from Ma, his sisters, and Reisel herself? Much ado about nothing. A stranger named Sydelle would be on the stage and he'd be in the audience. So what? Yet when he asked Reisel how she'd happened to pick this particular concert to treat him to his voice was hoarse.

In all innocence she answered, "Because they are playing Mozart your favorite," and it was true that his cousin Reisel would not bog herself down in petty detail like who was playing Mozart his favorite.

So in the front loge with stupidly trembling fingers he turned the program to the line-up, and . . . all boys.

He sat back weak.

The biographies gave the dates, and look—Hugh Critz, viola, had been the last to join up with Lenkowski, in '46. Lindstrom the second violin had been with him from the beginning. So she was home with the baby, or—that baby'd be around fifteen now—with the babies? She'd shed him and shed Fields to play housewife for Lenkowski, Danny's deep girl, his artist? What a lousy joke that would be. . . . Or she could be dead, Sydelle? Anything but that. Better housewife than dead if housewife was what she wanted. God, let her be well and happy, and the hell with himself.

The quintet appeared though, and if she was alive why wasn't she there? Lenkowski was still the boss but suaver, with graying temples. He showed less edge. He bowed, he even smiled, and he broke your heart with his Mozart in C minor, in C major. And, after the intermission and the *Adagio and Fugue*, what else would he conclude with but the G Minor Quintet Sydelle had sent Danny to in Chicago in his musical infancy when he hadn't cared that much for Mozart. Now old Mozart twisted you around, turned you inside out, all but extinguished you . . . and then left you smiling when he said goodbye. That was supposed to be a flaw, the happy ending of the G Minor, if you went by the heavy thinkers? Flaw my ass—that sign-off said "Mozart's the name!"

But suppose that the name is Share?

At the cloak counter the most honest man in the world helped Reisel on with her slender fur-trimmed beige and, "I have to make a stop," told a half truth.

The second she was out of sight down the escalator he hurried back into the auditorium and backstage where Lenkowski was holding court to a crowd—a mob—not like fifteen years ago. But shuffle the feet ahead and you get there.

"Beautiful, devastating," he thanked Lenkowski, "you wrecked me in Town Hall your first New York appearance and you finished me off tonight."

And Lenkowski really had mellowed, he was pleased. "Town Hall—the tempos were too fast in those days. Ah youth and impetuosity—as a rule to our sorrow." But when Danny jumped on the reminiscence with the wily question at age forty-nine about what had happened to that woman violist in the original quartet, Lenkowski—"Say, she may be underground for all I know"—turned his back and found himself a different admirer.

And wasn't that the sporting tune of a bastard dishing out alimony—or only child support more likely with Sydelle Danny's dear lightweight the folks just loved to push around? Oh God, good girl Sydelle! Underground to you Jack! She wasn't underground, and she wasn't with that bum any more either, or if she was she was unhappy.

How do you find out? You ask. Who do you ask? You ask her.

Sure—the escalator rolled down, but Danny was in the stars—this joy was ridiculous. What state of the union do you search for her in after Cleveland? She might have married again, she certainly would have changed. Yet what do people change to? To what they always were, only more so, like his father. And it had been incredible all this time that she should be walking, talking, eating, sleeping, and never with him, and after those two exploiters her every need was on his side. But say he was wrong. Then play it safe, stand on pride, keep popping off the blank cartridge women that rolled his way? Okay, only a goddam fool would still be in love fifteen years after the last insult. But first he'd drifted through school like a goddam fool, then he'd been a goddam fool and he'd gotten married, then he'd fallen in love and tossed it away like a goddam fool. So he was a goddam fool anyhow! Wishes were horses you don't bet on—elementary handicapping—but the way tonight had pushed itself at him! He hurried past dark cases of old-time costumes downstairs, and—God, Sydelle, oh Sydelle—he felt like a winner!

"Next comes my treat," he bubbled over at Reisel waiting patiently at the door. "Lindy's? Rumpelmayer's? Tavern-on-the-Green?"

"What has happened," she smiled at Share the open book, "to make you so happy?" He folded her arm in his and good old Reisel, she yanked it away tittering, "Have you become drunk Daniel?"

He laughed, "As good as, huh?" and outside with the cold air on his hot intoxicated face he hung at loose ends.

"Daniel, why are you just standing here?"

"Reisel," Danny laughed, "where did we leave the Cadillac?"